"This is the most successful Christian-fiction series ever."

PUBLISHERS WEEKLY

+ + +

"Combines Tom Clancy–like suspense with touches of romance, high-tech flash and Biblical references."

THE NEW YORK TIMES

+ + +

"Tim LaHaye and Jerry Jenkins . . . are doing for Christian fiction what John Grisham did for courtroom thrillers."

TIME

+ + +

"Wildly popular—and highly controversial."

USA TODAY

+ + +

"Call it what you like, the Left Behind series . . . now has a label its creators could have never predicted: blockbuster success."

ENTERTAINMENT WEEKLY

LEFT BEHIND SERIES

THE INDWELLING · THE MARK · DESECRATION

COLLECTORS EDITION III

EVIL'S EDGE

✠ ✠ ✠

TIM LAHAYE
JERRY B. JENKINS

Tyndale House Publishers, Inc., Carol Stream, Illinois

Visit Tyndale's exciting Web site at www.tyndale.com.

For the latest Left Behind news visit the Left Behind Web site at www.leftbehind.com.

TYNDALE, Tyndale's quill logo, and *Left Behind* are registered trademarks of Tyndale House Publishers, Inc.

Evil's Edge: Left Behind Collectors Edition III

Evil's Edge: Left Behind Collectors Edition III first published in 2010 by Tyndale House Publishers, Inc.

Designed by Dean H. Renninger

Published in association with the literary agency of Alive Communications, Inc., 7680 Goddard Street, Suite 200, Colorado Springs, CO 80920, www.alivecommunications.com.

Library of Congress Cataloging-in-Publication Data

LaHaye, Tim F.
Evil's edge / Tim LaHaye, Jerry B. Jenkins.
p. cm. — (Left behind series collectors edition ; 3)
ISBN 978-1-4143-3487-5 (pbk.)
1. Rapture (Christian eschatology)—Fiction. 2. Steele, Rayford (Fictitious character)—Fiction. 3. Christian fiction, American. 4. Fantasy fiction, American. I. Jenkins, Jerry B. II. Title.
PS3562.A315E95 2010
813'.54—dc22 2009049346

Printed in the United States of America

16 15 14 13 12 11 10
7 6 5 4 3 2 1

THE INDWELLING

✠ ✠ ✠

To our agent, Rick Christian,
who recognized the value of the idea and the potential
of the partnership and introduced us to each other

Monday of Gala Week

LEAH ROSE PRIDED herself on thinking under pressure. She'd been chief administrative nurse in a large hospital for a decade and had also been one of few believers there the last three and a half years. She had survived by her wits and eluded Global Community Peacekeeping Forces until finally having to flee and join the Tribulation Force.

But on the Monday of the week that would see the assassinations of the two witnesses and the Antichrist, Leah had no clue what to do. In disguise and under her alias, Donna Clendenon, she believed she had fooled authorities at the Belgium Facility for Female Rehabilitation (BFFR, or Buffer). She had passed herself off as Hattie Durham's aunt.

A squinting guard, whose nameplate read *Croix* and whose accent was unmistakably French, asked, "And what makes you think your niece is incarcerated here?"

"You think I'd come all the way from California if I had any doubt?" Leah said. "Everybody knows Hattie is here, and I know her alias: Mae Willie."

The guard cocked his head. "And your message can be delivered only in person?"

"A death in the family."

"I'm sorry."

Leah pursed her lips, aware of her artificially protruding teeth. *I'll bet,* she thought.

Croix stood and riffled through pages on his clipboard. "Buffer is a maximum security facility without standard visiting privileges. Ms. Durham has been separated from the prison population. I would have to get clearance for you to see her. I could give her the message myself."

"All I want is five minutes," Leah said.

"You can imagine how short staffed we are."

Leah didn't respond. Millions had disappeared in the Rapture. Half the remaining population had died since. Everybody was short staffed. Merely existing anymore was a full-time job. Croix asked her to wait in a holding area, but he did not tell her she would see no personnel, no inmates, or even any other visitors for more than two hours. A glass cubicle, where it appeared a clerical person had once sat, was empty. No one was there whom Leah could ask how long this might take, and when she rose to look for someone else, she found she was locked in. Were they onto her? Was she now a prisoner too?

Just before Leah resorted to banging on the door and screaming for help, Croix returned. Without apology, and—she noticed—avoiding eye contact, he said, "My superiors are considering your request and will call your hotel tomorrow."

Leah fought a smile. As if I want you to know where I'm staying.

"How about I call you?" Leah said.

"Suit yourself," Croix said with a shrug. *"Merci."* Then, as if catching himself: "Thank you."

Relieved to be outside, Leah drove around to be sure she wasn't being followed. With puzzling instructions from Rayford not to call him until Friday, she phoned Buck and brought him up to date. "I don't know whether to bolt or play it out," she said.

That night in her hotel room, Leah felt a loneliness only slightly less acute than when she had first been left behind. She thanked God for the Tribulation Force and how they had welcomed her. All but Rayford, of course. She couldn't figure him. Here was a brilliant, accomplished man with clear leadership skills, someone she had admired until the day she moved into the safe house. They hadn't clicked, but everyone else seemed frustrated with him too.

In the morning Leah showered and dressed and found something to eat, planning to see Hattie as soon as she had permission. She was going to call Buffer from her untraceable cell phone, but she got caught up watching on television as Carpathia taunted Moishe and Eli before the eyes of the world.

She sat, mouth agape, as Carpathia murdered the two witnesses with a powerful handgun. Leah remembered when TV cameras would have been averted in the face of such violence. Then came the earthquake that left a tenth of Jerusalem in rubble.

The GC global network showed quake scenes interspersed with footage of the silent witnesses badgered by the smirking Carpathia before their ignominious ends. The slow-motion pictures were broadcast over and over, and repulsed as she was, Leah could not turn away.

She had known this was coming; they all had—any students of Tsion Ben-Judah. But to see it played out shocked and saddened her, and Leah's eyes swam. She knew how it was to turn out, too, that they would be resurrected and that Carpathia would get his. Leah prayed for her new friends, some of whom were in Jerusalem. But she didn't want to sit there blubbering when she had work to do too. Things would get a lot worse than this, and Leah needed the training of performing under pressure to prepare herself and to convince herself she was up to it.

The phone at Buffer rang and rang, and Leah was at least warmed to know that the world government suffered just like the rank and file with the loss of half the population. Finally a woman picked up, but Leah couldn't get her even to acknowledge an employee named Croix.

"A French guard?" Leah tried.

"Ah, I know who you mean. Hold on."

Finally a man picked up. "Who are you holding for, please?" he said, in a hurry.

"Guard Croix," she said, "about six feet—"

"Croix!" the man hollered. "Phone!"

But he never came to the phone. Leah finally hung up and drove to the prison, leaving her phone in the car for safety.

At long last Croix ushered her into yet another private room. This one had a large window that Leah thought might be a two-way mirror. Again she feared her cover might have already been blown.

"I thought you were going to call," the guard said, pointing to a chair, ubiquitous clipboard in hand.

"I tried," she said. "This place is poorly run."

"Understaffed," he said.

"Can we get on with it?" Leah said. "I need to see my niece."

"No."

"No?"

Croix stared at her, apparently unwilling to repeat himself.

"I'm listening," she said.

"I'm not at liberty to—"

"Don't give me that," Leah said. "If I can't see her, I can't see her, but I have the right to know she's healthy, that she's alive."

"She is both."

"Then why can't I see her?"

Croix pressed his lips together. "She's been transferred, ma'am."

"Since yesterday?"

"I'm not at liberty to—"

"How long has she been gone? Where is she?"

He shook his head. "I'm telling you what I was told. If you'd like to get a message to—"

"I want to see her. I want to know she's all right."

"To the best of my knowledge, she's fi—"

"The best of your knowledge! Have you an inkling how limited your knowledge is?"

"Insulting me will not—"

"I don't mean to insult you, sir! I'm merely asking to see my niece and—"

"That's enough, Officer Croix," came a female voice from behind the glass. "You may go."

Croix left without a word or a look. Leah detected an Asian accent in the woman. She stood and stepped to the mirror. "So, what's next, ma'am? Am I to leave too, or will I get some word about my niece?"

Silence.

"Have I now become a prisoner too? Guilt by relation?"

Leah felt conspicuous and wondered whether anyone was behind the glass after all. Finally she marched to the door but was not surprised to find herself locked in again. "Terrific," she said, heading back toward the mirror. "What are the magic words that get me out of here? C'mon, lady! I know you're back there!"

"You will be free to go when we say you are free to go."

The same woman. Leah pictured her older, matronly, and clearly Asian. She raised her palms in surrender and plopped into a chair. She started and looked up when she heard a buzz in the door latch. "You may go."

Leah shot a double take at the mirror. "I may?"

"She who hesitates . . ."

"Oh, I'm going," she said, rising. "Could I at least see *you* on my way out? Please? I just want to know—"

"You're trying my patience, Mrs. Clendenon. You have received all the information you will get here."

Leah stopped with her hand on the doorknob, shaking her head, hoping to weasel something from the disembodied voice.

"Go, ma'am!" the woman said. "While you have the option."

Leah had given her best. She wasn't willing to go to prison for this caper. For another effort, maybe, another assignment. She would sacrifice her freedom for Dr. Ben-Judah. But for Hattie? Hattie's own doctor had died treating her, and she seemed barely grateful.

Leah moved briskly through the echoing corridors. She heard a door behind her and, hoping to catch a glimpse of the woman, turned quickly. A small, trim, pale, dark-haired woman in uniform turned and headed the other way. Could that have been her?

Leah headed for the main entrance but turned at the last instant and stepped behind a bank of phones. At least it looked like a bank of phones. She wanted to pretend to be talking on one while anyone who might follow her rushed out the door, but every phone was in shambles, wires hanging.

She was about to abandon her plan when she heard quick footsteps and saw a young Asian woman hurry out the front door, car keys jangling. Leah was convinced this was the same woman who had ducked away when she turned around. Now Leah was following *her.*

She hesitated inside the glass doors, watching as the woman trotted to the visitor parking lot and scanned the area. Apparently frustrated, she turned and walked slowly back toward the entrance. Leah nonchalantly exited, hoping to get a straight-on look at the woman. If she could get her to speak, she would know whether she had been the one behind the glass.

An employee of the GC and she's worse at this than I am, Leah thought, as the woman noticed her, appeared startled, then fought to act normal. As they neared one another, Leah asked where a washroom was, but the woman tugged her tiny uniform cap tighter onto her head and turned away to cough as she passed, not hearing or pretending not to.

Leah pulled out of the unattended lot and waited at a stop sign a quarter mile away, where she could see the prison entrance in her rearview mirror. The woman hurried out and hopped into a compact four-door. Determined to lose her, Leah raced off and got lost trying to find her hotel via side streets.

She called Rayford again and again. No way this could wait until Friday. When he didn't answer she worried that his phone might have fallen into the wrong hands. She left a cryptic message: "Our bird has flown the cage. Now what?"

She drove into the country, convinced no one was following her, and found her way back to the hotel at dusk. She had been in her room less than half an hour when the phone rang.

"This is Donna," she said.

"You have a visitor," the clerk said. "May I send her back?"

"No! Who is it?"

"'A friend' is all she'll say."

"I'll come there," Leah said.

She stuffed her belongings into a bag and slipped out to her car. She tried to peer into the lobby through the plate glass, but she couldn't see who was there. As she started the car, someone drove behind her and stopped. Leah was pinned in. She locked her doors as the driver emerged from the other vehicle.

As Leah's eyes adjusted to the light, she could see it was the same car the woman had driven from the prison. A knock made her jump. The woman, still in uniform, signaled her to lower her window. Leah lowered it an inch, her heart thudding.

"I need to make a show of this," the woman whispered. "Play your part."

My part? "What do you want?" Leah said.

"Come with me."

"Not on your life! Unless you want your car in pieces, get it out of my way."

The woman leaned forward. "Excellent. Now step out and let me cuff you and—"

"Are you out of your mind? I have no intention of—"

"Perhaps you cannot see my forehead in the darkness," the woman said. "But trust me—"

"Why should I—?"

And then Leah saw it. The woman had the mark. She was a believer.

The woman pointed to the lock as she removed handcuffs from a holster on her belt. Leah unlocked the door. "How did you find me?" she said.

"Checked your alias at several hotels. Didn't take long."

"Alias?" Leah said as she alighted and turned so the woman could cuff her.

"I'm Ming Toy," she said, leading Leah to the backseat of her car. "A believer comes all the way to Brussels to see Hattie Durham and uses her own name? I don't think so."

"I'm supposed to be her aunt," Leah said as Ming pulled out of the parking lot.

"Well, that worked on everybody else," she said. "But they didn't see what I saw. So, who are you and what are you doing here?"

"Would you mind if I double-checked your mark, Miss Toy?"

"*Mrs.* I'm a widow."

"Me too."

"But call me Ming."

"I'll tell you what you can call me as soon as I can check your mark."

"In a minute."

Ming pulled into a GC Peacekeeping station. "I need an interrogation room," she barked at the man behind the desk, still holding tight to Leah's left biceps.

"Commander," the man said with a nod, sliding a key across the counter. "Last door on the left."

"Private, no viewing, no bugs."

"That's the secure one, ma'am."

Ming locked the door, angled the lamp shade toward them, and released Leah from her cuffs. "Check me out," she said, sitting and cocking her head.

Leah gently held the back of Ming's head, knowing already that anyone who would let her do that had to be genuine. She licked her thumb and ran it firmly across the mark on Ming's forehead. Leah slumped into a chair across from Ming and reached for both her hands. "I can't wait to get to know you," she said.

"Likewise," Ming said. "Let's pray first."

Leah couldn't keep from welling up as this brand-new friend thanked God for their propitious meeting and asked that he allow them to somehow work together.

"First I'll tell you where Hattie Durham is," Ming said. "Then we'll trade stories, and I'll take you back to your hotel, tell my associates that you check out as Hattie's aunt, and let them think that you believe Hattie was transferred but that you don't know where."

"She wasn't transferred?"

Ming shook her head.

"Is she alive?"

"Temporarily."

"Healthy?"

"Healthier than when we got her. In fact, she's in quite good shape. Strong enough to assassinate a potentate."

Leah furrowed her brow and shook her head. "I'm not following you."

"They let her go."

"Why?"

"All she talked about was killing Carpathia. Finally they told her that as it was clear she had lost his baby, she was no longer a threat and was free to go, with a tidy settlement for her trouble. Roughly one hundred thousand Nicks in cash."

Leah shook her head. "They don't consider her a threat? She wants to kill him for real."

"They know that," Ming said. "In my opinion, they think she's dumber than she looks."

"Sometimes she is," Leah said.

"But not dumb enough to lead them straight to the rest of the Tribulation Force," Ming said. "The simplistic plan is that they follow her to the Gala in Jerusalem and to some sort of a rendezvous with one of you Judah-ites."

"I love that title. I'm a believer first, but also proudly a Judah-ite."

"Me too," Ming said. "And I'll bet you know Ben-Judah personally."

"I do."

"Wow."

"But, Ming, the GC is wrong about Hattie. She's crazy enough to go and try to kill Nicolae, but she has no interest in contacting any of us."

"You might be surprised."

"How so?"

"She didn't go to Jerusalem like they hoped. We've tracked her to North America. I think she's onto the GC and wants to get back to safety as soon as she can."

"That's worse!" Leah said. "She'll lead them to the safe house."

"Maybe that's why God sent you here," Ming said. "I didn't know what I was going to do to protect you people. Whom was I supposed to tell? You're the answer to my prayer."

"But what can I do? I'll never be able to catch her before she gets there."

"You can at least warn them, right?"

Leah nodded. "My phone's in my bag in my car."

"And my phones are all traceable."

They traded stories on the way back. Ming was twenty-two years old, a native of China. Her husband of two months had been killed a few minutes after the disappearances when the commuter train he was on crashed when the brakeman and several controllers vanished. She had joined the GC in a paroxysm of patriotism shortly after the treaty was signed between the United Nations and Israel. She had been assigned to the reconstruction administration in what used to be the Philippines, but there she had become a believer through the letters of her brother at home, now seventeen. "Chang's friends had led him to faith," she said. "He has not yet told my parents, who are very old school and very pro-Carpathia, especially my father. I worry about Chang."

Ming had applied for work in the peacekeeping forces, hoping for just this sort of opportunity to aid fellow believers. "I don't know how much longer I can remain inside undercover."

"How did you get to a position of authority over so many guards?"

"It's not so big a deal as it sounds. The population decimation didn't hurt."

"C'mon! You're in management."

"Well, in all humility, a stratospheric IQ doesn't hurt. That and wrestling," she added, seeming to fight a smile. "Two out of three falls."

"You're not serious."

"They know Greco-Roman. I know martial arts." Ming pulled into the hotel parking lot. "Call your friends right away," she said. "And stay away from Buffer. I'll cover for you."

"Thank God for you, Ming," Leah said, again overcome. They traded phone numbers. "The day will come when you need a safe place too. Keep in touch." They embraced, and Leah hurried to get her bag and get back into her room.

There was no answer at the safe house, and Leah worried it had already been compromised. Had it already been overrun? And what of her new friends? She tried Rayford's number, then the safe house, again and again.

Unable to reach anyone, Leah knew she had a better chance of helping the Trib Force in North America than from a Brussels hotel room. She found a flight and headed home that very night. All the way back she tried the safe house phone, to no avail.

1

BUCK BRACED HIMSELF with his elbow crooked around a scaffolding pole. Thousands of panicked people fleeing the scene had, like him, started and involuntarily turned away from the deafening gunshot. It had come from perhaps a hundred feet to Buck's right and was so loud he would not have been surprised if even those at the back of the throng of some two million had heard it plainly.

He was no expert, but to Buck it had sounded like a high-powered rifle. The only weapon smaller that had emitted such a report was the ugly handgun Carpathia had used to destroy the skulls of Moishe and Eli three days before. Actually, the sounds were eerily similar. Had Carpathia's own weapon been fired? Might someone on his own staff have targeted him?

The lectern had shattered loudly as well, like a tree branch split by lightning. And that gigantic backdrop sailing into the distance . . .

Buck wanted to bolt with the rest of the crowd, but he worried about Chaim. Had he been hit? And where was Jacov? Just ten minutes before, Jacov had waited below stage left where Buck could see him. No way Chaim's friend and aide would abandon him during a crisis.

As people stampeded by, some went under the scaffold, most went around it, and some jostled both Buck and the support poles, making the structure sway. Buck held tight and looked to where giant speakers three stories up leaned this way and that, threatening their flimsy plywood supports.

Buck could choose his poison: step into the surging crowd and risk being trampled or step up a few feet on the angled crossbar. He stepped up and immediately felt the fluidity of the structure. It bounced and seemed to want to spin as Buck looked toward the platform over the tops of a thousand streaking heads. He had heard Carpathia's lament and Fortunato's keening, but suddenly the sound—at least in the speakers above him—went dead.

Buck glanced up just in time to see a ten-foot-square speaker box tumble from the top. "Look out!" he shrieked to the crowd, but no one heard or noticed. He looked up again to be sure he was out of the way. The box snapped its umbilicals like string, which redirected its path some fifteen feet away from the tower. Buck watched in horror as a woman was crushed beneath it and several other men and women were staggered. A man tried to drag the victim from beneath the speaker, but the crowd behind him never slowed. Suddenly the running mass became a cauldron of humanity, trampling each other in their desperation to get free of the carnage.

Buck could not help. The entire scaffolding was pivoting, and he felt himself swing left. He hung on, not daring to drop into the torrent of screaming bodies. He caught sight of Jacov at last, trying to make his way up the side steps to the platform where Carpathia's security detail brandished Uzis.

A helicopter attempted to land near the stage but had to wait until the crowd cleared. Chaim sat motionless in his chair, facing to Buck's right, away from Carpathia and Fortunato. He appeared stiff, his head cocked and rigid, as if unable to move. If he had not been shot, Buck wondered if he'd had another stroke, or worse, a heart attack. He knew if Jacov could get to him, he would protect Chaim and get him somewhere safe.

Buck tried to keep an eye on Jacov while Fortunato waved at the helicopters, pleading with one to land and get Carpathia out of there. Jacov finally broke free and sprinted up the steps, only to be dealt a blow from the butt end of an Uzi that knocked him off his feet and into the crowd.

The impact snapped Jacov's head back so violently that Buck was certain he was unconscious and unable to protect himself from trampling. Buck leaped off the scaffold and into the fray, fighting his way toward Jacov. He moved around the fallen speaker box and felt the sticky blood underfoot.

As Buck neared where he thought Jacov should be he took one more look at the platform before the angle would obscure his view. Chaim's chair was moving! He was headed full speed toward the back of the platform. Had he leaned against the joystick? Was he out of control? If he didn't stop or turn, he would pitch twelve feet to the pavement and certain death. His head was still cocked, his body stiff.

Buck reached Jacov, who lay splayed, his head awkwardly flopped to one side, eyes staring, limbs limp. A sob worked its way to Buck's throat as he elbowed stragglers out of the way and knelt to put a thumb and forefinger to Jacov's throat. No pulse.

Buck wanted to drag the body from the scene but feared he would be recognized despite his extensive facial scars. There was nothing he could do for Jacov. But what about Chaim?

Buck sprinted left around the platform and skidded to a stop at the back corner, from where he could see Chaim's wheelchair crumpled on the ground, backstage center. The heavy batteries had broken open and lay twenty feet from the chair, which had one wheel bent almost in half, seat pad missing, and a footrest broken off. Was Buck about to find another friend dead?

He loped to the mangled chair and searched the area, including under the platform. Besides splinters from what he was sure had been the lectern, he found nothing. How could Chaim have survived this? Many of the world rulers had scrambled off the back of the stage, certainly having to turn and hang from the edge first to avoid serious injury. Even then, many would have had to have suffered sprained or broken ankles. But an elderly stroke victim riding in a metal chair twelve feet to concrete? Buck feared Chaim could not have survived. But who would have carried him off?

A chopper landed on the other side of the platform, and medical personnel rushed the stage. The security detail fanned out and began descending the stairs to clear the area.

Four emergency medical technicians crowded around Carpathia and Fortunato while others attended the trampled and the crushed, including the woman beneath the speaker box. Jacov was lifted into a body bag. Buck nearly wept at having to leave his brother that way, yet he knew Jacov was in heaven. He ran to catch up with the crowd now spilling into the streets.

Buck knew Jacov was dead. From the wound at the back of Carpathia's head, he assumed Nicolae was dead or soon would be. And he had to assume Chaim was dead too.

Buck longed for the end of all this and the glorious appearing of Christ. But that was still another three and a half years off.

✠ ✠ ✠

Rayford felt a fool, running with the crowd, the hem of his robe in his hands to keep from tripping. He had dropped the Saber and its box and wanted to use his arms for more speed. But he had to run like a woman in a long skirt. Adrenaline carried him, because he felt fast as ever, regardless. Rayford really wanted to shed the robe and turban, but the last thing he needed just then was to look like a Westerner.

Had he murdered Carpathia? He had tried to, intended to, but couldn't pull the trigger. Then, when he was bumped and the gun went off, he couldn't imagine he'd been lucky enough to find his target. Could the bullet have ricocheted off the lectern and into Carpathia? Could it also have passed through him and taken out the backdrop? It didn't seem possible.

If he had killed the potentate, there was certainly no satisfaction in it, no relief or sense of accomplishment. As he hurried along, the screams and moans of Carpathia's faithful all around him, Rayford felt he was running from a prison of his own making.

He was sucking wind by the time the crowd thinned and began to disperse, and when he stopped to bend at the waist, hands on his hips, to catch his breath, a couple hurrying past said, "Isn't it awful? They think he's dead!"

"It's awful," Rayford gasped, not looking at them.

Assuming TV cameras had caught everything, especially him with the gun raised, it wouldn't be long before he would be sought. As soon as he was away from the busy streets, he shed the garb and stuffed it in a trash barrel. He found his car, eager to get to Tel Aviv and out of Israel before it became impossible.

+ + +

Mac stood near the back of the throng, far enough from the gun that the report didn't reach his ears until after the massive crowd began to move. While others near him shrieked and gasped and pleaded to know what was going on, he kept his eyes on the stage, relief washing over him. So, he would not have to sacrifice himself and Abdullah to be sure Carpathia was dead. From the commotion down front and from his view of the platform via jumbo screens nearby, it was clear to Mac that Nicolae had suffered the massive head wound believers knew was coming.

Ever the professional, Mac knew what would be expected of him. He slid his cell phone from his jacket and dialed Tel Aviv Operations. "You got a pilot rated to shuttle the 216 to Jerusalem and is it light enough to land and take off on the short runway?"

"Already looking, sir, and it's light enough to do it. This is a tragedy."

"Yeah."

Mac dialed Abdullah. From the limited noise in the background, he could tell his first officer was not at the Gala. "You hear, Ab?"

"I heard. Shall I go get the Phoenix?"

"Hang loose; they're trying to get it here. I saw you leave the hotel. Where are you?"

"Doctor Pita's. I suppose I'll look suspicious finishing my meal when the big boss is dying and everyone else has run into the streets looking for a TV."

"Stick it in your pocket, and if you don't hear from me, meet me at Jerusalem Airport in an hour."

Mac made his way to the front of the plaza as the place emptied in a frenzy. He flashed his ID when necessary, and by the time he reached the platform, it was clear Carpathia was in the final throes of life. His wrists were drawn up under his chin, eyes shut tight and bleeding, blood trickling also from his ears and mouth, and his legs shook violently, toes pointed, knees locked.

"Oh, he's gone! He's gone!" Leon wailed. "Someone do something."

The four emergency medical technicians, portable monitors beeping, knelt over Carpathia. They cleared his mouth so they could administer oxygen, studied a blood pressure gauge, pumped his chest, cradled his head, and tried to stanch the flow from a wound that left them kneeling in more blood than it seemed a body could hold.

Mac peeked past the panicky Fortunato to see Carpathia's normally tanned hands and face already pale. No one could survive this, and Mac wondered if the bodily movements were merely posthumous reflexes.

"There is a hospital nearby, Commander," one of the EMTs said, which threw Fortunato into a rage. He had just made eye contact with Mac and seemed about to say something when he turned on the EMT.

"Are you crazy? These—these *people* are not qualified! We must get him to New Babylon."

He turned to Mac. "Is the 216 ready?"

"On its way from Tel Aviv. Should be able to lift off in an hour."

"An hour?! Should we helicopter him straight to Tel Aviv?"

"Jerusalem Airport will be faster," Mac said.

"There's no room to stabilize him in a chopper, sir," the EMT said.

"We have no choice!" Fortunato said. "An ambulance would be too slow."

"But an ambulance has equipment that might—"

"Just get him into the chopper!" Fortunato said.

But as the EMT turned away looking disgusted, a female colleague looked up at him. Carpathia was still. "No vitals," she said. "He's flatlined."

"No!" Leon bellowed, bullying his way between them and kneeling in Nicolae's blood. Again he leaned over the body, but rather than holding Carpathia to him, he buried his face in the lifeless chest and sobbed aloud.

Security Chief Walter Moon dismissed the EMTs with a nod, and as they gathered up their equipment and went for the gurney, he gently pulled Leon away from Carpathia. "Don't drape the body," he said. "Let's load 'im up now. Say nothing about his condition until we're back home."

"Who did this, Walter?" Fortunato whined. "Did we catch him?"

Moon shrugged and shook his head.

* * *

Buck ran toward the hostel. He dialed Chaim's number again, as he had all along the way. Still busy. The people in Chaim's house—Stefan the valet, Jacov's wife, Hannelore, and Hannelore's mother—had to have been watching on TV and were likely calling anyone they knew for news of their loved ones.

Finally, Hannelore answered. "Jacov!" she shouted.

"No, Hannelore, this is Greg North."

"Buck!" she wailed. "What happened? Where—"

"Hannelore!" Buck said. "Your phone is not secure!"

"I don't care anymore, Buck! If we die, we die! Where is Jacov? What happened to Chaim?"

"I need to meet you somewhere, Hannelore. If Chaim shows up there—"

"Chaim is all right?"

"I don't know. I didn't see him after—"

"Did you see Jacov?"

"Meet me, Hannelore. Call me from another phone and—"

"Buck, you tell me right now! Did you see him?"

"I saw him."

"Is he alive?"

"Hannelore—"

"Buck, is he dead?"

"I'm sorry. Yes."

She began to wail, and in the background Buck heard a scream. Hannelore's mother? Had she deduced the news?

"Buck, they're here!"

"What? Who?"

He heard a door smashing, a yell, another scream.

"GC!" she whispered fiercely. And the phone went dead.

* * *

Onboard the Phoenix 216, Nicolae Carpathia's personal physician examined him and pronounced him dead.

"Where were you?" Leon demanded. "You could have done something."

"Where I was supposed to be, Commander," the doctor said, "in the auxiliary trailer a hundred yards behind the platform. Security would not let me out, fearing more gunfire."

As the 216 taxied toward the runway, Leon came to the cockpit and told Abdullah, "Patch me through to Director Hassid at the palace, secure line."

Abdullah nodded and glanced at Mac as Fortunato backed out. The first officer made the connection and informed Leon over the intercom. With creative switch flipping, Abdullah allowed Mac to listen in, while muting the input button to keep out noise from the cockpit.

"You're aware of the awful news, David?" Leon said.

"I heard, yes, sir," David said. "How is the potentate?"

"He's dead, David . . ."

"Oh."

". . . but this is top secret by order of Chief Moon until further notice."

"I understand."

"Oh, David, what will we do?"

"We'll look to you, sir."

"Well, thank you for those kind words at such a time, but I need something from you."

"Yes, sir."

"Scramble the satellites to make it impossible for those who did this to communicate with each other by phone. Can you do that?"

A long pause. "Scrambling the satellites" was not the exact terminology, but David could produce Fortunato's desired result. "Yes," he said slowly. "It's possible, of course. You realize the ramifications . . ."

Mac whispered to Abdullah. "Call Buck, call Rayford, call the safe house. Leon's going to shut down communications. If they need to talk to each other, it has to be now."

"Tell me," Leon said.

"We're all served by the same system," David said. "It's the reason we've never been able to shut down the Judah-ites' Internet transmissions."

"So if they're shut down, we're shut down?"

"Exactly."

"Do it anyway. The landlines in New Babylon would still be operable, would they not?"

"They would, and this would not affect television transmission, but your long distance is all satellite dependent."

"So those of us in New Babylon would be able to communicate only with each other."

"Right."

"We'll get by. I'll let you know when to unscramble."

Two minutes later Leon called David again. "How long does this take?" he said. "I should not be able to reach you!"

"Three minutes," David said.

"I'll check back in four."

"You'll not reach me, sir."

"I should hope not!"

But four minutes later Leon was preoccupied with the doctor. "I want an autopsy," he said, "but zero leaks about cause of death." Through the reverse intercom bug, Mac heard Leon's voice catch. "And I want this man prepared for viewing and for burial by the finest mortuary technician in the world. Is that understood?"

"Of course, Commander. As you wish."

"I don't want the staff butcher in the palace, so whom would you suggest?"

"One who could use the business, frankly."

"How crass! This would be a service to the Global Community!"

"But surely you're prepared to reimburse—"

"Of course, but not if money is the primary concern. . . ."

"It's not, Commander. I simply know that Dr. Eikenberry's mortuary has been decimated. She's lost more than half her staff and has had to reorganize her business."

"And she's local?"

"Baghdad."

"I do not want Nicolae shipped to Baghdad. Can she come to the palace morgue?"

"I'm sure she'd be more than happy . . ."

"Happy?"

"Willing, sir."

"I hope she can work miracles."

"Fortunately his face was not affected."

"Still," Leon said, his voice husky again, "how do you hide the, the . . . awful injury?"

"I'm sure it can be done."

"He must look perfect, dignified. The whole world will mourn him."

"I'll call her now."

"Yes, please try. I'd like to know whether you're able to get through."

But he was not able. Global telephone communications were off the air. And Abdullah too had failed to reach anyone.

Mac was about to shut off the intercom bug when he heard Leon take a huge breath and let it out. "Doctor?" he said. "Can your mortician, ah—"

"Dr. Eikenberry."

"Right. Can she do a cast of the potentate's body?"

"A cast?"

"You know, some sort of plaster or plastic or something that would preserve his exact dimensions and features?"

The doctor hesitated. "Well," he said finally, "death masks are nothing new. A whole corpse would be quite an undertaking, pardon the expression."

"But it could be done?"

Another pause. "I should think the body would have to be dipped. The palace morgue has a large enough tank."

"It could be done then?"

"Anything can be done, Excellency. I'm sorry, I mean Commander."

Fortunato cleared his throat. "Yes, please, Doctor. Don't call me Excellency. At least not yet. And do arrange for a cast of the potentate's body."

2

BESIDE THE DESK in her hangar office, David stood facing Annie and holding both her hands.

"You're trembling," she said.

"I thought *you* were," he said. "You're not as scared as I am?"

"At least," she said. "What's going on?"

He sighed. "I just got a call from a mortician in Baghdad. Says she was told to go through me for large purchases. She wants several liters of some sort of a plastic amalgam delivered to the palace morgue as soon as possible."

"For?"

"I can only imagine. This stuff is used to make casts of faces, body parts, tire tracks, that kind of thing. But she wants enough to fill a tub the size of a whirlpool bath."

"She's going to make a cast of Carpathia's whole body?"

He shrugged. "That's my guess."

"Whatever for?"

"She didn't sound too sure herself. She kept asking how much water would have to be added to how much solution and if that would fill the stainless steel container. She also wanted to know how long I thought it would take that much solution to harden, how long it would remain pliable before drying, all that."

Annie slipped her hands around David's waist and laid her head on his chest. "Someone's put her up to it. Maybe to make a replica of the body so they can make him look better lying in state?"

He pondered that. "I just wonder if they've heard about the prophecy of his resurrecting and want to keep the real body somewhere convenient, just in case."

"They don't believe the prophecies, do they?"

"How could anyone not by this time?"

She looked up at him and shook her head. "What's going to happen around here when, you know . . ."

"It happens?"

"Yeah."

"It's not going to be pretty. I can't wait to see what Dr. Ben-Judah has to say about you-know-who when he's no longer really himself."

"You think there'll be any of the man left of him?"

David cocked his head. "His body, sure. Maybe he'll sound like himself and have the same mannerisms, but he's supposed to be indwelt, and indwelt means indwelt. When I was promoted, I moved into the quarters of that director who was reassigned to Australia, remember?"

"Yeah."

"It's the same place. Same walls, same bed, same lav, everything. It looks the same, but it's not. I'm the new dweller."

She held him tighter. "I don't want to know the new dweller of the potentate."

"Well, it'll be no more Mr. Nice Guy."

"Not funny," she said.

"They should be here any minute, babe."

"I know. My ears are tuned to the '16. I know how long it takes to get the hangar doors open and to position the forklift and winch. I hope security keeps its distance. Did you see all of 'em out there? Have you heard all the rules?"

"Have I! You'd think you were off-loading the body of the king of the world."

She snorted. "Tell you the truth, I'd like to drop the box and run over the whole thing with the forklift. Let's see *that* come back to life."

David tugged her toward the door. "What if he comes back to life while you're transporting the body?"

She stopped and closed her eyes. "Like I wasn't freaked out enough. You'd have to find me in heaven." A hum vibrated the office window. "You'd better go. They're about three minutes away."

* * *

Rayford could not believe his luck at Tel Aviv. He hurried past the busy counters and out a side exit toward the small-craft hangars. The Gulfstream sat gleaming in Hangar 3.

An armed guard doing double duty as manifest coordinator checked Marv Berry off his list and said, "Wait a minute, there's something else I'm s'posed to ask. Ah, yeah, flight plan reported to tower?"

"You bet," Rayford said, "but they weren't happy with how slow the small craft were being cleared, so I'd better keep you out of trouble by getting out of here quick."

"I 'preciate that," the guard said, clearly more comfortable with a gun than a pen. "They expect lots of passengers on the big birds tonight and want to get the little ones out of the way."

"Understandable," Rayford said. "I'll do my part."

"Wish I'd a been in Jerusalem tonight," the guard said as Rayford circled the Gulfstream, doing a quick preflight.

"Yeah?"

"I'd a killed somebody, guilty or not."

"That so?"

"Dang straight. Somebody'd pay for that. Who'd wanna go and kill our only hope?"

"I can't imagine."

"You're American, right, Mr. Berry?"

"You could tell?"

"Sure, me too."

"You don't say."

"Colorado," the young man said. "Fort Collins. You?"

"What're you doing here?"

"Wanted Gala duty. This is as close as I got. Hoped for potentate bodyguard, but I guess that's all political."

"Like everything else," Rayford said, pulling open the Gulfstream's door and steps.

"Need some help there, Mr. Berry?"

"Got it, thanks."

"Where'd you say you were from?"

I didn't, Rayford thought. "Kalamazoo," he said, mounting the steps and tossing in his bag.

"That's what, Midwest?"

Rayford hated the small talk, not to mention the delay, only slightly less than the prospect of being detained and put to death. "Michigan!" he called out, pulling the door.

"Hang on a second, sir," the guard said. "Squawk box is for me."

"I gotta go," Rayford said. "Nice talking to you."

"Just a minute, please," the young man said with a smile. "Another minute won't kill you, will it?"

It just might. "I've really got to go, son."

"Wyatt."

"Why?"

"Wyatt. That's my name."

"Well, thanks, Wyatt, and good-bye."

"Mr. Berry!"

"Yes, Wyatt."

"I'm not gonna be able to hear the box here if you fire up. Can't you give me a second?"

From the radio on Wyatt's makeshift desk in the middle of the hangar: "Officer 423, do you copy? Initiate code red screening effective immediately."

"This is Wyatt. You mean those thorough checks on everybody, even small craft?"

"Where are you, 423?"

"Small-craft Hangar 3, sir."

"Then that is what I mean, yes!"

Rayford quickly closed the door, but before he could settle into the cockpit, Wyatt came running. "Mr. Berry, sir! I'm going to have to ask you to step out of the craft!"

Rayford initiated the starting sequence, which only caused Wyatt to rush in front of the Gulfstream, waving, rifle dangling. He didn't appear alarmed or even suspicious. It was clear he simply thought Rayford couldn't hear him.

He motioned for Rayford to open the door. Rayford considered simply starting up as soon as Wyatt was clear of the front, hoping the GC was thin staffed enough and busy enough that they would ignore him. But he couldn't risk an air pursuit or gung ho Wyatt from Fort Collins shooting at him on the runway.

He moved to the door and opened it three inches. "What is it, Wyatt?"

"I've been instructed, sir, to do a thorough check and search of even small craft before departure tonight, due to what happened in Jerusalem."

"Even me, Wyatt? A small-town guy like you? An American?"

"Got to, sir. Sorry."

"Wyatt, you know the Gulfstream, don't you?"

"The Gulfstream, sir?"

"This aircraft."

"No sir, I don't. I'm not an aviation man. I'm a soldier."

Rayford peeked through the slivered opening. "If you knew this plane, Wyatt, you'd know that if the door opens all the way, I have to start the whole ignition sequence over."

"You do?"

"Yeah, some kind of a safety mechanism that keeps the engines from starting until the door is closed."

"Well, I'm sorry, but I have to—"

"I'm sorry, too, Wyatt, because the tower guys were complaining about you, and I was trying to keep you out of trouble, make you look good, by getting away quickly."

"But my commanding officer just told me—"

"Wyatt! Listen to me! You think I shot Carpathia?"

"'Course not. I—"

"I'd need you to teach me about weapons, for one thing."

"I could sure teach you, but—"

"I'll bet you could. And I could teach you to fly—"

"I have to—"

"Wyatt, I just heard on the radio that two wide-bodies are in landing sequence right now, with another waiting to take off. Now my perimeter flange is going to overheat if I don't get going, and you don't want a fire in here. Tell your boss I was already on my way out when you got the order; then we're both covered. You look quick, you avoid a fire, and you're still following orders."

Rayford kept a careful eye on Wyatt's hands and flinched when the young man moved his right. If he leveled that rifle at him, Rayford would have to comply. But Wyatt saluted and pointed at Rayford. "Good thinkin', sir. Carry on."

Rayford fired up the engines and maneuvered onto the tarmac. He couldn't wait to tell Mac about this one. He heard about other planes on a radio that wasn't on yet? Perimeter flange? Fire? Tsion taught that part of the population decimation might be God's way of removing his most incorrigible enemies in anticipation of the coming epic battle. Wyatt was living proof that the inept had survived. Rayford knew he wouldn't always enjoy such fortune.

"Ben Gurion Tower to Gulfstream!"

Rayford leaned forward and looked as far as he could in both directions, both on the runway and in the sky.

"Gurion Tower to Gulfstream, do you copy?"

He was clear.

"Gulfstream, you are not cleared! Remain stationary."

"Gulfstream to Tower," Rayford said. "Proceeding, thank you."

"Repeat, Gulfstream, you are *not* cleared!"

"Cleared by Officer 423, Tower."

"Repeat?"

". . . been . . . leared . . . two-three . . . wer."

"You're breaking up, Gulfstream! You are not cleared for takeoff. Repeat, not cleared!"

". . . nection . . . wer, thank y—"

"Do we have your flight plan, Gulfstream?"

". . . o copy, tow—"

"Flight plan?"

". . . icer fo—, two, thr—"

"If you can hear any of this, Gulfstream, be aware that satellite coordinates have been scrambled and there is only manual positioning. Copy?"

Rayford depressed and released the talk button rapidly, then held it halfway down, creating static on the other end. *No satellite capability?* For once he would be glad for that. He needn't worry about pursuit. If he was flying blind, so would the GC. Did that mean the phones were out too? He tried the safe house, then Laslos. Nothing. He only hoped he could connect with the Greek believers before he put down there. It made no sense to try to make it back to America. If Leah's message meant what he thought and Hattie was no longer in Belgium, she could have long since led the GC to the safe house. He only hoped his message had gotten to David's computer before the satellites went down.

\+ + +

Buck had been angry with his father-in-law before, but never like this. No contact? Nothing? What was he supposed to do, collect Leah from Brussels, and it was every man for himself? Now the phones didn't seem to be working.

Did he dare try to make it to Chaim's house and see what was going on? Why would the GC storm the place and force their way in? Were they too looking for Chaim? And why? Buck knew somebody already had to have the old man. Someone had spirited him, or his body, from the Gala site. No way a wheelchair-bound stroke victim could have made his own way out of that place with his contrivance in pieces on the ground.

Buck took a cab to the small place he had once used as an Israeli safe house. No one he recognized was living there. He walked several miles in the darkness through rubble, never far from the cacophony of sirens and the flashing light shows of emergency vehicles. When he finally arrived at Chaim's, the place was deserted and dark. Had everyone been taken away? Emergency personnel were stretched, of course, but if they expected Chaim, wouldn't someone be left to guard the place?

Buck crept to the back, suddenly aware of his fatigue. Grief and trauma did that to a person, he told himself. He had not gotten to know Jacov well, but how he had thrilled to the young man's coming to belief in Christ! They had kept up some, not as much as either had liked, due to the risk of discovery. And though he knew he would see Jacov at the Glorious Appearing—if not before—he dreaded having to break the news to Jacov's friend and coworker, Stefan.

Buck had the advantage of knowing, really knowing, this house. He feared he might be walking into a trap. He didn't think the GC knew he was in Israel, but one could never be sure. Maybe they lay in wait for Chaim or even Jacov. It was possible Jacov's death had not made the GC databases yet, though that was unlikely. But where was everyone else?

Buck found the back door unlocked, and he slipped in. A rechargeable flashlight was usually plugged into a socket near the floor, behind the food preparers' table. Buck felt for it and found it, but he didn't want to test it until he was confident no one was waiting to ambush him. He took it into the pantry and waited until he shut the door to turn it on. Then he felt foolish, reckless. He'd never been comfortable with the role he had been thrust into, still part journalist but also freedom fighter, raconteur. What kind of a swashbuckling Trib Force veteran backs himself into a closet with nothing more to defend himself with than a cheap flashlight?

He tried the light switch on the pantry wall. Nothing. So the power had been cut. Buck flipped the flashlight on, then off quickly. Something in his peripheral vision froze him. Did he dare shine the light that way? He let out a quavery breath. Who would lie in wait in a pantry?

Buck aimed the light that direction and turned it on. Just an unusual arrangement of boxes and cans. He doused the light and moved quietly to the door. Creeping through the kitchen into the dining room, the parlor, and then the front room, Buck held the flashlight in front of him as if it were on, but it served more like a blind man's cane. As his eyes began adjusting to the darkness, he became aware of pinpoints of light from the street, and he still heard sirens in the distance.

Later Buck would wonder whether he had smelled the blood before he heard it. Yes, heard it. He knew something was wrong as soon as he reached the front room. It was in the air. Heat? A presence? Someone. He stopped and tried to make out shapes. He felt his own heart, but something reached his ears more insistently even than that thumping. Dripping. *Drip, drip,* pause, *drip-drip, drip.* From two sources? Part of him didn't want to know, to see. He turned his back to windows at the front, pointed the flashlight toward the sounds, and braced himself, ready to defend himself with bare hands and the flashlight, if necessary.

He turned on the light but immediately shut his eyes to the horror. He dropped to his knees, the wind gushing from him. "Oh, God," he prayed. "No! Please!" Was there no end to the carnage? He would rather die than find his friends, his comrades (someday his own family?) like this. In the split second he had allowed himself to take in the scene, it became clear that two victims sat side by side in wood chairs, Hannelore on the left, her mother on the right. They were bound and gagged, heads tilted back, blood dripping into pools on the floor.

Buck did not want to reveal himself to anyone outside. Plainly, this scene was created to "welcome" someone home; certainly the perpetrators had no idea *he* would stumble upon it. Buck knelt before the chairs, repulsed by the sound of the drips. He knew if either of the women had survived, their respiration would have been noisy with their heads in that position. Still, he had to make sure. He lodged the flashlight between his knees, angled it toward the women, and turned it on. As he reached to check for Hannelore's pulse, the flashlight slipped and illumined her ankles, tied securely to the front legs of the chair. As he angled the light up again and tightened his knees to support it, he noticed her wrists tied behind her. A smallish woman, Hannelore's torso was stretched to allow her hands to go around the back of the chair. Great gushes of air rushed past Buck's gritted teeth.

He grabbed the flashlight and moved behind the chair to feel her wrist, but that put his arm in line with the blood dripping from her head. And though her wrist was warm, as he feared, there was no pulse.

Hannelore's mother, less than a foot away, was bound in the same position. A squat, heavy woman, her arms had been yanked into contorted positions to allow her wrists to be tied. She too was dead.

Who could have done this? And wouldn't Stefan, his Middle East maleness coming to the fore, have fought to the death to prevent it? Where could he be? Buck wanted to pan the light back and forth along the floor toward the front, but that might have been suicidal, he would be so obvious from the street. It was all he could do to keep from calling Stefan's name.

Chaim had not been home when Buck had talked with Hannelore on the phone. Did this massacre mean Chaim had arrived, or that he hadn't? Had Chaim himself been forced to witness this? Buck's first task was to locate Stefan, his second to check the entirety of the huge house for Chaim. If Chaim had not returned and this was all meant as a warning for him, could the place be staked out, surrounded? Perhaps it was.

Buck feared he would find not just Stefan's body, but also Chaim's. But how would Chaim have gotten there? Who might have caught him, rescued him, or helped him off that platform? And what was the purpose of murdering these innocents? Had they been tortured for information and eliminated once they provided it, or because they had not? Or was this simply vengeance? Chaim had been vitriolic in his revulsion of GC Peacekeepers, of the breaking of the covenant between the GC and Israel. Though he had never been a religious Jew, he expressed horror over the intrusion of the world government into the very affairs of the temple. First the Jews had been allowed to rebuild; then they were not allowed to conduct themselves the way they wished in the new temple.

But do you extinguish the household of a statesman, a national treasure, for such an offense? And what of the man himself? Buck's head throbbed, his chest felt tight, and he was short of breath. He was desperate to be with Chloe and Kenny and felt as if he could hold them tight for three and a half years. He knew the odds. Each had only a one in four chance of surviving until the Glorious Appearing. But even if he, or they, had to go to heaven before that, he didn't want it to be this way. No one deserved this. No one but Carpathia.

+ + +

It had been a long time since David had suffered such carping. On the way to his office from the palace hangar, past a full-dress color guard of pallbearers and a heavily armed ring of security personnel, his beeper had signaled a top-level emergency message. The call could have originated only locally, of course, but this sort of a code was reserved for life-and-death situations. He did not recognize the callback number but knew it was located in the palace proper.

Normally he would have called back immediately, fearing danger to Annie or himself, but he took a moment to trace the number against the personnel list and found that the call came from the Arts and Sciences wing. He had been there only once, knew virtually no one there, and had been so repulsed by what was considered artistic that he recalled rushing back to his quarters feeling soiled.

Wanting at least one more clue before replying, David called his own voice mail, only to be met by the foul, nasty rantings of a sassy *artiste.* David had not heard such profanity and gutter language since high school. The gist of the message: "Where are you? Where could you be at a time like this? It's the middle of the night! Do you even know of the murder? Call me! It's an emergency!"

David's beeper vibrated again—same number. He waited ninety seconds and called his voice mail again. "Do you know who I am? Guy Blod?!" The man pronounced *Guy* as *Gee* with a hard *G,* the French way, and *Blod* to rhyme with *cod,* as if Scandinavian. David had seen him scurrying around a few times but had never spoken with him. His reputation preceded him. He was the temperamental but lauded painter and sculptor, Carpathia's own choice for minister of the creative arts. Not only had he painted several of the so-called masterpieces that graced the great hall and the palace, but he had also sculpted many of the statues of world heroes in the courtyard and supervised the decorating of all GC buildings in New Babylon. He was considered a genius, but David—though admittedly no expert—considered his work laughably gaudy and decidedly profane. "The more shocking and anti-God the better" had to have been Blod's premise.

Part of David wanted Guy Blod to have to wait for a callback, but this was the wrong time to start puffing his anti-GC chest. He would take no guff from

Guy Blod, but he had to remain above suspicion and ingratiated to Fortunato. He dialed Blod as he settled behind his computer and began to program it to record directly from the morgue on a sound-activated basis.

As Blod answered, David noticed a list of messages on his computer. "This is Guy," he announced, "and you had better be David Hassid." He put the emphasis on the first syllable.

"It's *hah-SEED,*" David said.

"That should be easy enough to remember, Mr. Hayseed. Now where have you been?"

"Excuse me?"

"I've been trying to call you!"

"That's why I called you, sir."

"Don't get smart with me. Don't you know what's happened?"

"Nobody tells me anything, Mr. Blod." David chuckled. "Of course I know what's happened. Did it occur to you that that might have been why I was difficult to reach?"

"Well, I need stuff and I need it right now!"

"What do you need, sir?"

"Can you get it for me?"

"Depends on what it is, Blod."

"That's Mr. Blod to you, sweetie. I was told you could get anything."

"Well, almost."

"I have nowhere else to turn."

"I'll do my best."

"You'd better. Now come to my office."

"Excuse me?"

"Is this a bad connection? I said, come . . . to . . . my . . ."

"I heard you, sir, but I have many things on my plate tonight, as you can imagine, and I can't just—"

"You can do as you're told. Now get your tail over here, and I mean right now." *Click.*

David hung up and checked his messages. Most alarming was one from Rayford: "Our botanist reports the bird has flown. May need new real estate soonest. Signed, Geo. Logic"

David squinted at the screen for several seconds, wishing he could call someone at the safe house, or Rayford. He was tempted to put the satellites back in operation just long enough to do it, but he knew someone would discover that and he would have to answer for it. So Hattie was gone and the safe house was in jeopardy. He deleted the message and hacked his way into the mainframe database of abandoned, condemned, destroyed, and/or radioactive buildings in the Midwest. He looked at his watch when the phone rang. Six minutes had passed.

"What are you doing?"

"I'm sorry?"

"Is this David Hayseed?"

"This is Director Hassid, yes."

"Do you know who this is?"

"Yes! It sounds like Minister Blood. Haven't talked to you in ages. Good to hear from you again—"

"That's Blod, and did I or did I not tell you to get over here?"

"Is this multiple choice? I believe you did."

"Then why are you not here?"

"Let me guess. Because I'm here?"

"Agh! Listen here, you! Get over here this instant or—"

"Or what? You're going to tell my mom? I don't recall being subordinate to you, sir. Now if you have something you need me to procure for you, and you have clearance from the supreme commander—"

"A purchasing agent is not subordinate to a cabinet minister? Are you from Mars?"

"Actually Israel, sir."

"Would you stop calling me *sir*?"

"I thought *you* called *me,* sir."

"I mean quit calling me that!"

"What? *Sir?* I'm sorry, I thought you were male."

"You stay right where you are, Director. I'll be right over."

"That wasn't so hard, was it, Guy? I mean, it's you who wants to talk with me, not the other way 'round."

Click.

3

ROCKETING OVER THE Mediterranean in the middle of the night, Rayford had about a two-hour flight to Greece. For the first fifteen minutes he monitored the radio to be sure he was not being pursued or triangulated. But the radio was full of merely repetitious requests for more aircraft to help evacuate Jerusalem in light of the earthquake and the assassination. There were also countless calls for planes available to cart the mourning faithful to New Babylon for what was expected to become the largest viewing and funeral in history.

When the Gulfstream was far enough out over the water, local tower radio signals faded. Rayford tested that by trying to call his compatriots, to no avail. He switched off phone and radio, which left him in virtual silence at thirty-one thousand feet in a smooth-as-silk jet, most of the noise of the craft behind him.

Rayford suddenly felt the weight of life. Had it really been a mere three and a half years ago that he had enjoyed the prestige, the ease, and the material comfort of the life of a 747 captain for a major airline? He'd been no prize, he knew, as a husband and father, but the cliché was true: You never know what you've got till it's gone.

Life since the Rapture, or what most of the world called the disappearances, had been different as night and day from before—and not just spiritually. Rayford likened it to a death in the family. Not a day passed when he didn't awaken under the burden of the present, facing the cold fact that though he had now made his peace with God, he had been left behind.

It was as if the whole nation, indeed the whole world, lived in suspended mourning and grief. Everyone had lost someone, and not a second could pass when one was able to forget that. It was the fear of missing the school bus, losing your homework, forgetting your gym clothes, knowing you'd been caught cheating on a test, being called to the principal's office, being fired, going bankrupt, cheating on your wife—all rolled into one.

There had been snatches of joy, sure. Rayford lived for his daughter and was pleased with her choice of a husband. Having a grandchild, sobering though it was at this most awful time of history, fulfilled him in a way he hadn't known was possible. But even thinking about Chloe and Buck and little Kenny forced reality into Rayford's consciousness, and it stabbed.

With the Gulfstream on autopilot nearly six miles above the earth, Rayford stared into the cosmos. For an instant he felt disembodied, disconnected from the myriad events of the past forty-two months. Was it possible he'd, in essence, lived half a lifetime in that short span? He had experienced more emotion, fear, anger, frustration, and grief that day alone than in a year of his previous life. He wondered how much a man could take; literally, how much could a human body and mind endure?

How he longed to talk with Tsion! No one else had his trust and respect like the rabbi, only a few years older than he. Rayford couldn't confide in Chloe or Buck. He felt a kinship with T Delanty at the Palwaukee Airport, and they might become true friends. T was the kind of a man Rayford would listen to, even when T felt the need to rebuke him. But Tsion was the man of God. Tsion was one who loved and admired and respected Rayford unconditionally. Or did he? What would Tsion think if he knew what Rayford had done, starting with abandoning both Leah and Buck, but worse, wanting, intending, trying to murder the Antichrist, then perhaps doing so by accident?

Something about the altitude, the coolness he allowed in the cockpit, the tension he could postpone until overflying Greece, the comfort of the seat, and the artificial respite he enjoyed from his role as international fugitive, somehow conspired to awaken Rayford to what had become of him.

At first he resisted the intrusion of reality. Whatever comfort he had found in the buffering quality of life on the edge was stripped away when he allowed raw truth to invade. He told himself to stay with the program, to keep himself as well as his plane on autopilot, to let his emotions rule. What had happened to the scientific, logical Rayford, the one who had been left behind primarily due to that inability to accede to his intuitive side?

When he heard himself speaking aloud, he knew it was time to face the old Rayford—not the pre-Rapture man, but the new believer. He had wondered more than once during the past few months whether he was insane. Now talking to himself in the middle of the night in the middle of nowhere? Much as he hated the prospect, introspection was called for. How long had it been since he had indulged, at least honestly? He had questioned his sanity the past few months, but he seldom dwelt on it long enough to come to any conclusions. He had been driven by rage, by vengeance. He had grown irresponsible, unlike himself.

As Rayford allowed that to rattle in his brain, he realized that if he pursued this, turned it over in his mind like the marshmallows he had tried browning evenly as a child, it would not be himself he would face in the end. It would be God.

Rayford wasn't sure he wanted the blinding light of God in his mental mirror. In fact, he was fairly certain he didn't. But the hound of heaven was pursuing him, and Rayford would have to be thoroughly deluded or dishonest to turn and run now. He could cover his ears and hum as he did as a child when his mother tried to scold him. Or he could turn on the radio, pretending to see if the satellites had been realigned, or try the phone to test the global system. Maybe he could take the plane off autopilot and busy himself navigating the craft through trackless skies.

Down deep he could never live with himself if he resorted to those evasive tactics, so Rayford endured a shudder of fear. He was going to face this, to square his shoulders to God and take the heat. "All right," he said aloud. "What?"

+ + +

Buck straightened to relieve the aching in his joints from kneeling to check the lifeless women. Standing in the darkness of his old friend's sepulchral home, he knew he had never been cut out to be a hero. Brave he was not. This horror had brought a sob to his throat he could not subdue. Rayford was the hero; he was the one who had first come to the truth, then led the way for the rest of them. He was the one who had been rocked only temporarily by the loss of their first spiritual mentor but stood strong to lead.

What might Rayford have done in this same situation? Buck had no idea. He was still upset with the man, still puzzled over his mysterious self-assigned task that had left Buck and Leah on their own. Buck believed it would all be explained one day, that there would be some sort of rationale. It shouldn't have been so surprising that Rayford had grown testy and self-absorbed. Look what he had lost. Buck stubbornly left him on the pedestal of his mind as the leader of the Tribulation Force and as one who would act honorably in this situation.

And what would that entail? Finding Stefan, of course. Then challenging whoever was watching this house of death, fighting them, subduing them, or at least eluding them. Eluding didn't sound so heroic, but that was all Buck was inclined to do. Meanwhile, the most heroic he would get would be to finish the task inside—finding Stefan and Chaim, if they were there—and then running for his life.

The running part was the rub. It would be just like the GC—even decimated by population reduction, busy with the Gala, pressed into extraordinary service by the earthquake, and left in a shambles by the assassination—to dedicate an inordinate number of troops to this very house. It would not have surprised Buck an iota if the place was surrounded and they had all seen him enter, watched him find what he found, and now waited to capture him upon his departure.

On the other hand, perhaps they had come and pillaged and slaughtered and left the place a memorial husk.

Feeling ashamed, as if his wife and son could see him feeling his way in the dark, fighting a whimper like a little boy rather than tramping shoulders-wide through the place, Buck stepped on flesh. He half expected the victim to yelp or recoil. Buck knelt and felt a lifeless arm, tight and muscular. Was it possible the GC had suffered a casualty? They would not likely have left one of their own behind, not even a dead one.

Buck turned his back to the windows and switched on the flashlight again. The mess the enemy had left of Stefan made Buck's old nature surge to the fore. It was all he could do to keep from screaming obscenities at the GC and hoping any one of them was within earshot. Revolting as it was, Buck had to look one more time to believe what he saw. Stefan lay there, his face a mask of tranquility, eyes and mouth closed as if he were asleep. His arms and legs were in place, hands at his sides, but all four limbs had been severed, the legs at the hips, the arms at the shoulders. Clearly this had been done after he was dead, for there was no sign of struggle.

Buck dropped the light, and it rolled to a stop, luckily pointing away from the windows. His knees banged painfully on the floor, and when he threw his palms before him to break his fall, they splashed in thick, sticky blood. He knelt there on hands and knees, gasping, his belly tightening and releasing with his sobs and gasps. What kind of a weapon would it have taken and how long must the enemy have worked to saw through the tissue of a dead man until he was dismembered? And why? What was the message in that?

How would he ever tell Chaim? Or would his dear old friend be his next discovery?

* * *

At four o'clock in the afternoon Friday in Illinois, Tsion sat near the TV, trying to sort his emotions. He was still able to enjoy, if that was an appropriate word anymore, the ceaseless curiosity and antics of a one-year-old boy. Kenny cooed and talked and made noises as he explored, climbing, grabbing, touching, looking to his mother and to "Unca Zone" to see if he would get a smile or a no, depending on what he was doing.

But Kenny was Chloe's responsibility, and Tsion didn't want to miss a second of the constant coverage of the assassination. He expected news of Carpathia's resurrection and allowed himself only brief absences from the screen. He had moved his laptop to the living room, and his phone was close by. But his main interest was in Israel and New Babylon. It would not have surprised him if Carpathia was loaded onto his plane dead in Jerusalem and worshiped as he walked off under his own power in New Babylon.

Tsion was most upset at hearing nothing from other members of the Trib Force, and he and Chloe traded off trying to raise them, each of them, by phone. The last word they had heard from overseas was that Leah had not seen Hattie in Brussels, that she had told Buck Hattie was gone, and that she had not been able to communicate with Rayford. Since then, nothing.

Worried about the ramifications, Tsion and Chloe left most of the lights off, and they double-checked the phony chest freezer that actually served as an entrance to the underground shelter. Tsion normally left strategy and intrigue to the others and concentrated on his expertise, but he had an opinion on the security of the safe house. Maybe he was naïve, he told Chloe, but he believed that if Hattie were to give them away, it would be by accident. "She'll more likely be followed to us than send someone for us."

"Like she did with Ernie and Bo."

Tsion nodded.

"And who knows whom *they* might have told before they died?"

He shrugged. "If she was to give us up just by telling someone, she would have done it before she was imprisoned."

"If she *was* imprisoned," Chloe said. And suddenly she was fighting tears.

"What is it, Chloe?" Tsion asked. "Worried about Cameron, of course?"

She nodded, then shook her head. "Not only that," she said. "Tsion, can I talk with you?"

"Need you ask?"

"But, I mean, I know you don't want to miss anything on TV."

"I won't. Talk to me."

Tsion was alarmed at how much it took for Chloe to articulate her thoughts. They had always been able to talk, but she had never been extremely self-revelatory. "You know I will keep your confidences," he said. "Consider it clergy-parishioner privilege."

Even that did not elicit a smile. But she managed to shock him. "Maybe I've been watching too much TV," she said.

"Such as?"

"Those staged rallies, where everyone worships Carpathia."

"I know. They're disgusting. They refer to him as 'Your Worship' and the like."

"It's worse than that, Tsion," she said. "Have you seen the clips where the children are brought to him? I mean, we all know there's not a child among them as old as three years, but they're paraded before him in their little GC outfits, saluting over their hearts with every step, singing praise songs to him. It's awful!"

Tsion agreed. Day care workers and parents dressed the kids alike, and cute little boys and girls brought flowers and were taught to bow and wave and salute and sing to Carpathia. "Did you see the worst of it?" he asked.

Chloe nodded miserably. "The prayer, you mean?"

"That's what I mean. I was afraid of lightning."

Tsion shuddered, remembering the knockoff of the Lord's Prayer taught to groups of children barely old enough to speak. It had begun, "Our Father in New Babylon, Carpathia be your name. Your kingdom come. Your will be done. . . ." Tsion had been so disgusted that he turned it off. Chloe, apparently, had watched the whole debacle.

"I've been studying," she said.

"Good," Tsion said. "I hope so. We can never know enough—"

"Not the way you think," she said. "I've been studying death."

Tsion narrowed his eyes. "I'm listening."

"I will not allow myself or my baby to fall into the hands of the enemy."

"What are you saying?"

"I'm saying just what you're afraid I'm saying, Tsion."

"Have you told Cameron?"

"You promised you would keep my confidence!"

"And I will. I'm asking, have *you* told him your plans?"

"I have no plans. I'm just studying."

"But you will soon have a plan, because it is clear you have made up your mind. You said, 'I will not . . . ,' and that evidences a course of action. You're saying that if we should be found out, if the GC should capture us—"

"I will not allow Kenny or me to fall into their hands."

"And how will you ensure this?"

"I would rather we were dead."

"You would kill yourself."

"I would. And I would commit infanticide."

She said this with such chilling conviction that Tsion hesitated, praying silently for wisdom. "Is this a sign of faith, or lack of faith?" he said finally.

"I don't know, but I can't imagine God would want me or my baby in that situation."

"You think he wants you in *this* situation? He is not willing that any should perish. He would that you would have been ready to go the first time. He—"

"I know, Tsion. I know, all right? I'm just saying—"

"Forgive me for interrupting, but I know what you're saying. I just don't believe you are being honest with yourself."

"I couldn't be *more* honest! I would kill myself and commit inf—"

"There you go again."

"What?"

"Buffering your conviction with easy words. You're no better than the abortionists who refer to their unborn babies as embryos or fetuses or pregnancies so they can 'eliminate' them or 'terminate' them rather than kill them."

"What? I said I would com—"

"Yes, that's what you said. You didn't say what you mean. Tell me."

"I told you, Tsion! Why are you doing this?"

"Tell me, Chloe. Tell me what you are going to do to—" He hesitated, not wanting to alert Kenny they were talking about him. "Tell me what you're going to do to this little one, because obviously, you have to do it to him first if it's going to get done. Because if you kill yourself, none of the rest of us will do this job for you."

"I told you what I would do to him."

"Say it in plain words."

"That I will kill him before I let the GC have him? I will."

"Will what?"

"Kill him."

"Put it in a sentence."

"I will. I will . . . kill . . . my own baby."

"Baby!" Kenny exulted, running to her. She reached for him, sobbing.

Quietly, Tsion said, "How will you do this?"

"That's what I'm studying," she managed over Kenny's shoulders. He hugged her tight and scampered away.

"And then you will kill yourself, why?"

"Because I cannot live without him."

"Then it follows that Cameron would be justified in killing himself."

She bit her lip and shook her head. "The world needs him."

"The world needs you, Chloe. Think of the co-op, the international—"

"I can't think anymore," she said. "I want done with this! I want it over! I don't know what we were thinking, bringing a child into this world. . . ."

"That child has brought so much joy to this house—" Tsion began.

"—that I could not do him the disservice of letting him fall into GC hands."

Tsion sat back, glancing at the TV. "So the GC comes, you kill the baby, kill yourself, Cameron and your father kill themselves . . . when does it end?"

"They wouldn't. They couldn't."

"You can't. And you won't."

"I thought I could talk to you, Tsion."

"You expected what, that I would condone this?"

"That you would be sympathetic, at least."

"I am that, at the very least," he said. "Neither do I want to live without you and the little one. You know what comes next."

"Oh, Tsion, you would not deprive your global church of yourself."

He sat back and put his hands on his knees. "Yet you would deprive *me* of *your*self. You must not care for me as much as I care for you, or as much as I thought you did."

Chloe sighed and looked to the ceiling. "You're not helping," she said in mock exasperation.

"I'm trying," he said.

"I know. And I appreciate it."

Tsion asked her to pray with him for their loved ones. She knelt on the floor next to the couch, holding his hand, and soon after they began, Tsion peeked at a sound and saw Kenny kneeling next to his mother, hands folded, fingers entwined, eyes closed.

* * *

David found Guy Blod more outrageous and flamboyant in person. He showed up with a small entourage of similarly huffy and put-out men in their late thirties. Despite their differences in nationality, they could have been quints from the way they dressed and acted. David offered only Guy a chair across from his desk.

"This is what you call hospitality?" Guy said. "There are six of us, hello."

"My apologies," David said. "I was under the impression it was the responsibility of the *guest* to inform the *host* when uninvited people were coming."

Guy waved him off, and his sycophants glumly stood behind him with arms crossed. "The supreme commander has commissioned me to do a sort of bronzy iron thingie of Nicolae. And I have to do it fast, so can you get me the materials?"

They were interrupted by an urgent knock on the door. A woman in her late sixties, blue-haired, short, and stocky, poked her head in. "Miss Ivins," David said. "May I help you?"

"Excuse me," Guy said, "but we're in conference here."

David stood. "It's all right, Miss Ivins. You know Guy."

"Of course," she said, nodding sadly.

"And Guy, you know Vivian is—"

"Yes, the potentate's only living relative. I'm sorry for your loss, ma'am, but we—"

"How may I help you, ma'am?" David said.

"I'm looking for crowd control volunteers," she said. "The masses are already showing up from all over the world, and—"

"It's after midnight!" Guy said. "Don't they know the funeral isn't for at least two days? What are we supposed to do with them all?"

"Commander Fortunato is asking for any personnel below director level to—"

"That leaves me out, Vivian!" Guy said. "And Hayseed here too, unfortunately."

"How about your assistants, Guy?" David suggested.

"I need every last one of them for this project! Viv, surely you don't expect—"

"I'm aware of your assignment, Guy," Viv Ivins said, but she pronounced his name in the Western style, and he quickly corrected her. She ignored him. "I'm on assignment too. If either of you gentlemen could spread the word among your people, the administration would be grateful."

David returned to his seat and tapped out the notice to be broadcast to his workers' e-mail addresses as Miss Ivins backed out and shut the door.

"Aren't we efficient?" Guy said.

"We try," David said.

"I know what her assignment is," Guy said. "Have you heard?"

"I have enough trouble keeping up with my own."

David had acted uninterested enough that Guy turned to his own people and whispered, "That regional numbering thing." David was dying of curiosity but unwilling to admit it. Guy spun in his chair to face David. "Now, where were we?"

"I was about to check my catalog file for bronze and iron thingie suppliers, and you were going to be a bit more specific."

"OK, I'm gonna need a computer program that allows me to figure out how to do this. I'm going to be supplied by the coroner with a life-size cast of Carpathia's body—how ghastly—and I need to quadruple that in size. That means four times."

"Yeah, I recall arithmetic, Guy."

"I'm just trying to help. Truce?"

"Truce?"

"Start over, no hassles?"

"Whatever, Guy."

"Be nice."

"I'm trying."

"Anyhoo, I wanna make this like twenty-four-foot replica of Carpathia out of pretty much bronze, I think, but I want it to come out in a sort of ebony finish with a texture of iron. Ebony is black."

"I remember crayons too, Guy."

"Sor-*ry,* David! You don't want *any* help!"

"I'm going to need it if I'm to find you this material quickly. What do you think you need and how fast do you need it?"

Guy leaned forward. "Now we're getting somewhere. I want the thing to be hollow with about a quarter-inch to three-eighths-inch shell, but it has to be strong enough and balanced enough to stand straight without support, just like Nicolae would if he were that tall."

David shrugged. "So you make him to scale and cheat on the shoes if you have to, since an inanimate object won't make the unconscious balancing maneuvers to stay standing."

"Shoes!?"

"What, your statue will be barefoot?"

Guy giggled and shared the mirth with his clones. "Oh, David," he said, lifting his feet and spinning in his chair. "My statue will be *au naturel.*"

David made a face. "Please tell me you're joking!"

"Not on your life. Did you think the mortician was going to make a body cast of him in his suit?"

"Why not?"

Guy fluttered the air with his fingers and said, "Forget it, forget it, you wouldn't understand. You obviously have some hang-up about the human form and can't appreciate the beauty. You just—"

"Guy, I'm assuming this statue is to maintain a prominent place within the palace—"

"Within the palace? Dear boy! This will be THE *objet d'art* of history, my *pièce de résistance.* It shall stand in the palace courtyard not thirty feet from where the potentate lies in state."

"So the whole world will see it."

"In all its glory."

"And it's *your* masterpiece."

Guy nodded, appearing unable to contain his glee.

"So if I took a picture of something and then traced it, I could be an artist too?"

Guy looked disgusted. "You're about as far from an artist as I am from—"

"But what of this reproduction of a dead man's bare body is your work?"

"Are you just insulting me, or is that a sincere question?"

"Call it sincere. I really want to know."

"The concept! I con*ceived* it, David! I will supervise the construction. I will do the finish work on the face, leaving the eyes hollow. I was asked to create a huge statue to represent the greatest man who ever lived, and this came to me as if from God himself."

"You're on speaking terms with God?"

"It's just an expression, Hayseed. It's from my muse. Who can explain it? It's what I blame my genius on, the one thing that keeps me from unbearable ego. Can you imagine how embarrassing it is to be lauded for everything your hands create? I mean, I'm not complaining, but the attention becomes overwhelming. The muse is my foil. I am as overwhelmed at my gift—the gift from the muse, you see—as anyone else. I enjoy it as the masses do."

"You do."

"Yes, I do. And I can't wait to get to this one. I'm assuming I would have access to the GC foundry, as we won't have time to have this done off-site."

David shut one eye. "The foundry is on three shifts, seven days a week. We could have this more cheaply done in Asia, where—"

"Help me stay civil here, David, as it is clearly my fault for not clarifying. Supreme Commander Fortunato—who, in case you couldn't figure this out on your own, will likely be the new potentate once Carpathia is entombed—wants this monument in place no later than at dawn Sunday."

Guy stared at David, as if to let that sink in. It almost didn't. David looked at his watch. It was crowding 1:00 a.m. Saturday, Carpathia Standard Time. "I don't see it," he said, "but I don't imagine you can be dissuaded."

"Why, I believe we have begun to connect!"

Anything but that, David thought.

"Zhizaki," Guy said, "if you please."

With a flourish, an Asian with two-inch green nails produced a computer-generated schedule. It called for the procuring of materials and determining the manufacturing site by noon Saturday, concurrent with computer design by the artist and cast making by the mortician. By midnight Saturday, the foundry was to create a cast to the artist's specifications, produce the shell, and deliver it to the back of the palace courtyard. There Guy and his staff would do the finish work until the product was ready for positioning in view of the mourners just before dawn Sunday.

"That's more than ambitious, Guy," David said. "It's audacious."

"Audacious," Guy said with a faraway look. "Now there's an epitaph."

"You'll have to work with materials already on hand," David said.

"I assumed that. But we'll need you to override current projects, get this at the top of the list, and let me in there to make sure the consistency and the color are right."

"You'll have to wear protective clothing and a hard hat," David said.

Guy looked at his mates. "I love new clothes."

4

IT WAS TO RAYFORD'S advantage that the Global Community had rendered the whole of Greece virtually invisible. In realigning the world into ten regions with sub-potentates—which Tsion Ben-Judah insisted were "kingdoms with kings"—the United Holy Land States had appropriated Greece. Her potentate had lobbied for independence, as most countries' leaders had, then pleaded for membership as one of the United European States.

Carpathia himself had mollified the Greeks with a personal visit and several appearances, during which he took full responsibility for their inclusion in "his" region. Lukas (Laslos) Miklos had once regaled Rayford with a dead-on imitation of the potentate's Eastern-flavored Greek as he flattered the nation into compliance.

"You are a deeply religious people," Carpathia had told them, "with a rich place in the histories of many cherished belief systems. You are nearly as close to the cradle of civilization as you are to the United European States, so I personally argued for your inclusion as a Holy Land state. My own origins are not that far north of you. The line of demarcation that puts both my homeland and my current residence in the same region naturally includes Greece as well. I welcome you to 'my' region and trust you will enjoy the benefits from this area's housing the new world capital."

That had won over the majority of Greeks. One huge benefit to tribulation saints was that Greece seemed above suspicion as a spring of rebellion. The exploding church there went underground immediately, worried that it might otherwise draw the attention of the GC. Dr. Ben-Judah corresponded with nearly a thousand Greek evangelists he had identified as likely part of the prophesied 144,000 witnesses. These were Messianic Jews, many of whom had attended the great conference of witnesses in Israel and had returned to their homeland to win tens of thousands of converts to Christ.

Mr. and Mrs. Miklos's own local body of underground believers had mushroomed so that the original assembly had split many times and now met as more than a hundred "small groups" that weren't really so small. The new corporate church was too large to ever meet together without jeopardizing its clandestine identity. The witness-leaders of each faction met monthly for training and mutual encouragement, and of course the entire body counted itself part of the new worldwide band of believers, with Tsion Ben-Judah as its *de facto* cyberspace pastor-teacher.

The covert nature of the Greek church, while clearly not impeding its evangelistic efforts, served to keep from waving a red flag before the GC. Buck Williams's private investigations for his cybermagazine, *The Truth,* found—with the help of ultimate hacker David Hassid—that Greece was all but ignored by GC counterintelligence, security, and peacekeeping forces. The country was low maintenance. Most of the forces assigned there had been redeployed into Israel for the Gala and New Babylon for its aftermath.

Thus it was not a surprise to Rayford to find that the tiny airport in Ptolemaïs was not only closed and unmanned but also dark. He had neither the light power nor the confidence to land on an unlit runway without an instrument approach. He overflew the airfield a few times, not wanting to draw attention to himself, then headed south about twenty-five miles to Kozani and its larger airport. It too was closed, but one runway remained lit for emergencies and private cargo carriers. Rayford watched a wide-body international delivery craft put down, waited until it had taxied toward the colossal commercial hangars, then set his instruments for landing.

He didn't know how he would get hold of Laslos or find a ride to Ptolemaïs. Perhaps he would be close enough to use his phone without relying on satellite technology. He hated to bother the Mikloses at this hour, but he'd done it before. They always understood. In fact, it seemed they loved the intrigue of the underground, Mrs. Miklos as much as Lukas.

Rayford was strangely calm as he descended into Kozani. He believed he had made intimate contact with God during the flight, had communicated more directly, and felt more personally connected to heaven than he had in ages. This had come when Rayford finally heeded the Scripture "Be still, and know that I am God." After months of rationalizing, self-defense, and taking matters into his own hands, he had finally given up and sought God.

His first overwhelming emotion was shame. God had entrusted him, a brand-new believer, with a scope of leadership. God had used the gifts he had bestowed on Rayford to direct the little band of believers that had become known as the Tribulation Force.

Smarter people were in the Force, Rayford knew, including his own daughter and son-in-law. And where on earth was a more brilliant mind than that of Tsion Ben-Judah? And yet they all naturally looked to Rayford for leadership. He had not sought it, nor did he hoard it. But he had been willing. And as the Force grew, so did his responsibility. But though his capacity could have expanded with the scope of his charge, the illogical had invaded. The man who had prided himself on his pragmatism found himself living by his emotions.

At first, becoming attuned to his emotions had been revelatory. It had allowed him to care deeply for his daughter, to really grieve over the loss of his wife and son, and to understand how much he had loved them. It had allowed him to see himself for who he was, to understand his need for forgiveness, to come to Christ.

But, understandably, Rayford had found it difficult to balance his emotion and his intellect. No one could argue that he had been through more than his share of loss and trauma in three and a half years. But the emotion necessary to round him out as a new believer somehow overrode the levelheaded temperament that made him a natural leader. Never one for psychobabble, when Rayford opened himself to God that night, in his spirit he saw his failure for what it was: sin.

He had become selfish, angry, vengeful. He had tried to take God's place as defender and protector of the Tribulation Force. In the process, he had left them more vulnerable than ever to danger. As Rayford dared peek at himself in that spiritual mirror, he hated what he saw. Here was a man who had been wholly grateful to God for his forgiveness and love and salvation, now living as a maverick. He still called himself a believer. But what had happened to his dependence upon God, upon the counsel of his friends and relatives and spiritual mentors? What had happened to his love for the Bible and prayer, and for the guidance he had once found there?

As God seemed to shine the light of truth into his soul, Rayford pleaded for forgiveness, for restoration. Had his rage been sin? No, that didn't compute. The Scriptures counseled, "Be angry, and do not sin," so the anger itself was not wrong. What he did as a result of it clearly was. He had become consumed by rage and had allowed it to interfere with his relationship to God and to those he loved.

Rayford had become isolated, living out his private ambitions. He had fought to see through his tears as God showed him his very self in its rawest state. "I'll understand," he prayed, "if I have disqualified myself from any role with the Trib Force," but God did not seem to confirm that. All Rayford felt was an overwhelming hunger and thirst for the Bible and for instruction. He wanted to pray like this from now on, to constantly be in touch with God as he had been when he first became a believer. What that meant to his role as head of the Tribulation Force, he didn't know. More important was getting back to the basics, getting back to God.

Rayford found the cargo plane crew busy with their own work as he taxied a quarter of a mile north to park the Gulfstream. They barely looked up as he hurried past on foot, his bag slung over his shoulder as if he were headed somewhere specific. As soon as he emerged from the airfield's gated entrance and found a dark spot between road lamps, he phoned the Mikloses' home. Mrs. Miklos answered on the first ring.

"This is your friend from America," he said, and she immediately switched from Greek to her very limited English.

"Say code so I know," she said.

Code? He didn't remember any code. Maybe that was something among the local believers. "Jesus is the Christ, the Messiah," he said.

"That not code," she said, "but I know voice. Saw on television."

"You did? Me?"

"Yes. Did you shoot Carpathia?"

Rayford's mouth went dry. So the cameras had caught him. "No!" he said. "At least I don't think so. I didn't mean to. What are they saying?"

"Fingerprints," she said. "On gun."

Rayford shook his head. He had been so certain that if he shot Carpathia he would be immediately captured or killed that he had not even worried about fingerprints. He hadn't considered escaping. Some criminal *he* was! Why didn't he think to wipe the handle on his robe before dropping the weapon?

"Are they showing my face?" he asked.

"Yes."

He told her where he was and asked if Laslos was there.

"No. With our shepherd. Praying for you."

"I don't want to compromise you," he said. "I'll just fly on to America."

"Don't know *compromise,*" she said.

"Ah, sorry. Give you away. Get you in trouble. Be seen with you."

"Laslos would not leave you alone," she said. "I tell him. He call you."

Rayford hated the idea of jeopardizing Greek believers, but Laslos's English was better than his wife's, so perhaps Rayford would have an easier time dissuading him from becoming involved. He gave her the number and settled in to wait for the call in the shadows of the shrubbery off the makeshift road that led north out of the airport.

* * *

Upstairs in Rosenzweig's massive house, Buck used the flashlight sparingly as he searched for any sign of Chaim. From outside he heard noises in the underbrush that paralyzed him. He held his breath and crept to the window, peering down while desperate to stay out of sight. Someone signaled a few others, and their shapes moved about in the darkness. He couldn't imagine a scenario that would allow him to escape until it played out before his eyes.

Suddenly all GC Peacekeeping Forces were rallied for one purpose—to find a fugitive. And when the multi-language announcement came over rolling bullhorns, it was clear whom they were looking for.

"Attention, citizens and all Global Community personnel!" came the announcements. "Be on the lookout for American Rayford Steele, former GC employee wanted in connection with the conspiracy to assassinate Potentate Nicolae Carpathia. May be in disguise. May be armed. Considered dangerous. Qualified pilot. Any information about his whereabouts . . ."

Rayford? Conspiracy? Now the GC was grasping at straws.

From below, the GC Peacekeepers appeared to be arguing whether one or more should stay. Finally their leader barked at them and waved that they should follow. Buck waited a few minutes, then checked every window, staring into the night and listening for any enemy. He saw and heard nothing, but he knew time was his greatest adversary now.

He saved Chaim's workshop till last. It had no windows, so when he threw open the door, he didn't hesitate to shine the flashlight all about. It was empty, but it also looked different from when last he'd seen it. Chaim had shown him his handiwork, but now there was no evidence of that. The place was spotless. Even the vises had been unfastened from the workbenches and stored. The floor was clean, tools hung, counters spotless. It almost looked the way it would if someone were moving or had another function in mind for the room.

Buck backed out and closed the door. Something niggled at his mind, despite the taste of fear and revulsion in his throat. He tucked the flashlight into his pocket and carefully made his way to the front door. The casing had been shattered. Though he was sure the GC had done this and abandoned the place, Buck felt safer leaving the way he had come. As he moved toward the back door, he wondered who had cleaned Chaim's workshop for him. Had he done it himself before the stroke, or had the staff done it after it became clear he would be unable to engage in his hobby?

Buck felt his way through the sparse landscaping in the back and stopped frequently to listen for footsteps or breathing over the sirens and announcements from blocks away. He stayed out of the light and in the middle of earthquake rubble as much as he could until he found an area where the streetlamps were out.

He had to know for sure about Chaim before he could even think about trying to rendezvous with Rayford or Leah. But where should he start? Not that long ago, Buck would have tried to find him through Jacov, Hannelore, her mother, or Stefan. As he broke into a jog, heading for who knew where, tears dripped from his face.

\+ + +

Late Friday afternoon in Illinois, Chloe had been feeding Kenny in the other room when Rayford's photo—the one from his former GC ID—came on television. Tsion blanched and bolted for the set to turn it down and listen from up close. Tsion had been praying for Rayford, worried about him. When Rayford and Leah and Buck had left, Tsion thought he knew their various assignments and missions, and he feared playing mere shuttle pilot would not be enough for Rayford. He had been in the middle of so much action but was now, even more than the rest, merely a fugitive, having to stay out of sight.

Now what would he do? The news implied he had fired the weapon that may have killed Carpathia. How could one do that in such a crowd and escape? Never had Tsion so wanted to talk to Rayford, and never had he felt such a burden to pray for a man.

That compulsion was nothing new. It struck Tsion that he had spent more time in concerted prayer for Rayford than for any other individual. It was obvious why Rayford needed prayer now, of course, but when Tsion closed his eyes and covered them with a hand, he felt uncomfortable. He knew he would have to tell Chloe soon that her father was a suspect in the assassination—or the conspiracy, as the TV anchors called it—but that was not what made him fidgety. It seemed he was not in the proper posture to pray, and all he could make of that was that perhaps Rayford needed real intercession.

Tsion had studied the discipline of intercession, largely a Protestant tradition from the fundamentalist and the Pentecostal cultures. Those steeped in it went beyond mere praying for someone as an act of interceding for them; they believed true intercession involved deep empathy and that a person thus praying must not enter into the practice unless willing to literally trade places with the needy person.

Tsion mentally examined his own willingness to truly intercede for Rayford. It was mere exercise. He could not trade places with Rayford and become a suspect in the murder of the Antichrist. But he could affect that posture in his mind; he could express his willingness to God to take that burden, literally possible or not.

Yet even that did not assuage Tsion's discomfort. He tried dropping to one knee, bowing his head lower, then slipping to both knees, then turning to lay his arms on the seat of the couch and rest his head on his hands. He worried that Chloe would not understand if she saw him this way, suddenly not watching TV obsessively as he had since the assassination, but in a posture of total contrition—something foreign to his nature. He often prayed this way in private, of course, but Chloe would see this "showing" of humility so aberrational that she would likely feel obligated to ask if he was all right.

But these concerns were quickly overridden by Tsion's spiritual longings. He felt such deep compassion and pity for Rayford that he moaned involuntarily and felt himself sliding from the couch until his palms were flat on the floor.

His head now pressing against the front of the couch, his body facing away from the near silent TV, he groaned and wept as he prayed silently for Rayford. Having not come from a tradition comfortable with unusual manifestations, Tsion was startled by a sudden lack of equilibrium. In his mind's eye his focus had suddenly shifted from Rayford and his troubles to the majesty of God himself. Tsion at once felt unworthy and ashamed and impure, as if in the very presence of the Lord.

Tsion knew that praying was figuratively boldly approaching the throne, but he had never felt such a physical proximity to the creator God. Knees sliding back, palms forward, he lay prostrate, his forehead pressing into the musty carpet, nose mashed flat.

But even that did not alleviate his light-headedness. Tsion felt disembodied, as if the present were giving way. He was only vaguely aware of where he was, of the quiet drone of the television, of Chloe cooing and Kenny giggling as she urged him to eat.

"Tsion?"

He did not respond, not immediately aware he was even conscious. Was this a dream?

"Tsion?"

The voice was feminine.

"Should I try the phone again?"

He opened his eyes, suddenly aware of the smell of the old carpet and the sting of tears.

"Hm?" he managed, throat constricted, voice thick.

Footsteps. "I was wondering, should I try calling—Tsion! Are you all right?"

He slowly pulled himself up. "I'm fine, dear. Very tired all of a sudden."

"You have a right to be! Get some rest. Take a nap. I'll wake you if anything breaks. I won't let you miss anything."

Tsion sat on the edge of the couch, shoulders slumped, hands entwined between his knees. "I would be grateful," he said. He nodded toward the other room. "Is he all right for a minute?"

She nodded.

"You'd better sit down," he said.

Chloe looked stricken. "Was there news? Is Buck all right?"

"Nothing from Buck or Leah," he said, and she seemed to finally exhale. "But you need to know about your father. . . ."

* * *

David tried e-mailing Viv Ivins a list of those in his department who might be available for double duty over the next few days, but the message bounced back undeliverable. He would go past her office on the way to the hangar anyway, so he printed out the message and took it with him.

On the way he received a call from the foundry foreman. "You know what you're asking, don't you?" the man said.

"Of course, Hans," David said. "You have to know this didn't originate with me."

"Unless it's from Fortunato himself, I don't see how we can be expected—"

"It is."

"—to comply. I mean, this is way too—it is?"

"It is."

"'Nough said."

David slipped the printout into the slot on Viv Ivins's door, but it was not shut all the way and swung open. The small, dark office immediately brightened as the motion-sensitive light came on. The gossip around the palace was that on occasion, Carpathia's alleged aunt on his mother's side dozed for so long at her desk that her office went dark. If something woke her or caused her to move in her sleep, the lights came back on, and she resumed working as if nothing were awry.

David made sure she wasn't in there dozing, then reached to shut the door. But something on her desk caught his eye. She had laid out a map of the world, boundaries between the ten regions clearly marked. It was nothing he hadn't seen before, except that this was an old map, one drawn when the ten regions were members of the newly expanded United Nations Security Council. When Carpathia had renamed the one-world government the Global Community, he had also slightly renamed the ten regions. For instance, the United States of North America became the United North American States. Viv Ivins had not only handwritten these adjustments, but she had also added numbers in parentheses after each name.

David felt conspicuous and nosy, but who knew what significance this might hold for the Trib Force, the Judah-ites, tribulation saints around the world? He concocted his alibi as he moved toward the desk. If Viv were to return and catch him studying her map, he would simply tell the truth about the door tripping the light and the map catching his eye. How he would explain his scribbling the numbers, he did not know.

With one last look out her office window, David grabbed a business card from his wallet and wrote furiously in tiny script as he bent over Viv's map.

The United Holy Land States (216)*
The United Russian States (72)
The United Indian States (42)
The United Asian States (30)
The United Pacific States (18)
The United North American States (-6)
The United South American States (0)
The United Great Britain States (2)
The United European States (6)
The United African States (7)

David traced the asterisk after "The United Holy Land States" to the bottom of the map, where Viv, or someone, had noted in faint, tiny pencil marks "aka The United Carpathian States."

That was a new one. David had never heard another moniker for the Holy Land States. As he was straightening to leave he saw more pencil writing that appeared to have been erased. He bent close and squinted but needed more light. Dare he turn on Viv's desk lamp?

No. Rather, he held the whole map up to the ceiling light, knowing he would simply have to confess to pathological curiosity, if necessary. He only hoped that Viv, like nearly everyone else in the compound, was watching Carpathia's body being transported from the Phoenix 216 to the morgue. He was glad to miss that, knowing that most would hold hands or hats over their hearts, and he wasn't prepared to do that even as a ruse.

With the overhead light shining brightly through the map, David was barely able to make out the erasures. It appeared someone had written "Only caveat: H. L. highest, N. A. lowest."

David shook his head as he carefully replaced the map and headed out.

Viv Ivins was coming toward him. "Oh, David," she said, "I wish you could have seen the spontaneous outpouring of emotion . . ."

"I'm sure there'll be a lot of that over the next few days."

"But to see the workers, the soldiers, everybody . . . ah, it was moving. The salutes, the tears. Oh! Did I leave my light on?"

David explained the door tripping the motion sensor.

"And your list is in the door?"

He nodded and his phone rang, startling him so that he nearly left his feet.

"Carry on," Viv said.

It was Mac. David talked as he walked. "Half thought you'd be here to greet us," Mac said. "Corporal Christopher waited on the evidence until the pallbearers got the body out of here."

"The evidence?"

"I don't think I've ever seen pallbearers in dress unies carrying a big ol' wood crate like it was a polished mahogany casket. Where were you?"

"On my way, but what'd you say about evidence?"

"Annie's off-loading it now. Couple of huge plastic trash bags full of pieces of the lectern. And another crate with apparently the whole fabric backdrop off the stage. Moon wouldn't let us leave Jerusalem without it. You heard about the weapon, right?"

"'Course. And our friend."

"Funny thing, though, David."

"Yeah?"

"I'd better save this for in person."

\+ + +

"Rayford here."

"Mr. Steele!" came the easily recognized voice of Lukas Miklos. "Where are you?"

Rayford told him.

"Stay in the shadows but walk three kilometers north. We will pick you up north of the three-kilometer marker. When you see a white four-door slow and leave the road, run to us. If there is any traffic, we may pass and come back, but when we pull off, do not hesitate."

"We?"

"Our undershepherd and me."

"Laslos, I don't want you two to risk—"

"Nonsense! Do you have an alias and appropriate papers?"

"I do."

"Good. How fast can you walk?"

"How's the terrain?"

"Not the best, but don't get near the road until we get there."

"I'm starting now."

"Mr. Steele, we feel just like the prayer-meeting people from the New Testament, praying for Peter while he knocked on their door."

"Yeah," Rayford said. "Only he was coming *from* prison."

* * *

Exhausted, Buck sat behind a concrete wall, built decades before to protect Israel from shrapnel and mortar from nearby enemies. He was several blocks from the main drag, but close enough to hear the ever-present sirens and see the emergency lights bouncing off the low-riding clouds in the wee hours.

Think, think, think, he told himself. He didn't want to leave Israel without knowing where Chaim was. Buck knew of no other people Chaim might flee to or with if he had somehow survived. If Chaim had defied the odds, he would be looking for Buck as fervently as Buck was looking for him. They could not meet at the obvious places: Buck's hostel, Chaim's house, Jacov's apartment, Stefan's place. What would make sense to both of them?

Buck had never believed in extrasensory perception, but he sure wished there was something to it now. He wished he could sense whether the old man was all right, and if so, that he was trying to somehow communicate with Buck right then. As a believer, Buck was certain that clairvoyance was hogwash. But he had heard credible stories of people, particularly Christians, who somehow knew things supernaturally. Surely it wasn't beyond God's ability to perform such miracles, especially now.

Buck needed a miracle, but his faith was weak. He knew it shouldn't be. He had seen enough from God in three and a half years that he should never again doubt for an instant. What held him up now was that he was dead sure he didn't deserve a miracle. Weren't there bigger, more important things for God to worry about? People were dying, injured, lost. And there was the great supernatural battle between good and evil that Tsion wrote so much about, the conflict of the ages that had spilled out of heaven and now plagued the earth.

"I'm sorry to even ask," Buck prayed, "but at least calm me down, give me a clear mind just long enough to figure this. If Chaim is alive, let us run into each other or both think of a meeting place that makes sense."

Buck felt foolish, stupid, petty. Finding Chaim was noble, but involving God in such a trivial matter seemed, well, rude. He stood and felt the aches. He clenched his fists and grimaced. *Relax! Get hold of yourself! Think!*

But somehow he knew that was no way to open the mind. He had to really relax, and berating himself for being frantic would have the opposite effect. But how could he calm himself at a time like this, when it was all he could do to catch his breath and will his pulse to decelerate?

Maybe *that* was an appropriate request of God, a miracle enough in itself.

Buck sat back down, confident he was hidden and alone. He breathed deeply and exhaled slowly, shaking out his hands and stretching his legs. He laid his head back and felt the concrete wall against his hair and scalp. He let his head roll from side to side. His breathing became slower and more even; his pulse began to subside ever so slowly. He tucked his chin to his chest and tried to clear his mind.

The only way to do that was to pray for his comrades one by one, starting with his own wife and son, his father-in-law, and all the rest of the brothers and sisters who came to mind. He thanked God for friends now in heaven, including those whose bodies he had just discovered.

And almost before he knew it, he had calmed as much as a man could in that situation. *Thank you, Lord. Now what location would make sense? Where have Chaim and I been together that we would both think of?*

He pictured them at Teddy Kolleck Stadium, but that was too public, too open. Neither could risk it.

And then it came to him.

5

CHLOE FELL SILENT at the news. Tsion might have predicted tears, disbelief, railing against someone other than her father. She just sat, shaking her head.

Difficult as it had been to inform her, Tsion was oddly still reeling from what to him had felt almost like an out-of-body experience while praying. He had heard of those and pooh-poohed them as fabrications or drug-induced hallucinations on deathbeds. But this sensation, so real and dramatic that it had temporarily derailed his empathy and intercession on Rayford's behalf, was something else again. He had long advocated checking experience against Scripture and not the other way around. He would, he realized, have to remind himself of that frequently until the glow—which seemed too positive a word for the disturbing residue of the incident—receded into memory. A verse from the Old Testament teased his consciousness, and his mind wandered from the troubled young woman before him.

As Chloe had not yet responded, Tsion said, "Excuse me a moment, please," and brought his whole Bible text up onto his laptop screen. A few seconds later he clicked on Joel 2. He silently read verses 28 through 32, finding that he had been led to a passage that both illuminated his experience and might provide some balm to her as well.

I will pour out My Spirit on all flesh;
Your sons and your daughters shall prophesy,
Your old men shall dream dreams,
Your young men shall see visions.
And also on My menservants and on My maidservants
I will pour out My Spirit in those days.
And I will show wonders in the heavens and in the earth:
Blood and fire and pillars of smoke.
The sun shall be turned into darkness,
And the moon into blood,
Before the coming of the great and awesome day of the Lord.

And it shall come to pass
That whoever calls on the name of the Lord
Shall be saved.
For in Mount Zion and in Jerusalem there shall
be deliverance,
As the Lord has said,
Among the remnant whom the Lord calls.

Tsion looked up with a start when Chloe spoke at last. He detected no trauma in her voice, nothing that would have given away that she had just learned that her father was the most wanted fugitive in the world—except for her words themselves. "I should have seen it coming," she said. "He tried to divert me to Hattie, which wasn't hard. She never had any qualms about saying she wanted to kill Carpathia."

Tsion cleared his throat. "Why would he do it, knowing the death wound is only temporary anyway? Is your father capable of such an act?"

Chloe stood and peeked into the other room, where she was apparently satisfied with whatever Kenny was doing with his food. "I wouldn't have thought so until recently," she said. "He changed so much. Almost as dramatically as the difference in him before and after the Rapture. It was as if he had reverted into something worse than he had been before he became a believer."

Tsion cocked his head and sneaked a glance at the television. Nothing new. "I was aware of tension in the house," he said. "But I missed what you're talking about."

"The rage? You missed the rage?"

Tsion shrugged. "I *share* some of that. I still fight it when I think of my family—" His voice caught.

"I know, Tsion. But you have been a man of the Scriptures your whole life. This is new to Daddy. I can't imagine him actually standing there and doing it, but I'm sure he wanted to. If he did, it sure answers a lot of questions about where he's been and what he's been doing. Oh, Tsion! How will he get away? That they say he's at large makes me wonder if it's not just a lie, a smear campaign to make him and you and us look bad? Maybe he's a scapegoat."

"We can only hope."

She dropped into a chair. "What if he's guilty? What if he's a murderer? There's no exception to God's law if the victim is the Antichrist, is there?"

Tsion shook his head. "None that I know of."

"Then mustn't he turn himself in? Suffer the consequences?"

"Slow down, Chloe. We know too little."

"But if he *is* guilty."

"My answer may surprise you."

"Surprise me."

"Off the top of the head, I believe we are at war. In the heat of battle, killing the enemy has never been considered murder."

"But . . ."

"I told you I might surprise you. I personally would harbor your father from the GC if he shot Carpathia dead, even while urging him to seek God about himself."

"You're right," Chloe said. "You surprised me."

* * *

David watched Annie work from the corner of the hangar where Mac and Abdullah met him. "What's that smell?" he said.

"Yeah," Mac said, looking at Abdullah. "What *is* that?"

Abdullah shrugged, then held up an index finger. "Oh, I remember now, Captain," he said. "Your idea."

"I'm listening," Mac said.

Abdullah pulled a pungent pita sandwich from his pocket. "Hungry, anyone?" he said.

"Here's hoping I'll never be that hungry," David said, pointing to a trash barrel twenty feet away. Abdullah hit it with a hook shot, and somehow the thing didn't fly apart in the air.

Mac shook his head. "Next you're going to tell me you were an Olympic basketball player."

"Missed the trials," Abdullah said. "Active duty."

David caught Mac's what'd-I-tell-ya look.

"So, Ab," Mac said, "are you 'pout' because you never finished your dinner?"

Abdullah looked away, as if knowing he was being teased but not catching the whole drift. "If I am pout," he said, "it is because I am exhausted and want to go to bed. Is anyone sleeping around here? It seems everyone is about."

"Go," David said. "Don't make it obvious, but go to bed. I'm going to be good for nothing if I don't crash sometime soon too."

Abdullah slipped away. "You look whipped too, Mac," David said.

Mac nodded for David to follow him to his office, across the hall from Annie's. "They're making a big deal about finding Rayford's fingerprints on a Saber," Mac said as he settled into the chair behind his desk. "But who knows if he was even there?"

"I'll find out by listening in."

"I think I already did. The print trace, at least what they said about it on the plane, sounded legit. Israeli-based Peacekeepers found the weapon, bagged it, and immediately lifted prints and started comparing it against the global database. The only reason it took as long as it did was because they tested it against criminals first and against the former GC employee list last. But the funny thing is that nobody's talking about Rayford as the perpetrator."

David flinched. "When they've got him dead to rights?"

Mac showed both palms. "They must know something we don't know."

"Such as?"

"Well, Neon Leon has a bee in his bonnet for the three disloyal regional potentates. He keeps talking about a conspiracy. I mean, everybody hears a gunshot and heads for the hills. People jump off the stage. Carpathia is down and dying. The suspected weapon is found with a disgruntled former employee's prints all over it, and all Leon can talk about is a conspiracy. What does that tell you?"

David frowned and furrowed his brow. "That the shooter missed?"

Mac expelled a resigned breath through his nose. "That's my theory. If it was so cut-and-dried, why don't they just call Rayford the shooter?"

"In public they do."

"But in private they're still looking. David, something stinks here."

David heard Annie's office door and looked out through the blinds. She was doing the same, and he invited her over with a wave. She held up a finger and motioned that she had to make a call first. When she finally joined them, they brought her up to date.

"You still planning on listening in to the autopsy?" she said.

David nodded.

"Maybe you ought to patch in to the evidence room too."

"Didn't know we had one."

"We do now. They've cordoned off a section under the amphitheater. Lots of room, lots of light."

"Are you sure? That's next to where they've got Guy Blod fashioning a twenty-four-foot Carpathia statue."

"That's where I delivered the evidence. Two plastic bags, one wood crate. Hickman's got a crew of forensic experts scheduled for ten this morning."

David looked at his watch. "It *is* tomorrow already, isn't it? Well, looks like everything happens then, autopsy and all. Guess both sides need sleep first."

"I heard they're trying to start the viewing at dawn Sunday," Annie said. "That's tomorrow!"

"Bedtime, kids," David said.

* * *

Rayford felt grimy and groggy. Despite his fear and the knowledge that his life as a fugitive had escalated a thousand times over, he was buoyed by his eagerness to pray and to get back into the Bible. Maybe it was naïve to think he could elude the GC for long. His recklessness had probably cost him his hope for surviving until the Glorious Appearing. Even forgiven sin, he had learned, has its consequences. He just hoped he hadn't jeopardized the entire Tribulation Force, or worse, saints worldwide.

As he sat praying in the dust fifty yards off the road, the night air dried the sweat on his head and neck and chilled him. In his fatigue and misery he still felt closer to God than he had for months.

His phone chirped, and Rayford hoped against hope it would be someone from the Trib Force, ideally Chloe or Buck. It was Laslos. "Are you in place?"

"Affirmative."

"And you are . . . ?"

"Marvin Berry," Rayford said.

"Check," Laslos said. "We were at a spot about two kilometers back where we could see the entire stretch of road before us. There appears to be no other traffic. You should hear us inside thirty seconds and see our lights soon. Start moving toward the road as soon as you hear us. We will open the back door as we stop, and as soon as you are in and it is shut, we will turn around quickly and head north again."

"Gotcha."

"Repeat?"

"Um, OK!"

Eager to be in the presence of a friend and fellow believer, Rayford was almost giddy under the circumstances. He slapped his phone shut, then opened it again to try one more time to reach anyone long distance. When it was obvious he still could not, he rang off and realized he heard a vehicle. He began jogging toward the road, but something was wrong. Unless he was turned around, it sounded as if the car was coming from the south. Should he dial Laslos back and see if he had misunderstood? But how could he have? Ptolemaïs was north. The church had to be north. Surely Laslos had said he would be heading south.

The engine sounded much bigger than a small car's. Rayford skidded to a stop in the loose dirt, realizing he had nowhere to hide if a vehicle came upon him from the south. And it was becoming obvious that one was. It was loud and it was big and it was coming fast, but he saw lights only on the northern horizon. That had to be Laslos.

The bigger vehicle from the south would reach him first. Regardless who it was, they would likely stop to check out a walking stranger. Rayford spun, frantically looking for somewhere to hide. His shirt was light colored and might be detectable in the darkness. As the sound rushed toward him, Rayford dove face first to the ground, pulling his dark bag atop his back as he lay there. With his free hand he popped open his phone to warn Laslos to abort and keep going, but when he hit Redial, he got the long distance attempt again and realized he didn't even have Laslos's cell number.

He prayed Laslos would see the oncoming vehicle in time to keep from slowing and pulling off the road.

Rayford's phone rang.

"Yeah!"

"What is coming from the south with no lights?"

"I don't know, Laslos! I'm on the ground! Keep going, just in case!"

The vehicle flew past, and Rayford felt the rush of wind. He tried to get a look at the car but could determine only that it was Jeep-like. "That could have been GC!" he said into the phone.

"It was," Laslos said. "Stay right where you are! It doesn't appear they saw you. They will be able to see us behind them for miles, so don't move. We will come back when we feel it is safe."

"I'd feel safer back in the foliage," Rayford said.

"Better wait. They might be able to see movement. We will see if other GC vehicles are coming."

"Why are they speeding around without lights?"

"We have no idea," Laslos said.

\+ + +

Buck couldn't remember the name of the place, but it was one spot he and Chaim had been to together where no one would expect to see either of them. It took an hour to find an empty cab, and he was informed that any ride, regardless of distance, would cost one hundred Nicks.

Buck described the place to the driver and told him the general area. The man nodded slowly, as if it was coming to him. "I think I know place, or some like it. All work same when you want get, how do the Westerners say, medicated."

"That's what I want," Buck said. "But I have to find the right place."

"We try," the driver said. "Many closed, but some still open."

They rolled over curbs, around crumbled buildings, through dark traffic lights, and past accident scenes. The cabbie stopped at two bars that seemed to be doing land-office business, considering, but Buck recognized neither. "It's about the same size as this one, big neon sign in the window, narrow door. That's all I remember."

"I know place," the man said. "Closed. Want these, or other place?"

"I want the other one. Take me there."

"I know is closed. Closed weeks." He held up both hands as if Buck didn't understand. "Nobody there. Dark. Bye-bye."

"That's where I want to go," Buck said.

"Why you want to go where is closed?"

"I'm meeting someone."

"She won't be at closed place," he said, but he drove off anyway. "See?" he said, slowing at midblock nearby. "Is closed."

Buck paid him and hung around the street until the cab left, the driver shaking his head. He soon realized he was in sheer darkness, trees blotting out the clouds and far enough from the emergency action that no lights were visible. The cab lights had shown that the earthquake had leveled several buildings on the street. It was clear now that the power was out in the area.

Would Chaim have come here? *Could* he have? They had come here looking for Jacov the night he had become a believer, Chaim convinced he would be at his favorite bar, drunk as usual. They had found him there all right, and most assumed he *was* drunk. He was on a tabletop, preaching to his old friends and drinking buddies.

Buck was fast losing faith. If Chaim was alive, if he had been able to find someone to cart him around, how long would he have stayed on a deserted, dark, destroyed street? And was there really any hope that they might both have thought of this obscure establishment?

Buck pulled the flashlight from his pocket and looked around before it occurred to him that Chaim would not likely be in sight, at least until he was certain that it was Buck with the light. And how would Chaim know that? Buck stood in front of the closed bar and shined the light on his own face. Almost immediately he heard a rustle in the branch of a tree across the street and the clearing of a throat.

He quickly aimed the beam at the tree, prepared to retreat. Incongruously hanging out from under one of the leafy branches was a pajama leg, completed by a stockinged and slippered foot. Buck kept the faint beam on the bewildering scene, but as he moved slowly across the street, the foot lifted out of sight. The lower branch bent with the weight of the tree dweller, and suddenly down he came, agile as a cat. Standing there before Buck in slippers, socks, pajamas, and robe was a most robust Chaim Rosenzweig.

"Cameron, Cameron," he said, his voice strong and clear. "This is almost enough to make a believer out of me. I knew you'd come."

* * *

Another unlit GC vehicle raced past while Rayford lay in the dirt. All he could think of was the Prodigal Son, realizing what he had left and eager to get back to his father.

When the predawn grew quiet again, Rayford forsook caution and dashed for the underbrush. He was filthy and tried to brush himself off. Laslos and his pastor had to have seen the other GC vehicle and were playing it safe. Forty minutes later—which seemed like forever to Rayford—a small white four-door slid to a stop in the gravel. Rayford hesitated. Why had they not called? He looked at his phone. He had shut it off, and apparently the battery was too low to power the wake-up feature.

The back door opened. Laslos called, "Mr. Berry!" and Rayford ran toward the car. As soon as the door was shut, Laslos spun a U-turn and headed south. "I don't know where the GC is going, but I'll go the other way for now. Demetrius has a friend in the country nearby."

"A brother?"

"Of course."

"Demetrius?" Rayford said, extending his hand to the passenger. "Rayford Steele. Call me Ray."

The younger man had a fierce grip and pulled Rayford until he could reach to embrace him. "Demetrius Demeter," he said. "Call me Demetrius or brother."

* * *

Tsion was moved and took comfort in the verse that reminded him that during this period of cosmic history, God would pour out his Spirit and that "your sons and your daughters shall prophesy, your old men shall dream dreams, your young men shall see visions." The question was whether he was an old man or a young man. He decided on the former and attributed what he had felt on the floor to his drowsiness. He had apparently lost consciousness while praying and nearly slipped into a dream. If the dream was from God, he prayed he would return to it. If it was merely some sleep-deprived fancy, Tsion prayed he would have the discernment to know that too.

That the passage had gone on to reference the heavenly wonders and blood, fire, and smoke the world had already experienced also warmed Tsion. He had been an eyewitness when the sun had been turned into darkness and the moon into blood. He read the passage to Chloe and reminded her, "This is 'before the coming of the great and awesome day of the Lord.' I believe that refers to the second half of the Tribulation, the Great Tribulation. Which starts now."

Chloe looked at him expectantly. "Uh-huh, but—"

"Oh, dear one, the best is yet to come. I don't believe it was coincidence that the Lord led me to this passage. Think of your father and our compatriots overseas when you hear this: 'And it shall come to pass that whoever calls on the name of the Lord shall be saved. For in Mount Zion and in Jerusalem there shall be deliverance, as the Lord has said, among the remnant whom the Lord calls.' You know who the remnant is, don't you, Chloe?"

"The Jews?"

"Yes! And in Zion, which is Israel, and Jerusalem, where we know some of our own were, if they call upon the Lord, they will be delivered. Chloe, I don't know how many of us or *if* any of us will survive until the Glorious Appearing. But I am claiming the promise of this passage, because God prompted me to find it, that our beloved will all return safely to us this time."

"In spite of everything?"

"In spite of everything."

"Is there anything in there that says when the phones will start working again?"

\+ \+ \+

Leah Rose had landed in Baltimore and pondered her next moves. Finding Hattie Durham in North America was like pawing through the proverbial haystack for a needle someone else had already found. The GC was on Hattie's trail and clearly hoped she would lead them to the lair of the Judah-ites.

If Leah could get her phone to work, she would call T at Palwaukee and see if that Super J plane she had heard so much about was still at the airport and ready for use. On the other hand, if she could get through to T, she could have gotten through to the safe house and sent them running. Did she dare fly commercially to Illinois and rent a car under her alias?

She had no other choice. Unable to communicate except locally, her only hope was to beat Hattie to Mount Prospect. Finding the woman and persuading her to mislead the GC was just too much to hope for.

"How close can you get me to Gary, Indiana?" Leah asked at the counter, after waiting nearly a half hour for the one airline clerk.

"Hammond is the best I can do. And that would be very late tonight."

Having misled the young man about her destination, she switched gears. "How about Chicago? O'Hare and Meigs still closed?"

"And Midway," the clerk said. "Kankakee any help?"

"Perfect," she said. "When?"

"If we're lucky, you'll be on the ground by midnight."

"If we're lucky," Leah said, "that'll mean the plane landed and didn't crash."

The man did not smile. And Leah remembered: *We don't do luck.*

* * *

David lay in bed with his laptop, knowing he would soon nod off, but perusing again the abandoned buildings and areas in northern Illinois that might provide a new safe house for the stateside Trib Force. The whole of downtown Chicago had been cordoned off, mostly bombed out, and evacuated. It was a ghost town, nothing living within forty miles. David rolled up onto his elbows and studied the list. How had that happened? Hadn't the earliest reports said the attack on Illinois had been everything but nuclear?

He searched archives, finally pinpointing the day when the GC ruled the city and surrounding areas uninhabitable. Dozens had died from what looked and acted like radiation poisoning, and the Centers for Disease Control and Prevention in Atlanta had urged the ruling. Bodies lay decaying in the streets as the living cleared out.

Remote probes were dropped into the region to test radiation levels, but their inconclusive reports were attributed to faulty equipment. Soon no one dared go near the place. Some radical journalists, Buck Williams wannabees, averred on the Internet that the abandoning of Chicago was the biggest foul-up in history, that the deadly diseases were not a result of nuclear radiation, and that the place was inhabitable. *What if?* David wondered.

He followed the cybertrails until he was studying the radiation probe results. Hundreds had been attempted. Not one had registered radiation. But once the scare snare was set, the hook had sunk deep. Who would risk being wrong on a matter like that?

I might, David thought. *With a little more research.*

He had just studied the skyline of Chicago and become intrigued by the skyscraper that had been built by the late Thomas Strong, who had made his fortune in insurance. The place was a mere five years old, a magnificent eighty-story tower that had housed Strong's entire international headquarters. Pictures of the aftermath of the bombing showed the top twenty-six stories of the structure twisting grotesquely away from the rest of the building. The story-high red letters STRONG had slid on an angle and were still visible during the daytime, making the place look like a stubborn tree trunk that refused to cave in to the storms that leveled most of the rest of the city.

David was about to hack into the blueprints and other records that might show if any of the rest of the structure had been left with any integrity when his laptop beeped, announcing a news bulletin from Global Community headquarters.

His eyes were dancing as it was, so he bookmarked where he had been and determined to go to sleep after checking the bulletin. It read:

"A spokesman for Global Community Supreme Commander Leon Fortunato in New Babylon has just announced that satellite communications have been restored. He asks that citizens employ restraint so as not to overload the system and to limit themselves to only emergency calls for the next twelve hours.

"The spokesman also has announced the decision, reportedly made by Fortunato alone, to rename the United Holy Land States. The new name of the region shall be the United Carpathian States, in honor of the slain leader. Fortunato has not announced a successor to his own role as potentate of the region, but such a move is expected under the likelihood that the supreme commander be drafted into service as the new Global Community potentate."

David wondered why he had been asked to interfere with telephone capability and someone else had been asked to reverse it.

6

RAYFORD FOUGHT TO STAY awake in the warm backseat of Laslos's small car. Pastor Demetrius Demeter pointed the way to the rustic cabin in the woods, some twenty kilometers south of Kozani. Laslos avoided any talk of Rayford's guilt or innocence but took it upon himself to cheerfully bring Rayford up to date on the growth of the underground church in northern Greece.

Rayford apologized when a snore woke him.

"Don't give it another thought, brother," Laslos told him. "You need your rest, regardless of what you decide."

Suddenly the car was off the highway and onto an unpaved road. "You can imagine what a great getaway is this cottage," Demetrius said. "The day will come when we, or it, will be found out, and it will be lost to us."

Rayford had gotten only a brief glimpse of the young man when the car door was open. Thin and willowy, it appeared he might be as tall as Rayford. He would have guessed Pastor Demeter at about thirty, with a thick shock of dark hair, deep olive skin, and shining black eyes. He was articulate in English with a heavy Greek accent.

The cottage was so remote that one either came there on purpose or found it while hopelessly lost. Laslos parked in the back where they also entered, using a key Demetrius pulled from under a board near the door. He grabbed Rayford's bag from the car, over his protests. "There's nothing I need from there until I get back home, thanks," Rayford said.

"You must spend at least one night here, sir," Demetrius said.

"Oh, imposs—"

"You look so tired! And you have to be!"

"But I must get back. The stateside people need the plane, and I need them."

Laslos and Demetrius wore heavy sweaters under thick jackets, but Rayford didn't warm up until Laslos had a fire roaring. Laslos then busied himself in the kitchen, from which Rayford soon smelled strong tea and looked forward to it as he would have a desert spring.

Meanwhile, in a small, woodsy room illuminated only by the fire, Rayford sat in a deep, ancient chair that seemed to envelop him. The young pastor sat across from him, half his face in the dancing light, the other half disappearing into the darkness.

"We were praying for you, Mr. Steele, at the very moment you called Lukas's wife. We thought you might need asylum. Forgive my impudence, sir, as you are clearly my elder—"

"Is it that obvious?"

Demetrius seemed to allow himself only the briefest polite smile. "I would love to have you tell me all about Tsion Ben-Judah, but we don't have time for socializing. You may stay here as long as you wish, but I also want to offer you my services."

"Your services?" Rayford was taken aback, but he couldn't shake the feeling that he and Demetrius had immediately connected.

"At the risk of sounding forward or self-possessed," Demetrius said, intertwining his fingers in his lap, "God has blessed and gifted me. My superiors tell me this is not unusual for those of us who are likely part of the 144,000. I have loved the Scriptures since long before I was aware that Jesus fit all the prophecies of the Coming One. It seemed all my energies were invested in learning the things of God. I had been merely bemused by the idea that the Gentiles, specifically Christians, thought they had a corner on our theology. Then the Rapture occurred, and I was not only forced to study Jesus in a different light, but I was also irresistibly drawn to him."

Pastor Demeter shifted in his chair and turned to gaze at the fire. The fatigue that had racked Rayford, which he now realized would force him to at least nap before trying to return to the States, seemed a nuisance he would deal with later. Demetrius seemed so earnest, so genuine, that Rayford had to hear him out. Laslos came in with steaming mugs of tea, then returned to the kitchen to sit with his, though both men invited him to stay. It was as if he knew Rayford needed this time alone with the man of God.

"My primary gift is evangelism," Demetrius said. "I say that without ego, for when I use the word *gift,* I mean just that. My gift before becoming a believer was probably sarcasm or condescension or pride in intellect. I realize now, of course, that the intellect was also a gift, a gift I did not know how to exercise to its fullest until I had a reason."

Rayford was grateful he could just sit and listen for a while, but he was also amazed he was able to stay awake. The fire, the chair, the situation, the hour, the week he had had all conspired to leave him in a ball of unconsciousness. But unlike in the car, he was not even aware of the temptation to nod off.

"What we who have been called find fascinating," Demetrius continued, "is that God has seemed to streamline everything now. I'm sure you've found this in your own life. For me the sense of adventure in learning of God was magnified so that my every waking moment was happily spent studying his Word. And when I was then thrust into a place of service, giftings that might have taken decades to develop before were now bestowed as if overnight. I had had my nose in the Scriptures and commentaries for so long, there was no way I could have honed the skills the Lord seemed to pour out upon me. And I have found this true of my colleagues as well. None of us dare take an iota of credit, because these are clearly gifts from God. We can do nothing less than gleefully exercise them."

"Such as?" Rayford said.

"Primarily evangelism, as I said. It seems most everyone we talk with personally is persuaded that Jesus is the Christ. And under our preaching, thousands have come to faith. I trust you understand I say this solely to give glory to Jehovah God."

Rayford quickly waved him off. "Of course."

"We have also been given unusual teaching and pastoring skills. It is as if God has given us the Midas touch, and not just us Greeks."

Rayford was lost in thought and nearly missed the humor. He just wanted to hear more.

"But most fascinating to me, Mr. Steele, is a helpful, useful gift I would not have thought to ask for, let alone imagine was either necessary or available. It is discernment, not to be confused with a gift of knowledge—something I have witnessed in some colleagues but do not have myself. Frankly, I am not envious. The specific things God tells them about the people under their charge would weigh on me and wear me down. But discernment . . . now, that has proven most helpful to me and to those I counsel."

"I'm not sure I follow."

Demetrius leaned forward and set his mug on the floor. He rested elbows on knees and stared into Rayford's face. "I don't want to alarm you or make you think this is some kind of a parlor trick. I am not guessing, and I am not claiming that any of this is a skill I have honed or mastered. God has merely given me the ability to discern the needs of people and the extent of their sincerity in facing up to them."

Rayford felt as if the man could look right through him, and he was tempted to ask questions no one could answer unless God told them. But this was no game.

"I can tell you, without fear of contradiction, that you are a man who at this very moment is broken before God. Despite the news, I have no idea whether you shot Nicolae Carpathia or tried to. I don't know if you were there or had the weapon in question or if the Global Community is framing you because they know your allegiances. But I discern your brokenness, and it is because you have sinned."

Rayford nodded, deeply moved, unable to speak.

"We are all sinners, of course, battling our old natures every day. But yours was a sin of pride and selfishness. It was not a sin of omission but of willful commission. It was not a onetime occurrence but a pattern of behavior, of rebellion. It was an attitude that resulted in actions you regret, actions you acknowledge as sin, practices you have confessed to God and have repented of."

Rayford's jaw was tight, his neck stiff. He could not even nod.

"I am not here to chastise you or to test you to see if what I discern is correct, because in these last days God has poured out his gifts and eliminated the need for patience with us frail humans. In essence, he has forsaken requiring desert experiences for us and simply works through us to do his will.

"I sense a need to tell you that your deep feelings of having returned to him are accurate. He would have you not wallow in regret but rejoice in his forgiveness. He wants you to know and believe beyond doubt that your sins and iniquities he will remember no more. He has separated you from the guilt of your sins as far as the east is from the west. Go and sin no more. Go and do his bidding in the short season left to you."

As if knowing what was coming, Demetrius reached for Rayford's cup, allowing Rayford to leave the comfort of his chair and kneel on the wood floor. Great sobs burst from him, and he sensed he was in the presence of God, as he had been in the plane when it seemed the Lord had finally gotten his attention. But to add this gift of forgiveness, expressed by a chosen agent, was beyond what Rayford could have dreamed for.

Fear melted away. Fatigue was put in abeyance. Unrest about the future, about his role, about what to do—all gone. "Thank you, God" was all he could say, and he said it over and over.

When finally he rose, Rayford turned to embrace a man who an hour before had been a stranger and now seemed a messenger of God. He might never see him again, but he felt a kinship that could only be explained by God.

Lukas still waited in the tiny kitchen as Rayford spilled to Demetrius the whole story of how his anger had blossomed into a murderous rage that took him to the brink of murder and may have even given him a hand in it.

Demetrius nodded and seemed to shift and treat Rayford as a colleague rather than a parishioner. "And what is God telling you to do now?"

"Rest and go," Rayford said, feeling rightly decisive for the first time in months. For once he didn't feel the need to talk himself into decisions and then continue to sell himself on them, carefully avoiding seeking God's will. "I need to sleep until dawn and then get back in the game. As soon as I can get through by phone, I need to be sure Buck and Leah are safe and go get them, if necessary."

Laslos joined them and said, "Give me that information. I will stand watch until dawn, and I can try the phones every half hour while you are sleeping."

Demetrius interrupted Rayford's thanks by pointing him to a thick fabric couch and a scratchy blanket. "It is all we have to offer," he said. "Kick your shoes off and get out of that shirt."

When Rayford sat on the couch in only undershirt and trousers, Demetrius motioned that he should lie down. The pastor covered him with the blanket and prayed, "Father, we need a physical miracle. Give this man a double portion of rest for the hours available, and may this meager bed be transformed into a healing agent."

Without so much as a pillow, Rayford felt himself drifting from consciousness. He was warm; the couch was soft but supportive, the stiff blanket like a downy comforter. As his breathing became rhythmic and deep, his last conscious thought was different from what it had been for so long. Rather than the dread fear that came with life as an international fugitive, he rested in the knowledge that he was a child of the King, a saved, forgiven, precious, beloved son safe in the hollow of his Father's hand.

✣ ✣ ✣

Buck and Chaim sat in an abandoned, earthquake-ravaged dwelling in the middle of a formerly happening Israeli neighborhood where crowded bars and nightclubs once rocked till dawn. With no power or water or even shelter safe enough for vagrants, the area now hosted only an enterprising journalist and a national hero.

"Please douse that light, Cameron," Chaim said.

"Who will see us?"

"No one, but it's irritating. I've had a long day."

"I imagine you have," Buck said. "But I want to see this walking, breathing miracle. You look healthier than I've ever seen you."

They sat on a crumbling concrete wall with remnants of a shattered beam protruding from it. Buck didn't know how the old man felt, but he himself had to keep moving for a modicum of comfort.

"I am the healthiest I have been in years," Chaim exulted, his accent thick as ever. "I have been working out every day."

"While your house staff feared you were near death."

"If they only knew what I was doing in my workshop before dawn."

"I think I know, Chaim."

"Thinking and knowing are different things. Had you looked deep into the closet, you would have seen the ancient stationary bicycle and the dumbbells that put me in the fighting trim I am in today. I laboriously moved my chair through the house so they could hear the whine of it if they happened to be up that early. Then I locked myself in there for at least ninety minutes. Jumping jacks and push-ups to warm up, the dumbbells for toning, the bike for a hard workout. Then it was back inside the blanket, into the chair, and back to my quarters for a shower. They thought I was remarkably self-reliant for an old man suffering from a debilitating stroke."

Buck was not amused when Chaim stiffened his arm, turned one side of his mouth down, and faked impaired speech with guttural rasping.

"I fooled even you, did I not?"

"Even me," Buck said, looking away.

"Are you offended?"

"Of course I am. Why would you feel the need to do that to your staff and to me?"

"Oh, Cameron, I could not involve you in my scheme."

"I'm involved, Chaim. I saw what killed Carpathia."

"Oh, you did, did you? Well, I didn't. All that commotion, that trauma. I couldn't move. I heard the gunshot, saw the man fall, the lectern shatter, the backdrop sail away. I froze with fear, unable to propel my chair. My back was to the disturbance, and no one was coming to my aid. I shall have to chastise Jacov for his failure to do his duty. I was counting on him to come to me. My other clothes were in the back of the van, and I had a reservation at a small inn under an alias. We can still use it if you can get me there."

"In your pajamas?"

"I have a blanket in the tree. I wrapped it around myself, even my head, as I ran to the taxis. I had not expected to have to do that, Cameron, but I was prepared for all exigencies."

"Not all."

"What are you saying?"

"I'll try to get you to your hotel, Chaim, and I may even have to hide out there with you myself for a while. But I have bad news that I will tell you only when we are there. And only after you tell me everything about what happened on the platform."

Chaim stood and reached for the flashlight, using it to find his way to a man-size hole in the wall. He leaned against the opening and switched off the light.

"I will never tell anyone what happened," he said. "I am in this alone."

"I didn't see it happen, Chaim, but I saw the wound and what caused it. You know I couldn't have been the only one."

Chaim sighed wearily. "The eye is not trustworthy, my young friend. You don't know what you saw. You can't tell me how far away you were or how what you saw fits into the whole picture. The gunshot was a surprise to me. That your comrade was even there was also a shock, and him as a suspect now!"

"I find none of this amusing, Chaim, and soon enough you won't either."

Buck heard the old man settle to the ground. "I did not expect that much chaos. I hoped, of course. That was my only chance of getting away from there with everyone else. When Jacov did not arrive—because of the panic caused by the gunshot, I assume—I leaned on that control stick and headed for the back of the platform, clutching my blanket like a cape. I rolled out of the chair at the last instant, and it went flying. I wish it had landed on one of the regional potentates, who were by then limping away. I tossed my blanket over the side, then rolled onto my belly and threw my feet over, locking them around the support beam. I shinnied down that structure like a youngster, Cameron, and I won't even try to hide my pride. I have scrapes on my inner thighs that may take some time to heal, but it was worth it."

"Was it?"

"It was, Cameron. It was. Fooling so many, including my own staff. Doctors, nurses, aides. Well, actually, I didn't fool every aide. As Jacov and a young nurse's aide were lifting me into the van after my last visit to the hospital, she stalled, locking my wheels and straightening my blanket while Jacov went to get behind the wheel. Just before she closed the door, she leaned close and whispered, 'I don't know who you are or what your game is, old man. But you might want to remember which side was affected when you came in here.'"

Chaim chuckled, which Buck found astounding under the circumstances. "I just hope she was telling the truth, Cameron, that she didn't know who I was. Celebrity is my curse, but some of the younger ones, they don't pay so much attention. I looked desperately at her as she shut the door, hoping she would wonder if it were she who had forgotten. I stayed in character, but if my face flushed it was from embarrassment and not frustration over my lack of ability to speak or walk. She was right! I had stiffened my right arm and curled my right hand under! What an old fool!"

"You took the words right out of my mouth, Chaim. Get your blanket, and let's find a cab."

Without a word, Chaim switched on the flashlight, hurried to the tree, tossed the light back to Buck, and leaped, grabbing the low branch and pulling himself up far enough to grab the blanket. He wrapped it around his head and over his shoulder, then affected a limp and leaned on Buck, chuckling again.

Buck moved away from him. "Don't start that until you need to," Buck said.

* * *

Leah Rose awoke with a start and looked out the window. Cities were rarely illuminated in the night anymore, so she had no idea where she was. She tried looking at her watch, but couldn't focus. Something had awakened her, and suddenly she heard it again. Her phone. Could it be?

The one lone flight attendant and the rest of the dozen or so passengers seemed asleep. Leah dug in her bag for the phone and pressed the caller ID button. She didn't recognize the number, but her comrades had assured her the phone was secure. She would not jeopardize them if she answered, even if her number had fallen into the wrong hands.

Leah opened the phone and tucked her head behind the back of the seat in front of her. She spoke softly but directly. "This is Donna Clendenon."

A brief silence alarmed her. She heard a male inhale. "I'm sorry," he began with a Greek accent. "I am calling on behalf of, ah, Mr. Marvin Berry?"

"Yes! Is this Mr. Miklos?"

"Yes!"

"And are you calling from Greece?"

"I am. And Mr. Steele is here. And what is it that those filled with demons cannot say?"

Leah smiled in spite of herself. "Jesus is the Christ, the Messiah, and he will return in the flesh."

"Amen! Rayford is sleeping but needs to know you are safe and how to find y—"

"I'm sorry, Mr. Miklos, but if the phones are working, I have an emergency call to make. Just tell Rayford that I am nearly home so not to worry about me, but that he needs to locate Buck."

* * *

Tsion experimented with five-minute catnaps every few minutes, fearing he would otherwise sleep through the resurrection of the Antichrist. With Chloe and the baby asleep elsewhere in the safe house, the experiment was not working well. He found himself popping awake every fifteen or twenty minutes, desperate to be sure he had missed nothing. There had been no repeat of his dreamlike state while praying for Rayford, and he began to wonder if it had been more related to praying than sleeping. He also began to wonder how long Carpathia was supposed to remain dead. Was it possible he had been wrong all along? Was someone else the Antichrist, yet to be murdered and resurrected?

Tsion couldn't imagine it. Many sincere believers had questioned his teaching that Antichrist would actually die from a wound to the head. Some said the Scriptures indicated that it would be merely a wound that made him appear dead. He tried to assure them that his best interpretation of the original Greek led him to believe that the man would actually die and then be indwelt by Satan himself upon coming back to life.

Given that, he hoped he had been right about Carpathia. There would be no doubt of the death and resurrection if the body had begun to decay, was autopsied, embalmed, and prepared to lie in state. If Carpathia were dead even close to twenty-four hours, few could charge him with faking his demise. Too many eyewitnesses had seen the man expire, and though the cause of death had not yet been announced, that was forthcoming. The world, including Tsion, had to believe the gunshot provided the kill.

The TV carried yet another airing of an earlier pronouncement of grief and promised vengeance from Leon Fortunato. Tsion found himself nodding and dozing until the phone woke him.

"Leah! It's so good to hear your voice. We have been unable to reach—"

She interrupted and filled him in on Hattie and the danger posed to the safe house. Tsion stood and began pacing as he listened. "We have nowhere else to go, Leah," he said. "But at the very least we had better get underground."

They agreed that she would call if she got near the safe house and was sure no one was casing the place. Otherwise, Leah would keep her distance and try to find Hattie. How, she said, she had no idea.

Despite his weariness, Tsion was suddenly energized. He was responsible for Chloe and Kenny, and though the macho stuff was usually left to Rayford or Buck, he had to act. He trotted up the stairs and grabbed a few clothes from his closet and a stack of books. He returned to the first floor and piled these near the old chest freezer that stood next to the refrigerator.

Tsion added his laptop and the TV to the pile, then outed every light in the place except the single bulb hanging from the ceiling in the hall bath. He carefully pushed open the door to Buck and Chloe's bedroom, knocking softly. He did not hear Chloe stir, and he could not see her in the darkness. He knocked again and whispered her name.

When he heard a quick motion from the crib on the far wall, Tsion fell silent, holding his breath. He had hoped not to wake the baby. Clearly, Kenny was pulling himself up to stand. The crib rocked, and Tsion imagined the little guy with his hands on the railing, rocking, making the crib squeak. "Mowning! Ga'mowning, Mama!"

"It's not morning, Kenny," he whispered.

"Unca Zone!" Kenny squealed, rocking vigorously.

And with that, Chloe awoke with a start.

"It's just me, dear," Tsion said quickly.

Twenty minutes later the three of them were relocated underground, having lifted aside the rack of smelly, spoiled food in the freezer that led to the stairs. Kenny, beaming from his playpen, had loved seeing his mother and Tsion reappear downstairs every few minutes with more stuff. He was not so happy when they muscled his crib down there and he had to make the switch.

Fortunately the underground was large enough that Tsion could set up the TV in a spot where the light and sound did not reach Chloe and Kenny's sleeping quarters. He monitored the doings from New Babylon, but every time he had need to venture into the other part of the shelter, he heard Chloe groggily trying to talk Kenny into going back to sleep.

He poked his head through the curtain. "How about he watches TV with me until he falls asleep again, hmm?"

"Oh, Tsion, that would be wonderful."

"Unca Zone!"

"TV?" Tsion said as he lifted the boy from the crib.

Kenny kicked and laughed. "TV, Unca Zone! Video!"

"We'll watch my show," Tsion whispered as he carried him to his chair.

"You show!" Kenny said, holding Tsion's face in his hands. Tsion was transported to when his relatives had been toddlers and sat in his lap as he read or watched television. Kenny was quickly bored with the repetitious news, but he quit asking for a video and concentrated on tracing the contours of Tsion's ears, squeezing his nose, and rubbing his palm back and forth on Tsion's stubble. Eventually he began to blink slowly, tucked a thumb in his mouth, and turned to settle into the crook of Tsion's elbow. When his head lolled over, Tsion gently carried him back to bed.

As he tucked a blanket around Kenny he heard Chloe turn and whisper, "Thank you, Unca Zone."

"Thank you," he said.

+ + +

"Why didn't you just go straight to the hotel?" Buck asked Chaim as he tried to flag down a cab.

"I was lucky enough the cabbie didn't recognize me. How was I going to fool a desk clerk? I was counting on Jacov to get me in. Now I'm counting on you. Anyway, how would we have found each other?"

"How *did* we find each other?" Buck said.

"I couldn't think of any other place you might look, except at my home, and I didn't expect you to risk that. I don't think anybody is there anyway. I haven't been able to raise anybody."

Buck was struck by that unfortunate choice of words.

"They're there, Chaim."

"You *did* go there? Why don't they answer? Did Jacov make it back? I expected he would call me."

Buck spotted a cab sitting a couple of blocks off a busy thoroughfare. Grateful he didn't have to answer Chaim directly yet, he said, "Wait here, and keep that blanket over your face."

"You workin'?" he asked the cabbie.

"Hundred and fifty Nicks, only in the city."

"A hundred, and my father is contagious."

"No contagious."

"OK, a hundred and fifty. We're only going to the Night Visitors. You know it?"

"I know. You keep old man in back, and don't breathe on me."

Buck signaled to Chaim, who shuffled over, hidden in the blanket. "Don't try to talk, Father," he said, helping him into the backseat. "And don't cough on this nice young man."

As if on cue, Chaim covered his mouth with the blanket and both hands and produced a juicy, wheezing cough that made the driver look quickly into the rearview mirror.

The Night Visitors was dark, not even an outside light on. "Are they closed?" Buck said.

"Only for now," the driver said. "Probably open again at dawn. One-fifty. I gotta go."

"Wait until I see if I can rouse anybody," Buck said, getting out.

"Don't leave him in here! I gotta go. Money now!"

"You'll get your money when we get a room."

The driver slammed the car into Park and turned it off, folding his arms across his chest.

7

BUCK'S PHONE RANG as he was trying to peer through the front window of the Night Visitors. "Laslos!" he said, stepping around the corner of the building and into the shadows. The cabbie honked, and Buck signaled him to wait a minute.

"Get this man out of my cab!"

"Five minutes!" Buck said.

"Fifty more Nicks!"

"He's there with you, Lukas?" Buck said. "How am I supposed to—does he know he's wanted here—he does? . . . Is Leah with him? . . . Oh, that's good. We need a way out of here, and there's no way he can risk coming back. Never mind. I'll handle that. Listen, does he have to see anyone before he takes off? . . . You can't be sure airport personnel won't be on alert. His face is on international TV every few minutes. Do you know anyone who can give him a new look? . . . He'll need new papers too. Thanks, Laslos! I have to call my wife."

Buck dialed Chloe, but her phone rang and rang.

When he returned to the cab, the driver was out and screaming. "Now! Go! No more this man in my car!"

Buck paid him and helped Chaim out, pushing him into an alley while he banged on the windows and door and tried to rouse the manager.

* * *

Tsion heard something upstairs and ran to the utility box to shut down the power. If the GC searched the place, it would be clear someone had been living there recently, as food in the refrigerator would still be fresh and lots of personal belongings remained. But if they found power meters still spinning, they would know someone was still there somewhere.

Tsion held his breath in the darkness. It was a phone! Had Chloe forgotten to bring hers down? He rushed to the stairs, pushed the plywood away from the bottom of the freezer, pushed up the smelly rack, and lifted himself out. He felt his way to Chloe's room and followed the sound to her phone. Just as he reached it, it stopped ringing. The caller ID showed Buck's code. Tsion hit the callback button, but Buck's phone was busy.

* * *

While continuing to bang with one hand, Buck speed-dialed David Hassid with the other. He got only David's machine. When he hung up, his call button was illuminated. His caller ID showed he had received a call from Chloe's phone. He was about to call her back when a light came on in the Night Visitors, followed by slamming, stomping, and cursing.

"We have a reservation!" Buck shouted.

"You'll have a bullet if you don't shut up!" came the voice from inside. "We closed at midnight and we open again at six!"

"You're up now, so give us our room!"

"You lost your room when you didn't show up! Who are you, Tangvald or Goldman?"

Buck whispered desperately to Chaim, "Who are we?"

"Do I look like a Tangvald?"

"Goldman, and my father is sick. Let us in!"

"We're full!"

"You're lying! You held two rooms till you went to bed and then gave them both away?"

"Leave me alone!"

"I'll knock until you let us in!"

"I'll shoot you if you knock once more!"

The light went out. Buck put his phone in his pocket and banged on the door with both fists.

"You're a dead man!"

"Just open up and give us a room!"

More swearing, then the light, then the door opened an inch. The man stuck his fingers out. "Five hundred Nicks cash."

"Let me see the key."

The man dangled it at the end of a six-inch block of wood. Buck produced the cash, and the key came flying out. "Around back, third floor. If I didn't need the money, I'd have shot you."

"You're welcome," Buck said.

The room was a hole. A single bed, one straight-back chair, and a toilet and sink. Buck pulled out his phone and sat in the chair, pointing Chaim to the bed. As Buck tried Chloe's phone, Chaim kicked off his slippers and stretched out on the bed, atop the ratty spread and under his own blanket.

"Tsion!" Buck said. "No, don't wake her. . . . Underground? That's probably good for now. Just tell her I'm all right. I need to get hold of T. May need him to get Chaim and me out of here. . . ."

"I'm not going anywhere," Chaim mumbled from the bed. "I'm a dead man."

"Yeah," Buck said to Tsion, "just like you and me. . . . Kenny OK? . . . We'll keep in touch."

Buck couldn't get an answer at Palwaukee Airport or on T's cell phone. He put his phone away and took a deep breath, kicking his bag under the chair. "Chaim, we have to talk," he said. But Chaim was asleep.

+ + +

Rayford awoke with a start just after dawn, feeling refreshed. He grabbed his bag and padded past a dozing Demetrius to the bathroom, smelling breakfast from the kitchen. While in the tiny bathroom, however, he heard tires on the gravel and pulled the curtain back an inch. A small pickup pulled into view.

Rayford leaned out the door and called to Laslos. "Company," he whispered. "You expecting anyone?"

"It's all right," Laslos said, setting a pan of food on the table and wiping his hands on an apron. "Get a shower and join us for breakfast as soon as you can."

Rayford tried to run hot water in the sink. It was lukewarm. Laslos interrupted with a knock. "Don't shave, Mr. Steele."

"Oh, Laslos, I really need to. I've got several days of growth and—"

"I'll explain later. But don't."

Rayford shrugged and squinted at himself in the mirror. He was due for a haircut, more and more gray appearing at his temples and in the back. His beard was salt-and-pepper, which alarmed him. Not that he cared so much about gray in his mid-forties. It was just that it had seemed to happen almost overnight. Until this morning, he had felt every one of his forty-plus years. Now he felt great.

The shower, a trickle from a rusty pipe, was also lukewarm. It made him hurry, but by the time he scrubbed himself dry with a small, thin towel and dressed, he was ravenous. And curious. He emerged eager to get going, but also intrigued by yet another guest at the table, a pudgy man a few years older than he with slick, curly black hair and wire-rimmed glasses.

Rayford leaned past Laslos and Demetrius and shook the man's hand. The mark of the believer was on his forehead, so Rayford used his own name.

The man looked at Laslos and shyly back at Rayford.

"This is Adon, Mr. Steele," Laslos said. "He speaks no English, but as you can see, he is a brother."

As they ate, Laslos told Rayford about Adon. "He is an artist, a skilled craftsman. And he has brought with him contraband items that could get him locked away for the rest of his life."

Adon followed the conversation with blank eyes, except when Laslos or Demetrius broke in to translate. Then he shyly looked away, nodding.

As Laslos cleared the table, Demetrius helped Adon bring in his equipment, which included a computer, printer, laminator, digital camera, dyes, hair clippers, even a cloth backdrop. Rayford was positioned in a chair under the light and near the window, where the early sun shone in. Adon draped a sheet around him and pinned it behind his neck. He said something to Laslos, who translated for Rayford.

"He wants to know if it is OK to make you bald."

"If you all think it's necessary. If we could get by with very short, I'd appreciate it."

Laslos informed Adon, whose shyness and hesitance apparently did not extend to his barbering. In a few swipes, he left Rayford's hair in clumps on the floor, leaving him with a quarter inch of dark residue such as Rayford had not seen since high school. "Mm-hmm," Rayford said.

Then came the dye that made what was left of the hair on his head look like the lightest of the gray in the long stubble on his chin.

Adon spoke to Laslos, who asked Rayford if he wore glasses.

"Contacts," Rayford said.

"Not anymore," Laslos said, and Adon produced a pair that completed the look.

Adon asked for Rayford's documents, shot a few pictures, and got to work on the computer. While he transformed Rayford's papers with the new photograph, Rayford stole away to the bathroom for a peek. The shorter, grayer hair and the gray stubble added ten years. In the glasses, he hardly recognized himself.

The technology allowed Adon to produce old-looking new documents in less than an hour. Rayford was eager to get going. "What do I owe you?" he said, but neither Laslos nor Demetrius would translate that.

"We'll be sure Adon is taken care of," Laslos said. "Now, Pastor is going to ride back to Ptolemaïs with him, and I will drop you at Kozani. I called ahead to have your fuel tanks topped off."

* * *

David sat bleary-eyed before his computer in New Babylon, his phone turned off. He had programmed the autopsy to be recorded on his own hard drive and anything from the evidence room to go onto Mac's computer. Meanwhile he continued to study the Chicago skyscraper he felt had potential as a new safe house. If he was right, it could accommodate hundreds of exiles, if necessary.

The Strong Building was a technical marvel, wholly solar powered. Giant reflectors stored enough energy every day to run the tower's power plant for weeks. So even a several-day stretch without bright sunlight never negatively impacted the building.

It was clear to David that neither the foundation nor at least the first thirty-five or so stories had been compromised by the damage above. The building appeared to have suffered a direct hit, but the impact had knocked the top half of the floors away from the rest of the structure rather than sending them crashing through those below. The question was what had happened to the solar panels and whether there was any way people could live in the unaffected portion of the structure without being detected.

It took David more than two hours of hacking through a morass of classified layers of information before he was able to turn his code-breaking software loose on the gateways that led to the mainframe that controlled the Strong Building. Reaching that point gave him a thrill he couldn't describe, though he would try to describe it later to Annie.

David was amazed that satellite phone technology got him as far as it did, and he had to wonder how much untapped energy was still operative in the condemned city. The longer everyone else remained convinced the place was radioactively contaminated, the better for him and the Tribulation Force. At every cybergateway along the path, he planted warnings of high radioactive levels. And while he was at it, he launched a robotic search engine that found all the original probe readouts and changed more than half of them to positive results. Civilian and GC planes were automatically rerouted so they couldn't fly over Chicago, even at more than thirty thousand feet.

David had to feather his way through the Strong Building mainframe by trial and error, seeing if he could remotely control the heating and cooling system, the lights, phones, sanitation system, elevators, and security cameras. The best video game in history would not have been more addictive.

The state-of-the-art monitoring system clearly reflected how much of the building was malfunctioning. More than half the elevators were off-line due to incomplete circuits. David clicked on More Information and found "Undetermined error has broken circuits between floors 40 and 80." He checked two dozen elevators that serviced the first thirty-nine floors and found that most appeared in running order.

By the time he had played with the system for another forty-five minutes, David had determined which security cameras worked, how to turn on lights on various floors, then the cameras, to show him whether the elevators would run, open, and shut. From nine time zones away, he was running what was left of a skyscraper in a city that had been abandoned for months.

Recording his keystrokes in a secure file, David fired up the camera on the highest floor he could find, the west end of the thirty-ninth. It showed water on the floor, but the mainframe indicated that it was being successfully redirected to keep it from flooding the floors below. He maneuvered the camera to show the ceiling and blinked. There was no ceiling, only a three-sided shell of the building that rose maybe another ten stories and revealed the inky sky, moon shining, stars twinkling.

So the Strong Building had been designed to withstand the worst nature could offer and had largely survived even what man threw at it. David stayed with his search until he found cameras that gave him a good view of what now served as the roof of the tower. By the time he had saved most of the information, he had an idea what the place looked like. In essence, it was a modular tower that appeared mortally wounded but had a lot to offer. Unusual in a modern skyscraper, the blueprints showed an inner core of offices hidden from outside view, surrounding the elevators on every floor. Here was unlimited floor space, water, plumbing, power, light—all undetectable by anyone who dared venture into an area that had been officially condemned and rendered off-limits anyway.

The open top appeared large enough to accommodate a helicopter, but David couldn't determine remotely whether the new roof by proxy, which at first appeared to be the ceiling of the thirty-ninth floor, would support significant weight. He found parking underneath the tower, though debris from the top floors blocked two of the main garage entrances. It was a long shot, but David believed that if he could get the stateside Trib Force to the place, they could find ways in and out of that underground carport.

And that gave him another idea. The last rain of bombs to hit Chicago had come with little warning. Employees and residents of tall buildings fled to the streets, but no one would have been allowed below ground with buildings falling. Underground garages would have been automatically sealed off with the city so gridlocked. How many vehicles might still be in that garage? David clicked away until he found the underground security cameras and the emergency lighting system. Once he had the lights on in the lowest level, he panned one of the security cameras until the vehicles came into view. Six levels below the street, he found more than a dozen cars. The problem, of course, was that drivers would have had the keys.

David kept trying cameras at different levels, looking for valet parking. He struck pay dirt near the elevators on the first level below the street. Nearly fifty late-model and mostly expensive cars, at least one of them a Hummer and several others sport-utility vehicles, were parked in the vicinity of a glassed-in shack clearly labeled Valet Parking. David manipulated the closest camera until he could make out a wall next to the cash register, replete with sets of keys. It was as if this place was made for the Trib Force, and he couldn't wait to send someone in to investigate. David wondered how soon he and Annie might be living there.

A call startled him. It was the director of the Global Community Academy of Television Arts and Sciences, an Indonesian named Bakar. "I need your help," the man said.

What else was new?

"Fire away," David said, shutting down his computer with everything saved and hidden.

"Moon is all over me about why we didn't bring back the videodiscs from the Gala. I thought we had. Anyway, we have them secured now, and I had arranged to have them flown here commercially. Walter tells me now that he'll have my job if those discs are out of GC hands for one second."

"Who's got 'em, Bakar?"

"One of our guys."

"Can't he just bring them?"

"Yeah, but he'd have to fly commercially."

"So? He's still not letting the discs out of his sight."

"Commercial flights are full coming here, and Moon doesn't want to wait."

"So you want us to send a plane for one guy?"

"Exactly."

"Do you know the cost of that?"

"That's why I'm begging."

"How did I get so popular all of a sudden?"

"What?"

"Nothing. Be at the hangar by ten this morning."

"Me?"

"Who else?"

"I don't want to go, Director. I want our guy picked up."

"I'm not going to have our sleep-deprived first officer fly a multimillion-dollar, er, Nick, fighter to Israel *and* have to find your guy, Bakar. You're going to ride along so Mr. Smith doesn't have to leave the cockpit. And I won't charge you the thousands for fuel."

"I appreciate it, Director. But couldn't I just have my guy be at a certain place and—"

"Earth to Bakar! This is a seller's, or I should say giver's, market, sir. You make

Smith go alone and I'll charge you depreciation on the jet, fuel, *and* his time. And his time is not cheap."

"I'll be there."

"I thought you would."

David called Abdullah.

"I was up anyway," Abdullah said. "I was hoping something would take me away from here today."

"You know how to work a disc-copying machine?"

"I don't know, boss. Is it more complicated than a fighter-bomber? Of course."

"I'm sending one with you. When Bakar finds his guy, you take the discs into the cockpit and tell them regulations say you have to personally log all cargo. Copy them, tag them as logged, and give them back to the TV boys."

"And bring you the copies."

"We're on the same page, Smitty."

David was next to giddy about the Trib Force all being in touch with each other via phone. He would feel better when he knew Buck was out of Israel and that Rayford was also on his way home, but David was unaware he had a message to call Buck.

* * *

Rayford shook Laslos's hand with both of his, got his promise to again personally thank Pastor Demeter and Adon, then loped into the airport and to the hangar. His head felt cool with so little insulation, but he didn't want to keep running his hand over it for fear of making it obvious that it was new to him.

A tower official met him at the Gulfstream. "You must be Mr. Berry."

"Yes, sir."

"Here's your fuel bill. Your papers?"

Rayford dug them out and paid his bill in cash.

"Lot of currency to have on your person, Mr. Berry," the man said, shuffling through Rayford's documents.

"A risk I'm willing to take to keep from going bankrupt again."

"Credit cards do you in, did they, sir?"

"Hate 'em."

"Wow, this picture looks like it was taken today."

Rayford froze, then forced himself to breathe. "Yeah?"

"Yes, look here. Karl! Come look at this!"

A mechanic in coveralls wandered over, looking peeved that he had been interrupted.

The official held Rayford's ID photo next to Rayford's face. "Look at this. He got this, let me see here, eight, nine months ago, but his hair's the same length and, if I'm not mistaken, he's wearing the same shirt."

"Sure enough," the mechanic said, leaving as quickly as he had come. Rayford watched to make sure he wasn't going to call someone, but he just moseyed back to the engine he'd been working on.

"Yes, that's something," the man said. "Did you notice that?"

"Nope," Rayford said. "Lemme see that. Well, I'll be dogged. I *had* just got a haircut when this was taken, but 'course the hair doesn't grow much anymore, anyway. And that probably *is* the same shirt. I don't have that many."

"Your own plane and not that many shirts? There's priorities for you."

"My own plane, I wish. I just drive 'em for the company."

"And what company's that, sir?" The man handed back his documents.

"Palwaukee Global," Rayford said.

"What do you transport?"

"Just the plane today. They had too many this side of the ocean."

"That so? You could pick up some business running from Jerusalem to New Babylon this week, you know."

"I heard. Wish I had the time."

"Safe flight."

"Thank you, sir." And thank you, Lord.

\+ + +

At ten in the morning in New Babylon, David strolled past the makeshift evidence room, pretending to be checking progress on the nearby Carpathia statue. He knew if he appeared to be snooping on the evidence, Intelligence Director Jim Hickman would shoo him. But Hickman also liked to impress, and allowing a colleague an inside look seemed to make him feel special.

David slowed as he walked by, hoping to run into Jim. Not seeing him, he knocked at the door. An armed guard opened it, and David spotted Jim across the room with a technician on his knees in the middle of a fifteen-by-one-hundred-foot drapery. "Don't want to bother anybody," David said. "Just want to make sure Director Hickman and his team have everything they need. I'll call him in his office."

"I'm in here, David!" Hickman called.

"Oh! So you are!"

"Let 'im in, Corporal! Come over here, David. Slip your shoes off. I wanna show you something."

"I don't want to intrude."

"Come on!"

"If you insist. This is fascinating."

"You haven't seen anything yet."

But David had. Three techies in the corner were hunched over the remains of the wood lectern. They had magnifying lamps and large tweezers, similar to what the technician had in the middle of the drape. He wore a helmet with a light on it and hand-held his magnifier.

"Look at this, David," Hickman said, motioning to him. "Got your shoes off?"

"I can come right out there where you are?"

"If I say you can, and I do! Now come on, time's a-wastin'."

David got to within about ten feet of Hickman and the techie when Jim said, "Stop and look down. Whoever was shootin' at this thing had to know what he was doin'. Looks like it went right through the middle. I mean, I never even knew Steele was a shooter, but to get a round, one round, to go through that pulpit dealie and then through the center of this curtain, well . . ."

"What am I looking at here, Jim?" David said, staring at a strange configuration about ten feet in diameter.

Hickman rose and limped over, joining David at the edge of the pattern. "Gettin' old," he said, grunting. "Now look here. The bullet coming from a weapon like that creates a mini tornado. If a real Kansas twister had the same relative strength, it would mix Florida and Maine with California and Washington. This one popped an eight-inch hole through the curtain there—you can see it from here."

"Uh-huh."

"But what you see at your feet is the effect it had on fibers this far from the center."

The force of the spinning disk had ripped the individual threads out of place and yanked them uniformly to create the huge twisted image.

"Now, c'mere and look at this."

Hickman led David to the top of the curtain, where brass eyeholes were set six inches apart along the whole one-hundred-foot edge. "Hooks went through these holes to suspend the whole thing from the iron piping."

"Wow," David said, astounded at the damage. The eight holes on either side of the center had been ripped clean, brass casings and all. The next several dozen were split apart, then more on each side had mangled hooks still attached, all the way to the ends, where the eyeholes were intact but the hooks were missing.

"Just ripped this thing away and sent it flying into the distance."

"Director!" the techie called.

Hickman started toward the middle again, but David hung back until Hickman motioned him to follow.

"Bullet residue," the techie said, holding a tiny shard of lead between slender forceps.

"Bag that up. Ten'll get you twenty we can trace it to the Saber we found."

The technician began dropping pieces into a plastic bag. "I hate to say it, sir, but fragments like this will be almost impossible to positively match with—"

"Come on now, Junior. We've got eyewitnesses who say a guy in a raghead getup took the shot. We found the gun, got a match on the prints, and we know who the guy is. We found his disguise in a trash can a few blocks away. The fragments'll match all right, even if the lab work is inconclusive. This guy's definitely part of the conspiracy."

"Conspiracy?" David said, as they moved to the corner where the lectern pieces lay.

"We think the gunshot was diversionary," Hickman whispered.

"But this Steele guy is being accused—"

"Is a suspect, sure. But we're not sure the bullet even came close to Carpathia."

"What? But—"

"Carpathia didn't die from a gunshot wound, David. At least not solely."

"What then?"

"Autopsy's going on right now. We ought to know soon. But let me tell you somethin' just between you, me, and the whatever: Fortunato's no dummy."

David could have argued. "Yeah?"

"If it turns out the kill wound came from the platform, wouldn't that be highly embarrassing?"

"If one of his—our own did it, you mean."

"'Xactly. But the public doesn't know that. The only video that's been shown so far only shows the victim hittin' the deck. People think he got shot. Leon sees that we blame this on the disgruntled former employee, and then he has us deal with the insurrection privately. And by dealin' with it, well, you get my drift."

The technicians digging through the remains of the lectern produced several bullet fragments, some big as a fingernail.

"This sure is fascinating stuff, Jim."

"Well," Hickman said, slowly running his hand through his hair, "it helps if you're a trained observer."

"You're nothing if not that."

"Right as rain, Hassid."

8

LEAH SAT FITFULLY at what was left of the tiny airport in Kankakee. When her phone rang and Rayford identified himself, she was speechless. "I have so much to talk to you about," he said, "so much to apologize for."

"I'll look forward to that," she said flatly. In truth she was more eager to get to the safe house and see Tsion than she was to talk to Rayford. "Thanks for leaving me stranded, but I guess I can see why. Did you kill Carpathia?"

"I just got a call from David Hassid, who seems pretty sure I didn't. I wanted to. Planned to. But then I couldn't do it."

"So what about the gun with your prints? You weren't the shooter?"

"I was, but it was an accident. I was bumped."

"Be glad I'm not on your jury."

"Leah, where are you?"

She told him and filled him in on her plan to fly to Palwaukee and perhaps get a ride with T to near the safe house, where they would try to determine if anyone was casing it. "Problem is, nothing is going that way tonight, and in the morning it's exorbitant. I may hitchhike."

"See if T will come get you. If it's too far to drive, he can fly."

"I hardly know him, Rayford. When will you be here?"

"I should hit Palwaukee about nine in the morning."

"I'll wait for you then, I guess."

"That would be nice."

Leah sighed. "Don't get pleasant on me all of a sudden. I can't pretend I'm not irritated with you. And getting yourself in even deeper trouble with the GC, what was that all about?"

"I wish I knew," he said. "But I *would* like the chance to talk to everyone face-to-face."

"Thanks to you, that's looking more and more remote. You know Tsion and Chloe and the baby are underground now?"

"I heard."

"And nobody knows where Hattie is."

"But someone told you she was in the States?"

"It's a big place, Rayford."

"Yeah, but I still can't see her giving us up."

"You have more faith than I."

"I agree we need to be careful."

"Careful? If I do get T to take me to Mount Prospect, or if I wait for you, who knows we're not walking into a trap at the safe house? It's a miracle it wasn't found out long before I joined you."

Rayford ignored that, and Leah felt mean. She meant every word, but why couldn't she cut him some slack?

\+ + +

David checked in with Annie—who said she was headed back to bed—then invited Mac to join him in his office to see what was happening in the morgue. They settled close to the computer, and David started by listening live. Dr. Eikenberry was into a routine of announcing for the record the height and weight of the body and her plans for embalming and repair.

"There was some kind of a hassle right at the start," Mac said. "People say she was yelling, demanding the doctor. Can you go back without messing up the recording you're doing now?"

David pinpointed when the microphones in the morgue first detected sound. The time showed just after eight o'clock in the morning, and the recording began with a key in the door and the door opening. It was clear the mortician had two assistants with her, a man and a woman, and both sounded young. She called the young man Pietr and the young woman Kiersten.

The first spoken words were Dr. Eikenberry's. She was swearing. Then, "What is this? They leave the crate in here? Get someone to get it out of here. I'm going to work on this table and I want room. I'm assuming there are no more bodies in storage?"

"I'm here with you, Doc," Pietr said. "I wouldn't know."

"Check, would you? Kiersten, call someone to get rid of the crate."

In the background Kiersten could be heard talking tentatively to the palace switchboard operator. In the foreground, Pietr could be heard slamming a door. "You're not gonna be happy, ma'am."

"What?"

"There are *no* bodies in here."

"None?"

"None."

"You're telling me Carpathia is not in there either?"

"None means none, ma'am."

She swore again. "Kiersten! Get somebody in here with a crowbar. They left the body in this crate all night? I'll be surprised if he doesn't stink."

After several minutes of muttering, a male voice: "You asked for a crowbar, ma'am?"

"Yes, and someone who knows how to use it."

"I can do it."

"You're a guard!"

"Crowbars are nothing. You want the box opened?"

"Put your weapon down, soldier. Why do they send *you* to do this?"

"Security. They don't want anybody in here but you and your staff."

"Well, I appreciate that, but . . ."

David and Mac heard the crate being torn open.

"No casket?" the doctor said. "Get him into the fridge."

"In the bag or out?" Pietr said.

"In," she said. "I don't even want to think how much blood he's lost in there. I'm not starting till ten, per instructions, but let's get ready."

Several minutes passed with minimal conversation, much of it related to their finding the plastic amalgam and her instructing her assistants how and where and when to have it ready. "You think this winch can handle a man his size?"

"Never saw a portable one before," Pietr said. "We'll make it work."

David fast-forwarded until he heard conversation and stopped only when it seemed meaningful. Finally he was at the ten o'clock point, and the cooler was opened again. Dr. Eikenberry switched on a recorder and spoke into a microphone David had seen hanging from the ceiling when he helped deliver her supplies.

"This is Madeline Eikenberry, M.D. and forensic pathologist, here in the morgue at Global Community Palace in New Babylon with assistants Pietr Berger and Kiersten Scholten. They are bringing to the table the body of Nicolae Jetty Carpathia, age thirty-six. We will remove the corpse from the body bag into which it was placed following his death approximately fourteen hours ago in Jerusalem, cause to be determined."

David and Mac heard the transfer of the bag from gurney to examining table. "I don't like the sound of that," Dr. Eikenberry muttered. "It feels as if he may have nearly bled out."

"Yuck," Kiersten said.

"Could you spell that for the transcriptionist, dear?" the doctor said. Then, "Oh, no! Oh, my! Agh! Keep it off the floor! Pietr, make sure it drains through the table. What a botch! OK, transcriptionist, you know what to leave out. Pick up here. The body was not properly prepared for transfer or storage, and several liters of blood have collected in the bag. The body remains dressed in suit and tie and shoes, but a massive wound about the posterior head and neck, which will be examined once the deceased is disrobed, appears to be the exit area for the blood."

It sounded to David as if Carpathia's clothes were being cut off. "No apparent anterior wounds," Dr. Eikenberry said, as the sound of spraying water came through. "Let's turn him over. Oh! Be careful of that!" She swore again and again. "Get his doctor in here now! And I mean now! What in the world is this? I was told nothing of this!"

The footsteps must have been Kiersten's running to the door to have someone look for the doctor, because Pietr could be heard as clearly as the doctor. "I thought you were to look for a bullet entry wound."

"So did I! Is someone trying to kill us?"

More spraying, grumbling, and mumbling. Finally the door opened again. Hurried footsteps. "Doctor," Eikenberry began, "why wasn't I told of this?"

"Well, I, we—"

"Turning over a man with this kind of a weapon still in him is ten times more dangerous than a cop sticking his bare hands in a perp's pocket without checking for needles or blades first!"

"I'm sorry, I—"

"You're *sorry*? You want to help pull this out? Ah, never mind. Just tell me if there's anything else I should have known."

The doctor sounded thoroughly intimidated. "Well, to tell you the truth—"

"Oh, please, at *least* do that. I think it's about time, don't you?"

"Uh-huh, well, you know you're to look for bullet—"

"Damage, wounds, yes. What?"

"The fact is, the EMTs are of the opinion—"

"The same ones who prepared, or I should say left unprepared, a body like this?"

"That wasn't their fault, ma'am. I understand the supreme commander was pushing everyone to get the body out of there."

"Go on."

"The EMTs believe you will find no bullet wounds."

A pregnant silence.

"Frankly, Doctor, I don't care what we find. I'll give you my expert opinion, and if there are also bullet holes, I'll include that. But can you answer me one thing? Why does everybody think there was a shooter, and why is that former employee pretty much being charged in the media? Because his prints were found on a weapon that *didn't* shoot Carpathia? I don't get it."

"As *you* said, ma'am, if you'll pardon me, it isn't your place to care about the cause of death, but only to assess it."

"Well, I'd say about an, oh, say, fifteen- to eighteen-inch, ah, what would you call this, Doctor, a big knife or a small sword?"

"A handled blade, certainly."

"Certainly. I'd hazard a guess that this whatever-it-is entering about two inches below the nape of the neck and exiting about half an inch through the crown of the skull, that certainly didn't enhance the victim's health, did it?"

"No, ma'am."

"Doctor, do you really not know why I wasn't informed of this major, likely lethal, wound?"

"I know we didn't want to prejudice you."

She laughed. "Well, you certainly succeeded there! As for nearly slicing open my assistants and me, what do you say to that?"

"I guess I thought you'd see the, ah, sword."

"Doctor, the man was swimming in his own blood! He was on his back! We transferred him the same way, disrobed him, hosed him down, saw no entry or exit wounds on the anterior, and naturally, flipped him to examine the posterior wounds. What do you think I was expecting? I saw the news. I heard the gunshot and saw the people running and the victim fall. I had heard the scuttlebutt that there may have been a conspiracy, that one of the regional potentates may have had a concealed weapon. But I would have appreciated knowing that the man would look like a cocktail wiener with a sword poking through him."

"I understand."

"Do you see the damage this weapon did to significant tissue?"

"Not entirely."

"Well, unless we find bullets in the brain or somewhere else above the neck, it alone killed him."

Water was spraying again. "I see no bullet holes, do you?"

"No, ma'am."

"Pietr?"

"No."

"Kiersten?"

"Nope."

"Doctor?"

"I said no."

"But this blade, and I'll be able to tell you for sure when I get in there, appears to have gone through vertebrae, perhaps spinal cord, the membrane, the brain stem, the brain itself, the membrane again, and then come out the top of the skull, all none the worse for wear."

"That would be my observation too, ma'am."

"It would?"

"Yes."

"Your expert opinion."

"I'm no patholog—"

"But you know enough about the anatomy to know that I should not be surprised if I have guessed the internal damage fairly accurately?"

"Right."

"But more important, that this weapon appears as lethal now as it must have before it was thrust?"

"I'm afraid so."

"You see what I'm driving at?"

"I think so."

"You think so. One of us unsuspecting pathologists so much as brushes a finger against that blade, and we're sliced."

"I'm sorry—"

"And while the victim may be one of the most respected men in the history of the world, we don't know yet, do we, what might be in his blood? Or what might have been on the hands of the perpetrator. Do we?"

"We don't."

"Do you notice anything unusual about the blade, sir?"

"I don't know. I've never seen one quite like it, if that's what you m—"

"Simpler than that, Doctor. The cutting edge is facing out."

"You're sure there's only one cutting edge?"

"Yes, and do you know how I know? Because I was fortunate enough to catch my finger there when we turned over the body. Look here, at the top of his head. As we turned him, my hand went behind the head, and hidden there in the hair was the half-inch protrusion of the blade. As soon as it came in contact with my gloved index finger, I flinched and pulled away. Had I done that on the other edge, I daresay it would have cut my finger off."

"I see."

"You see. Do you also see our challenge in removing the weapon?"

A pause. "Actually, if it is as strong and sharp as you say, removal should be fairly simple. You just pull it back out the way it entered, and—"

"Doctor, may I remind you that the cutting edge is facing away from the body."

"I know."

"Then unless we are precise to a millimeter, the blade could cut its way out vertically. Cardinal rule of forensic pathology: Do as little damage to the body as possible so it is easier to determine how much trauma was actually inflicted from without."

"Ah, Madeline, if I could have a word."

"Please."

"Privately."

"Excuse us," she said, obviously looking at her assistants. Footsteps.

"Madeline, I apologize for any part I played in this dangerous situation. But we have been friends a long time. I sold the supreme commander on you because I wanted you to have the honor and the income. I resent being berated in front of your subordinates and—"

"Point well taken. I'll say nice things about you when you're gone. And I do appreciate the assignment. I don't know what the benefits are to a mortician asked to evaluate the most famous victim in history, but I do owe you thanks for that."

"You're welcome," he said flatly, and David heard him leave.

Pietr and Kiersten returned. "Wow," Pietr said.

"Wow is right," Dr. Eikenberry said. "That man?"

"Yes."

"That doctor who just left?" she clarified.

"Yes."

"I must tell you, he is a complete idiot."

The mortician told the transcriptionist to please disregard everything since the turning of the body and to pick up at that point. She explained how she had irrigated the entire wound area and found "just the one entry and one exit wound, with weapon still in place. The entry wound is considerably larger than the exit, and nearly all the blood flow came from the neck, though understandably there is evidence of blood exiting through eyes, nose, mouth, and ears as well. That the entry wound is clearly larger, while the blade itself is not that much wider there, indicates that the weapon was dug and twisted aggressively. The skull would have held the top of the weapon in place, but the bottom appears to have been flexible enough to inflict severe trauma."

David looked at Mac and exhaled. "Rayford's in the clear. I mean, he might get busted for shooting *at* Carpathia, but he couldn't have killed him."

Mac shook his head. "Sounds to me like Carpathia was murdered by one of his own people."

"It sure does," David said. "There was talk of one of the potentates with something in his coat, but I want to see the videodiscs."

* * *

Buck awoke late morning, stiff and sore. The sun blinded, but Chaim remained asleep. Buck took a closer look at Chaim's ratty blanket. The inside was blood encrusted, and he wondered how the old man could stand it. He also worried that some of the blood might be Chaim's own.

Buck carefully tugged at the blanket to see if any blood stained Chaim's pajamas. But Chaim held tight and turned over, exposing his back. No wounds or stains that Buck could see.

"You awake?" the old man mumbled, still facing away from Buck.

"Yes. We have to talk."

"Later."

"Now."

"Why don't you go find me some clothes? I need to get home, and I can't go like this."

"You don't think the GC is waiting for you there?"

Chaim rolled over to face Buck, squinting against the sunlight. "And why would they be? Where's my phone? I want to call the house, talk to Jacov."

"Don't."

"Why not?"

"Don't, Chaim. I know the truth. I know what happened."

"You saw nothing! No one saw anything!"

"You can't admit to me what I know already? What kind of a friend are you?"

Chaim got up and relieved himself, then returned to sit wearily on the bed. His white hair pointed everywhere. "You should be happy," he said.

"Happy?"

"Of course! What do you care how the deed was done, so long as it was done?"

"I care because *you* did it!"

"You don't know that. And what if I did?"

"You'll die for it, that's what! You think I want that?"

Chaim cocked his head and shrugged. "You're a better friend than I, Cameron."

"I'm beginning to think so."

Chaim chuckled. "I can't cheer you, eh?"

"Tell me how you did it, Chaim."

"The less you know, the less you have to answer for."

"Oh, don't be naïve! You've been around too long for that. I have to answer for everything. I have to be grateful for facial lacerations, because if I had not suffered them, I would have had to change my appearance anyway. Telling me you murdered Carpathia won't add much to my plate. They have enough on me, manufactured and otherwise, to put me away on sight. So, tell me."

"I'm telling no one. This is mine alone."

"But you know you can't go home."

"I can tell my people where I am, that I am all right."

"You must come to the States with me."

"I can't leave my country, my staff."

"Chaim, listen to me. Your staff is dead. They were tortured and massacred last night by the GC, probably trying to get to you."

Chaim looked up slowly, his hair casting wild shadows on the far wall. "Don't talk crazy," he said warily. "That is not amusing."

"I wouldn't joke about that, Chaim. Jacov was killed by a blow to the chin that broke his neck. A guard hit him with the butt end of an Uzi when he tried to rush to you."

Chaim put a hand over his mouth and sucked in a noisy breath. "Don't," he said, his words muffled. "Don't do this to me."

"I didn't do it, Chaim. You did it."

"He's dead? You know for certain he's dead?"

"I checked his pulse myself."

"What have I done?"

"Hannelore and her mother and Stefan are gone too."

Chaim stood and moved toward the door as if wanting to leave but knowing he had nowhere to go. "No!" he wailed. "Why?"

"Someone had to know, Chaim. Someone had to have seen you. Surely you didn't expect to get away with it."

Chaim's knees gave way and he hit the floor hard, a high-pitched cry in his throat. "You checked the pulses at my home too?"

Buck nodded.

"That was not smart. You could have been killed too."

"And *my* death would have been your fault too, Chaim. Look what's happened!"

Chaim turned and leaned over the bed, still kneeling. He buried his face in his hands. "I was willing to die," he managed. "I didn't care about myself. The sword was perfect and fit into the tubing of my chair just so. No one knew. Not even Jacov. Oh, Jacov! Jacov! What have I done to you? Cameron! You must kill me! You must avenge those deaths!" He stood quickly and opened the window. "If I lose my nerve, you must push me! Please, I cannot bear this!"

"Shut the window, Chaim. I'm not going to kill you, and I won't let you kill yourself."

"I'll not turn myself in to those swine. I wouldn't give them the satisfaction! Oh, I *will* kill myself, Cameron. You know I will!"

"You'll have to try without me present. I love you too much, Chaim. I will die before you do to keep you from going to hell."

"Hell? If God would send me to hell for murdering such a monster, I will go happily. But he *should* send me to hell for what I did to my people! Oh, Cameron!" He collapsed onto the bed, rolling into a fetal position and groaning as if about to burst. Suddenly he sat up, seeming eager to relive the deed.

"I was going to leap from my chair at just the right moment, weapon in hand. He is so much taller, I had been practicing my jumping. I was going to leap as high as I could and, with both hands on the handle, drive the blade down through the top of his head. The whole world would see and know.

"There were all those shenanigans on the stage, people standing, sitting, moving, laughing. I joined in, measuring the distance, seeing where I could maneuver the chair. When he came to greet me and lift my hand, I came close to reaching across my body to lift out the sword and plunge it into his heart. But my angle was wrong. I would not have had the leverage to get the blade out, let alone to thrust it where I needed to.

"I was rolling toward him finally as he moved my way. My plan was to turn quickly at the last minute and trip him. Then I would leap from the chair and kill him. But just as he got near me, the gun went off. At first I thought I had been detected and that his security guards had shot me. But he lurched my way, away from the sound of the gun and the shattering lectern.

"I could see that he was about to tumble into my lap, so I quickly withdrew the blade. I didn't have time even to orient it in my hands. I pointed it straight up and held steady as he fell back onto it. I held firm and tried to scrape the brain from his evil head. He jerked, and I let go. He rolled to my feet. It was chaos. People came running. I steered away and, for an instant, I thought I had gotten away with it. The timing! The shot! I could tell it came from the crowd, and as I ran away I wondered if it might be mistaken for a two-person crime.

"I had plotted an unlikely escape just on a lark. And here I am. Who would have believed it?"

Buck sat shaking his head. Chaim rolled back over, moaning. "You're right," he whispered. "It's all on me. I did this to them. Oh, no, no, no . . ."

Buck heard voices below the window. Three vagrants sat sharing a bottle. "Which of you would like a fifty-Nick note?" he called down.

Two waved him off, but a young drunk stood quickly. "What I gotta do?"

"Buy me some clothes and shoes with this twenty, and when you bring 'em back, keep the change and get another fifty."

The other two laughed and tried to sing. The young drunk squinted and let his head fall back. "How do you know I won't run off with your twenty?"

"My risk," Buck said. "Your loss. You want twenty or fifty?"

"Gimme," the man said, reaching. Buck let the bill flutter down, which brought the other two to their feet to compete for it. The younger shoved them away and got it easily. Buck felt better about his chances when the man turned back to him and said, "What size?"

+ + +

"No deal," Abdullah said on the phone.

"What's the problem?" David said.

"The guy had the fear of God in him. Wouldn't let those discs out of his sight. I didn't even get the machine out of my bag. He said he'd stand there and watch while I logged them in, if I had to."

"I just hope they're not bringing them here to destroy them. They're the only hope of exonerating Rayford."

"Exonerating? What's that mean?"

"Getting him off the hook."

"No, sir," Abdullah said. "He didn't even have to pull the trigger to be guilty. He drew down on Carpathia. What more do they need? He needs to stay as far away from here as he can."

9

Seven Hours Later

DAVID HATED GETTING so little time with Annie, but he knew their exile was fast approaching. Then, if they could pull it off, they would be together as much as they wanted—and probably a long, long way from New Babylon.

What an incredibly beautiful city New Babylon would have been under other circumstances. Carpathia had employed the best architects and landscapers and designers and decorators. And except for the absence of any God-honoring works of art, the place looked magnificent, particularly at night. Great colored spotlights accented the massive, crystalline buildings. Only since the recent decimation of another huge percentage of the population and the resulting personnel shortages had the place begun to evidence the lack. It took longer for refuse removal or for lights to be repaired. Yet still the skyline was stunning, a man-made marvel.

As dusk crept over the horizon, David sat listening to Fortunato, Hickman, and Moon through the bug in Carpathia's office. He couldn't tell whether Leon was actually in Nicolae's chair, but it sure sounded like it. They were watching the videos that had been brought back from the Gala. David sat with his head in his hands, using earphones to be sure to catch every detail. He wished he could see the videos, but that was not his call.

They played and replayed and replayed clips that included the gunshot. "See?" Moon said. "He's right down there, stage right, about three or four deep, there! See? Pause!"

"I see it, Walter," Leon said. "Good thing we've got fingerprints. I would not have been able to tell who that was in a million years."

"Good getup," Hickman said. "The gray hair stickin' out of the turban. Nice touch. Robes. I woulda thought he was an Arab."

"Some kinda raghead anyway."

They all chuckled.

"Rayford Steele," Leon said softly. "Who'd have believed that? Wouldn't murder be against his religion?"

Laughter. Silence. Then, "I don't know." It was Hickman. "Maybe he convinces himself it's a holy war. Then I guess everything goes."

"Fact is," Moon said, "he missed."

"You look close," Hickman said, "and he had a better shot earlier. He fires then, he's our guy. But I don't think he even meant to shoot when he did."

"What're you talking about?"

"Look. Slow motion, well, back it up a second first. Look! Right there! Somebody bumps him. A little person. A woman? Can you zoom?"

"I don't know how to run these crazy machines," Leon said. "We oughta get Hassid in here."

"You want me to call him?"

"Maybe. Just a minute. Here, OK. Slow and zoomed. What do you see?"

"There!" Hickman said again. "She trips, loses her balance or somethin'. Ha! Who's that look like? Wally, who's that remind you of?"

"Nah."

"No? Come on! Who am I thinkin' of?"

"I know who you're thinking of, but we've got her eyeballed in North America. Probably trying to get to her sister's funeral. She doesn't know it was a month ago."

They chuckled again, and David picked up the phone. "Rayford," he said, "maybe Hattie's *not* on her way to the safe house yet. GC's tracked her out west, trying to make her sister's funeral."

"That's a relief. Maybe we're OK for a while."

"Don't get overconfident. I uploaded a whole bunch of stuff to Chloe's computer so you can see your new digs, if you need 'em. Where are you?"

"Well, I was about to put down at Palwaukee when I heard from Leah. I'd been having trouble reaching T to see if he could go get her in Kankakee, southeast of here. She never got him either, so I'm on my way to get her. We'll come back here and use Buck's car to see if we can get to the safe house."

"Call Tsion first. Last time I talked to him he said he thought he heard car noises."

"That's not good."

"Tell me about it," David said. "Hey, Leah might need a new alias."

"Yeah? Why?"

"She's been asking around about Hattie using that Clendenon name. They might try to follow her to Hattie."

"They're already onto Hattie. They don't need Leah."

"Whatever you say, Rayford. Just a thought."

"I appreciate it."

"You'd better be careful. They're going to try to pin this on you." David told him of the autopsy and evidence investigation.

"So I missed, just like you thought?"

"Looks pretty sure at this point."

"Then how can they pin it on me?"

"What, they're obligated to the truth? If you didn't do it, someone on the platform did."

"My money's on one of the three insurgent kings," Rayford said. "Probably Litwala."

"Even if you're right, you're a less embarrassing assassin than somebody behind Nicolae. I'll bet you're the scapegoat."

* * *

Buck had sat with the morose Chaim Rosenzweig the whole day. The old man had alternately slept and wept, threatening suicide. Buck wanted to go out and find them something to eat, but he didn't dare leave Chaim. The drunk came back to toss a bundle of used clothes up to the window, but he wasn't interested in more money to find food. Once he had his fifty, he was gone.

Buck called the desk. "Anybody down there that could bring us some food for a fee?"

"What, you think we got room service?"

"Just tell me if you know anybody who wants to make a few Nicks."

"Yeah, OK. When the concierge gets off his break, I'll send 'im up. You'll recognize him by his tuxedo."

Amazingly, ten minutes later someone knocked tentatively. Buck wished he had a gun. "Who is it?"

"I'll get you food," a man said. "How much?"

"Ten."

"Deal."

Buck sent him out for local fare. It was all he could do to get Chaim to eat a few bites. Presently, David called.

"Is it true?" he asked. "About Chaim?"

Buck was stunned. "What about him?"

"That he's dead, burned up at his home along with his whole staff?"

"You know that's not true, David. Hasn't anyone told you I'm with him?"

"I'm just telling you what's on television."

"So that's how they're going to spin it? Hero statesman dies in a fire. That keeps him out of the conspiracy?"

"They're convinced one of the three insurgents did it," David said, "but that would be bad for morale. What's Chaim's theory? He was right there."

"We need to talk about this later, David. I need to get him out of here."

"How?"

"I finally got hold of T. He's bringing the Super J. I directed him to a blocked-off road. We have to be there when he puts down so he can be in the air again before anyone's the wiser. We'll have to stop in Greece for fuel, though—wouldn't want to risk it over here."

* * *

Tsion was alarmed. Chloe was proposing madness. "Can I trust you with Kenny," she said, "that you won't fall asleep?"

"I would give my life for that child, you know that. But you must not go. This is foolishness."

"Tsion, I can't sit here doing nothing. I have informed everybody in the co-op generally what's going on, but there's little I can do until the buying-selling restrictions are sanctioned. Don't keep me from doing something worthwhile."

"I am not your superior, Chloe. I could not deprive you of anything. I'm just urging you to think this through. Why must you go? And why must it be now? Cameron's car is at the airport. If you take the Suburban, you leave me with no vehicle."

"You have nowhere to go, Tsion. You can't outrun the GC anyway. Your best bet is to stay right here, listen for them, turn the power off if you hear them, and become invisible."

Tsion threw up his arms. "I cannot dissuade you, so do what you are going to do. But don't be long."

"Thank you. And promise me you will do anything but let Kenny fall into GC hands."

"I would die first."

"I want *him* to die first."

"That I will not do."

"You would let them take him."

"Over my body."

"But don't you see, Tsion? That's how it will be! You'll be a martyr, but you will still have lost Kenny to the enemy."

"You're right. You'd better stay here."

"Nice try."

"This is not a smart thing to do in broad daylight."

"I'll be careful."

"Too late. You're already being reckless."

"Good-bye, Tsion."

* * *

"What do you make of this?" Hickman was saying as David listened in.

"Ramblings," Leon said. "Hallucinations. Gibberish. Not uncommon in such a situation."

"But first he said that about thinking he had done all you asked. What was that about?"

"Nicolae was not addressing me! I have never, would never, could never ask him to do anything! Anyway, if he was talking to me, it would indicate that he thought I had attacked him."

"But then what is his obsession with the—what does he call it?"

"The veil? Or the vale? What?"

"Listen. Listen to what he says."

David pressed both earphones close and listened carefully. After Carpathia's first lament, which echoed through the sound system, the PA system appeared to have failed, but his next words were picked up through the videodisc machine mike. "The veil," Carpathia rasped. "Was it rent in twain from the top to the bottom?" Carpathia struggled to make himself understood. "Father," he managed. "Father, forgive them, for they know not what they do."

David shuddered.

The exchange reminded him of something he and Mac had heard from the morgue. He called Mac. "What was it Dr. Eikenberry said about reports of Nicolae's last words?"

"Just that it would have been impossible."

"That's what I thought. Once she got in there and saw the damage, she said he wouldn't have been able to speak, right?"

"Exactly."

David re-cued the recording and found it.

"Well," Dr. Eikenberry said, "this gives the lie to the 'last words' business, doesn't it?"

"It sure does," Pietr said. "Unless he could speak supernaturally."

He and the doctor and Kiersten laughed. "This man could not have said a word," Dr. Eikenberry concluded. "Maybe they want to invent something for posterity, but no one had better ask me if it was possible."

\+ + +

A few minutes after nine in the morning, Central Standard Time, Rayford put the Gulfstream down in Kankakee. He had told Leah to watch for a smallish jet and to be ready to board quickly. But as he taxied by the terminal, he saw her sleeping in a chair by the window.

He left the jet whining on the tarmac, knowing how conspicuous that would look to ground control, and sprinted into the terminal. "Donna!" he said, as he approached. "Donna Clendenon!"

She jumped and squinted at him. "Do I know you?" she said, clearly terrified.

"Marv Berry," he said, grabbing her bag. "We've got to go."

"Hi, Marv," she whispered. "You've got to tell a girl when you get a makeover."

Rayford heard some kind of warning through the PA system, and a couple of orange-vested officials started his way. He ignored them and was airborne quickly, certain that Kankakee had no GC pursuit craft and little interest in a small jet flyer who had boorishly violated their protocols.

He told Leah, "All I get out of Palwaukee is a tower guy who says T is not there and won't be back until tomorrow, and that he's not at liberty to say where he went."

"I got the same. What do you make of it?"

"I don't know. Wish there was someone in his church I could ask. But T and I have never needed to communicate through third parties. He's usually reachable by cell. He's always wanted to be in on the action, and I need someone to go and ferry Buck and Chaim over here. I'm tempted to call Albie and see if he can find someone."

"Now there's a name I haven't heard," Leah said.

"Albie? Long story. Good guy."

"So tell me."

"Not until you and I clear up a few things."

"Until you do, you mean," she said.

Rayford told her what had happened to him in Israel, on the flight to Greece, and in Greece. "I know that sounds a little too convenient," he said, "and I wouldn't blame you if you thought I just made it up to—"

"Made it up?" she said, obviously emotional. "If you made that up, you'd burn in hell."

"So, will you be the first to forgive me?"

"Of course. And I need to apologize too. I—"

"You've done nothing close to what I did," Rayford said. "Forget it."

"Don't brush me off, Rayford. I feel awful about how I've responded to you."

"Fair enough. We're even."

"Don't be flippant."

"I'm not. You can imagine how I feel about—"

"I'm not saying I was as terrible as you," she said wryly.

* * *

David responded to an announcement that all GC management personnel from director level and above were to report immediately to the small theater in the education wing. What now?

As dozens crowded into the room, Fortunato stood at the lectern like a professor. "Quickly now, quickly please, find your seats. I've been informed that more than a million people are in New Babylon already with probably at least two million more to come. Our social services are being taxed to their limits, and these people have no outlet for their grief. I want to know if there is any reason we cannot put the body of the potentate in position even this evening and begin the procession past the bier. We're estimating that not half the mourners will stay for the burial, which may have to be postponed as well. Do we have adequate lighting?"

Someone shouted yes.

"And concessions? Stations with water, food, medical services?"

"Could be in place within an hour!" someone said.

"Good. The bier itself and its pedestal?"

"Pedestal is finished and waiting."

"Bier is finished! Per specifications."

"Really?" Fortunato said. "I was told there was some question whether it could be vacuum sealed—"

"Solved, with a little help. Once the body is, ah, placed inside, the air can be quickly removed and the hole secured. The stopper is a hard rubber compound that will be screwed into the Plexiglas—"

"Thank you, we can skip the details. The entire container is transparent?"

"Yes, sir. And on the pedestal it will sit nearly fifteen feet off the ground."

"Yet the mourners will have access . . . ?"

"Via stairs leading up one side and down the other. They will, of course, be unable to touch the glass, as they will be separated from it by approximately five feet with velvet ropes and, um, armed security."

"Thank you," Fortunato said. "Now there are certain details I would like us all to hear, except those of you who need to supervise construction of the restoring stations. You may be excused now, and let's shoot for an 8:00 p.m.

start time. Let's get the word out to the people so they can begin assembling. Yes, Mr. Blod."

Guy had been waving and now stood.

"I'm afraid my statue will not be ready until dawn, as originally planned. We're making progress, and I believe it will be stunning, but even the initial goal was nearly impossible."

"No problem. You may go now too, and we'll all look forward to your handiwork."

As Guy rushed from the room, Leon called upon Dr. Eikenberry to come to the microphone. "It has been her difficult duty to prepare for burial the body of our beloved leader. As she is a loyal citizen of the Global Community and was a great admirer of the potentate, you can imagine what an emotional task this was. I have asked her to report on her findings and summarize the challenges she faced to allow the mourners to have one last encounter with His Excellency in as dignified and memorable a manner as possible, under the circumstances."

Dr. Eikenberry had lost the severe look David had seen when he first met her. Her white coat was gone, and she seemed to have applied fresh makeup and had her hairdo softened. He wondered when she had had time for that.

"Thank you, Supreme Commander," she began. "This has indeed been a most difficult and emotional day for me and my assistants, Pietr Berger and Kiersten Scholten. We treated the body of Nicolae Carpathia with utmost reverence and respect. As expected, the cause of death was severe brain trauma caused by a single bullet from a Saber handgun. The projectile entered the potentate's body just below the nape of his neck in the posteri—in the back and exited through the top of the crani—through the top of his head. The particularly devastating power of this type of projectile destroyed two vertebrae, severed the spinal cord, obliterated the brain stem and posterior of the brain, and left residual damage to the carotid artery and much of the soft tissue in the throat.

"Because of the spinning bullet, the back of the neck and head were laid open, causing the greatest challenge for repair and reconstruction. Without getting into the details, the gaping wound has been stapled and stitched, camouflaged with wax and putty and coloring and a minimum of artificial hair. If the result contributes to an appropriate farewell to the greatest leader the world has ever known, I am grateful and consider it a privilege to have served the Global Community this way."

Amid tears and sustained applause, Dr. Eikenberry began to leave, then returned to the podium with an index finger raised. "If I may add one thing," she said. "There is recorded evidence that His Excellency's last words were an expression of forgiveness to the perpetrator of this heinous crime. Forgiveness has long been ascribed to the divine, and as a medical professional, I must tell you why I concur with this assessment. Besides the *sentiment* of those last words, I can tell you that there is no human explanation for the potentate's ability to speak at all, given the physical damage. Truly this was a righteous man. Truly this was the son of god."

+ + +

At Palwaukee Rayford tried in person to get more information out of the tower fill-in. "I'm sorry, sir," the man said. "But not only am I not at liberty to tell you, I couldn't if I wanted to. He didn't tell me where he was going but only when he expected to return."

"Do you know who I am?"

"No, sir."

"You haven't seen me around here, don't know I'm a friend of T's?"

The man squinted at Rayford, and Leah cleared her throat. "He, ah, may not recognize you."

Rayford couldn't believe his own stupidity. "Listen, son, I have permission to take an associate's vehicle, but he neglected to leave the keys with me. I need to know you won't feel obligated to phone any authorities if I were to hot-wire the car."

The man's look was not as reassuring as his words. "I won't even be looking your direction."

"He doesn't trust you," Leah said as they strode to the Land Rover.

"Why should he? I wouldn't either. See? Even forgiven sin has its consequences."

"Do we have to spiritualize everything?" Leah said, but Rayford could tell she was bemused. Once they were on the road, she said, "We're not going straight to the safe house in broad daylight, are we?"

"Of course not. We have a stop first."

He drove to Des Plaines and the one-pump gas station run by Zeke and Zeke Jr. Zeke emerged quickly but hesitated when he saw Rayford. He looked past him to Leah. "I recognize the vehicle," he said. "But not the occupants."

"It's me, Zeke. And this is Leah."

"That wasn't Z's handiwork, was it?"

"Hers was."

"Humph. Not bad. Yours either. Need auto work?"

"Yup."

Zeke ignored the pump and opened the ancient garage door. Rayford pulled in, and he and Leah got out so Zeke could raise the car on the rack. Then the three of them took a hidden staircase to the basement, where Zeke Jr. looked up expectantly. "'Sup?" he said.

"You know me?" Rayford said.

"Not till you spoke, but I woulda got it. Wha'dya need?"

"New ID for her."

Zeke Jr. stood, rolls of fat jiggling under his black vest and shirt. "Gerri Seaver," he said.

"Excuse me?"

"How's Gerri Seaver sound?"

"How does she look?" Leah said.

Zeke grabbed a file. "Like this."

"You're a genius," she said. The blonde was roughly her age, height, and weight. "I don't know how you do it."

"Lots more to choose from these days," he said shyly. He directed her to a sink and gave her the chemicals necessary to make her a blonde. She and Rayford drove off two hours later with foodstuffs, a full tank, and Leah in a scarf over wet, freshly bleached hair. Her dental appliance had been changed, as had the color of her contacts. In her purse was a wallet with documents to match.

"I'm going to take the northern route," Rayford said. "That'll give us a good look at any other traffic."

"Unless they're hidden."

"Not too many places to do that," he said. "Shall we wait till dark too?"

"You're asking me?"

"We both live or die by the decision," he said.

"That helps."

He phoned the safe house. Tsion answered. "She's where? . . . Tell me she's not! . . . Oh, Tsion! What about the radiation, the—"

Tsion told him what David had told them about the radiation. Rayford pulled over and covered the mouthpiece. "We're waiting till dark," he said, popping a U-turn.

"Where to till then?"

"Chicago, and watch our backs in case you were right about tower boy."

Rayford phoned Chloe and eschewed any pleasantries. "Where are you?" he said.

"Palos area," she said. "I'm guessing, where the Tri-State used to intersect Harlem."

"Ninety-fifth Street?"

"Uh-huh."

"What now? You going the rest of the way on foot?"

"I may have to."

"That'll take hours!"

"What else have I got to do, Dad?"

"At least wait for us. You're more likely to give us away than Hattie is. We've got both vehicles out in the daytime. On foot you'll stick out like a sore thumb. We're as exposed as we've ever been."

"Just tell her what to do, Rayford," Leah said. "You're back in charge, remember?"

"What?" Chloe said.

Rayford covered the phone. "She's a married adult, Leah, not my little girl anymore."

"But she's subordinate to you in the Trib Force. Do what you have to do."

"Chloe?"

"Yes?"

"Stay put until we can find you. We're not doing this thing until after dark."

10

BUCK WAS HAVING A CRISIS of conscience. It would have been one thing to be harboring Carpathia's assassin, had it been Rayford or another misguided believer for whom the deed could have at least been rationalized as an act of war. But Chaim?

He professed no faith, no acrimony toward Carpathia from a spiritual standpoint. The man had committed first-degree murder, and regardless of what Buck thought about the victim, it was a crime.

"So, what are you going to do?" Chaim pressed him as they languished at the Night Visitors hotel in Jerusalem. "Turn me in? Abandon me? Your conscience can't take what I did to your worst enemy. I cannot abide what I have done to my dearest friends. They died for me."

"Greater love hath no man . . ."

"You've quoted that before, Cameron, and I know where you want to go with it. But they had no choice. Perhaps they would have died for me voluntarily, but this was my doing. I forced their deaths."

"Would you have done the same for them? Would you have died for them?"

"I'd like to think I would. I should now."

"Stop talking like that."

"You think I am not sincere? The only things standing in the way are you and my cowardice."

"Cowardice? You planned the assassination for months, virtually told me you were going to do it by showing me your blade making—I don't know where my head was—and you pulled it off according to plan. Right or wrong, it was hardly evidence of cowardice."

"Ach!" Chaim waved him off. "I am a fool and a coward, and the blood of my people is on my hands."

Buck paced. "Because the GC are already announcing that you're dead, they can kill you without explanation."

"Let them. I deserve it. I'm a murderer."

Buck turned the chair backward and straddled it. "What happens when your victim comes back to life? Then what is your crime? Attempted murder? What if there is no evidence of the wound you inflicted?"

"You're talking crazy now, Cameron."

"It's going to happen, Chaim."

"I know you say that, and Tsion says that. But come now. The man was in my lap when I thrust the blade into his brain. For all practical purposes, he was dead before he hit the floor. He could not have survived it. You can't really believe he is coming back to life."

"What if he does?"

Chaim waved him off again.

"Don't do that. You're an intellectual, a lifelong student and teacher and scientist. Humor the debate. What if Carpathia comes back to life?"

Chaim rolled on the bed and turned his back to Buck. "Then I guess you'll all be right; I'll be wrong. You'll win."

"You're not pretending that it has actually happened."

"You said yourself I have a thinking man's brain. I find it impossible to consider impossibilities."

"That's why we've never gotten through to you? All our arguing and pleading . . . ?"

"You've gotten through more than you know, Cameron. I have come from atheism to agnosticism and finally to belief in God."

"You believe?"

"In God, yes. I told you that. Too many things have happened that can be explained no other way."

"Then why not Carpathia's resurrection?"

"You can't tell me that you yourself actually believe this," Chaim said.

"Oh, yes, I can. And I do. You forget I was there when Eli and Moishe came back to life after three days in the hot sun."

"You believe what you want to believe."

Buck looked at his watch. "I wish it would get dark. I want out of here."

"You should leave me, young friend. Distance yourself from me. Pretend you never met me."

Buck shook his head, though Chaim was still turned away from him. "Can't do that," he said. "We go back way too far."

"I was merely the subject of an article. We didn't have to become friends."

"But we did. And now I love you and can't let you go. You think you have nothing else to live for—"

"True enough."

"But you do. You do! You know what I fear for you, Chaim?"

"You're afraid I will die in unbelief and go to hell."

"There's something more frightening. What if you wait too long to change your mind and God hardens your heart?"

"Meaning?" Chaim rolled over to face him.

"Meaning that you finally decide it's true and want to give yourself to Christ, but you had already pushed God past where he would allow you to come back."

"Explain to me how that fits with your view of a loving God who is not willing that any should perish."

"I don't understand it myself, Chaim. I'm new at this. But Dr. Ben-Judah teaches that the Bible warns about just that during the end times. Be careful that you don't go too far, that you don't ignore too many warnings and signs."

"God would do that?"

"I believe so."

"To me?"

"Why not?"

Chaim let his head rest on the mattress, then covered his face with his arms.

"Ready to engage in the debate?" Buck pressed.

"I'm tired, Cameron."

"You slept well."

"I slept. Not well. How could I?"

"I can't imagine. But this is too important for you to brush aside."

"You have pleaded with me before! I have heard every argument from you and from Tsion. I could make your case for you!"

"Then think about what may happen to you. Say I get cold feet and abandon you. Even if you are a coward and unable to take your own life, someone is going to take it for you. Then what?"

"I like to believe death is the end."

"It's not," Buck said.

"Listen to the new believer, full of knowledge. You can't know."

"Chaim. If all this stuff that has amazed you and made you believe God is real, why shouldn't heaven and hell be real? If there's a God, why would he want you to die and disappear into nothingness? It makes no sense."

"You're repeating yourself."

"You're holding out, Chaim. You're like the fainthearted who want one more sign. I just don't want you to wait past the point of no return."

"Ach!"

"Just think about it, will you? What it would mean if the prophecy were fulfilled, Nicolae was the Antichrist, and he resurrected from the dead."

"I don't want to think about it. I want to die."

"You wouldn't if you believed what I believe."

"That, I agree with."

"You do?"

"Of course. Who would want to go to hell?"

"You don't have to, Chaim! God has—"

"I know! All right? I know! Stop talking."

"I will, but just consider—"

"Please!"

"—how you would feel if Nicolae—"

"For the love of—"

"I'll shut up now, Chaim. But—"

Buck's phone rang.

"Maybe there is a God," Chaim said. "The patron saint of phones has saved me."

"This is Buck."

"Buck, is it really you?"

"Hattie!" Buck stood so quickly his chair bounced away. "Where are you?"

"Colorado," she said.

"You're on a secure phone?"

"One thing I absconded with, one of those from your friend on the inside."

"I'm listening."

"The GC think I'm dumber than I am. They released me from prison, gave me money, and then followed me here. I know they were disappointed I didn't go to Israel, but I wanted to see if any of my family was left."

"And?"

Her voice caught. "No. Not for a while. But you know where they hope I'll go now."

"Exactly where I hope you won't go."

"Buck, I have nowhere else to turn."

He ran a hand through his hair. "I'd love to help you, Hattie, but I—"

"I understand. I had my chance."

"That's not it. I—"

"It's all right, Buck. You owe me nothing."

"It has nothing to do with owing you anything, Hattie. I'm in the middle of a situation myself, and until you can shake the GC, I can't advise that you head back to the safe house. Everybody's welfare is at stake."

"I know," she said, and he heard the terror in her voice. "Would you please tell everyone that I never told anyone where they were?"

"Hattie. You as much as put Bo and Ernie on our doorstep."

"They couldn't have found their way back there. Anyway, they're both dead, and if they had told anyone, you'd have been raided by now."

"What will you do, Hattie?"

"I don't know," she said wearily. "Maybe I'll just run these goons on a wild-goose chase until they get tired of me. Heaven knows they gave me enough money."

"They're not going to let you out of their sight. And don't think they couldn't patch in even to this call."

"They're watching my car. They think I'm eating."

"Good time to slip away?"

"Too open. I've got to get them to somewhere more densely populated. Maybe Denver."

"Be careful."

"Thanks for nothing."

"Hattie, I'm sorry. I—"

"I didn't mean that, Buck. I was trying to be funny. Nothing's funny anymore, is it?"

"If you shake them and are sure, try me again. We may not be at the same place, but if we can accommodate you . . ."

"You would, wouldn't you?"

"Of course we would. You know us."

"Yes, I do. You all were better than I deserved. I'd better get off."

"Yeah. I s'pose you've heard they're trying to pin the assassination on Rayford."

"I heard. Has to be a frame-up. He probably wasn't even there."

"He was there, but he didn't do it."

"You don't have to convince me. Rayford kill somebody? Not in a million years. I know him better than that. Listen, just tell everybody I'm safe and so are they and thanks for everything I didn't deserve."

"Hattie, we all love you and are praying for you."

"I know you are, Buck."

+ + +

David, stunned at the difference between Dr. Eikenberry's public pronouncements and the autopsy, frantically searched his database for a meeting between her and Fortunato prior to the meeting with management. He had to know what approach Leon had used, in case Leon tried the same with him. Via his hard drive, he bounced all over the compound but had no luck. He did, however, come upon a private meeting between Leon and an unidentified male in a conference room near Carpathia's office.

". . . and how long have you been working for us, sir?"

"Almost from the beginning, Mr. For—Supreme Commander."

"And you're from?"

"Greenland."

"You enjoy your work?"

"Until the assassination, yes."

"The shooting?"

"Well, I meant the stabbing. The assassination of those two guys at the Temple Mount, that was exciting. I mean, to see His Excellency put them in their place . . ."

"But you didn't enjoy your job so much when you saw the potentate himself murdered."

"No, sir. I kept the camera right on him, but it was the hardest thing I've ever done."

"You know the autopsy is finished, and it was the gunshot that killed the potentate."

David could not decipher the response, but it sounded like a snort.

"But there was only one gunshot, Commander—"

"There was only one needed, son. It was a weapon identical to the one His Excellency used on the troublemakers at the Wailing Wall."

"I understand that, but from where I sat, above stage left, I saw the wood speaker's thing—"

"The lectern."

"Yeah, that. I saw that get hit and the curtain go flying. No way that bullet also hit the potentate. He was closer to me."

"Nevertheless, it has been determined that—"

"Excuse me, Commander, but the real murder happened right below me, and I saw it happen."

"And you have reviewed this?"

"Watched it over and over. Couldn't believe it."

"And you discussed it with whom?"

"Just my boss."

"That would be Mr. Bakar?"

"Yes, sir."

Footsteps. A door opening. More faintly: "Margaret, would you have Mr. Bakar join us, please? Thank you."

The door shut and David heard Leon's chair. "Look into my eyes, son. There, yes. You trust me, do you not?"

"Of course."

"When your superior gets here, I am going to tell you both what you saw and what you will remember."

"Excuse me?"

"I am going to tell you what you saw and what you will remember."

"But, sir, I know what I—"

"You understand that I will soon become the new potentate, don't you?"

"I assumed that, yes, sir."

"You did?"

"I think most people assume that."

"Do they?"

No response.

"Do they?" Leon repeated. "Don't just nod. Tell me."

The young man's voice sounded hollow. "Yes."

"You understand that my new title will be Supreme Potentate and that I must also be addressed as Excellency?"

"Yes, Commander."

"You may try out the new title now."

"Yes, Excellency."

"And you realize that I will not only be worthy of worship, but also that worship of me will be mandatory."

"Yes, Excellency."

"Call me Potentate. Supreme Potentate."

"Yes, Supreme Potentate."

"Would you like to kneel before me?"

Silence. Then a knock and a loud sigh from Leon. The door opening. "Excuse me, Commander, but Mr. Bakar is currently engaged in—"

"Margaret!" Leon hissed fiercely. "Do not interrupt me again!"

"I'm, sorry, sir, I—"

"I don't want apologies and I don't want to hear that my subordinates have more important things to do! The next person through this door had better be Mr. Bakar, and for your sake, it had better be within ninety seconds."

"Right away, sir."

The door. The chair. "Now then, son, where were we?"

"I was worshiping you, Supreme Potentate." Another chair.

"That's it. Yes, kneel before me and kiss my ring."

"I see no ring, sir."

"Kiss my finger where the ring will soon be."

A quick knock and the door opening. Bakar's voice: "Forgive me, Commander, I—what the devil is going on?"

"Sit, Director."

"What's he doing on the floor?"

"He was just about to tell me what was on the videodisc you brought back from Jerusalem."

"You've seen it, haven't you, Supreme Commander?"

"Of course, but it seems there's a discrepancy between what he and I saw and what you apparently saw."

"Oh?"

"Yes," Fortunato said. "Return to your chair and tell your boss what you saw."

"I heard the gunshot and saw the potentate's head snap back."

"I get it," Bakar said. "A joke. Now the gun killed him? We all know that's not true."

"It's true," the cameraman said.

"Yeah, I was born yesterday and went blind today."

"Did you go blind, Bakar?" Leon said soothingly.

"Wha—?"

"Lean across the table here and let me see your eyes."

"My eyes are fine, Le—er, Commander. I—"

"Bakar, are you listening to me?"

"Of course, but—"

"Are you listening?"

"Yes!"

"Are you listening? Really listening?"

Silence.

"I have your attention now, don't I, Bakar?"

"You do, sir."

"Bakar, you understand that I will soon become the new potentate, don't you?"

David could stand to listen no more and clicked away from the feed. He stood, dizzy and sick to his stomach. He called Annie and apologized for waking her.

"What is it, David?" she said.

"I need you," he said. "Meet me soon, before I get called in to see Fortunato."

+ + +

Rayford and Leah agreed to meet Chloe in a mostly destroyed banquet hall that had been turned into a dimly lit, dingy bar. They were ignored, sitting in a dark corner, huddled against wind that gusted through huge gaps in the wall.

Rayford and Chloe embraced, but he wasted little time chastising her. "This is more dangerous than staying put, even if Hattie leads the GC right to the safe house. There's a chance they won't find the underground."

"We need the new place, Dad," she said. "And I'm tired of doing nothing."

"Granted, but let's not get crazy."

Leah's phone chirped. "This is, um, Gerri Seaver."

"Oh, I'm—I'm sorry. I—" *Click.*

"Oh, no!" Leah said. "That was Ming, I'm sure of it."

"Hit Callback," Rayford said.

\+ + +

Any doubts Buck had about Chaim's physical condition were erased when they finally left the Night Visitors. Chaim knew exactly where they were headed. He had ripped from one clean corner of his blanket a piece large enough to fit under his hat and extend down the back of his neck and both sides of his face. His nondescript shirt and blowsy pants made him look like any other Israeli day laborer, and he had replaced his slippers with boots.

Buck had a tough time keeping up with him. He jogged as Chaim walked quickly, and though the man was a foot shorter and more than thirty years older, he wore Buck out.

"We get to America and what, I'm holed up with Tsion and you? I won't need to kill myself. You'll both talk me to death."

"There's nothing we could say that you haven't heard already," Buck said, gasping and grateful that that comment had made Chaim stop briefly.

"Now there's the truest thing I've heard all day."

"That's not so," Buck said, slow to start moving again when Chaim took off.

"What?" Chaim said, a step and a half ahead.

"The truest thing you heard today was that you are lost!"

Again Chaim stopped and turned. "I'm lost?"

"Yes!"

In the dim light in the middle of the ravaged City of God, Buck saw the pain in his friend's face.

"You don't think I know I'm lost?" Chaim said, incredulously. "If there's one thing I do know, one thing I am certain of, it is that I am lost. Why do you think I would sacrifice myself to murder the greatest enemy my country has ever had? I did not expect to survive! I was ready to go! Why? Because I am lost! Nothing to live for! Nothing! My farewell act was to be of some benefit to Israel. Now the deed is done and I am here and yes, I am lost!"

Buck was desperate that Chaim not give them away with his ranting. But that was only one reason he approached his dear friend, arms outstretched, and embraced him.

"You don't need to be lost, Chaim. You don't need to be."

And the old man sobbed in Buck's arms.

11

"DON'T HANG UP. It's Leah." She had moved out to the Land Rover to make the call.

"It sounded like you," came the voice Leah never felt fit the delicate Ming Toy. "But who is Gerri something?"

"We international fugitives have to keep changing identities, Ming. If it weren't for the intrigue, what would be the appeal?"

"I don't know how you keep your sense of humor. This is too dangerous, too frightening for me."

"You handle it well, Ming."

"I called with a question. Your friend, Williams?"

"Buck, yes."

"No, not Buck. Longer name."

"Cameron?"

"Yes! Where's his family?"

"West somewhere, why? I think only his father and brother are still around."

"I don't think they're around either. There was lots of talk at Buffer today about what happened to Dr. Rosenzweig's house and his people. They don't know where he is, but they're making it look like everybody died in the fire."

"Yes?"

"They're saying the same thing will happen to Cameron Williams's people if they don't give him up."

"His relatives don't know where he is!" Leah said. "He's smarter than to give them that kind of information."

"Leah, they may already be dead. This was supposed to happen right away."

"What was?"

"Torture. Dismemberment. They tell or they are killed. Then comes the fire to cover it up."

"I don't know what to do."

"Just have your friend check on them. Maybe he can warn them in time."

"I will, Ming. How are you doing? Ready to come see us? Whoops! Hang on." Leah slid down in the seat as two uniformed GC officers strolled by. They stopped right next to the Rover, chatting and smoking. "Ming," Leah whispered, "can you still hear me?"

"Barely. What's going on?"

"I've got company. If I don't say anything, you'll know why."

"If you need to hang up—"

"I'd rather stay on with you. Let me give you Rayford Steele's number in case I get caught. He'll answer to Marvin Berry."

"Got it."

Leah felt the vehicle rock. "They're leaning against the car," she said. "Luckily all the windows are tinted except the windshield."

"Where are you?"

"Illinois."

"I mean in the car."

"Floor of the front seat. Wish I were daintier. The gearshift is killing me."

"They don't see you?"

"Don't think so. I can hear them plain as day."

"What?"

Leah didn't want to speak louder. The Peacekeepers were trading wild party stories. She wanted to say, "Yeah, and I'm the Easter bunny," but she lay still.

"This hunk of junk looks like it's been through a war," one said.

"It has, stupid. It's old enough to have been through the war and the earthquake."

"Tough make."

"Not as tough as the Land Cruiser."

"No? Same company?"

"Toyota."

"Really?"

"Expensive."

"More than this?"

"Quite a bit more."

"No kiddin'? This thing's loaded. I think it's got a GPS."

"This rig? Nah."

"Betcha."

"How much?"

"Ten-spot."

"You're on."

"Oh, no," Leah whispered, "they're coming to the front."

"You need me to call Rayford?"

But Leah didn't answer. She tucked the phone between the seats and pretended to sleep.

"See, isn't that the positioning system right there. Hey! She all right?"

"Who? Oh, man! Door's unlocked. Ask her."

A rap on the window. "Hey, lady!"

Leah ignored it, but moved slightly so they wouldn't think she was dead. When one opened the passenger door, she sat up, trying to look groggy. "Hey, what's the deal?" she said. "You want me to call a Peacekeeper?"

"We are Peacekeepers, ma'am."

"There a law against a girl getting some shut-eye?"

"No, but what're you doin' on the floor? Backseat's wide open."

"Trying to stay out of the sun."

She sat up in the seat, desperate to remember her new address and hometown. Zeke Jr. had reminded her more than once to memorize it as soon as possible. She hated being so new at this part of the game.

"This your vehicle?"

"Borrowing it."

"From?"

"Guy named Russell."

"That a first or last name?"

"Russell Staub."

"He know you're borrowing it?"

"'Course! What're you driving at?"

"Run a check on it," one told the other, who immediately got on his phone. "Where's he from, ma'am?"

"Mount Prospect."

"What're you doing all the way down here?"

She shrugged. "S'posed to meet some friends."

"We're gonna find this Rover registered to a Staub in Mount Prospect, right?"

She nodded. "I don't do his paperwork for him, but that's whose it is and that's where it's from."

"You got any ID, ma'am?"

"Yeah, why?"

"I'd like to see it."

"You've come a long way from wondering if I was all right to accusing me of stealing a car."

"I didn't accuse you of anything, lady. You feeling guilty about something?"

"Should I be?"

"Let me see your ID."

Leah made a show of digging through her purse even after she had located the new documents so she could take a last peek at the new information.

"This your current address, Miss, ah, Seaver?"

"If it says Park Ridge, it is."

"You're a long way from home too."

"Only because there are hardly any roads anymore."

"That's the truth."

"Staub, Mount Prospect," the other officer said. "No outstandings and no reports."

Leah raised her eyebrows, her pulse racing. "Satisfied?"

He handed back her ID. "Don't be out and about without something to do, ma'am. Why don't you get this vehicle back to the owner and get on home."

"Can't I get a drink first, in case my friends show up?"

"Don't be long."

"Thank you." She pushed open the car door and saw Rayford and Chloe on their way out, concern on their faces. "Oh, there they are now! Thanks again, officers!"

\+ + +

Annie had hurried to David's office. They pretended it was a normal superior/subordinate meeting, and he quickly told her what he had heard.

She paled. "That sounds like what Buck Williams went through with Carpathia at the UN."

"But who knew Fortunato could do that?"

"Is *he* the Antichrist?" Annie said.

David shook his head. "I still think it's Carpathia."

"But he's really dead, David. I mean really. How long was he in that bag and in that box? I thought he was supposed to come back to life right away."

"Dr. Ben-Judah thought so too," he said. "What do we know? If we had this stuff figured out, we probably would have figured out the rest and wouldn't have been left behind."

David's secretary buzzed him. "The supreme commander would like to see you."

Annie grabbed his hands. "God," she whispered, "protect him on every side."

"Amen," David said.

\+ + +

Buck and Chaim sat shivering in a ditch at the far north end of a deserted and blocked-off road. Only a small stretch remained smooth, and Buck began to wonder whether it was long enough for the Super J. The jet might be able to land and take off without attracting attention, but if T had to circle or take more than one shot at it, who knew?

Worse, the stretch was unlit. T would use his landing lights only as much as he had to, counting on Buck to guide him in by phone. That meant Buck would have to stand at one end of the makeshift runway or the other. He opted for the front end so he could talk T through coming straight over his head, then he could spin and try to keep him straight until he landed. Buck would transmit the GPS coordinates listed in his phone to T's phone. The only danger was T's coming in too low too quickly. Buck would have to leap out of the way. Still, that seemed easier than trying to elude a plane careening toward him at the other end.

"This is a lot of trouble for someone who doesn't want to leave," Chaim said.

"Well, *I* want to leave even if you don't."

Buck's phone rang, and he assumed it was T, though he had not heard the plane yet. It was Rayford.

"We have a situation here," Rayford said, quickly bringing him up to date on Chloe. "The question is whether now is the time to talk."

"It's not," Buck said. "But in a nutshell, what's up?"

"Wouldn't do that to you, Buck. Call us when you're in the air or in Greece. And greet the brothers for us."

"Will do," Buck said, puzzled at Rayford's new tone. It was as if he were talking to his old father-in-law.

"Chloe sends her love and wants to talk with you when you have time."

"Thanks. Me too."

"I love you, Buck."

"Thanks, Ray. I love you too."

\+ \+ \+

David realized how petrified he was when he nearly blundered by heading straight toward the conference room upon reaching the eighteenth floor. "He in there?" he said, trying to mask his anxiety.

"No," Margaret said, clearly puzzled. "He's with Messrs. Hickman and Moon in his office. They're expecting you."

I will not kneel, David vowed. *I will not worship or kiss his hand. Lord, protect me.*

Leon and the other two directors huddled around a TV monitor. Leon still appeared grief stricken. "Once we get His Excellency into the tomb," he said, his voice thick with emotion, "the world can begin approaching some closure.

Prosecuting his murderer can only aid in achieving that. Watch this with us, David. Tell me if you see what we see."

David approached the monitor, certain Fortunato could hear his heartbeat and see the flush of his face. He nearly missed the chair, then settled in awkwardly.

Shot from above, the videodisc was crystal clear. At the sound of the gunshot from Carpathia's left, he had turned and run into the wheelchair as Chaim rolled toward him. Chaim grabbed at the metal back support over his left shoulder and quickly produced what appeared to be a two-foot sword. As Nicolae tumbled atop him, Chaim whipped the weapon in front of him, holding it with both hands, point up, sharp edge facing away from the potentate.

Chaim lifted his forearms as Carpathia's body met the blade, and the sword slipped into his neck and straight through the top of his head as easily as a bayonet would slice a watermelon. Carpathia's hands shot to his chin, but David kept his eyes on Chaim, who violently twisted the handle at the base of Nicolae's neck. He let go as Carpathia dropped, then quickly steered stage left and sat with his back to the dying man.

"Well?" Leon said, peering at him. "Is there any doubt?"

David stalled, but all that served was to make the other two glance at him.

"Cameras don't lie," Leon said. "We have our assassin, don't we?"

Much as he wanted to argue, to come up with some other way to interpret what was clear, David would jeopardize his position if he proved illogical. He nodded. "We sure do."

Leon approached him, and David froze. The supreme commander took David's face in his fleshy hands and looked deep into his eyes. David fought the urge to look away, praying all the while that he would do the right thing and hoping that Annie was continuing to pray too. Like Nicolae, here was a man with clear mind control over unbelievers. He felt his pulse in his ears and wondered if Leon could detect his panic through his fingers.

"Director Hassid," Leon said, eyes boring into his. "Rayford Steele shot dead our beloved potentate."

Rayford? Hadn't they watched the same video?

Leon would be suspicious if David agreed too quickly.

"No," David said, "the disc was clear. Dr. Ro—"

"A stroke victim and a great loyal statesman would be incapable of such an act, would he not?"

"But—"

Fortunato's sweaty palms still cupped his cheeks. "The only killing weapon was the Saber in the hands of Rayford Steele, who shall have to pay for his crime."

"Rayford Steele?" David said, his voice cracking like a junior high schooler.

"The assassin."

"The assassin?"

"Look again, David, and tell me what you see."

David was terrified. He had not noticed anyone switching discs, yet this version indeed showed Rayford firing at the stage. David wondered if he was weaker than Buck had been three and a half years before. Was it possible that Leon *could* make him see something that wasn't there? He stared, unblinking. Time seemed to stand still.

Someone had to have changed the disc while he was distracted in Leon's hands. This was no concoction, no mind game. For while this showed the gunshot, it also showed Nicolae falling into Chaim's lap.

"Slow it down," David said, trying to mimic the flat voices he had heard earlier. He believed his ruse was failing miserably, but he had no choice but to play it out.

"Yes, Walter," Leon said. "Show the fatal shot again and slow it down."

David fought for control, determined to watch the lectern, the curtain, the kings. As soon as the flash of fire and the puff of smoke appeared at the end of the Saber, the lectern split, and the pieces hurtled toward the ten kings. The curtain seemed to twist on itself from the middle and shoot into the distance. Chaim appeared to come from behind the falling potentate and steer toward the center of the stage. The angle was wrong for seeing what he had actually done.

To his disgust, David had to submit a second time to Leon's hands on his face. "Well?" Leon said, peering at him. "Is there any doubt?"

This time David could not stall. He was suddenly aware of Leon's overbearing cologne. How had he missed that before?

"Cameras don't lie," Leon said. "We have our assassin, don't we?"

David nodded, forcing Leon to loosen his grip. "We sure do," he managed. "Steele must pay."

+ + +

"I hate this," Leah said as the three sat inside again. "It's nerve-racking. We shouldn't be out during the day. Too many things can go wrong."

"You shouldn't have gone to the car," Chloe said.

Leah cocked her head and gave Chloe a stare. "*I* shouldn't have gone to the car? I'm not the reason we're here, dear."

"I didn't ask you to come," Chloe said.

"Stop," Rayford said. "This gets us nowhere. Now, Chloe, I'm sorry, but this was a monumentally stupid thing to do."

"Dad! We need to get to the new place."

"And we have to check it out, but we're way past where we can get away with being out one second more than necessary, except at night."

"All right! OK! I'm sorry!"

Leah reached for her hand. "Me too," she said, but Chloe pulled away.

"C'mon, don't do that," Leah said. "I shouldn't have said that, and I'm sorry. We have to be able to work together."

"We need to get out of here," Rayford said. "Those guys think we're just friends in here for a drink. We can't stay till dark."

"We should get closer to Chicago," Chloe said.

"That'll look *more* suspicious," Rayford said, "unless we can find a place where we could leave the cars out of sight and still be able to walk into the city."

"Where the L tracks end now?" Chloe suggested.

"They end everywhere," Leah said. "Totally shut down, right?"

"Well," Chloe said, "the tracks are torn up heading in from the south, and then they're OK in the city, but they're closed."

Rayford looked to the ceiling. "So how about we find a place to hide the cars down that way, coming in from separate directions, then follow the tracks into the city."

Leah nodded. "Good idea."

Chloe said, "That's what I thought."

+ + +

"If you're where I think you are," T said, "it looks impossible."

"You can see the road?" Buck said. "Why can't I hear you?"

"Wind, maybe, but you'll hear me soon. I'm already lower than I want to be, but I sure hope I'm looking at the wrong road."

"There's only one possibility in this area," Buck said. "If you see any stretch of open road, you're looking at us."

"Buck, do you have any idea how long it takes for one of these to stop? An aircraft carrier would be easier."

"Any options?"

"Yeah! I land at Jerusalem Airport or better yet, Tel Aviv, and we hope for the best."

"It would be more efficient for Chaim to commit suicide right here than to risk that, T. They're looking for him."

"I'm willing to try this, Buck, but it sure seems an uninspired way to become a martyr."

"I hear you."

"Thanks."

"I mean I literally hear you. Flash your landing lights. . . . I see you! You're way to my right!"

"Adjusting."

"More. More! More! There! No, a little left now! Hold."

"I see nothing!"

"Use your lights when you need to. That'll help me too."

"I don't like what I'm not seeing." The landing lights came on and stayed on this time. "Now I don't like what I *am* seeing."

"You seem high. I thought you were too low."

"I was lower than I wanted to be with all those emergency lights off to the left down there. Let's hope they're too busy to look up."

"You still seem high."

"I am. But I still don't see you either."

"If you stay up there, I'm safe. You gonna go 'round again?"

"Negative. I have one shot and I'm going to make it work."

"You'd better start dropping."

"Here I come."

Buck put his phone down and waved, though he couldn't imagine T seeing him from that angle. The plane drifted right, and Buck tried to signal T back to center. With his lights still on, T should have been able to see that for himself.

As the Super J screamed past him, Buck grabbed his phone and shouted, "You straight?"

"Straight as I can get! No way this works! Too steep! Too fast!"

"Abort?"

"Too late!"

Buck shut his eyes as the plane dropped and the hot exhaust swept past him. He covered his ears, knowing that would never block the sound of the impact. But what he heard wasn't a plane crash. He thought he detected the screech of tires over the din of the jets, but that may have been wishful thinking. He peeked through the dust and exhaust to see the plane bounce a couple of feet, the red exhaust flame pouring out the sides as the plane used reverse thrust in a desperate attempt to slow down.

The next impact resounded like a rifle shot. White smoke billowed from beneath the craft, and the plane began spinning wildly—the landing lights illuminating the ditch and grass, then shining toward him. Suddenly the lights went off, but he could hear the jets continue to run. The noise abated except for the whine of the engine, but Buck no longer saw anything. The plane had to be facing him. He had not heard the fuselage break up, as he had feared if T couldn't stop.

He ran toward the plane, amazed to see Chaim beside him, keeping pace.

+ + +

The New Babylon night was warm and dry. Spotlights from a dozen angles bathed the palace courtyard, nearly bright as day. Nothing would compete with the merciless, cloudless, sun-filled daytime sky, but until then, everyone could clearly see all there was to see.

David and Annie were among the hundreds of employees allowed—or in their case assigned—to file past the bier ahead of the pilgrims from around the globe. The couple waited on the steps while ten pallbearers—four men on each side and one at each end—solemnly carried in the draped Plexiglas box, accompanied by a live orchestra playing a dirge. From behind the barricades an eighth of a mile away, the mourning began. Employees began to wail too. The men gently placed the bier atop the pedestal and carefully positioned it. A technician, with what appeared to be a portable vacuum cleaner tucked under one arm, knelt between one of the end men and a side man and screwed a pressure gauge into the rubber stopper at the foot end. He checked the readout twice, then hooked a hose to the stopper, twisted a dial, and ran the suction machine for two seconds. He checked the pressure once more, removed everything but the stopper, then hurried away.

The eight side men backed smartly away while the two on the ends removed the shroud. Annie seemed to recoil. David was stunned. He had expected Carpathia to appear lifelike. The work of Dr. Eikenberry had been astounding, of course, as there was no evidence of trauma. Yet somehow, even in a dark suit, white shirt, and striped tie, Carpathia appeared more lifeless than any corpse David had ever seen.

The bier itself was shaped like an old-fashioned pine box, the torso area expanding to contain Carpathia's robust physique. The lid was two inches thick and bolted to the sides with huge, stainless steel screws that bit deep into the plastic, pulled the casket gasket tight, and were secured at their undersides by self-locking washers and screws.

The lid was not three inches above Carpathia's face, and as people passed, they could lean over the velvet ropes and see their breath on the top. If this was Carpathia, he would be closer to his people in death than he had ever been in life.

David had listened to the revised autopsy report wherein all references to the sword and its damage were omitted and the bullet trauma was added. At the end of that, Dr. Eikenberry had launched a clinical play-by-play as she secured the eyelids with adhesive and stitched the lips with invisible thread.

David was curious and wanted a closer look. Fortunately, the cluster in front of them paused for more than a minute. David leaned forward and studied the remains, knowing this probably made him look grief stricken. He wondered if this was really Carpathia. The body looked stiff, cold, pale. Could it be a wax figure? Might the resurrection occur in the morgue refrigerator? The vacuum-sealed Plexiglas bier certainly would not be conducive.

Carpathia's hands were more lifelike and convincing. Left was draped over right at the waist, and they looked manicured and only slightly paler than in life. They rested within a quarter inch of the transparent lid. David almost wished the man were worthy of this display.

David was stunned when several ahead of him made religious gestures, from crossing themselves to bowing. A woman nearly toppled as she gave in to tears, and David wondered what the outcry from the public would be like if GC personnel reacted like this.

Three armed guards stood on the other side of the bier. When any mourner touched the glass, the closest guard leaned over and wiped the prints away, polishing, polishing.

Finally the line moved, and David tried to guide Annie for a closer look. She surreptitiously stiffened, and he let her stay outside him as they passed. The man behind David collapsed to his knees upon full view of the body and moaned in a foreign tongue. David turned to see it was Bakar.

Annie left, still looking exhausted, and David moved atop an observation deck that had been fashioned as the second floor of one of the medical tents. He watched as the barricades were pulled away and the crowd slowly began to move toward the bier.

Someone hurrying around the outside of the courtyard distracted David, heading toward where the evidence room had already been dismantled. It was a woman carrying a bulky, paper package. He scampered down and excused himself through the crowd to get to the area from the opposite direction of the woman.

When he arrived he saw her, Dr. Eikenberry, hurrying back the way she had come. Guy Blod stood there with the package. He looked at David and shrugged. "We're going to make dawn," he said. "Thanks to your help."

David didn't want to be pals with Guy. But he did want to know what was in the package. "What've you got there, Minister Blod?"

"Just something she said the supreme commander wants in the statue."

"*In* the statue?"

Guy nodded. "Which means it has to go in now, because once we weld this together, the only things that will get inside it will have to be smaller than the eyeballs, nostrils, or mouth. I mean, at four times life-size, they'll be plenty big, but . . ."

"May I?" David said, reaching for the package.

"Whatever," Guy said. "It's going to burn anyway."

"Burn?"

"Or melt. The hollow legs will be an eternal furnace; don't you love it?"

"What's not to love?" David said, peeking through a corner of the paper. In his hands was the real murder weapon.

12

AS RAYFORD FOLLOWED Leah and Chloe out of the ersatz bar, one of the GC Peacekeepers was coming in. "You wouldn't be Ken Ritz, would you?"

Rayford fought for composure and noticed Leah stiffen and Chloe shoot the man a double take. With a furtive nudge, Rayford urged Chloe to keep moving and hoped Leah would do the same.

"Who's askin'?" Rayford said.

"Just yes or no, pardner," the guard said.

"Then no," Rayford said, brushing past.

"Hold on a second there, pop." Rayford preferred *pardner.* "Let me see some ID."

"I told you I'm not whoever you're looking for."

The guard stood in the doorway with his hand out. Rayford showed his papers.

"So, Mr. Berry, you *know* Ken Ritz?"

"Can't say that I do."

"How about your friends?"

"Guess you'd have to ask them."

"No need to be a smart aleck."

"My apologies, but how would I know about them if I don't know him?"

The guard nodded his dismissal, and as Rayford emerged, he heard him calling out in the bar: "Ken Ritz in here? R-I-T-Z!"

Leah and Chloe waited by the Rover while the other guard had one foot on the bumper of the Suburban. He was on the phone.

Rayford walked nonchalantly to the driver's side of the Rover, and the three climbed in. As he pulled away, Rayford said, "Well, so much for the Suburban."

"Thanks to me," Chloe said. "Go ahead and say it, you two. This is all my fault."

\+ \+ \+

Chaim's bravado had finally cracked. Buck thought it might have been due to exhaustion from the running, but for whatever reason, the old man was in a panic. Buck was strangely encouraged. There was little more difficult than rescuing someone who didn't care to be rescued. At least Chaim retained a degree of self-preservation. It was a start.

The Super J sat at a severe angle with a blown tire. The door swung down and T leaned out. "You must be Dr. Rosenzweig," he shouted.

"Yeah, hey, hi, how are ya," Chaim said with a wave. "You know we got people coming, and you've got a flat tire?"

"I was afraid of that," T said. He reached to shake Rosenzweig's hand.

"Save the introductions until the GC shoots us," Chaim said. "We've got to get out of here. Have you taken off in a plane with only one tire?"

"We're not going to outrun anybody on foot. Let's give this a try."

Buck stepped up behind Rosenzweig and tried to guide him up the stairs. He wouldn't be moved. "This is lunacy, Cameron! There's barely enough road here to take off if the plane was healthy."

"You ready to turn yourself in?"

"No!"

"Well, we're leaving. You coming or taking your chances?" Buck pushed past him up the steps. He grabbed the handle and set himself to lift the door. "Last call," he said.

"There's *no* chance on the plane," Rosenzweig whined. "We're all going to die."

"No, Chaim," Buck said. "Our *only* chance is in the air. Have you given up?"

Rosenzweig leaped aboard as T muscled the plane to the end of the road, turned around, and gave it full throttle. Buck and Chaim, listing far to the left, buckled themselves in. Buck prayed. Chaim muttered, "Lunacy, lunacy. No chance. No hope."

With the engines screaming, the plane was shuddering, though they weren't moving. Buck didn't know what T was doing. As he released the brake and maneuvered the controls, the Super J teetered crazily as it shot down the road.

At the other end the pavement had been twisted and tossed up onto its side to form a four- or five-foot barrier. As they hurtled straight toward it, Buck knew T had to find the right combination of speed and runway to pull this off. Buck couldn't tear his eyes from the barrier. Chaim sat with his head between his legs, hands clasped behind his head. He moaned, "Oh, God, oh God, oh God," and Buck had the impression it was a sincere prayer.

It seemed there was no way the J would get enough lift to clear the barrier. T seemed to be doing everything he could to keep the plane level, but the imbalance had to be affecting speed too. At the last instant T seemed to abandon balance and put all his efforts into thrust. The jet lifted off the road, then dropped, and the tire chirped on the pavement before lifting yet again.

Buck grimaced and held his breath as they swept toward the barrier. T must have rolled just enough to avoid a direct hit, because the plane lurched right, and something underneath slammed the barrier. Now they were in no-man's-land.

"God forgive me!" Chaim shouted as the jet was tossed back to the left, then dipped and nearly crashed as T pulled out all the stops. The tail seemed to drag, and Buck couldn't imagine how it stayed airborne. They headed for a grove of trees, but it was as if T knew he couldn't afford the drag that a turn would require. He seemed to set the jet at the shallowest possible angle to clear the trees. That was their one chance to get airborne, and if successful, the Super J would rocket into the night toward Greece. T would have to worry later about conserving fuel and landing on one tire.

Buck sat with fists clenched, eyes shut, grimacing, fully expecting to hit the trees and crash. He was pressed back against his seat, his head feeling the g-forces as the Super J broke into open sky. He allowed his eyes to open, and in his peripheral vision, Chaim remained hunched over, now lamenting in Hebrew.

Buck unstrapped but found himself struggling to step toward the cockpit against the acceleration and upward deck slope. "You did it, T!"

"Lost what was left of that bad tire, though," T said. "Think we lost the whole wheel assembly. I thought we were going down."

"Me too. That was some takeoff."

"I've got about two hours to decide how to land. I know one-wheel landings can be done, but I'd almost rather pull up the one good wheel and go in belly first."

"Would this thing take it?"

"Not like a big one would. I'd say we're fifty-fifty for success either way."

"That's all?"

T reached for Buck's hand. "I'll see you in heaven, regardless."

"Don't say that."

"I mean it. If I didn't believe that, I'd have taken my chances with the GC back there."

Buck started when Chaim spoke, and he realized the Israeli was standing right behind him. "You see, Cameron? I was right! I should not have come! Now we have a one-in-two chance of surviving, and you two are just fine, knowing where you're going. . . ."

"I wouldn't say I'm fine, Chaim," Buck said. "I'll be leaving a wife and son."

"You've already given up?" T said. "I said we've got a fifty-fifty chance of landing successfully. Even a crash landing doesn't have to be fatal."

"Thanks for that cheery word," Buck said, turning to head back to his seat.

"Pray for me," T called after him.

"I will," Buck said.

"So will I," Chaim said, and Buck shot him a look. He didn't appear to be kidding.

After Rosenzweig was buckled in, Buck leaned over and clapped him on the knee. "You don't have to be afraid of death, you know. I mean dying, yeah, I'm afraid of that too, afraid it'll hurt, that I might burn. I hate leaving my family. But you're right. T and I know where we're going."

Chaim looked terrible, worse than Buck had seen him since the night before. He couldn't make it compute. Chaim had seemed almost giddy after escaping the Gala. Then he was suicidal after hearing about Jacov and his family and Stefan. But now he looked grave. So, he was human after all. Despite all the talk of suicide, he was afraid to die.

Buck knew he had to be as forthright with Chaim as he had ever been. "We may meet God tonight, Chaim," he began, but Rosenzweig immediately made a face and waved him off.

"Don't think I wasn't listening all these years, Cameron. There is nothing more you can tell me."

"Still you refuse?"

"I didn't say that. I just said I don't need to be walked through this."

Buck couldn't believe it. Chaim said that as if he were going to do "this" on his own.

"I do have one question, however, Cameron. I know you don't consider yourself an expert like Dr. Ben-Judah, but what is your best guess about how God feels about motives?"

"Motives?"

Chaim looked frustrated, as if he wished Buck caught his drift without Chaim having to explain. He looked away, then back at Buck. "I know God is real," he said, as if confessing a crime. "There has been too much evidence to deny it. I can't explain away any of the prophecies, because they all come true. The evidences for Jesus as Messiah nearly convinced me, and I had never been a Messiah watcher. But if I were to do what you and Tsion have been pleading with me to do for so long, I confess it would be with the wrong motive."

Except for the likelihood that they might be dead within a couple of hours, Buck wished Tsion was with them right then. He wanted to ask Chaim what his motive was, but he sensed he would lose him if he interrupted.

Chaim pressed his lips together and hung his head. When he looked up again, he seemed to fight tears. He shook his head and looked away. "I need to think some more, Cameron."

"Chaim, I've pleaded with you before to not run out of time. Clearly I'm on solid footing to say so now."

Suddenly Rosenzweig leaned over and grabbed Buck's elbow. "That's the very issue! I'm scared to death. I don't want to die. I thought I did, thought it was the only answer to being a murderer, even if I believed I was just in killing the man. But I did it with forethought, with months of forethought. I planned it, fashioned my own weapon, and saw it through. I have no pity, no sympathy for Nicolae Carpathia. I came to believe, as you do, that he was the devil incarnate."

That wasn't quite accurate, but Buck held his tongue. While believers were convinced Carpathia was the Antichrist and deserved to be killed and stay dead, they knew that he would not literally be Satan incarnate until he came back to life. Whether he deserved to live again or not, that was what was prophesied.

"It's hard for me to fathom that I might have been in God's plan from the beginning. If it is true that Carpathia is the enemy of God and that he was supposed to die from a sword wound to the head, I feel like Judas."

Judas? A nonreligious Jew knows the New Testament too?

"Don't look so surprised, Cameron. Everyone understands what a Judas is. Someone was to betray Jesus, and it fell to Judas. Someone was to murder Antichrist, and while I cannot say it actually fell to me, I took the job into my own hands. But say it *was* my destiny. Though apparently God *wanted* it done, it certainly was not legal. And look at what it has cost me already! My freedom. My peace of mind, which, I admit, is only a distant memory. My loved ones.

"But Cameron, can God accept me if my motive is selfish?"

Buck squinted and turned to look out the window. The dim, sparse lights of Israel receded fast. "We all come to faith selfish in some ways, Chaim. How could it be otherwise? We want to be forgiven. We want to be accepted, received, included. We want to go to heaven instead of hell. We want to be able to face death knowing what comes next. *I* was selfish. I didn't want to face the Antichrist without the protection of God in my life."

"But Cameron, I am merely afraid to die! I feel like a coward. Here I did this rash thing, which many would say took courage and even strength of character. At first I took pride in it. Now I know, of course, that God could have used anyone to do it. He could have caused something to pierce Carpathia's head during the earthquake. He could have had a political rival or a crazy man do it. Perhaps he did! Part of it was compulsion, especially perfecting the weapon. But I had motives, Cameron. I hated the man. I hated his lies and his broken promises to my homeland. I hated even what he did to the practicing Jews and their new temple, even though I did not count myself among them.

"I am without excuse! I am guilty. I am a sinner. I am lost. I don't want to die. I don't want to go to hell. But I fear he will cast me out because I squandered so many opportunities, because I resisted for so long, because I suffered even many of the judgments and still was cold and hard. Now, if I come whimpering to God as a child, will he see through me? Will he consider me the little boy who cried wolf? Will he know that down deep I am merely a man who once had a wonderful life and enjoyed what I now see were bountiful gifts from God—a creative mind, a wonderful home and family, precious friends—and became a crazy old fool?

"Cameron, I sit here knowing that all you and Tsion and your dear associates have told me is true. I believe that God loves me and cares about me and wants to forgive me and accept me, and yet my own conscience gets in the way."

Buck was praying as he had not prayed in ages. "Chaim, if you told God what you're telling me, you'd find out the depth of his mercy."

"But, Cameron, I would be doing this only because I'm afraid I'm going to die in this plane! That's all. Do you understand?"

Buck nodded. He understood, but did he know the answer to Chaim's question? People through the ages had all kinds of motives for becoming believers, and surely fear was a common one. He'd heard Bruce Barnes say that people sometimes come to Christ for fire insurance—to stay out of hell—only to later realize all the benefits that come with the policy.

"You said yourself that I don't consider myself an expert," Buck said, "but you also said you knew you were a sinner. That's the real reason we need Jesus. If you weren't a sinner, you'd be perfect and you wouldn't need to worry about forgiveness and salvation."

"But I knew I was a sinner before, and I didn't care!"

"You weren't staring death in the face either. You weren't wondering whether you might end up in hell."

Rosenzweig rubbed his palms together. "I was tempted to do this when I was suffering from the locust attack. I knew that was a prophesied biblical event, but I also knew that becoming a believer would not speed my recovery. You told me that yourself. And relief would have been my only motive then, as I fear it is now. What I should do, intellectually, is wait and see if I survive this landing or this crash or whatever it is we're going to do. If I am not facing imminent death, I won't be so suspicious of my own intentions."

"In other words," Buck said, "'get me out of this and I'll become a believer'?"

Chaim shook his head. "I know better than to bargain with God. He owes me nothing; he need not do one more thing to persuade me. I just want to be honest. If I would not have come to the same conclusion on the ground or in a plane with two good tires, then I should not rush into it now."

Buck cocked his head. "Friend, rushing into this would be the last way I would describe you. My question is, why do you feel in any more danger now than you did on the ground, or than you will feel if we land safely?"

Chaim raised his chin and shut his eyes. "I don't. The GC has already announced my death and is now free to exterminate me without the nuisance of publicity. That's why I found myself running to this plane. I don't need to tell you the dread of living in exile."

"But whatever motive you have now, you will also have if we survive. Nothing changes."

"Maybe I'll lose the urgency," Rosenzweig said, "the sense of imminence."

"But you don't know that. They may have to foam the runway, bring out the emergency vehicles, all that. You can't hide under a blanket or claim to be contagious when we leave the plane. And you can't hide in the lav until the coast is clear. You're going to be as exposed and as vulnerable as ever, safe landing or no."

Chaim held up a hand and slowly closed his eyes. "Give me a minute," he said. "I may have more questions, but just leave me alone a moment."

That was the last thing Buck wanted to do just then, but neither did he want to push Chaim away. He settled back, amazed at how smooth was the ride that might lead them to eternity.

\+ \+ \+

Kenny Bruce took long afternoon naps, and Tsion looked forward to that. He loved the boy and had had a lot of fun with him for the last fourteen months, even in cramped quarters. He was a good-natured, though normal, kid, and Tsion loved teasing him and playing with him.

Kenny could be wearying, however, especially for one who had not been around infants for nearly twenty years. Tsion needed a nap himself, though he was still desperate not to miss whatever was going to happen in New Babylon.

"Mama?" Kenny asked for the dozenth time, not troubled but curious. It was unusual for her to be gone.

"Bye-bye," Tsion said. "Home soon. Getting sleepy?"

Kenny shook his head, even as he rubbed his eyes and appeared to be trying to keep them open. He yawned and sat with a toy, soon losing interest. He lay on his back, feet flat on the floor, knees up. Staring at the ceiling, he yawned, turned on his side, and was soon motionless. Tsion carried him to the playpen so he wouldn't fuss if he awoke before Tsion did. There were plenty of things to keep him occupied there.

Tsion settled before the TV again and put his feet up. The underground was cool, so he draped a blanket over himself. He tried to keep his eyes open as the GC CNN pool camera remained trained on the transparent coffin and the endless line of the mourning faithful from around the world.

Knowing that young David Hassid and his lady friend Annie Christopher were there, along with who knew how many other believers, he began silently walking through his prayer list. When he closed his eyes to pray for his comrades and his cybercongregation (more than a billion now), he felt himself nodding and his brain longing for sleep.

He peeked at the digital clock on the videodisc player atop the TV. He set the machine to record, just in case he fell asleep and was unable to wake up in time for "the" event. As he settled back in to try to pray, knowing full well he would drift off, the clock showed 12:57 in the afternoon.

Tsion began praying for Chloe, Leah, and Rayford, whom he knew were in the state. Then he prayed for T, Rayford's friend, who was presently unaccounted for. Then Cameron, always in the middle of something and who knew where. As his mind drifted to his old friend and professor, Dr. Rosenzweig, Tsion began feeling a tingle, much like when he had tried to intercede for Rayford.

Was it fatigue, a hallucination? So disconcerting, so real. He forced his eyes open. The clock still read 12:57, but he felt as if he were floating. And when he let his eyes fall shut again, he could still see plain as day. The cramped cellar was cool and musty, the sparse furniture in its place. Kenny slept unmoving in the playpen, blanket still tucked around him.

Tsion saw this from above now, as if in the middle of the room. He saw himself asleep on the couch. He had heard of out-of-body experiences but had never had one, or dreamed one. This didn't seem like a dream, didn't feel like one. He felt weightless, moving higher, wondering if the joists from the flooring above would conk him on the head as he rose and whether that would hurt a floating, hallucinating, dreaming, praying, or sleep-deprived man. He wasn't sure what kind of a man he was right then, but despite his incredible lightness of being, he felt as conscious and aware as he had ever been. Though he knew he was unconscious, he had never been so attuned to his senses. He could see clearly and feel everything from temperature to the air moving over the hair on his arms as he ascended. He heard every noise in the house, from Kenny's breathing to the refrigerator kicking on as he passed it.

Yes, he had drifted through the first floor, but he could still see Kenny and neither worried nor felt guilty about leaving him. For he saw himself too, still on the couch, knowing that if Kenny needed him, he could return as quickly as he had left.

The fall air was crisp above the house, yet he was glad he was in shirtsleeves. It was not uncomfortable, but he was so aware of everything . . . feeling, seeing, hearing—the wind through the dead-leafed trees. He even smelled the decaying leaves on the ground, though no one burned them anymore. No one did anything anymore that used to be mundane. Life was about surviving now, not about incidentals. If a task did not put food on the table or provide shelter, it was ignored.

In an instant Tsion instinctively shot his arms out for balance and felt as if he had returned almost to his sleeping form in the underground. But the house, the half-destroyed village of Mount Prospect, the northwest suburbs, the twisted ribbons that used to be highways and tollways, the whole Chicago area had become minuscule beneath him.

Would he soon grow colder, lose oxygen? How could it be that he was this far from home, now looking at a blue globe that reminded him of the hauntingly beautiful pictures of earth from the moon? Daylight turned to night, but the earth was still illuminated. He felt as if he were in the deep recesses of space, maybe on the moon. Was he on the moon? He looked about him and saw only stars and galaxies. He reached for the earth, because it seemed to recede too quickly. In a strange way, though he could not see it anymore, he sensed he and Kenny still slept in Mount Prospect at the safe house.

He was soon able to see the planets as he drifted, drifted, farther and farther from all that he knew. How fast could he be going? Such physical questions seemed pedestrian, irrelevant. The question was, where was he and where was he going? How long could this go on?

It was so, so strange and wonderful, and for the briefest instant, Tsion wondered if he had died. Was he on his way to heaven? He had never believed heaven was on the same physical plane as the universe, somewhere rocket men could go if they had the resources. And at the same time he had never before felt so thoroughly alive. He was not dead. He was somewhere in his mind, he was convinced.

In an instant, as he seemed to hang weightless in space, it seemed he accelerated yet again. He raced through the vast universe itself, with its numberless galaxies and solar systems. The only sound was his own breathing, and to his amazement, it was rhythmic and deep, as if, as if, as if he were asleep.

But he wondered how so puny a mind could dream such a vista. And as if a switch had been pulled, the darkness turned to the brightest light, obliterating the utter darkness of space. Just as the stars disappear in the light of the sun, so everything he had passed on his way to this plateau vanished. He hung motionless in soundless, weightless animation, a sense of expectancy coursing through him.

This light, like a burst of burning magnesium so powerful as to chase even a shadow, came from above and behind him. Despite the sense of wonder and anticipation, he feared turning toward it. If this was the Shekinah glory, would he not die in its presence? If this was the very image of God, could he see it and live?

The light seemed to beckon him, to will him to turn. And so he did.

13

RAYFORD DROVE AS CLOSE as he could to the Chicago city limits, staying on a rebuilt collar road that had ominous warning signs its entire length, prohibiting traffic beyond its northern line. Patrolling GC cars ignored the sparse traffic, so Rayford looked for a turn that would appear to take him into a local area but which might lead him off-road to the city.

He felt as conspicuous and obvious as he had in a long time, bouncing over dusty lots and through closed forest preserves in the middle of the day. But he detected no tail. He parked the Land Rover beneath a crumbling former L station. He and Chloe and Leah sat in the shade, Rayford beginning to feel the fatigue that had preceded his wonderful sleep in Greece.

"This is my fault," Chloe said. "I was impatient and stupid and selfish. No way we can walk into Chicago until tonight. And how far is it? Twenty miles to the Strong Building? It'll take hours."

Leah shifted in her seat. "If you're looking for someone to argue with you, I can't. I'm not trying to be mean, but we're going to sit here until dark. Then we're going to walk at least five hours to what, check out our next safe house?"

Chloe sat shaking her head.

"We're not walking anywhere," Rayford said. "I know this town like the back of my hand. When it's good and dark, we're going to drive to the building with our lights off. The GC aren't keeping people out of here for fun. They really believe it's contaminated. If we have to turn on the lights now and then to keep from getting swallowed up in a hole and some surveillance plane spots us or some heat detector locates us, at worst they'll warn us to get out. They're not coming in after us."

"No, Dad," Chloe said. "The worst that will happen is that they force us out and figure out who you are."

"They would keep their distance and check us for radiation first."

"And finding none, there goes our whole plan."

"There's enough to think negatively about these days," Rayford said. "Let's think positive. Bad enough I have to give Buck the news about his family soon."

"Let me do that, Dad."

"Are you sure?"

"Absolutely. When he calls, let me talk to him."

But when Buck called, it was clear this was still not the time to give him news like that. Rayford watched as Chloe seemed to disintegrate on the phone. "Thank you, sweetheart," she said. "Thanks for telling us. We'll be praying. I love you too, and Kenny loves you. Call me as soon as you can. Promise me."

Chloe rang off and quickly brought Rayford and Leah up to speed.

"So that's where T is," Rayford said. "Good thinking on Buck's part. We need to pray for them right now."

"Especially for Chaim," Chloe said. "He sounds close."

"Landing on one wheel is risky," Rayford said, "but it can be done. I think this is T's first time in a Super J, though."

"What kinds of odds would you give them?" Leah said, then appeared to regret asking, realizing Chloe could lose her husband within the next twenty minutes.

"No, I want to know too," Chloe said. "Really, Dad. What are their chances?"

Rayford stalled but saw little value in getting Chloe's hopes up. "About one in two," he said.

* * *

Chaim called for Buck, who had joined T in the cockpit. Buck went back and knelt near Chaim's seat. "One more question," Rosenzweig said. "Dare I test God?"

"How?"

"Tell him I want to believe, offer him what's left of my life, and just see if he'll accept me in spite of my selfish motive."

"I can't speak for God," Buck said. "But it seems to me if we're sincere, he'll do what he promised. You already know that this is about more than mere believing, because you believe now. The Bible says the demons believe and tremble. It's a decision, a commitment, a receiving."

"I know."

"We're about fifteen minutes out, Chaim, give or take circling and getting some tower help. Don't stall."

"But you see?" Chaim said. "That just contributes to my problem. I won't be any more just because my time may be running out. I may be even less."

"Let God decide," Buck said.

Chaim nodded miserably. Buck didn't envy his having to work this out while wondering how long he had to live. Chloe and Kenny were at the forefront of

Buck's mind, and knowing he would see them again in three and a half years regardless did nothing to abate his desperation not to leave them.

He headed back to the seat next to T. "I've decided to land at an airport south of Ptolemaïs called Kozani. I've decided that I might have a better shot trying a belly landing than trying to put down on one wheel. No telling how strong that one is, or how good a pilot I am. If I'm not perfect, we bounce and that's it. Going in flat will allow me to land at the slowest possible speed and hope for the best."

"You've got to really be smooth, don't you?"

"Tell me about it."

"You gonna fly over low first and see if they can get a look at the wheels?"

T pointed to the fuel gauge, buried on empty. "You tell me."

"Well, that could be good news, couldn't it?"

"How so?" T said.

"If we crash, we don't burn."

"If we crash, Buck, you're going to want to burn. You're going to wish we were vaporized."

* * *

Tsion felt such a sense of peace and well-being that he didn't want this to end, dream or not. He knew he should be terrified to turn and face the light, but it was the light itself that drew him.

He did not move as if in water or in a vacuum. He didn't have to move his limbs. All he had to do was will himself to turn, and he turned. At first Tsion believed he was looking into a bottomless crevice, the only dark spot in a wall of bright white. But as he backed away from the image, so real he believed he could touch it, other dark spaces of relief came into view. As his eyes adjusted to the light, he pulled back far enough to make out a face. It was as if he dangled between the nose and cheekbone of some heavenly Mount Rushmore image.

But this was neither carved from stone nor made of flesh and bone. Huge and bright and strong, it was also at once translucent, and Tsion was tempted to will himself to pass through it. But as it should have been frightening and was not, he wanted to see the whole. If a head, then a body? He pulled back to see the face ringed with hair massive as prairie grass. It framed a face kindly and yet not soft, loving and yet confident and firm.

Tsion knew beyond doubt he was imagining this, and at the same time it was *the* most sensory-rich experience of his life. It burned into his mind's eye, and he believed he would never forget it nor experience anything like it again as long as he lived.

His voice nearly failed him, but he managed to croak, "Are you Jesus the Christ?"

A rumble, a chuckle, a terrestrial laugh? "No," came a gentle voice that surrounded him and, coming from a mouth that size, should have blown him into oblivion. "No, son of the earth, I am merely one of his princes."

Tsion pulled back farther to take in the scope of this beautiful heavenly being. "Gabriel?" he whispered.

"Gabriel and I are as brothers, child. He announces. I command the heavenly host."

It came to Tsion at once. The great sword long as the Jordan, the breastplate big as the Sinai. "You are Michael! The prince who shall defend my people, the chosen ones of God."

"You have said it."

"Prince of God, have I died?"

"Your time has yet to come."

"May I inquire more?"

"You may, though I prefer righteous warfare to conversation. Gabriel announces. I engage in battle."

"A selfish question, sir. Will I remain until the Glorious Appearing?"

"It is appointed unto men once to die, and—"

"But will I die before the—"

"That is not for you to know, created one. It has no bearing on your obligation to serve the Most High God."

Tsion wanted to bow to this being and to the truth he spoke. He could not believe he had interrupted Michael the archangel, one of only two named angels in all of Scripture.

"Why am I here if I am not dead?"

"You have much to learn, teacher."

"Will I learn the identity of Antichrist, the enemy of God?"

Michael seemed to grow stony, if that were possible for an angel. It was as if the mere mention of Antichrist had stoked his bloodlust for battle. He spoke again: "Antichrist shall be revealed in the due time."

"But, sir," Tsion said, feeling like a child, "is not now the due time?"

"We measure past, present, and future with different rods than you, son of earth. The due time is the due time, and to the prudent and watchful ones, the revelation will be clear."

"We'll know for sure the identity of the . . . of the enemy?"

"So I have spoken."

"Teach me all I am here to learn, great prince who stands watch over the sons of Abraham, Isaac, and Jacob."

"Stand silent," the angel said, "observe, and give ear to the truth of the war in heaven. Since the calling up of the righteous dead and alive, the enemy has competed with the hosts of heaven for the remaining souls of men.

"The evil one, that old serpent, has had access to the throne of the Most High since the beginning of time, until now, the appointed time."

What was he saying? That Tsion was there to witness the end of Satan's access to the throne, where for millennia he had exercised his power to accuse the children of God? Tsion wanted to ask how he earned so great a privilege, but Michael put a finger to his lips and beckoned with his other hand for Tsion to look past him to the very throne room. Tsion immediately fell prostrate in what seemed the midair of the extended universe. He saw only one figure, bigger, brighter, and more beautiful than Michael himself.

Tsion covered his eyes. "Is it the Lamb of God who takes away the sin of the world?"

"Silence, son of earth. This is neither Son nor Father, whom you will not see until *your* due time. Before you is the angel of light, the beautiful star, the great deceiver, your adversary, Lucifer."

Tsion shuddered, repulsed, yet unable to look away. "Is this the present?" he asked.

"Eternity past and future are the present here," Michael said. "Listen and learn."

Suddenly Tsion was able to hear the beautiful angel plead his case before the throne, which was beyond Tsion's view.

"Your so-called children are beneath you, ruler of heaven," came the persuasive mellifluous tones of the eternal solicitor. "Abandon them to me, who can fashion them for profit. Even after being called by your name, their natures reek with temporal desires. Allow me to surround myself with these enemies of your cause, and I will marshal them into a force unlike any army you have ever assembled."

From the throne came a voice of such power and authority that volume was irrelevant: "Thou shalt not touch my beloved!"

"But with them I shall ascend to a throne higher than yours!"

"No!"

"They are weak and ineffective in your service!"

"No!"

"I can salvage these hopeless wrecks."

"Thou shalt not."

"I beseech you, ruler of heaven and earth—"

"No."

"Grant me these or I will—"

"No."

"I will—"

"No."

"I will destroy them and defeat you! I shall bear the name above all other names! I shall sit high above the heavens, and there shall be no god like me! In *me* there shall be no change, neither shadow of turning."

Suddenly from Tsion's right he saw the flash in the eyes of Michael the archangel, and he spoke with great emotion. "God, the Father Almighty," he shouted, causing the evil one to look his way in disgust, then anger, "I beseech you allow no more blasphemy in the courts of heaven! Grant that I destroy this one and cast him out of your presence!"

Yet Michael apparently neither heard nor sensed the permission of God. Lucifer glared with contempt at Michael, smirking, laughing. He turned back to face the throne.

"Michael, your master shall not assign you an impossible task! He knows I am right about the sons of God. He will eventually concede them to me. You are a fool, weak and unable to face me on your own. You shall lose. I shall win. I shall ascend—"

But as Tsion watched and listened, Lucifer's voice changed. It became high-pitched and whiny, and his persona began to change. As he railed and begged and challenged and blasphemed, the voice from the throne continued to deny him. His bright shining robe lost its luster. His face curled into a hideous mask of scales. His hands and feet disappeared, and his garment fell off, revealing a slimy, writhing, coiling serpent. His eyes sank under deep hoods and his voice became a hiss, then a roar as he seemed to transform himself.

His hands and feet reappeared, but his fingers and toes had turned to great horned appendages. He dropped to all fours. His words had vanished into flaming breaths, and he paced before the throne with such anger that Tsion was glad Michael stood between him and this dragon.

His head grew horns and a crown appeared upon it, and suddenly his whole being turned fiery red. As Tsion watched in horror, the beast grew six more heads with crowns and a total of ten horns. Pacing and growing ever larger with each step, the beast shook itself in rage and threatened the throne and they that sat upon it.

And the voice from the throne said, "No."

With a great roar and stomping and shaking of its heads, the dragon postured threateningly and appeared to want to advance on the throne. Michael stepped that way, and the voice again said, "No."

Michael turned to Tsion. "Behold," he said, pointing behind Tsion.

Tsion turned to see the figure of a woman with clothes as bright as the sun. While Michael's brightness had nearly blinded him and Lucifer proved brighter still, the woman . . . the woman appeared as if clothed in the sun. It seemed she stood on the moon itself, and on her head was a wreath made of twelve stars.

Tsion was transfixed and felt a great kinship with the woman. He wanted to ask Michael who she was. Mary? Israel? The church? But he could not speak, could not turn. He was aware that the hideous seven-headed dragon was behind him but that Michael stood between him and that danger.

The woman was pregnant, her great sun-clothed belly causing her to turn and cry out in labor pains. She grimaced and her body convulsed in contractions, and as she held her abdomen as if about to give birth, the dragon leaped from his place before the throne, clearing Michael and Tsion and pouncing before the woman.

His great tail swept a third of the stars from the heavens, and they plummeted to the earth. And now he crouched before the woman who was ready to give birth, seven mouths open and salivating, tongues darting, ready to devour her child as soon as it was born.

She bore a male child who was caught up to God. The dragon watched in rage as the child was transported to the throne, and when he turned back to the woman, she had fled. He rose up to give chase, and Michael the archangel said, "Behold."

Tsion turned to watch him use both mighty hands to pull the golden sword from its sheath and swing it in a high arc over his head. Immediately he was joined by a heavenly host of warrior angels, who fell in behind him as the dragon's angels also mustered behind him.

Tsion had so many questions, but Michael had led the charge against the dragon. Perhaps Gabriel the announcer was close by. Tsion opened his mouth to ask, but when he said, "Who is the woman?" his words sounded plain to him and he felt enclosed. "Who is the woman?" he repeated, and his words woke him with a start.

He sat up and his blanket slid off. The TV still showed the slow moving line of mourners, bathed in the eerie palace courtyard spotlights. Tsion stood and peered into the playpen where Kenny slept, having not moved. He sat back down and stared unbelieving at the videodisc player clock. It read 12:59.

+ + +

Movement in the cabin caught Buck's eye. In the darkness he saw Chaim unstrap himself and awkwardly kneel in the aisle, his elbows on the armrest. Buck touched T's arm and nodded back. T looked and glanced at Buck, who raised both fists and bowed his head. He turned sideways so he had one ear facing the cabin. The man who had been so endearing and so stubborn was finally on his knees.

"Oh, God," Chaim began, "I have never before prayed believing that I was actually talking to you. Now I know that you are there and that you want me, and I don't know what to say." He began to weep.

"Forgive me for coming to you only because I am afraid for my life. Only you know the truth about me, whether I am sincere. You know better than I. I know that I am a sinner and need your forgiveness for all my sins, even for murder, regardless that the victim was your archenemy. Thank you for taking the punishment for my sins. Forgive me and receive me into your kingdom. I want to give you all of myself for the rest of my days. Show me what to do. Amen."

Buck looked back to where Chaim remained kneeling, his head buried in his arms. "Cameron?" he called, his voice muffled.

"Yes, Chaim?"

"I prayed, but I'm still scared!"

"So am I!"

"Me too!" T said.

"You tested God?" Buck said.

"I did. I guess I won't know his decision until we crash and I wake up in heaven or hell."

"Oh, the Bible says we can know."

"It does?"

"It says his Spirit bears witness with our spirit that we are children of God. What does your spirit say?"

"My spirit says to land carefully."

Buck laughed in spite of himself. "Chaim, there is a way we can know in advance. Do you want to know?"

"With all my heart."

"T, turn the lights on back there."

\+ \+ \+

David stood atop the observation tower again, watching the line. With a couple of hours to go before midnight, the air was cool enough to keep the crowd calm. The next day was expected to be over one hundred degrees, and he worried about health and tempers. The funeral was to begin in twelve hours, but David couldn't imagine the crowds having completely passed by the bier that soon.

From his perch he could see the final touches on the massive, black, hollow, iron and bronze image of the late potentate, made from a postmortem body cast.

Guy Blod seemed about to burst, supervising the last welds and the winching of it into place. Guy would stand on a scaffold and do the final sanding and polishing himself, planning to have workmen roll the finished product near the bier sometime before dawn.

Fortunato and his lackeys were making the rounds, and Leon had a couple of folded sheets of paper in his hand and seemed to be taking copious notes. He and his entourage visited the statue-making operation, where Guy broke long enough to animatedly point out the features and accept accolades from the supreme commander.

The Fortunato juggernaut moved to the middle of the long line, where many had been waiting for hours. People bowed and knelt and kissed his hands. Often he lifted them and pointed up to the bier, and they stood nodding and gesturing.

Leon checked the various concession tents and stands, none of which would open until daybreak. When he got to the stand beneath where David stood, David's worst fears were realized. "Anyone seen Director Hassid?" Leon said.

While his people were shaking their heads, someone in the tent said, "He's upstairs, Commander."

"With whom?"

"Alone, I think."

"Gentlemen, wait for me, would you?"

He mounted the steps, and David felt the whole structure sway. David acted as if he was not expecting anyone and had not heard anyone come up.

"Director Hassid, I presume," Fortunato said.

David turned. "Commander."

"Want to join our little group, David? We're just greeting the people."

"No, thanks. Long day. I'm about to turn in."

"I understand," Leon said, pulling the pages from his pocket. "Have time to give me a little input?"

"Sure."

"I'm getting pressure from a few people in Rome for a memorial service for Pontifex Maximus. Remember him?"

Leon had asked that seriously, as if David wouldn't remember the head of the one-world faith who had died within the week. "Of course," David said.

"Well, he seems to have faded from most people's memories, and I'm inclined to leave it that way."

"Not have the service, you mean?"

"You agree?" Fortunato said.

"I'm just asking."

"Well, I agree with you that we probably shouldn't have it."

That wasn't what David had said, of course, but there was no sense squabbling. Fortunato was likely eliciting the same forced ideas from everyone around him, and he would eventually find himself "acquiescing" to the counsel from his staff.

"I would like spiritual matters centralized here in New Babylon for good, and I believe there is a place for a personal expression of faith better than what that amalgam gave us."

"Everyone seemed to go for that all-faiths-into-one idea, Commander."

"Yes, but with mounting evidence that Potentate Carpathia deserves sainthood, and the possibility that he himself was divine, I believe there's a place for worshiping and even praying to our fallen leader. What do you think?"

"I think you will prevail."

"Well, thank you for that. David, I have found you a most capable and loyal worker. I want you to know that you can name your role in my regime."

"Your regime?"

"Surely you don't see anyone else in line for Supreme Potentate."

David was tempted to tell him who the potentate would be very soon. "No, I don't suppose."

"I mean, if you do, tell me. I have people watching the three dissident kings closely, and I think Litwala has a lean and hungry look. You know where that's from, Hassid?"

"Shakespeare. *Julius Caesar*."

"You *are* well read. What role would motivate you?"

"I'm happy where I am, sir."

"Really?"

"Yes."

"Well, how would you respond to a healthy raise and a title change, say special assistant to the supreme potentate?"

David knew this would all be moot soon. "I wouldn't oppose it," he said.

"You wouldn't oppose it!" Fortunato laughed. "I like that! Look at this list of people who want to say a few words at the funeral tomorrow." He swore. "Self-serving sons of the devil."

Takes one to know one, David thought.

"You want to say a few words?"

"No."

"Because I could squeeze you in."

"No, thank you."

"It'd be no problem, give you some visibility."

"No."

"Going to get some rest, eh?"

"Yes, sir."

"And you'll be back when?"

"Daybreak, I imagine."

"Hmm."

"Problem, sir?"

"I was looking for someone from our level to be here when the statue is put in place."

"Blod's a minister."

"Yeah, but, you know."

David didn't know, but he nodded nonetheless.

"Could you be there, David?"

"Whatever you say, sir."

"Attaboy."

+ + +

Buck moved into the cabin as Chaim rose and turned to face him. He looked exhausted and was tearstained. Chaim now had his back to the armrest he had leaned on, and it caught him just above the knee. Buck put a hand on each of Chaim's shoulders, and the old man lurched back and plopped into the seat, his feet on Buck's knees.

"So, you saw it, did you?" Buck said.

"Yes!" Chaim said, rising. "And you can see mine?" He maneuvered until he was directly under a light, and he held a shock of white hair out of the way.

"I sure can, Chaim. You didn't believe us all this time, did you? That we could see each other's marks, I mean."

"Actually, I did believe you," Chaim said. "Not all of you would have lied to me. I was so jealous."

"No more."

"So God knew my heart."

"Apparently."

"That in itself is a miracle."

"Prepare for descent," T hollered.

"I can't say I'm any less scared," Chaim said.

"I'm scared too, friend, but a lot less than I would be if I didn't know my destination."

14

LEAH WAS TIRED and bored, despite being fascinated by the change in Rayford and the relationship between him and his daughter. Even with the windows open and a chilly breeze coming through, the Land Rover was cramped and oppressive.

When her phone rang and it was Ming, she was alarmed but glad for the diversion.

"I am going to get to see my parents and my brother again," Ming said.

"That's great. How? Where?"

"At the funeral."

"You're going?"

"And so are they. I called to tell them I had been assigned crowd control and they insisted on coming."

"Well, that's good, isn't it?"

"Leah, I am so worried about my parents. They do not know about either Chang or me being believers. They were *such* admirers of Carpathia that they are sick with grief. I want to tell them and persuade them, but it would take a miracle."

"It's always a miracle, Ming. We'll pray with you that it will happen."

"You don't know my father."

"I know, but God is bigger than any of that. How are you getting to New Babylon? I heard all flights were full."

"Military transport. I don't know how my family found seats, except that my father has a lot of influence with the GC. His business contributes more than 20 percent of its profits to New Babylon. They are expecting another million people there tomorrow. I'm telling you, Leah, even prisoners here are mourning Carpathia."

"When you're there, look up David Hassid and Annie Christopher."

"Believers?"

"Of course. Keep up the front. Pretend to argue with them. They'll notice your mark and play along to protect you. Introduce your brother. I'll tip them off that your parents don't know. Hey, any more news on Hattie or on Cameron Williams's family?"

A pause.

"You can tell me, Ming."

"Well, it's sort of good news and bad news."

"Shoot."

"The Williamses' home burned and two bodies were discovered, identified as Cameron Williams's father and brother."

"And?"

"This is unconfirmed, Leah, but there is some evidence that they may have become believers."

"That will be so helpful if Buck could know that for sure."

"I'll see what I can find out without being too obvious, but someone said the murders and the torching had to wait because they were at a church-type meeting."

"Does that mean the GC knows where the church meets?"

"Likely. They know more than most believers want to think."

"We've got to warn that church."

* * *

Buck listened to T talk on the radio to the tower at Kozani. "Very low on fuel. I may make one test pass, but I'd better go for it."

"On the downside, Super Juliet, we have no foam and no prospects to get any soon."

"Roger that."

"You have friends in high places, Juliet."

"Repeat?"

"You have new equipment coming."

"I'm not following you, tower."

"Man named Albie. Know him?"

"Heard of him. Friend of a friend."

"That's what he said. He's delivering a plane for you, assuming yours is going to need some rehab."

"Roger. What's he bringing?"

"No idea."

"How's he going to get back?"

"I believe he's planning to do the fix on yours and take it in trade."

"He'd better be bringing something pretty nice."

"Just hope yours is worth trading after you scrape our runway."

"Roger."

Buck looked at T. "Do you believe that? Rayford had to set that up."

"Wonder when Albie's expected."

Buck shook his head. "He's got a lot longer flight than we do, and who knows where he's getting the craft?"

"I can't wait to see it."

"I can't wait to see if we survive."

"I believe we will," T said. "We'll take a look at the situation, and slide her in there nice and smooth."

"I love the confidence in your voice."

"Must be my acting background."

"Don't say that."

"Truth is, Buck, I need both of you strapped in in the very back seats. I'll call out altitude readings. By fifty feet, you should be braced and tucked, but you can get into that position anytime after you hear one hundred feet. Got it?"

Buck nodded.

"We're close. Get Chaim ready."

Buck stood and was moving into the cabin when T said, "Oh, no!"

"What?"

The interior lights went dark. Battery-operated emergency lights eerily illuminated the control board.

"What's happening?" Chaim called out. "Someone talk to me."

"Let's just say we won't have to jettison fuel," T said. "Get strapped in now, back seats, and don't talk to me till we're on the ground."

"I'm ready for heaven!" Chaim said. "But tonight I prefer asphalt to gold, if you don't mind."

"Shut up, Doctor," T said, and he called the tower on batteries. "Mayday, Kozani tower, this is the Super J, and we're out of fuel, repeat, out of fuel. On battery backup, landing lights may not be fully operational."

"Roger, Juliet," came the response, as Buck settled in across the aisle from Chaim. "Cleared to land."

"Roger," T said. He started to talk to himself as he went through all the emergency procedures. He looked too busy to talk on the radio. "Let's see here, emergency engine shutdown, then set up the best glide speed. The one gear will not come up, so forget that. Better do a partial gear-up landing checklist."

T's hand flew all over the panels, and Buck could see from the back through the front window that the airport boundary fence was going to be a problem.

"Approach, can you call off altitudes for Juliet?" T said to approach control, also on tower frequency.

"No problem, Juliet, one thousand and holding below glide path."

T worried out loud how he was going to control the plane on the ground with only one gear. "Nine hundred . . . eight hundred . . . seven . . . six . . . five-fifty." He concentrated on keeping the best possible glide airspeed, in a desperate attempt to make the field.

"Runways are clear, emergency teams in place, Juliet," the tower reported. "Four hundred . . . below glide path . . . looks like you will land short . . . watch out for the boundary fence, Juliet."

"Roger," T said. "Three hundred . . . two . . ."

* * *

Tsion stood and stretched and checked on Kenny. He felt as if he'd been out for hours, yet he was as weary as when he nodded off. While he was determined not to miss anything in New Babylon, he knew he needed sleep. He sat back down and settled in, hoping, praying he would again be transported to the very portals of heaven. He didn't know what to call what had happened to him or how to assess it, but it had been the privilege of a lifetime. He was left with so many questions and so much more to come. But before he slept he again felt compelled to pray for his brothers and sisters on the front lines.

* * *

David headed for his quarters, phoning Guy on the way. "I'd like to see the positioning of the statue when you're ready."

"Now?"

"I say, when you're ready. The regular schedule will be fine."

"You're asking permission?"

"I'm just saying I'd like to watch. There a problem with that?"

"I don't need my hand held."

"Believe me, Guy, I don't want to hold your hand."

"Protocol demands that you not refer to me by my first name."

"Sorry, Blood."

"It's Blod, and my last name isn't appropriate either!"

"Oh, I don't think it's that bad."

"Ooh! My title is Minister!"

"Sorry, Reverend Minister. But your supreme commander and mine wants a liaison from administration present when you move naked boy into position."

"How rude and tacky."

"That's sort of what I thought, but I'm surprised you agree."

"David!"

"Ah, Director Hassid to you, Minister Blood. Anyway, he chose me, so don't leave home without me."

"David! *I* am a minister, therefore *I* qualify as a liaison from administration. You just stay in bed until you can be civil."

"Sorry, Minnie, but I have a direct order. If you want to contest it, you may take it up with him."

"Just wait till he hears what you called the potentate."

"Oh, if you tell him that, please clarify that I was referring to your statue. And you might add that you yourself admitted it was—what did you say?—rude and tacky."

"Five a.m., Hayseed, and we're not waiting for you."

"Oh, good. I'd hate to miss that. Have a nice day."

\+ + +

Buck knew he should have his head buried, as Chaim did, but he was too curious. He leaned out into the aisle where he could see through the cockpit. The plane was too steeply nose down, and clearly T was going to try one last maneuver to somehow clear the south fence, which preceded about a hundred yards of grass and then the runway. It struck Buck that most of the tire marks on the runway were at least a quarter mile from the edge of the pavement and only a couple of others showed nearer, none of them really close to the grass. He would not bet T could get the Super J over the fence, let alone into the grass, forget the runway proper.

"Your landing gear is down, Juliet! Repeat, down! Full gear down on right, partial assemblage on left! Good luck!"

"We don't do luck!" Buck shouted, as the fence disappeared from view. "God, do your thing through T!"

"Roger!" T shouted as he yanked on the stick; the plane bucked ever so slightly, clearing the fence, then swept tail first onto the grass.

The impact slammed Buck so deep into his seat that he felt it in every fiber of his being. Chaim had let out a terrific grunt on impact, and it seemed his face was near his shoes. Buck wished he'd been in the same position, because he felt soft tissue give way from his tailbone to his neck, and he was sure both shoulders had nearly been torn from their sockets. He felt it in his feet, ankles, and knees, and the plane was still nose up as the rear tore through the sod.

That meant at least one more impact was to come, but Buck couldn't imagine they would feel it in the back, at least not the way they felt the first one.

The angle and speed T had brought the plane in on somehow carried the craft all the way to the runway on its tail. When the tail hit the edge of the runway, the nose slammed down in a shower of sparks so fast that the front half of the fuselage tore away from the back and the two huge pieces of airplane went sliding and scraping, spinning in opposite directions.

Buck was aware of sky and pavement and lights and hangars and sparks and noise and dizziness, until the g-forces were too much and he felt himself losing consciousness. "Lord," he said as blissful darkness invaded his brain, "I can recover from this. Leave me here awhile. Chloe, I love you. Kenny . . ."

* * *

Exhausted as he was, David could not sleep. He lay in his quarters, wondering why he got such joy out of tormenting Guy Blod. He couldn't shake from his memory Rayford's story of having tormented Hattie Durham's friend Bo, and how Bo had eventually committed suicide. Sure, Guy was a case, and David enjoyed beating him in a battle of wits and sarcasm. But was he laying groundwork for ever having a positive influence on the man? Guy's becoming a believer seemed remote, but who would have guessed David himself would have ever come to faith? A young Israeli techie with street smarts, he had been a skeptical agnostic his whole life. Could he start over with Guy, or would the man laugh in his face? Regardless, he had to do the right thing.

David tapped out a love message for Annie, telling her that while he agreed they should not even think about children until after the Glorious Appearing, he still wanted to marry her. Her response would determine his next move in the relationship.

He took one last look at messages and e-mail and thought he had an idea where every Trib Force member was. All absent and accounted for, he decided. By now Buck and Chaim ought to be in Greece. He wondered what Chaim was doing for identification.

With a brief prayer for Tsion, who he hoped would get back to his daily Internet studies and commentaries soon, David fell into bed. He asked forgiveness for how he had treated Guy Blod and asked God to give him special compassion for the man. Of course it would not be safe for him to declare himself a believer to a GC insider yet, but he didn't want to shut the door to opportunities once he and Annie had escaped.

* * *

Buck's eyes flew open, and he feared he might be going into shock. The night air hit him like a polar blast, though he knew it was not that cold. He could not even see his breath. He sat in the jagged back half of the Super J, staring straight down the runway to the front half, which faced him about half a mile away. He had to get out, get to T, make sure he was OK. T had saved their lives. What a masterful job of flying the lifeless bird!

Chaim! Buck looked to his left to find the old man still curled upon himself, bent all the way forward, the back of his head pressed against the seat in front of him. How could he have not broken his neck? Did Buck dare move him?

"Chaim! Chaim, are you all right?"

Rosenzweig did not move. Buck gently touched Chaim's back and noticed that his own hand quivered like the last leaf on a maple tree. He clasped his hands together to control himself, but his whole body shuddered. Was anything broken, punctured, severed? It didn't appear so, but he would be sore for days. And he must not allow himself to slip into shock.

Worried about Chaim, Buck unstrapped himself and reached for his right wrist, which was by Chaim's foot, his hands tightly wrapped around the ankles. He could not loosen Chaim's grip, so he forced his fingers between Chaim's leg and wrist. Not only did he have a pulse, but it was strong and dangerously fast.

Buck heard footsteps and shouting as three emergency workers appeared, demanding to know if there were any survivors. "I need a blanket," he said. "Freezing. And he needs someone who knows what they're doing to get him out of here and check for neck injuries."

"Blood," one of the men said.

"Where?" Buck said.

"The man's shoes. Look."

Blood dripped from Chaim's face to his shoes.

"Sir!" they called to him. "Sir!" Turning to Buck, one said, "What is his name?"

"Just call him Doctor. He'll hear you."

Someone tossed Buck a blanket, and he saw more workers sprinting down the runway to the other half of the plane. He tried to stand. Everything hurt. His head throbbed. He was dizzy. He pulled the blanket around himself, feeling every muscle and bone, and staggered out the front of the wreckage to solid ground. He stood there, swaying, assuring everyone he was all right. He had to get to T. There was nothing he could do for Chaim. If the worst he had was a racing pulse and facial lacerations, he should be all right. It was too late to tell him not to use his own name.

Buck started toward the other end of the runway, but he moved so slowly and shook so much that he wondered if he could make it. The ground beckoned and almost took him several times. But though he knew he had to look like a drunk, he kept forcing one foot in front of the other. An emergency medical technician ran toward him from the cockpit half and another came from the tail end. As they got close to Buck, he thought they were going to carry him the rest of the way. He would not have resisted.

But they ignored him and shouted to each other. The one from behind him told the other, "Old guy back there looks like the Israeli who died in a house fire last night."

"He gets that a lot," Buck said, realizing that neither heard him.

"How's the pilot?" the first EMT said, but Buck didn't hear the response.

"What'd he say?" he called after the man, who was now running for the cockpit.

"He didn't!"

Buck hadn't seen the man shake his head in response either, but maybe he hadn't been watching carefully enough. At long last he arrived at the front end of the plane. No one was working on T. That could be good or bad. He heard someone call for a body bag.

That couldn't be. If he and Chaim had survived the jolt, surely T had. He was in better shape than either passenger. One of the workers tried to block Buck's way into the plane, but Buck gave him a look and a weak shove, and the man knew there would be no dissuading him. "Please don't touch the body," the man said.

"It's not a body," Buck slurred. They had for sure misread this one, hurriedly misdiagnosed whatever the problem was. "It's a friend, our pilot."

The cockpit portion had come to rest directly by a huge runway lamp, which filled the wreckage with light. Buck saw no blood, no bones, no twisted limbs. He stepped behind T, who was sitting straight up, still strapped in. His left hand lay limp on his lap, his right hung open-palmed in the space between the seats. T's head hung forward, chin on his chest.

"T," Buck said, a hand on his shoulder, "how we doin', pal?"

T felt warm, thick, and muscly. Buck put a finger to the right pressure point in the neck. Nothing. Buck felt the blanket slide from his shoulders. He slumped painfully into the seat across from T and grabbed the lifeless hand in both of his. "Oh, T," he said. "Oh, T."

The rational part of his brain told him there would be more of this. More friends and fellow believers would die. They would reunite within three and a half years. But though he didn't know T the way Rayford had, this one still hurt. Here was a quiet, steady man who had risked his life and freedom more than once for the Tribulation Force. And now he had made the ultimate sacrifice.

"We need to remove the body and the wreckage, sir. I'm sorry. This is an active runway."

Buck stood and bent over T, taking his head in his arms. "I'll see you at the Eastern Gate," he whispered.

Buck dragged his blanket out of the plane but could walk no farther. He tried to sit on the edge of the runway but couldn't catch himself and rolled on his back. A stiff breeze chilled the back of his neck, and he didn't have the energy to protest when he felt a hand in his pocket. "Anyone meeting you here, Mr. Staub?"

"Yeah."

"Who?"

"Miklos."

"Lukas Miklos, the lignite guy?"

"Yeah."

"He's in the terminal. Can you make it?"

"No."

"We'll get a gurney out here."

Buck watched as T's body was lifted out in a bag. "Take care of the old guy back there," Buck managed, pointing the other way.

"We've got the old man," someone said. "Bloody nose and a jittery heart, but he'll make it."

And Buck was out again.

\+ + +

The skies began to darken in Chicago at around seven, but Rayford decided to wait until eight to venture out. He wanted the skies black and no one even looking their direction. The city had been abandoned, condemned, and cordoned off for months, and it wouldn't have surprised him to know that not even a leftover drunk walked those streets. Radiation or not, decaying bodies littered many streets. It might be a safer place to hide out, but it was not going to be a fun place to live.

He pulled slowly from under the L platform with his lights off, hoping to kick up as little dust as possible. There would be no shooting straight into the Loop on the Dan Ryan. Nothing was as it once was.

Between separate bombing raids and the great earthquake, some reconstruction had been attempted, but these were meant to be shortcuts, two-lane roads that cut straight through the city. But only a few were even half finished, so the most direct route anywhere was as straight a line as you could point—over, under, around, and through the natural and man-made obstacles in the best four-wheel-drive vehicle you could find.

Rayford guessed he had between fifteen and twenty miles to drive, his lights off most of the way, traveling at around ten miles an hour. "I hope this is all David says it is," he said.

"Me too," Chloe said. "For my sake. Of course, I watched his little cybertour of the place. If it's half what it looks like, it's going to be as close to ideal as we can find."

Leah was asleep.

* * *

David showed up at the statue construction site a few minutes after five in the morning, Carpathia Time. Guy started in with something sarcastic about how now they could finish their work. David held up both hands. "Sorry if I held you up. Minister Blod, a word, please?"

Guy seemed so shocked that David had addressed him with proper protocol in front of his staff that he dropped what he was doing and joined him several feet away. David thrust out his hand, and Guy, clearly suspicious, shook it tentatively. "I want to apologize for speaking inappropriately to you, sir. I trust you'll find me helpful and not a hindrance to your work from here on."

"What?"

"I said I want to apologize—"

"I heard you, Hayseed. I'm waiting for the punch line."

"That's all I had to say, sir."

"I'm waiting for the other shoe to drop!" Guy said in a singsong tone.

"That's all, sir. Will you forgive me?"

"I'm sorry?"

"I said, that's all, sir—"

"I heard you; I'm trying to digest this. The supreme commander put you up to this, didn't he? Well, I didn't squeal on you. C'mon, who made you do this?"

David would have loved to have said "God" and blown Guy's mind. "No outside influence, Minister Blod. No ulterior motives. Just want to start over on the right foot."

"Well, count me in, mister!"

"Is that an acceptance of my apology?"

"It's whatever you want it to be, soldier!"

"Thanks. No sense holding up the work any longer."

"I should say not. We're ready to roll in five."

15

BUCK STRUGGLED TO OPEN his eyes. He had never felt so beat-up.

The dawn sun peeked through the blinds in a small infirmary, he wasn't sure where. He had awakened to the quiet praying of three men who sat holding hands. One he recognized as Lukas Miklos. The others were a tall, dark-haired man about his own age and an older, smaller, Middle Easterner.

"How are you feeling, my friend?" Lukas said, approaching.

"I've been better, Laslos, but you're a sight. Where are we, and how is Chaim?"

Lukas stepped closer and whispered. "Chaim will be all right, but we had to come up with an alias for him. His nose was severely damaged and his jaw broken. So he has not spoken, and medical personnel are not suspicious, only curious. He is being operated on right now. Our document forger pulled off the impossible, so . . ."

"And our pilot is gone, right? I wasn't hallucinating."

"That is correct. Praise God he was a believer. His papers identified him as Tyrola Mark Delanty. Was this an alias, or—?"

"Didn't need an alias. He ran a small airport near us and was able to evade suspicious eyes."

Laslos nodded. "The GC will not allow bodies to be transported internationally. Let our church handle the burial."

Buck rolled his shoulders and rotated his head. Pain shot through his neck. "What's your guy going to do about Chaim's picture?"

Lukas looked over his shoulder. "Look what we planted after surgery." He showed Buck an ID with the photograph nearly scraped off, a bit of white hair peeking through the top. "Doesn't that look like it went through the crash? We tried to persuade officials to postpone surgery until the swelling reduced, but they're short staffed here, like everywhere. Meanwhile, he's Tobias Rogoff, a retired librarian from Gaza on his way to North America on a charter flight, the same one you're on."

"Does he know this?"

"We told him a few hours ago. Our story is that the charter insurance company has contracted with Albie Air to guarantee the completion of the trip as soon as you two are airworthy."

"I'm airworthy now," Buck said, looking over Laslos's shoulder toward the little Middle Easterner. "You must be Albie."

"I am, sir," he said with a thick accent and a slight bow. "Your father-in-law and your friend Mr. McCullum and I go way back. Also Abdullah Smith."

"How well I know. I did not expect to see your mark. Is my father-in-law aware?"

Albie shook his head. "This was very recent, within the week. I tried to contact Rayford, but I found him impossible to connect with. Of course, now I know why."

"And how did you come to faith, sir?"

"Nothing dramatic, I'm afraid. I have always been religious, but Rayford and Mac and Abdullah all urged me to at least consider the writings of Dr. Ben-Judah. Finally I did. You know what reached me? His assessment of the difference between religion and Christianity."

"I know it well," Buck said, "if you're referring to his contention that religion is man's attempt to reach God, while Jesus is God's attempt to reach man."

"The very argument," Albie said. "I spent a couple of days surfing the archives of Dr. Ben-Judah's Web site, saw all his explanations of the prophesied plagues and judgments, then studied the prophecies about the coming Christ. How anyone with a functioning mind could read that and not—"

"Forgive me, Albie," Laslos said, "but we must keep moving. We should tell you, Buck, that Dr. Rosenzweig's eyes danced at the prospect of a new identity. We don't know how long it will be before he can speak, but it's clear he can't wait to playact as someone else."

Buck slid off the side of the bed. "Are we near the airport?"

Laslos shook his head. "We're north of Kozani. Albie has flown the new craft to Ptolemaïs, and when you and, ah, Tobias are healthy, you'll leave from there. Meanwhile, as soon as we can get you out of here, you'll stay with us at the same safe house where we harbored Rayford."

"We have not met," Buck said, reaching past Laslos's hand to shake hands with the tall, willowy one.

"I'm sorry," Laslos said. "Pastor Demeter."

The pastor said, "Mr. Williams, I answered your phone a while ago and talked to your wife. She and your father-in-law are checking out a new safe house, and she was very relieved to hear that you and Chaim are alive. Naturally, they are distraught over Mr. Delanty, particularly Rayford. Mrs. Williams wants to talk with you as soon as you are able."

"I want to get home soon," Buck said. "Albie, I'll bet you weren't planning on flying that far, were you?"

"I have nothing to return to Al Basrah for, Mr. Williams. Could you use another craft and another pilot?"

"Oh, I think the Trib Force might find room for the best black-market contact in the world."

Demetrius handed Buck his phone. As Buck dialed, Laslos explained that so far they had not seemed to arouse suspicion on the parts of the local GC. "They believe Demetrius works for me and that you are an American come to study the business."

Chloe didn't like the plan. "Get out of there, Buck," she told him. "We've found *the* perfect safe house. Even my curmudgeon father hopes so. Chaim is smart, but this clandestine stuff is not his game. Let us get you two healthy here."

"You may be right, Chlo'," he said. "What time is it there? I've got to call my dad."

She paused. "Buck, it's after eight in the evening and earlier out west, but that was one of the reasons I wanted to talk with you."

He read it in her voice.

"Dad?"

"Yes."

"And—"

"Your brother too, Buck. I'm so sorry."

"How?"

"GC."

"Looking for us?"

"That's what we understand."

"But they didn't know where we are! That's why I never told them!"

"I know, sweetheart. There may be some good news too."

"What?"

"Our source tells us that the first attempt to get information out of them had to be postponed. They were at church."

"Chloe, don't."

"It's true, Buck. Leah found a believer at Buffer who has access to these schemes, and she says that's from a reliable source."

"Why wouldn't Dad have told me?"

"Maybe the timing wasn't right."

"I wish I could know for sure."

"Leah is trying to reach the church so they know what happened and can be on guard. She'll ask for the truth about your dad and brother."

* * *

Rayford had had to stop driving when news came of T's death. He walked a couple of blocks in the darkness, and when Chloe asked if she could walk with him, he thanked her but added, "I need a few minutes, hon."

Chicago was, naturally, a mess. Buildings in piles, rotting carcasses, vehicles crashed or burned. It seemed an appropriate ambience for Rayford's sojourn.

The hardest thing about living during this period, he decided, was the roller coaster of emotions. He would never get used to the shock of loss and the necessity to telescope mourning into minute slivers so it could be dealt with and yet one could get on with the business at hand.

In the past, with each death of someone close to him, Rayford had rehearsed the ever-growing list in his mind. He didn't do that anymore. He wondered if a person had a limit, some finite reservoir of grief that would eventually peter out and leave him with no tears, no regret, no melancholy. He stopped at what was once a corner and leaned over, hands on his knees. His grief supply was still stocked, and the pain of the loss gushed from him.

Hard as it was, Rayford had to condense the bereavement caused by yet another aching amputation into a few brief hours. He was not allowed to dwell on it, to jot his memories, to console a widow, to break the news to a congregation. There would be no wake, no funeral, not even a memorial service, at the rate they were going. T's church was likely to have one, of course, but there was no way Rayford dared attend. Who knew who might be watching, lying in wait?

Not enough of his comrades in the Tribulation Force really knew T. There would be little reminiscing. He was gone. They would see him in heaven. Now what was next on the crisis docket? It was unfair, unnatural. How was a person supposed to function this way and stay sane?

Rayford was grateful for his own return to what Dr. Ben-Judah liked to call the "first love of Christ," that wonderful season when the plan of salvation and the truth of grace are fresh and new. He was thankful for the counsel of Demetrius Demeter and the refreshing rest and new sense of resolve he enjoyed.

And now this. The thrill ride. He'd had enough ups for twenty-four hours, apparently. He had been due for some downs.

As usual when in a stretch like this, Rayford tried cataloging what he still had to be thankful for. Without fail, every blessing in his life had a name attached: Chloe, Kenny, Buck, Tsion, Leah, her new friend he hadn't yet met, the two Zekes, Chaim, David and Annie, Mac, Abdullah, Laslos and his wife, Demetrius, Albie. Rayford wondered why Albie had been so eager to help in Greece and what it was he was so eager to tell him, but only in person.

Rayford had to fight the knowledge that while his list might expand, it also had to suffer attrition. He had already lost so many, including two wives. He would not allow himself to think about losing more relatives.

When he returned to the Rover, Leah reported that she had reached the leader of the house church Buck's father and brother had attended. "I told him I'd love it if he could talk directly to Buck and he said he'd be happy to, but I didn't feel right about giving out Buck's number."

"That was wise," Rayford said. "Let Buck decide that. His phone is secure, but this pastor's is likely bugged if they just had a GC cleansing. Try Buck and give him the pastor's number. Let him work out the contact."

A few minutes later Rayford parked near Strong's and they cased the place, only to find it secure. The three of them sat on the sidewalk with their backs to the cold brick, and Rayford pulled out his phone.

* * *

Something about the New Babylon predawn David never liked. Maybe Israel was lusher. Both were desert areas, but the hour before daybreak in Israel had always invigorated him, made him look forward to the promise of the day. The dry, windless heat of New Babylon mornings, beautiful as the sunrises could be, David found suffocating.

Watching Guy Blod put the finishing touches on the huge image of Nicolae Carpathia did little to cheer David. Not a hundred feet away, hundreds of thousands of grieving pilgrims from all over the world moved in slow silence, waiting hours for their few seconds before the sarcophagus. It was sad enough that these blind, lost, misled minions clearly worried about their future due to the loss of their beloved leader. But here behind great curtains, Guy and his assistants rhapsodized over the finished product.

"Care to look close?" Guy asked David as he glided down on a motorized scaffold.

Not really, David wanted to say, but how would he explain passing on such a so-called privilege? He shrugged, which Guy interpreted as affirmative, and the sculptor sang out instructions.

"There's only room for one on the scaffold, and you have to run the controls yourself. Be careful! The first time I did it I nearly knocked over one of my own creations!"

Guy showed David the controls, which consisted primarily of a joystick and speed selector. He was tempted to point the thing at the statue's head, shoot up, and knock it over. As David tentatively and jerkily practiced maneuvering the scaffold before rising, Guy hollered his cautions. "Careful of the smoke! The fire is lit under the knees, and the face has the only exhaust."

"Why didn't you wait until it was in place to start the fire?"

"We don't want to distract the crowds. This sort of art is a duet between sculptor and viewer, and my goal is that they participate in the illusion that the statue is alive."

"Twenty-four feet high and made of metal?"

"Trust me, this works. People will love it. But it would spoil everything if they saw us dumping in the stuff for the fire."

"What are you using for fuel?" David asked.

"A form of shale," Guy said. "For kindling, onionskin paper."

"Where'd that come from?"

"Every tribe and nation!" Guy said, and his people laughed. "Seriously, we have an unlimited supply of holy books from all over the world, the last contribution of the late Pontifex Maximus. He shipped from Rome all the holy texts that had been confiscated and donated from the various religions and sects when the one-world faith was established."

David was repulsed, now certain he didn't want the closer look, but he was stuck. "Note the handiwork on the way up!" Guy said. What was there to see but polished black iron? "You can touch, but be careful! It's delicately balanced!"

Nearly two and a half stories up, David could hardly hear Guy anymore. Smoke wafted out the eyes, nostrils, and mouth of the quadruple-size image of Carpathia. It was uncanny. Though from that close the illusion was lost that the eyes were real, the features, having been made from the actual cast of the body, were perfect replicas.

David was high enough to see past the statue to the horizon, where the sun's pinks were just beginning to wash the sky. Suddenly he flinched and backpedaled, hitting the safety bar just above his waist. The whole scaffold shuddered, and he feared it might topple.

"Hey!" one of Guy's assistants hollered.

"What's going on up there?" Guy yelled. "You all right?"

David waved. He didn't want to admit what he'd heard, what had made him jump. He steadied himself and listened. A low rumble, echoing as if from the belly of the image. Muffled and sonorous, it was clearly Carpathia's timbre. What was it saying, and how had they gotten it to do that? A chip? A disc player? A tape?

He felt the vibration again, heard the hum, cocked his head to listen. "I shall shed the blood of saints and prophets."

David whipped the control so the scaffold lurched down about five feet and stopped, swaying again. "How did you do that?" he called down.

"Do what?"

"Get a recording in there!"

Silence.

"Well, how did you? Where's the hardware, and what does the phrase mean?"

Guy was still staring up at him, obviously holding out.

"Guy!"

"What?"

"What didn't you hear? Do I have to repeat everything?"

"What didn't I hear? I didn't hear anything but you, David. What the devil are you talking about?"

David began his slow descent. "The thing talks. How did you do it? Tape loop? Disc? What? And won't the heat or smoke destroy it?"

Guy rolled his eyes at his people. He whispered, "What are you, serious?"

"You know blamed well I'm serious, Guy."

"So we're back to first names, are we?"

"Can we not get hung up on that right now, Minister-Director-Poten-take-your-choice Blod? The thing speaks. I heard it twice, and I'm not crazy."

"If you're not crazy, you're mistaken."

"Don't tell me I didn't hear what I heard!"

"Then you're hearing things, Director Hassid. This thing hasn't been out of my sight since the shell was delivered. This isn't a theme park. I don't want giant talking action figures. OK? Are we all right now? May I have them start moving my big boy into position?"

David nodded and stepped back to let a monstrous forklift move in behind the statue. His phone chirped, and as soon as he answered he heard a tone indicating another call. "This is Director Hassid; hold please," but as he punched in the other call heard, "Dav—!" and recognized Fortunato's voice.

"This is Director Hassid; hold please," he said again, switching back to Fortunato. "Sorry, Commander. I'm watching the moving of the statue, and—"

"I'm sure that'll succeed without you, David. I'd appreciate not being put on hold in the future." David knew he should apologize again to keep up appearances, but he was dwelling on how important his getting up before 5:00 a.m. was to Fortunato last night and how incidental it was now. "We've got a situation here," Leon continued. "I need you in the conference room on eighteen as soon as possible."

"Anything I need to bring or be thinking about?"

"No. Well, yes. Captain McCullum's schedule."

"Oh, he's—"

"Tell me when you get here, David. Quickly, please."

David switched to his other call. "That busy that early, huh, kid?" Rayford said.

"Sorry. What's up?" David walked backward as he talked, watching the statue emerge from the preparation room and become visible to the crowds. The murmuring grew louder as people nudged each other and pointed. The statue leaned back against the forks of the truck, and not until it came into the beams of the spotlights did it become apparent to all that it was, as Guy had so delicately put it, *au naturel.*

Oohs and *aahs* rose from the crowd; then they began applauding and soon cheering.

"What in the world is going on there?" Rayford said.

David told him. "I think they've waited so long to see the body that they would worship trading cards if we passed them out." Rayford told David what had happened in Greece. "I'm so sorry, Captain Steele. I only talked to Mr. Delanty a few times by phone, but I know you two were close."

"This is a hard one, David. They don't get any easier. Sometimes I feel like an albatross. The people who get close to me are soon gone."

David told him he was on his way to a mysterious meeting, and they debriefed each other again on what had happened at the Gala. "No matter what they say, sir, it's clear the shooting was accidental and that the bullet totally missed Carpathia."

"That doesn't make me any less of a scapegoat, but—"

"Oh, Captain, wait a second . . ."

"I hear the crowd. What happened?"

"Oh, man, it almost toppled over! They set down the statue, and it rocked forward! People were diving out of the way. The forklift guy moved up to sort of catch it on its way back so it wouldn't fall that way, and that just made it rock forward again! I don't know how it didn't go over. It's settled now, and they're nudging it straight. Oh, man!" He told Rayford of the built-in furnace but said nothing about what he'd heard.

"That jostling must have stoked the fire, because the smoke is really pouring out now. You know they're burning Bibles, among other holy books, in there?"

"No!"

"Sir, I'm heading inside now, and I never asked what you called about."

"I'm at the new safe house, David."

"Yeah? How is it?"

"It looks fabulous, but we have one problem. It must lock automatically in emergencies. We can't get in. Can you unlock it from there?"

David was near the elevator. "I can't talk here, sir, so let me just say yes, I'll get to that as soon as this meeting is over. I wish I could say when that will be."

* * *

Tsion took a call from Chloe, informing him it was likely they would be back very late. "Any evidence of GC nosing around?"

"None," he said, but he did not add that he had been 93 million miles from Mount Prospect for at least two minutes.

She spoke briefly to Kenny, who kept wanting to pull the phone from his mouth and "see Mama." Finally he said, "Lub-you-too-see-ya-lader-bye-bye."

"Tsion, I appreciate this more than you know," Chloe said.

"He's easy," he said. "And you know I love him."

She told Tsion what to feed Kenny and to put him to bed at nine. Much as he had enjoyed the baby, that was good news. Kenny often slept through the night.

* * *

David had not given himself time to worry what the big meeting was about. He just hoped he would not be in there alone with Fortunato. David was the last to arrive. A dozen directors and above were there, including television personnel, most yawning and rubbing their eyes.

"Let's get started, people," Leon began. "We have a crisis. No one is leaving New Babylon. Despite the decimated population in the last three and a half years, hotels are jammed and people are even agreeing to double up, two whole families in each room. Others are sleeping in the street, under lean-tos. The airport is crowded with big jets. They bring in capacity loads for the viewing, but they're canceling most outbound flights for lack of interest. You know what's happening, don't you?"

"The viewing is not meeting their felt needs," a woman said. David recognized her as Hilda Schnell, head of Global Community Cable News Network.

"I'm glad it was you who answered, Hilda," Leon said. "We need your help."

"What can *I* do? I'm staying for the funeral too."

"We were not prepared for this size crowd," Leon said. "This will be twice as large as the Jerusalem Gala."

Hilda said, "I still don't understand how GC CNN can help. Even at the Gala we merely—"

"Bear with me," Leon said. "As you know, we already pushed back the funeral and burial to accommodate the crowds. We assumed that a million or so people would still be waiting to view the body by the time we were ready for the ceremony. With more than three million here already, another estimated million on their way, and virtually no one leaving, we have to regroup. Where are the big screens we used in Jerusalem, and do we have more?"

Someone from Event Programming said they were in storage in New Babylon and that there would be enough—supplemented by smaller monitors—to handle the larger crowd. "But," he added, "that will require a lot of man-hours and, of course, a layout scheme. The way the courtyard is cordoned off now will certainly not handle a crowd that size, especially if the ones who have already passed by the bier stay for the funeral, and I can't imagine why they're still in the city if that is not their plan."

"My point exactly," Leon said. "I already have engineers on the new schematic. And let me be clear: Laborers are starting to rearrange barricades, chairs, crowd control ropes, and so forth. All this work will go on with no interruption of the viewing process. If the line has to be moved, that should be able to be done in an orderly fashion without stopping the procession.

"My question for you, Ms. Schnell, is whether your equipment can feed that many monitors. Some people, naturally, will be hundreds of yards from the podium."

"We don't worry about that, Commander," Ms. Schnell said. "We concern ourselves with providing the best visual and audio coverage of the event for television and leave it to your event organizers to make it work for their purposes."

Leon stared at her, expressionless. "What I am suggesting, madam, is that you *do* worry about it. We have singers, dancers, speakers, and the like to make this ceremony appropriate, not only to the occasion and the size of the live crowd, but also to the stature of the one we honor."

"Yes, sir."

"Yes, ma'am?"

"Just tell us what you want, sir."

"Thank you."

"Thank you for the privilege."

Now Fortunato was smiling. "That the big screens from Jerusalem are already here, Director Hassid, eliminates my need for one of your pilots to go get them. If we could make use of your entire hangar crew, cargo staff, pilots and all, in crowd control, I would appreciate it. Viv Ivins will be coordinating that, so let her know how many are available and who they are.

"The new times for the ceremony and burial are noon and 2:00 p.m. today respectively. Some dignitaries' speeches may be shortened, but those times are firm and may be announced effective immediately. Ms. Schnell, I'm assuming this event supersedes all other programming so that the entire globe may participate, including those who reach the airport in time to watch on television but too late to be here in person."

She nodded.

David fidgeted, knowing Rayford, Chloe, and Leah were waiting to get into the Strong Building. He wasn't certain he could remotely unlock a door, but he'd rather have been studying that than sitting through a logistics meeting. Fortunato soon left the details in the hands of his engineers, and David hurried out.

On the way to his office, he saw the laborers already at work refashioning the massive courtyard into a vista that would accommodate the expected flood of humanity. According to the snatches of news reports he caught on the monitors lining the hallways of the palace complex, Leon was right. People of every ethnic background were interviewed at the airport, in line, and on the streets. Nearly every person expressed a desire to attend the funeral, even if they had already passed by the body.

"This was the greatest man who ever lived," a Turkish man said through an interpreter. "The world will never see another like him. It is the worst tragedy we will ever face, and we can only hope that his successor will be able to carry on the ideals he put forth."

"Do you believe Nicolae Carpathia was divine in any sense?" the reporter said.

"In every sense!" the man said. "I believe it's possible that he was the Messiah the Jews longed for all these centuries. And he was murdered in their own nation, just as the Scriptures prophesied."

As David settled in behind his computer in the privacy of his office, he left on the TV monitor hanging from the ceiling in the corner. GC CNN had followed that interview with a live feed from Israel, where thousands were listening to enthusiastic preachers, running forward, falling on their knees, and then shouting of their new allegiance to Jesus the Messiah.

The Jerusalem correspondent had with her a religious expert, who attempted to explain. "In the vacuum created by the deaths of both the head of the One World Faith and the supreme potentate of the Global Community, whom many considered every bit as much a religious as a political figure, spiritually hungry people are rushing to fill the gap. Longing for leadership and bereft of the one man who seemed to fit the bill, they now find attractive this fairly recent craze of ascribing to the historical figure of Jesus the Christ the qualifications of the Messiah Israel has awaited so long.

"This phenomenon existed in small pockets of conservative fundamentalist Christian sects but was fueled shortly after the vanishings by Dr. Tsion Ben-Judah, an Israeli biblical scholar. He had been commissioned by the State of Israel to clarify the prerequisites of the prophesied Messiah for the modern Jew.

"Dr. Ben-Judah created an uproar, particularly among Jews, when at the end of the live, globally televised airing of his views he announced that Jesus the

Christ was the only person in history to fulfill all the Messianic prophesies, and that the vanishings were evidence that he had already come."

David was impressed that the "expert," while clearly not agreeing with what was going on, had an accurate handle on the issue. Having studied under Tsion on the Net for so long, David knew that this further outbreak of evangelism in Israel would also spawn many more false christs and second-rate antichrists. Dr. Ben-Judah had often cited Matthew 24:21-24 in urging his followers—now referred to as Judah-ites—to beware:

> *For then there will be great tribulation, such as has not been since the beginning of the world until this time, no, nor ever shall be. And unless those days were shortened, no flesh would be saved; but for the elect's sake those days will be shortened.*
>
> *Then if anyone says to you, "Look, here is the Christ" or "There!" do not believe it. For false christs and false prophets will rise and show great signs and wonders to deceive, if possible, even the elect.*

By now David was deep into the labyrinthine inner workings of the Strong Building. While whirring through the many security pass gates using code breakers of his own design, he had a phone tucked between his cheek and shoulder.

"Captain Steele," he said, "if I can do this, I'm going to get you in through one of the parking garage's inner doors. The gates will be down, but you can walk around those and get to the elevators."

"We were that far," Rayford said. "The glass doors leading to the elevators are the ones we need opened. We could break the glass, but we're afraid that would set off an alarm."

"Who'd hear it?"

"I know, but usually those kinds of alarms are attached to all sorts of interrelated devices. Like at the airport, you force your way through the wrong door, and certain systems automatically shut down."

"Bingo," David said.

"Excuse me?"

"You're in."

"We're not even on that side of the building."

"Well, get there," David said. "I can't wait to hear what you find. Listen, good news: The designers of this building did two very nice things, as if they knew we were coming. First, the electrical panel room and the telephone room, both of which are traditionally on the top floor or even above in some spire, are located on the first floor, one up from where you'll enter. Second, I think I have detected why the structure is so sound below where the bomb damage is. The blueprints show what's called a 'closure for stack effect' every fifteen floors or so. It happens that there is just such a closure one floor beneath where the bomb damage occurred. This closure acts as a new roof for the building. I'm not certain yet, but you may be able to land a helicopter there, if you can deal with the complications of a three-sided opening above that."

"Helicopter?" Rayford said. "We're in the garage, by the way."

"I can see you."

"You can?"

"See the monitor up in the corner to your right?"

The three waved at David and he almost waved back, forgetting this was not a two-way visual feed.

"Yep. I see you. The door directly in front of you should be unlocked. And yes, I said helicopter before."

"Where am I going to get one of those?"

"I don't know," David said. "Know anybody in purchasing anywhere?"

"We also need to start thinking about a new air base, closer to here. Different anyway. We have no friends at Palwaukee anymore."

"How was Kankakee?"

"Might work. How about we have Albie set up there as a small private transport company, maybe serving Laslos, who's still considered legit by the GC? Then we can come and go as we please out of there with no questions asked. And we can chopper our way up here when we need to."

"I like the way you think, Captain Steele."

"I like the options you provide, David."

"I'll try to keep track of you floor by floor with the various monitors," David said. "But I may have to leave you abruptly too. You know where I am."

Leah and Chloe appeared to be working well together. Though David could hear only Rayford, he could see the women checking out sight angles from various windows.

"Leah wants to talk with you, David. Here she is."

"You're looking at blueprints?"

"Online," he said, "yeah."

"Am I seeing this right? Are we not visible from the street, at least where we are now?"

"Affirmative."

"And what if we turn on lights?"

"That I wouldn't do."

"What if we spray painted the windows black?"

16

BY TEN O'CLOCK Saturday night in Illinois, Tsion had survived two messy operations: feeding and changing Kenny. The boy was now sound asleep in his crib in the other room, and Tsion had turned the sound off on the television. He merely glanced at it occasionally, tired of the endless repetition.

How many times had he seen Rayford's photograph and history and the grave conclusion on the part of Global Community Security and Intelligence forces that he was the lone assassin, the lone gunman? Rayford was also constantly referred to as a committed Judah-ite. Tsion knew, because he knew the Tribulation Force, that Rayford Steele had ceased to exist. He would neither make himself obvious to the public nor leave a trail in his own name. Tsion prayed that would preserve Rayford for as long as possible.

Tsion pored over his Bible texts and commentaries, trying to make sense of the vivid dream. He pleaded with God for another of the same, but short of that, he wanted to understand the one he'd had. Scholars were divided on who the sun-clothed woman was, the one who wore a garland of stars and used the moon as her footstool.

Clearly she was symbolic, as no woman was that large or had a child in space. Some believed she represented womankind as mentioned in Genesis when God told Satan that the woman would produce a child whose heel Satan might bruise, but who would crush his head. That was a prophecy of the Christ child, and of course that woman turned out to be Mary. Yet further details of this symbolic woman indicated that she might symbolize Israel. The Christ came from Israel, and Satan pursued and persecuted God's chosen people even to the present day.

As Tsion studied the biblical texts about Lucifer and his being cast out from heaven, he became convinced that when he had seen the dragon sweep a third of the stars from the skies and they fell to earth, he was witness to eternity past. The Scripture often referred to angels, righteous or fallen, as stars, so he believed this was a picture of when Lucifer was first cast down due to his sin of pride.

Yet Tsion also knew that Satan, even up to the halfway point of the

Tribulation—where Tsion believed history stood right then—had been granted access to the throne of God. He was the accuser of believers, yet when he pursued the woman and her child to devour them, a great battle was to be waged in heaven and he would be cast out for good.

Tsion was not aware he had fallen asleep again. All he knew was that the trip from the underground safe house into the chilly night air took less getting used to this time. He didn't worry about temporal things. He could see Kenny sleeping in his crib and himself dozing on the couch as clearly as he could see the oceans and continents of the beautiful blue planet. How peaceful it looked from up here, compared to what he knew was happening down there.

When he arrived at the appointed place, the woman had left her footstool. The sun-garment was gone with her, of course, as was the garland of stars. Yet brightness enveloped Tsion again, and he was eager to ask questions before this all faded and he awoke. Though Tsion knew it was a dream, he also knew it was of God, and he rested on the promise of old men dreaming dreams.

Tsion turned to the brightness, marveling again at the size and majesty of the angel. "Michael," he began, "is the woman Mary or—"

"Michael is engaged in battle, as you will soon see. I am Gabriel, the announcer."

"Oh! Forgive me, Prince Gabriel. Can you tell me, who is the woman? Is it Mary, or is it Israel?"

"Yes and yes."

"That was not as helpful as I had hoped."

"When you ponder it, you will find it so."

"And the twelve stars on her head. Do they represent the tribes of Israel?"

"Or . . . ?" Gabriel prodded.

"Or the . . . the apostles?"

"Yes and yes."

"Somehow I knew you were going to—so these things mean whatever we want or need them to mean?"

"No. They mean what they mean."

"Uh-huh."

"Son of earth, did you see what the male child bore in his hand?

"I'm sorry, I did not."

"A rod of iron, with which he shall rule the nations."

"So clearly he is Jesus . . ."

"The Christ, the Messiah, Son of the living God."

Tsion felt unworthy even to hear the description. He felt as if he were in the very presence of God.

"Prince Gabriel, to where has the woman fled?"

"Into the wilderness where God has prepared a place for her, where she will be safe for three and a half years."

"Does this mean God has prepared a place in the wilderness for his chosen people, where they too will be safe during the Great Tribulation?"

"You have said it."

"And what of the dragon?"

"He is enraged."

"And Michael?"

Gabriel gestured behind Tsion. "Behold."

Tsion turned to see a great battle raging. Michael and his angels wielded great double-edged swords against fiery darts from the dragon and his evil angels. The ugly hordes advanced again and again against Michael's mighty forces, but they could not prevail. As his comrades retreated behind him, the dragon fled to the throne. But it was as if a colossal invisible door had been slammed in his face. He fell back and tried to advance again to the place he had enjoyed before the throne. But from the throne came an insistent, "No. There is no longer a place here for you. Be gone!"

The dragon turned, his anger nearly consuming him. With his seven heads grimacing and gnashing their teeth, he gathered his own around him, and they all tumbled toward the earth. And Gabriel announced in a loud voice, "So the great dragon was cast out, that serpent of old, called the Devil and Satan, who deceives the whole world; he was cast to the earth, and his angels were cast out with him." And now louder still, with great joy: "Now salvation, and strength, and the kingdom of our God, and the power of his Christ have come, for the accuser of our brethren, who accused them before our God day and night, has been cast down. And they overcame him by the blood of the Lamb and by the word of their testimony, and they did not love their lives to the death. Therefore rejoice, O heavens, and you who dwell in them! Woe to the inhabitants of the earth and the sea! For the devil has come down to you, having great wrath, because he knows that he has a short time."

"What happens now?" Tsion said.

Gabriel looked at him and folded his arms. "The dragon will persecute the woman who gave birth to the child, but God will protect her. In his wrath the dragon will make war with the rest of her offspring, those who keep the commandments of God and have the testimony of Jesus the Christ."

Michael stood next to Gabriel now, his great sword sheathed, his warriors dispersed. Tsion could not speak. He opened his mouth to form words of gratitude, but he was mute. And he awoke. It was still ten o'clock.

* * *

By nine in the morning Carpathia Time, New Babylon was a sea of people. Opportunists had set up shop on every road that led to the palace courtyard. Sellers of chairs, sunblock, umbrellas, bottled water, food, and souvenirs preyed on the pilgrims. Some merchants were run off by GC Peacekeepers, only to set up again a quarter mile away.

It was clear the forecasted one hundred degrees would be surpassed before noon. A canopy was erected behind the bier to protect both it and the armed guards from the relentless sun. Still, mourners and officials dropped right and left and were ferried to medical tents, where they were hydrated and fanned and sometimes doused with water.

David returned to his perch above one of the med tents, though it had been moved more than two hundred yards from the courtyard to make room for the crowds. Barriers, ropes, and makeshift fences forced people to snake back and forth in an agonizingly slow path to the bier. Street entertainers, jugglers, clowns, strippers, and vendors tried to keep people occupied. Here and there scuffles broke out, quickly quelled by the Peacekeepers.

Laborers continued to swarm, finalizing the reconstruction that would allow hundreds of thousands more in the courtyard. The huge screens were in place and operating, as were countless monitors surrounding the palace. When the ceremony was about to begin at noon, the line would be stopped and millions would fan out from the speaker's platform next to the coffin to more than a mile away.

From his spot David heard bands practicing, choirs rehearsing, dance troupes going through their paces. With binoculars he saw Annie manning her station nearly a half mile away. His phone chirped. It was a Peacekeeper at the airport.

"Director Hassid, I have a family here from China looking for their daughter, a GC employee named Ming Toy."

"Yes?"

"They say she told them to contact you or Cargo Chief Christopher if they could not find their daughter. She's come from Buffer in Brussels."

"Do they know where she is positioned here? It's all numbered, you know."

The guard covered the phone and asked them. "No," he said. "They said they thought their daughter was trying to get assigned near Ms. Christopher."

"Ms. Christopher is stationed at marker 53."

"Thank you, sir."

David kept his field glasses trained on Annie and saw when the red-uniformed Asian approached and they embraced. They engaged in what appeared an animated conversation, and Annie grabbed her phone. David's erupted again. "Hi, babe," he said. "Ming's parents and brother are on their way from the airport and will look for her at your station. Did she get assigned—"

"David!" Annie whispered fiercely. "North American GC has identified the safe house!"

"What?!"

"Ming overheard it. She couldn't let me know before because they gathered everyone's phones for security."

"Call Tsion! I'll call Steele."

\+ + +

Rayford believed the new safe house might be the greatest gift God had bestowed on the Trib Force since the arrival of Tsion Ben-Judah. Several floors had been left virtually unblemished, and all the systems worked. There were more bathrooms than the occupants could ever use, and every service imaginable. It wasn't a home, of course, so beds would have to be brought in or fashioned. But the place could hold hundreds, maybe more. He didn't know how reasonable it was to think a whole lot of people could hide out there undetected, but he dreamed of inviting every dispossessed believer he knew: Leah's friend from Brussels, maybe her brother from China, Albie, maybe the Mikloses one day, all the insiders from New Babylon. A guy could dream.

He and Leah and Chloe were headed back toward Mount Prospect just after midnight, Central Standard Time, when David called with the news. "Annie's calling Tsion," David said. "He's got to get out of there."

"There are certain things we have to have," Rayford said. "And Tsion doesn't have wheels."

"Captain, he's got to get out of there now."

"We have to go get him, David. Any way you can tell where we might run into GC?"

"Not in time to help you. You might have to take some risks."

"We'll also try to get Tsion on the phone. Who knows where the GC is or when they might strike? Our underground is a pretty good cover."

\+ + +

Tsion thanked Annie and rushed to shut off the power, trying to keep from hyperventilating. He felt his way in the dark and filled two pillowcases with necessities. The TV would stay. He gathered up essential medicines, a few reference works, and all the laptops, baby stuff, a handful of clothes, whatever he could fit into the bulging slipcases. He left enough room at the tops to tie them together and left them at the bottom of the stairs. There was only one way out of the shelter, and that was the way he had come in. Even if he were to throw a blanket over Kenny and lug him and the stuff out into the garage, that would be the second place the GC would look.

His best hope, he knew, was to hear the GC come in upstairs, pray that they would be stopped by the spoiled food in the phony freezer, find no one, and move on. Then he would be ready to flee as soon as the others arrived.

Chloe called, nearly hysterical. "Tsion," she said, "if the GC gets to the cellar, you have to promise me—"

"I'll protect the baby with my life."

"You have to promise me, Tsion, please! Under my mattress is a syringe with a potassium cyanide solution. It'll work quick, but you have to inject it directly into his buttocks. You can do it right through the diaper. It doesn't have to be perfect; it just has to be decisive and sure."

"Chloe! Get hold of yourself! I'm not going to harm Kenny!"

"Tsion," she cried, "please! Don't ever let them have my baby!"

"I won't. But I'll not—"

"Please!"

"No! Now let me do my work! I have to watch and listen. For now, Kenny is down and out. God is with us."

"Tsion!"

"Good-bye, Chloe."

Tsion went to the edge of the underground with the thinnest barrier to the outside and stood listening for engines. Or footsteps. Doors. Windows. So far, nothing. He hated being trapped. He was tempted to lug Kenny and the stuff to the garage, then make a break for it if the GC broke into the house. It was foolishness, he knew. He'd get nowhere on foot. His more-than-lifelike dream had put him on a first-name basis with the archangels of God, yet there he stood, cowering in a corner. He guessed Rayford was, at best, nearly an hour away. And if he happened to arrive when the GC was already there, Rayford would have to disappear.

Tsion prayed the GC had decided to take its time, to come the next day or the next week.

+ + +

Until he sat in a cramped jet for a transatlantic flight, Buck didn't realize how extensive were his injuries. He felt twenty years older, wincing and sometimes yelping when he moved.

A couple of hours after Albie had taken off in a refurbished Jordanian fighter, the type with which Abdullah was most familiar, Buck had gotten word from Leah about the pastor who wanted to speak with him. He told her to give the man his number but to be sure he called from a public phone. The resulting conversation was one bright spot in a harrowing weekend.

"Your brother was the instigator," the pastor told him. "He confronted your father about his stubborn insistence that he was a believer and always had been. Your brother visited our house church by himself the first two or three times, and to hear your father tell it, he finally came just to avoid being alone. Mr. Williams, it took a long time for your father to get the picture."

"It would."

"Your brother less so. It was as if he were ready. But he knew better than to push your father. One of the biggest obstacles was that he knew one day he would have to admit that you were right and he was wrong."

Buck fought tears. "That's Pop all right. But why—"

". . . didn't your brother call? Two reasons. First, he wanted your dad to be the one to share the news. Two, he was scared to death they were going to somehow give you away. He knew well your position and how dangerous it was, or I should say is."

"Only calling from a bugged phone would have caused a problem."

"But he didn't know that. I just want you to know, sir, that your dad and your brother became true believers, and I'm sure they're with God right now. They were so proud of you. And you can tell Dr. Ben-Judah that he has at least one church out here that could lose its pastor and never skip a beat. We all love him."

Buck assured him he would tell Tsion.

They were an hour from Palwaukee when Buck got the call from Chloe about the safe house. While Chaim lay across the backseat, humming in agony over his various ailments, Albie seemed to grow more and more agitated as he realized what was going on.

"How was the safe house compromised?" he said. "Did Miss Durham finally give you up?"

"We don't know, Albie. All we know for sure is that Dr. Ben-Judah and our baby are there without transportation, and we have no idea how far away the GC is or whether Rayford can get there in time."

"And you have a new safe house, somewhere to go if you can get them out of there."

"Yes."

"Grab my bag from behind my seat."

Buck pulled it up, deciding it weighed more than Albie. "What have you got in this thing?"

Albie was all business. "Open, please."

The top layer consisted of Albie's underwear.

"Dig, please. Find sidearm and holster."

Buck dug past what looked like a GC uniform. "Is this what I think it is?"

Albie nodded with a pleased look. "See cap. Check rank."

Buck whistled. "Deputy commander? Where did you get this?"

"No questions, no obligations."

"C'mon, did you used to work for the GC?"

"Better not to know."

"But did you?"

"No, but no more questions."

"Just where did you—"

"I have my sources. Sources are my life. Call Rayford. Tell him to meet us at Palwaukee."

"He shouldn't get to the safe house?"

"We need a vehicle. We need it as bad as Rayford needs it."

"How so?"

"Watch and learn. At Palwaukee, where can I change into the uniform?"

"You're going to—?"

"You don't ask. You only answer."

"There's a spot," Buck said. "I can show you."

"Anywhere we can leave Tobias Rogoff?"

"I wouldn't, now that we don't really know anyone there."

"OK. Find my papers. Dig deeper. Between the fake bottom of bag and the real bottom."

Buck found Albie's straight ID, then, right where he said, a worn leather pouch.

"Open, please. How many of us will be in the vehicle, six?"

Buck thought and confirmed that.

"And Mr. Rogoff needs a whole seat to self."

"Maybe not."

"Hope not. Too crowded. Find the papers to go with the clothes."

Buck leafed through until he found documents proving Albie's high-level role with the GC Peacekeeping Force. The picture, in snappy uniform, was of Albie but over a different name.

"Marcus Elbaz?" Buck said.

"Deputy Commander Elbaz to you, citizen," Albie said with such conviction that for a moment Buck thought he was truly upset. Buck saluted and Albie matched him. "Call Steele now."

\+ + +

Rayford was heartsick that Chloe was so determined to kill Kenny rather than see him fall into the hands of the enemy. And yet as a father, he could identify with her passion. It terrified him that she had thought it through to the point where she had an injection prepared.

Rayford had found a way back to a short stretch of unobstructed open road without making it obvious he had emerged from a restricted area. Now he had to find shortcuts and pick his way around debris and craters while careful not to violate any traffic laws. When he was free of other traffic he would make up for lost time and get to the safe house at the highest speed he could muster, his and his passengers' heads banging the roof of the Land Rover or not.

Buck's call was puzzling, and Rayford demanded to talk with Albie.

"What's the deal, friend? What're you up to?"

"Do you trust me, Captain Steele?"

"With my life, and more than once."

"So trust me now. You get to Palwaukee and be waiting for us. Then be prepared to get me to the safe house fast as you can. I'll explain roles as we go. If we're lucky, we beat the GC and we get the rabbi and the baby out. If we engage, everything depends on me."

\+ + +

Tsion prayed as he waited, but God did not grant the request to calm his fears. He'd had close calls in his day, but waiting for the enemy was the worst. He tiptoed around, watching, listening. Then he found the TV and bent to turn it on. He would only watch. But it would not come on. *Of course!* He smacked himself in the head. He had turned off the main power.

\+ + +

David hated this more than all the rest that came with working undercover in the enemy camp: knowing all that was happening half a world away, yet being powerless to do anything but warn and open the occasional skyscraper door.

There was nothing more he or Annie or Ming could do from New Babylon. The players were in their places and the dangers real. All they could do was wait to hear how it turned out.

Ming's parents and brother were reunited with her at marker 53, and David was struck by the formalities. As he watched through binoculars, Ming and Chang embraced enthusiastically and emotionally. Ming kissed her mother lightly on the cheek, and she and her father shook hands. Then came more animated conversation and soon Annie was on the phone again.

"Mr. Wong is insulted that you are not here to greet him."

"Well, I can hardly do anything about th—"

"David, just come. Can you?"

17

"I TRUST ALBIE," Rayford said, "but I don't like this."

"What do you think he's up to?" Chloe said.

"I don't know. He's a pretty shrewd guy. The problem is that we have only one vehicle."

"Thanks for reminding me," Chloe said.

"I just wish he'd make arrangements for another car at Palwaukee. I don't like leaving Tsion and Kenny like this."

Leah, strapped in in the backseat, pressed her hands against the ceiling to keep herself from bouncing too high. "How much farther, Daddy?" she said.

Chloe made a face, but Rayford said, "At least one of us is keeping a sense of humor."

✝ ✝ ✝

"David," Buck said on the phone, "Albie wants to talk with you. What's happening there? I hear the crowd."

"Let's just say I've pulled rank and appropriated an administrative golf cart. I'm on my way to mollify a public relations problem. At least I get to see Annie. Where are you guys?"

"Not sure. I'll let you talk to the pilot."

Buck handed the phone to Albie and listened as he peered out the window.

"David, my friend, good to talk with you again. I'm going to enjoy working with you. . . . We're within forty minutes of Palwaukee. If I represent myself as GC, will they ask for a security code? . . . They will? Is there one I can use?" He covered the phone. "Buck, write this down . . . OK, go ahead . . . zero-nine-two-three-four-nine. Got it. . . . So, anything that starts with zero-nine will be OK in the future and will go back through you for clearance. Good . . . helicopter? Yes, we sure could! You can do that? . . . GC? Perfect! . . . I'll tell the tower it will be delivered when? . . . OK! I know we will meet one day soon."

* * *

David was struck by the variety in the crowds that lined the route to the courtyard. People of every ethnic background slowly moved toward the palace—young and old, wealthy and poor, colorfully dressed. Many appeared shell-shocked, as if they truly didn't know what they would do without Nicolae J. Carpathia to lead them through such a tumultuous time.

David called Mac. "Where are you, Captain?"

"Sector 94. Fun work."

"People must love that uniform."

"Yeah, they want to know if I know the supreme commander personally."

"And I'm sure you tell them how thrilled you are that you do."

"What do you want, David?"

"I need you to make a couple of calls for me. Get hold of the tower at Palwaukee and—you got a pencil?—refer to security code zero-nine-two-three-four-nine. Tell 'em they'll be hearing from one of our people who needs to hangar an Egyptian fighter there. Someone will be picking him up along with two passengers, and they must not be detained for clearances and paperwork. We will handle all that from New Babylon. Then call our base in Rantoul."

"Illinois?"

"Right. Tell them we need a chopper in Brookfield, Wisconsin, but all they have to do is get it as far as Palwaukee and we'll take it from there. Tell Palwaukee Tower that too. Can you do that?"

"Gee, I don't know, David. I'm better in the cockpit than on the phone. What's shakin' where you are?"

"Tell ya later. Get on those calls and we'll talk."

David arrived at sector 53, where Annie was keeping the peace and keeping people moving. She answered questions about the times of the ceremony and the burial and also told people how far it was to water, shade, medicine, and the like. In public, of course, she had to be formal with David.

"Welcome, Director Hassid. I would like you to meet our very special guests from China. This is Mr. and Mrs. Wong, their daughter Ming Toy, who works with us in Belgium, and their son, Chang."

David bowed and shook hands all around. Mr. Wong was plainly unhappy. "What language you speak?" he said.

"Primarily English," David said. "Also Hebrew."

"No good," Mr. Wong said. "No Asian language?"

"I'm sorry, no."

"You know German? I know German. English not good."

"No German. I apologize."

"We talk?"

"I'd be honored, sir."

"You forgive bad English?"

"Certainly. Perhaps your daughter can translate."

"No! You understand."

"I'll try."

"You insult no meet me at airport. I tell you through daughter we come."

"I did get that word secondhand, sir, but I was too busy here. I apologize and ask your forgiveness."

"VIP! I VIP because of business. Give lots money to Global Community. Very big patriot. Global patriot."

"You are well known here, sir, and your daughter is highly regarded. Please accept my apologies on behalf of the entire GC management team for our inability to welcome you in the manner you deserve."

"Son work for you someday. Not old enough yet. Only seventeen."

David glanced at Chang and noticed the mark of the believer on his forehead. "I will look forward to having him as a colleague when he's eighteen, sir. More than you can know."

"Whole family so sorry for Nicolae. Great man. Great man."

"I'll pass along your sentiments to the supreme commander."

"I meet supreme commander!"

"Have you?"

"No! I want meet!"

"I'm sorry, but we have been asked not to arrange any more personal meetings for him this week. You understand. Too many requests."

"Special seat! You arrange special seat?"

"Oh, I don't know. That would be diff—"

Mr. Wong shook his head as his wife took his arm as if to calm him. "No meet at airport. No meet supreme commander. Way back in line. You get us up front?"

"I'll see what I can do."

"No! You get special seat for funeral. We want in courtyard."

"I'll see what I can do."

"You see now. Tell us now. Take us now."

David sighed and got on the phone. "Yes, Margaret, do we have anymore VIP seating at all? . . . I know . . . I know . . . three."

"No! Daughter sit with us too. And you! Five."

"Five, Margaret . . . I know. I'm in a bit of a bind here. I'll owe you . . .

just inside the court? That sounds fine, but I'm expected with administrative personnel in the—"

"We sit with you! You can do! Four join you in good seat."

"I'm having trouble appeasing him, Margaret. . . . It's not your problem, no. . . . Yes, it's mine. What's the best you can do? . . . He did? Well, there you go. We can kill two birds, as they say. I owe you. . . . I know. Thanks, Margaret."

David turned back to them. "It seems the sculptor wrongly arranged for his assistants to sit with him in the management section, and the supreme commander's office is going to reverse that."

"I no understand. We sit there?"

"Yes. The sculptor is going to be 'honored' by standing next to the statue and having his assistants with him."

"We sit with you or not?"

"Yes, you sit with me."

"Good! Daughter too?"

"Yes."

"Good! Her new friend here too?" he pressed, pointing at Annie.

"Ah, no. I wish."

"I really can't, Mr. Wong," Annie said. "I must stay here during the ceremony."

"OK, us then."

* * *

In the wee hours of Sunday morning, Rayford barreled in to Palwaukee Airport in a cloud of dust. The place was deserted except for a light in the tower. The only lit runway was one that accommodated jets. Rayford laid his head on the steering wheel. "I just pray we're doing the right thing," he said. "To have been so close to the safe house and not check on Tsion and Kenny . . ."

Leah leaned forward. "And yet if the GC nose around there and *don't* discover the underground, we might give our people away by showing up."

"I know," he said, "but I just—"

"No!" Chloe said. "Dad's right. We need to take our chances and get there and get them out. You know what the GC are doing to Judah-ite sympathizers. They killed everybody in Chaim's house and burned it. They killed Buck's dad and brother and burned their place. What happens if they don't find Tsion and Kenny but burn the place anyway, because it's obvious we'd been living there? How would they get out? Tsion would come running right up into a burning house."

"Chloe," Rayford said, "I feel like we should play out Albie's scheme here, whatever it is."

"He can't know our situation."

"Buck has filled him in. And he's right that it makes no sense for some of us to go to the safe house while others wait here for a ride. This way, if it's obvious the GC haven't been there yet, we need to get what we can and get out of there. That'll make eight of us, including the baby, so we won't have room for much else."

"Surely Tsion will think to bring the computers and necessities."

Rayford nodded.

"I'd better call him one more time," Chloe said. "He may not think to bring the notebooks with the co-op stuff."

"You don't have that on your computer?" Leah said.

Chloe gave her a look. "I always keep hard-copy backups."

"But you've got it on disks too, right?"

Chloe sighed and ignored her. And phoned Tsion.

* * *

David let the Wong family pile into the two-seat golf cart, first pointing Ming Toy to the front seat next to him and Dad, Mom, and Chang to the back bench. But Mr. Wong wouldn't budge, muttered something about "seat of honor," and Ming joined her mother and brother in the back. Mr. Wong sat straight, chest out, with a solemnly proud look as David carefully steered the cart through the throng toward the palace courtyard.

"They are not seating dignitaries until 11:30," David said. "They'll begin with the ten regional potentates and their entourages, then headquarter management personnel and their guests."

"They seat you right away," Mr. Wong said confidently. "And we with you."

"They'll follow protocol."

"I talk to Supreme Commander Leon Fortunato. He make sure we seat right away."

"He's greeting dignitaries and getting set for the processional now, Mr. Wong. Let's just get to the staging area, and I'm sure they'll accommodate us in due time."

"I want sit now, good view, ready for program." He turned and grabbed his son's knee. "This spectacular, ay? You work here someday, make proud, serve Global Community. Honor memory of Carpathia."

Chang did not respond.

"I know you want to, Son. You not know how say it. Be patriot like me. Duty. Honor. Service."

David pulled up to a corral area where lesser dignitaries were already being led to a line that would eventually fill the VIP area. Manning the gate was Ahmal, a man from David's department.

"We'll take care of the cart," Ahmal said. "You and your guests wait under the canopy by section G."

"Thanks, Ahmal."

"You no introduce! You rude host!"

"My apologies," David said. He introduced the family, emphasizing Mr. Wong's support of the GC.

"An honor, sir," Ahmal said, raising a brow at David.

"We sit now."

"No, sir," Ahmal said. "You're being asked to wait in line at section—"

"Big supporter of Carpathia, Fortunato, GC no wait in line. No one sitting in seats. We sit there now."

"Oh, sir, I'm sorry. There'll be a processional. Very nice. Music. You all file in."

"No! Sit now!"

"Father," Ming said, "it will be better, nicer, to come in all at the same time."

Mrs. Wong reached for her husband's arm, but he wrenched away. "I go sit! You no want sit now, you stay! Where seat?"

Ahmal looked to David, who shook his head.

"Mr. Ahmal! Check sheet! Where I sit?"

"Well, you're going to be in D-three, sir, but no one—"

"I sit," he said, pushing past, daring someone to stop him.

"He's only going to embarrass himself," David said. "Let him go."

Mr. Wong caused a stir in the crowd when he moved up the steps to the permanent amphitheater seating and began looking for his chair. Even people at the viewing platform were distracted and looked to see who was being seated already. Assuming he was someone important, some applauded, causing others to do the same. Soon everyone was aware that an Asian was in the VIP section, and they shaded their eyes to see if they recognized him.

"Must be the Asian States potentate," someone near David said.

Mr. Wong acknowledged the crowd with a nod and a bow.

"He old fool," Mrs. Wong said, and her son and daughter erupted into laughter. "We wait with Mr. Director Hassid."

"I'm afraid I'll have to join you later," David said. "Will you be all right?"

Mrs. Wong looked lost, but Ming took her hand and assured David they would be fine.

David went behind the stage to check progress on the technical aspects. Everything seemed to be in place, though there was a water shortage. The temperature was already 106 and climbing. GC personnel wore damp rags under their caps. Singers, dancers, and instrumentalists moved into place. Banks of monitors kept TV technicians aware of what was happening.

David went up steps that led to the bier from the back, passing armed guards every few feet. He slipped in behind the canopy that kept the coffin and the guards out of the sun, which was directly overhead now. As he squinted out at the courtyard and beyond, the pavement emitted shimmering waves of heat, and the line moved more and more slowly. David saw many looking at their watches and deduced that they were trying to worm their way into up-front positions for the funeral ceremony.

Once mourners were unwillingly urged past the bier, they would not be hurried away. They slowed, lingered, hoping to be stalled for the start of the festivities like some massive game of musical chairs.

David peered past the armed guards to the glass coffin, wondering how it would hold up in this heat. The vacuum seal looked secure and was checked every hour on the hour by the technician. Would the heat soften the box? Build up steam like a pressure cooker? David looked for signs that the heat affected the makeup, wax, or putty Dr. Eikenberry had used. How embarrassing if the real body was cooling in the morgue when the phony one reached its melting point and turned into a pool before the world.

"Stop the line, please!" came the directive from a bullhorn down and behind David's right. Two guards hurried that way and stepped in front of a Dutch couple who had observed the occasion by appearing in native costume. They looked as if they regretted it already, red-faced, sweating, and panting. They seemed pleased, however, at being left first in line some one hundred feet before the stairs. As they waited and the crowd behind them slowly came to a standstill of realization as well, the several dozen mourners ahead of them continued.

When they had passed and started down the stairs on the other side, a wave of silence invaded the entire area. Everyone looked to the courtyard with expectancy, the only movement the last of the mourners, trying to clear the exit stairs. They did not want to leave, but the program would not start until they did.

The stragglers finally reached the bottom and many sat directly on the pavement. They found it so hot that they began taking off garments to sit on.

With everyone in place and still, the silence of four million plus was eerie. David slipped back down the steps behind the platform and saw that the staging area was full, everyone in place from Fortunato to his ministers and all ten regional potentates with their entourages. After that, high-ranking GC personnel filled the line all the way out of the courtyard.

From David's left, someone with a clipboard and headset signaled the director of the orchestra. With men in tuxedos and tails and women in full-length black dresses, the one hundred members of the orchestra mounted the back steps and made their way out onto the platform at stage left. Sweat poured from their faces, and great dark stains spread under their arms and down their backs. Once seated, they brought instruments into position and waited for their cue.

"Ladies and gentlemen," came the announcement over the massive public-address system, echoing in the courtyard, resounding for nearly a mile, and followed by instant translation into three other major languages. "Global Community Supreme Commander Leon Fortunato and the administration of the one-world government would like to express sincere thanks and appreciation for your presence at the memorial service for former Supreme Potentate Nicolae J. Carpathia. Please honor the occasion by removing head coverings during the performance by the Global Community International Orchestra of the anthem, "Hail, Carpathia, Loving, Divine, and Strong."

As the orchestra played the dirge, weeping broke out among the crowd until great sobs filled the courtyard. The Global Community vocal band filed in, singing praises to Nicolae. Eventually a troupe of dancers, who seemed to move in slow motion and show remarkable balance, emoted with the music and the mournful groaning of the audience. As they performed, the VIPs filed in to subdued but sustained applause.

David finally made his way to the seat next to Mr. Wong, who gazed beatifically at the stage, tears streaming, both hands clutching his heart. David shaded his eyes and wondered if he himself was prepared to sit in this kind of heat for two hours. They were stage left with a clear view of the podium and coffin, about thirty feet away.

When the music finally ended, orchestra, singers, and dancers moved out and Fortunato and the ten potentates, grim-faced, moved into position one row up and behind the bier. One more joined the three armed guards who had stood behind it, and they moved two to each end of the casket.

The great screens and monitors showed a montage of Carpathia's life, beginning with his fifth birthday party in Romania, hugging his parents at high school graduation while holding some sort of trophy in each hand, being presented an award in college, winning an election in Romania, taking office as president there, speaking at the United Nations three and a half years before, and presiding over various major functions after that. The music that accompanied the visuals was poignant and triumphant, and people began to clap and cheer.

They reached fever pitch when Nicolae was shown announcing the new name of the one-world government, cutting the ribbon on the majestic palace, and welcoming people to the Gala just the week before in Jerusalem. Now fighter jets screamed in from the east and rumbled low over the event as the montage showed Carpathia mocking and challenging the two witnesses at the Wailing Wall. The crowd shouted and screamed with glee as he shot them dead. Of course, the show did not include their resurrections, which had been denounced as a myth.

The crowd fell silent as the jets swept out of earshot and the music again turned melancholy. The screens showed Carpathia back at the Gala, beginning with a long shot that showed much of the devastation from the earthquake. As the camera zoomed in on Nicolae, it changed to slow motion as he responded to the welcome of the crowd, introduced Chaim Rosenzweig, and joked with the potentates. Gasps and moans greeted the super-slow-motion replay of his turning away from a white puff of smoke in the crowd, tumbling over Dr. Rosenzweig, and lying there as the crowds fled.

The montage showed Nicolae being loaded onto a helicopter, GC logo emblazoned on the side, and here artistic license came into play. The screens showed the chopper lifting off from the stage, banking left between scaffolds and past great banks of lights, and almost disappearing into the darkness. The aircraft seemed to fly higher and higher until it pushed past the clouds and into the vastness of space.

Higher and higher it went, to the delight of the largest live crowd ever assembled, until the helicopter itself seemed to fade. Now all they saw on the big screens were space and a large image taking shape. The fighter jets returned, but no one watched. They just listened and watched as the screen morphed into the image of a man wide as the heavens. Standing in midair among the planets in dramatic dark suit, white shirt, and power tie, feet spread, arms folded across his chest, teeth gleaming, eyes flashing and confident, was Nicolae Carpathia, gazing lovingly down on the faithful.

The image froze under Nicolae's benevolent gaze, and the roar from the crowd was deafening. All stood and wildly cheered and clapped and whistled. David had to stand to avoid being conspicuous, and while he clasped his hands in front of him he glanced at Ming and Chang, who stood stone-faced, Chang with a tear rolling. David realized that no one was watching anyone else anyway, so complete was the devotion to Carpathia.

The symbolism could not be lost on anyone. He may have been murdered. He may be dead. But Nicolae Carpathia is alive in our hearts, and he is divine, and he is in heaven watching over us.

When finally the image disappeared and the music faded, Leon Fortunato stood at the lectern, his emotion-gripped face filling the screen. As Leon spread his notes before him, David noticed he was wearing a resplendent dark suit, white shirt, and power tie. It didn't work as well for poor Leon, but he apparently assumed his succession to the throne of the world, and he was giving the look all he had.

* * *

"I want to know if it was Hattie who gave us away," Chloe said as the Egyptian jet came into view.

"We can't know that," Rayford said, "unless she tells us. We can't contact her, remember? It's a one-way street right now."

Once the jet touched down, the light in the tower went off and a fat, older man came chugging down the stairs and out the door. Here was a guy with a job to do, and he was going to do it. "You're here to pick up GC personnel, am I right?" he hollered.

"Affirmative," Rayford said.

"Your number match mine? Zero-nine-two-three-four-nine?"

"Absolutely," Rayford said.

"Stay put, please. The airport is officially closed, and I must get the jet hangared and these people accommodated with dispatch."

He hurried off to the edge of the runway and went through a series of gyrations with his clipboard that would have been more effective with a flashlight as he tried to guide Albie toward the hangars.

This amused Rayford, who figured Albie had hangared as many small craft as anyone alive, and he watched as the jet steered a course straight at the tower man. He ran off the runway as the craft whined past and finished his signals with a flourish as if Albie had done precisely what he asked.

As the man ran to be sure the plane got into the hangar, Chloe shot past him. Rayford headed that way too as Leah waited by the car. It didn't take Rayford long to overtake the man, who clearly hadn't run around like this in ages.

The door of the plane, which was parked next to the Gulfstream, popped open, and Albie was the first one off. Rayford couldn't believe it. Albie had a presence, a strut. He looked a foot taller. Carrying his big leather bag, he pointed at the man and said, "You in charge here?"

"Yes, I—"

"Zero-nine-two-three-four-nine, GC, Deputy Commander Marcus Elbaz, requesting service as arranged."

"Yes, sir, Mr., er, Captain, Commander Deputy Commander, sir."

Albie said, "These people are with me. Let them help with my passengers. Refuel the plane overnight, check?"

"Oh, yes, check, sir."

"Now where can I change clothes?"

As the man pointed to a dark office at the end of the hangar, Chloe met Buck coming off the plane. "Careful, babe, careful," he said, as she wrapped her arms around him.

"Let's go, Buck," she said. "We've got to get to Kenny."

"Aliases," he whispered. "Help with Dr. Rogoff. He's had surgery."

Rayford climbed aboard to help with Chaim, who grinned stupidly at everyone and kept pointing to his forehead. "Welcome to the family, Doctor," Rayford said, and Chaim's grin turned to a grimace as he put weight on sore limbs and was helped off the plane.

Rayford noticed that everyone was on edge with the tower man around, but that was quickly taken care of when Albie emerged in uniform. Amazing.

"We're all set then, are we, sir?" Albie said.

"All set. I'll secure the door. We're not expecting any more air traffic tonight. I stay on the grounds, so I'll personally be responsible for the security of your aircraft."

"Both of them. The Gulfstream is ours too."

"Oh, I was unaware of that. No problem."

"Thanks on behalf of the Global Community. Now we have to go."

Leah had driven the Land Rover across the runway and into the hangar. She stayed behind the wheel while Rayford got in behind her and pulled Chaim in from the other side as Albie pushed. Chaim was plainly in agony as he slid across the seat, but once in and supported on both sides, he laid his head back.

Chloe sat next to Leah in the front with Buck on her right. As Leah backed up to pull out of the hangar, Chloe put her arm around her. "Thanks for bringing the car over. And forgive me."

"It's all right, Chloe," Leah said. "Just tell me you didn't get the potassium chloride idea from any of my texts."

"I did, but right now I'm glad I know Tsion would never hurt Kenny."

Leah sped back the way she had come and headed for the exit. Rayford turned to see the tower man securing the hangar door, and as they reached the road, the runway lights went out.

"OK," Albie said, "we need to get a few things out of the way first. Madam driver?"

"Leah, sir."

"Yes, ma'am, could you turn on the overhead light back here?"

Leah fumbled for it, and Buck reached to flip the switch. Albie took off his uniform cap and turned toward Rayford. "With little time to talk, just look, Captain." Rayford stared and blinked. The mark. "Don't say anything right now," Albie said. "There's too much to do. You can turn the light off. All right, next order of business. Captain Steele, will you surrender command to me, just for tonight?"

"You have a plan?"

"Of course."

"Carry on."

"How far are we from the safe house?"

"Less than half an hour."

"All right. Here's the plan."

18

DAVID WAS STRUCK by the fact that Leon, for all his sanctimony, seemed genuinely moved. No doubt he revered Carpathia and was more than the typical sycophant. Clearly he was jockeying for position as new supreme potentate, but here also was a man who grieved the loss of his friend and mentor and champion. And while he did not have the polish, the panache, the charisma of his predecessor, Leon knew how to milk the moment.

"If you'll all be seated, please," he began, his voice so thick with emotion that thousands seemed to involuntarily cover their mouths to contain their own crying. David, his own uniform heavy with sweat, lifted one foot to cross his legs and felt the stickiness on the ground. The heat had made his rubber soles tacky.

Fortunato made a show of collecting himself and smoothing his notes with meaty hands. "Nicolae Jetty Carpathia," he began in just above a whisper, "excuse me." He wiped a hand across his mouth. "I can do this. I will do this, with your patience. Nicolae Carpathia was born thirty-six years ago, the only child of two only children, in a tiny hospital in the town of Roman, Romania, in the eastern foothills of the Moldavian Carpathian Mountains, a little more than two hundred kilometers north and slightly east of Bucharest."

Fortunato paused again to clear his throat. "The young Nicolae was a precocious and extremely bright child with avid interests in athletics and academics, primarily languages, history, and science. Before the age of twelve he won his first election as president of the Young Humanists. He was a stellar high school student, a celebrated debater and speaker, and valedictorian, repeating that honor at university.

"Mr. Carpathia excelled as an entrepreneur and began public service early, becoming a member of Romania's Lower Parliament before age twenty-five. His devotion to pacifism brought both criticism and praise and became the hallmark of his life's work.

"Mr. Carpathia once told me that he believed the zenith of his career, even after being swept in as president of Romania as a young man at the behest of his predecessor, was his invitation to address the United Nations some three and a half years ago.

"Honored beyond expression, the young head of state worked hard on his presentation, outlining the history of the UN, employing every one of its languages, and memorizing his speech in its entirety. Little did he know that just prior to his appearance at the General Assembly, the earth would suffer its greatest calamity, the tragedy we all know now as the day of the vanishings.

"Stripped of our children and babies—" Fortunato paused again—"and countless friends and relatives and neighbors, the world family grieved as one. We were not aware then of the truth that only a man such as Nicolae Carpathia could bring to light: that the phenomenon that brought such bereavement was preventable, one rooted in our war technology. All we knew when the Romanian president stepped to the podium at the United Nations was that we were terrified to the point of immobility. Despairing of the future, regretting the past, we prayed in our own ways to our own gods for someone to take us by the hand and lead us through the minefields of our own making and into the blessedness of hope.

"How could we have known that our prayers would be answered by one who would prove his own divinity over and over as he humbly, selflessly served, giving of himself even to the point of death to show us the way to healing?"

The crowd could not contain itself and burst into applause. Several times Leon held up a hand, but they would not be silenced. Applause turned to cheering, and then they rose, sector by sector, until again everyone was standing, clapping, cheering, mourning their slain leader.

David was nauseated.

* * *

"Give me the rough layout of the safe house," Albie said, "where it stands, what's around it, any other buildings, roads in and out."

"I don't know if you have anything similar in your country, Albie," Rayford said. "But picture a subdivision, a housing development maybe thirty years old that has been tossed into a blender. The roads were ripped up and twisted out of the ground, and so many of the homes and businesses in that area were demolished that after rescue efforts, the area was abandoned. Best we can determine, no one lives within three miles of the place. We took over half of a badly damaged duplex, two homes in one. We expanded a cellar to make an underground hiding place, which we didn't need—at least that we knew of—until now. We rigged our own makeshift well and solar power plant, and took various routes to the place that made it look as if we could have been headed anywhere."

"What else is on the property?"

"About fifty paces from the back door is a barnlike garage that originally served both halves of the duplex. We hid our vehicles in there. We are now down to one, and this is it, so the garage is empty."

"And the other half of the residence?"

"Empty."

"Other dwellings in the area?"

"Pretty much piles of rubble that have never been hauled away."

"What hides you?"

"Besides that no one comes to that area except by mistake, there are mature trees and lots of open fields beyond our place."

"And the usual route from the airstrip takes you into the area from what direction?"

"We use various routes to keep from attracting attention, almost always travel by night, but usually find ourselves coming in from the south."

"Miss Leah," Albie said, "if you find an inconspicuous place to stop, please do." Away from paved roads already, Leah pulled into a shallow gully between two small groves of trees. "Thank you. Now, Captain Steele, your best guess of how the GC would approach the house, if they wanted to surprise."

Rayford searched for a scrap of paper and drew an aerial view of the place. "They'd come through the trees at the north," he said. "Buck, what do you think?"

Buck studied the schematic, then showed it to Chloe and Leah. They all nodded.

"All right, Leah," Albie said. "Come in from the south as usual. As far away from the safe house as you can, drive without lights. Stop about half a kilometer away, ideally where you can see the safe house but someone there would not likely see you."

"Half a kilometer?" Leah said.

"About three-tenths of a mile," Chloe said. "There's a little rise about that far away, isn't there, Dad? Just past where we turn to head toward Des Plaines?"

"Yeah, and we notice it because the rest of the whole area is so flat."

"Let's get there quickly," Albie said. "Lights off as soon as you're confident."

+ + +

As Fortunato held forth, alternately bringing the masses to their feet and making them weep, David surreptitiously pulled his binoculars from a side pocket. Leaning forward, elbows on knees, he trained the glasses on the great crowds seated just past the courtyard. He found the placard that read Sector 53 and carefully panned, looking for Annie. At first he didn't see her but was then intrigued to see a pair of binoculars pointed his direction. Despite hands and glasses covering her face, he could tell it was Annie.

They stared at each other through the lenses, then tentatively waved with just their fingers. David, with his hand still on the binoculars, held up one finger, then four, then three. She mirrored the message, their code for the number of letters in each word: *I love you.*

"I shall have some closing remarks as well," Leon said, winding down. "But I want to give your representatives from every global region the opportunity to express their thoughts before interment in the palace mausoleum. We've requested these be kept brief due to the weather, but we also want these potentates to speak from their hearts. First, from the United Russian States, Dr. Viktor . . ."

\+ + +

"Captain Steele," Albie said, "call Tsion and tell him who I am so I may speak to him without his suspicion."

Tsion answered on the first tone. "Tsion, it's me. We're within a half mile of you. Are you OK?"

"So far. Kenny is asleep. I'm packed and ready to go and feeling claustrophobic. I want out of this place."

"Tsion, I'm giving the phone to my dear friend and new believer, Albie. You've heard me mention him before."

"Yes! And he is one of us now?"

"Thanks to your teaching, which we can discuss later. He is using the name Marcus Elbaz and posing as a Global Community Peacekeeping deputy commander."

\+ + +

Tsion sat on the steps in the darkness, phone to his ear, the two tied-together packed pillowcases at his feet. All he had to do was grab them in one hand and the baby in the other, and he could be up through the freezer and out the door in seconds. But for now, he had no transportation and no idea whether the GC was waiting to ambush him.

He had heard so much about Rayford's black-market friend, he could hardly believe he was about to speak with him.

"Dr. Ben-Judah?"

"This is Tsion, yes. Albie?"

"Sir, I want to get right to business, but I must tell you, I owe you my soul."

"Thank you, sir. It appears I may soon owe you my life."

"Let's hope so. Tell me, have you heard anyone, anything, that might tell you the GC are nearby?"

"To tell you the truth, I nearly phoned Rayford about half an hour ago. It may have been paranoia, but I heard vehicles."

"Close?"

"Not very, but they were north of here. What frightened me was that they were intermittent."

"Meaning?"

"Starting, stopping, moving. I didn't know what to make of it."

"You don't usually hear any cars or trucks?"

"Right."

"And you've heard nothing since about thirty minutes ago?"

"About that."

"All right, listen carefully. Do you recognize the sound of the Land Rover? I mean, could you confidently distinguish it from, say, a GC Jeep?"

"I believe I could."

"Would you hear it plainly if it came between the house and the garage?"

"Certainly."

"And you can hear garage sounds? Doors opening and closing?"

"Yes, but these aren't typical American garage doors. They are manual and they swing like barn doors."

"All right. Thank you. If in the next fifteen minutes you hear what sounds like the Land Rover, it will be us. Any other noises or sounds, please let us know immediately."

* * *

Each potentate was greeted by music from his region and wild demonstrations from his people. Some had their people largely together; others saw them spread throughout the crowd. Most of the speakers echoed the sentiments of the potentate of the United Russian States, who listed Carpathia among not only the greatest heads of state and military leaders the world had ever known, but also among the most revered religious leaders and even deities of various faiths and sects.

The Asian leader, the second potentate to speak, said, "I know I speak for every citizen of my great region when I say that my reverence for His Excellency, the supreme potentate, has only increased in his death. I worshiped his leadership, his vision, his policies. And now I worship the man himself. May his fame and legend and glory only grow, now that he is again in heaven from whence he came!"

The potentate of the United Indian States intoned that "while we once believed that a good man comes back at a higher level, and thus that a bright star like Nicolae Carpathia would be guaranteed the role of a Brahman, he himself taught us—with his brilliant vision for a one-world faith—that even such traditional religious views have lost their currency. Even those who have come to believe that when you are dead, you are dead, and there is nothing more, have to admit—and I say this directly to Nicolae Carpathia—you will live for as long as we live. For you will always be alive in our hearts and in our memories."

Though the throng responded enthusiastically, David was intrigued that Fortunato seemed to feel the need to clarify, or at least modify, the effect of that speech. Before introducing the potentate from the United African States, Enoch Litwala, Fortunato took the floor briefly.

"Thank you for those sentiments, Potentate Kononowa. I appreciated the reference to the one-world church, which shall reappear here in New Babylon as an even better expression of a pure, united religion. Ironic, isn't it, that of the two sects most resistant to the ideas of a unified faith, one saw our great leader fall in its own homeland, and the other was responsible for his assassination.

"I do not blame the Israelis, as they are a valued part of the United Carpathian States. They cannot be held responsible for the climate engendered by their stubborn Orthodox Jews, most of whom have resisted to this day the inclusive invitation of the one-world faith. And then the Judah-ites! Espousing such exclusivistic, close-minded doctrines as there being but a single path to God! Should we be surprised that the very assassin of our beloved potentate is a leading member of that cult?"

With that pronouncement and the attendant applause, the great black statue to Leon's left began to smoke profusely, the wisp of black vapor becoming billowing clouds. Leon seemed to take this in stride, quipping, "Even Nicolae the Great has to agree with that.

"But seriously, before our African potentate comes, let me reiterate. Any cult, sect, religion, or individual who professes a single avenue to God or heaven or bliss in the afterlife is the greatest danger to the global community. Such a view engenders divisiveness, hatred, bigotry, condescension, and pride. I say to you with the confidence of one who sat in the presence of greatness every day for the last several years, there are many ways to ensure eternal bliss, if anything is eternal. It is not by walling yourself and your comrades off in a corner claiming you have the inside track to God. It is by being a good and kind human being and helping others.

"Nicolae Carpathia would have been the last person in the world to espouse a one-way religion, and look how he is revered. We will worship him and his memory for as long as we are alive. And that, my friends, will keep him and his ideals alive."

David wondered if the crowd would ever get as sick of itself as he was of the predictable clapping and cheering.

Enoch Litwala cast a pall on the proceedings when his inappropriately brief and lukewarm tribute fell flat. All he said was, "As potentate of the great United African States, it falls to me to express the sentiments of my people. Please accept our sincere condolences to the leadership of the Global Community and to those of you who loved the deceased. The United African States opposes violence and deplores this senseless act by a misguided individual, ignorantly believing what has been spoon-fed him and millions of others who refuse to think for themselves."

With that, Litwala sat, catching even Leon off guard. Two other tributes were lukewarm, which David thought made it obvious who were the loyal and the disloyal among the potentates.

* * *

Albie leaned forward and whispered to Rayford, "Come with me. Leah, watch for my signal. If I wave, proceed slowly, lights off. If I call again, stand by for instructions, but be prepared to come fast, lights on, and be sure to stop short of Rayford and me."

"I'm coming with you," Chloe said. "Our baby is in there."

"Just as well," Albie said without hesitation. "Three is better anyway."

They crept from the Rover toward the safe house. Rayford saw Chloe's look in the low light, one of fierce determination that was more than just that of a protective mother. If they were going to engage the enemy, she plainly wanted in on it.

Rayford was aware of the cool air, the sound of his steps in the sparse underbrush, and his own breathing. He felt great melancholy about the safe house as they approached. It had become his base, his home, despite all the places he had been. It had housed his family, his friends, his mentor. And he knew if he had the opportunity to step inside it once again, it would likely be for the last time.

* * *

When the last potentate had spoken, the crowd grew restless. From all over the courtyard and beyond, people stood en masse, ready to once again begin the processional past the bier. But Fortunato was not finished.

"If you'll bear with me a few more minutes," he said, "I have additional remarks I believe you will find inspirational. It should be clear to even the most casual observer that this is more than a funeral for a great leader, that the man who lies before you transcends human existence. Yes, yes, you may applaud.

Who could argue such sentiments? I am pleased to report that the image you see to my left, your right, though larger than life, is an exact replica of Nicolae Carpathia, worthy of your reverence, yea, worthy of your worship.

"Should you feel inclined to bow to the image after paying your respects, feel free. Bow, pray, sing, gesture—do whatever you wish to express your heart. And believe. Believe, people, that Nicolae Carpathia is indeed here in spirit and accepts your praise and worship. Many of you know that this so-called man, whom I know to be divine, personally raised me from the dead.

"And now, as your new leader in the absence of the one we all wish were still here, allow me to be forthright. I am no director, but let me ask the main television camera to move in on my face. Those close enough can look into my eyes. Those remote may look into my eyes on the screen."

David knew what happened to people who allowed themselves to be caught in Fortunato's gaze. He looked left, past the Wongs, who appeared enraptured, and reached to touch Chang and motion with his head to Ming. When they looked at him he shook his head imperceptibly and was grateful they both seemed to understand. They averted their gaze from Fortunato's.

"Today," Fortunato intoned, "I am instituting a new, improved global faith that shall have as its object of worship this image, which represents the very spirit of Nicolae Carpathia. Listen carefully, my people. When I said a moment ago that you may worship this image and Nicolae himself if you felt so inclined, I was merely being polite. Silence, please. With global citizenship comes responsibility, and that responsibility entails subordination to those in authority over you."

There was such deathly silence that David doubted if anyone so much as moved.

"As your new ruler, it is only fair of me to tell you that there is no option as it pertains to worshiping the image and spirit of Nicolae Carpathia. He is not only part of our new religion, but he is also its centerpiece. Indeed, he has become and forever shall *be* our religion. Now, before you break your reverie and bow before the image, let me impress upon your mind the consequences of disobeying such an edict."

Suddenly, from the statue itself—with its great expanses of black smoke now nearly blotting out the sun—came a thundering pronouncement: "I am the lord your god who sits high above the heavens!" People, including Guy Blod and his assistants, shrieked and fell prostrate, peeking at the image. "I am the god above all other gods. There is none like me. Worship or beware!"

Fortunato suddenly spoke softly, fatherly. "Fear not," he said. "Lift your eyes to the heavens." The massive dark clouds dissipated, and the image appeared serene once more. "Nicolae Carpathia loves you and has only your best in mind.

Charged with the responsibility of ensuring compliance with the worship of your god, I have also been imbued with power. Please stand."

The masses stood as one, appearing terrified, eyes glued to Leon or to his image on the screens. He gestured grandly behind him, past the glass coffin and the guards, past the ten potentates, three of whom glared stonily. "Let us assume that there may be those here who choose, for one reason or another, to refuse to worship Carpathia. Perhaps they are independent spirits. Perhaps they are rebellious Jews. Perhaps they are secret Judah-ites who still believe 'their man' is the only way to God. Regardless of their justification, they shall surely die."

The crowd recoiled and many gasped.

"Marvel not that I say unto you that some shall surely die. If Carpathia is not god and I am not his chosen one, then I shall be proved wrong. If Carpathia is not *the* only way and *the* only life, then what I say is not *the* only truth and none should fear.

"It is also only fair that I offer proof of my role, in addition to what you have already seen and heard from Nicolae Carpathia's own image. I call on the power of my most high god to prove that he rules from heaven by burning to death with his pure, extinguishing fire those who would oppose me, those who would deny his deity, those who would subvert and plot and scheme to take my rightful place as his spokesman!"

He paused dramatically. Then, "I pray he does this even as I speak!"

Leon turned to face the ten potentates and pointed at the three who opposed him. Great beams of fire burst from the cloudless skies and incinerated the three where they sat. The other seven leaped from their seats to avoid the heat and flames, and even the guards backpedaled.

The crowd shrieked and wailed, but no one moved. No one ran. Every soul seemed paralyzed with fear. And the fire that left the three smoldering in tiny piles of ash disappeared as quickly as it had come.

Fortunato spoke again: "Faithful patriots of the Global Community from the three regions formerly led by men of lying tongues, take heart. Their replacements have already been selected in meetings I have enjoyed with the spirit of Nicolae Carpathia himself. The Global Community shall prevail. We shall reach our goal of utopian living, harmony, love, and tolerance—tolerance of all but those who refuse to worship the image of the man we esteem and glorify today!"

It was clear Fortunato expected applause, but the gathered were so stunned, so filled with terror that they merely stared. "You may express yourselves," Leon said with a smile. Still no one moved. His eyes narrowed. "You may express your agreement," he said, and tentative clapping began.

"You need not fear your lord god," he said, as the applause continued. "What you have witnessed here shall never befall you if you love Nicolae with the love that brought you here to honor his memory. Now before the interment, once everyone has had a chance to pay last respects, I invite you to come and worship. Come and worship. Worship your god, your dead yet living king."

* * *

Rayford followed Albie's signal and fanned left while Chloe was sent right. The three, about thirty paces apart, advanced upon the safe house from two hundred yards away. They watched for signs of GC. Had they been there? Were they yet there? Were they coming?

Suddenly Albie dropped into the grass and signaled Rayford and Chloe to do the same. He had taken a call. Then he signaled them to join him.

"Tsion hears the engine noises again," he whispered. "Coming from the north, only steady this time, as if advancing." He spoke as he dialed Leah. "We're going to beat them to the safe house on foot, so be ready to run, and if we encounter GC, stay a step or two behind me. Leah? Give us about ninety seconds, then come fast with lights on. Just be careful not to overtake us. When we stop, you stop as close to the garage as you can. Stay in the vehicle with the lights on and don't worry if you see GC Jeeps coming the other way."

Albie slapped the phone shut, unholstered his sidearm, bounced to his feet, and said, "Let's go."

As Rayford loped along in the darkness, wondering how many minutes he might have left on earth, he was impressed that Chloe had no trouble keeping pace. He also wondered at the strange difference in Albie. He'd always been resourceful, but was there something else about him now, besides his new profession of faith?

Rayford wondered, why had he not assured himself of the integrity of Albie's mark? Could he be sure of anything he saw under the dim interior light of the Rover, a wounded old man between him and Albie?

19

MR. WONG DROPPED to his knees next to David, weeping and crying out in his native tongue. His wife sat rocking, fists clenched, eyes closed, appearing more stunned than convinced.

Ming and Chang sat with hands covering their eyes, appearing to pray. To anyone else, it might appear they were praying to the new god of the world, but David knew.

He found it surreal that as Fortunato backed away from the lectern and joined the seven remaining potentates, they seemed to ignore the piles of ashes. They solemnly shook hands with their new leader, appearing to congratulate him on his speech and his display of power.

The security chief instructed his people to remove the barricade from in front of the single-file line. The couple in Dutch garb first refused to move toward the bier, but those behind them began to jostle and push, urging them on. The couple smiled with embarrassment, each clearly wanting the other to go first. They finally locked arms and shuffled along with mincing steps, seeming to want to see Carpathia's body but afraid of not only the gigantic speaking and smoke-belching statue, but also the seats behind the bier, three of which contained only ashes.

Fortunato and the remaining seven stood in front of the row of seats, just far enough behind the coffin to stay out of the guards' way and so that mourners would not be tempted to shake their hands or speak with them. It appeared to David that it suddenly came to Leon why people were shy about approaching. He turned first to one side and then the other and asked the potentates to move away from him.

Then he stepped back and, with a flourish, swept the ashes from each of the three seats, brushing and tidying them with his big hands. This stopped the processional and made anyone close by stare in amazement. With a satisfied look, Leon turned back to face the bier and motioned that the seven should rejoin him. As they did he clapped and rubbed his hands together, and the residue fell away. He and the potentates enjoyed a chuckle.

* * *

Three sets of headlights appeared on the horizon, maybe a half mile beyond the safe house. Rayford had feared this day, when the GC would swoop down upon them. He worried he would be gone or sleeping or unaware. How bizarre to be here and see it happening.

Albie and Chloe had picked up the pace and sprinted now. Rayford tried but found himself suddenly awkward and feeling his age again. "Closer to me now, Captain Steele," Albie called out, then hollered the same to Chloe.

Rayford and Chloe closed ranks, now ten or twelve feet on either side of Albie and about four feet back. Behind them the roaring Land Rover came bouncing over the terrain, projecting eerie shadows on the safe house.

It seemed to Rayford that the three vehicles advancing from the other way had slowed and separated. He and Albie and Chloe stopped between the old garage and the house, and Leah skidded the Land Rover to Chloe's right, next to the garage. "Hold," Albie said quietly. "Hold and maintain positions."

"We're vulnerable, Albie," Rayford said.

"Deputy Commander Elbaz, Mr. Berry," Albie said. "And you have ceded command to me, have you not?"

"Temporarily," Rayford said ruefully. If Albie was legit, he could take it as a joke. If Rayford had stupidly fallen for something and had sacrificed the Tribulation Force to a lapse in judgment, he was saying he would wrest back command and not go down without a fight.

The headlights before them now spread out, the vehicle to Rayford's left heading farther that way, angling toward them and stopping about seventy-five yards away. The one in the middle advanced closer, maybe fifty yards away. And the one to the right mirrored the one on the left.

"Hold," Albie said again. "Hold."

"We're targets here," Rayford said.

"Hold."

"I don't feel good about this," Chloe said.

"Hold. Trust me."

Rayford held his breath. *I wish I could. Lord, tell me I did the right thing.*

Rayford started when he heard someone jump out of the center vehicle, equipment jangling as he hit the ground, and move toward the house. While he could still see all three sets of headlights, Rayford lost behind the house the silhouette of the soldier hurrying their way.

"Hold."

"I'm holding, Alb—Deputy Commander, while they have an armed man on the other side of the house. What if he torches the place? What if the others join him? They have clear shots at us, while they're protected by trees and the house."

"Silence, Mr. Berry," Albie said. "We are outmanned twelve to three."

Rayford felt a deep foreboding. *How would he know that?*

"And unless one of you is packing," Albie added, "we are out-armed twelve to one."

"So, what," Chloe said, "we're surrendering? I'll die first."

"You might if you don't let me handle this."

Rayford had gone from suspicion to fear and now to full-blown dread. He had walked his charges into the biggest trap imaginable. Wasn't it Albie himself who had once counseled to never trust anyone? They could be dead or in prison within half an hour.

"Global Community squadron leader!" Albie shouted, his voice deep and clear and louder than Rayford had ever heard it. "Show and identify yourself! I am GC Deputy Commander Marcus Elbaz, and that is an order!"

* * *

David guessed the temperature at 110 degrees. He couldn't remember being out at midday in New Babylon when it was this hot. He removed his uniform cap and wiped a sleeve across his brow. He was dripping. There was no wind. Just the relentless sun, the body heat of four million people, and the acrid smoke from the imposing statue.

The image began to move as if an earth tremor made it sway and bounce, but nothing else was affected. All eyes turned toward it in terror and word spread quickly throughout the courtyard that something was happening. For a long minute the thing seemed to vibrate in place. Then it rocked, and the smoke began to billow once more.

The image soon glowed red hot, and the smoke poured out so fast that it again formed clouds that darkened the sky. The temperature dropped immediately, but going from daylight to dusk so quickly made many fall to their faces.

The image roared, "Fear not and flee not! Flee not or you shall surely die!"

The blackness covered the sky in the immediate area, but when David sneaked a glance at the horizon, it remained light. At the edges, all the way around as he turned, lightning burst from the low-riding smoke and struck the ground. Seconds later the thunderclaps rolled in, shaking the area.

"Flee not!" the image shouted again. "Defy me at your peril!"

Leon stood with his arms folded, gazing at the statue as the seven potentates dropped to all fours, wide-eyed. The armed guards fell to their knees.

People at the far edges of the crowd turned and ran, only to be struck by lightning as the rest of the throng watched in horror. "You would defy *me?*" the statue roared. "Be silent! Be still! Fear not! Flee not! And behold!"

People froze in place, staring. The smoke stopped rising, yet the sky remained dark. It formed itself into roiling, growing black clouds mixed with deep reds and purples.

David, secure in his faith and believing he knew what was going on, still found himself shaking, shuddering, heart ablaze.

"Gaze not upon me," the statue said, now with no smoke coming from its face. As it cooled it faded from orange to red and back to black. It no longer moved. "Gaze upon your lord god."

It was as if the statue had shrunk, David thought, but it had merely become still, silent, and cold. People slowly rose, and all eyes turned upon the glass coffin where Carpathia, unmolested, remained reposed. Millions stood in the quickly cooled desert, the sky pitch, horrifying clouds churning. The people folded their arms against the sudden chill. Shoulders hunched, they stared at Carpathia's lifeless body.

* * *

"I have eleven Peacekeepers with weapons trained on you, sir!" came the reply from the far corner of the safe house. "I'll need to see some identification!"

"Fair enough!" Albie called back. "But be prepared with your own, as I am your superior officer!"

"I suggest we meet on your side of the house with weapons holstered!"

"Agreed!" Albie said, making a show of returning his sidearm to its strapped sheath on his belt.

"And your aides?"

"Same as yours, sir," Albie said. "Weapons trained on you."

The squadron leader stepped out from behind the house with his weapon secured, arms away from his body, hands empty. Albie stepped toward him with purpose. "Excellent approach, sir. I'm reaching for my papers now."

"As am I."

The squadron leader pulled a flashlight from behind his belt and they compared documents. "Sorry for the confusion, Deputy Commander," the young man said. "Do I know you?"

"You should, Datillo. I likely taught you. Where did you train?"

"BASALT, sir. Baltimore Area Squadron Leadership Training."

"I only guest lectured there. I was at Chesapeake."

"Yes, sir."

"Squadron Leader Datillo, may I ask what you're doing here?"

Datillo pulled order papers from his pocket. "We were led to believe this was headquarters of a Judah-ite faction, maybe even *the* central safe house. Our orders were to lay siege to it, apprehend any occupants, determine the whereabouts and identities of any others, and destroy the facility."

"Torch it?"

"Affirmative, sir."

Suddenly Albie moved closer to the young squadron leader. "Datillo, where did these orders come from?"

"I assumed New Babylon, sir."

"You assumed. Did you check them with the regional director?"

"No, sir, I—"

"Datillo, do you know what time it is?"

"Sir?"

"Do we not both speak English, Datillo? It's not my mother tongue, but it's yours. Is my accent too thick for you, son?"

"No, sir."

"Do you know what time it is?"

"After 0400 hours, sir. Requesting permission to check my watch."

"Granted."

"It's 0430, sir."

"It's 0430, Datillo. Does that mean anything to you?"

"Mean anything, sir?"

"Listen to me, Squadron Leader. I'm going to tell you this outside the listening range of your subordinates, though you don't deserve it. I'm going to resist the temptation to inform North American States Midwest Regional Director Crawford that you did not check orders through him before proceeding. And I'm even going to give you a pass on your *unbelievable* lack of awareness of the time zone differences between North America and the Carpathian States. I ask you again, Squadron Leader Datillo, what is the significance of 0430 hours?"

"I beg your pardon, Deputy Commander, and I appreciate your lenience on the other matters—particularly not embarrassing me in the presence of my subordinates. But, sir, I am drawing a complete blank on the time issue."

"Honestly," Albie said, "I don't know where they get you kids or what you're doing during basic training. Did you or did you not sit in any of my guest lectures at BASALT?"

"I honestly don't recall, sir."

"Then you didn't, because you wouldn't have forgotten. And you would know what time it is in New Babylon when it's 0430 in your part of the world."

"Well, if you mean do I know the time difference, yes sir, I do."

"You do."

"Yes, sir."

"I'm listening."

"At this time of the year, there's a nine-hour time difference."

"Very good, Datillo. What time does that make it in New Babylon right now?"

"Uh, let's see, they're later than we are, so it's, ah, 1330 hours."

"Do I have to walk you through this, son?"

"I'm sorry, sir. I'm afraid so."

"What is today, Squadron Leader?"

"Saturday, sir."

"You lose. Try again. It's after midnight, officer."

"Oh, yeah, it's Sunday morning already."

"Which makes it what in New Babylon?"

"Sunday afternoon."

"It's Sunday afternoon in New Babylon, Datillo. Ring any bells?"

Datillo's shoulders slumped. "It's the funeral, isn't it, sir?"

"Ding-ding-ding-ding! Datillo hits the jackpot! You're aware of the moratorium on combat-related activity anywhere in the world during the funeral, are you not?"

"Yes, sir."

"And every GC directive requires CPR, correct?"

"Concrete Peacekeeping Reasoning, yes, sir."

"And the CPR behind this directive?"

"Um, that no untoward publicity crowd out the funeral as the top news story."

"There you go. Now, Datillo, I can tell you're an earnest young man. You and your people are going to evacuate this area. You may return at 1000 hours and torch this place, if I leave it standing. My people and I were onto this location long before you were, and we have already apprehended the occupants and evacuated the building. I have a crew here to comb the residence for evidence, and we should be finished by dawn. Do not return until 1000, and if you see smoke on the horizon before that, you'll have no need to come then either. Have I made myself clear?"

"Yes, sir. Any way my people and I can assist, sir?"

"Only by following orders and leaving now. And I'll make a deal with you, son. You don't tell your superiors of the serious mistakes you made this morning, and I won't either."

"I appreciate that, sir."

"I know you do. Now move out."

Datillo saluted and trotted back to the middle Jeep. It popped a U-turn, as did the other two before falling in line behind it. And they raced off in the darkness.

+ + +

The sky was so black that the lights of the palace courtyard came on automatically. The TV lights were trained on the coffin, and David was sure every eye but his was too. He searched and searched sector 53 for Annie, praying she would stand strong. He couldn't locate her.

David turned back. Heat waves shimmered off the statue in the comparatively chilly air. The potentates appeared paralyzed. Even Fortunato had paled and wasn't moving, his gaze on the casket. A rim of light along the horizon looked like the rim of hair on a bald man. Clouds of ebony and other deep shades, produced by smoke from the statue, hung ominously over the immense gathering. People stood stock-still, riveted. Brilliant lights bathed the platform.

David's eyes were drawn to the body. What was that? Almost imperceptible movement? Or had it been his imagination? He had imagined a corpse's chest rising and falling at a funeral before. But until now, Carpathia's body hadn't given even the illusion of life.

Carpathia's left index finger lifted an inch off his wrist for an instant, then fell again. A few people gasped, but David assumed most had not seen it. Then it rose and fell twice. Next it lifted half an inch, uncurling as if pointing.

One of the potentates apparently saw that and recoiled, trying to back away but falling over a chair. As he scrambled to his feet and tried to exit, lightning struck ten feet from him and knocked him back to where he had been. He stood shakily and brushed himself off, reluctantly looking at Carpathia again.

Now the index finger twitched, and all the potentates stiffened. The guards went into assault position, as if prepared to shoot a dead body. Carpathia's hands separated and rested at his sides. Those close enough began to weep, their faces contorted in terror. It seemed they wanted to escape but could not move.

Those ahead of David edged closer, careful to keep someone between them and the bier. Those in front held their ground or tried to step back, but no one behind them would have that.

Now it was clear that Carpathia's chest did rise and fall. Many fell to their knees, hiding their eyes, crying out.

Nicolae's eyes popped open. David stared, then tore his gaze away to see even Leon and the kings trembling.

The corpse's lips separated, and Nicolae lifted his head until it pressed against the Plexiglas lid. Everyone within a hundred yards of the coffin, including

Fortunato, collapsed, covering their faces but, David noticed, most peeking through intertwined fingers.

As if stretching, Carpathia tilted his head back, grimaced, and lifted his knees until they too met the lid of the casket. He straightened his left leg until his heel met the large rubber stopper and forced it free with a loud *thwock!* The plug flew out and knocked the cap off one of the prostrate guards. He dropped his weapon and rubbed his head as the projectile bounced and rolled and finally stopped under a chair.

With the vacuum seal broken, Carpathia slowly brought his hands to his chest, palms up, heels of his hands resting on the underside of the lid. Moans and gasps and shrieks came from the crowd for as far as David could see and hear. Everyone was on the ground now, either peering at the screens or trying to see the platform.

Carpathia lifted his knees again, ripping the massive stainless steel bolts free of the glass. Then he pushed mightily until the top end shattered loose. The lid, more than eighty pounds of Plexiglas, flew away from the coffin, bolts flying, and smashed into the lectern, knocking it over and taking the microphone with it.

Carpathia catapulted himself to a standing position in the narrow end of his own coffin. He turned triumphantly to face the crowd, and David noticed makeup, putty, surgical staples, and stitches in the box where Nicolae's head had lain.

Standing there before now deathly silence, Nicolae looked as if he had just stepped out of his closet where a valet had helped him into a crisp suit. Shoes gleaming, laces taut, socks smooth, suit unwrinkled, tie hanging just so, he stood broad-shouldered, fresh-faced, shaven, hair in place, no pallor. Fortunato and the seven were on their knees, hiding their faces, sobbing aloud.

Nicolae raised his hands to shoulder height and said loudly enough for everyone to hear, without aid of a microphone, "Peace. Be still." With that the clouds ascended and vanished, and the sun reappeared in all its brilliance and heat. People squinted and covered their eyes.

"Peace be unto you," he said. "My peace I give you. Please stand." He paused while everyone rose, eyes still locked on him, bodies rigid with fear. "Let not your hearts be troubled. Believe in me."

Murmuring began. David heard people marveling that he was not using a microphone, but neither was he raising his voice. And yet everyone could hear.

It was as if Carpathia read their minds. "You marvel that I speak directly to your hearts without amplification, yet you saw me raise myself from the dead. Who but the most high god has power over death? Who but god controls the earth and sky?"

Hands still raised, he spoke gently. "Do you still tremble? Are you still sore afraid? Fear not, for I bring you good tidings of great joy. It is I who loves you who stands before you today, wounded unto death but now living . . . for you. For you.

"You need never fear me, for you are my friends. Only my enemies need fear. Why are you fearful, O you of little faith? Come to me, and you will find rest for your souls."

David nearly fainted from nausea. To hear the words of Jesus from this evil man, whom Dr. Ben-Judah taught was now indwelt, Satan incarnate, was almost more than he could take.

"Only he who is not with me is against me," Carpathia continued. "Anyone who speaks a word against me, it will not be forgiven him. But as for you, the faithful, be of good cheer. It is I; do not be afraid."

David searched for Annie again, knowing that no one around him was even aware he was not paying attention to Carpathia. How he wished he could see her, know she was all right, communicate to her that she was not alone, that other believers were here.

"I want to greet you," Carpathia said. "Come to me, touch me, talk to me, worship me. All authority has been given to me in heaven and on earth. I will be with you always, even to the end."

The line that had frozen in place still did not move. Carpathia turned to Fortunato and nodded, gesturing to the guards. "Urge my own to come to me." Slowly the guards rose and began to nudge the people toward the stairs again. "And as you come," Carpathia continued, "let me speak to you about my enemies. . . ."

\+ + +

Tsion had sat praying as vehicles approached the safe house from two directions. "Is this the end, Lord?" he said. "I so long to come to you. But if it is not the due time for my beloved brothers and sisters and me to give our lives for you, give us all strength and wisdom."

The vehicles stopped, and he heard shouting. Tsion moved to the corner of the cellar where he could hear. A Middle Eastern GC commander was calling out a squadron commander. Tsion tried to slow and regulate his breathing so he could hear every word. Was that Albie, the one he had just spoken to, pretending to be GC? Or *was* he GC? He was so convincing, so knowledgeable. How could a man know so much about systems and procedures without being on the inside? Or perhaps he once was and had turned. Tsion could only hope.

Whatever he was, Albie had driven off the squadron commander and his men, and Tsion knew his friends would now come for him. His first order of business? He turned the power back on and fired up the TV. His phone rang.

"Dr. Ben-Judah," Albie said, "are you down there and all right?"

"I am fine and watching the funeral on TV. Come down and see."

"Do you want to come and let us in?"

"Break in! I don't want to miss this, and we're not staying anyway, are we?"

Albie chuckled and the back door was kicked in. Footsteps. The freezer door opened, the rack pulled aside, footsteps on the stairs. Albie entered, followed by Chloe, who raced to pull Kenny from his crib and smother him with kisses. Then Rayford, looking grave even as he embraced Tsion.

"The others are coming," Rayford said.

"Yes, yes, and praise God," Tsion said. "But watch this. A great storm has invaded the palace courtyard, and I am convinced the hour is near."

Buck limped gingerly down the stairs and found Chloe and Kenny. Leah followed, carefully aiding Chaim. Bandaged, mute, and fragile, still he forced a grin when he saw Tsion, and the countrymen embraced. "I praise the Lord for you, my brother," Tsion said. "Now sit and watch."

"We want to get this done before dawn, people," Albie said. "I don't think our young friend will return until ten, but we'd better not test him."

"Are we really going to torch this place once we've got what we want?" Rayford said.

Tsion tried to shush them, but both ignored him. He turned up the TV. "This seems pretty risky," Buck said, emerging from the bedroom with Chloe and Kenny, "partying down here with GC in the area."

"I believe the indwelling is about to occur," Tsion announced.

"Put a videodisc in, Tsion!" Rayford said. "We've got work to do and fast."

"I am confident Albie's ruse was successful," Tsion said. "At least I hope so."

Rayford approached him. "Doctor," he said, "I'm back and I'm in charge, and I need to pull rank, despite my respect for you. Record that and let's get packing."

Tsion read such confidence and also concern in Rayford that he immediately popped in a disc. "Chaim, you can't work in your condition. Monitor this for me until we have to go." He hurried upstairs.

"Bring only what you can carry on your lap," Rayford announced. "Tying stuff atop the car would attract too much attention."

As Tsion busied himself, he worried about Rayford. It was natural for them all to be relieved and yet worried they were not out of the woods yet. Rayford was plainly agitated about something. After Tsion gave his room one last cursory glance for any indispensables, he saw Rayford pull Albie into Buck and Chloe's empty first-floor bedroom.

\+ + +

"You all know me as a forgiving potentate," Carpathia said, as the masses began to queue up once more to file past him. This time they would have the weird experience of touching and chatting with a man who had been dead nearly three days and who still stood in the remains of his own coffin.

"Ironically," he continued, "the person or persons responsible for my demise may no longer be pursued for murder. Attempted murder of a government official is still an international felony, of course. The guilty know who they are, but as for me, I hereby pardon any and all. No official action is to be taken by the government of the Global Community. What steps fellow citizens may take to ensure that such an act never takes place again, I do not know and will not interfere with.

"However, individual would-be assassins aside, there are opponents to the Global Community and to my leadership. Hear me, my people: I need not and will not tolerate opposition. You need not fear because you came here to commemorate my life on the occasion of my death, and you remain to worship me as your divine leader. But to those who believe it is possible to rebel against my authority and survive, beware. I shall soon institute a program of loyalty confirmation that will prove once and for all who is with us and who is against us, and woe to the haughty insurrectionist. He will find no place to hide.

"Now, loyal subjects, come and worship."

20

RAYFORD PULLED ALBIE into Buck and Chloe's bedroom by his elbow. As he was shutting the door he saw Chaim staggering toward Tsion, gesturing, grunting through his bandages and wired jaw, trying to get Tsion to follow.

Rayford's phone rang. "Stay put," Rayford told Albie. Then, into the phone, "Steele here."

"Rayford, it's Hattie!" She was near hysterics.

"Where are you?" he said.

"The less you know the better, but get your people out of the safe house."

"Why?"

"They're onto you. Don't ask me how I know. And Carpathia has come back from the dead. Did you see?"

"No."

"It's all true, isn't it, Rayford?"

"Of course it is, and you knew that almost as soon as most of us did. I didn't think doubt was why you were holding out."

"It wasn't, totally. But I was still holding out hope that it couldn't all be just the way Dr. Ben-Judah said."

"What're you going to do about it, Hattie? You know how we all feel about it and about you."

"Nothing right now, Rayford. I just wanted to warn you."

"Thanks, but now *I'm* warning *you.* Don't wait any longer."

"I have to go, Rayford."

"Dr. Rosenzweig has made his decision."

"I've really got to—what? He has? He was supposed to be dead. Is he there? May I talk with him?"

"I'll have him call you when he's able."

"I don't want my phone ringing at the wrong time."

"Then call us back tomorrow, Hattie, hear? We'll all be praying you do the right thing."

* * *

David did not know where Viv Ivins had been sitting. Surely she had been in the VIP section, but he did not notice her until she appeared at Carpathia's side. Fortunato was to her right, so as people swept past they encountered first Leon, then Viv, and finally Carpathia. It was as if this setup was designed to put people at ease. They need not fear a recently dead man who wanted to touch and be touched.

Leon gently pushed them to Viv, who said something soothing and guided them quickly past Carpathia. He seemed to be looking each one in the eye and cooing something as he grasped his or her hand with both of his. No one was allowed to pause, and all seemed overcome as they floated away. Many swooned and some passed out. David did some quick figuring. If Nicolae gave, say, three million people five or six seconds apiece, it would take more than 200 twenty-four-hour days. Surely those who waited more than a few hours would give up.

* * *

"Can this wait, Captain Steele?" Albie said.

Rayford blocked his path. "Why, Albie?"

"Don't *you* want to see what's happening on the news?"

"I'll watch the replay."

"So, you want to see it too."

"Of course," Rayford said. "But I'm starting to wonder if we want to see it for the same reason."

"What are you saying?"

"What is your real name?"

"You know my name, Rayford."

"May I check your mark?"

Albie squinted at him. "In my culture, that is a terrible insult. Especially after everything we have been through."

"Your culture never had the mark before. What's the insult?"

"To not be personally trusted."

"You yourself advised me to trust no one."

"That's a principle, my friend. You think I would fake and lie to you about something I know to be so real to you?"

"I don't know."

"Then you had better check my mark. You could not insult me further."

"Take it as a compliment, Albie. If you're for real, you were so convincing as a GC commander that you made me wonder."

"I must have."

"You did. How did you know we were outmanned twelve to three?"

"I do my homework. It's part of the job. How do you think I outlived the average black marketer by two times? I'm careful. I don't just find a uniform and affect an identity without learning the nuances."

"How did you know three Jeeps carried four Peacekeepers each?"

"That is GC protocol. Night patrols are called squadrons and have a leader, three vehicles, and eleven subordinates. By day they travel in pairs."

"Uh-huh. And BASALT?"

"Never heard of it. I was glad he explained."

"Guest lecturing?"

"Made it up."

"Chesapeake?"

"Guessing. Hoping. I had read something about a GC training facility there. I'm glad I was so convincing, Rayford, because our lives depended on it. It's what I do."

"Midwest Regional what-did-you-call-him, Director—"

"Director Crawford, right."

"And you know him from . . . ?"

"A directory I thought it would behoove me to familiarize myself with."

"You've never met him?"

"How would I?"

"You're still a closet hater of Carpathia?"

"Out of the closet soon, I hope. I don't enjoy long-term playacting. Satisfied?"

"How did you know about the funeral moratorium and, what did you call it? CPR?"

"I read."

"You read."

"You should know that about me."

"I think I need to know a lot more about you."

Now Albie was mad. "I won't pretend not to be deeply offended," he said, ripping off his uniform cap and slamming it to the floor. Rayford was suddenly aware that they alone remained on the main floor and he heard no footsteps above. Everyone must have been huddled around the television in the underground shelter.

Albie unstrapped his gun and drew it, Rayford retreating until the back of his head hit the bedroom door. Albie turned the weapon around so he was holding the barrel. He thrust it at Rayford. "Here," he said. "Shoot me if I am a liar."

Rayford hesitated.

"Go on, take it!"

"I'm not going to shoot you, Albie."

"Even if I'm a phony? Even if I've turned on you, lied to you? Compromised you? Even if I was GC after all? Let me tell you, Captain Steele, if that *were* true about me and I were *you,* I would shoot me without remorse." He stood offering the weapon. "But I will say this. If I *were* GC, this is where and when I would shoot you too. And I would kill every one of your comrades as they rushed from the underground. Then I would secure the place and let Squadron Commander Datillo burn the evidence to the ground. What will it be, Captain Steele? This is a limited offer. Hadn't you better check me to see if you signed the death warrants of all your friends? Or will you risk their lives to keep from insulting me further?"

Rayford would not reach for the gun, so Albie tossed it on the bed. Rayford wished he had taken it, not sure whether he could beat Albie to it now if he had to. Albie took a step closer, making Rayford flinch, but Albie merely stuck his forehead in Rayford's face.

"Touch it, rub it, wash it, put petrol on it. Do whatever you have to do to convince yourself. I already know who I am. If I'm phony, shoot me. If I'm real, assume I have turned command back over to you. Either way, you could not have offended me more."

"I don't mean to offend you, Albie. But I must—"

"Just get on with it! If you are to be the leader, take command!"

* * *

David scanned the far reaches of the crowd where carts zigzagged with bullhorns, advising the people that the GC regretted to inform them that "only those already inside the courtyard will be able to greet His Excellency personally. Thanks for understanding, and do feel free to remain for final remarks in an hour or so."

David searched and searched for Annie, finally telling the Wong family he had to go.

Mr. Wong, his face ravaged by tears and exhaustion, said, "No! You get us into receiving line."

"I'm sorry," David said. "They've closed the line."

"But we in courtyard! VIP seat! You make happen."

"No," David said, leaning close. "You're the VIP. You make it happen."

As the older man sputtered, David squeezed Mom's shoulder and embraced both Ming and Chang, whispering in their ears, "*Jesus* is risen."

Both responded under their breath, "He is risen indeed."

* * *

"Forgive me, Albie," Rayford said. "Please don't be insulted."

"You have already insulted me, my friend, so you might as well put your mind at ease."

"I'm trying to put *your* mind at ease, Albie."

"That will require more of an apology than you have the time or energy or, I may say, insight to give. Now check the mark, and let's get out of here."

Rayford reached for Albie, who seemed to stiffen. A loud rap on the door made them both jump. Tsion poked his head in. "My apologies, gentlemen, but Carpathia has resurrected! You must come see!"

Rayford retrieved the gun.

"Keep it," Albie said, as they headed downstairs.

"But that would insult you even more."

"I told you, I cannot be more deeply insulted."

Rayford reached back awkwardly, holding the gun out to Albie.

Albie shook his head, grabbed the gun, and slammed it into its holster. As he snapped the strap he said, "The only thing more offensive than not being trusted by an old friend is your simpering style of leadership. Rayford, you and those you are responsible for are entering the most dangerous phase of your existence. Don't blow it with indecision and poor judgment."

* * *

Buck held the sleeping baby while Chloe finished packing. He heard Rayford and Albie descending and wondered why they were empty-handed after having been upstairs for so long. Maybe they had already carried stuff to the car.

"Did you see this, Dad?" he said, nodding toward the TV where GC CNN played and replayed the most dramatic moments from New Babylon.

"Better not refer to me informally in front of the rest of the Force," Rayford whispered, as he stared at the TV.

Buck cocked his head. "Whatever you say, Captain Steele."

He limped to where Chloe had gathered their essentials, traded the baby for a bundle, and slowly made his way out to the Land Rover. The coolness of the predawn refreshed him, though he caught himself sniffing the air and listening. The last thing he wanted, after the bizarre story of Albie's ruse, was to hear those GC Jeeps returning. What if the squadron leader was braver than Albie gave him credit for and he risked embarrassment and even reprimand to check out the story? He'd be back with more help, and they could all be imprisoned or killed and the place destroyed.

Buck worried about some of his injuries. He had pain in both legs that felt sharper than soft tissue damage, so he worried about broken bones. He was certain he'd also cracked a rib or two and couldn't imagine that Chaim hadn't as well. They shared whiplash trauma, even though their heads had first been driven forward.

Buck caught a glimpse of himself in the cracked outside rearview mirror of the Rover as he stepped away from the vehicle. Was it possible he was only thirty-three? He felt even worse than he looked, and he looked fifty. A fabric burn on his forehead he hadn't even noticed in the hospital had formed a large, ugly scab that was tender to the touch. That had to have come from the first impact and the forcing of his head into the back of the seat in front of him. Deep lacerations from dropping into a woody bush at the Jerusalem Airport what seemed eons ago had healed as high-ridged scars with crimson centers that covered his chin, cheeks, and forehead.

Worse, his eyes had that world-weary look, a deep fatigue that combined survival desperation, love and concern for his wife and child, and the sheer exhaustion of living as a fugitive and enduring searing personal losses. He took a deep breath that brought stinging pain to his ribs. He wondered where he might next sleep, but he didn't wonder if he would sleep well.

Buck would have returned inside to help, but in his condition he was more help staying put. The others began to straggle out under heavy bundles, except for Tsion who had just two full pillowcases tied together over one shoulder and was supporting Chaim on his other arm.

Albie, the last out, was on the phone. Rayford arranged the seating. He put Chloe, Kenny, Leah, Tsion, and Chaim in the backseat, where they were barely able to close the doors. Buck would ride shotgun in the front with Albie in the middle and Rayford driving. First, however, Rayford and Albie stood between the garage and the house—Albie still on the phone—and Rayford beckoned Buck with a nod.

"The chopper is at Palwaukee," Albie reported. "And the shuttle pilots are on their way back to Rantoul in the trail plane. You want my advice, Captain?"

"You bet."

"I say we go directly to the airstrip and put the wounded and as much of the luggage in the chopper as we can. Then you can fly the chopper to the new safe house, and someone else can drive."

"And you?"

"I should take the fighter to Kankakee. You can pick me up there later in the chopper, and I can fly the Gulfstream into Kankakee."

"How about torching this place?" Rayford said.

"You have materials?"

"Kerosene and gasoline in the garage. Some flares."

"That would do it. Have you left anything incriminating inside?"

"Not that I can think of. You, Buck?"

Buck shook his head. "I'd light 'er up."

"That's me too," Rayford said. "Just in case. Leave 'em nothing to find."

Albie looked at his watch. "I think we're pressing our luck. Let the GC waste time digging through it, and then *they* can cook it. We need to be gone from here as soon as we can."

"You're the expert," Rayford said. "You want a vote, Buck?"

"I'm with you, D—ah, Captain."

At Palwaukee Albie stayed in character and informed the in-residence tower man that the procurement of the chopper and the fuel for the fighter and Gulfstream should all be kept under the same GC order number. Greasy haired and short on sleep, the big man seemed as thrilled as he had been hours before to be doing his duty to the GC and particularly to the deputy commander.

"Did you see the news, sir?" the man said. "The wonderful, wonderful news?"

"Did I ever," Albie said. "Thanks for your kindness. Now we must be off."

"My pleasure, Deputy Commander, sir! A pleasure indeed. If you ever need anything else, don't hes—"

Buck was left to nod to the man. Albie was off to the freshly refueled jet, and Rayford to the chopper.

* * *

David searched and searched for Annie, unable to raise her on the phone and not willing to holler for her over the midafternoon crowds. Finally he rushed back to his office, flipped on the TV so he could catch Carpathia's final remarks, and got on his computer to be sure the new safe house was accessible.

He called Rayford, who filled him in on everything since they had last spoken. "I *can* trust Albie, can't I, David?"

"Albie? He was your find, wasn't he? We've been working fairly closely lately. I think he's the best, and you and Mac always said he was. Anyway, he's one of us now, right?"

"Right."

"If you doubt him, check his mark."

"Apparently you don't insult Middle Eastern men that way."

"Hey! Captain! You're talking to one."

"Would someone checking your mark insult you?"

"Well, I suppose if you did, after knowing me so long. I mean, I don't think you ever have."

"If I can't trust you, David, who can I trust?"

"I'd say the same about Albie, but you're the one who needs to feel right about it. We're getting in pretty deep with him, looks like."

"I've decided to take the risk."

"That's good enough for me. Let me know when you get to the Strong Building. You going to try to put down inside the tower?"

"Not with this load. I'll keep the chopper as inconspicuous as I can so it won't be seen from the air."

"The most you'd have to worry about would be satellite shots, because no planes are flying low enough to shoot anything meaningful. But if you get unloaded and can determine before daybreak that the chopper can be housed way up inside there, you'd better do it."

"Roger."

"I'm unlocking everything in the place for you. I'd get in, get settled, and stay quiet and out of sight."

"We need some black spray paint."

"Can do. Where should I ship it?"

"Kankakee, I guess."

"You got it. Rayford? How is Tsion?"

"Chaim and Buck are the banged-up ones."

"But they're going to be all right, right?"

"Looks like it."

"Tsion is the one I worry about. We need him online and doing what he does best."

Rayford guessed he was halfway to the safe house. "I hear that, David. I just hope we can transmit out of the new place like we could out of the old."

"Should be able to. When the day comes for Mac and Smitty and Annie and me to get out of here, we'll come and set up the greatest communications center you can imagine. Hey, you've got your laptop, right?"

"I had left it in Mount Prospect. I'll get back online in Chicago."

"Good, because I sent you a list I found, made by a woman named Viv Ivins, Carpathia's oldest confidante. It shows the ten kingdoms with their new names, but it also has a number assigned to each one. There has to be some significance, but I can't decipher it, at least not yet."

"You haven't put one of your fancy computer programs on it by now?"

"Soon, but I don't care what it takes or who figures it out. I just want to know what it means and whether there's any advantage to our knowing it."

"We'll take a shot at it. For now it's going to be great to be back together, all in one place, getting caught up with each other, getting acquainted better with the newcomers, and reestablishing some order."

"I'll know when you get in. I've got my cameras on."

With his computer set, David wanted to return his attention to finding Annie. There were a thousand reasons she might be hard to locate, but he'd rather not consider any of them. He stood and stretched, noticing that the TV picture had changed. The network had switched from a wide shot of the receiving trilogy of Leon, Viv, and Nick and now moved in on Nicolae.

He had stepped down a few rows and looked directly into the camera. In spite of himself, David could see why the man was so riveting. Besides the rugged, European handsomeness, he really sold the care and compassion. David knew he was insidious, but his smarminess didn't show.

The announcer said, "Ladies and gentlemen of the Global Community, your Supreme Potentate, His Excellency Nicolae Carpathia."

Nicolae took one step closer to the camera, forcing it to refocus. He looked directly into the lens.

"My dear subjects," he began. "We have, together, endured quite a week, have we not? I was deeply touched by the millions who made the effort to come to New Babylon for what turned out to be, gratefully, not my funeral. The outpouring of emotion was no less encouraging to me.

"As you know and as I have said, there remain small pockets of resistance to our cause of peace and harmony. There are even those who have made a career of saying the most hurtful, blasphemous, and false statements about me, using terms for me that no person would ever want to be called.

"I believe you will agree that I proved today who I am and who I am not. You will do well to follow your heads and your hearts and continue to follow me. You know what you saw, and your eyes do not lie. I am also eager to welcome into the one-world fold any former devotees of the radical fringe who have become convinced that I am not the enemy. On the contrary, I may be the very object of the devotion of their own religion, and I pray they will not close their minds to that possibility.

"In closing let me speak directly to the opposition. I have always, without rancor or acrimony, allowed divergent views. There are those among you, however, who have referred overtly to me personally as the Antichrist and this period of history as the Tribulation. You may take the following as my personal pledge:

"If you insist on continuing with your subversive attacks on my character and on the world harmony I have worked so hard to engender, the word *tribulation* will not begin to describe what is in store for you. If the last three and a half years are your idea of tribulation, wait until you endure the Great Tribulation."

THE MARK

✠ ✠ ✠

To Linda and Rennie,
with gratitude

1

IT WAS MIDAFTERNOON in New Babylon, and David Hassid was frantic. Annie was nowhere in sight and he had heard nothing from her, yet he could barely turn his eyes from the gigantic screens in the palace courtyard. The image of the indefatigable Nicolae Carpathia, freshly risen from three days dead, filled the screen and crackled with energy. David believed if he was within reach of the man he could be electrocuted by some demonic charge.

With the disappearance of his love fighting for his attention, David found himself drawn past the jumbo monitors and the guards and the crowds to the edge of the bier that had just hours before displayed the quite dead body of the king of the world.

Should David be able to see evidence that the man was now indwelt by Satan himself? The body, the hair, the complexion, the look were the same. But an intensity, an air of restlessness and alertness, flowed from the eyes. Though he smiled and talked softly, it was as if Nicolae could barely contain the monster within. Controlled fury, violence delayed, revenge in abeyance played at the muscles in his neck and shoulders. David half expected him to burst from his suit and then from his very skin, exposed to the world as the repulsive serpent he was.

David's attention was diverted briefly by someone next to Carpathia, and when he glanced back at the still ruggedly handsome face, he was not prepared to have caught the eye of the enemy of his soul. Nicolae knew him, of course, but the look, though it contained recognition, did not carry the usual acceptance and encouragement David was used to. That very welcoming gaze had always unnerved him, yet he preferred it over this. For this was a transparent gaze that seemed to pass through David, which nearly moved him to step forward and confess his treachery and that of every comrade in the Tribulation Force.

David reminded himself that not even Satan himself was omniscient, yet he found it difficult to accept that these eyes were not those of one who knew his every secret. He wanted to run but he dared not, and he was grateful when Nicolae turned back to the task at hand: his role as the object of the world's worship.

David hurried back to his post, but someone had appropriated his golf cart, and he found himself peeved to where he wanted to pull rank. He flipped open his phone, had trouble finding his voice, but finally barked at the motor-pool supervisor, "I had better have a vehicle delivered within 120 seconds or someone is going to find his—"

"An electric cart, sir?" the man said, his accent making David guess he was an Aussie.

"Of course!"

"They're scarce here, Director, but—"

"They must be, because someone absconded with mine!"

"But I was going to say that I would be happy to lend you mine, under the circumstances."

"The circumstances?"

"The resurrection, of course! Tell you the truth, Director Hassid, I'd love to get in line myself."

"Just bring—"

"You think I could do that, sir? I mean if I were in uniform? I know they've turned away civilians not inside the courtyard, and they're none too happy, but as an employee—"

"I don't know! I need a cart and I need it now!"

"Would you drive me to the venue before you go wherever it is you have to g—"

"Yes! Now hurry!"

"Are you thrilled or what, Director?"

"What?"

The man spoke slowly, condescendingly. "A-bout-the-res-ur-rec-tion!"

"Are you in your vehicle?" David demanded.

"Yes, sir."

"That's what I'm thrilled about."

The man was still talking when David hung up on him and called crowd control. "I'm looking for Annie Christopher," he said.

"Sector?"

"Five-three."

"Sector 53 has been cleared, Director. She may have been reassigned or relieved."

"If she were reassigned, you'd have it, no?"

"Checking."

The motor-pool chief appeared in his cart, beaming. David boarded, phone still to his ear. "Gonna see god," the man said.

"Yeah," David said. "Just a minute."

"Can you believe it? He's got to be god. Who else can he be? Saw it with my own two eyes, well, on TV anyway. Raised from the dead. I saw him dead, I know that. If I see him in person, there'll be no doubt now, will there? Eh?"

David nodded, sticking a finger in his free ear.

"I say no doubt, eh?"

"No doubt!" David shouted. "Now give me a minute!"

"Where we goin', sport?"

David craned his neck to look at the man, incredulous that he was still speaking.

"I say, where we going? Am I dropping you or you dropping me?"

"I'm dropping you! Go where you want and get out!"

"Sor-*ry!*"

This wasn't how David normally treated people, even ignorant ones. But he had to hear whether Annie had been reassigned, and where. "Nothing," the crowd-control dispatcher on the phone told him.

"Relieved then?" he said, relieved himself.

"Likely. Nothing in our system on her."

David thought of calling Medical Services but scolded himself for overreacting.

Motor-pool Man deftly picked his way through the massive, dispersing crowd. At least most were dispersing. They looked shocked. Some were angry. They had waited hours to see the body, and now that Carpathia had arisen, they were not going to be able to see him, all because of where they happened to be in the throng.

"This is as close as I hope to get in this thing then," the man said, skidding to a stop so abruptly that David had to catch himself. "You'll bring it back round then, eh, sir?"

"Of course," David said, trying to gather himself to at least thank the man. As he slid into the driver's seat he said, "Been back to Australia since the reorganizing?"

The man furrowed his brow and pointed at David, as if to reprimand him. "Man of your station ought to be able to tell the difference between an Aussie and a New Zealander."

"My mistake," David said. "Thanks for the wheels."

As he pulled away the man shouted, "'Course we're all proud citizens of the United Pacific States now anyway!"

David tried to avoid eye contact with the many disgruntled mourners turned celebrants who tried to flag him, not for rides but for information. At times he was forced to brake to keep from running someone down, and the request was always the same. In one distinct accent or another, everyone wanted the same thing. "Any way we can still get in to see His Excellency?"

"Can't help you," David said. "Move along, please. Official business."

"Not fair! Wait all night and half the day in the blistering sun, and for what?"

But others danced in the streets, making up songs and chants about Carpathia, their new god. David glanced again at the monstrous monitors where Carpathia was shown briefly touching hands as the last several thousand were herded through. To David's left, guards fought to block hopefuls from sneaking into the courtyard. "Line's closed!" they shouted over and over.

On the screen, pilgrims swooned as they neared the bier, graced by Nicolae in his glory. Many crumbled from merely getting near him, waxing catatonic. Guards held them up to keep them moving, but when His Excellency himself spoke quietly to them and touched them, some passed out, deadweights in the guards' arms.

Over Nicolae's cooing—"Good to see you. Thank you for coming. Bless you. Bless you."—David heard Leon Fortunato. "Worship your king," he said soothingly. "Bow before his majesty. Worship the Lord Nicolae, your god."

Dissonance came from the guards stuck with the responsibility of moving the mass of quivering, jellied humanity, catching them as they collapsed in ecstasy. "Ridiculous!" they grumbled to each other, live mikes sending the cacophony of Fortunato, Carpathia, and the complainers to the ends of the PA system. "Keep moving. Come on now! There you go! Stand up! Move it along!"

David finally reached sector 53, which was, as he had been told, deserted. The crowd-control gates had toppled, and the giant number placard had been trampled. David sat there, forearms resting on the cart's steering wheel. He shoved his uniform cap back on his head and felt the sting of the sun's UV rays. His hands looked like lobsters, and he knew he'd pay for his hours in the sun. But he could not find shade again until he found Annie.

As crowds shuffled through and then around what had been her sector, David squinted at the ground, the asphalt shimmering. Besides the ice-cream and candy wrappers and drink cups that lay motionless in the windless heat was what appeared to be residue of medical supplies. He was about to step from the cart for a closer look when an elderly couple climbed aboard and asked to be driven to the airport shuttle area.

"This is not a people mover," he said absently, having enough presence to remove the keys before leaving the vehicle.

"How rude!" the woman said.

"Come on," the man said.

David marched to sector 53 and knelt, the heat sapping his energy. In the shadows of hundreds walking by, he examined the plastic empties of bandages, gauze, ointment, even tubing. Someone had been ministered to here. It didn't have to have been Annie. It could have been anyone. Still, he had to know. He made his way back to the cart, every seat but his now full.

"Unless you need to go to Medical Services," he said, punching the number into his phone, "you're in the wrong cart."

* * *

In Chicago Rayford Steele found the Strong Building's ninth floor enough of a bonanza that he was able to push from his mind misgivings about Albie. The truth about his dark, little Middle Eastern friend would be tested soon enough. Albie was to ferry a fighter jet from Palwaukee to Kankakee, where Rayford would later pick him up in a Global Community helicopter.

Besides discovering a room full of the latest desktop and minicomputers—still in their original packaging—Rayford found a small private sleeping room adjacent to a massive executive office. It was outfitted like a luxurious hotel room, and he rushed from floor to floor to find the same next to at least four offices on every level.

"We have more amenities than we ever dreamed," he told the exhausted Tribulation Force. "Until we can blacken the windows, we'll have to get some of the beds into the corridors near the elevators where they can't be seen from the outside."

"I thought no one ever came near here," Chloe said, Kenny sleeping in her lap and Buck dozing with his head on her shoulder.

"Never know what satellite imaging shows," Rayford said. "We could be sleeping soundly while GC Security and Intelligence forces snap our pictures from the stratosphere."

"Let me get these two to bed somewhere," she said, "before I collapse."

"I've moved furniture in my day," Leah said, slowly rising. "Where are these beds and where do we put them?"

"I wish I could help," Chaim said through clenched teeth, his jaw still wired shut.

Rayford stopped him with a gesture. "If you're staying with us, sir, you answer to me. We need you and Buck as healthy as you can be."

"And I need you alert for study," Tsion said. "You made me cram for enough exams. Now you're in for the crash course of your life."

Rayford, Chloe, Leah, and Tsion spent half an hour moving beds up the elevator to makeshift quarters in an inner corridor on the twenty-fifth floor. By the time Rayford gingerly boarded the chopper balanced precariously on what served as the new roof of the tower, everyone was asleep save Tsion. The rabbi seemed to gain a second wind, and Rayford wasn't sure why.

Rayford left the instrument panel lights on and, of course, the outside lights off. He fired up the rotors but waited to lift off until his eyes had adjusted to the darkness. The copter had twenty feet of clearance on each side. Little was trickier—especially to a fixed-wing expert like Rayford—than the shifting currents inside what amounted to a cavernous smokestack. Rayford had seen choppers crash in wide-open spaces after merely hovering too long in one place. Mac McCullum had tried to explain the physics of it, but Rayford had not listened closely enough to grasp it. Something about the rotors sucking up air from beneath the craft, leaving it no buoyancy. By the time the pilot realized he was dropping through dead air of his own making, he had destroyed the equipment and often killed all on board.

Rayford needed sleep as much as any of his charges, but he had to go get Albie. There was more to that too, of course. He could have called his friend and told him to lie low till the following evening. But Albie was new to the country and would have to fend for himself outside or bluff his way into a hotel. With Carpathia resurrected and the GC naturally on heightened alert, who knew how long he could pull off impersonating a GC officer?

Anyway, Rayford had to know whether Albie was "with him or agin him," as his father used to say. He had been thrilled to see the mark of the believer on Albie's forehead, but much of what the man had done in the predawn hours confused Rayford and made him wonder. A wily, streetwise man like Albie—one who had provided so much at high risk to himself—would be the worst kind of opponent. Rayford worried that he had unwittingly led the Tribulation Force into the lair of the enemy.

As the chopper rumbled through the shaft at the top of the tower, Rayford held his breath. He had carefully set the craft as close to the middle of the space as he could, allowing him to use one corner for his guide as he rose. If he kept the whirring blades equidistant from the walls in the one corner, he should be centered until free of the building.

How vulnerable and conspicuous could a man feel? He imagined David Hassid having miscalculated, trusting old information, not realizing that the GC itself knew Chicago was safe—not off-limits due to radiation. Rayford himself had overheard Carpathia say he had not used radiation on the city, at least initially. He wondered if the GC had planted such information just to lure in the insurgents and have them where they wanted them—in one place for easy dispatch.

With his helicopter free of the tower, Rayford still dared not engage the lights. He would stay low, hopefully beneath radar. He wanted to be invisible to satellite surveillance photography as well, but heat sensing had been so refined that the dark whirlybird would glow orange on a monitor.

A chill ran up his back as he let his imagination run. Was he being followed by a half dozen craft just like his own? He wouldn't hear or see them. They could have waited nearby, even on the ground. How would he know?

Since when did he manufacture trouble? There was enough real danger without concocting more.

Rayford set the instrument panel lights at their lowest level and quickly saw he was off course. It was an easy fix, but so much for trusting his brain, even in a ship like this. Mac had once told him that piloting a helicopter was to flying a 747 as riding a bike was to driving a sport utility vehicle. From that Rayford assumed that he would do more work by the seat of his pants than by marrying himself to the instrument panel. But neither had he planned on flying blind over a deserted megalopolis in wee-hour blackness. He had to get to Kankakee, pick up Albie, and get back to the tower before sunup. He had not a minute to spare. The last thing he wanted was to be seen over a restricted area in broad daylight. Detected in the dead of night was one thing. He would take his chances, trust his instincts. But there would be no hiding under the sun, and he would die before he would lead anyone to the new safe house.

+ + +

In New Babylon frustrated supplicants had formed a new line, several thousand long, outside the Global Community Palace. GC guards traversed the length of it, telling people that the resurrected potentate would have to leave the courtyard when he had finished greeting those who happened to be in the right place at the right time.

David detoured from his route to Medical Services to hear the response of the crowd. They did not move, did not disperse. The guards, their bullhorned messages ignored, finally stopped to listen. David, looking puzzled, pulled up behind one of the Jeeps, and a guard shrugged as if as dumbfounded as Director Hassid. The guard with the loudspeaker said, "Suit yourselves, but this is an exercise in futility."

"We have another idea!" shouted a man with a Hispanic accent.

"I'm listening," the guard said, as the crowd near him quieted.

"We will worship the statue!" he said, and hundreds in line cheered.

"What did he say? What did he say?" The question raced down the line in both directions.

"Did not Supreme Commander Fortunato say we should do that?" the man said.

"Where are you from, my friend?" the guard asked, admiration in his voice.

"Méjico!" the man shouted in his native tongue, and many with him exulted.

"You have the heart of the toreador!" the guard said. "Let me check on it!"

The news spread as the guard settled in his seat and talked into his phone. Suddenly he stood and gave the man a thumbs-up. "You have been cleared to worship the image of His Excellency, the risen potentate!"

The crowd cheered.

"In fact, your leaders consider it a capital idea!"

The crowd sang and chanted, edging closer and closer to the courtyard.

"Please maintain order!" the guard urged. "It will be more than an hour before you will be allowed in. But you *will* get your wish!"

David shook his head as he executed a huge U-turn and headed to the courtyard. People along the way called out to him. "Is it true? May we at least worship the statue?"

David ignored most of them, but when clusters moved in front of his speeding cart, he was forced to brake before slipping around them. Occasionally he nodded, to their delight. They ran to get in a line that already stretched more than a quarter mile. Would this day ever end?

2

RAYFORD MENTALLY KICKED himself. He had vastly underestimated the time and his ability to pick up Albie, settle on the disposition of both the fighter jet and the Gulfstream, and get back to the new safe house before sunrise. The sun was already toying with the horizon. He patted his pants pocket for his phone. He felt for it in his flight bag, his jacket, on the floor.

He wanted to swear, but since coming to his senses just days before, Rayford acknowledged that he needed a return to discipline. He had learned from an old friend in college something he had then rejected as too esoteric and way too touchy-feely. His broad-minded friend had called it his "opposite trigger" mode, and while in it, he forced himself to respond in ways diametrically opposed to how he felt. If he wanted to shout, he whispered. If he wanted to smack someone, he gently caressed his or her shoulder.

Rayford hadn't thought about that old friend or his crazy idea until the lonely, emotional flight from the Middle East to Greece and then to the United North American States. And now he decided to try it. He wanted to swear at himself for being shortsighted and for losing his phone. Instead, he surveyed his mind for an opposite response. One opposite of swearing was blessing, but whom would he bless? Another was praying.

"Lord," he began, "once again I need some help. I'm mad at myself and have few options. I'm exhausted, but I need to know what to do."

Almost instantly Rayford remembered that Albie had his phone. Albie had a phone of his own, too, but in the bustle and grabbing of various items, Rayford had entrusted his to his friend. Sometime soon he would have to get someone to rig a radio base in the safe house with a secure channel to the chopper so he could communicate directly. Meanwhile, he couldn't tell the rest of the Tribulation Force where he was or that he would not be returning until at least late that same evening.

Neither could he determine whether Albie was all right. He would have to simply land, using his alias with the tower, and hope Albie was waiting for him.

* * *

David left messages on Annie's phone and tried every other source he could think of that might know her whereabouts. Medical Services was too busy to look her up on their computers. "She wouldn't be in the system yet," he was told, "even if she were here."

"You're not swiping bar codes on the badges of employees as they are admitted?"

"They're not actually being admitted, Director. Everybody goes to triage, the living are treated, and the dead pronounced. Cataloging them is low on the priority list, but we'll eventually get everyone logged in."

"How will I know if she's there?"

"You may come look, but don't interfere and keep out of the way."

"Where's triage?"

"As far east as you can go from our main tent. We try to start 'em in the shade of three tents, but we're out of space and they're in and out of there as fast as we can move 'em."

"Mostly sunstroke?" David said.

"Mostly lightning, Director."

* * *

"Tower to GC chopper! Do you copy?"

"This is GC chopper, Kankakee," Rayford said, trying to cover that he was rattled. "My apologies. Asleep at the stick here."

"Not literally, I hope."

"No, sir."

"State your business."

"Uh, yeah, civilian under the authority of Deputy Commander Marcus Elbaz."

"Mr. Berry?"

"Roger."

"Deputy Commander Elbaz asks that we set your mind at ease about your phone."

"Roger that!"

"Cleared for landing to the south where he will meet you in Hangar 2. You can appreciate we're shorthanded here. You can handle your own securing and refueling."

Ten minutes later Rayford asked Albie how long he thought he could keep up the ruse on the GC. "As long as your comrade Hassid is in the saddle at the palace. He's a remarkable young man, Rayford. I confess I had to hold my breath more than once here. They were tough, short of personnel as they are. I had to go through two checkpoints."

Rayford squinted. "They let me in without a second glance, and I hadn't even contacted the tower."

"That's because you're with me and a civilian."

"You convinced 'em, eh?"

"Totally. But I have to hand it to your friend. Not only does he have me on the international GC database with name, rank, and serial number, but he also has me assigned to this part of the United North American States. I'm here because I'm supposed to be here. I check out better than most of the legitimate GC personnel."

"David's good," Rayford said.

"The best. I blustered and acted impatient and pretended they would get in trouble if they detained me too long. But they were unmoved—until the second checkpoint ran me through the computer and reached David's database. Someday he'll have to tell me how he does that. He entered all of my information, and when my papers matched with what they saw on the screen, I was gold. Then I began barking orders, telling them to pave the way for you, that we had urgent business and must be on our way."

Rayford told Albie it would be impossible to return to the safe house until dark and that he might as well carry him back to Palwaukee so he could move the Gulfstream to Kankakee.

"Would you rather have some fun?" Albie said. "You want to see if GC has torched your old safe house yet and do it for them if not?"

"Not a bad idea," Rayford said. "If they just burned it, fine, but if they start combing it for evidence, I worry what we might have left."

"They don't have the personnel for that," Albie said, moving toward the helicopter. "Fueled up?"

Rayford nodded.

"The fighter is too, ready whenever we need it." Albie slung his bag over his shoulder, dug in it for Rayford's phone, and tossed it to him.

"Three unanswered calls," Rayford muttered as they boarded the chopper. "Hope everything's all right in Chicago. When did the calls come?"

"All three about half an hour ago, one right after the other. None showed phone numbers, so I didn't think I should answer for you."

They were strapped in now, but Rayford said, "I'd better check with the safe house."

Tsion answered groggily.

"I'm sorry to wake you, Doctor," Rayford began.

"Oh, Captain Steele, it's no trouble. I only just fell asleep. Chloe's phone, it was ringing and ringing, and she was sound asleep. No one roused; they are so exhausted. I was not able to get to it in time, but when it rang again, this time I hurried and carried it to a quiet place. Rayford, it was Miss Durham!"

"You're sure?"

"Yes, and she sounded desperate. I pleaded with her to tell me where she was and reminded her that we all love her and care about her and are praying for her, but she wanted only to talk to you. She said she had tried your phone, and I told her I would try too. I tried twice to no avail. Anyway, you have her number."

"I'll call her."

"And you'll let me know."

"Tsion, get some rest. You have so much to do, setting up your computer area, teaching Chaim—"

"Oh, Rayford, I am so excited about that that I can barely contain myself. And I have so much to communicate to my audience on the computer. But you must call Miss Durham, and yes, you're right. Unless there is a compelling reason why we should know, you can tell us when you return. Frankly, I expected you by now."

"I miscalculated, Tsion. I can't return until the sky is black. But I am available by phone now."

"And you have connected with your Middle Eastern friend."

"I have."

"And is he all right, Rayford? Forgive me, but he seemed preoccupied."

"Everything's fine here, Doctor."

"He is a new believer too, correct?"

"Yes."

"And he will be staying with us?"

"That's likely."

"Then I will look forward to training him as well."

+ + +

David was aghast at Medical Services. He had visited their indoor facility many times, which, despite their thinning ranks, was pristine and shipshape. What had begun as the main first-aid station, which serviced dozens of others throughout the area during the Carpathia wake, now looked like a mobile army surgical hospital.

The rest of the first-aid stations were being dismantled and leftover injured taken either to the courtyard triage center or into the indoor facility.

Row upon row of makeshift cots snaked across the courtyard. "Why aren't you moving these people inside?" David said, tugging at his stiff collar.

"Why don't you manage your area and let us manage ours," a doctor said, turning briefly from an ashen victim of the heat.

"I don't mean to criticize. It's just that—"

"It's just that we're all out here now," the doctor said. "At least most of us. The majority of the treatable cases are heatstroke and dehydration, and most of the casualties are lightning victims."

"I'm looking for—"

"I'm sorry, Director, but whoever you're looking for, you're going to have to find on your own. We don't care about their names or their nationalities. We're just trying to keep them alive. We'll deal with the paperwork later."

"I had an employee stationed at—"

"I'm sorry! It's not that I don't care, but I can't help you! Understand?"

"She would have known how to avoid sun- or heatstroke."

"Good. Now, good-bye."

"She was at sector 53."

"Well, you don't want to hear about five-three," the doctor said, turning back to his patient.

"What about it?"

"Lots of lightning victims. Big bolt there."

"Where would the victims have been taken?"

The doctor was finished talking with David. He nodded to an assistant. "Tell him."

A young man in scrubs spoke with a French accent. "No specific place. Some came in here. Some were treated in that sector. Some inside."

David started on the cart but soon abandoned it to jog down the line of victims. This would be impossible. How could he tell who was who? Annie was in uniform, and while he was sure he could recognize her, with only shoes peeking out from sheets soaked to cool patients, he would have to check each face. And he would be interfering with the medical treatment.

As he trotted along in the heat, David reached in his belt for his water bottle and found it empty. His throat was parched, and he knew his thirst trailed by several minutes his real need for water. When had he last taken a swig? When had he eaten? When had he slept?

The huge screens showed Viv Ivins, Leon Fortunato, and Nicolae Carpathia moving the pilgrims along, cooing to them, blessing them, touching them. The waves of heat from the asphalt made David's uniform cling to him like a single, damp weight. He stopped and bent to catch his breath, but his throat felt swollen, his mouth unable to produce saliva, his windpipe constricted. *Dizzy. Annie. Light-headed. Hot. Annie. Spinning. Thirst. Hands red.*

David pitched forward, his cap sliding off and tumbling before him. His mind told him to reach for it, but his hands stayed planted above his knees. *Break your fall! Break your fall!* But he could not. His arms would not move. His face would take the brunt of it. No, he could tuck his chin.

The top of his head smacked the pavement, the jagged asphalt digging through his hair to his scalp. He shut his eyes in anticipation of the pain, and white streaks shot past his eyes. Hands still on his knees, his seat in the air, he slowly, slowly rolled sideways and crashed onto his hip. He opened his eyes and saw his own blood trickle past his face, quickly coagulating in a pool on the baked pavement. He tried to move, to speak. Unconsciousness pursued him, and all he could think of was that he was next in a long line of victims.

+ + +

"You want me to fly while you make your call?" Albie said.

"Maybe you'd better," Rayford said. They switched places as he punched in Hattie's number. She answered in a hoarse, panicked whisper on the first sound.

"Rayford, where are you?"

"I don't want to say, Hattie. Talk to me. Where are you?"

"Colorado."

"Specifically."

"Pueblo, north end, I think."

"GC has you?"

"Yes. And they're going to send me back to Buffer." Rayford was silent. "Don't leave me hanging, Rayford. We go back too far."

"Hattie, I don't know what to say."

"What?!"

"What do you want me to do?"

"Come get me! I can't go back to Belgium! I'll die there."

"What do you expect me to do?"

"The right thing, Ray."

"In other words, jeopardize my life and expose the Force to—"

Click.

Rayford couldn't tell whether she hung up because he had insulted her or because she heard someone coming. He told Albie the conversation.

"What are you going to do, my friend?"

Rayford stared at Albie in the emerging light and shook his head. "That woman has caused us no end of grief."

"But you care for her. You've told me before."

"I have?"

"Bits and pieces. Maybe Mac told me."

"Mac doesn't know her."

"But he knows you, and you talk, no?"

Rayford nodded. "We know they let her out of Buffer, thinking she—"

"Buffer?"

"Belgium Facility for Female Rehabilitation."

"Ah, I'd better remember that."

"Anyway, we know they were hoping she would lead them to us at the gala in Jerusalem, but she—"

"Excuse me, Rayford, but do you want me to set a course over the old safe house or just head directly for Palwaukee?"

"Depends on whether I decide to go to Colorado."

"Your choice, but if I may say so, I expected you to be more decisive. I am just playacting, yet I appear more of a leader than you are. Your people admire and respect you—it's obvious."

"They shouldn't. I—"

"You've reconciled with them, Rayford. They forgave you. Now become their leader again. What are you going to do about this Hattie Durham? Decide. Tell me, tell the people in the Strong Building, and do it."

"I don't know, Albie."

"You'll never *know*. Just weigh your options, consider the pros and cons, and pull the trigger. Either way, the old safe house is fewer than ten minutes out of the way. Start with a small decision."

"Let's have a look at it."

"Good for you, Rayford."

"Don't patronize me, Albie. We're in a GC chopper. We won't look suspicious anyway."

"But you've made a decision. Now think aloud about the more important one. Are we going to Colorado?"

"I was saying, rather than lead the GC to us, she went straight there. Her family is gone, but maybe she thought she could hook up with friends in Colorado. Who knows? I couldn't even tell you whether her confounding the GC was a stroke of genius or dumb luck, but I'd lean toward the latter."

"So she may be leading *you* to *them* rather than the other way round."

Rayford turned away from Albie and looked out the window, praying silently. It hadn't been that many years since his lust for Hattie Durham had almost cost him his marriage. He took the blame for that, but since then she had been nothing but trouble. He and the others in the Tribulation Force had loved her and counseled her, provided for her, pled with her to receive Christ. But she would not be persuaded, and she pulled dangerous stunts that compromised the safety of the Force. For all he knew, she was the reason the GC had finally discovered the safe house.

Rayford's phone chirped. "Hattie?"

"I heard footsteps. They've got me in a small room in a bunker about an hour south of Colorado Springs."

"I'm a long way from there."

"Oh, thank you, Rayford. I knew I could count—"

"I haven't decided what I'm going to do, Hattie."

"Of course you have. You won't leave me here to be sent back to prison or worse. What do I have to do, promise to become a believer?"

"Not unless you mean it."

"Well, if you *don't* come for me, you can kiss that idea good-bye."

Rayford slapped his phone shut and sighed. "What an idiot!"

"Her?" Albie said. "Or you for considering what you're considering?"

"Her! This is such a transparent attempt by the GC to lure one of us out there. Once they get me, they hold me ransom for information on the rest of the Force. Who they really want, of course, is Tsion. The rest of us are irritants. He's the enemy."

"So your choice is between this Miss Durham and Tsion Ben-Judah? You want my vote?"

"It's not that easy. We want her for the kingdom, Albie. I mean, we all really do."

"And you think if you abandon her now, she'll never believe."

"She said as much."

"This may sound cold, and I admit I'm new to this, but it's her choice, isn't it? You're not making the decision for her."

"Going out there would be the dumbest thing I've ever done. They've caught her, detained her, threatened to take her back to prison, and yet they leave her with her phone. I mean, come on."

Albie scanned the horizon. "Then your decision is easy."

"I wish."

"It *is.* Either you don't go, or you consider all your resources."

"What does that mean?"

"There's one it seems you've forgotten. Maybe two."

"I'll bite."

"Assign David Hassid to find out exactly where they have her and have him send through an order from a bogus commander to keep her there until further notice. You call her back and tell her you're not coming. Make her and whoever is listening in believe it. You just show up, surprise attack, just when both she and the GC think you have abandoned her."

Rayford pursed his lips. "Maybe you ought to be in charge of the Trib Force. But surprising them doesn't guarantee success. I'll still likely be killed or detained myself."

"But you've forgotten another resource."

"I'm still listening."

+ + +

"Sir? Director? Are you all right?"

"He's out."

"His eyes are open, Doctor."

"He fell on his head, Medicine Woman."

"I've asked you not to call me th—"

"Sorry. I don't know how you handled fallen braves on the reservation, but this one couldn't even break his fall. He couldn't shut his eyes if he wanted to."

"Help me get him onto—"

"There you go again, sweetie. I'm not an orderly."

"And there *you* go again, *Doc*tor! We can let him lie here and bleed to death, or I can remind you that our patients way outnumber the help."

David's tongue was swollen, and he could not maneuver it to form the word. All he wanted was water, but he knew his head required attention too.

"Spray!" the dark nurse called out, and someone tossed her a bottle. She sprayed three bursts of lukewarm water directly into David's face, and he couldn't even blink. Compared to the heat of the asphalt, which he estimated at 120 degrees, the water felt icy. A few drops reached his mouth and he panted, trying to drink them in.

The doctor and nurse gently rolled him to his back, and in his mind he was squinting against the harsh sun. Yet he knew his eyes were wide open and burning. He wanted to plead for another spray, but he felt paralyzed. The nurse mercifully laid his cap over his face, and when feeling returned, he tried not to move so as to keep the cap in place.

If he could find his voice he would plead for Annie, but he was helpless. She was probably somewhere looking for him.

When David was lifted to a canvas cot, the hat slipped off his face, but he was able to blink and was soon under the shade of a crowded tent. He had been assigned the last sliver of shadow. "Critical?" someone asked.

"No," the doctor said. "But sew that head up soon."

The first syringe that plunged into his scalp made his whole body jerk and shudder, but still he could not call out. In seconds the top of his head was numb. "You can do this?" the doctor said.

The nurse said, "It's not exactly cosmetic, is it?"

"Give him threads like a football—I don't care. He can always wear a hat."

In truth, David didn't care what his head looked like, and it was a good thing, because the nurse quickly shaved an inch on each side of the laceration, splashed more liquid on him, and began opening a huge needle.

"How bah?" David managed, his tongue lolling.

"You'll live," she said. "Strictly superficial. Tough skull. But you really yanked the flesh away from the bone. Five inches at least, laterally at the top."

"Watah?"

"Sorry."

"Little?"

She quickly removed the top of the spray bottle, which had an inch of water left in it. "Open up."

Most of it ran down David's neck, but it loosened his tongue. "Looking for Chief Christopher," he said.

"Don't know him," she said. "Now hold still."

"*Her.* Annie Christopher."

"Director, I've got about five minutes for you, and if you're lucky, I'll find an IV to rehydrate you. But while I'm sewing, you're going to have to shut up and hold still if you don't want to look worse."

+ + +

"Do you see what I see?" Albie squinted into the distance.

Rayford followed his gaze and was surprised by a gush of emotion. A black tower of smoke billowed several hundred feet in the air. "You think?" he said.

Albie nodded. "Gotta be."

"Get as close as you can," Rayford said. "That was my home for a long time."

"Will do. Now, you going to use every resource available? Or did I waste my money on this uniform and all the credentials?"

3

BUCK AWOKE AT NOON, Chicago time, and felt twice his age. As had been true every day since the Rapture, he knew exactly where he was. In the past it was not uncommon to wake up in a foreign city and have to remind himself where he was, who he was, and what he was doing there. No more. Even when exhausted and injured and barely able to function, somehow the self-preservation flywheel kept spinning in his otherwise unengaged mind.

He had slept soundly, but at the first flutter of his eyelids and that initial glance at his watch, he knew. It all made sense in a ludicrous way. Buck stared at the wall next to an elevator in a bombed-out skyscraper in Chicago, heard muffled voices from around the corner, smelled coffee and a baby. Kenny had his own aroma, a fresh, powdery sweetness that Buck conjured when they were far apart.

But Kenny was here, barricaded from the outer hallways exposed to the windows that let in the midday sun. Buck rolled to his back and propped himself up on his elbows. Kenny had apparently given up trying to climb the makeshift barrier and sat contentedly playing with one of his loose shoelaces.

"Hey, Kenny Bruce," Buck whispered. "Come see Daddy."

Kenny's head jerked up, and then he went to all fours before righting himself and toddling to the bed. "Da-da."

Buck reached for him, and the chubby bundle climbed atop him and stretched out on his stomach and chest. Buck let his head fall back again and wrapped his arms around Kenny. The boy seldom had the patience to simply rest in his father's arms, but now he seemed almost ready to nap himself. With the baby's tiny heart beating against his own, Buck wished he could lie there forever.

"Da-da bye-bye?" Kenny said, and Buck could not stop the tears.

+ + +

Rayford had made a decision, several in fact. After watching the old safe house burn to the ground, he instructed Albie to turn back to Kankakee, where they would fly the GC fighter to Colorado.

"Now you're talking, Captain," Albie said.

"Now I'm talking," Rayford groused. "Now I'm probably getting us all killed."

"You're doing the right thing."

Unable to reach David in New Babylon, Rayford left a message asking him to get back to them with Hattie's exact whereabouts. He also asked David to inform GC personnel holding her that, should their current operation fail, they should keep Hattie there until assigned personnel could come for her.

David often overrode other GC systems to send such directives in a way that they could not be traced back to him. He was the one who assigned security codes to keep such transmissions from "enemies of the Global Community," so he was also able to use the channels without detection. "As soon as you can," Rayford recorded on David's private machine, "get back to Albie and me to confirm you've paved the way for us."

Before long Rayford would have to transmit his picture, with his new look and name, to David Hassid so the young Israeli could "enlist" him in the GC Peacekeeping Forces too. Meanwhile, he and Albie would put down at what was once Peterson Air Force Base, appropriate a GC Jeep David would reserve, follow his directions to this bunker, if that's what it was, and pick up the prisoner.

By the time Albie had stalled his landing until the fighter was short of fuel, Rayford had been dozing more than two hours. Albie woke him with the news that they had not yet heard back from David.

"Not good," Rayford said, placing yet another call to New Babylon. No answer. "You have a computer, Albie?"

"A subnotebook, but it's got satellite capability."

"Programmed to communicate with David?"

"If you've got his coordinates, I can make it work."

Rayford found the machine in Albie's flight bag. "Batteries are low," he said.

"Plug in to the plane's power," Albie said. "I don't do heavy-duty stuff on batteries anyway."

"Keep the power on after we land," Rayford said. "This could take a while."

Albie nodded and got on the radio to the GC outpost. "GC NB4047 to Peterson Tower."

"You ought to know we're now Carpathia Memorial, GC," came the reply.

"My mistake, tower," Albie said. "First time here in I don't know how long." He winked at Rayford, who glanced up from his computer work. Albie had never been in the States before.

"Gonna hafta take the *Memorial* out of our name, aren't we, 4047?"

"Come back?"

"He is risen."

Albie rolled his eyes at Rayford. "Yeah, I heard. That's something, eh?"

"You're supposed to reply with 'He is risen indeed.'"

Rayford pantomimed sticking his finger down his throat. Albie shook his head. "Well, I sure believe that, tower," he said, glancing at Rayford and pointing up.

"Business here?"

"Deputy Commander with confidential orders."

"Name?"

"Marcus Elbaz."

"One moment."

"Low on fuel, tower."

"Short on people here, Commander Elbaz. Give me a minute."

"We're putting down either way," Albie told Rayford, who was busy pecking in the details that would orient Albie's computer global-positioning hardware to a satellite that would link him directly with David's computer.

"There you are, sir," the tower said. "I see you on the system."

"Roger."

"Don't have you assigned out this way, though. You been to Kankakee?"

"That's where I came from."

"And your business here?"

"Repeat, confidential orders."

"Oh, yes, sorry. Anything we can help with?"

"Refueling and a ground vehicle should have been arranged."

"As I say, sir, we don't have your disposition here. We can refuel you, no problem, with the proper authorization code. Ground transportation is scarce."

"I'll trust you to figure something out."

"We're very shorthanded and—"

"You mentioned that."

"—and frankly, sir, there's no one here near your rank."

"Then I expect whoever's in command to obey my order for transportation."

A long pause.

"I'll, uh, pass that word along, sir."

"Thank you."

"And you're cleared to land."

* * *

David awoke in the palace hospital, his head throbbing so he could barely open his eyes. He shared a room with two sleeping patients. His clothes had been removed, and he lay there in a flimsy gown, an IV in his hand, his watch on a stand next to him. Holding it before his bleary eyes was almost more than he could bear. Twenty-one hundred hours. It couldn't be!

He tried to sit up and was aware of bandages around his head and over his ears. He heard his own pulse and felt pain with every beat. It was dark outside, but a silent TV monitor showed pilgrims still in the courtyard, passing by, kneeling, bowing, worshiping, praying to the gigantic statue of Nicolae.

On David's other side was the remote control. He didn't want to wake the other patients, but the captioning system was in Arabic. He fiddled with it until it changed to English, and the captions merely represented songs piped into the courtyard as people slowly passed by the image. He stared as the camera pulled back to show the immense crowd, seemingly as big as for the funeral, snaking a mile outside the palace.

David panicked. He had been away from his phone and computer longer than he had been in months. He craned his neck looking for a phone, and the pain nearly drove him to his pillow again. He pulled a cord ostensibly connected to the nurses' station, but no one came. He knew the ratio between nurses and patients was ridiculously low, but surely they knew he was a director. That should count for something.

However they were hydrating him was working, because he had to relieve himself in a bad way. No bedpan for him. He played with the controls on the side of the bed until one railing lowered. He grimaced as he swung his legs off the side, pausing to let the throbbing subside and catch his breath.

Finally he put both hands on the edge of the bed and eased himself to the floor. The marble was incongruously cold for such a hot part of the world, but it felt good. He stood, swaying, dizzy, waiting for his equilibrium to catch up. When he felt steadier he stepped toward the bathroom, reminded by a tug at his wrist that he was still hooked to the IV. He stepped back and wiggled the metal stand on rollers away from the wall and the end of the bed, but as he dragged it with him, it caught.

A monitor cord was plugged into the wall. He tried to remove it, but it wouldn't budge from the connection or the stand. David knew there had to be some simple trick to it. Maybe it was screwed opposite of normal or you had to push to pull it, or something. All he knew was, he had to go. Painful as it might be, he yanked at the tape, which pulled hairs on his hand, then pulled the needle out with one motion. The sting brought tears to his eyes, and as the solution dripped on the floor, he made one feeble attempt to turn the stopper, then just tied the cord and headed for the bathroom.

Within seconds he heard the alarm informing the nurses' station that an IV had come loose. He opened the closet on his way back, and though his clothes were there, his phone was not. His mind nearly went blank from pain and fear. Was this the end? Would someone dial back the numbers of Trib Force members who may have tried to reach him? He could have already been discovered. Should he just find Annie and get out of there? What if she was already dead? She would want him to escape and not risk his life in a vain attempt to be sure of her.

Not a chance. He would not leave without her or without knowing for sure whether she was dead.

"What are you doing out of bed?" It was not a nurse but a female orderly.

"Bathroom," he said.

"Back to bed," she said. "What have you done with your IV?"

"I'm fine," he said.

"We have bedpans and—"

"I already went—now just—"

"Sir! Shh! I can hear you and so can everyone else on this floor. Your roommates are sleeping."

"I just need—"

"Sir, do I need to get someone in here with restraints? Now quiet down!"

"I am being quiet! Now—" Suddenly David realized the bandages over his ears made him talk louder.

"Sorry," he said. "I'm Director Hassid. I need to find—"

"Oh! *You're* the director. Are you a lightning victim?"

"Yeah, I took a bolt right through the top of my head, but here I stand."

"You don't have to—"

"Sorry. No, I just fainted in the heat, and I'm fine."

"You had surgery."

"Minor, now—"

"Sir, if you're the director, I'm supposed to tell someone when you're awake."

"Why?" And why had she asked about the lightning? Was Annie a victim, and did they somehow connect him with her? He didn't want his mind to run away with him.

"I don't know, sir. I just do what I'm told. Six nurses and two aides are handling this whole floor, and some floors have fewer staff than that, so—"

"I need to know where my phone is. I carry it with me, and it's not in my uniform. I know you're going to tell me to stay away from my uniform anyway, but—"

"On the contrary, sir. You were sponge bathed when you were brought here, and if you're ambulatory, I think you're supposed to get dressed."

"You think?" This couldn't be right. Something was wrong. David had been sure he'd have to sneak out, but now he was being given the bum's rush?

"I'll get my supervisor, but you might as well start getting dressed. Can you do it yourself?"

"Of course, but—"

"Get started then. I'll be right back. Or she will."

David had overestimated his strength. He pulled his stuff from the closet and sat in a chair to dress, but he was soon short of breath and dizzier than ever. His whole head felt afire, and it seemed his wound was oozing over both ears, but when he felt under the bandaging, he felt nothing. He didn't want to think about the first time that dressing came off.

With his uniform on and only socks and shoes to go, David opened the door wider to get light from the hall. He peered into the mirror and shuddered. Still in his mid-twenties with smooth, clear, dark skin and nearly black hair and eyes, he had often been mistaken for a teenager. Never again. When had he aged so?

His face looked thin and drawn and, yes, his color lighter. He lowered his head and peeked atop it where the bandaging evidenced blood and ooze. The outer wrapping extended over his ears and beneath his chin, reminding him of dental patients from old movies. David's head seemed to push against the tight wrapping, and when he gingerly put on his uniform cap, he knew it was more than his imagination. He couldn't be sure how thick the bandages were, but between that and the swelling of his head, his cap rode atop him as if several sizes too small. Any thought of covering the effects of his stitching to avoid attention was hopeless. Maybe he could find a bigger—much bigger—cap, but there was no way to hide the wrap that extended under his chin anyway.

The supervising nurse knocked gently and stepped in as David was pulling on his socks. She was a bottle blonde, tall and thin, about twice his age. He had to straighten up to breathe and let the pain subside every few seconds.

"Let me help you," she said, clearly Scandinavian, kneeling and putting on his socks and shoes and tying them. David was so overwhelmed he nearly wept. Could she be a Christian? He wanted to ask. Anyone with a servant spirit like that was either a believer or a candidate.

"Ma'am," he said, trying to remember to talk softly. She looked up at him and he studied her forehead, searching, hoping for the mark of the believer. None. "Thank you."

"You're welcome," she said quickly. "Happy to help and wish I could help more. If I had my way, you would be with us a couple more days at least, maybe more."

"I'd just as soon leave. I—"

"Oh, I'm sure you would. No one wants to stay, and who can blame them?

All the excitement, the resurrection, and all. But the potentate has called a meeting of directors and above, his office, at 2200 hours. You are expected."

"I am?"

"When his office was told you had succumbed to the heat and had been injured and operated on, we were informed that if you were alive and ambulatory, you were to be there."

"I see."

"I'm glad someone does. You, sir, should be a patient. I wouldn't be running around so soon—"

"I was told this was superficial, minor surgery."

"Minor surgery is an operation on someone else. You've heard that, I'm sure. You know a nurse did the procedure, and good as she was, she was pressed into duty—"

"Do you know who that was? I'm pretty sure she was Native—"

"Hannah Palemoon," she said.

"I wonder if she's got my phone. It was in my—"

"I doubt it, Director. You'll find your wallet and keys and ID unmolested. We know better than to confiscate things from someone at your level."

"I appreciate that, but—"

"No one took your phone, sir. Could you have dropped it where you fell, left it in your vehicle?"

David cocked his head. Possible, but unlikely. He had not been talking on the phone when he fell, best he could remember, so it would have been in his pocket. "Where would I find Nurse Palem—"

"I told you, Director. She would not have your phone, and I'm not going to tell you where she is. We're working twenty-four on and twenty-four off here, and she's off. If she's like me, she sleeps the first twelve of those twenty-four hours off, and she ought to be allowed to."

David nodded, but he couldn't wait to get back to his computer and look her up in the personnel directory. "Ma'am, I have to find an employee I'm worried about. Name's Annie Christopher. Cargo chief of the Phoenix but assigned crowd control at sector 53 today."

"That's not good."

"So I've heard. Lightning there?"

"Bad. Several deaths and injuries. I can check to see if she's in our system. You might check the morgue."

David flinched. "I'd appreciate it if you'd check your system."

"I will, sir. Then you had better get to your quarters and relax before your meeting. You know as well as I do you're in no condition to be sitting at a table, thrilling as it may be to meet with a man who was dead this morning and is alive tonight. Follow me." She led him to the nurses' station, where she searched the computer. "No Christopher," she said, "but our entries have been hopelessly delayed."

"She would have had an employee badge," David said.

"And it should have been swiped by a wand."

"So the morgue?" he said, again trying to cover his emotion.

"Look on the bright side," she said. "Maybe she wasn't a victim at all."

That would almost be worse, David decided. Why could he not reach her, and why would she not have tried to reach him? Well, maybe she had. He had to find his phone before the meeting.

* * *

"Nothing," Rayford said. "David hasn't accessed his computer for hours, and I'm getting no answer on his phone. Now it's not even letting me leave a message, as if he's turned it off."

"Strange," Albie said. "So Pueblo doesn't even know we're coming."

"And we're not going if we don't know where it is."

"We'll find out."

"You're a resourceful guy, Albie, but—"

"I love the impossible. But you're the boss. I need your permission."

"What's your plan?"

"To find out if your new look and ID work."

"Oh, boy."

"C'mon, man. Confidence."

"The plan, Albie."

"I'll be the ranking officer down there. I blame the computer delay on all the excitement or the incompetence in New Babylon. Who can argue that? You're with me. If they demand ID, you've got it. You're no longer just a civilian helping out, though. You're a recruit, a trainee."

"Uh-huh."

"Not only do I insist on a car, but I'll get out of them the location of the bunker."

"This I've got to see."

"I love showing off."

Rayford slapped Albie's computer shut. "Tell me about it."

* * *

Kenny Bruce tried to tug Buck toward the barrier, as if knowing his dad could get him past it. But Buck was anchored to the bed. He felt as if he'd survived a plane crash. Or hadn't. It was as if his spine were compacted, every muscle, bone, joint, and tendon tender. He sat there trying to muster the strength to rise and stretch and make his way to his wife and the others.

Kenny, apparently resigned to patience, climbed onto his father's lap and put a hand on each side of his face. He looked into Buck's eyes and said, "Mama?"

"We'll see Mama in a minute, hon," Buck said. Kenny traced Buck's deep facial scars with his stubby fingers. "They don't bother you, do they, bud."

"Da-da," Kenny said. "Mama."

Presently Buck rose, lifting Kenny as he went. The boy spread his legs and settled in over Buck's hip, his arms around him, head on Buck's chest. "Wish I could take you with me everywhere I go," Buck said, limping, stiff legged, and gimpy.

"Mama, Da-da."

"Yep. We're goin', bud."

Buck prepared himself for the always embarrassing welcome saved for the last person to rise, but when he came into view of everyone else in the safe house, he was virtually ignored. Leah sat bundled in a robe, leaning back against a wall, dozing, her bleached-blonde hair with red roots wrapped in a towel. Chaim stared at the tabletop before him, his head in his hands, a straw in his coffee cup. Tsion stood beside a window, out of view from the outside just in case, head bowed, softly praying.

Chloe paced, phone pressed to her ear, tears streaming. She looked directly into Buck's eyes as if to let him know she was aware he was there, and when Kenny tried to wriggle down to get to her, Buck whispered, "Stay with Daddy a minute, hmm?"

Chloe was saying, "I understand, Zeke. . . . I know, sweetie, I know. God knows. . . . It'll be all right. We'll come get you, don't you worry. . . . Zeke, God knows. . . . It'll be after dark, but you stay strong, hear?"

She finally rang off, and everyone looked to her. "Big Zeke was busted," she said.

"Zeke Sr.?" Tsion asked. Zeke Jr. was much bigger than his father, but still they were known as Big Zeke and Little Zeke.

She nodded. "GC goons got him this morning, cuffed him, charged him with subversion, took him away."

"How'd they miss Zeke Jr.?" Buck asked, finally letting Kenny down.

"Zeke!" Kenny said, giggling.

Chloe shrugged. "Their underground was better hidden than ours, and I don't think Little Zeke ever showed his face outside."

"Zeke!" Kenny said.

"Little Zeke coming here?" Leah said.

"Where else would he go? He says GC is staking out the place, picking up people who stop for gas."

"How's he know?"

"He's got some kind of a monitor rigged up that he used to keep track of his dad. That's how he knew Big Zeke had been arrested. He knows his dad won't give him up, but he also knows he can't stay there. He's packing."

"Yeah," Buck said, "all he'd need is for the GC to find all his files and document-making paraphernalia."

"It will be good to have him here," Tsion said. "He will be safe and can do so much for so many. Cameron, how are you feeling?"

"Better than Chaim, apparently."

The old man lifted his head and tried to smile. "I'll be OK," he mouthed through his clenched jaw. "No capers for me. Eager to study and learn."

Tsion moved away from the window. "And me with a student who cannot talk. You must listen and read. You will be an expert about our own people before you know it. God's chosen people. What a thrill to teach it. I will use the same material in my cyberlesson, wherein I expose Carpathia as the Antichrist."

"Coming right out with it, are you?" Buck said.

"Absolutely," the rabbi said. "The gloves are off, as you Americans so like to say. There is no longer any question about him, nor should there be. I am persuaded that Leon is his false prophet, and I will say that too. Those who have ears will not be deceived. It will not be long before the Satan-indwelt beast will take out his rage against the Jews."

Chaim held up a hand. Buck could barely make out the labored, muffled question. "And what are we to do? We are no match for him."

"You will see, my friend," Tsion said. "You will learn today not only the history of the Jews, but their future as well. God will protect his people, now and forevermore."

"I like being a believer already," Chaim managed.

"Buck," Chloe said, stepping close to embrace him, "we have to plan Zeke's rescue."

"Just what I need today, another mission."

"You slept, didn't you?"

"Like a dead man."

"Don't say that."

"Well . . ."

"It's you or me, pal," Chloe said. "If you need another day of recup—"

"I'll be ready," Buck said.

"I can help," Leah said. "I'm fit."

"Maybe the two of you, then," Chloe said. "I've got to get news to the co-op, keep everybody working together."

"We're going to need a pilot," Buck said. "Put the GC chopper down right in the middle of their stakeout, chide 'em for missing a suspect, and we arrest Zeke Jr. and bring him here. What? What's with all the looks?"

"We don't have a chopper today or tonight, hon," Chloe said. "Probably not until tomorrow night, and we don't dare risk making Zeke wait that long."

"OK, so where's the helicopter and your dad? And Albie?"

4

DAVID HURRIED TO HIS office and phoned Annie. No answer. Then he called the motor pool. The man who had originally brought him his cart was off duty, but the one he reached told him, "No, sir, no phone. Nothing was left in there. We found the cart but not you, and my boss was pretty mad until he traced you to Medical Services. You OK?"

"Fine."

"Need the cart?"

"No."

"Anything I can do fo—"

But David had hung up. He flipped open his computer and saw urgent messages flashing from the code words and numbers he knew belonged to his comrades in the Tribulation Force. He would get to those when he could, but for now, before the infernal meeting, he had to get his phone back and find out where Annie was.

His watch read 2135. He searched the GC database for Personnel, Medical, Nursing, Female, under *P.* There it was: "Palemoon, Hannah L., room and extension 4223." A groggy hello greeted the fifth ring.

"Nurse Palemoon?"

"Yeah, who's this?"

"I am so sorry to be calling so late and sorry to wake you, but—"

"Hassid?"

"Yes, forgive me, but—"

"I have your phone."

"Oh, thank G—goodness! Is it on?"

"No, sir, I turned it off. Now are you coming to get it so I can get back to sleep?"

"Could I? If you don't mind terribly, I—"

"I gotta show you something anyway."

What in the world? Was he being set up? Why would she be so willing to have him come and get it? And why did she take it in the first place? To be safe, he jumped back on the computer and fired up the bugging device that would record their conversation in the corridor outside her room.

As he backed out of that program he saw the blinking signals for his urgent messages again. Looked like Rayford and Albie had been desperately trying to reach him. He didn't have time to deal with them, but what if they had heard from Annie? He had to peek.

The requests stunned him. He was way late for helping Albie and Rayford in Colorado, but his fingers flew over the keyboard anyway. His head ached, his wound oozed, and he blinked furiously. He entered the numbers to override the Peacekeeping security codes. Under his phony name as a high-level GC unit commander in New Babylon, he assigned Marcus Elbaz to Carpathia Memorial Airstrip in Colorado Springs. He also authorized him to temporarily appropriate a vehicle with which to take custody of an escapee from the Belgium Facility for Female Rehabilitation, currently incarcerated at a bunker on the north end of Pueblo. A few more keystrokes derived the exact coordinates of that facility and the name of the deputy director in charge—Pinkerton Stephens. Fortunately, Stephens was lower ranked than Deputy Commander Elbaz.

David would work on name, rank, and serial number for Rayford later, hoping the two of them could bluff their way past the GC in the meantime. It was 2150, Hannah Palemoon was waiting, and he couldn't be late for the big meeting. Healthy and in shape it would have been a challenge to get to her room, retrieve his phone, and get to Carpathia's office in time, but wounded as he was, he couldn't imagine it.

He could phone Fortunato at the last minute and explain he would be a few minutes late, coming from his hospital bed. But neither did he want to miss any of that meeting. As he locked his door and strode quickly toward the elevator, he wobbled and had to grab the wall. *Catch your breath,* he told himself. *Late is better than not there at all.*

+ + +

"Give me my razor," Albie said. "It's going to be hard to pull this off if I'm out of regulation."

"You'll be on the ground in less than a minute," Rayford said.

"I have a copilot, do I not?"

Rayford pulled Albie's electric razor from his bag and took over the landing as Albie shaved and tightened his tie. When ground control confirmed the landing, Albie responded, then whipped off the headphones and put on his uniform cap. When they disembarked, Rayford was struck again how the diminutive Middle Easterner seemed taller, more commanding.

"I can point you to the refueling area so you can tank up before takeoff, Commander Elbaz."

"You can't do it for me while I'm on assignment?"

"Sorry, sir, we're shorthan—"

"I know. Carry on."

Rayford stayed a step behind Albie as they made their way to the offices, hoping that once David got him enlisted as a GC Peacekeeper, he would give him an even higher rank. How could he supervise a man who outranked him in disguise?

The officer at the desk saluted and said, "I told my chief you weren't in the computer, so you're on your own for ground transportation. If you'll give me your fueling order number, however, I can clear you for that when—"

"Excuse me?" Albie said.

"You'll have to refuel yourself, because—"

"I know all that. I need a vehicle for an important assignment, and I need it now. You expect me to rent a car?"

"Sir, I'm just telling you what my chief said. I—"

"Get him out here."

"He's a her, sir."

"I don't care if he's a gorilla. Get him, or her, out here."

The airstrip chief appeared before the deskman buzzed her. She saluted but did not smile. "Judy Hamilton at your service, Commander."

"Not enough at my service, I'm afraid."

"I can do only what I can do, sir, but I'm open to suggestions."

"Do you have a vehicle?"

"None available, sir."

"I need it for half a day, tops."

"None, sir."

"You personally?"

"Me, sir?"

Albie sighed loudly through his nose. "You understand English, Hamilton? Do-you-personally-have-a-vehicle?"

"I have not been issued GC wheels, sir."

"I didn't ask you that. How do you get to work?"

"I drive."

"Then you must have a vehicle."

"My own, yes, sir."

"That would be what *personal* means, Ju-dy. I will be borrowing your personal vehicle this afternoon, and the Global Community will be indebted to you. In fact, we will be indebted at the rate of one Nick per mile."

She raised a brow. "The manual says half that, sir."

"I'm aware of that," Albie said. "I'll authorize it due to your cooperation."

"No demerits for stupidity, sir?"

"Only for insubordination, Hamilton, which is one way I define sarcasm."

"So you'll pay me a Nick a mile for the use of my car."

"You catch on quickly."

"No."

"No?"

"No, you'll not be using my car."

"I beg your pardon, Hamilton?"

"I have a meeting in Monument in two hours, and C-25 has been open only a week, and not all lanes. I need to leave now."

"And you believe your meeting takes precedence over that of a deputy commander?"

"It does today, sir, because of your attitude."

"You are denying me the use of your car?"

"You catch on quickly."

Albie squinted at her, reddening. "You're going on report, Hamilton. You will be disciplined."

"But surely not this afternoon. And you will be disciplined as well."

"I?" Albie said.

"How long has it been since the resurrection of the potentate, yet you greeted neither my deskman nor me with the new phrase."

"I have been busy and up for hours."

"You don't know that we greet each other with 'He is risen,' to be responded to by 'He is risen indeed'?"

"Of course, but—ma'am, I also need to know the exact location of the facility on the north end of Pueblo where—"

"You don't have full orders, sir?"

"Unfortunately not."

"Corporal, check the computer again. Let me see what we do have on Deputy Commander Elbaz and whether we can add bluster and bullying to his profile."

"Hamilton, I—"

She silenced him with a hand.

"Hey," the deskman said, "this wasn't here before. Straight from the brass in New Babylon. Look."

Hamilton peered and blanched at the screen. Rayford let out a breath. The woman cleared her throat. "It appears everything is in order, Commander. I, uh, would like to propose a truce."

"I'm listening."

"You're cleared for a vehicle too, and we will find you one, though I will be happy to use the Jeep if you still care to use my car."

"You would let me?"

"I will not only let you use the car, but I will also agree not to report your breach of protocol if you will keep between us your opinion of my insubordination."

✣ ✣ ✣

Buck and Chloe left the baby in Leah's care while Tsion and Chaim studied. The couple made their way to the basement of the tower, where Buck had parked the Land Rover among many other vehicles.

"We can be grateful this place had the ritzy clientele it did," Chloe said. "Look at these rigs."

Buck had to smile at the difference between them and the filthy, banged-up Rover, which wasn't so old. He smacked a palm atop it, and it echoed throughout the parking garage. "Ol' Bessie saw us through a lot, didn't she?"

Chloe shook her head. "*She?* You men and your penchant for attributing female characteristics to your cars."

Buck leaned back against a pillar and beckoned Chloe to him. He enveloped her. "Think about it," he said. "I couldn't pay the car, or women, a higher compliment."

"Keep digging. You'll need a backhoe in a minute."

"Not if you think about it."

She leaned back and cocked her head, pointing to her temple. "Hmm, let's see if ol' Charley and I can figger this out. Callin' mah brain by a man's name is the biggest compliment I can pay it and men."

"C'mon," Buck said. "Think what that car's been through with us. It got us through traffic when the war broke out. Kept you alive when you sailed it into a tree, no less. Rode with me into a crevice in the earth and back out again, not to mention up, over, and through every obstacle."

"You're right," she said. "No man could have done that."

"You and Charley figger that out all by yourselves?"

"Yep. And wanna know what else? I think a Humvee is the way to go this time."

"We got one?"

"Two. Down around the corner near the luxury cars."

She pulled him to a darker area of the underground structure. "All the spaces are numbered, and they coincide with the key Peg-Board in the attendant's shack. There's hardly a car in here with less than half a tank of gas, and most of 'em are full."

"People must have been prepared."

"Some were listening to the rumors of war, apparently."

Buck tapped her head. "Thank you, Charley." He surveyed the selection of vehicles—dozens of them, mostly new—and let out a low whistle. "When God blesses, he blesses." But Chloe had grown quiet. "Whatcha thinking?" he said.

She pursed her lips and buried her hands in her jacket pockets. "About what fun we would have had if we'd been lovers at any other time in history."

He nodded. "We wouldn't have been believers."

"Someone might have gotten to us. Look at us. This is the most fun I've had in ages. It's like we're in a free car dealership and it's our turn to pick. We've got a beautiful baby and a free sitter, and all we have to do is decide what model and color car we want."

She rested against a white Hummer and Buck joined her. She shook her head. "We're older than our years, wounded, scarred, scared. It won't be long before our days will be spent looking for ways to just stay alive. I worry about you all the time. It's bad enough living now, but I couldn't go on without you."

"Yes, you could."

"I wouldn't want to. Would you, without me? Maybe I shouldn't ask."

"No, Chlo', I know what you mean. We have a cause, a mission, and everything seems crystal clear. But I wouldn't want to go on without you either. I *would.* I'd *have* to. For Kenny. For God. For the rest of the Force. Like Tsion says, for the kingdom. You'd have been the best thing that ever happened to me even if you weren't my whole life. But you are. Let's watch out for each other, keep each other alive. We've got only three and a half years to go, but I want to make it. Don't you?"

"'Course."

She turned and held him tightly for a long minute, and they kissed fiercely.

+ + +

When David finally mince-stepped his way down the fourth floor of the employee residence tower, he found room 4223 open a crack, a sliver of light peeking out. He was about to knock when a dark hand poking out the end of a quilted robe thrust his phone out at him.

"Thanks, ma'am," he said. "I've got to run."

"Ma'am?" Nurse Palemoon said. "I can't be *that* much older'n you, boy. How old *are* you?"

"Why?"

She opened the door and leaned wearily against the jamb. Her hair was in a ponytail, and her eyes looked sleepy behind puffy cheeks. David was surprised how short she was. "I'm not even thirty yet," she said, "so quit with the ma'am, all right?"

"Fair enough. Listen, I'm late for a meeting. I wanted to thank you, and—"

"I said I wanted to show you something."

"So you did. What? And why did you take my phone?"

"Well, that's sort of what I wanted to show you."

David didn't want to be rude, but what was this game? She just stood there, arms folded, gazing at him with raised brows. "OK," he said. "What?"

She didn't move. *Oh, brother,* he thought. *She's not trying to make a move on me. Please!*

He slipped the phone in his pocket and gestured with both palms raised. "Oh!" she said. "You're in the dark."

I sure am.

She straightened and flipped a switch just inside the door. The tiny light above her door illuminated them both. She matched his gesture and he stopped breathing. *You've* got *to be kidding!* Plain as the nose on her face, the mark was clear on her forehead.

"Check it," she said. "I wouldn't blame you. I *know* yours is real. I rubbed it with alcohol."

David looked up and down the hall, asked her to forgive him, licked his thumb, and pressed it against her forehead as she leaned in to him. He looked both ways one more time and leaned down to embrace her briefly. "Sister," he whispered. "I am glad to see you! I didn't know we had *any*body in Medical."

"I don't know of anyone else," she said. "But as soon as I saw your mark and knew your rank, I thought of your phone."

"You're brilliant," he said.

"You're welcome. I'll be back in touch."

"I'm sure you will."

"And thanks, Nurse P—"

"Hannah," she said. "Please, David."

On his way back to the elevator he checked his phone. There were several messages, none from Annie. He would visit the morgue only as a last resort. He speed-dialed the supreme commander's office and reached Sandra, the assistant Carpathia and Fortunato had shared.

"Glad to hear you're up and about," she said. "They're expecting you. I'll tell them you'll be a few minutes."

\+ + +

Assuming that because David had finally gotten Albie's clearance into the system he might also have passed along the location of the Pueblo bunker, Rayford jogged to the fighter to grab Albie's computer on their way out.

"This used to be an interstate," he said, driving Judy Hamilton's nondescript minivan south on C-25. "Until everything got renamed for St. Nick."

Albie was accessing data. "It's here," Albie said. "The interchanges and exits are still under construction, so watch for a hard left into Pueblo. I'll tell you from there. *Humph.* Pinkerton Stephens. There's a handle for you. The man we want to see there."

"Heard of him?"

Albie shook his head. "Ask me tomorrow."

A few minutes later they passed the Quonset-hut-style building deep off a side road. Rayford said, "Question. Why not come in here with a GC Jeep—complete the image?"

"Surprise. You told Ms. Durham in no uncertain terms you were not coming, knowing they were listening. They're not expecting anyone. Let them wonder who's pulling in. I show up in uniform, outranking everyone; they don't recognize the civilian. They'll worry more about impressing us than making up a story. Anyway, I don't want to transport this woman in an open Jeep, do you?"

Rayford shook his head. "You really think we'll surprise 'em?"

"Only briefly. The gate guard will let them know brass is coming."

Rayford popped a U-turn and headed for the entrance. The guard at the gate asked him to state his business. "Just chauffeuring the deputy commander here."

The guard stooped to get a look at Albie, then saluted. "An appointment with whom, sir?"

"Stephens, and I'm late, if you don't mind."

"Sign here, please."

Rayford signed "Marvin Berry," and they were waved on.

As they entered the front office, a woman at the desk was listening to a strange voice over the intercom. It was high-pitched and nasal, and Rayford couldn't tell if it came from a man or a woman. "A deputy commander to see me?" the voice said.

"Yes, Mr. Stephens. I checked the name with the GC database and the only Marvin Berry employed by us is not in Peacekeeping. He's an elderly fisherman in Canada."

"I smell a rat," the voice said.

So it's a man, but what's the matter with him? Rayford wondered.

"One moment, sir," the woman said, standing when she noticed the deputy commander behind Rayford. "Is your name Berry?"

"Berry's my driver," Albie barked. "Look up Elbaz on your computer. None of my family knows how to fish."

"Mystery solved, Mr. Stephens," the woman announced over the intercom. "The gate guard had the driver sign."

"Incompetent!" Stephens's weird voice sang into the squawk box. "Send him in!"

"The guard?"

"The deputy commander!"

She pointed to the first door on the left down a short hallway, but when Rayford moved to follow, she said, "Only the deputy commander, please."

"He's with me," Albie said. "I'll clear it with the boss."

"Oh, I don't know."

"I do," Albie said. He stopped at the door and knocked.

"Come in," came the disembodied voice.

"Come in?" Albie repeated in a whisper. "Is he going to be embarrassed when he realizes he didn't open the door to a superior officer."

Albie pushed the door open, stepped in, and hesitated, causing Rayford to bump into him. "Sorry," Rayford mumbled. He could not see Stephens, but he heard the whine of an electric motor.

"Forgive the lack of protocol," came the voice as Stephens's wheelchair rolled into view. Rayford was taken aback. The man had one leg, the other a stump just above the knee; his right hand had small protrusions in place of fingers, and the other hand, though whole, had clearly suffered severe burns. "I'd stand, but then, I can't."

"Understood," Albie said, hesitantly shaking the man's partial hand.

Rayford did the same, and they followed Stephens's gesture to two chairs that filled the small office. What was it about the face? Stephens's neck was permanently red and scarred, as were his cheekbones and ears. He was clearly wearing a toupee. Except for the lips, the middle of his face—chin, nose, eye sockets, and the center of his forehead—seemed all of one piece, the color of a plastic hearing aid.

"Don't know you, Elbaz," Stephens said, almost like a man with no tongue or no nose. "You, Berry, you look familiar. You GC?"

"No, sir."

"I'm here on business," Albie said. "I don't have a hard copy of my orders, but—"

"Excuse me, Deputy Commander, but I'll get to you. You got a minute?"

"Well, sure, but—"

"Just give me a minute. I mean, I know you outrank me and all, but unless you're in an unusual hurry, bear with me. Your story checks out. I'll give you all the help I can on whatever you need. Now, Berry, were you *ever* GC?"

Rayford, disconcerted by the wasted body and the voice, hesitated. "No, uh, no, sir. Not Peacekeeping anyway."

"But something."

"I didn't mean to say that."

"But you did. You were GC connected some way, weren't you? You look familiar. I know you or of you, or I'll bet I know a friend of yours."

Albie gave Rayford a look, and Rayford quit talking. Regardless of the question, Rayford merely stared at the man, racking his brain. Where would he have run into a Pinkerton Stephens, and how could he forget him if he had?

"I was a whole man then, Mr. Berry. If that's your real name."

Rayford grew more uncomfortable by the second. Had they been set up? Would he ever get out of here? And what of Hattie? Albie seemed to have stiffened and was no more comfortable than he.

Stephens cocked his head for one more lingering glance at Rayford, then turned to Albie. "Now then, Deputy Commander Elbaz. What might be your business with me?"

"I've been assigned to take custody of your prisoner, sir."

"And who told you I had a prisoner?"

"Top brass, sir. Said the subject was uncooperative, that some plan or mission failed, and that we were to return her to Buffer."

"Buffer? What's that?"

"You know what that is, Stephens, if you are who you say you are."

"Doesn't make sense that half a man would be in a leadership role in the GC?" Stephens said.

"I didn't say that."

"But it doesn't add up, does it?"

"Can't say it does."

"Never saw another like me in the ranks, have you, Elbaz?"

"No, sir, I haven't."

"Well, I'm legit whether you like it or not, and you're going to have to deal with me."

"Happy to, sir, and when you check me out, you'll see that everything is in order, and—"

"Did I say I was housing a prisoner here, Deputy Commander?"

"No, sir, but I know you are."

"You know I am."

"Yes, sir."

"Buffer is a female rehab facility, sir. Were you under the impression I had a female incarcerated here?"

Albie nodded.

"Does this look like a detention center to you?"

"They take different forms during different times."

"Indeed they do. Is there a reason, sir, why you did not greet me with the new protocol?"

"I've been having trouble remembering that, Mr. Stephens."

"Indeed? Do you realize, sir, that you have a smudge on your forehead?"

Albie jerked. Rayford felt a chill. A GC Peacekeeper could see Albie's mark? Things tumbled into place so fast that Rayford could barely keep up. How much had been compromised? Albie knew everything!

"I do?" Albie said innocently. He swiped at his forehead with his palm.

"There, that's better," Stephens said.

Albie slowly moved his hand until it rested on his sidearm. If only Rayford had one.

"Gentlemen," Stephens enunciated carefully past his awful sound, "if you'll do me the kindness of following me, I'd like us to start over in a new room. This time we'll begin with the proper protocol—what do you say?"

He rolled past Rayford and Albie, reached for the door, swung it open, and sped through before it slammed on him. Albie rose and grabbed it, and Rayford followed him down the hall. Albie unsnapped the strap that held the 9 mm in its holster. Rayford wondered if he had time to peel off and get out the front door to the van before Albie knew he was gone. He hesitated, hoping the whir of the chair would cover him if he made the decision.

But Albie turned and motioned Rayford to walk in front of him, behind the fast-moving chair. Even if he could escape, Hattie was history. He had no choice but to stay and play it out.

5

BUCK SETTLED ON the white Hummer, confirmed it had a full tank, checked the tires, found the keys, checked the engine, and fired it up.

"What shall we name her?" Chloe said.

"This is a big, ol' muscle car," he said. "It's got Chloe written all over it."

It would be hours before dark, and they would be in touch with Zeke frequently to discover what he knew about the positioning of the GC stakeout. They were looking for rebels who gassed up at his dad's station, not expecting Zeke Jr. to even be there. But could Buck get him out of there without their seeing?

Kenny was down for a nap, and Leah was reading when they returned. "Tsion said you could join him and Chaim," she said. "And Chloe was going to involve me in the co-op stuff."

"I've got to start communicating with everyone," Chloe said, setting up her computer as Leah pulled up a chair. Buck moved up one floor to Tsion's hideaway.

What a spot he had set up for himself. In a room just big enough for a U-shaped desk, Tsion had what amounted to a cockpit, where he was within arm's length of whatever he needed. With his computer before him and his commentaries and Bible on a ledge above, he was ready. Buck was struck by how few books he had brought with him, but Dr. Ben-Judah explained that most of what he needed had been scanned onto his massive hard drive.

Chaim sat in a comfortable chair looking less than comfortable. He had been hurt worse than Buck in the plane crash, yet he sat weeping tears of apparent joy, as Tsion rushed to teach him.

"Much of this you have heard from your youth, Chaim," the rabbi said, "but now that God has opened your eyes and you know Jesus is the Messiah, you will be amazed at how it all comes together for you and makes sense."

Chaim rocked and wept and nodded. "I see," he said over and over. "I see."

Buck sat transfixed, hearing in a gush much of what he had learned over the past three-plus years from Tsion's daily cybermessages. At times the rabbi himself would be overcome and have to stop and exult, "Chaim, you don't know how we prayed for you, again and again, that God would open your eyes. Do you need a break, my brother?"

Chaim shook his head but held up a hand, trying to make himself understood despite the wired-shut jaw. "God is opening my eyes to so many things," he managed. "Cameron, come close. I must ask you something."

Buck looked at Tsion, who nodded, and he pulled his chair closer to Chaim's. "I always wondered why you had not come to Nicolae's first meeting with his new leadership team at the United Nations. Remember?"

"Of course."

"Forgive me for spitting on you, Cameron, but I cannot speak another way just now."

"Don't give it a second thought."

"I could not fathom it! The privilege of a lifetime, the opportunity no self-respecting journalist could miss. You were invited. I invited you! You said you would come, and yet you did not. It was the talk of New York. You were demoted because of it. Why? Why did you not come?"

"I was there, Chaim."

"No one saw you there! Nicolae was disappointed, enraged. Everyone asked about you. Your boss, what was his name?"

"Steve Plank."

"Mr. Plank could not believe it! Hattie Durham was there! You were the one who introduced her to Carpathia, and yet you were not there when she expected you."

"I was there, Chaim."

"I was there too, Cameron. Your place at the table was empty."

Buck was about to say again that he was there, but he suddenly realized what was happening and why Chaim would bring this up again after so long. "Your eyes truly are being opened, aren't they, Chaim?"

The old man put a quivering hand on Buck's knee. "I could not understand it. It made no sense. Jonathan Stonagal had embarrassed Nicolae by going after you. Nicolae shamed him into committing suicide, and he killed Joshua Todd-Cothran in the process."

Buck wanted to say he had seen it and that was not the way it had happened, but he waited.

"None of it made sense," Rosenzweig whined. "None of it. But the eyes don't lie. Stonagal grabbed the gun from the security guard, shot himself and his colleague with him."

"No, Chaim," Buck whispered. "The eyes don't lie. But the Antichrist does."

Rosenzweig began to shiver until his whole body shook. He pressed his hands against his tender face to stop the quivering of his lips. "Why were you not there, Cameron?"

"Why would I not have been there, sir? What could have kept me away?"

"I cannot imagine!"

"Neither could I."

"Then why? Why?"

Buck did not respond. He had quit trying to convince the old man. "I was assigned to be there; my boss expected me to go."

"Yes, yes!"

"It was the mother of all cover stories for the largest circulation magazine in history. It was the apex of my career. Would I have thrown that away?"

Rosenzweig shook his head, tears falling, hands trembling. "You would not."

"Of course I wouldn't. Who would?"

"Maybe you had come to believe Nicolae was Antichrist and you didn't want to be exposed to him?"

"By then I knew, yes, or I thought I did. I would not have gone in there without the protection of God."

"And you did not have it?"

"I had it."

"And so why not go? You would have been the only one there with God's hand upon you."

Buck merely nodded. Rosenzweig's eyes cleared, and it appeared he was studying something a thousand miles away. His pupils darted back and forth. "You were there!"

"Yes, I was."

"You were there, weren't you, Cameron?"

"I was, sir."

"And you saw it all!"

"I saw everything."

"But you did not see what the rest of us saw."

"I saw what really happened. I saw the truth."

Chaim's hands fluttered beside his head, and through clenched teeth he described what he had once seen and what he now saw anew. "Nicolae! Nicolae murdered those men! He made Stonagal kneel before him, stuck the weapon in the man's ear, and killed the both of them with one shot!"

"That's what happened."

"But Nicolae told us what we had seen, told us what we would remember, and our perception became our reality!"

Chaim turned around and knelt, resting his fragile head in his hands, elbows on the seat of his chair. "Oh, God, oh, God," he prayed, "open my eyes. Help me to always see the truth, your truth. Don't let me be led by a madman, deceived by a liar. Thank you, Jehovah God."

Slowly he stood and embraced Buck, then turned to face Tsion. "Truly Nicolae is Antichrist," he said. "He must be stopped. I want to do whatever I have to do."

Tsion smiled ruefully. "May I remind you that you already tried?"

"I certainly did, but not for the reasons I would try today."

"If you think you know the depths of the depravity of the man," Tsion said, "wait till we get to what he has in mind for God's chosen people."

Chaim sat and reached for a pad of paper. "Skip to that, Tsion. Please."

"In due time, my friend. Just a few thousand more years to go."

\+ + +

Despite his pain, David was rested. He could have used more, but he had slept the sleep of the drugged, and his mind—at least—felt refreshed. Unfortunately, that made it hard for him to separate his dread over Annie from his wariness over the indwelt Carpathia. He had been in the presence of evil many times, but never in the company of Satan himself. He breathed a prayer for Annie, thanks for Nurse Palemoon, for Tsion who had taught him that Satan—though more powerful than any human—was no match for the Lord God. "He is not omniscient," Tsion had taught. "Not omnipresent. Deceiving, persuasive, controlling, beguiling, possessive, oppressive, yes, but greater is he that is in you than he that is in the world."

"They're waiting for you," Sandra told him. "Apparently the risen potentate did not want you to miss a thing."

"Well, good then."

"And with your arrival, I leave. And that's good too. Long day."

"You and me both."

"Feeling all right? Heard you took a tumble."

"Better."

"Good night, Director Hassid. And, oh yes. He is risen."

David stared at her and was struck by the plainness of her forehead compared to that of the beautiful, dark sister he had just met. "He is risen indeed," he said, meaning just what he said.

He knocked and entered and was dazed when not only Carpathia and Fortunato stood, but all the other managers too. "My beloved David," Carpathia began, "how good that you were up to joining us."

"Thank you," David said as Intelligence Director Jim Hickman pushed out a chair for him.

"Yes," Hickman said. "How good it is!" He beamed, peeking at Carpathia as if to see whether he had pleased the boss. The potentate pursed his lips and squinted, ignoring Hickman. To David it appeared purposeful. Hickman was Fortunato's choice, and Carpathia had scarcely hidden his opinion of the man as a buffoon.

The team of two dozen, plus Nicolae and Leon, sat around a huge mahogany table in Nicolae's office, the first time David had been there for this size of a meeting. David felt a dark foreboding as he sat and was shaken to see a well-worn Bible on the table in front of Nicolae. Everyone else sat when David did, but Carpathia remained standing. The man seemed energized, his breath coming quickly in great gasps that whistled through his teeth. It was as if he were a football player caged in the locker room before kickoff of a championship game.

"Gentlemen and ladies," he began, "I have a new lease on life!"

The room exploded with laughter, and when it waned, Nicolae was still laughing. "Trust me, there is *nothing* like waking from the dead!"

The others nodded and smiled. David was aware of Security Chief Walter Moon's gaze, so he offered a cursory nod.

"Oh, I was dead, people, lest anyone wonder." They shook their heads. "Mr. Fortunato, we should publish photographs from the autopsy, the coroner's report, the rising itself. There will always be skeptics, but anyone who was there knows the truth."

"We know," several said.

David felt evil emanating so pervasively from Carpathia that he sat rigid and worried he might faint. Suddenly Nicolae faced him. "Director Hassid, you were there."

"I was, sir."

"You had a good view?"

"Perfect, sir."

"You saw me rise from the dead."

"I'll never deny it."

Carpathia chuckled warmly. He strode to his desk and stood behind the huge, stuffed, red leather chair. He caressed it, then massaged it deeply. "It is as if I am seeing this for the first time," he said to twenty-four pairs of admiring eyes. "Leon, what is directly above my office?"

"Why, nothing, sir. We are on eighteen, the top floor."

"No utility room, no elevator-maintenance area?"

"Nothing, sir."

"I want more room, Leon. Are you taking notes?"

"Yes, sir."

"What do you have so far?"

"Autopsy photos, coroner's report, the rising."

"Add the expansion of my office. I want it twice as high, with a transparent ceiling that exposes me to the heavens."

"Consider it done, Excellency."

"How soon?" Carpathia said. "Who would know that?" Fortunato pointed at the construction director, who waved a tentative hand. "Yes, sir," Nicolae pressed, "and may I assume this would be top priority?"

"You bet your life," the man said, and Carpathia nearly collapsed in laughter.

"Let me tell you something, Director. I know you must displace me for a few days because of the mess it will be to raze and raise this ceiling. But I want this done as fast as humanly possible, and do you know why?"

"I have an idea, sir."

"Do you?"

The man nodded.

"By all means, let us hear it!"

"Because I don't believe you are human anymore, and you could do it faster than my team on its best day."

"Only God bestows such wisdom, Director."

"I believe I am in his presence, Potentate."

Nicolae smiled. "I believe you are too." He turned and gestured to all. "When I lay there dead for three days, my spirit was so strong and powerful that I knew, I knew, I knew my time would come. When death had enjoyed victory over me long enough, I willed myself to live again. I raised myself, people. I raised myself back to life."

A murmur filled the room as the men and women approved aloud and pressed their hands together as if praying to him or worshiping him.

Nicolae picked up the Bible in what seemed to David a loving manner. "You may wonder what this is doing here," he said. He opened it and let it plop spine first onto the table. "This is the playbook of those who oppose me. This is the holy book of those who do not recognize me and who will not, despite what they saw with their own eyes." He slammed a fist onto the book. "This holds the lies about the chosen people of God and the supreme lie that there is one above me."

His team, save one, murmured disapproval.

Carpathia stood back from the end of the table and folded his arms, legs spread. "We shall use their very blueprint to bring them to their knees. The Jews who worship their coming Messiah in their own Holy Land, in their beloved city where they deigned slay me. I shall return there triumphant, and they will have one opportunity to repent and see the light.

"And the Judah-ites, who believe Messiah already came and went, who believe Jesus is their Savior—and whom I see nowhere; do you?—also trace their heritage to Jerusalem. If they want to see the true and living god, let them journey there, for that is where I shall soon be. If the sacred temple is the residence of the most high God, then the most high god shall reside there, high on the throne.

"In the city where they slew me, they shall see me, high and lifted up."

Many directors raised fists of victory and encouragement.

"Now, some plans. As I have left no doubt in any thinking person's mind about who I am, I no longer feel the need for a buffer between my team and me. While my dear comrade, Supreme Commander Leon Fortunato, has ably assisted me since first I came to power, I have need of him now in another crucial role, one he has already accepted with enthusiasm. What was once nobly attempted and ultimately failed shall now be consummated in success and victory.

"The Enigma Babylon One World Faith failed because, despite its lofty goal of unifying the world's religions, it worshiped no god but itself. It was devoted to unity, yet that was never achieved. Its god was nebulous and impersonal. But with Leon Fortunato as Most High Reverend Father of Carpathianism, the devout of the world finally have a personal god whose might and power and glory have been demonstrated in the raising, *of himself,* from the dead!"

Many applauded and Carpathia motioned to Leon to rise and speak as he himself backed away but remained standing.

"I am deeply humbled by this assignment," Leon said, moving to Nicolae, dropping to his knees, and kissing the potentate's hands. He rose and moved back to the head of the table. "Let me clarify, not that His Excellency needs any help from a mere mortal, that the very name of the new religion was my idea. It was no stroke of brilliance. What else could we call a faith in which the object of our worship is His Excellency?

"The outpouring of emotion from the citizens this very day spurred the idea that we should reproduce the image of His Excellency, the great statue, and erect it in all the major cities throughout the world. Plans have already been sent out, and each city is required to have the image constructed. They will be only a quarter of the size of the original, which as you know, is four times life-size. It doesn't take a scientist to figure out, then, that the replicas will be exactly life-size.

"While our beloved potentate lay dead, he imbued me with power to call fire from the sky to kill those who would oppose him. He blessed me with the power to give speech to the statue so we could hear his own heart. This confirmed in me the desire to serve him as my god for the rest of my days, and I shall do that for as long as Nicolae Carpathia gives me breath."

"Thank you, my beloved servant," Nicolae said as Leon sat. "Now, blessed comrades, I have written assignments for one and all. These were prepared just before my demise and now will make more sense than ever to you. First, one of my oldest and dearest friends, a woman closer to me than a relative, shall explain something to you. Ms. Ivins, if you would come."

Viv Ivins, prim and proper, her blue-gray hair piled atop her head, made her way to the head of the table and embraced Nicolae. As she passed out file folders with each director's name inscribed on them, Nicolae said, "Many of you know that Ms. Ivins helped raise me. Indeed for many years I believed she was my aunt—we were that close. She has been working on a project that will help me put in place certain unfortunately necessary controls on the citizenry. Most people are devoted to me—we know that. Many who were not or who were undecided are now decidedly with us, and, you will agree, for good reason.

"But there are those factions, primarily the two that I have already mentioned, who are not loyal. Perhaps now they have seen the error of their ways and will henceforth be loyal. If so, they will have no trouble with the safeguards I feel must be initiated. I am asking those loyal to the Global Community, specifically to me and to the unified faith, to willingly bear a mark of loyalty."

Walter Moon stood. "Sir, I beg of you, allow me to be the first to bear your mark."

"Let us not get ahead of ourselves, brother," Nicolae said. "You may just get your wish, and while I am touched by your sentiment, how do you know that I will not brand you with an iron like a head of cattle?"

Moon spread his hands on the table and bowed his head. "As you, my lord, are my witness, I would endure it and bear it with endless pride."

"My, my," Nicolae said, "if Director Moon's sentiment is shared by the populace, we shall need no enforcement measures, shall we?"

David peeked at his packet and fanned the pages until his eye fell on a startling word. "Guillotines?" he said aloud before he could stop himself.

"Now we *are* ahead of ourselves," Nicolae said. "Needless to say, such would be a last resort and I pray it will never be needed."

"I would gladly offer my head," Moon rhapsodized, "if I should be so foolish as to deny my lord."

Nicolae turned to David. "You are responsible for technical purchasing, correct?"

David nodded.

"I do not imagine we have an adequate supply of immediate-response mechanisms for the reluctant. We must study the expected need and be prepared. As I have said, my loftiest dream is that not one would refuse the loyalty mark. Ms. Ivins, please."

"The first page of your folders," she began, in a precise and articulate tone with a hint of her native Romanian dialect, "long before you reach the guillotines—" she paused for the chuckling, in which David did not join—"is a listing of the ten world regions and a corresponding number. It is the product of a mathematical equation that identifies those regions and their relationships to His Excellency the Potentate. The loyalty mark, which I shall explain in detail, shall begin with these numbers, thus identifying the home region of every citizen. The subsequent numbers, embedded on a biochip inserted under the skin, will further identify the person to the point where every one shall be unique."

Suddenly, as if in a trance, Leon rose and began to speak. "Every man, woman, and child, regardless of their station in life, shall receive this mark on their right hands or on their foreheads. Those who neglect to get the mark when it is made available will not be allowed to buy or sell until such time as they receive it. Those who overtly refuse shall be put to death, and every marked loyal citizen shall be deputized with the right and the responsibility to report such a one. The mark shall consist of the name of His Excellency or the prescribed number."

With that, Leon dropped heavily into his chair. Viv Ivins smiled benevolently and said, "Why, thank you, Reverend," which caused all, including Leon, to laugh.

David was afraid his crashing heart and shaking hands would make him conspicuous. What if someone got the bright idea to apply the mark to the inner circle that very night? He might be in heaven before Annie knew he was dead.

"We have settled on the technology," Viv continued. "The miniature biochip with the suffix numbers embedded in it can be inserted as painlessly as a vaccination in a matter of seconds. Citizens may choose either location, and visible will be a thin, half-inch scar, and to its immediate left, in six-point black ink—impossible to remove under penalty of law—the number that designates the home region of the individual. That number may be included in the embedded chip, should the person prefer that one of the variations of the name of the potentate appear on their flesh."

"Variations?" someone asked.

"Yes. Most, we assume, will prefer the understated numbers next to the thin scar. But they may also choose from the small initials—no bigger than the numbers—*NJC.* The first or last name may be used, including one version of *Nicolae* that would virtually cover the left side of the forehead."

"For the most loyal," Nicolae said with a grin. "Someone like, oh, say, Director Hickman, for instance."

Hickman blushed but called out, "Sign me up, Viv!"

"The beauty of the embedded chip is twofold," she continued. "First, it leaves the visible evidence of loyalty to the potentate, and second, it serves as a method of payment and receipting for buying and selling. Eye-level scanners will allow customers and merchants to merely pass by and be billed or receipted."

Several whistles of admiration sounded. David's head throbbed. He raised his hand.

"Director Hassid," Viv said.

"What are you looking at in the way of timing?"

"Worried that your head won't take any more invasion just now?" she said, smiling.

"I had an IV in the hand too."

"Not to worry," she said. "While the potentate and the former supreme commander see value in employees serving as examples to the world, you will have thirty days, beginning tomorrow, to fulfill your obligation."

"I'll do it tonight," someone said, "and I'm not even Hickman!"

A month, David thought. *A month to get out of Dodge.* What would become of him and Annie and Mac and Abdullah? And Hannah Palemoon?

Viv said that over the next few days she would be sure each director knew his or her part in the rollout of images of Carpathia and the application of the mark of loyalty. Meanwhile, she said, "His Excellency has a closing comment."

"Thank you, Viv," Nicolae said. "Allow me to tell you just one story of a family I met today, and you know I met thousands. We have such a nucleus of loyal citizenry! This was a beautifully loyal Asian family named Wong."

David fought to maintain his composure.

"Their daughter already works for us at Buffer in Brussels. The parents are well-to-do and great supporters of the Global Community. The father was quite proud of his family and of his record of loyalty. But I was most impressed with the seventeen-year-old son, Chang. Here is a boy who, according to his father, loves me and everything about the world as we see it today. He wants nothing more than to work for me here at the palace, and though he has another year of high school, would rather bring his talents our way.

"And such talents! I will arrange for the completion of his schooling here, because he is a genius! He can program any computer, analyze and fix any procedural or operational or systems problem. And this is not just a proud father talking. He showed me documents, grades, letters of recommendation. This kind of boy is our future, and our future has never looked brighter."

That boy, David thought, *would die before he took the mark.*

6

AS RAYFORD FOLLOWED the wheelchair down the hall, barely able to breathe, his mind reeled with his mistakes. Were it somehow possible to extricate himself from this, he would be the most decisive leader the Tribulation Force could imagine.

They repaired to an office even smaller than the original. Pinkerton Stephens opened the door and neatly pivoted his chair so he could hold it open and leave room for Rayford and Albie to enter. He pointed Rayford to a steel gray chair near the wall, facing a desk of the same color and material. Albie sat to Rayford's left.

Stephens let the door shut and locked it, breathed something nasally about the room being secure and not bugged, then steered himself to the other side of the desk, plowing a standard chair out of the way. He maneuvered his wheelchair up to and under the desk, leaned forward and rested his elbows atop it, and folded his hand and a half under his chin.

Part of Rayford could hardly bear to look at the man; another part could not take his eyes off him. "Now then," Stephens began slowly, "Deputy Commander Elbaz—if that's your real name—you may restrap your sidearm and keep your hand off it. We're both on the same team, and you have nothing to fear. As for you, Mr. Berry, while you may be out of uniform and likely using an alias yourself, neither do you have anything to fear. You are about to be pleasantly surprised to find that the three of us are on the same team."

Rayford wanted to say, "I doubt it," but feared he would emit no sound if he tried.

"Shall we start over, gentlemen?" Stephens said.

If only . . . , Rayford thought.

"Mr. Elbaz, as the superior officer, I believe it falls to you to begin our session with the proper protocol."

"He is risen," Albie said, miserably in Rayford's opinion.

"Who is risen indeed?" Stephens responded, and Rayford attributed the mispronunciation to the man's malady, whatever it was. Albie just stared at Stephens. Rayford noticed that while Albie had taken his hand off his gun, he had not fastened the strap. Rayford wondered if he could grab the gun, kill them both, and get away with Hattie.

"Commander Elbaz, you have business here, and I will let you get to it after I satisfy the curiosity on both your parts. I realize that I am difficult to look at, that you both have to be wondering what happened to me, and that as hard as I have worked on my speech, I am difficult to understand. Have either of you ever seen someone with most of his face missing?"

Both shook their heads, and Stephens placed his good thumb beneath his chin. "Once I remove my prosthesis, I will be unable to be understood at all, and so I will not attempt to speak."

Snap!

Rayford flinched as Stephens unsnapped the plastic covering under his chin.

Snap! Snap!

As he continued, it became clear that the prosthesis was all one piece that substituted for most of his chin, nose, eye sockets, and forehead. It was held in place by metal fasteners embedded in what was left of the original facial bones. Stephens kept it in place with his stubfingered hand and said, "Prepare yourselves; I won't make you look long."

Albie held up a hand. "Mr. Stephens, this is unnecessary. We have business here, yes, and I don't see the need to—"

He stopped when Stephens pulled the piece away from his face, revealing a monstrous cavity. Only what was left of his lips hinted at anything human, and Rayford fought to keep from covering his own eyes. The man had no nose and his entire eyeballs were exposed. Through gaps in his forehead, Rayford believed he could see through to the brain.

Rayford could breathe again when Stephens refastened the appliance. "Forgive me, gentlemen," he said, "but just as I assumed, neither of you really saw what I wanted you to see."

"And what was that?" Albie said, clearly shaken.

"Something that explains what I see on your faces."

"I'm lost," Rayford said.

"Oh, but you're not," Stephens said with a twisted smile. "You once were lost, but now you're found. Would you like me to remove the prosthesis again and—"

"No," Rayford and Albie said in unison. And Albie added, "Just get to the point."

Pinkerton folded his hands beneath his chin again, and his eyes seemed to bore into Albie. "How did I respond when you said, 'He is risen'?"

Albie seemed to have regained his voice and composure. "Sounded like you said, 'Who is risen indeed?'"

"That's what I said. What's your answer?"

Albie shifted and cleared his throat. "I believe the protocol is that I say, 'He is risen,' and that you respond, 'He is risen indeed.'"

"Fair enough, but my question remains. Who is risen indeed?"

So, Rayford concluded, *somehow he's onto me.* And yet he sat silent, knowing a moment of truth had arrived and waiting to see what would come of it.

"Humor me one more time, Commander."

Albie sighed and glanced at Rayford. Albie's phony mark sure looked real. "He is risen," Albie muttered.

"Who is risen indeed?" Stephens said, forcing another smile through the misshapen lips.

"Oh, for Pete's sake!" Albie said. "I'm tired of this game."

"Christ!" Stephens whispered excitedly. "Come on, brothers! The answer to the question is 'Christ!' Christ is risen indeed! I see the marks of the believer on both your foreheads! You missed mine for the horror of the rest of my face. Now look!"

He unfastened the prosthesis from the top this time and merely peeled it back. Rayford and Albie leaned forward, and there, amidst the gore, the mark was clear. As Stephens reapplied the piece, Rayford turned and grabbed Albie's head in both hands. He cupped the back with his left hand and rubbed the forehead hard with his right.

"Satisfied?" Albie said, smiling.

Rayford felt like jelly. He flopped back in his chair, panting and unable to move.

"So who are you anyway?" Stephens said.

Rayford leaned forward, "I'm—"

"Oh, I know who you are. I knew almost immediately, though I like the new look. But who's this character?"

Albie introduced himself.

Stephens leaned forward and shook his hand. He nodded to Rayford. "I've got Mr. Steele completely dumbfounded, don't I?"

"That's an understatement," Rayford said.

"You and I both worked for Carpathia at the same time, Rayford, and before that your son-in-law worked for me."

"Steve Plank?"

"In the flesh, or what's left of it. Crushed, chopped up, burned, and left for dead by the wrath of the Lamb earthquake. I'd been on the edge for weeks, reading Buck's stuff, realizing things about Carpathia. I decided that if Buck and other believers were right about a global earthquake, I was in at the sound of the first tremor. I was praying the prayer as the building came down."

Rayford shook his head. "But why the ruse—why work for the GC again?"

"It came to me in the hospital. No one, including me, knew who I was. When my memory returned, I made up a name and a history. That was twenty-one months ago, and all through a year of therapy and rehab, I had time to think about where I wanted to land. I wanted to take Carpathia down from the inside."

"But why not tell anyone? Everyone thought you were dead."

"The best secrets are kept between two people, providing one of them is dead. One of the most shameless stunts Carpathia pulled was how he treated Hattie Durham. I got myself into the Peacekeeping Force and kept my eye on her till I tracked her out here. I prayed this day would come. I'll follow orders, obey the rules, do my job, and you'll rescue her."

+ + +

David panicked. After sitting through the surreal performance by Carpathia, Fortunato, and Viv Ivins, he was in line to leave with the others. But Carpathia stood by the door, accepting embraces, handshakes, kisses, and bowing from each director. The shameless Hickman fell to his knees and wrapped his arms around Nicolae's knees, weeping loudly. The potentate rolled his eyes and gave Fortunato a look that would have put a wart on a gravestone.

When he was about sixth in line, David prayed desperately. What was he to do? In the flesh he wanted to fake whatever he had to fake in order to not be found out and jeopardize the rest of the Force. But he could not, would not, bow the knee to Antichrist. It was impossible that his breach of etiquette would go unnoticed. From what he could tell, it appeared he would be the only director who did not gush over the resurrected leader.

"God, help me!" he prayed silently. Was this the end? Should he merely bolt now and hope for the best? Or shake Carpathia's hand and say something neutral: "Glad you're feeling better after that dying thing"? "Welcome back"?

Except for his obvious disgust with Hickman, Carpathia oozed graciousness and humility as his people poured on the sugar. "Oh, thank you. I am grateful for your partnership and support. Great days ahead. Yes. Yes."

Now second in line, David was nauseated. Literally. His tender scalp vibrated against the bandages with every beat of his heart. He tried to pray, tried to be sensitive to what God wanted him to do. But as the director in front of him finally pulled away from a long embrace of the potentate, David stood there blankly.

Carpathia spread his arms and said, "David, my beloved David."

David could not move and sensed the turning heads of those nearby. Carpathia looked puzzled, seeming to beckon him. David said, "Pothen—potenth—Exshell—"

and pitched forward. His last image before crashing to the floor, head banging the marble, was that he had vomited all over Carpathia.

* * *

"How you doing, Zeke?" Buck said.

He pictured the all-black-wearing, flabby forger huddled underground at his dad's one-pump filling station in ravaged Des Plaines. "I'm OK," came the whispered reply. "I been watchin' TV to keep from gettin' bored, and I got all kinds of food down here. Kinda dark though. And 'course there's nothing on but all this Carpathia junk."

"Have you been keeping an eye on the GC?"

"Yeah, every time I hear a car I scoot over to my monitor and watch what they do. Some of these people aren't even our real customers. They just see the pump and stop in. Then the GC car swings over from across the road and parks right in front of 'em."

"A Jeep?"

"No, it's a little four door, a dark compact."

"Good."

"Why's that good, Mr. Williams?"

"Because when I come for you, I'm going to be in a white Hummer, and it'll squash a compact like a bug."

"It's not a VW, sir. It's—"

"That was just an expression, Zeke."

"Oh, I getcha."

"So they don't pull up in front *and* behind the car?"

"No, there's only one GC car over there. I looked."

"You did?"

"Yeah. I know I shouldn't've, but I was real bored, so I sneaked up the stairs where I was still in the dark and could see across the way. You know this road never really got rebuilt. They threw some asphalt on it a little over a year ago, but there was no real base, so it went to potholes and now it's just chunks of pavement. We don't get much traffic."

"You don't think the GC knows you're there, do you?"

"Nope, and I'm real sure they don't know there's a basement. There didn't use to be. Dad and I dug it ourselves."

"Where's the debris?"

"Out back, through the door at the back of the service bay."

"Hmm, never noticed it. How close are the secret stairs to the underground?"

"Maybe ten feet. It's kinda hidden in the corner."

"So if I was to drive to the back of the station, I'd see a door right about in the middle of the building, a door you could get to by sneaking up the stairs and moving about ten feet along the back wall."

"Yeah."

"So if you knew exactly when I was coming, you could sneak out the back without the GC stakeout guys seeing you."

"They'd probably see you, though."

"I'll worry about that. We don't want them to know you were ever in the underground. You come out and crawl in the back and I'll have a blanket you can hide under."

"I'll have a lot of my stuff."

"That's OK. If they see me and stop me, I'll bluff my way out of it, but I'm going to try to do it in a way where they won't even know I'm there."

A beep told Buck he had another call. It was Rayford. "Zeke, let me call you back. It could be a while, so be packed." He pushed the button. "Buck here."

"Buck, you're not going to believe who I just prayed with."

"Hattie?"

"No, you'd never guess."

+ + +

David awoke in the palace hospital during the wee hours to someone caressing his hand.

"Don't speak," she whispered. It was Nurse Palemoon. "You're a celebrity."

"I am?"

"Shh. It's all over the palace that you blew chunks on Carpathia."

David was on an IV again. He felt better. "Did you change my dressing?"

"Yes, now be quiet."

"I thought you were off duty."

"So did I, but I was yanked in here because I was the one who had stitched you up, and you know no doctor was going to be dragged out of bed."

"Hannah, I've got to get out of here."

"No, you should have been with us a few days anyway, and now you've got the chance."

"I can't and neither can you." He quickly whispered what he had learned at the meeting. "We've got to be out of here before thirty days from today or be prepared for the consequences."

"I'm prepared, David. Aren't you?"

"You know what I mean. I've got to find my fiancée and my pilots, and if you know of any other believers—"

"Fiancée? You're attached?"

"The Phoenix cargo chief, Annie Christopher."

"I don't know what to tell you, David. If she were here, she'd be in the system by now."

"Would you check again for me? And see if you can get Mac McCullum and Abdullah Smith to visit me."

\+ + +

"That's quite an alias, Albie," Plank said. "You want me to report that a Deputy Commander Elbaz came in here with the proper credentials and that I followed the letter of the law?"

"I'm so visible on the GC database, no one will even question it," Albie said. "They'll probably wonder why they haven't met me yet."

"And soon enough," Rayford said, "I'll be enlisted and we'll make sure Albie reports to me. I just worry about compromising our inside guy, the one who sets this stuff up for us."

"How will they trace it to him or even to the palace?" Albie said.

"I don't know. Maybe he's precluded that, but we'll have to let him know what's happening."

Plank led them out the door and down the hall, past the receptionist and into the cell area. "I heard a noise back there a minute ago," Mrs. Garner called out from the desk.

"Trouble?"

"Somethin' banging, that's all."

Plank led the men to Hattie's door and knocked but heard no response. "Ma'am," he called out, "GC personnel are here to transport you back to Buffer." He winked at Rayford and Albie. "May I come in, ma'am?"

Plank fished for his key ring, unlocked the door, and pushed it open about an inch until it met resistance. Albie and Rayford stepped forward to help, but Plank said, "I got this."

He backed up his chair, then threw it forward, bashing into the door and pushing past the bed that had been wedged against it. "Oh, no!" he said, and Rayford stepped over him, driving his shoulder into the door to force his way in.

The room was dark, but when he flipped the light switch, sparks startled him from the ceiling where the fixture had been. Light from the hall showed the fixture now on the floor, knotted at the end of a sheet. The other end was tight around Hattie's neck, and she lay there twitching.

"Tried to hang herself from a flimsy light," Plank said, as Albie leaped past him and slid up to Hattie on his knees. He and Rayford dug and tore at the sheet until it came loose. Rayford gently turned her on her back, and she flopped like a dead woman. As his eyes grew accustomed to the dark, he saw that hers were open, pupils dilated.

"She was moving!" Albie whispered, grabbing her belt and lifting her hips off the floor. Rayford plugged her nose, forced her mouth open, and clamped his mouth over hers. Her tiny frame rose and fell as he breathed into her, and Albie applied pressure to help her breathe out.

"Shut the door," Albie told Plank.

"You don't need the light?"

"Shut it!" he whispered desperately. "We're going to save this girl, but nobody but us is going to know it."

Plank steered his chair to push the bed out of the way, then shut the door.

"She's got a pulse," Albie said. "You OK, Ray? Want me to take over?"

Rayford shook his head and continued until Hattie began to cough. Finally she gulped in huge breaths and blew them out. Rayford sat heavily on the floor, his back against the wall. Hattie cried and swore. "I can't even kill myself," she hissed. "Why didn't you let me die? I can't go back to Buffer!"

She collapsed in tears and lay rocking on the floor on her knees and elbows.

"She doesn't recognize anybody," Albie said.

Hattie looked up, squinting. Rayford leaned over and turned on a small lamp. "No, I don't," she said, peering at Albie and glancing at Rayford. "I know Commander Pinkerton here, but who are you losers?"

Albie pointed to Rayford. "He saved your life. I'm just his loser friend."

Hattie sat in the middle of the floor, her knees pulled up, hands clasped around them. And she swore again.

"You're not going to Buffer, Hattie," Rayford said finally, and it was clear she recognized his voice.

"What?" she said, wonder in her voice.

"Yeah, it's me," Rayford said. "There are no secrets in this room."

"You came?" she squealed, scrambling to him and trying to embrace him.

He held her away. She looked at Plank. "But . . ."

"We're all in this together," Rayford said wearily.

"I almost killed myself," Hattie said.

"Actually," Albie said, "you did."

"What?"

"You're dead."

"What are you talking about?"

"You want out of here? You want the GC off your back? You go out of here dead."

"What are you saying?"

"You called your old friend to rescue you. He refused. You were despondent. When you gave up hope and were convinced you were going to Buffer, you lost all hope, wrote a note, and hung yourself. We came to get you, discovered you too late, and what could we do? Report the suicide and dispose of the body."

"I *did* write a note," she said. "See?" She pointed to a slip of paper that had fallen off the bed.

Rayford picked it up and read it under the lamp. "Thanks for nothing, old FRIENDS!!!" she had written. "I vowed never to go back to Buffer, and I meant it. You can't win them all."

"Sign it," Rayford said.

Hattie massaged her neck and tried to clear her throat. She found her pen and signed the note.

"How long can you hold your breath?" Albie asked.

"Not long enough to kill myself, apparently."

"We're going to wheel you out of here under a sheet, and you're going to have to look dead when we load you on the plane too. Can you pull that off?"

"I'll do whatever I have to." She looked at Plank. "You're in on this too?"

"The less you know, the better," he said. He glanced at Albie, then Rayford. "She never needs to know, far as I'm concerned." They nodded.

Plank told them to leave the sheet the way it was, with the light fixture still embedded in one end. "Use the other sheet from the bed to cover her, and do it now."

Rayford ripped the sheet from the bed, and Hattie lay on the bare mattress. He floated the sheet atop her and let it settle. Plank opened the door. "Mrs. Garner!" he called, "we've had a tragedy here!"

"Oh my—"

"No, don't come! Just stay where you are. The prisoner hanged herself, and the GC will dispose of the remains."

"Oh, Commander! I—is that what I heard?"

"Possibly."

"Could I have done something? Should I have?"

"There's nothing you could have done, ma'am. Let's let these men do their work. Bring the gurney from Utility."

"I don't have to look, do I, sir?"

"I'll handle it. Just get it for me. I'll dictate a report later."

Despite her ashen countenance and protestations, Rayford noticed that Mrs. Garner watched the "body" until it was loaded into the minivan. He was amazed at Hattie's ability to look motionless under that sheet.

Plank agreed to call ahead to the former Carpathia Memorial Airstrip to clear the way for Deputy Commander Elbaz and his driver to pull Judy Hamilton's vehicle right up to their fighter jet in order to load a body for transport. No, they would not need any assistance and would appreciate as little fuss as possible over it.

Hattie slipped back under the sheet a few miles from the airstrip, and though curious eyes peered through the windows, Rayford and Albie carried her aboard without arousing undue suspicion.

7

BUCK PULLED THE HUMMER out of the garage under the Strong Building after dark, lights off. He had spent the afternoon rigging up a special connection to the brake lights and backup lights. Once in regular traffic outside Chicago, he didn't want to risk getting stopped for malfunctioning rear lights, but neither did he want those lights coming on when he braked at Zeke's place.

Zeke himself was an expert at this and walked Buck through it by phone. It would be great when Zeke was tucked away at the new safe house, available to help with just those kinds of details. The brake lights were now disengaged, so with his lights on or off, Buck would have to manually illuminate them when applying the brake. A thin wire led from the back, through the backseat and up to the driver's side. If he could just remember to use it.

No one knew how frequently, if ever, the GC invested the time, equipment, and manpower to overfly the quarantined city their own databases told them was heavily radioactive. It didn't make sense that anyone would be near the place. If the readings were true—which David Hassid and the Tribulation Force knew was not the case—no one could live there long.

Still, Rayford's plan was to come and go in his helicopter from the tower in the dark of night. And Buck, or anyone else coming or going, would do the same from the garage. It was tricky going, because no light sources—outside the Strong Building—were engaged in the city. Unless the moon was bright, seeing anything in the dark was almost impossible on what used to be those miles of city streets.

Buck pulled away slowly, the gigantic Hummer propelling itself easily over the jagged terrain. He wanted to get used to the vehicle, the largest he had ever driven. It was surprisingly comfortable, predictably powerful, and—to his delight—amazingly quiet. He had feared it would sound like a tank.

Driving around Chicago in the dark was no way to familiarize himself with the car. He needed open road and the confidence that no one was paying attention. Half an hour later he hit the city limits and took the deserted frontage road that would deliver him into the suburbs without detection. He turned on his lights and set the manual brake light switch where he could reach it with his left hand.

Near Park Ridge a rebuilt section actually had a few miles of new pavement and a couple of working traffic lights. The rest of northern Illinois seemed to have regressed to the earliest days of the automobile. Cars made their own trails through rubble, and rain sometimes made those routes impassable.

Buck saw a couple of GC squad cars, but traffic was light. When he felt safe, he tested the power of the Hummer and practiced several turns at varying speeds. The faster he went and the sharper he turned, the more violently his body was pressed against the safety belt. But it seemed nothing would make the Hummer tip. Buck found a deserted area where he was sure no one could see him and tried a couple of fast turns even on inclines. The Hummer seemed to ask for more. With its superwide stance, its weight, and its power, it had unmatched maneuverability. Buck felt as if he were starring in a commercial.

He floored the vehicle, got it up to near eighty on packed dirt, slammed on the brakes, and turned the wheel. The antilock system kept him from skidding or even hinting at going over. He couldn't wait to compete with whatever toy the GC was using in its stakeout in Des Plaines.

Buck had to calm himself. The idea was to pick up Zeke undetected. He considered stopping at the station like a normal customer and ramming the GC as they came to investigate. But they had phones and radios and a communications network that would hem him in. If he could find a way to approach the station from the back, lights out, they might never see him, even after he pulled away with his quarry.

His phone chirped. It was Zeke. "You close by?" the young man said.

"Not far. What's up?"

"We're gonna hafta torch this place."

"Why?"

"Once they figure they've busted every rebel that used to gas up here, they're going to torch it anyway, right?"

"Maybe," Buck said. "So why not let them?"

"They might search it first."

"And find what?"

"The underground, of course. I can't even think about gettin' all the stuff outta here that could give my dad away."

"What more can they do to him?"

"All they got him on now is sellin' gas without GC approval. They fine him or make him sit a month or two. If they find out me and him was runnin' a rebel forgery biz outta here, he becomes an enemy of the state."

"Good thinking." Buck never failed to be amazed at the street wisdom of the unlikely looking Zeke. Who would have guessed that the former druggie-biker-tattoo artist would be the best phony credentials man in the business?

"And remember, Mr. Williams. We were feedin' people outta here too. Groceries, you name it. Well, you know. You bought a bunch of 'em. OK, here's what I'm thinkin'. I rig up a timer to a sparking device. You know, it ain't the gas that burns anyway."

"I'm sorry?" Buck felt stupid. He had been a globe-trotting journalist, and a virtual illiterate was trying to tell him gasoline fires aren't what they seem?

"Yeah, it's not the gas that burns. When I was workin' above ground, helpin' Dad in the station when it was legal and all, I used to toss my cigarettes in a bucket of gas we kept in the service bay."

"No, you didn't."

"I swear."

"Lit cigarettes?"

"Swear to—I mean, honest. That was how we put 'em out. They'd hiss like you was tossin' 'em into a bucket o' water."

"I'm confused."

"We kept gas in there to clean our hands on. Cuts grease, you know. Like if you just did an axle job and now you gotta go fill a tank or write on a credit card receipt or something."

"I mean I'm confused about how you could throw a cigarette into a container of gasoline."

"Lots of people don't know that or don't believe it."

"How'd you keep from blowing yourselves to kingdom come?"

"Well, if the bucket of gas was fresh, you had to wait awhile. If you saw any of that shimmerin' of the fumes over it, like when you first pour it in there, or when you're fillin' your tank, well, you don't want any open flame of any kind near that."

"But once it sat and the, uh, shimmering fumes were gone?"

"Then we tossed our cigarette butts in there."

"So, it's the fumes."

"Yeah, it's the fumes what burns."

"I get it. So, your thoughts?"

"See, Mr. Williams, it works the same in an engine. Like a fuel-injected engine shoots a fine spray of gas into the cylinders and the spark plugs spark and burn it, but they're not burning the spray."

"The spray is emitting fumes and that's what's, in essence, exploding in the cylinder," Buck said.

"Now you've got it."

"Good. I'm heading your way, so cut to the chase."

"OK. I moved two huge boxes of stuff out by the pile of dirt in the back, and I got one big canvas bag. All my files, my equipment, everything is there. Even had room for some food."

"We have plenty of food, Zeke."

"Never have enough food. Anyway, the stuff's out there waitin'. I figure if you don't get seen comin', I can be waitin' for ya and load my stuff in there real quick before I jump in."

"Sounds like a plan. Back to the torching."

"Yeah. I've got auto parts down here. I cut a feed from the pipe that leads to the storage tank, which runs right by the wall we dug out here, and I hook a fuel injector to it. When I leave, I turn the spigot, the gas runs through the fuel injector and starts sprayin' gasoline."

"And pretty soon the underground is filled with gas."

"Fumes."

"Right. And you, what, toss a match down the stairs on your way out to the car?"

Zeke laughed.

"Shh."

"Yeah, they can't hear me. But no, tossing a flame down here then would blow me all the way to Chicago. Save you a trip, eh?"

"So how do you ignite it?"

"Put a spark plug on a timer. Give myself five minutes or so, just in case. At the right time, kaboom."

"Kaboom."

"Bingo."

"Zeke, even if I agreed, you'd never have time to rig that all up. I'm not ten minutes away."

"I figured you'd agree."

"And so—?"

"It's all done."

"You're kiddin' me."

"Nope. If you're ten minutes away, I'll set the timer for fifteen, and when I leave I'll open the spigot."

"Hoo, boy, you're resourceful."

"I know how to do stuff."

"You sure do, but do me a favor."

"Name it."

"Set the timer for five, but don't start it until after you've turned the spigot on your way out. Deal?"

"Deal."

"Oh, and one more thing. Make sure I'm there before you open that spigot."

"Oh, yeah, right. That would be important."

"Kaboom, Zeke."

"Bingo."

"Call you when I get there."

* * *

"Her name is not in our system, David," Nurse Palemoon said. He tried to sit up and she shushed him. "That doesn't have to mean the worst."

"How can you say that? The sun is coming up, and I haven't heard from her. She'd communicate with me if she could!"

"David, you must calm down. This room is empty but not secure. Your friends are on their way, but you can't trust anyone else."

"Tell me about it. Hannah, you have got to get me out of here. I can't stay here another few days. There is so much I have to do before leaving New Babylon."

"I can supply you with extra meds and dressings and try to make sure you're set, but you're going to be sore."

"I'm not worried about that. Will you—" His throat caught and he couldn't say it. "Ah, would you—"

"You want me to check the morgue?" She said it with such compassion that he nearly broke down.

He nodded.

"I'll be right back. If your friends get here while I'm gone, remind them there are ears everywhere."

* * *

Rayford and Albie and their human cargo from Colorado put down at a tiny airstrip near Bozeman, Montana, rather than try to get back to Kankakee without sleep. Albie bluffed and blustered the tiny GC contingent at the strip, who bought his story of transporting a criminal and let the three of them borrow a Jeep to get into town.

Such as it was. Bozeman had been left with few amenities, but one was a nearly deserted motel where they rented two rooms. "I don't guess we have to worry about you bolting," Rayford told Hattie.

"Compared to Buffer," she said, "the new safe house sounds like heaven."

"You'll be in for the pitches of your life," he said. "There are more of us, and you're going to be our prime target."

"I might just listen for once," she said.

"Don't say that lightly."

"I don't say anything lightly anymore."

Hattie had a million questions about Pinkerton Stephens, but Rayford and Albie told her only that "he is one of us." Then she wanted Albie's story, and he told of becoming a believer after a lifetime as a Muslim. "You know who I mean when I mention Tsion Ben-Judah then?" he said.

"Do I know?" she said. "I know him personally. Talk about a man who loves the unlovable . . ."

"Are you speaking of yourself, young lady?"

She snorted and nodded. "Who else?"

"Let me tell you something. I was unlovable. I was no kind of husband or father. My whole family is dead now. I was a criminal, and the only people who cared about me paid me well to get what they needed for illegal acts. I began to justify my existence when my black marketing was used to oppose the new evil world ruler. But I would not have called him Antichrist, would not even have known the term. I was in the same business when the world was merely chaotic, not so evil. My god was cash, and I knew how to get it.

"When Mac and Rayford needed my services, I took some comfort in the fact that they seemed to be good people. I was no longer just helping criminals. I watched them, listened to them. They were outlaws in the eyes of the Global Community, but to me that was a badge of honor.

"When all the predictions Mac and Rayford had told me began coming true, I could not admit to them I was intrigued. More than that, I was scared. If this were all true, then I was an outsider. I was not a believer. I began monitoring the Internet messages of Dr. Ben-Judah without telling my friends. I was full of pride still. What struck me hardest was that Dr. Ben-Judah made it so clear that God was the lover of sinners. Oh, I knew I was that. I just could hardly accept that anyone would love me.

"I downloaded a Bible to my computer and would switch back and forth between it and Dr. Ben-Judah. I was able to see where he was getting his information, but his insights! Those had to come from God alone. What I was learning went against everything I had ever heard or been taught. My first prayer was so childish that I would never have prayed it aloud in front of another living soul.

"I told God I knew I was a sinner and that I wanted to believe that he loved me and would forgive me. I told him that the Western religion—for that is what it sounded like to me—was so foreign to me that I did not know if I could ever understand it. But I said to the Lord, 'If you are really the true and living God, please make it plain to me.' I told him I was sorry for my whole life and that he was my only hope. That was all. I felt nothing, maybe a little foolish. But I slept that night as I had not slept in years.

"Oh, do not misunderstand me. I was *not* sure I had gotten through to God. I was *not* sure that he was, in fact, who Dr. Ben-Judah and the others believed him to be. But I knew I had done all I could. I had been honest with myself and honest with him, and if he was who I hoped he was, he would have heard me. That was the best I could expect."

Albie sat back and inhaled deeply.

"That's it?" Hattie said. "That's all?"

He smiled. "I thought I would pause and see if I had bored you to sleep yet."

"You two are the ones who were up all night. Tell me what happened."

"Well, I awoke the next morning with a feeling of expectancy. I didn't know what to make of it. Before I could even eat, I felt a deep hunger and thirsting—there is no other word for it—for the Bible. I believed with my whole being that it was the Word of God, and I had to read it. I pulled it up on my computer and read and read and read and read. I cannot tell you how it filled me. I understood it! I wanted more of it! I could not get enough. Only after midday, when I was weak from hunger, did I realize I had not eaten yet.

"I thanked God over and over for his Word, for his truth, for answering my prayer and revealing himself to me. Occasionally I would break from my Bible reading and check to see if Dr. Ben-Judah had posted anything new. He had not, but I followed some of his links to a site that walked the reader through what the rabbi calls the sinner's prayer. I prayed it, but I realized that it was what I had already done. I was a believer, a child of God, a forgiven, loved sinner."

Hattie appeared unable to speak, but Rayford had seen her this way before. Many had told her their stories of coming to faith. She knew the truth and the way. She simply had never accepted the life.

"There is a reason I wanted to tell you that story," Albie said. "Not just because I want to persuade you, which I do. Those among us who have found the truth long for everyone else to have it. But it was because of what you said about yourself. You said Dr. Ben-Judah was one who loved the unlovable. He does, of course. This is a Christlike quality, a Jesus characteristic. But then you referred to yourself as unlovable, and I identified with you.

"But more than that, Ms. Durham, if I may use a phrase of Dr. Ben-Judah's. Often he will say that this or that truth 'gives the lie' to certain false claims. Have you heard him say that, and do you know what it means?"

She nodded.

"Well, it applies to you, dear woman. I have just met you, and yet God has given me a love for you. Rayford and his family and friends speak often of you and their love for you. That gives the lie to your claim that you are unlovable."

"They shouldn't love me," she said, just above a whisper.

"Of course they shouldn't. You know yourself. You know your selfishness, your sin. God should not love us either, and yet he does. And it is only because of him that we can love each other. There is no human explanation for it."

Rayford sat praying silently, desperately, for Hattie. Was it possible she was one who had for so long rejected Christ that God had turned her over to her own stubbornness? Was she unable to see the truth, to change her mind? If that were true, why did God plague Rayford and his friends with such a concern for her?

Suddenly she rose and stepped to Rayford. She bent and kissed the top of his head. She turned and did the same to Albie, cupping his face in her hands. "Don't worry about me tonight," she said. "I'll be here in the morning."

"You have no reason not to be," Albie said. "You are not really in our custody. In fact, you are dead."

"Anyway," Rayford said, standing and stretching, "where would you bolt to? Where would you be safer than where we're taking you?"

"Thanks for saving my life," she said as she turned to head for her room.

When she shut the door, Rayford said, "I just hope this wasn't for nothing."

They heard her door open and shut and her moving about in her room.

"It wasn't," Albie said.

Rayford was bone weary, but as he disrobed for bed he thought he heard something over the sound of Albie's shower. From the adjoining room he thought he heard voices. He moved closer to the wall. Not voices, just one. Crying. Sobbing. Wailing. Hattie, muffled, apparently with her face buried in a pillow or blanket.

As he drifted off to sleep half an hour later in the bed across from Albie's, Hattie's laments still wafted through the wall. Rayford heard Albie turn and pat his pillow, then settle back. "God," the little man whispered, "save that girl."

* * *

Buck drove straight past the little filling station, pretending to not notice the GC stakeout car amidst a small grove of trees across the road. He didn't even slow, so as not to attract attention. If he had to guess, he thought just two GC guards were in the car.

He phoned Zeke. "Any more activity?"

"Nope. Was that you what just passed? Nice rig."

"I'm going to circle way around and see if I can come in from the back with my lights off. Might take ten minutes. I'll call you when I'm in position."

Buck drove until he couldn't see even the outline of the station in his rearview mirror, assuming the GC could no longer see him either. He cut his lights and took a right, slowly feeling his way over rough ground. He was a couple of miles from the station, and he wanted to be sure he didn't find a hidden fence or culvert that would mess up the Hummer.

At one point, after taking two more rights and thus heading in the general direction of the back of the station, he felt the vehicle dip and hoped he hadn't found a hole too deep to pull out of. When the front grille hit something solid, he hit the brakes and briefly turned on the headlights. He shut them off again quickly, hoping the GC hadn't seen anything in the distance. Buck saw that he needed to back up and swing left around a five-foot-high or so mound of dirt and boards.

He wanted to turn on his brights and be able to see if anything else obstructed his path to the back of the station, but he didn't dare. By the time he could make out the shape of the place, he slowed to just a few miles an hour and crept along in the uneven dirt, bouncing, jostling, and—he hoped—not sending up too much dust. It was a starry night, and if the GC noticed anything blocking the sky, they were sure to come nosing around the back.

Buck phoned Zeke.

"I hear you," Zeke said.

"You *hear* me? From inside? That can't be good."

"That's what I was thinking. You ready for me?"

"Better come quick. Carrying anything?"

"Yeah, one more bag. Figured I might as well not leave anything I could bring."

"Good thinking. Come on."

"Gotta open the spigot and turn on the timer."

"For how long?"

"Five minutes."

"Anything on the monitor?"

"They're just sittin'."

"Good. Let's go."

Buck knew he could come back the way he came, and though the ride would be pretty rugged, he estimated he could do as much as 40 mph. But in case the GC could hear the Hummer as well as Zeke could, he jumped out and started loading the car to save time.

The inside light stayed dark as he opened the door to get out, and he left it open. He opened the back door on the far side and crept around to start lifting. The first box was almost too heavy, and it was all he could do to not cry out under the weight. He heard Zeke coming up the stairs.

Buck lugged the box onto the backseat from the car door farthest from the station's back door, feeling every sore fiber from his recent ordeal. When he got back around the car to grab the other box, figuring Zeke could load the bag he was carrying and the one on the ground at the same time, he nearly ran into the young man, startling him.

Zeke grunted. Buck tried to shush him, but Zeke dropped his bag and lurched back inside, slamming the door. Buck heard him lumbering down the stairs. Now they were making way too much noise.

Buck yanked open the station door and called out desperately, as quietly as he could, "Zeke, it's just me! C'mon, man! Now!"

"Oh, man!" Zeke hollered. "I thought it was them! The timer's goin', the gas is spittin'. And they're comin', Buck! I can see 'em on the monitor!"

Buck turned and opened the back door nearest the station. He picked up the bag that had been waiting and the one Zeke had dropped and hurled them across the backseat. He left the door open and jumped behind the wheel, slamming his door and putting the Hummer in gear. Zeke barreled out and dove into the backseat, knocking one of the bags out the other side, where Buck had left the door open.

Buck floored the accelerator, but Zeke yelled, "We can't leave that bag! It's got lots of stuff we need!"

The door had started to close when Buck took off, but when he hit the brakes, it swung the other way and creaked against the hinges. "Get it!" he screamed, and Zeke scrambled over the stuff and out onto the ground, his foot dragging a bag out too. And here came the GC mobile around the station in front of Buck.

"Go! Go!" Zeke yelled, forcing himself into the backseat with both heavy bags tucked under his arms.

The door was still open, but Buck had to move. He gunned the engine and slammed into the GC car, driving it back against the station as his back door shut. The guards had weapons out and appeared to be reaching for door handles. Buck knew he couldn't outrace bullets, so he threw the Hummer into Reverse, floored it, and the monstrous vehicle climbed the hill of debris near the door.

Buck stopped at the top as they teetered some twelve feet above their pursuers. He shifted into Drive, and when the GC saw the vehicle start to move, they lowered their weapons and dove out of the way. The Hummer dropped almost vertically, ramming the hood of the little car and blowing both of its front tires.

The engine gushed water and steam, and Buck could tell he had rendered the GC vehicle useless.

Rather than look for the guards, he merely backed up six feet, whipped the wheel right, and sped off into the night. Zeke had somehow gotten the door shut, but neither he nor Buck had time to buckle in. As the Hummer lurched across the plains at high speed, both men were thrown around like rag dolls, their heads hitting the ceiling, their shoulders banging the doors.

Buck skidded to a stop.

"What?" Zeke demanded.

"Buckle up!"

They both did and off he flew again. Fewer than five minutes later, as Buck found a route that would lead them back to Chicago, the sky behind them went from night to day in a massive orange ball of flame. A few seconds later the sound and the shock rocked the car anew. Buck, high from the adrenaline, knew how close they had come to dying.

Zeke, laughing like a child, kept turning in his seat and looking back at the flaming horizon. "Well," he said, cackling, "so much for that job!"

8

MAC AND ABDULLAH sat sullenly in David's hospital room, whispering. "Thirty days?" Mac said over and over. "Hard to believe."

"No way of staying around here," Abdullah said. "Not that I'll miss it. Well, in some ways I will."

"I know I will," David said, coming to full attention whenever he heard footsteps in the corridor. "So much we can do from the inside that we'll never be able to pull off from the outside."

Mac let out a sigh that made him sound old and tired. "David, this may sound like I'm kissin' up to the boss, but you know I wouldn't kiss up to you if you were the potentate. But we both know you can do anything technologically. Get yerself healthy and do whatever you got to do to keep tabs on this place from anywhere in the world. Isn't that doable?"

"Theoretically," David said. "But it won't be easy."

"Somehow you've got this place bugged, sliced, and diced. Why can't you access computers here the way you did that buildin' in Chicago where we're all likely gonna wind up?"

David shrugged. "It's possible. I can't imagine psyching myself up to get it done. Not without Annie." David caught the glance between Mac and Abdullah. "What?" he said. "You know something you're not telling me?"

Mac shook his head. "We're just as worried as you. Makes no sense. No way she wouldn't let you know where she was, if she could." He paused and a twinkle played at his eyes. "Unless she locked herself in that utility room again."

David laughed in spite of himself. Annie was one of the most disciplined, buttoned-down employees he'd ever had, but one out-of-character stunt she pulled would hang over her head as long as she lived.

The way Hannah Palemoon knocked at the half-open door told David way more than he wanted to know. A sob rose in his throat. Mac stood and David nodded to him. "Come in," Mac said.

David tried to ignore the small, corrugated box in Hannah's hands and desperately searched her face for some trace of optimism. She approached slowly and set the box near David's feet. "I am so sorry," she said, and David collapsed inside.

His pain, his fatigue melted away, overwhelmed by grief and loss too great to bear. He groaned and drew his fists up under his chin, turning from his friends, rolling onto his side, drawing his knees up, and folding in on himself.

"Lightning?" The question forced its way past his constricted throat.

"Yes," Hannah whispered. "There would have been no pain or suffering."

Grateful for that, David thought. *At least not for her.*

"David," Mac said huskily, "me and Smitty will be right outside—"

"I'd appreciate it if you could stay," David managed, and he heard them sit again.

"I have a few of her personal effects," Hannah said. David tried to sit up, feeling the cursed dizziness. "It's just her purse and phone, jewelry, and shoes."

David finally sat up and put the box between his knees. His breath caught at the charred smell. The phone had melted in spots. One shoe had scorched holes in the heel and toe.

"I have to see her," he said.

"I wouldn't recommend it," Hannah said.

"David, no," Mac urged.

"I have to! She's not really gone and never will be unless I know for sure. This is her stuff, but did you see her, Hannah?"

The nurse nodded.

"But you didn't know her. Had you ever seen her before?"

She shook her head. "Not that I know of. But, David, I don't know how to say this. If the woman in the morgue were my best friend, I wouldn't recognize her."

The sobs returned and David pushed the box toward the end of the bed, shaking his head, his fingers pressed lightly against his temples, tender and fiery to the touch. "You know she was my first love?"

No one responded.

"I had dated before, but—" he pressed a hand over his lips—"the love of my life."

Mac stood and asked Abdullah to shut the door. He pulled the hanging curtain around the bed so the four of them were cocooned in the dim white light. Mac lay a hand gently on David's shoulder. Abdullah reached for a knee. Hannah gripped David's sheet-covered foot.

"God," Mac whispered, "we're long past asking why things happen. We know we're on borrowed time and that we belong to you. We don't understand this. We don't like it. And it's hard for us to accept. We thank you that Annie didn't suffer," and here his voice broke and became barely audible. "We envy her because she's with you, but we miss her already, and a part of David that can never be replaced has been ripped away. We still trust you, still believe in you, and want to serve you for as long as you'll let us. We just ask that you'll come alongside David now, unlike you ever have before, and help him to heal, to carry on, to do your work."

Mac could not continue. Abdullah said, "We pray in the name of Jesus."

"Thank you," David said, and he turned away from them again. "Please don't go yet." As he lay there, his friends still by the bed inside the curtain, he realized that there would be no formal funeral for Annie and that even if there was—because she was an employee—he would have to conduct himself as a somber superior, not as a grieving lover. When he was forced to separate himself from this place, he didn't want it to reflect upon her and call into suspicion everyone she knew or spent time with.

He heard the drape being opened again. Hannah put the box under the head of the bed, and Mac and Abdullah returned to their chairs. "You need sleep," Hannah said. "You want me to get you something?"

He shook his head. "I'm sorry, Hannah, but I really have to see her. Can you unhook me and help me down there?"

She looked as if about to refuse him, but he saw the light of an idea come to her eyes. "You're sure?" she said.

"Absolutely."

"It won't be easy."

"And this is?"

"I'll get a wheelchair and I'll pull the IV along with us."

+ + +

Zeke was wearing his trademark getup when Buck presented him to the Tribulation Force at the new safe house and introduced him to Tsion. "When the boss gets back, we'll make you a full-fledged member," Buck said. "But meanwhile, find yourself some privacy and appropriate whatever you need to settle in, make yourself at home, and become part of the family."

"By all means," Tsion said, embracing the fleshy young man. In thick-soled, square-toed, black motorcycle boots, black jeans, black T-shirt under black leather vest, Zeke was a stark contrast to the sweatered, corduroyed rabbi, standing there in his Hush Puppies. "Welcome and God bless you."

Zeke was awkward and shy, and while he shook hands all around and lightly returned hugs, he stared at the ground and mumbled replies. Soon enough, however, he was exploring, unpacking, moving a bed, setting up his stuff. An hour later he returned to the central meeting place near the elevators. "This place is really uptown," he said.

"Literally," Leah said, clearly bemused by the man who had once changed her entire look and given her a new identity.

Zeke stared at her, and Buck got the impression he didn't know what she meant but was afraid to admit it. As if to cover his embarrassment and change the subject, Zeke dug in both back pockets and one vest pocket for huge rolls of twenty-Nick bills, which he slapped noisily on the table. "I intend to earn my keep," he said. "Put this here in the pot."

"You might want to wait until it's official," Buck said. "Rayford will be here tomorrow night and—"

"Oh, it's all right. Consider it a donation, even if I get voted out or blackballed or whatever."

"I don't see that happening," Chloe said, burping the sleeping Kenny Bruce on her shoulder.

"Oh, man!" Zeke said quietly, noticing the baby. He approached slowly and reached carefully toward Kenny's back. "Can I?"

"You may," Chloe said. "Your hands clean?"

Zeke stopped and turned his hands before his eyes. "They have to be for my kinda work. Can't smudge the new IDs, you know. They look dirty, 'cause I work on engines and stuff, but they're just stained."

He bent at the knees before Chloe and gently put his meaty hand on Kenny's back. His fingers nearly stretched from shoulder to tiny shoulder. Zeke lightly touched the boy's feathery hair.

"Sit and you can hold him," Chloe said, as the others watched. Buck was especially amused by Chaim, whose eyes filled.

"Want a turn?" Buck whispered.

"It's been so long," Chaim whispered, trying to make himself understood. "It would be a privilege."

Somehow Kenny slept through everyone's turn, even Tsion's. He was last and quickly passed Kenny back to Chloe, as he was overcome. "My children were teenagers when they . . . when they . . . but the memories . . ."

+ + +

"We need to identify a body," Hannah Palemoon said, pushing David's wheelchair and pulling his IV to the desk just inside the morgue.

"Sign in," a bored older woman said.

"Forget it," Hannah said. "The system is behind by several days. Nobody'll ever check anyway."

The woman made a face. "Less work for me," she said. "I'm just filling in."

David's heart raced as Hannah pushed him past rows and rows of bodies as far as the eye could see—on gurneys, in lateral refrigerators, and sheet-wrapped head to toe, shoulder to shoulder on the floor. "She's not one of these, is she?"

"Next room, around the corner."

Hannah steered him to the foot end of a covered body on a bed. He took a deep, quavery breath. Hannah lifted the sheet from one foot and peered at the toe tag to make sure she had the right corpse. "You're sure you want to do this?"

He nodded, though now not so sure.

She showed him the tag thin-wired to the big toe. It bore Annie's name and rank and serial number all right, plus date of birth and date of death. The foot was swollen and discolored, but no doubt hers. David reached to envelop it with both hands and was struck by the cold stiffness.

It was the other foot whose shoe had showed lightning damage. David began pulling the sheet from it, ignoring Hannah when she cleared her throat and said, "Uh, David . . ."

He recoiled at the damage. The heel was split wide and the big toe mangled. He covered her feet and dropped his head. "You're sure she never felt that?"

"Positive."

"Fortunato was given the power to call down fire from heaven on those who didn't worship the image."

"I know."

"I could have easily been struck."

"Me too."

"Why her?"

Hannah did not answer. David tried to wheel himself between beds to the other end of the body. His IV stretched. "Let me," Hannah said, and she pushed him slowly. When he reached for the sheet, Hannah reached over his shoulder and put a hand on his forearm. "You may want to look only at her face," she said. "There was severe cranial trauma."

He hesitated.

"And David? For some reason no one closed her eyes. I tried, but with time and rigor mortis . . . well, a mortician will have to do that."

He nodded, panting. His head throbbed, and when he was able to control his breathing again, David lifted the sheet and brought it down to her neck, careful not to look. With another deep breath, his eyes traveled to hers.

For an instant it didn't look like Annie. Her eyes were fixed on something a million miles away, her face bloated and purple. Burns on her ears and neck evidenced where her necklace and earrings had been.

He sat staring at her for so long that Hannah finally said, "OK?"

David shook his head. "I want to stand."

"You shouldn't."

"Help me."

She pushed the IV stand around the chair so it was next to him. "Use that to brace yourself. If the room starts to spin, sit again."

"Starts?"

She locked the wheels and put a hand on his back, guiding as he rose. He pushed with his left hand on the arm of the chair and pulled with his right on the stand. Finally, up and wobbly, Hannah's hand still on his back, David cupped Annie's cheek with his free hand. Despite the cool rigidity, he imagined she could feel his caress. In spite of himself, he leaned over her until he could see past where a tuft of hair had been pushed up in front. Behind that was a silver dollar–sized hole that exposed her brain.

David shook his head and carefully sat again. He didn't want to think what a lightning bolt through her body would have done to vital organs. He now believed Hannah that Annie never would have known what hit her.

Hannah pulled David's chair and left him at the foot of the bed. He sat with his head in his hands, unable to produce more tears. He heard Hannah rearranging the sheet and carefully re-covering Annie, almost as if she were still alive, and it struck him as sweet and thoughtful.

As she wheeled him out, he whispered his thanks.

"I wish I had known her," Hannah said.

+ + +

Rayford had briefed Buck and Chloe and Tsion the night before, so when a phone woke him at dawn in Montana, he assumed it was one of them. As he reached to answer, however, it was not his cell but the room phone. He had not given out that number, so who would be calling? The desk? Was someone onto them? Should he identify himself as Rayford Steele or Marvin Berry?

Neither, he decided. "Hello?"

"Ray," Hattie said, "it's me. I'm awake, I'm up, I'm starved, and I want to get going. You?"

He groaned and glanced at the other bed. Albie was sound asleep. "You're a little too chipper for me," he said. "I'm asleep, I'm in bed, I'm not hungry, and there's no sense leaving so early that we get to Kankakee before dark. We can't go to the safe house until after that anyway."

"Oh, Rayford! C'mon! I'm bored. And I'm dead, remember? I need a new identity, but I'm as free as I've been in years, thanks to you! How 'bout some breakfast?"

"We can't be too obvious or public."

"Are you going to go back to sleep, really?"

"Back? I never woke up."

"Seriously."

"No, I probably won't. Someone in the next room is up banging around anyway."

She knocked on the wall. "And I'll keep banging until I get company for breakfast."

"All right, dead girl. Give me twenty minutes."

"I'll be outside your door in fifteen."

"Then you'll be waiting five."

Rayford was glad his showering and dressing hadn't wakened Albie. He peeked out the window and saw nothing and no one. Out the peephole in the door he saw Hattie stretching in the sun, just beyond the shadow caused by the second-floor walkway. He peeked through the curtain. The place was otherwise deserted.

Rayford stepped out, and Hattie nearly lunged at him. "Let me see, let me see!" she said, staring at him. "I can see yours!" she said. "That means you can see mine! Can you?"

His eyes were still adjusting to the sun, but as she pulled him out of the shadow by the door, it hit him. His knees buckled and he almost fell. "Oh, Hattie!" he said, reaching for her. She leaped into his arms and squeezed him around the neck so hard he finally had to push her away so he could breathe.

"Does mine look like yours?" she said.

He laughed. "How would I know? We can't see our own. But yours looks like every other one I've seen. This is worth waking Albie for."

"Is he decent?"

"Sure. Why?"

"Let me."

Rayford unlocked the door and Hattie burst in. "Albie, wake up, sleepyhead!"

He didn't stir.

She sat on the bed next to him and bounced. He groaned.

"C'mon, Albie! The day is young!"

"What?" he said, sitting up. "What's wrong?"

"Nothing will ever be wrong again!" she said, taking his face in her hands and pointing his bleary eyes toward her. "I'm just showing off my mark!"

9

BUCK AWOKE AT DAWN and made the rounds, checking on everyone. He smiled at Zeke's domain and was grateful it was private. Zeke had worked until after midnight arranging his area, getting his computer and other equipment set up. Zeke snored loudly, but when Buck peeked in, he found Zeke on the floor next to his bed. *Each to his own.*

Leah's door was shut and locked. She had been up late on a call from Ming Toy, who had returned to Buffer frantic about her parents' staying in New Babylon until her brother could find a position with the GC.

Chloe had been on her computer until after Kenny was in bed, coordinating the international co-op. She urged the tens of thousands of members to watch for Tsion's next missive, wherein he planned to discuss the importance of their readiness when the buying/selling edict would go into effect. He would also be asking volunteer pilots and drivers to bring small planes and vehicles into Israel for a secret mission.

The only other two Trib Force members were awake and working. Chaim was hunched over a stack of books, several of them open, assigned by Tsion. He looked up with twinkling eyes when Buck poked his head in. Buck seemed to understand his constricted speech better than the others.

"Miss Rose, the redhead," Chaim said.

"Leah."

"Yes, she is a trained nurse, you know."

Buck nodded.

"She tells me she can remove the wires when I am ready. Well, I am more than ready. A man my age cannot lose this much weight this fast. And I want to be able to speak clearly!"

"How is everything else?"

"On my body, you mean? I am an old man. I've survived a plane crash. I should complain? Cameron, this building is a gift from God! What a luxury! If we have to live in exile, this is where to live. And what young Tsion has given me to read, well . . . I call him young because he was once my student, but you knew that. There are times, Cameron, when the Scriptures are like an ugly mirror to me, showing me again and again my bankrupt soul. But then I rejoice at the redemption, *my* redemption! The story of God, the history of his people, it is all coming alive to me before my eyes."

"Did you remember to eat?"

"I don't eat. I drink. Agh! But yes, thank you for asking. I am now drinking in the truth of God."

"Carry on."

"Oh, I will! Tsion was looking for you, by the way. Did he find you?"

"No. I'm on my way to him now."

Buck moved up a floor and found Dr. Ben-Judah with his fingers flying over the computer keyboard. He didn't want to disturb him, but the rabbi must have heard him. Without looking up or slowing, he said, "Cameron, is that you? So much to do. I shall be busy all the day, I fear. Dark as the days are, my joy is complete. Prophecy comes alive by the minute. Did you see what Master Zeke did for me? A precious lad!"

Buck looked again. Tsion had not only a main computer but also two laptops networked to it on each side. "No more switching back and forth between programs," Tsion sang out. "Bibles on one, commentaries on the other. And I am writing to my people in the middle!"

"Glad to get back to it?"

"You cannot imagine."

"Don't let me slow you."

"No, no! Come in, Cameron. I need you." He finally stopped and hit the Print command. Pages began piling in the printer output tray. Tsion swiveled in his chair. "Sit, please! You must be my first reader today."

"I'd be honored, but—"

"First, tell me. What news from our brothers and sisters in the field?"

"We know little. We haven't heard from David Hassid, except secondhand through Rayford, since the Carpathia resurrection."

"And what did you hear then?"

"Only that Ray and Albie had trouble raising him. They needed him to pave the way for a scheme they were pulling, trying to get Hattie Durham back from the GC. At the last minute he must have gotten their messages, because the stuff came through and the mission was accomplished."

Tsion nodded, pursing his lips. "Praise the Lord," he said quietly. "She is coming back to us then?"

"Tonight. We expect Ray and Albie and Hattie after dark."

"I will pray for their safety. And we must continue to pray for her, of course. God has given me such a weight of care for that woman."

Buck shook his head. "Me too, Tsion. But if ever there seemed a lost cause . . ."

"Lost cause? Cameron, Cameron! You and I were lost causes! All of us were. Who was a less likely candidate than Chaim? We pleaded and pleaded with him, but who would have believed he would eventually come into the kingdom? Certainly not I. Don't give up on Miss Durham."

"Oh, I haven't."

"With God, all things are possible. Have you taken a close look at this young man you brought home last night?"

"Zeke? Oh, yeah."

"Clearly this was not a churchgoing boy. He is so delightful, so bright! Shy, bashful, uneducated. Almost illiterate. But what a sweet, gentle spirit! What a servant's heart! And, oh, what a mind! It would take him the next three and a half years to read one of the many books Chaim will finish by tomorrow, and yet he has proclivities for this technical stuff that I could not learn in a lifetime."

Buck smacked his palms on his thighs and began to rise. "Don't let me keep you."

"Oh, you're not! My mouth is keeping me from it. If you are not too busy today, I could use your help."

Buck sat back down, and Tsion handed him a sheaf of papers from the printer. "I have many pages to go, but I need a first impression. I will not transmit these until I know they are right."

"They are always right, Tsion. But I'd love to get the first look at them."

"Then begin! I will try to stay ahead of you. And if I start talking again, feel free to become parental with me."

That'll be the day, Buck thought. He tapped the papers even and settled back to read. Every so often Tsion printed out the next several pages, and Buck idly pulled them from the printer as he read, sitting, standing, pacing. All the while he thanked God for the gift of Tsion Ben-Judah and his incredible mind.

To: The beloved tribulation saints scattered to the four corners of the earth, believers in the one true Jehovah God and his matchless Son, Jesus the Christ, our Savior and Lord

From: Your servant, Tsion Ben-Judah, blessed by the Lord with the responsibility and unspeakable privilege of teaching you, under the authority of his Holy Spirit, from the Bible, the very Word of God

Re: The dawn of the Great Tribulation

My dear brothers and sisters in Christ,

As is so often true when I sit to write to you, I come in both joy and sorrow, with delight but also soberness of spirit. Forgive me for the delay since last I communicated with you, and thank you each and every one for the expressions of concern for my welfare. My comrades and I are safe and sound and praising the Lord for a new base of operations. And I always want to remember to also thank God for the miracle of technology that allows me to write to you all over the world.

Though I have met few of you personally and look forward to that one day, either in the millennial kingdom or in heaven, I feel deeply that family bonds have been created by our regularly sharing the deep riches of Scripture through this medium. Thank you for your continued prayers that I will remain faithful and true to my calling and healthy enough to continue for as long as the Father himself gives me breath.

I ask that all of you who have volunteered to translate these words into languages not supported by the built-in conversion programs begin to do that immediately. As I have been unable to write to you for several days, I anticipate that this will be a longer than usual communiqué. Also, as always, in those areas where computers or power sources are scarce and this message is reproduced as hard copy, I ask that those responsible feel free to do so free of charge with no credit necessary, but that every word be printed as it appears here.

Glory to God for news that we have long since passed the one-billion mark in readership. We know that there are many more brothers and sisters in the faith who are without computers or the ability to read these words. And while the current world system would, and does, deny these figures, we believe them to be true. Hundreds of thousands join us every day, and we pray you will tell more and more about our family.

We have been through so much together. I say this without boasting but with glory to God Almighty: As I have endeavored to rightly divide the Word of Truth to you, God has proven himself the author over and over. For centuries scholars have puzzled over the mysterious prophetic passages in the Bible, and at one time I was one of those puzzled ones. The language seemed obscure, the message deep and elusive, the meanings apparently figurative and symbolic. Yet when I began an incisive and thorough examination of these passages with an open mind and heart, it was as if God revealed something to me that freed my intellect.

I had discovered, strictly from an academic approach, that nearly 30 percent of the Bible (Old and New Testaments together) consisted of prophetic passages. I could not understand why God would include these if he intended them to be other than understandable to his children.

While the messianic prophecies were fairly straightforward and, indeed, led me to believe in Jesus as their unique fulfillment, I prayed earnestly that God would reveal to me the key to the rest of the predictive passages. This he did in a most understated way. He simply impressed upon me to take the words as literally as I took any others from the Bible, unless the context and the wording itself indicated otherwise.

In other words, I had always taken at its word a passage such as, "Love your neighbor as yourself," or "Do unto others as you would have them do unto you." Why then, could I not take just as straightforwardly a verse which said that John the Revelator saw a pale horse? Yes, I understood that the horse stood for something. And yet, the Bible said that John saw it. I took that literally, along with all the other prophetic statements (unless they used phrases such as "like unto" or others that made it clear they were symbolic).

My dear friends, the Scriptures opened to me in a way I never dreamed possible. That is how I knew the great Seal Judgments and Trumpet Judgments were coming, how I was able to interpret what form they might take, and even in what sequence they would occur.

That is how I know that the Bowl Judgments are yet to come, and that they will be exponentially worse than all those that came before. That is how I knew that these plagues and trials were more than just judgments on an unholy and unbelieving world. That is how I knew that this whole period of history is also one more evidence of the long-suffering, loving-kindness, and mercy of God himself.

Believers, we have turned a corner. Skeptics—and I know many of you drop in here now and then to see what we zealots are up to—we have passed the point of gentility. Up to now, while I have been forthright about the Scriptures, I have been somewhat circumspect about the current rulers of this world.

No more. As every prophecy in the Bible has so far come to pass, as the leader of this world has preached peace while wielding a sword, as he died by the sword and was resurrected as the Scriptures foretold, and as his right-hand man has been imbued with similar evil power, there can be no more doubt:

Nicolae Carpathia, the so-called Excellency and Supreme Potentate of the Global Community, is both anti-Christian and Antichrist himself. And the Bible says the resurrected Antichrist is literally indwelt by Satan himself. Leon Fortunato, who had an image of Antichrist erected and now forces one and all to worship it or face their own peril, is Antichrist's false prophet. As the Bible predicted, he has power to give utterance to the image and to call down fire from heaven to destroy those who refuse to worship it.

What's next? Consider this clear prophetic passage in Revelation 13:11-18: "Then I saw another beast coming up out of the earth, and he had two horns like a lamb and spoke like a dragon. And he exercises all the authority of the first beast in his presence, and causes the earth and those who dwell in it to worship the first beast, whose deadly wound was healed. He performs great signs, so that he even makes fire come down from heaven on the earth in the sight of men. And he deceives those who dwell on the earth by those signs which he was granted to do in the sight of the beast, telling those who dwell on the earth to make an image to the beast who was wounded by the sword and lived. He was granted power to give breath to the image of the beast, that the image of the beast should both speak and cause as many as would not worship the image of the beast to be killed. He causes all, both small and great, rich and poor, free and slave, to receive a mark on their right hand or on their foreheads, and that no one may buy or sell except one who has the mark or the name of the beast, or the number of his name.

"Here is wisdom. Let him who has understanding calculate the number of the beast, for it is the number of a man: His number is 666."

It won't be long before everyone will be forced to bow the knee to Carpathia or his image, to bear his name or number on their forehead or right hand, or face the consequences.

Those consequences? Those of us without what the Bible calls the mark of the beast will not be allowed to legally buy or sell. If we publicly refuse to accept the mark of the beast, we will be beheaded. While it is the greatest desire of my life to live to see the Glorious Appearing of my Lord and Savior Jesus the Christ at the end of the Great Tribulation (a few days short of three and a half years from now), what greater cause could there ever be for which to give one's life?

Many, millions of us, will be required to do just that. While it conjures in us age-old self-preservation instincts and we worry that at that hour we will be found lacking courage, loyalty, and faithfulness, let me reassure you. The God who calls you to the ultimate sacrifice will also give you the power to endure it. No one can receive the mark of the beast by accident. It is a once-and-for-all decision that will forever condemn you to eternity without God.

While many will be called to live in secret, to support one another through private markets, some will find themselves caught, singled out, dragged into a public beheading, to which the only antidote is a rejection of Christ and a taking of the mark of the beast.

If you are already a believer, you will not be able to turn your back on Christ, praise God. If you are undecided and don't want to follow the crowd, what will you do when faced with the mark or the loss of your head? I plead with you today to believe, to receive Christ, to envelop yourself with protection from on high.

We are entering into the bloodiest season in the history of the world. Those who take the mark of the beast will suffer affliction at the hand of God. Those who refuse it will be martyred for his blessed cause. Never has the choice been so stark, so plain.

God himself gave name to this three-and-a-half-year period. Matthew 24:21-22 records Jesus saying, "For then there will be great tribulation, such as has not been since the beginning of the world until this time, no, nor ever shall be. And unless those days were shortened, no flesh would be saved; but for the elect's [that's you and me, believer] sake those days will be shortened."

In all God's dealings with mankind, this is the shortest period on record, and yet more Scripture is devoted to it than any other period except the life of Christ. While the Hebrew prophets referred to this as a time of "vengeance of our God" for the slaughter of the prophets and saints over the centuries, it is also a time of mercy. God goes to extreme measures to compress the decision-making time for men and women before the coming of Christ to set up his earthly kingdom.

Despite that this is clearly the most awful time in history, I still say it is also a merciful act of God to give as many souls as possible an opportunity to put their faith in Christ. Oh, people, we are the army of God with a massive job to do in a short time. May we do it with willingness and eagerness, and the courage that comes only from him. There are countless lost souls in need of saving, and we have the truth.

It may be hard to recognize God's mercy when his wrath is also intensifying. Woe to those who believe the lie that God is only "love." Yes, he is love. And his gift of Jesus as the sacrifice for our sin is the greatest evidence of this. But the Bible also says God is "holy, holy, holy." He is righteous and a God of justice, and it is not in his nature to allow sin to go unpunished or unpaid for.

We are engaged in a great worldwide battle with Satan himself for the souls of men and women. Do not think that I lightly advance to the front lines with this truth, not understanding the power of the evil one. But I have placed my faith and trust in the God who sits high above the heavens, in the God who is above all other gods, and among whom there is none like him.

Scripture is clear that you can test both prophet and prophecy. I make no claim of being a prophet, but I believe the prophecies. If they are not true and don't come to pass, then I am a liar and the Bible is bogus, and we are all utterly without hope. But if the Bible is true, next on the agenda is the ceremonial desecration of the temple in Jerusalem by Antichrist himself. This is a prediction made by Daniel, Jesus, Paul, and John.

My brothers and sisters of Jewish blood, which I proudly share, will cringe to know that this desecration shall include the sacrificing of a pig on the sacred altar. It also includes blasphemy against God, profanity, derogatory statements about God and Messiah, and a denial of his resurrection.

If you are Jewish and have not yet been persuaded that Jesus the Christ of Nazareth is Messiah and you have been deceived by the lies of Nicolae Carpathia, perhaps your mind will be changed when he breaks his covenant with Israel and withdraws his guarantee of her safety.

But he shows no favoritism. Besides reviling the Jews, he will slaughter believers in Jesus.

If this does not happen, label me a heretic or mad and look elsewhere than the Holy Scriptures for hope.

Thank you for your patience and for the blessed privilege of communicating with you again. Let me leave you on a note of hope. My next message will concern the difference between the Book of Life and the Lamb's Book of Life, and what those mean to you and me. Until then, you may rest assured that if you are a believer and have placed your hope and trust in the work of Jesus Christ alone for the forgiveness of sins and for life everlasting, your name is in the Lamb's Book of Life.

And it can never be erased.

Until we meet again, I bless you in the name of Jesus. May he bless you and keep you and make his face to shine upon you, and give you peace.

When Buck looked up from reading, his eyes moist, he was surprised to see that Tsion had slipped out without his knowledge. Despite the length of the rabbi's message, Buck knew that if the rest of the constituency was as thirsty for the truth as he was, they would welcome it and hang on every word. And a difference between the Book of Life and the Lamb's Book of Life? He had never heard of such a thing and couldn't wait to learn more.

He stood and stretched, the pages still in his hand. As he left he saw a note on the door. "Cameron, I welcome any suggestions. If you think it acceptable, feel free to hit Enter to post it on the Web site."

It may have seemed a small thing, a utilitarian task. But to Buck it was a monumental honor. He hurried to Tsion's computer, brushed the cordless mouse to clear the screen saver, and with great relish hit the key that broadcast Tsion's words to a global audience.

\+ \+ \+

Rayford offered to give Albie a break and pilot the fighter back to Palwaukee. His friend had done the bulk of the "flying and the lying," as they called it, and both could be grueling. Deceiving the enemy was tightrope work, and until David Hassid was able to get Rayford a phony rank, ID, and uniform, Albie was always in the hot seat.

It worked out best this way, though, because Hattie would have worn Rayford out during the flight, had he been free to listen. He heard most of it anyway, of course, but he was glad for the busyness of flying so he didn't have to maintain eye contact and match her energy.

He was thrilled beyond words for her and couldn't wait to see the faces of the rest of the Tribulation Force later that evening. More than that, he was happy for the whole Force. More than once, he, and he knew the others too, had given up hope for Hattie.

Albie was too new a believer to counsel her much, but she asked him to tell her again and again about the hunger for the Bible God had seemed to plant in his heart. "I don't know if that's what I have yet," she said, "but I'm sure curious. Do you have a Bible I can read?"

Rayford's was packed away somewhere at the safe house, and Albie said he did not have one. But then he remembered. "I have one on my hard drive!"

"Oh, good," she said, until he fired it up and she discovered it was in his native language. "Now my understanding *that* would be a miracle!" He tried his decoding conversion software on it, but it didn't support his language.

"Something to look forward to this evening," he said.

"Among other things. You know, Albie, I owe a lot of those people some serious apologies."

"Yes?"

"Oh, yes. I'll hardly know where to begin. If you only knew."

"There was a time," he said, "when I would have been most curious. Captain Steele can attest that there is something in the black marketer akin to a pathological gossip. We are quiet and do not say much, but oh, how we love to listen. But do you know, I would rather not hear of the offenses you may have committed against those who love you so much."

"I don't care to talk about them either."

"You can hope that your new brothers and sisters won't either. A wise man once counseled me that apologies must be specific, but now that I am a believer, I am not sure I agree. If your friends know that you are sorry, deeply remorseful, and that you mean it when you apologize, I expect they will forgive you."

"Without making me rehash everything so they'll know I know what I did?"

Albie cocked his head and appeared to be thinking. "That doesn't sound like a born-again response, as Dr. Ben-Judah would call it. Does it?"

She shook her head. "That would be like rubbing it in."

Rayford's phone rang. The area code was Colorado. "Yeah," he said.

"Ah, Mr. Berry?" It was the unmistakable voice of Steve Plank.

"That's me."

"Are you maintaining my anonymity with the dear departed?"

"I am indeed, Mr. Stephens. I'm assuming we're on a secure connection?"

"Absolutely."

"Then I am happy to tell you that she has come back from the dead, both physically and spiritually."

Silence.

"Did you catch that, Pinkerton?"

"I'm speechless, and that's new for me. Are you serious?"

"Roger."

"Wow! Better still keep my confidence, but pass along my best and a big welcome to the family."

"Will do."

"I have good news for you too. I reported to the brass the unfortunate incident in the detention area, and they said to just dispose of the body and send in the paperwork. I asked 'em where I was supposed to do that—with the body, I mean—and they said they'd just as soon not know. I guess there's more'n enough corpses to deal with everywhere so we luck out on this one."

"You know the irony, don't you, Pink?"

"Tell me."

"The GC pretended she was dead once too."

"I remember that. She must be the woman with nine lives."

"Well, three anyway. And now she has all she needs."

"Amen and roger that. Keep in touch."

When they arrived within airspace of Kankakee, Albie got on the radio to talk to the tower. He identified himself as Commander Elbaz and asked permission to load a body into his chopper for "proper disposition."

"We have no extra personnel to help with that, Commander."

"Just as well. We're not totally sure of the cause of death or any potential contagions."

"It's you and Mr. Berry and the deceased?"

"Roger, and the paperwork has been filed with International."

"Consider yourselves processed. Oh, stand by, Commander. I've been reminded that a shipment has arrived for you from New Babylon."

"A shipment?"

"It's stamped Confidential and Top Secret. About half a skid. I'd say two hundred pounds."

"Can it be delivered to the chopper?"

"We'll see what we can do. If we've got a free man and a forklift, what say we load her for ya?"

"Obliged."

Half an hour later, as Rayford and Albie carried Hattie to the chopper under a sheet, she whispered, "Anyone around?"

"No, but hush," Rayford said.

"I need a new identity. This is really getting old."

"Shut up or I drop you," Albie said.

"You wouldn't."

He pretended to let his end slip, and she cried out. "You two are gonna get us busted," Rayford said.

Once she was loaded, Rayford told her to stay out of sight until they were airborne. He got behind the controls again because he knew the way and Albie had not performed a landing inside a bombed-out skyscraper before.

Before Rayford lifted off, Albie turned and reached over the hidden Hattie and began unfastening the skid and boxes until he found a gross of black spray paint cans. The snapping of plastic fasteners and wrap made Hattie ask, "What in the world are you doing?"

"Just clearing the trapdoor so Rayford can eject you if you don't behave."

\+ + +

A full day had passed in New Babylon, and David felt well enough to leave the hospital. Hannah came to change his dressing. "How are we doing?" she asked, peering into his eyes.

"Nurses all use the collective *we*, don't they?"

"We're trained in it."

"Physically I feel a hundred percent better."

"You'll still have to take it easy."

"I've got a desk job, Hannah."

"You also have a ton of stuff to do fast. Pace yourself."

"I don't feel like doing it anyway."

"Do it for Annie."

"Touché."

With his new bandage in place, she put her hands gently over his ears. "I wasn't trying to be mean, David. I mean it. I know your heart is broken. But if you wait for that pain to go away before doing what you have to do, it'll be time to get out of here."

He nodded miserably.

"You're going to be OK, David," she said. "That sounds trite now, but just knowing you a little makes me certain."

He wasn't so sure, but she was trying to help.

"I've been thinking," she added.

Uh-oh. "Glad somebody's up to that."

"I knew I wanted to be a nurse when I was a veterinarian's aide in high school."

He raised his eyebrows. "I'm expecting some joke about me as a patient."

"No jokes. It's just that one of the things our office offered was the injection of biochips into pets so they could always be found and identified."

"Yeah?"

"Isn't that what you said the GC is going to do to everybody?"

He nodded.

"And I'm sort of an expert in that, and now you know it."

"Guess I'm still too medicated, Hannah. Spell it out for me."

"Aren't they going to need to train people in how to do this and send experts here and there to supervise it?"

He shrugged. "Probably, sure. What? It looks like a plum job, a way to see the world? You want a letter of recommendation?"

She sighed. "If you weren't hurting, I'd smack you. Give me some credit. You think I'd want to teach people how to apply the mark of the beast? Or that I'd want to watch while they do it? I'm looking for a way we can all get out of here without making it obvious why we left. You want to be among Carpathia's top ten most wanted?"

"No."

"No, so you get in there with Viv Ivins and offer the services of your pilots and even a nurse you know who has some background in this stuff. Get us sent somewhere to get the ball rolling, whatever. You're the one with the creativity. I'm just shooting wild here."

"No, keep going. I'm sorry. I'm listening now."

"You get us all on the same plane, maybe a big expensive one, because the bigger the lie, the more people want to believe it. Crash it somewhere, like the middle of an ocean, where it would be more trouble than it's worth to confirm we're all dead. We hook up with the rest of your friends, but we're not constantly looking over our shoulders for GC."

"I like it."

"You're not just saying that?"

"I wouldn't. It's a stroke of genius."

"Well, it's a thought."

"A great thought. Let me run it past Mac and Abdullah. They're good at finding holes in schemes and—"

"I already did. They liked it too."

"Anything left for me, or can you keep everybody in the palace healthy and stitched up and do my job too?"

She bit her lip. "I was just trying to help."

"And you did."

"But we both know I can't do your job. Nobody can. So I mean it when I say you have to channel your grief into productivity and do it for Annie. It's the only way to make any sense out of this. Mac tells me the Tribulation Force sees you as second in importance only to Dr. Ben-Judah."

"Oh, come on."

"David! Think about it. Look what you've done here. It doesn't have to fizzle when we all leave if you can figure a way to keep it going from anywhere."

+ + +

When Buck's phone rang, he assumed it would be Rayford, telling him he and Albie and Hattie were close. But it was Mac McCullum.

"Hey, Mac!" he said, holding up a hand to quiet the others. Buck had to sit when he heard the news. "Oh, no. No. That's awful. . . . Oh, man . . . how's he doing? . . . Tell him we're with him, will you?" Buck's face contorted and he couldn't control his tears. "Thanks for letting us know, Mac."

Chloe rushed to him. "What, Buck? What's happened?"

10

"EXCUSE ME, RAYFORD," Hattie said, a hand on each of his shoulders as he directed the chopper over Chicago toward the Strong Building. Albie was dozing.

Rayford slipped off one headphone so he could hear her, and she let her hands slip to the top of his chair. "I'm worried about how I'm going to be received."

"Are you joking? I can think of three who will be overjoyed."

"I've been terrible to them."

"That was before."

"But I should apologize. I don't even know where to begin with you. Planting that stuff about Amanda. Making you all wonder about her."

"But you admitted that, Hattie."

"I don't remember apologizing for it. That seems so weak compared to what I did."

"I won't say it wasn't an awful time for me," he said. "But let's put it behind us."

"You can do that?"

"Not by myself."

"Chloe really lost patience with me."

"With me too, Hattie. And I deserved it."

"She forgave you?"

"Of course. Love forgives all."

Hattie fell silent, but Rayford felt the pressure of her hands on the back of his chair. "Love forgives all," she repeated, as if mulling it over.

"That's from the Bible, you know. First Corinthians 13."

"I didn't know," she said. "But I hope to learn fast."

"Want another one? I'm doing this from memory, but there's a verse in the New Testament—more than one, I think—that quotes Jesus. He basically says that if we forgive others, God will forgive us, but if we don't forgive others, neither will God forgive us."

Hattie laughed. "That puts us over a barrel, doesn't it? Like we don't have a choice."

"Pretty much."

"You think I should find that verse and memorize it so I can quote it to them when I get there? Tell them they'd better forgive me, if they know what's good for them?"

Rayford turned and raised an eyebrow at her.

"I'm kidding," she said. "But, um, you think they all know that verse?"

"You can bet Tsion does. Probably in a dozen languages."

She sat quiet awhile. Rayford pointed out the Strong Building in the distance and rapped lightly on Albie's knee with his knuckles. "You might want to be awake for this, friend."

"I'm nervous," Hattie said. "I was all psyched up, but now I don't know."

"Give them some credit," Rayford said. "You'll see." He hit the button on his phone to call Buck and handed it to Hattie. "Tell Buck the next sound he hears will be us."

* * *

Buck had told Chloe the news about Annie, then gathered everyone in the safe house to tell them. None had met her, of course, but Tsion, Buck, Chloe, and Leah had had enough interaction with David that they felt they knew Annie. Chaim and Zeke were brought up to speed; then they all prayed for David and Mac and Abdullah. Zeke asked if they would mind praying for his father too.

"I don't know 'xactly where they took him, but I know Dad, and he ain't gonna be cooperative."

"David says they're going to try out the mark on prisoners first," Buck said.

"Dad would die first."

"That might be the price."

"Ten to one he'd take a couple of 'em with him," Zeke said.

Buck's phone rang, and he was grateful when Chloe reached for it.

"Hattie?" she said. "Where are you guys? . . . That close? See you in a few then. . . . Yeah, we heard Dad and Albie found a, um, friend on the inside. You ought to be grateful for all the time and expense and effort that went into—well, I don't know if you realize how risky that was. And investing Dad and Albie's time and an aircraft—I mean—it's not like you did anything to deserve it. I'm not trying to be mean, I'm just saying . . . don't start the waterworks with me, Hattie. We go back too far. For all we know the old safe house is ashes now because of—Yeah, we can talk about it when you get here. . . . Of course I still care about you, but you may not find all of us as soft as my dad. There's a delicate balance here and a lot more people than before. Even in a place as huge as this, it's not easy living together, especially with people who have a history of putting *their* needs ahead of everybody el—OK, all right. We'll see you in a minute."

\+ + +

Hattie clapped the phone shut and slapped it into Rayford's hand. "I take it that wasn't Buck," he said.

"She hates me!" Hattie said. "This is a bad idea. You should have left me there, let them take me back to Buffer and take my chances. I might not have lasted, but at least I'd be in heaven."

"Should we have let you kill yourself too? Then where would you be?"

"Chloe didn't sound like she's going to forgive me. Ah, I don't blame her. I deserve it."

Rayford felt Hattie sit back and she muttered something.

"Can't hear you," he said, maneuvering toward the building.

"I said she probably only said what I would have if the shoe was on the other foot."

\+ + +

Hannah Palemoon had dressed David's wound differently, applying a tight-fitting bandage that adhered to the shaved part of his head and did not touch his hair. It aided the stitches in keeping his scalp together for fast healing, she told him, and he didn't need the layers of gauze covering his ears and extending under his chin anymore. He felt almost normal except for the residual pain—much less—and the itching he knew he had to ignore. The best he could do was to gently press around the edges of the bandage, but as the stitches would not be removed for at least another two days, he had to be careful.

Still, his cap fit again. He stopped by his quarters for a fresh uniform, checked the mirror, and realized how incongruous he looked. His youthful, Israeli features and dark complexion went well with the tailored, formfitting garb of the senior GC staff. But as he studied his visage, he wondered if any of the Nazis he'd seen in history books hated the swastika on their snappy uniforms as much as he hated the insignia of the Global Community. How he would love abandoning the whole look. And it wouldn't be long.

He stopped with his hand on the inside door handle. Though he was better, he still felt the fatigue of one whose body was trying to heal itself. Part of him wanted to stretch out on the bed and not move for twelve hours, to simply lie there in his grief and embrace the gnawing emptiness. David found some solace in Hannah's insistence that Annie would not have suffered even for a split second. But why couldn't the power that obliterated her nervous system and baked her vital organs also destroy the longing in him she could now never fulfill? No lightning bolt of any magnitude could extinguish a love so pure.

He bowed his head and prayed for strength. If he had, say, two months, he might have allowed himself the luxury of another day or two to take the hardest edge off his pain. But even the time he had was not really enough for all he had to do. *For Annie,* he told himself as he headed for his office. And he would remind himself of that every few minutes for as long as it took to keep himself going.

His relegating Annie to a sacred, protected part of his mind was not helped when he encountered Viv Ivins in the corridor outside his office. "I need to see you," she said in her crisp, delicate voice and Romanian accent. "My office or yours?"

He was so glad she had not begun with the obligatory "He is risen," which he and Mac and Abdullah and Hannah had decided they would respond to with "He is risen indeed," privately knowing they were referring to Christ. Perhaps Vivian eschewed the formality because technically she was outside the hierarchy. She did not even wear a uniform, though her light blue, dark blue, black, charcoal, and gray suits were uniform enough. She wore sensible shoes, and her blue-gray hair was teased into a helmetlike ball.

Giving David the option of meeting with her in his own office was unusual, for while Ms. Ivins bore no official title, everyone knew she was akin to the boss's daughter, or, in this case, the boss's aunt. She was not a blood relative, as far as anyone knew, but Carpathia himself made it plain that she was as close to him as anyone in the world. She had been a dear family friend and had, from almost the beginning, helped his late parents raise their only child.

She did not overtly lord it over anyone that she had clout without title. There was simply an unspoken knowledge between her and everyone. What she wanted she got. What she said went. Her word was as good as Carpathia's, and so she didn't have to assert herself. She employed her understood power in the same way everyone else accepted it.

"Please," David said, "come in." He enjoyed the brass of having someone so close to Carpathia sitting in his office, not six feet from the computer he used to subvert the potentate's efforts.

His assistant greeted him with a concerned look as he passed. David merely said, "Good morning," but she slowed him with, "Are you all right?"

"Better, Tiffany, thanks," he said.

When she noticed his visitor, she lurched to her feet. "Ms. Ivins," she said.

Viv merely nodded. David held the door for her, and once she was inside and he shut it, she stood waiting for him to pull out a chair for her. He imagined saying, "Is your arm broken?" But there was almost as much feminist power in her expecting his chivalry as there would have been in her not doing so.

"I heard you say you were feeling better," she said, opening a folder in her lap and pulling a pencil from behind her ear. "So I won't belabor that. I trust you're able to get past your unfortunate incident with His Excellency?"

"Throwing up on the leader of the world, you mean?" he said, eliciting a grimace from her. "Except that such news travels fast and I doubt there is an employee in New Babylon not aware of it, yes, I try not to dwell on it."

"Senior management understands," she said.

He wanted to ask if they understood that barfing on the big boss was actually an answer to a desperate prayer to be spared from pretending to worship him.

Viv made a tiny check mark after her first listed item. David wondered what she might have written there as the discussion point. Regurgitation?

"Now then," she said, "a few more items. First, your new immediate superior will be James Hickman."

"My area will report to Intelligence?"

"No, Jim has been promoted to supreme commander to replace Reverend Fortunato."

David mused that having had *Intelligence* in Hickman's previous title was similar to Fortunato now having *Reverend* in his. "Surely this was Leon's, er, Commander Fortunato's choice, not the potentate's."

David detected the hint of a smile, but Viv wouldn't take the bait. "So Jim will be relocating to Leon's old office?" he said.

"Please don't get ahead of me, Mr. Hassid. And I would urge you to use titles or at the very least *Mister* when you refer to personnel at such levels. You shall be expected to refer to Mr. Hickman as Supreme Commander and Mr. Fortunato as Reverend or Most High Reverend."

Do I get a vote? David wondered. He might rather have vomited on Leon than call him Most High anything. He bit his tongue to keep from asking Viv, er, Ms. Ivins, whether it had been Hickman's groveling that won him his promotion. Or perhaps that performance was in gratitude for a move that had already been put in place.

"And no," Viv continued, "the new supreme commander will not be moving into Reverend Fortunato's old office. Mr. Hickman will be sharing space with His Excellency's assistant."

"*Real*-ly," David said. "Seems Sandra's kind of cramped as it is."

"How shall I put this? Though Mr. Hickman will have the same title Mr. Fortunato had, the job may not have quite the same range of influence."

"Meaning?"

Viv appeared frustrated, as if she were seldom asked to be more precise. "Mr. Hassid, it should be obvious to everyone that a leader whose deity has been publicly affirmed would not have need for the same level of assistance he may have in the past. Mr. Fortunato was, in essence, the chief operating officer to His Excellency's chief executive officer. Mr. Hickman's role will be more that of facilitator."

Like sergeant-at-arms or town crier? David wanted to say.

"And, of course, you are aware of Reverend Fortunato's new duties."

More than you are. But False Prophet *may not look right on the business card.* "Refresh me."

"He will be the spiritual head of the Global Community, directing homage to the object of our worship."

David nodded. To cover any unconscious look that might have given him away, he said, "And, what, ah, is to become of Leon's, excuse me, Reverend Fortunato's old office?"

"It will become part of the potentate's new quarters."

"Oh! I knew he wanted to expand upward. But out as well?"

"Yes, it should be magnificent. One of the benefits, so far anyway, of his resurrected body is that he is apparently immune to the need for sleep. Busy twenty-four hours a day, he needs variety in his work environment."

"Uh-huh." *That's all we need. Satan with no downtime.*

"The potentate's new office will be spectacular, Director Hassid. It will encompass both his and Mr. Fortunato's old spaces, as well as the conference room, and above the ten-foot walls will extend another thirty feet of windows to a clear roof."

"Sounds impressive, all right."

"I'm sure you will have your share of audiences with him," she said, "though you will more often meet with the new supreme commander."

"If I were the potentate, I would want an office large enough to allow plenty of distance between him and me."

"I don't understand."

"You know, the throwing up thing."

"Oh, yes. I get it. Amusing." But she did not appear amused.

"Will Mr. Hickman have a meeting area, or will we have to keep our voices down so as not to disturb the potentate's assistant?"

"I'm sure between the two of you, you'll be able to work something out. For instance, meeting here. Oh, my, look at the time. I have several other appointments, so you'll forgive me if I plunge ahead."

No, time's up. Get out. "Certainly, Ms. Ivins. I understand."

"During your incapacity, we were unable to wait on several important issues. We needed to get orders placed for several technical purchases that involve international shipping and manufacture."

David had to concentrate to keep from making a face. He knew exactly what she was talking about, and he had hoped he could stall such requisitions and frustrate the potentate's efforts.

"Technical purchases?" he said.

"Biochip injectors. And, of course, loyalty enforcement facilitators."

Loyalty enforcement facilitators!? Why not just call them cranium and trunk separators? "Guillotines, you mean?"

That made her wince. "Director, please. That has such an eighteenth-century sound to it, and you can understand why we want to avoid any language that bespeaks violence or conjures images of beheading and the like."

And the like? "Begging your pardon, ma'am, but do we not assume that people will recognize the guillotines, or loyalty enforcement facilitators, for what they are? What else might they be used for, halving cabbages?"

"I don't find that the least bit amusing."

"I don't either, but let's call a blade a blade. People see a heavy, angled, razor-sharp edge waiting to be triggered from the top of a grooved track, with a head-shaped yoke at the bottom over a handy basket, and my guess is they'll have a clue what it's about."

Ms. Ivins shifted in her chair, made another check mark on her list, and said, "I shouldn't put it so crassly. But my guess—no, my sincere belief—is that these will hardly, if ever, be used at all."

"You really think so?"

"Absolutely. They shall merely serve as a tangible symbol for the seriousness of the exercise."

"In other words, willingly express your loyalty or we chop your head off."

"That will not need to be said."

"I should guess not."

"But, Mr. Hassid, I wager that only the most unusually hard cases, so few and far between that they will be newsworthy for their uniqueness, will result in complete consummation of the enforcement."

I'd hate to see incomplete consummation of the enforcement. "You're confident, then, that all opposition has been eradicated."

"Of course," she said. "Who in their right mind could see the resurrection of a man dead three days and not believe in him as God?"

* * *

Rayford did not get the reception he expected, and Chloe hurried to him to explain it. He was staggered by the news of Annie. The three sat, stunned as the rest, and most, it appeared, avoided eye contact with Hattie.

"What do we hear from David?" Rayford said. "Is he all right?"

"We heard from Mac," Buck said. "Worse is that David collapsed from heat exhaustion or sunstroke or something, and that just delayed his finding out about Annie."

Rayford sat shaking his head. He knew more and more of this would be their lot, but it never seemed to get easier.

"Not everybody knows everyone else here," he said finally, and made cursory, subdued introductions.

"'Scuse me," Zeke said, "but is it OK if I ask a dumb question?"

"Anything," Rayford said.

"No offense, lady," he said to Hattie, "but I didn't expect to see a mark on you."

Tsion stood, lips trembling, and approached her. "Is it true, dear one?" he said, putting his hands on her shoulders. "Let me look at you."

Hattie nodded, her eyes darting to Buck and Chloe, who stared, wide-eyed.

Tsion embraced her, weeping. "Praise God, praise God," he said. "Lord, you take one away and send one anew." He opened his eyes. "So, tell us. When? How? What happened?"

"Not twenty-four hours ago," she said. "It wasn't just one thing, but all of you caring about me, loving me, pleading with me, praying for me. If you have not heard Albie's story, though, make sure you do soon."

She leaned close and whispered in Tsion's ear.

"Certainly," he said. "Chaim, Zeke, Albie, Leah, let's let our new sister have a few moments with the Steele family, shall we? There will be plenty of time for getting acquainted."

The others rose and followed Tsion as if they understood, though Zeke looked puzzled. When it was just the four of them, Hattie stood as Rayford, Buck, and Chloe sat. "I'm so happy for you," Chloe said, "and I mean it even if I sound stunned. I am. I wish you'd told me on the phone before I went off on you."

"No, Chloe, I deserved that. And I don't blame any of you for being shocked. I'm a little shocked myself. But I have so much to explain. Well, not to explain, because who can explain rottenness? But to apologize for it. I was so awful to you, all of you at different times. I don't know how you could ever forgive me."

"Hattie," Chloe said, "it's all right. You don't have to—"

"Yes, I do. And Chloe, one thing you need to know is that something you said to me a long time ago never left me. I couldn't get it out of my mind, though I tried over and over. It was when I visited you at Loretta's house and I accused you all of just trying to change my mind about an abortion and of only really loving me if I bought into the whole package and agreed with everything you said. Remember?"

Chloe nodded.

Hattie continued. "Even though you were so much younger than me, you told me that you all wanted to love me the way God loved me, and that was whether I agreed with you or not. No matter what I did or what I decided, you would love me because that was the way God loved you, even when you were dead in your sins."

"I don't remember being that articulate," Chloe said, her eyes filling.

"Well," Hattie said, "you were right. God loved me at my lowest. And to think I almost killed myself before he finally got to me."

"They don't know that story," Rayford reminded her. And she told them everything, from the time the GC in Colorado apprehended her to that very moment.

"I was so worried that you would never forgive me," she concluded.

Chloe stood to embrace her. Then Buck did. "You've never forgiven me for something that was worse than anything you ever pulled, Hattie."

"What?"

"I introduced you to Nicolae Carpathia."

She nodded, smiling through tears. "That *was* pretty bad," she said. "But how could you know? He fooled almost everybody at first. I wish I'd never laid eyes on him, but I also wouldn't trade a thing about my life now. It all pointed to today."

+ + +

David was antsy. He wanted Viv Ivins to leave so he could get started on his real chores. She rattled on about Fortunato.

"He'll move into Peter Mathews's old office, but nothing will be the same there. There's no Enigma Babylon One World Faith anymore, because there's no enigma. We know whom to worship now, don't we, Mr. Hassid?"

"We sure do," he said.

"Now," she said, "there is one more item. You're aware that you lost an employee the other day?" She flipped a page in her notebook and read, "'Single, white, female, twenty-two, almost twenty-three, Angel Rich Christopher.' Rich is apparently a family name."

David held his breath and nodded.

"Lightning victim," Viv added. "One of several."

"I was aware of that, yes."

"I just wanted to tell you that if you were planning any sort of memorial, I'd advise against it."

"I'm sorry?"

"We have simply lost too many employees to make it practical to give them all their moments, if you will."

David was offended, especially for Annie. "I, uh, have attended other such ceremonies. They have been short but appropriate."

"Well, this one would not be appropriate. Understood?"

"No."

"No?"

"I'm sorry, I don't understand. Why would it not be appropriate to remember a coworker who—"

"If you would think about it for just a moment, you would likely understand."

"Save me the time, please."

"Well, Mr. Hassid, Miss Christopher was apparently struck by lightning when the now Reverend Fortunato was calling down fire from heaven on those who refused to recognize His Excellency the Potentate as the true and living God."

"You're saying her death proves she was subversive. That Fortunato killed her."

"God killed her, Director. Call it subversive or whatever you will, it is obvious to all who were present—and I know you were—that only skeptics suffered for their unbelief that day."

David pursed his lips and scratched his head. "If we are not memorializing employees who did not recognize Nicolae Carpathia as deity, I understand and will comply."

"I thought you would, sir." She rose and waited for David to open the door for her. "Good day to you, Director. You know I am always available, should you need anything at all."

"Well, there is one more thing."

"Name it."

"The biochip injectors you mentioned. Are they similar to the type used for inserting the same into household pets?"

"I believe they are, with certain modifications."

"One of the nurses who attended me happened to mention that she got her start in medicine as a veterinarian's assistant. I wonder if she has any experience with that kind of technology that might be helpful to us."

"Good thinking. Give me her name and I'll check it out."

"I don't recall offhand," he said. "But it should be easy enough to find out. I'll call you with it."

As soon as Viv was gone, David phoned Hannah. "I'll be giving your name to Viv Ivins. Expect a call."

"Got it."

He told her of the prohibition against even a moment of silence in his department for Annie.

"That's perfect," she said. "David, she would wear that like a badge of honor. If being honored made it appear she was a Carpathia loyalist, you'd have to answer to her in heaven someday."

11

FOR THE NEXT SEVERAL DAYS in the safe house, Rayford quietly observed the group dynamics and took notes. Tsion and Chaim spent most of their time studying. Leah seemed bored with helping Chloe with the international co-op, and while she got acquainted with Hattie, Hattie was getting on everyone's nerves. Everyone's except Zeke's. He mostly kept to himself and didn't appear affected by personal idiosyncrasies.

Rayford asked Tsion to lead the group in a brief Bible study each day, and they prayed together. Everyone was also expected to log on to Tsion's daily cybermessage. Each took a turn spray painting the insides of exposed windows until all the floors they were using were invisible to the outside, even with lights on.

A week after Rayford had brought Hattie into the safe house, he called a meeting to officially insert Chaim, Zeke, Albie, and Hattie into the Tribulation Force. They watched the Internet and television for information on when and how the mark of loyalty would be administered. And Buck was back in full swing with his *The Truth* cyberzine. With his international contacts and his ability to write stories that had a ring of authenticity without exposing believers in high places, Buck's was the most popular site on the Net, except for Tsion's. Through contacts Chloe lined up in the co-op, Buck enlisted underground printers all over the world who risked their lives publishing *The Truth* and Tsion's messages for those without access to computers.

Hattie evolved from a hesitant newcomer to the vivacious, excited believer she had been that first morning in Bozeman. Rayford enjoyed her spirit, and it seemed Tsion did too. The others' eyes seemed to glaze over each time she exulted over something anew. Something had to give. The Trib Force had plenty of space and privacy, but even in a massive skyscraper, cabin fever set in.

Fresh air was a problem. The building ventilation system worked fine, but other than the occasional slightly opened window that brought in crisp, fall breezes, everyone longed for time outdoors in the daylight. Too risky, Rayford told them, and even Kenny Bruce was taken out only after dark.

One by one his comrades came to Rayford in private, and while they carefully avoided bad-mouthing each other, all had similar requests. Each wanted an assignment, something away from the safe house. They wanted to be proactive, not waiting for Nicolae and the GC to be the only ones on the offensive.

All but Zeke, that is, who seemed content with his role. He inventoried the tools and supplies necessary to outfit the best forgery and phony identification operation possible. "I'm not a book readin' kind of a guy," he told Rayford, "but I can see what's coming."

"You can?"

Zeke nodded. "Dr. Ben-Judah is training Chaim what's-his-name to go back to Israel. That means I gotta work on a new ID for him, and not just on paper. He's gotta look like somebody else, because everybody knows him all over the world."

Rayford could only nod.

"You can't change a guy's height and weight, and I'm no plastic surgeon. But there's things you can do. He's got that Einstein hair thing goin' now, and he shaves. I'd bald him and dye his eyebrows dark. Then have him grow a big bushy beard or maybe muttonchops and a mustache, and make them dark too. He'll look younger and kinda hip, but mostly he won't look like himself. We gotta get rid of the glasses or change 'em drastically. Then I'd give him colored contacts. If he can get along without a prescription, I got plenty he can choose from."

"Uh-huh," Rayford said. "Zeke, what makes you think he's going back to Israel?"

"Oh, he isn't? Well, my mistake then. I just figured."

"I'm not saying you're wrong. I just wondered why you figured that."

"I don't know. Somebody's got to go, and you guys have never wanted to risk Dr. Ben-Judah."

"Somebody's got to go to Israel? Why?"

Zeke furrowed his brow. "I don't know. You can tell me if I'm wrong 'cause a lot of time I am, but Dad says I've got intuition. I try to figure out Zion's messages each day, but like I say, readin's not my thing. I don't think I ever read a book all the way through, except maybe a parts manual and then only over about six years. But Zion makes those daily message things pretty easy to understand for a smart guy. I'm sayin' he's smart, not me. Most smart guys think they're explainin' something, but they're the only ones who understand it. You know what I mean?"

"Sure."

"Well, what I'm gettin' from Zion lately is that Carpathia is up to somethin'. And it has to do with Jerusalem. Zion says the Bible says the Antichrist is not only gonna pull a fast one on the Jews, he's also gonna brag about it right in their own temple and defile it somehow and break his promise."

"I think you've pretty much got that down, Zeke. How does Chaim play into it?"

"Zion says God's preparin' a safe place for the Jews to run off to, but they got to have a leader. Zion can lead 'em on the Net, but they need somebody there, somebody they can see. He's gotta be Jewish. He's gotta be a believer. He's gotta be popular or at least be able to get people to follow him. And he's gotta know a lot of stuff. The only person that's gonna know more than Zion pretty soon will be Chaim. And no way I think *Zion's* goin' over there."

"It's just as dangerous for Chaim, isn't it, Zeke?"

"Well, I don't know who'd be worse in Carpathia's mind, the guy who's tellin' the whole world Carpathia's the devil himself or the guy what ran a sword through his brain. But the fact is, we—I mean us believers—could probably get along without Chaim if we had to. But we're in trouble without Zion."

Zeke looked troubled for having said it.

Rayford stood and paced. "Well, Zeke, your dad's right about your intuition. You've hit this nail on the head."

"Then I'm gonna be asked to help send him over there as, what's his new name?"

"Tobias Rogoff."

"Right. As him?"

"You are."

"Don't you think a lot of people will recognize his voice and his body type? People notice hands too. I might have to work on that."

"Yes, there will be people who know right away who he is. And if David is right that there is tape showing him murdering Carpathia, I can see the GC showing that to the world. But Carpathia himself has already pardoned his attacker."

"But Carpathia also said he can't control what other citizens might do to the guy, so Chaim would be livin' on borrowed time, don't you think?"

"If he can get to the safe haven with the Jews, I think he will be supernaturally protected."

"That would be cool."

"You said you weren't a plastic surgeon. Are there less invasive ways to change someone's appearance?"

Zeke nodded. "There's dental gizmos."

"Appliances."

"Right. I used one on Leah, and I've got plenty more. We can really change the look of a man's teeth and jaw."

"How about one whose jaw is wired shut?"

"Even better. Leah's going to take out those wires soon. I think we can make him look like somebody else. Then he has to dress different than he ever has, maybe walk different. I can get him to do that just by adding a little somethin' to one of his shoes. I'll be ready when he is."

* * *

David dealt with his grief by working every waking moment and then crashing hard till he had no choice but to sleep. He assigned Mac and Abdullah the task of planning their disappearance, as conceived by Hannah. Meanwhile, he planted far and wide in the complex access numbers that would allow him, with the right keystrokes, to hack into the system and monitor the goings-on as fully as he was able to do now, at least for as long as the current system was used.

David found listening in on Nicolae and Leon and Hickman almost addictive, but he also enjoyed hearing what Security Chief Walter Moon had to say. While it was unlikely Moon would become a believer, who could know for sure? If he did, it would have to be before the initiation of the mark on employees, because, as Tsion taught, Scripture was clear that that was a once-and-for-all decision. But Moon, from what David could gather, shared openly with both his assistant and his most trusted subordinate that he believed he had been overlooked for the role of supreme commander. He spent most of his time swearing, ironically, "on a stack of Bibles," that he wouldn't have taken the job if it had been offered. But the opposite was so obviously and patently true that even his confidants felt free to tell him, "Of course you would have, and it should have gone to you."

David daydreamed of having Moon on his side, a grouser within the palace who had the potential for subversion.

The new intelligence director, replacing Jim Hickman, was a Pakistani named Suhail Akbar. A devout Carpathia supporter, he was a behind-the-scenes kind of guy, quiet and slow to voice an opinion but with a résumé that far outstripped his former superior's for experience and training. David feared he was bright enough to be a problem. *Bright* was not an adjective ever applied to Hickman.

"It is crucial," David e-mailed Mac one afternoon following a heavy day of hacking and setup for a future of the same, "that we leave no room for questioning our loyalty to the GC and to Carpathia specifically. I challenge the brass occasionally for the very purpose of keeping them from suspecting me, and I believe they do suspect those who seem blindly loyal. I want them to ask themselves, Why would Hassid challenge us and yet stay and serve so capably if he is not simply trying to make the place the best it can be?

"Mac, we have to plan ahead, plant the problem that will explain our demise and cost the GC some plum pieces of equipment. I wouldn't mind seeing the plane go down with a few million Nicks' worth of biochip injectors and even loyalty enforcement facilitators. Wonder if guillotines are listed that way in the top-end headchopping paraphernalia catalogs? Sorry for the gallows humor; it's no laughing matter. Praise God he can make glorified bodies even of those saints who have been dismembered, cremated, or lightning struck.

"At the risk of insulting your intelligence, I must caution against even considering wasting the Phoenix 216. Much as I would love to tweak Carpathia's nose with the loss of his precious ride, we have way too much invested in the bugging system, which I am now able to access even from outside the plane. For whatever time God allows us the freedom to listen in, I can imagine no greater source of information. I have developed a program that can even track the position of the craft via satellite. It is always fun and enlightening, isn't it, when Nicolae thinks he's in a wholly secure environment and lets his hair down? The bluster and posturing among his people is one thing, but to hear him cackle and admit to his most trusted aides the very things he denies everywhere else, well, that's when it's worth it.

"Speaking of that, he has a meeting scheduled with Hickman, Moon, Akbar, and Fortunato that I plan to tape. If you think his go-rounds with just Leon were hilarious, wait till you hear this. I'll upload it to you. Remember the unique secure code for all this privileged information and secure transmissions. Should anyone, yourself included, try to access these files with the wrong code, I have programmed in a bug so nasty that it really should be called a monster. This is a creature that ignores the software programs and attacks the hardware.

"If I hadn't developed it myself, I wouldn't have believed it. This thing will literally intercept the impulses being relayed from point to point in the processor, carry them to the power source, whether battery or AC, and draw the current into the motherboard itself. If there were an incendiary device in there, I could get a computer to literally blow up in a hacker's face. Given that all that is in there is plastic and metal, the best I can do is produce a lot of heat, smoke, and some melting. Regardless, the victim computer is irreparable after that.

"More later, confrere. I'll look for something concrete from you and Abdullah within forty-eight hours. Meanwhile, it's less obvious and risky for you to have occasion to run into Hannah than for me to. Keep her warm and courageous as a compatriot and assure her that we will get out in time and have productive years left to devote to the cause of the kingdom."

+ + +

Rayford, who had been kept up-to-date by David once he was up and around again, worried about the calendar. He had been noodling the most effective roles for each member of the Force, and the prospect of a sudden infusion of four members displaced from the palace had both its up- and downsides. Were he to bring them all to Chicago, he would add to the base of operations two pilots, a nurse, and one of the world's greatest computer geniuses. Clearly he had the room, but he wondered if having virtually everybody in one place was the most efficient use of resources.

Not just for their own psyches but also for the sake of the two-pronged overall mission—stymieing Carpathia where possible and winning as many people to the kingdom as they could—it might make more sense to spread the talent around the globe. Hattie and Leah were restless and eager for assignments. Chloe was resigned to staying, because of Kenny and the work of the co-op, but Buck needed live exposure to what was going on to make his cyberzine as effective as it could be.

Rayford and Albie needed all the pilots they could get, but planes weren't plentiful either. If he and the insightful if inarticulate Zeke were right about what Tsion was up to, thousands of pilots and planes would have to be recruited from around the world to airlift Jewish believers to safety. Veteran pilots like Mac and Abdullah could help make that happen.

But in an instant in the middle of the night, Rayford went from thinking he had more than two more weeks to think and plan how to best make use of the New Babylon contingent to realizing he had to act quickly. Time was a luxury he never had enough of, but an emergency threw everything into turmoil.

Rayford's phone rang, but no one was there. He checked the readout. A message from Lukas (Laslos) Miklos. "Have been found out," it read. "Pastor and my wife detained, among others. Pray please. Help please."

The underground church in Ptolemaïs was the largest in Greece and likely the largest in the United Carpathian States. Up to now the local GC presence had not been a problem. The Greek believers had been careful, Rayford knew from personal experience, but even they feared GC Security and Intelligence sources could not look the other way much longer. Part of the reason they felt they had been ignored was that local GC leadership believed Carpathia wanted the region that bore his name to have the lowest reported incidence of insurgence of the ten global supercommunities.

Whatever public relations sensitivities Carpathia had exhibited before his assassination, since his resurrection his emphasis had been on enforcement. Apparently, Rayford deduced, the new Carpathia would rather eradicate the opposition within his own duchy than pretend it didn't exist. Rayford would ask David to check into the situation and see what would be served by a Trib Force party showing its face over there.

Rayford had known Mrs. Miklos to be a quiet, deeply spiritual woman. But Laslos had told him she was also opinionated, stubborn, and brave. She was not the type to back down if confronted over the exercise of her beliefs by those in authority. Rayford imagined the GC storming a meeting and Mrs. Miklos resisting and even putting up a fuss rather than allowing her pastor, Demetrius Demeter, to be taken into custody.

But Rayford didn't want his imagination to run away with him. He would find out what he could from David and perhaps take a run over there with Albie. Or perhaps with Buck. He hated the idea of leaving the Trib Force without so much as a helicopter pilot.

+ + +

David was keying in his coordinates to listen to Carpathia's meeting with Hickman and the others when he got a call from Rayford regarding a GC vs. underground church skirmish in Greece. "I'll let you know what I find out," he told Rayford. David phoned Walter Moon, but before Walter answered, David was surprised to be paged to Hickman's office.

His office? Hickman shared space with Carpathia's assistant. And didn't Hickman have a meeting with Carpathia soon? David hung up and called Hickman. The assistant, Sandra, answered. "Hassid here. Was I just paged?"

"Yes, sir. The supreme commander would like you to meet with him in the conference room, eighteenth floor."

David found a mess. Though the workday was moments from being over and Sandra was packing up to leave, workmen still jammed the area. Drills, saws, hammers, dust, scaffolds, ladders, materials everywhere.

"They're not going to relocate you while they're working?" David said.

"Apparently not," Sandra said, and she marched off.

Hickman opened the door to a conference room that was not long for this world and waved David in. "Hurry and let me get this door closed, Hassid. Less sawdust."

The new supreme commander, a Western version of Fortunato with even less class, offered a fleshy hand and shook David's enthusiastically. "Yeah, hey, how ya doin'? He is risen, huh?"

"Huh," David said, and when Hickman shot him a double take, he added, "Indeed."

Hickman appeared nervous and in a hurry. David thought he could pry information from him by playing dumb. "So, just about the end of your day, hmm? How's it been, sharing space with—"

"Never mind that," Hickman said, sitting and letting his generous belly push past his unbuttoned uniform jacket. "Got a meeting coming up with the big guys, and I'd rather not go in there unprepared."

That'll be the day, David thought. "How can I help?" he said.

"We all up-to-date, up to snuff, on track, on target, on course?"

David shook his head, amazed. "All of the above, I guess. What are we talking about?"

Hickman grabbed a dog-eared pad and riffled through a couple of pages. "Guillotines, syringes?"

"You mean loyalty enforcement facilitators and biochip injectors?"

"Yeah, thanks!" Hickman said, scribbling. "I *knew* Viv had some special names for those. You know, Hassid, basically I was a cop. I'm honored and everything, but I gotta prove to His Majesty, ah, His Excellency, that I can handle this. That I'm not in over my head."

"You feel you are?"

"What I feel is that my loyalty and my devotion to the potentate will make up for any lack of experience I've had at this level of management. Now where are we on these things? What can I tell him?"

"That we're on track, on pace."

"Good. I can count on you then."

"Oh, can you ever, J—, er, Supreme Commander."

"Ah, you can call me Commander when it's just you and me. Keep it formal in public, of course."

"Of course."

"By the way, do you purchase livestock too?"

"You mean foodstuffs? No, that would be Food Services."

"No, this is live. I don't need food. I need a live animal."

"Still not my area, I'm afraid. Rolling stock, avionics, computers, communications hardware. That's my game."

"Who's going to help me procure a pig?"

"A pig, sir?"

"Huge and live, Hassid."

"I have no idea."

Hickman stared at him, apparently not accepting the dodge.

"I could look into it," David said. "But—"

"I knew I could count on you, David. Good man. Let me know first thing in the morning, 'cause the word I get is that the big man is going to assign me that today."

"Oh, you haven't even heard from him about it yet?"

"No, this is what you'd call a heads-up from a colleague who cares."

"Really?"

"Oh, yeah. Guy like me tends to accumulate friends all up and down the corporate ladder. Buddy told me today he was in on a meeting with Fortunato and Carp—oh, forgive me! I know better'n that. I should never use those names, especially in front of a subordinate. I'm gonna direct you to disregard that, Hassid, as your superior officer."

"Jury will disregard, sir."

"Yeah, good. Anyhow, this guy's in a meeting with His Excellency and the Most High Reverend, and he says they're agitated—you know what that means? Exercised, I guess you'd say."

"Understood, Commander."

"They're upset, up in arms, whatever you wanna call it, about the Judah-ites."

"I've heard of them, sir."

"I know you have. Their top guy, who Peacekeeping thought they had flushed out and sent packin', turns up now in a new place—we don't know where, which doesn't have Carp—the potentate, any too cheery, if ya know what I mean—and this Judah guy's turnin' out more and more of this anti-Carpath—well, I guess, yeah, it's OK in that context. This guy's disseminatin' anti-Carpathia stuff everywhere. He's predictin' and says the Holy Bible prophesies that Antichrist—which is what he calls His Excellency, imagine—is gonna defile the temple and sacrifice a pig on the altar."

"You don't say."

"I *do* say, and while I wasn't there, my buddy tells me the potentate is fiery mad; I mean he's hoppin'."

"I can imagine."

"Me too. He says to the Reverend, he says somethin' along the lines of, 'Oh, yeah, well, maybe I *will* show them.' You know how he talks, never usin' contractions and like that."

"I do."

"So, and this is the genius of Nicolae Carpathia, if you'll forgive the familiar reference. He's gonna like, get this, *fulfill* this prophecy—the one in the Bible and the one by Ben Judah-ite, or, um—"

"Tsion Ben-Judah."

"Right! He's gonna sacrifice a pig on the altar of the temple in Jerusalem on purpose, knowing what the guy and the Holy Bible are sayin'. Sorta in yer face, wouldn't you say?"

"That's for sure." *In God's face, no less.*

"Well, see I don't know this yet, you follow?"

"Sure. It's on the QT from your buddy."

"Exactly. But when he, you-know-who, asks me can I get him a pig, I want to be able to tell him no problem. Can I tell him that? You're going to check with, with, ah, your people or whatever, and I'm gonna get him this pig, right?"

"I'll do my best, sir."

"I knew you would. Hot dog, you're good."

"You said that on purpose, didn't you, sir?"

"What's that?"

"Talking about a pig, and you said 'hot dog.'"

Hickman disintegrated into gales of laughter, then tried to pretend he had indeed said it on purpose. When he regained control, he said, "You know what I want, Hassid?"

"Tell me."

"I want a pig, are you ready—?"

"I'm ready."

"—big enough for His Excellency to ride."

"Sir?"

"You heard me. I want the biggest pig you've ever seen in your life. Big as a pony. Big enough to put a saddle on, not literally, but you know what I mean."

"Not sure I do, Commander."

"I'm tryin' to earn a few points here, understand, Director? Just like you're doin' without tryin', 'cause you're just that good. But I wanna be able to suggest to His Excellency that if he's gonna take the gloves off and go toe-to-toe with his worst enemies, he oughta go 'em one better."

Take the gloves off to go toe-to-toe? Annie would have loved that mixed metaphor. "One better?"

"He ought to ride that pig into the temple!"

"Oh, my." David could not imagine Carpathia, even at his basest, lowering himself to such a spectacle.

"Oh, my is right, Hassid. You read the Bible?"

"Ever?"

"Yeah."

"Some."

"Well, isn't there a story about Jesus ridin' into Jerusalem on a donkey and people singin' and throwin' leaves and whatnot?"

"I was raised Jewish."

"So no New Testament for you. Well, anyway, there is that story, I'm pretty sure. Picture His Excellency havin' fun with that. Ridin' a pig with people paid to sing and throw stuff."

Lord, please! "I can't imagine."

"I can come up with 'em, can't I, Hassid?"

"You can, sir."

"Hey, I'd better get in there. Get on that pig for me, will ya? I'm gonna tell him it's as good as got."

"I'll let you know."

David was on his way out the door when Hickman called after him. "I forgot to tell you," he said, turning pages on his pad again. "There's a gal in Medical Services, a nurse. Here it is. She used to be a vet or something and she's shot biochips into dogs and cats."

"You don't say," David said.

"You might want to check her out, see if we can take advantage of her expertise. You know, in training people how to do this."

"I'll check her out. What's the name?"

"I don't think I have it right, Hassid. Some kind of a funny name. You'll be able to track her down."

"I'll ask for the nurse with the funny name, sir."

12

RAYFORD COULDN'T SLEEP. Pacing various floors in the cavernous Strong Building, he happened by Chaim's room. The door was wide open, and in the darkness he noticed the old man's silhouette. Chaim sat motionless on the bed, though Rayford knew he had to hear and see him in the corridor. Rayford poked his head in.

"You all right, Dr. Rosenzweig?"

A loud sigh through the wire-bound clenched teeth. "I don't know, my friend."

"Want to talk?"

A low chuckle. "You know my culture. Talk is what we do. If you have time, come in. I welcome you."

Rayford pulled up a chair and sat facing Chaim in the darkness. The botanist seemed in no hurry. Finally, he said, "The young woman takes my wire out tomorrow."

"Leah, yes. You can't tell me you're worried about that."

"I can hardly contain myself waiting."

"But something else is on your mind."

Chaim fell silent again, but soon he began panting, then leaned to his pillow where he was racked with great sobs. Rayford pulled his chair closer and laid a hand on the man's shoulder. "Talk to me."

"I have lost so much!" Chaim wailed, and Rayford strained to understand him. "My family! My staff! And it is all my fault!"

"Little is our fault anymore, sir. Carpathia is in charge of everything now."

"But I was so proud! So skeptical! Tsion and Cameron and Chloe and you and everyone who cared about me warned me, tried to persuade me. But oh, no, I was too intellectual. I knew better!"

"But you came to the Lord, Chaim. We must not live in the past when all things have become new."

"But look where I was not that long ago! Tsion is joyful in spite of it all, so happy for me, so encouraging. I dare not tell him where my mind is."

"Where is it?"

"I am guilty, Captain Steele! I could do as you say, put the past behind me, if all I was dealing with was my pride and ignorance. But it led me down paths I never believed I would walk. My dearest, most trusted friends are dead because of me. Slaughtered in my house!"

Rayford resisted platitudes. "We have all lost much," he whispered. "Two wives and a son for me, many friends—too many to think about or I'd go mad."

Chaim sat up again, wiping his face with both hands. "That is my problem, Rayford. I have gone nearly mad with grief, but mostly remorse. I murdered a man! I know he is Antichrist and that he was destined to die and come back to life, but I didn't know that when I committed the act. I murdered a man who had betrayed my homeland and me. Murder! Think of it! I was a beloved statesman, yet I stooped to assassination."

"I understand rage, Chaim. I wanted to murder Carpathia myself, and I knew exactly who he was and that he would not stay dead."

"But I premeditated it, Captain, planned it many months in advance, virtually invented and manufactured the weapon myself, faked a stroke just to get myself in proximity to him without suspicion, then finished the job exactly as I had envisioned it. I am a murderer."

Rayford leaned forward and rested his elbows on his knees, head in his hands. "You know I almost saved you the work."

"I don't understand."

"You heard a gunshot before you attacked Carpathia."

"Yes."

"My gun."

"I don't believe you."

Rayford told him the story of his own anger, personality change, plotting, the purchase of the weapon, his determination to do the deed.

Chaim sat shaking his head. "I can hardly believe that the two people who dared attack Nicolae are in the same room. But in the end you could not do it. I did it with enthusiasm, and even up to the time I finally saw my need for God, I was glad I did it. Now I suffer such regret and shame I can barely breathe."

"Can you take no solace in the fact that this was destiny, and that you cannot be guilty of murdering a man who is alive?"

"Solace? I would give all I own for a moment of peace. It isn't *whom* I did this to, Rayford. It is *that* I did it. I did not know the depth of my own wickedness."

"And yet God has saved you."

"Tell me, is one supposed to *feel* forgiven?"

"Good question. I have faced the same dilemma. I have full faith in the power of God to forgive and forget, to separate us from our sins as far as the east is from the west. But I'm human too. *I* don't forget and thus often I don't appropriate the forgiveness God extends. Because we feel guilty does not mean God does not have the power to absolve us."

"But Tsion tells me I may have a greater destiny, that I just might be the one to be used to lead my believing countrymen to safety from Antichrist. How could he say that and how could I do such a thing when I feel the way I do?"

Rayford stood. "Perhaps the fallacy is in thinking it would have to be *you* who accomplishes this."

"I would love to be out from under the weight of it, but as Tsion says, who else? He himself cannot risk it."

"I'm saying it's something God is going to do, through you."

"But who am I? A scientist. I am not eloquent. I don't know the Word of God. I barely know God. I was not even a religious Jew until just days ago."

"Yet as a child you must have been exposed to the Torah."

"Of course."

"If Tsion is right, and not even he is sure, this could be your burning-bush experience."

"No one will ever see me as Moses."

"Are you willing to let God use you? Because if Tsion is right and you do what he thinks you should do, you *would* be a modern-day Moses."

"Ach!"

"You could be used of God to flee the evil ruler and take your people to a safe haven."

Chaim moaned and lay down again.

"Moses pled the same case you're pleading," Rayford said. "The question is whether you are willing."

"I know."

"You're right. You were depraved. We all were, until Christ saved us. God can make a miracle of your life."

Chaim mumbled.

"I'm sorry?" Rayford said.

"I said I want to be willing. I am willing to be willing."

"That's a start."

"But God is going to have to do something in me."

"He already has."

"But more. I could no more accept this assignment now than I could fly. The person who accepts this duty must have a clear conscience, confidence that comes only from God, and communication ability far beyond what I have ever possessed. I was able to hold forth in a classroom, but to speak to thousands as Tsion has done, to publicly oppose Antichrist himself, to rally the masses to do what is right? I don't see it. I just don't."

"But you are willing to trust God to work?"

"He is my only hope. I am at the end of myself."

* * *

At high noon Carpathia Time in New Babylon, David left the palace and went outside for the first time in days. He was to have his stitches removed at two that afternoon, and he looked forward to seeing Hannah Palemoon again, even in a sterile setting where they might not be able to converse freely.

The heat reminded David of the day of Nicolae's resurrection. It didn't seem right to stroll the grounds of the spectacular palace without Annie. His pain was so raw and the ache so deep that it made his scalp wound fade to insignificance. Hannah had told him that the removal of the bandage would be worse than the removal of the stitches. His uniform cap protected the wound from the sun, but David's body began to heat up in his dress uniform, and the memories of his trauma floated back.

The decimation of the world's population was reflected in the workforce at GC headquarters. What had once been its own bustling metropolis was now a shell of itself. The crowds that used to consist of enthusiastic employees were now made up of tourists and pilgrims, necks craned to catch a glimpse of someone famous.

In the distance David saw visitors crowded around one of the outdoor TV monitors that broadcast GC news twenty-four hours a day. He moseyed over and stood unnoticed at the back. The new Most High Reverend of Carpathianism, Leon Fortunato, held forth from his new office.

David could only shake his head. Leon stood before a pulpit-type lectern, but his height had seemed to change. A husky, swarthy man a tick under six feet tall, Leon wore a long burgundy and navy robe that flattered his physique. But when the late Peter Mathews—in a gaudy, silly-looking robe—had stood at the same podium, he had looked shorter than Leon, despite that he was several inches over six feet. Leon had to be standing on some sort of box or platform!

He reported on the worldwide competition to see which locales and regions led in the race to complete their replicas of the Carpathia statue. Of course, the United Carpathian States had an insurmountable lead, but the rest of the world competed for second place.

The report was dotted with feeds from all over the globe, showing how many communities had tried to make unique their version of the statue. Regulations stipulated that the replicas had to be at least life-size and monochromatic, but none could be as large as the original. Past that, local committees were free to exercise creativity. Most of the statues were black, but many were gold, some crystal, some fiberglass, one green, one orange, and several were twice life-size (or half the size of the original). Fortunato seemed particularly pleased with those two and announced plans to personally visit those sites.

"In the interest of full disclosure, it falls to me to report that while Israel has several replica statues in cities as disparate as Haifa and Tel Aviv, Jerusalem has not even begun theirs." Leon switched into his deep bass, solemn voice. "Speaking under the authority of the risen potentate, I say woe! Woe and beware to the enemies of the lord of this globe who would thumb their noses in the face of the most high!"

Here he switched to Uncle Leon mode, sounding like a beloved relative reading a bedtime story. "But you know, while I have been imbued with power from on high to perform all the miracles that our beloved leader performs, and whereas I have proven this power by calling down fire from heaven to destroy the disloyal, your lord, His Excellency, is the embodiment of love and forgiveness and long-suffering. Against my counsel and better judgment, though I defer to his divine wisdom, the Supreme Potentate has asked me to announce that he knows he has devout followers in the capital of the Holy Land. Their loving lord shall not forget those loyal pilgrims, suffering under the insanity and subversion of the very leaders who have been charged with responsibility for the spiritual health of their souls.

"One week from today, the object of our adoration shall personally visit his children in Jerusalem. He will be there not only to deal forthrightly with those who oppose him—for he is, besides being a loving god, a just god—but also to bless and accept worship and praise from the citizens otherwise without voice.

"As your global pastor, let me urge the countless oppressed Carpathianists living under the thumb of misguided rebels in Jerusalem to bravely show your support to the one worthy of all honor and glory when he arrives in your home city. May it be a triumphal entry like none before it. Let me, on his behalf, personally guarantee your safety and protection against any form of retribution you might otherwise have suffered for your doing the right thing in the face of powerful opposition.

"We know that the leadership there has a thin majority of Judah-ites and Orthodox Jews who risk the vengeance of their god by continuing with their suicidal lunacy. Unless they see the error of their ways and come on bent knee to beg forgiveness of their lord, new leadership will be in place before His Excellency leaves that great city.

"And to those who swear that the temple is off-limits to the potentate himself, I say, dare not come against the army of the lord of hosts. He is a god of peace and reconciliation, but thou shalt have no other gods before him. There shall not be erected or allowed to stand any house of worship anywhere on this planet that does not recognize His Excellency as its sole object of devotion. Nicolae Carpathia, the potentate, is risen!"

The crowd around the TV shouted the customary response, and David said silently, "Jesus the Christ is risen indeed."

Fortunato reminded the world that within two days, all statues must be completed and open for worship. "And, as you know, the first one hundred cities with finished and approved units will be the first to be awarded loyalty mark application centers."

Leon had aides bring into view a flip chart he could reach from whatever he was standing on, and David noticed that as they came into view, his proximity made him look seven feet tall. Fortunato used a pointer to show the standard mark application facility. It contained a staging area, where several thousand at a time would be herded through crowd-control barriers, entertained by taped speeches from Carpathia and Fortunato. Every four minutes, a replay would show Fortunato's calling down fire from heaven on dissidents and Carpathia's actual resurrection. He paused to let the tape roll, and David had to look away. The tourists cheered the broadcast.

Fortunato returned to his demonstration drawing. The citizens would feed into a dozen or two dozen open-air booths—depending on the size of the city and the crowd—where they would be asked to decide on the design and size of their mark and whether they wanted it on their foreheads or the backs of their right hands.

"A friendly reminder," Fortunato said with a grin. "Should you procrastinate on your decision or forget due to your excitement, the standard injection will be made on your right hand, depicting the prefix that identifies your region, next to the thin scar that evidences injection of the biochip.

"We have been asked repeatedly how we are precluding counterfeit marks. While it may be impossible for any but highly skilled and trained observers to tell a fake mark from the real, biochip scanners cannot be fooled. We are so confident of the 100 percent reliability of this technology that anyone whose biochip is not authenticated by a scanner will be subject to execution without appeal. A readable, implanted biochip will be required for standard trade and commerce.

"And yes, we will have loyalty enforcement facilitators at every mark application site."

To David's surprise, this announcement was illustrated by footage of a huge, gleaming guillotine, and Fortunato actually punctuated it with a hearty laugh. "I can't imagine any citizen of the Global Community having to worry about such a device, unless he or she is still mired in the cult of the Judah-ites or Orthodox Judaism. Frankly, only the blind or those without access to television have not seen the resurrection of our god and ruler, so I can't imagine skeptics remain outside Jerusalem. Well, as you can see," and he laughed again, "they will not remain long."

Fortunato then hefted a huge stack of letters and printouts. "These, my friends, are applications from those who want to be first to show their loyalty to His Excellency by proudly having their marks applied right here in New Babylon. Any citizen from any region may have his or her mark applied here, though the code number will coincide with your home region. There is a limit to the number we can accommodate, so get your application in quickly or plan to have yours applied in your local center.

"Does the application hurt? It does not. With technology so advanced and local anesthesia so effective, you will feel only the pressure of the biochip inserter. By the time any discomfort would have passed, the anesthetic will still be working.

"Bless you, my friends, in the name of our risen lord and master, His Excellency the Potentate, Nicolae Carpathia."

\+ + +

Rayford returned to his bed drowsier but still unable to sleep. He spent an hour noodling assignments for the Force and finally concluded that Albie and Buck ought to go to Greece. He needed to stay for the sake of morale, and Buck needed to be able to expose the close-mindedness of the Carpathia regime.

With that settled, Rayford drifted off, planning to get Buck yet another new ID from Zeke in the morning and assign David a little more way-paving from his perch in New Babylon.

\+ + +

David informed the head of Food Services that Supreme Commander Hickman had need of the largest live pig available for Carpathia's Israel visit. Then he stopped in his office to check his computer before his appointment with Hannah. He found an urgent e-mail from Ming Toy.

"I did not know whom else to write to," she said. "I was distraught to hear of your loss and can only pray God's strength for you. I cannot imagine your pain.

"Mr. Hassid, have you seen my family since I left there? Last I heard, they had not seen you. I am most troubled. They have been awarded free accommodations until Chang has been processed for employment, and my father is thrilled beyond words. Mother is silent as usual, but I have heard directly from Chang, and he is desperate. He says the last thing he wants is to work for the GC, yet my father insists. Having his son serve Carpathia is the highest honor he can imagine.

"Chang has heard that all employees will receive the mark within a few weeks, but there is a rumor that new employees hired during this time may be the first to have it applied. Have you heard that? Could it be true? It makes sense in its own way. Why hire someone without knowing up front that they are loyal? And it saves their losing work time later just to stand in line for their marks.

"Father is insistent that Chang initiate his paperwork through Personnel immediately and is eager to see him among the very first to take the mark, especially if Father can witness this himself. Chang is ready to admit to my father that he is a believer in Jesus and, yes, could accurately be called a Judah-ite, but he is afraid of two things. One, that Father would report him, and two, that he would demand to know the truth about me. Trust me, Mr. Hassid; I know my father. He would sell us both out to prove his loyalty to Carpathia and the GC.

"I am urging my brother not to admit anything to Father, and yet I do not know how long he can avoid being tested to the ultimate. The only way to keep from officially applying for work there is to run away or tell my father the truth. Can you help in any way? I am sorry to trouble you with this during such a terrible time for you.

"Rest assured that I am praying for you. And while I assume you know this, Leah reports that your compatriots in the safe house are also upholding you daily.

"With utmost respect and honor, your sister in Christ, Ming Toy."

David called Personnel. "Can you give me the status on a Chang Wong?"

"Yes, sir. Impressive résumé. Mentioned publicly, at least among the brass, by Carpathia. A no-brainer. He's going to work here as soon as we can get him processed. Only question is where. I suppose you want him; everybody else does."

"Can't say for sure. Just wondering."

"Your area makes the most sense. You wouldn't turn him down, would you?"

"Too early to tell, but I'm not a follower. Just because everybody wants him doesn't mean I should be desperate to snag him."

"True enough. But he'd be an asset."

"What's next?"

"Don't know. We expected him yesterday. It's in his court. He completes the paperwork, makes his app official, and we make an offer."

"And if he accepts?"

"He's in."

"He's not graduated high school."

"We have tutors. He could *teach* high school."

"When would he start?"

"A few days. Delay would be because of the new freeze. You saw that, right?"

"No."

"Should have it in your e-mail."

David didn't want to appear too eager. "I'll find it. Thanks."

"You want this kid if we can get him?"

David had to think fast. If he got him and then David and the others disappeared, the kid could be found out as an enemy of the state. But if their disappearance looked like an accident, there would be no suspicion of them or anyone they associated with. On the other hand, if taking the mark was prerequisite to hiring, the issue was moot. The kid would refuse, the father would turn him in, end of story. David would not be under suspicion for wanting him or spending time with him.

"Would I be able to do a preliminary with him?"

"Interview? Hmm. Not protocol, but I don't see the harm."

"Where's he staying?"

"Four-oh-five-four."

That close to Hannah. Wonder if she knows? "Thanks."

David hurried to the hospital. Hannah greeted him professionally and asked the typical questions about bleeding, discomfort, and pain. Then she asked him to follow her to a private room for removal of the stitches.

"You look OK but distracted," she said, dousing his head with disinfectant and soaking the bandage.

"Can't imagine why," he groused.

"Sarcasm? Remember, I'm on your side."

"Did you know the Wongs are staying on your floor?"

"Who are the Wongs?"

David smacked himself in the forehead.

"Terrific," she said. "So much for sterility. Close your eyes." He obeyed and she doused him again. "So, who *are* the Wongs?"

He told her the story.

"What're you going to do?" she said.

"Bug their room."

"You can do that?"

"I can do anything."

"I'm gathering that. But how?"

"I'd tell you, but then—"

"Yeah, I know, you'd have to kill me." She looked embarrassed to have said that with his having just lost his fiancée. "I'm sorry," she whispered.

"My fault," he said. "I started it."

She lightly tugged at the bandage, making his eyes water. "Bear with me," she said, squirting more liquid.

"That stuff supposed to make it easier?"

"We tell ourselves that," she said. "Fortunately, you had a good surgeon. Oh, yeah, it was me. I cut enough hair that all we're dealing with is scalp and wound and stitches. Imagine if there was hair too."

"I don't want to think about it."

"Think about something else and I'll hurry."

"You can't just yank it?"

"Not with stitches. Those have to come out the right way. If I pull one out with the bandage, you're on the ceiling. Now try to get your mind on something else."

"Like what?"

She stopped and put her wrists on her hips, careful to keep her gloved hands from touching anything. "David, I hardly know you. How would I know what you have to think about?"

He shrugged.

"Think about freedom," she said. "About being away from here forever."

"You call that freedom? It's just another form of prison."

"I've been wondering about that," she said. "It has to be less tension, don't you think?"

"Different kind, I guess. Ow!"

"Sorry. Be brave. Tell me more."

"Well, we won't have to worry about who's watching and listening and whether my secure e-mail and phone connections have been compromised. We won't have to worry that we've already been found out and they're just letting us hang ourselves and expose others before they arrest us."

"That's what I was thinking," she said.

"But we'll never be free again. We'll be fugitives."

"So you've already ash-canned my idea."

"No, why? I assigned it to Mac and Abdullah."

"Because if it works, no one's even looking for us. We get new IDs, change our looks, and start over."

"But without the loyalty mark."

She hesitated. "Well, yes, there is that. Hold on. There we go." She held before his eyes the long bandage in a pair of surgical scissors. Besides disinfectant, it showed his blood and the imprint of his wound, two staples, and several stitches.

"Can I ask you something?" he said. "Totally off the subject."

"You mean *may I?*"

"Ah, one of those. Showing off your education."

"Sorry. Incurable."

"I guess we'll need a grammar cop at the safe house, in case Tsion and Buck are out. Anyway, why do you people think we want to see that stuff? The yucky bandage, I mean."

"Yucky?" She morphed into baby talk. "Does he hate to see that yucky stuff?"

"Doctors and nurses are forever doing what you just did. Just remove it and toss it. You think I need to see it or I won't pay?"

She shrugged.

"You all must just love this stuff," he said. "That's all I can figure. By the way, you never said anything about staples."

"You just answered your own question."

"I'm lost."

"I showed you so you know what's next. The stitches are separate, so they come out individually. It's not one of those deals where I cut or untie and then the whole thing just sort of tickles as it comes looping out. It won't hurt, but there are several. And there are two staples that have to stay in till the stitches are out, just in case, to hold everything together. When the stitches are gone, I'll know whether the scar can contain that big brain of yours. Then I have to get under each of those two staples, one at a time, with a wire cutter."

"You're joking."

"No, sir. I cut through the staple—"

"Ouch."

"Not if you don't flinch."

"You're the one who'd better not flinch."

"I'm good. I promise. Then I grip each remaining end, that would be two for each staple, and slowly curl it out."

"That's got to hurt."

She hesitated.

"I needed a real fast 'Not at all' right there."

"I admit you'll feel it more than the stitches. It's a bigger invasion, thus a busier evacuation."

"A busier evacuation? You could be in management."

"What *should* I say? The big, yucky staple displaced more tissue than the itty-bitty stitchies. If any of the scar tissue adhered to the metal, you may feel it give way."

"I don't like the sound of 'give way.'"

"What a wuss! It won't even bleed. And if I feel it's too early and it would cause trauma, we'll put it off."

"Not unless it would kill me. I mean it, Hannah. I want to be done with this."

"You don't want any reason to have to come back and talk to me."

"It's not that."

"No," she said dismissively, obviously feigning insult. "I can take it. I don't know any other believers with reasons to come around, but that's all right. Just leave me here to suffer alone."

"Get on with it."

"Shut up and I will. Now think about something else."

"Can you talk while you work?"

"Oh, sure. I told you I was good."

"Then tell me your story while you do this."

"Story's longer than the procedure, David."

"Then take your time."

"Now there! That was a sweet thing to say."

13

HANNAH PALEMOON'S STORY actually took David's mind off what she was doing. And she did take her time, pausing between each stitch. She teased him by showing him the first, but his look stopped her.

She had been raised on a Cheyenne reservation in what was now known as the United North American States. "You wouldn't believe the misconceptions about Native Americans," she said.

"Never been to the States, even when it was just the United States of America. But I read about it. They called you Indians because of Columbus's mistake."

"Exactly. He thinks he's in the West Indies, so we must be Indians. Now it's Indian this, Indian that. Indian tribes. Cowboys and Indians. Indian nation. Indian reservation. The Indian problem. American Indians—that was my favorite. And of course, anyone who hadn't visited the reservation assumed we lived in tepees."

"That's what I would have guessed," David said. "From pictures."

"The pictures are from the tourist sites. They want to see old Native American culture; we're happy to show it. Dress in the old garb, dance the old dances, sell 'em anything they want made from colorful beads. They didn't want to see our real homes."

"Not tepees, I take it."

"Just like any other depressed economy. Multifamily units, tiny houses, house trailers. And the tourists didn't want to know that my dad was a mechanic and my mom worked in the office of a plumbing company. They'd rather believe we were part of a raiding party, drank firewater, or worked in a casino."

"Your parents really didn't?"

"My mother liked to play the slots. Dad lost a paycheck one night playing blackjack. Never went back."

"And you were a vet."

"Vet's assistant, that's all. My uncle, my mother's brother, was self trained. Didn't have to be licensed or certified or any of that other stuff, like on the outside. Unless you wanted business from the outside, and he didn't. And he wasn't into weird stuff either. Tourists asked if he danced and chanted and brought dead pets back to life. He was a good reader, read everything he could find on patching up animals, because he loved them and there were so many of them."

"You didn't want to be a vet?"

"Nope. I read all the books about Clara Barton and Florence Nightingale. Did well in school, especially science, and was encouraged by a teacher to take advantage of opportunities for Native Americans at state universities. Went to Arizona State and never looked back. Cost me more because I wasn't from Arizona, but I wanted distance between me and the reservation."

"Why?"

"I wasn't ashamed or anything. I just thought I had more opportunity outside. And I did."

"Where did you hear about God?"

"Everywhere. There were Christians on the reservation. We weren't churchgoers, but we knew a lot who were. That teacher used to talk to me about Jesus. I wasn't interested. She called it 'witnessing,' and that sounded way too weird for me. Then at university. They were everywhere. You could get witnessed to walking to class."

"Never intrigued you?"

"Not enough to go to any meetings. I was afraid I would wind up in a cult or a multilevel-marketing scheme. The big thing with those kids was getting people to admit they were sinners and that they couldn't do anything about their sin. Tell you the truth, I never felt like a sinner. Not then."

"So, wrong approach for you."

"Not their fault. I *was* a sinner, of course. I was just blind to it."

"What finally made the difference?"

"When I found out who disappeared in the vanishings, I was mad. Those churchgoers I knew. Christians from university. My high school teacher."

"So you must have had an inkling."

"An inkling? I knew. People were saying God did this, and I believed them. And I hated him for it. I thought about those people and how sincere and devout they were, how they cared enough for me to tell me something that made me think they were strange. I didn't want any part of a God who would remove them and leave me here. I wanted a hero, someone to believe in, but not him. Then I saw all the news about Carpathia. The Bible talks about how so many will be deceived? I was at the top of the list. Bought the whole package. Found out he needed medical people, hopped the next plane to New York. Wasn't so sure about moving on to this beautiful, godforsaken desert, but I was still loyal then.

"I started getting squirrelly about Carpathia when he started sounding like a politician, trying to put everything in the best light. He never seemed genuinely remorseful about all the chaos and the loss. I didn't agree with him when he said all this proved that God couldn't have been behind the disappearances, because why would a loving God do that? I believed God *had* done it, and it proved he wasn't so loving after all."

Hannah finished her stitch-removal work, stripped off and discarded her rubber gloves, washed and dried her hands, and pulled on another pair of gloves. She sat on a stool next to David. "Still have the staples, but we can both use a break."

"Somebody had to lead you to God. I'm dying to know where you met another believer here."

"Didn't know there was one till I saw your mark plain as day as you lay there on the ground. I tried wiping it off, then almost danced when I realized what it was. I couldn't see mine and had never seen another, just read about it."

"Where?"

"Remember when we were told that Tsion Ben-Judah's Web site was contraband?"

"'Course."

"That was all I needed to hear. I was there. It was all Greek to me until he predicted the earthquake. First, it happened. Second, my whole reservation was swallowed up. Lost everybody. Mom, Dad, two little brothers, extended family. I'll bet we were one of the only places in the world that had no survivors. Zero."

"Wow."

"You can imagine how I felt. Grief-stricken. Alone. Angry. Amazed that the weird guy on the Net got it right."

"Can't imagine that convincing you, though. Seems you would have been madder than ever at God."

"In a way, I was. But I really began to see the light about Nicolae. You were here then, right? You heard the rumors."

David nodded.

"People said he bullied his way onto a chopper on the roof of the old headquarters building—which I have no problem with. I probably would have done the same. Self-preservation instinct and all that. But no calls for help. No orders for more rescue craft. People hanging on the struts of his chopper, screaming, pleading for their lives. He orders the pilot off the roof. Probably couldn't have saved anybody anyway, the way the thing went down. But you've got to try, don't you? Isn't *that* true leadership?

"Then he was phony again. The remorse didn't ring true. I just started doing my job and forgetting my idealism, but I couldn't tear myself away from the Ben-Judah site. Then millions and millions joined in, and so many of them became believers. I read about the mark of the sealed believer, and I was envious. I wasn't sure I wanted in yet, but I wanted to be part of some family.

"But you know what got to me about Tsion? Listen to me, calling a man like that by his first name. But that's just it. He's clearly one of the most brilliant scholars ever born. But he had a way of putting the cookies on the lower shelf for people like me. I understood what he was saying. He made it plain and clear. And he was transparent. He lost his whole family in a worse way than I did.

"He was so loving! You could sense it, feel it right through the computer. He prayed for people, ministered to them the way the best doctors do."

"And that was what finally persuaded you?"

"Actually, no. I believed he was sincere, and I came to believe he was right. But all of a sudden I went scientific on him. I was going to take this slow, not rush into anything, study it carefully. Well, he starts predicting these plagues, and here they come. Didn't take me long after that. People suffered. These were real. And he knew they were coming."

"Did you ever see yourself as a sinner?"

She stood and found the small wire cutters.

"Uh-oh," David said.

"Just relax. Listen to the nice lady's story." She gently pressed her fingers on each side of the staple and eased the cutting edge of the clippers in. With both hands she forced the handles together, and the staple broke with a snap.

David jumped.

"You still with us?" she said.

"Didn't feel a thing. Just scared me."

"Story of my life." She snapped the other while continuing. "Tsion warned us—you know this; surely you're part of the readership."

David nodded. "I've spoken to him by phone."

"You have *not!*"

He nodded.

"Don't nod with loose staples in your head. And if you lie to me again, I'll twist 'em for you."

"I'm not lying."

"I know you're not. That's what makes me *so* jealous."

"You know you're going to get to meet him someday."

"Better bring a mop and bucket. You can just squeegee me off the floor and pour me down the drain."

"Me too."

"But you know him already! You're best buds."

"Just by phone."

She mimicked him. "Just by phone. Blah, blah, blah. Yeah, we talk. He calls once in a while. 'How ya doin', Dave? Just finished my message.'"

David had to laugh and quickly realized it was the first time since . . .

"Anyway," she continued, pulling the ends of one staple neatly from his scalp. "See? Good timing, good technique. Uh-oh, do I see brain oozing there? Nope. Must be empty."

David shook his head. "The story, Hannah."

"Oh, yeah. Tsion promises us that if we start reading the Bible, it'll be like a mirror to us and we might not like what we see. Remember that?"

"*Do* I?"

The other staple came out just as easily. She made a show of presenting it to him, and he waved it away. "I didn't have a Bible and you don't exactly see them lying around here anywhere. But Tsion had that site where you could call up the whole Bible in your language. Well, not Cherokee, but you know. So I'm reading the Bible on the Net in the wee hours."

"And couldn't get enough of it?"

"Um, no. I did it wrong. I didn't read his little guide on where to start and what to look for. I just started in at the beginning and I loved all those stories in Genesis, but when I got into Exodus, and then—what's the next one?"

"Leviticus."

"Yeah. Ugh! I'm wondering, where's the mirror? I don't like what I'm seeing, all right, but it's no mirror. Finally, I go into his site where you can ask questions. Only a million people a day do that. I didn't expect him to answer personally, of course, and he didn't. Probably was on the phone with his pal Dave. But somebody pointed me to that guide place. I start with John and then Romans and then Matthew. Talk about desperate for more and seeing yourself! My besetting sin, the way Tsion described it, was pride. I was my own god. Captain of my own destiny. I got to that *Romans Road* thing, taking you down the path of being born in sin, separated from God, his gift is eternal life . . . man, I was there. Stayed up all night and didn't even feel the effects working a full shift the next day. Wanted to tell everybody, but wanted to stay alive too."

Hannah doused David's head with disinfectant and dabbed it dry with a clean towel. "I'm going to cover you with Betadyne now, friend, so you don't look like a skunk with a lateral stripe. You'll still look funny, but not from so far away. And we'd better get out of here before they send in a search party."

"Just a minute."

"Hmm?" She was dabbing at his head again.

"Just wanted to thank you. I needed to hear that. Those stories never get old."

"Thanks, David. Can you imagine how long I've wanted to tell someone that? Oh, and one more thing."

"Yeah?"

"Say hey to Tsion for me?"

* * *

"You don't either," Buck said.

"I do too!" Zeke said. "C'mere, look."

Buck followed Zeke to his room, turning to give Rayford and Chloe a do-you-believe-this? look. Sure enough, just as Zeke had claimed, hanging in his closet were four soiled, wrinkled GC uniforms. "Where in the world?"

"After that horsemen deal," Zeke said, "remember?" Buck nodded. "Dead GC all over the place. Dad cruised me around in the middle of the night, trying to stay ahead of the recovery teams. I didn't like yankin' clothes off dead bodies, but Dad and me both thought they were gifts from God. I got their IDs and everything, but you can't use the same name as goes with the uniform."

"I can't?"

Zeke sighed. "These guys turned up missin'. Unless somebody identified their naked bodies, they're listed as AWOL or unaccounted for. You show up with their name, rank, and serial number, who do you think they're gonna pin the murder on? Or the swipin' of the uni?"

"I get it."

"Yeah, huh?"

"So, what do you do, put a new name patch on? Make a new ID?"

"Yeah, only I mix and match. Well, here, first see if this one fits. It's the biggest I got."

"I can see already it's going to be short."

"But look at the cuffs in the shirt, the pants, and the jacket. They leave lots of hem in 'em so they won't have to make custom-made duds for everybody."

"You do tailoring work too, Zeke?"

"Not in front of everybody, and I don't brag on it, but yeah. I do everything. Full-service shop."

Buck found the trousers about two inches short and the waist snug. The shirt was close but needed another inch in the sleeves. Same with the jacket. The cap was way too small. Buck shook his head when Zeke rummaged around and found his sewing kit. It was all he could do to keep from bursting out laughing when the big kid popped a half dozen straight pins in his mouth and knelt to do his work.

"What do you mean, you mix and match?"

"Well," Zeke said around the pins, "your ID is probably gonna be from a dead civilian. You've already done your own facial surgery, not on purpose, but you did. I'll dye your hair dark, use dark contacts, and shoot a picture to go with the new papers. You want to find someone you like? You've seen my files before. You pulled Greg North out of that stack. Grab a few. Pick someone about your same size and everything. The less I have to change, the better."

"Can you give me a rank above Albie's?"

"No can do," Zeke said. "See the shoulders and the collar on that jacket? That's your basic Peacekeeper. If your collar had another stripe or two and stuck straight up instead of layin' flat, you could be as high as a commander."

"And you can't do that much tailoring."

"That's big-time work. I'd hafta charge you double."

Buck smiled, but Zeke roared. "Did you almost check your wallet to see if you could handle it?"

"Almost."

"Dad says I'm a card." Zeke was suddenly sober.

"Know where your dad is yet?"

Zeke shook his head. "Didn't like what I saw on TV, though. Something about startin' that mark thing with guys they've got behind bars already. Use 'em as test cases." He shook his head.

"Your dad won't take the mark."

"Oh, I know that. No way. Never. Which means I'll probably never see him again."

"Don't think that way, Zeke. There's always hope."

"Well, maybe, and I'm prayin'. But I'll tell ya when there's no more hope, and that's when they line these guys up for the mark. They get a choice, right?"

"That's what I understand."

"Dad won't even think about it. He's already got a mark. I've seen his and he's seen mine—that's how we know. And he won't start wonderin' if he can have both and stay alive. He'd never do a thing that looks like he's a Carpathia guy. He'll say, 'No you don't,' and they'll thump 'im right there. I don't know how they're gonna kill 'em in jails, whether they've got gill-o-teens or if they just shoot 'em. But that's how Dad's gettin' out of jail. In a box."

\+ + +

On the way back to his office, David felt strangely warmed and encouraged. He loved Hannah's personality and way of expressing herself. She would be a good friend. She was older than he but didn't act like it. He had begun to wonder if there was an oasis of good feeling anywhere.

David worked his magic on the computer, patching in to the bug in room 4054. He slipped on earphones and found himself in the middle of a heated argument. He heard the television and Mrs. Wong pleading, "Shh! TV! Shh! TV!"

Her husband shouted back in Chinese. David knew there were many dialects, but he didn't understand even one. It soon became clear that father and son were arguing and that the mother wanted to watch television. The only words David could make out from the males were an occasional *GC* and *Carpathia.* The son was soon in tears, the father berating him.

David recorded the conversation in the unlikely event he could download voice-activated software that would not only recognize the language and the dialect, but would also convert it to English or Hebrew, his two languages.

Suddenly he heard the father speak more harshly than ever, the son pleading and—it sounded like—collapsing in tears. The mother pleaded for quiet again, the father barked at her, and then it sounded to David as if someone picked up a phone and punched buttons. Finally, English!

"Missah Akbar, you speak Chinese? . . . Pakistani? Me no. English OK, OK? . . . Yes, Wong! Question for you. New worker get loyalty mark first, yah? . . . OK! How soon? . . . Not till then? . . . Maybe sooner, OK! Mrs. Wong and me get too? OK? Son, Chang Wong, want be first to get mark."

The boy cried out in Chinese, and it sounded as if Mr. Wong covered the phone before screaming at him. Someone left the room, David assumed Chang, and slammed a door.

"Missah Akbar, you do mark on boy, mother, father? . . . You no do? Who? . . . Moon? Walter Moon? . . . Not Moon himself? . . . Moon people, OK! Son first! Picture! Take picture son! . . . When? . . . Yes. I talk to Moon people. Bye-bye."

David heard Mr. Wong call out something more calmly, and then something from Chang, muffled. The father was angry again and had the last word. Then he whispered something in Chinese to his wife. She responded with what sounded like resignation.

David wondered if Chang had told his father why he would refuse the mark, or if he simply said no. When the apartment was silent except for the television, David saved the file and forwarded it to Ming Toy with a request. "If it's not too much trouble or too painful, it would help me to know what was said here. I'm guessing your father is pressuring Chang to get himself hired and to be among the first to take the mark. I'll try other sources inside to see how soon they're going to start administering the mark, but help me with this at your earliest convenience, if you would. I regret eavesdropping, but I'm sure you want to preclude this disaster too."

David dialed 4054. Mr. Wong answered. "Chang, please?"

"You want Chang Wong?"

"Yes, please."

"Talk to him about GC job?"

"Yes, sir."

"You Mr. Moon?"

"No. David Hassid. I met you last week."

"Yes! Mr. Hassid! Chang work for you?"

"I don't know yet. That's what I'd like to talk to him about."

"He here. You talk to him. You in computers, yes?"

"Much of my area is computers, yes."

"He best. He help you! Work for you. You talk to him. Wait . . . Chang!" He switched to Chinese, and the boy argued from the other room. Finally he came to the phone.

"Hello," the boy said, sounding as if he'd lost his best friend.

"Chang, it's David. Just listen. Your sister told me what was going on. Let me try to help. It will get your father off your back if you get interviewed by a director, right?"

"Yes."

"It'll buy us some time. You don't worry, OK?"

"I'll try not to."

"Don't say anything, but we might even find a way to get you out of here."

"Before the mark?"

"Don't say that, Chang. Just play along for now. Understand?"

"Yes, David."

"Call me Mr. Hassid, OK? We can't sound like friends, and we sure don't want to sound like fellow believers, brothers, right?"

"Right, Mr. Hassid."

"Thataboy, Chang. Let's do this right. You call my assistant tomorrow and arrange for an appointment with me. I'll tell Tiffany to expect your call, and you tell her I asked you to call her. All right?"

"Yes, sir."

"Everything will be all right, Chang."

"I hope so."

"You can trust me."

"Yes, Mr. Hassid."

14

RAYFORD AND THE OTHERS were invited to listen in as Tsion grilled his former professor and mentor on the history of God's chosen people. Chaim, with the wire finally out of his mouth, slowly worked his jaw and rubbed his face, clearly relieved. He was not animated, however, and hard as it seemed Tsion tried, Chaim appeared still tormented by the same things he had discussed with Rayford a few nights before.

"Come, come, Chaim!" Tsion said. "This is exciting, dramatic, miraculous stuff. This is the greatest story ever told! I know where God has provided a place of refuge for his children, but I am not going to tell you until you are ready. You must be prepared in case God calls you to be a warrior for the Lord, to go into a battle of words and wit. Your knowledge would help carry you, but God would have to be your strength. I believe that if he confirms in your heart that you shall be his vessel, he will empower you with supernatural abilities to fight the satanic miracles of Antichrist. Can you envision the victory, my friend? How I wish I were the one going!"

"How I wish that too," Chaim said.

"No, no! If you are God's man in God's time, you must never want out of this most sacred duty and calling! The history of this country carries much discussion of a manifest destiny. Well, my brother, if ever a people had a manifest destiny, it is our people! Yours and mine! And now we include our Gentile brothers who are grafted into the branch because of their belief in Messiah and his work of grace and sacrifice and forgiveness on the cross. Jesus is Messiah! Jesus is the Christ! He is risen!"

"He is risen indeed," Chaim said, but he did not match Tsion's energy.

"Do you hear yourself?" Tsion mimicked Chaim, mumbling, "He-is-risen-indeed. No! *He is risen, indeed!* Amen! Praise the Lord! Hallelujah! You could go to Jerusalem, a leader of men, a conqueror! You would stand up to the lying, blaspheming enemy of the Lord Most High. You would expose Antichrist to the world as the evil man indwelt by Satan and rally the devout believers to repel the mark of the beast!

"Oh, Chaim, Chaim! You are learning so much. That old brain is still good, still facile, still receptive. You are getting this—I know you are! If not you, who shall go? You seem uniquely qualified, but much as I dream it, I cannot presume to make this assignment. How I wish *I* were the one and could be there in person to see it! If it is you, I will want every detail. Should the forces of evil come against you and you should be overwhelmed by the power of the enemy, God would provide a way, a place, and you, you my friend, would lead the people to that place. And the Lord God himself would protect you and care for you and watch over you and provide for you. Do you realize, Chaim, that God has promised that it will be as in the days of old? Think of it! Weak and frail and wicked as they were, unfaithful, ignorant, impatient, and dallying with other gods, the God of the universe himself catered to the children of Israel.

"Do you understand what that means? You could lead your people, *his* people, to a place that will be almost impossible to go into or out from. If you were to be there until the Glorious Appearing of the Christ, what would you eat? What would you wear? The Bible says God himself will provide as he did in the days of old! He will send food, delicious, nourishing, fulfilling food! Manna from heaven! And do you know about your clothes?"

"No, Tsion," Chaim said wearily, a tease in his voice, "whatever you do, *do not* neglect to tell me about my clothes."

"I won't! And you will be grateful, not to mention amazed. If I amaze you, will you admit it?"

"I will admit it."

"Promise me."

"My word is my bond, my excitable young friend. Amaze me and I will say so."

"Your clothes will not wear out!" Tsion stopped with a flourish, his hands in the air.

"They won't?"

"Are you amazed?"

"Maybe. Tell me more."

"Now you want to hear it?"

"I always want to hear it, Tsion. I am just unworthy. Scared to death, unqualified, unprepared, and unworthy."

"If God calls you, you shall be none of those! You would be Moses! The Lord God of Abraham, Isaac, and Jacob would go before you, and the glory of the Lord would be your rear guard."

"I would need a rear guard? Who would be chasing me?"

"Not Pharaoh's army, I assure you. But if it were, God would make a way for you to escape. Carpathia's hordes would be pursuing you. And for all his talk of peace and disarmament, who has access to the residue of the world's weapons, surrendered willingly to the lying purveyor of peace? But if you needed the Red Sea parted yet again, God would do it! For what have we learned, my little Hebrew schoolchild?"

"Hmm?"

"Hmm? Don't *hmm?* me, Chaim! Tell the rabbi what you learned about the great stories, the miracles from the Torah."

"That they are not just stories, not just examples, myths for our encouragement."

"Excellent. But rather, what are they? What are they, my star pupil?"

"Truth."

"Truth! Yes!"

"They actually happened."

"Yes, Chaim! They happened because God is all-powerful. He says they happened—they happened. And if he says he will do it again, what?"

"He will."

"He will! Oh, the privilege, Chaim! Deal with your fears. Deal with your doubts. Give them to God. Offer yourself in all your weakness, because in our weakness we are made strong. Moses was weak. Moses was nobody. Moses had a speech impediment! Chaim! Moses, the hero of our faith, had less to offer than you do!"

"He was not a murderer."

"Yes he was! You forget! Did he not kill a man? Chaim, think! Your mind, your conscience, your heart tells you God cannot forgive you. I know the guilt is fresh. I know it is grievous. But you know, down deep, that God's grace is greater than our sin. It has to be! Otherwise we all live in vain! Is anything too hard for God? Anything too big for him? Any sin too great for him to forgive? It would be blasphemy to say so. Chaim! If you are the one who can commit a sin too great for God to forgive, you are above God. That's how we can wallow in our sin and still be guilty of pride. Who do we think we are, the only ones God cannot reach with his gift of love?

"He found you, Chaim! He pulled you from the miry clay! Humble yourself in the sight of the Lord, and he will lift you up!"

"Back to my clothes," Chaim said. "I could wear clothes from now until Jesus comes again, and they wouldn't wear out?"

Tsion sat back and waved dismissively. "Chaim, if he can save you and me, of all people, forgive us our sins, bring us back from spiritual death, this clothes thing is one of his lesser miracles. Forget the extra buttons, the patches, the thread. Go there with something you like, because you'll still be wearing it when this is all over."

* * *

David had pushed the limits of his ability to virtually set up the entire GC compound for his own remote computer monitoring. He breathed a prayer of thanks to God for allowing him to focus and work in spite of his grief. Mac and Abdullah were set to visit him in an hour to finalize the escape plan that included David and Hannah, and all four had agreed to carefully watch for believers they had been unaware of. It was already apparent that the brilliant teenager, Chang Wong, might be tagging along. David just had to figure out how to pull it off.

While awaiting word from Ming Toy, David checked his archives for meetings he had recorded but never listened to. In his Carpathia file was the one with Suhail Akbar, Walter Moon, Leon Fortunato, and Jim Hickman the day he himself had chatted with Hickman. David felt a chill as he prepared to eavesdrop, and he did a quick walk-through of his area to make sure everyone was gone for the day. He could close a program and shut down with a single keystroke, but still he didn't want to be surprised by the wrong person.

Something Hannah had asked a few days before haunted him too. She had said, "How do you know there isn't someone just as technically astute as you are who is doing exactly what you're doing?"

"Such as?" he had said.

"Monitoring you, maybe."

He had brushed it off. He had developed antihacking programs, antibugging devices. He had electronic ears everywhere and believed he could hear if someone breathed a word of something like that. It was impossible, wasn't it? Surely the brass wouldn't be so free to speak if they thought he was listening in. And if they were onto him, it seemed they would have shut him down long before this.

David believed the security chips he'd inserted in his phones and e-mail programs were impenetrable, and he had tried to explain it to Hannah.

"I don't pretend to have a clue, David. Maybe you *are* the top computer genius alive, but ought you not be very careful?"

"Oh, I am."

"You are?"

"You bet."

"But you tell me of phone calls and e-mails between you and your compatriots in the States."

"Not traceable. Not hackable."

"But you trace others. You hack others."

"I'm good."

"You're living on the edge."

"There's no other way to live."

Hannah had dropped it with a shrug. He believed the only reason she raised the issue was because she cared, and she was, after all, a civilian when it came to technology. But he almost wished she hadn't planted the seed of curiosity in his mind. With every message, every transmission, every phone call, he got the niggling feeling that someone somewhere could be looking over his shoulder. Everything he knew told him it couldn't be, but there was no accounting for intuition. He ran continuous checks on his programs, searched for intruders. So far so good, but Hannah had spooked him. If nothing else, it would keep him on his toes.

David had begun the Carpathia meeting recording before he went to see Hickman, so he discovered several minutes of Carpathia alone in his office. The last time he had listened in that way he had heard Nicolae praying to Lucifer. Now, Nicolae *was* Lucifer. Did Satan pray to himself?

No, but he did talk to himself. At first David merely marveled at the fidelity of the sound. He had merely arranged a simple intercom system to both transmit and receive, based on his commands, but it worked better than he had hoped. He heard when Nicolae sighed, cleared his throat, or even hummed.

That was the strangest part. Here was a man who apparently did not sleep. Yet he seemed to exude energy, even when alone. David heard movement, walking, things being arranged. In the background he heard the workers he had encountered just outside Carpathia's office.

"Hmm," Carpathia said softly, as if thinking. "Mirrors. I need mirrors." He chuckled. "Why deprive myself of the joy others luxuriate in? They get to look at me whenever they want."

He pushed the intercom button and his assistant answered immediately. "Excellency?" Sandra said.

"Is that foreman still out there?"

"He is, Lordship. Would you like to speak with him?"

"No, just pass along a message. Better yet, step in a moment."

"My pleasure," she said, as if she meant it with all of her being. Sandra had always seemed so cold and bored to David that he wondered how she interacted with Carpathia. She was more than twenty years his senior. David heard the squeak of a chair, as if Carpathia had sat.

Simultaneous with a soft knock, the door opened and closed. "Your Excellency," she said, to the sound of rustling.

"Sandra," Carpathia said, "you need not kneel every time you—"

"Pardon me, sir," she said, "but I beg of you not to deprive me the privilege."

"Well, of course not, if you wish, but—"

"I know you don't require it, sir, but to me it is a privilege to worship you."

He sighed without a trace of impatience, David thought.

"What a beautiful sentiment," he said at last. "I accept your devotion with deep satisfaction."

"What may I do for you, my lord?" she said. "Do me the honor of asking anything of me."

"Merely that I want several full-length mirrors in the remodeled office. I will leave it to those in charge of such matters to position them, but I believe it would add a nice touch."

"I couldn't agree more, sir. I shiver at the thought of multiple images of you in here."

"Oh, well, I thank you. Run along and deliver that message now."

"Right away, sir."

"And then you may go for the day."

"But your meeting—"

"I will welcome them. Do not feel obligated."

"As you wish, sir, but you know I would be more than happy—"

"I know."

The door opened and shut, and it sounded as if Carpathia rose once more. Just loud enough for David to hear he said, "I too shiver at the thought of multiple images of me, you homely old wench. But you do know how to make a man feel worshiped."

Now it sounded as if he was moving chairs into position. "Akbar, Fortunato, Hickman, Moon. No, Moon, Akbar, ah . . . must let Leon wonder about his proximity and access, keep him nimble. Hickman needs assurances. All right."

Back to his intercom. "Are you still out there, Sandra?"

"Yes, sir."

"Before you go, get Mr. McCullum on the phone for me, please."

David froze, then chastised himself. He didn't care that Nicolae communicated with Mac. If David couldn't trust Mac, he couldn't trust anyone.

"Captain McCullum," Carpathia said a few minutes later. "How good to speak with you. You are aware, are you not, that 10 percent of all weapons of war were ceded to the Global Community when we were known as the United Nations? . . . The rest were destroyed, and I am satisfied that our monitoring has confirmed that this was largely carried out. If any munitions remain, they are few and are likely in the hands of factions so small as to pose little threat. My question to you is, do you know where we stockpiled the armaments we received? . . . You had nothing to do with that? . . . Well, yes, of course *I* know,

Captain! The question is merely probative. You are former military, you are a pilot, and you get around. I want to know if the word has leaked out where we inventory our weapons. . . . Good. That is all, Captain."

Clearly, Mac had told Nicolae he had no idea where the weapons were. As far as David knew, that was the truth. But what a massive operation that had to have been, and how was it pulled off without word getting out? And what might Carpathia be planning now?

"Gentlemen!" Carpathia said a few minutes later, welcoming the four visitors. "Please, come in."

"Allow me to be the first to kneel before you," Leon said, "and kiss your hands."

"Thank you, Reverend, but you are hardly the first."

"I meant at this meeting," Fortunato whined.

"And he won't be the last!" Hickman said, and David actually heard the smack of his lips.

"Thank you, Supreme Commander. Thank you. Chief Akbar? Thank you. Chief Moon? My thanks. Oh, Reverend, no, please. I would appreciate it if you would sit here."

"Here?" Leon said, clearly surprised.

"A problem?"

"I will sit anywhere His Excellency wishes, of course. I would even stand, if you asked."

"I'd kneel for the whole meeting," Hickman said.

"Right here, my friend," Carpathia said, devoting much time and energy to putting people where he wanted them.

"Sir?" Leon began when they were settled. "Have you been able to sleep, get some rest?"

"You are worried about me, Reverend?"

"Of course, Excellency."

"Sleep is for mortals, my friend."

"Well spoken, sir."

"I'm sure mortal, boys, er, gents," Hickman said. "Slept like a rock last night. Out of shape, I guess. Gotta do something about this gut."

An awkward silence.

"May we begin?" Carpathia said. Hickman muttered an apology, but Nicolae was already addressing Intelligence Chief Akbar. "Suhail, I have become convinced that the location of our armaments remains confidential. Would you concur?"

"I would, sir, though I confess it baffles me."

"Baffles is right!" Hickman said. "Seems to me we had hundreds of troops involved in this thing and—oh, my bad, I'm sorry. I'll wait my turn."

David could only imagine the look Carpathia must have given Hickman. He had to have known whom he was putting in such a lofty position. Having Hickman share space with Sandra and become primarily an errand boy with a big title proved Carpathia knew exactly what he was doing.

"Peacekeeping Forces prepared to go on the offensive, Chief Moon?"

"Yes, sir. Ready to deploy, anywhere and everywhere. We can crush any resistance."

"An update, Reverend?"

"On loyalty mark, Jerusalem, religion?"

"Jerusalem, of course," Carpathia said, dripping sarcasm.

Leon was clearly hurt. "On top of it all, Excellency," he said. "Program is prepared, loyalists ready, should be a triumphal entry in every sense of the word."

"Commander Hickman," Carpathia said condescendingly, "you may put down your hand. You need not ask for the floor here."

"I can just jump in then?"

"No, you cannot just *jump in.* You have each been invited here because I need updates from your areas."

"Well, I'm ready. I have that. I—"

"And when I want your input, I shall call on you. Understood?"

"Yes, sir; sorry, sir."

"No need to apologize."

"Sorry."

"Suhail or Walter, what kind of resistance may we expect in Jerusalem?"

There was a pause, during which, David assumed, the two were looking at each other to avoid interrupting.

"Come, come, gentlemen," Carpathia said. "I have a planet to rule." He chuckled as if joking, but it wasn't funny to David.

Akbar began, slowly and articulately. David thought that in another setting, Suhail could have been an effective intelligence chief. "Frankly, Potentate, I do not believe the Judah-ites will show their faces. I am not discounting the effectiveness of their movement. Their numbers still seem large, but they are an underground cause, networked by computers. You will not likely see the mass public rally similar to the one at Kolleck Stadium when Tsion B—"

"I recall it well, Akbar. Tell me, is part of the reason they are not likely to make a fuss in Jerusalem because many of their ranks have been dissuaded by seeing a *real* resurrection—one that does not require blind faith?"

Silence, except for the clearing of a throat. David assumed it was Suhail's.

"No?"

"Surprisingly not, sir. That would certainly have persuaded me of your deity, except that I was already convinced of it."

"Me too!" Hickman said. "Sorry."

"Of course," Fortunato said, "I had personal experience that proved it. And now—well, it's not my turn, is it?"

"The truth is, Excellency," Akbar continued carefully, "our monitoring of the Judah-ite Web site reveals they are even more entrenched. They believe, ah, that your resurrection proves the opposite of what is so patently obvious to thinking people."

David flinched when he heard a loud bang on the table, the rolling back of a chair, and a string of expletives from Carpathia. That was something new. The Nicolae of before always kept his composure.

"Forgive me, Holiness," Akbar said. "You understand that I am merely reporting what my best analysts—"

"Yes, I know that!" Carpathia spat. "I just do not understand what it is going to take to prove to these people who is worthy of their devotion!" He swore again, and the others seemed to feel obligated to grumble loudly about the lunacy of the skeptics. "All right!" Carpathia said finally. "You think they will just snipe at us from the comfort of their hiding places."

"Correct."

"That is unfortunate. I was so hopeful of gloating in their faces. Any confirmation that they are harboring Rosenzweig?"

David held his breath through another pause.

"I admit we're stumped," Walter Moon said. "We traced a few leads from people who thought they saw him running, taking a taxi, that kind of a thing. We know for sure that stroke was phony."

"You can say that again," Nicolae said.

"Dang straight!" Hickman offered. "Sorry."

"He deceived me," Nicolae added. "I have to give him that."

"Um, sir," Moon continued. "I, ah, am not second-guessing you, but . . ."

"Please, Walter."

"Well, you did pardon your attacker, maybe before you knew who he was."

Carpathia roared with laughter. "You do not think I knew who murdered me? I lift that limp arm of his to start the applause and a few seconds later I lurch away from the sound of a gun, he chops my feet from under me with that infernal chair, and the next thing I know I am in the lap of a madman. Well, I knew instantly what was happening, though I may never know why. But he was no frail old man. There was no stiff arm and no limp arm, no scrawny senior citizen. He rammed that blade into me, and I could hear him gutting my skull. The man was hard as a rock and strong."

"Ought to put out a worldwide all points bulletin and use all our resources to bring him in," Hickman said. "Got him on tape! Show it to the world!"

"In due time," Carpathia said, calmer now, and it sounded to David as if Nicolae had sat and joined them again. "I pardoned him, knowing that a world of loyal subjects would relish avenging me, should he ever show his face. Needless to say, we shall not prosecute a crime when that event occurs."

"Needless to say," Hickman parroted.

"And," Carpathia said, "where are we with the accomplice?"

"The nut with the gun?" Moon said. "We don't think he was Middle Eastern. Found his getup and the weapon. Matches the bullet. No prints. No leads. You're convinced they were working together?"

Carpathia sounded flabbergasted. "Convinced? I am not the law-enforcement expert here, but the timing of those two attacks was just a little too coincidental, would you not agree?"

"I would," Hickman said. "I worked that case and—"

"Proceed," Nicolae said.

"I figure they were hedgin' their bets. If one of 'em didn't get ya, the other one would. Guy with the gun could have been a diversion, but he's lucky he didn't kill anybody."

Akbar cleared his throat. "You're aware there's a connection between Ben-Judah and Rosenzweig?"

"Tell me," Nicolae said.

"Ben-Judah was once a student of Rosenzweig's."

"You don't say," Nicolae said, and it was the first time David had heard him use a contraction. "Hmm. Find Ben-Judah, and you find Rosenzweig."

"That's what I was thinkin'," Hickman said.

"I'm ready for your report, James."

"Me? Mine? You are? Oh, yes, sir. Um, everything's on track. Injector thingies, beheaders, er, um, jes' a minute. Viv, ah, Ms. Ivins gave me the correct terminology here, bear with me. Loyalty confirmation facilitators. Got those comin' or goin', depending. They're on their way here and there and wherever we need 'em. Not all of 'em, certainly. Some are being made as we speak, but we're on schedule. I found a nurse here that has experience shooting biochips into . . . into . . . well . . . dogs, I guess. But she's going to help train. And I've got a lead on your pig."

"My pig?"

"Oh! Not, I mean, if you don't need a pig, they'll just butcher it and use it here. But if you needed a pig, I'm pretty sure we've got a big one ordered."

"What would I want a pig for, James?"

"It's not that I heard . . . or knew . . . I mean . . . that you actually need a pig for anything, really. But if you ever did, just let me know, all right. You need one? For anything?"

"Who has been talking to you, Commander?"

"Um, what?"

"You heard me."

"Talking to me?"

Carpathia was suddenly shouting, cursing again. "Mr. Hickman, what is said in these meetings in my private office is sacred. Do you understand?"

"Yes, sir. I would never—"

"Sacred! The security of the Global Community depends on the confidentiality and trustworthiness of the communications in here. You've heard the old expression, 'Loose lips sink ships'?"

"Yeah, I have. I know what you mean."

"Someone told you there was a discussion in this room about my need for a pig."

"Well, I'd rather not—"

"Oh, yes, you had rather, Mr. Hickman! Violating the sacred trust of the potentate of the Global Community is a capital offense, is it not, Mr. Moon?"

"Yes, sir, it is."

"So, James, the next thing out of your mouth had better be the guilty party, or *you* will pay the ultimate price for the transgression. I'm waiting."

David could hear Hickman whimpering.

"The name, Commander. If I hear that he is your friend or that you'd rather not say or anything other than who he is, you are a dead man."

Still Hickman struggled.

"You have ten seconds, sir."

Hickman took a labored breath and coughed.

"And now five."

"He's—he's—a—"

"Mr. Moon, are you prepared to take Mr. Hickman into custody for the purpose of exec—"

"Ramon Santiago!" Hickman blurted. "But I beg of you, sir, don't—"

"Mr. Moon."

"Please! No!"

David heard Moon on his cell phone. "Moon here. Listen, take Santiago into custody. . . . Right, the one from Peacekeeping . . . right now . . . yes. Till I get there."

"You'll let me handle it personally, Walter?"

"As you wish."

"No! Please!"

"James, when it is announced tomorrow that a Peacekeeping deputy commander has been put to death, you at least will understand the gravity of the rules, won't you?"

David heard assent through Hickman's sobs. Apparently that wasn't good enough for Carpathia.

"Won't you, *Supreme* Commander?"

"Yes!"

"I thought so. And yes, I have need of a pig. A big, fat, juicy, huge-nostriled beast so overfed that it will be too lethargic to throw me, should I choose to ride it through the Via Dolorosa in the *Holy* City. Tell me, Hickman. Tell me about my pig."

"I haven't actually seen it yet," Hickman said miserably, "but—"

"But you understand my order."

"Yes." His voice was shaky.

"Big, fat, and ugly?"

"Yeah."

"I didn't hear you, James. Stinky? May I have him smelly?"

"Yeah."

"Whatever I want?"

"Yes!"

"Are you angry with me, my loyal servant?"

"Uh-huh."

"Well, thank you for your honesty. Do you understand that I want an animal that could accommodate my fist in either nostril?"

David jumped at the knock on his door. Mac and Abdullah had arrived.

15

BUCK FELT HIS AGE and was embarrassed to disembark in Kozani, Greece, with a severe case of jet lag that didn't seem to bother the older Albie. And Albie, of course, had done all the flying.

"Use it to your advantage," Albie said.

"How so?"

"It should make you cranky."

"I'm pretty even."

"Well, quit that. You're just being polite. Your natural instinct, when you'd rather be in bed, is to be testy, short, irritable. Go with it. GC Peacekeepers are macho, in charge. They have an attitude."

"So I've noticed."

"Don't ask—don't apologize. You're a busy man, on assignment, with things to do."

"Got it."

"Do you?"

"I think so."

"That didn't sound so macho."

"I've got to be that way with you too?"

"At least practice, Buck. You Americans, I swear. I had to shame your father-in-law into being the leader he was born to be. You're an international journalist and you can't playact to get things done?"

"I think I can."

"Well, show me. How did you get the big stories, get access to the best interview subjects?"

"I used the power of my position."

"Exactly."

"But I was working for *Global Weekly.*"

"More than that. You were Buck Williams, *the* Buck Williams of *Global Weekly.* It may have been your talent and your writing that made you *the* Buck Williams, but once you were him, you walked with confidence, didn't you?"

"I guess."

"I guess," Albie mocked. "Come on, Buck! You strutted!"

"You want me to strut?"

"I want you to get us a vehicle to drive to the detention center where Pastor Demeter and Mrs. Miklos and several others from their church are incarcerated."

"But wouldn't it be easier for you?"

"Why?"

"You're the superior officer. You outrank everybody we'll run into."

"Then take advantage of that. I'll be the one everybody sees but no one mentions. They will only salute. You speak with my authority. And you're wearing that beautiful uniform, tailored at *Chez Zeke*."

"I'll try."

"You're hopeless."

"I can do this."

"You're not giving me confidence."

"Watch me."

"That's what I'm afraid of. I'll be watching you get found out. Prove me wrong, Buck."

"Outta my way, old man."

"That's the spirit."

"You going to have them refuel us while we're in Ptolemaïs?"

"No, Buck, you are."

"C'mon. I don't know all that plane stuff."

"Just do it. From this point on, I am an angry, jet-lagged, ill-tempered deputy commander, and I don't want to speak."

"So it's all on me?"

"Don't ask me. I'm mute."

"Are you serious?"

But Albie wouldn't answer. The twinkle faded from his eyes and he set his jaw, scowling as they marched from the jet to the terminal, about twenty-five miles south of their destination. Buck accosted the first corporal he saw. "English?" he asked the young man.

"'Course. 'Sup?"

"I need you to hangar that aircraft and refuel it while my commanding officer and I are on assignment up the road."

"Yeah? Well, I want you to shine my boots while I'm sleeping."

"I'll pretend I didn't hear that, son."

"Yeah, good. Me too."

He started to leave and Buck swung him around with a grab of his shoulder. "Do it."

"You think I know how to jockey a plane? I'm ground forces, pal. Get some other lackey to do it."

"I'm telling you. Find someone who knows how to do it and have it done by the time we get back, or suffer the consequences."

"You gotta be kiddin' me!"

Albie had kept his back to the conversation, and Buck was convinced he was trying not to laugh aloud.

"You got that, son?" Buck said.

"I'm outta here. I'll take my chances. You don't even know my name."

"Well, *I* do," Albie said, spinning to face the boy, suddenly ashen. "And you'll do what you're told or you'll be walking back to your hometown in civilian clothes."

"Yes, sir," the boy said, saluting. "Right away, sir."

"Don't let me down, boy," Albie called after him.

Buck gave Albie a look. "Thought you were mute."

"Somebody had to bail you out."

"He was my own rank!"

"That's why you refer to me! I've got the clout, but you've got to use it. Try again."

"What now?"

"I told you. We need a vehicle."

"Ach!"

Buck strode into the terminal, which was crawling with GC. With the crackdown on the underground churches, it would be a noisy area for a while. "Give me your papers," he told Albie.

"What for?"

"Just do it! Hand 'em over!"

"Now you're talking."

Buck stepped to the front of a line of GC Peacekeepers. "Hey!" the first in line shouted.

"Hey yourself," Buck said. "You a deputy commander or are you escorting one? Because if you're not, I'd appreciate your standing down."

"Yes, sir."

Buck raised an eyebrow at Albie, then spoke to the GC officer at a desk behind a window. "Corporal Jack Jensen on behalf of Deputy Commander Marcus Elbaz, here on assignment from the USNA. Need a vehicle for transport to Ptolemaïs."

"Yeah, you and a thousand other guys," the officer said, lazily looking over their IDs. "Seriously, you're about two hundredth in line."

"Seems to me we're near the top, sir, begging your pardon."

"How come your superior officer is USNA? He looks Middle Eastern."

"I don't do the assigning, pal. And I wouldn't recommend getting into it with him. No, better yet, it would be fun. Tell *him* he looks Middle Eastern and that you're questioning his base of operations. Go ahead. Really."

The officer pursed his lips and slid the IDs back under the window. "Something basic do ya?"

"Anything. I could push for something fancy, but we just want to get in and get out. Anyway, tell you the truth, Elbaz has been so touchy today, I don't think he deserves a nicer ride. We'll take whatever you've got."

The officer slid Buck a set of keys attached to a manila ticket. "Show this at the temporary motor pool behind the exit gate."

As they headed that way, Albie mimicked Buck. "He's been so touchy today, I don't think he deserves a nicer ride. I oughta bust you down to Boy Scout."

"You do and *you'll* be walking home in civilian clothes."

* * *

"Carpathia's up to something," Mac said, sitting next to Abdullah in David's office.

"I am going to be so glad to say good-bye to this place," Abdullah said.

David shifted in his chair. "Tell me about it."

"Well, don't you want to get out of here too?"

"I'm sorry, Smitty," David said. "I was talking to Mac."

"Oh! A thousand pardons."

"Watch him now," Mac said. "He'll be pout in a New Babylon second."

"I am not pout! Now stop teasing!"

Mac smacked Abdullah on the shoulder and the Jordanian smiled. "Anyway," Mac said, turning back to David, "Carpathia calls me a little while ago and asks me do I know where his weapons are. 'Course, I don't, but I'd sure like to. Tell you somethin', guys, people can talk all they want about the miraculous rebuilding Carpathia did all over the world. But nothin', and I mean nothin', compares to him getting all those countries to destroy 90 percent of their weapons and give him the other 10, and then him storin' 'em somewhere that nobody ever talks about."

"Loose lips sink ships," David repeated.

"You think people know but won't say?"

"Obviously."

"How does he keep a secret that big among so many people?"

"I think I just heard how," David said, and he briefed Mac and Abdullah on it.

Abdullah sat shaking his head. "Nicolae Carpathia is a bad man."

Mac looked at Abdullah and then at David. "Well, yeah! I mean, come on, Smitty. You just come to that conclusion, or have you known all along and just been keeping it from us?"

"I know you are teasing me," Abdullah said. "Just wait until I know your language good."

"You'll be dangerous; that's a fact."

David's cell phone rang. He flipped it open and held up an apologetic finger. "It's Ming," he said.

"Should we go?" Mac said.

David shook his head.

"They were fighting over what you assumed they were fighting over," she said. "My father wants Chang to take a job right away with the GC and be among the first to take the mark. Chang swears he will never take the mark."

"Did he tell your father why?"

"No, and I am coming to see that he never can unless my father himself somehow becomes a believer. I have not lost faith and I keep praying, but until that happens, Chang cannot tell him. He would expose us."

"Does your mother know?"

"No! She would eventually tell him. I'm afraid she is so intimidated that she would not be able to stand up to him in the end. David, you cannot let Chang get a job there, especially if new employees are the first to get the mark."

"It appears that prisoners are going to be first, but yes, new employees soon. As they are hired, apparently. And even the rest of us within a couple of weeks."

"What are you going to do, David? You and your friends?"

"We're talking about that now. Obviously, we run or we die."

"Can you take Chang with you?"

"Kidnap him?"

Ming was silent. Then, "Did you hear yourself, David? You want to leave him to take the mark or be beheaded for refusing so you won't run the risk of kidnapping him? Please! Kidnap him! For one thing, he will go willingly."

"I'm supposed to interview him for a job tomorrow."

"Then either find a way to eliminate him, discredit him as a potential employee, or tell him where to meet you when you escape."

"The latter is more likely. What could possibly disqualify him? He looks like a gold mine to any department, especially mine."

"Make something up. Say he has AIDS."

"And let your father kill him himself?"

"Well, how about a genetic defect?"

"Does he have one?"

"No! But work with me."

"I'm not a doctor, Ming. It would just stall things."

"That's better than nothing."

"Not if it makes me look suspicious. We're hoping to get out of here without their suspecting we are subversives."

"Great idea. Tell them you want to take Chang with you to check him out before hiring. Then, whatever happens to you happens to him. He's free and he can help you wherever you go."

"Maybe."

"It *has* to work, David. What choice is there?"

"What if they don't go for it? What if they say no, just hire him, give him the mark, and *then* take him on assignment?"

"You have to try. He's brilliant, but he's a child. He can't fend for himself. He can't even defend himself against my father."

"I'll do the best I can, Ming."

"That sounds like an excuse after everything fails."

"I'm sorry, but I can't do better than the best I can do."

"David, he's my brother! I know he's not your flesh, but can you pretend? If it was Annie, would you do your best? Or would you do whatever you had to do to save her?"

David couldn't speak.

"Oh, David! Forgive me! That was so wrong of me! Please! That was cruel."

"No. I—"

"David, please blame that on my fear and my situation."

"It's all right, M—"

"Please tell me you forgive me. I didn't mean that."

"Ming, it's all right. You're right. I understand. You put it in perspective for me. Count on me. I will do whatever I have to do to protect Chang, all right?"

"David. Do you accept my apology?"

"Of course."

"Thank you. I'll be praying for you and loving you in the Lord."

When David rang off, Mac said, "What in the world did she say, man? You looked more like me than like an Israeli there for a second."

David told him.

"Tell you what," Mac said, "and Smitty you speak for yourself on this, but if that boy's a believer and he's got the mark to prove it, he's with us. And anybody else we can find before we get out of here. Right, Smitty?"

"Right, I think. If I understand. Other believers here all go with us, yes. Of course. Right?"

"That's what we're saying."

"Mac, a question. Who else would speak for me?"

* * *

On the drive north, Buck used a secure phone to call Lukas (Laslos) Miklos. The man was distraught. "Thank you for coming, but there is nothing you can do. Surely you did not bring weapons."

"No."

"You would be so hopelessly outnumbered anyway that you would never get out alive. So why the trip? What can you do?"

"I wanted to see it firsthand, Laslos. Expose it to the world through *The Truth.*"

"Well, forgive me, Brother Williams. I love your magazine, and I read it almost as religiously as Dr. Ben-Judah's messages. But you go to all the time and trouble and expense and danger to come all the way here, and it is for a magazine article? Did you know that the guillotines have arrived?"

"What?"

"It's true. I would pass it off as a rumor myself if it weren't for the brothers and sisters who told me. The GC is carting them through town in open trucks so the people can see the consequences of thinking for themselves. We are part of the United Carpathian States, a name I have to spit when I say. Nicolae is going to make an example of us. And you are here to write an article!"

"Brother Miklos, hear me. You knew there was nothing we could do. We would make matters only worse if we tried to free your wife and pastor and fellow believers. But I thought you'd want to know we were here so we can tell you—if we get in—what the conditions are, how their spirits are, whether they have any messages for you."

Silence. Then Buck heard Laslos weeping.

"Are you all right, my friend?"

"Yes, brother. I understand. Forgive me. I am upset. It is all over the television that the guillotines will be set up first in the prisons, then at the mark sites. It is just a matter of days for us now. But it could be just hours for the prisoners. Please tell my wife I love her and am praying for her and long to see her again. And tell her that if I don't see her again in this life, I will meet her in heaven.

Tell her," and he began to weep aloud, "that she was the best wife a man could have and that, that I love her with all my heart."

"I will tell her, Laslos, and I will bring you any message she may have as well."

"Thank you, my brother. I *am* grateful you have come."

"Do you know where she and the others have been taken?"

"We have an idea, but we dare not go looking or we will all be rounded up. You know our church is made up of many, many small groups that are not so small anymore. When the GC raided the main one, they took my wife and Pastor D and about seventy others, but they missed more than ninety other *groups.*"

"Wow."

"That is the good news. The worst of it is that apparently some in the original group have cracked under the strain. I can tell you without question it would not have been my wife or my pastor, but someone was tortured or scared or deceived into telling of the other groups. More raids have begun, and now they dare not meet at all. It is only a miracle I was not at the meeting with my wife, but if she becomes a martyr, I'll wish I was there to die with her."

* * *

"We came up with a question, besides a suggestion, David, and Smitty was very helpful on this, by the way," Mac said. "We tease him about the language, but that's a pretty shrewd brain in there. That's a compliment, Abdullah."

"Well, hey, cowpoke, I know that much right now!"

"I guess if I can make fun of Jordan, he can make fun of Texas. Really burned me there, didn't he? Anyway, the question is this: Do we want to play this out to the end, assumin' you're gonna have an inside track on *exactly* when employees have to take the mark? Or do we want some wiggle room?"

David thought about it. "It's more than wiggle room, Mac. It's part of the impression. If we wait till the last second and still try to make it look like we were killed, the timing alone is going to make it suspicious."

"That's what I said!" Abdullah said. "Isn't that what I said, Mac? I said that."

"That's what he said. Good point. OK, if we're going to do this sooner than the actual deadline, we have lots of options. Peacekeeping just started shipping its first loads of—what are they calling those contraptions now? Loyalty somethin's or other."

"Call 'em what they are," David said.

"OK, they shipped guillotines into Greece last night."

"Not from here," David said. "I would have known that."

"No, these were actually manufactured in Istanbul and driven down. Pretty soon they'll be flyin' 'em here and there, and you know we'll be pressed into service. You ought to pick a particularly strategic place you want to see or a shipment you want to monitor, find a reason to bring Hannah and Chang what's-his-name, and I'll have to requisition a Quasi Two."

"A Two? How will you justify that? We want to avoid suspicion. You can fit two pilots and three passengers in something cheaper than a 15-million-Nick aircraft."

"Yeah, but let's say we want to take a huge load of guillotines and skids of biochips and injectors."

"I'm listening. Still need more ammo to justify a Two."

"Well, let's say it's somewhere that St. Nick hisself is gonna be."

"Tell him who thought of that," Abdullah said.

"I think you just did, big mouth."

"Big mouth?"

"Teasin', Smitty. Slow your camel down now."

David cocked his head. "Are you thinking what I think you're thinking?"

"Is this a game?" Abdullah said.

"We are," Mac said. "Jerusalem."

David sat considering the possibilities. "I pass the word up the line that we want to be there, bring the injection expert and my best new computer prospect. We want to carry the maximum cargo load in an impressive craft that will look good for the potentate, play to his ego."

"You think he's egotistical?" Mac said, as seriously as if he meant it.

David smiled.

"Is he joking again?" Abdullah said. "Not enough cloth in Jordan to make a turban for Nicolae's head."

Mac threw his head back and laughed.

David was still deep in thought. "And the Quasi Two can be flown remotely."

"Just about any plane can nowadays, but I've got lots of experience with these."

"So we land somewhere out of sight on our way there. Then, from the safety of the ground, you fly that very expensive jet, with all that precious cargo—except us—in it, nose down right into the middle of one of the deepest bodies of water we can find."

"With people watching."

"Come again?"

"Let 'em see it! You wanted us to think about a logical explanation for the accident. Well, forgive the painful subject, but we recently lost our cargo chief. She would have prohibited that much weight on that particular plane, but me bein' a veteran, I thought it would handle it. Flyin' it remote and also broadcasting from it remote, I start hollerin' about a weight shift, cargo rolling, hard to control, Mayday, good-bye cruel world."

"You guys are brilliant."

"Thank you."

"Both of us," Abdullah said. "Right?"

"Of course," David said.

"Just thought of one more good one," Abdullah said.

"Hold on now, Smitty," Mac said. "Is this new to me?"

"Slow down your pony. You'll like it. You want to do this in front of people, do it in Tel Aviv. Carpathia is flying through there. Do air show for him and crowds. Crash into Mediterranean, so deep they know we're dead and plane is too deep to bother with search."

"And where are we supposed to be during all this?" Mac said. "It's going to be awfully hard to hide in Tel Aviv with Carpathia and all his crowds."

"We don't take off from Tel Aviv. We come straight from here to show, only they don't know we stopped in Jordan. I know that place. We can land where no one sees. Send plane to Tel Aviv, do show, crash."

"From how far away do you think I can remotely fly that plane, Smitty?"

"Sort of not remote. Take off remote, but flight plan, tricks, everything programmed into computer."

Mac looked from Abdullah to David. "He may just have something there."

"Really?" David said. "You can program the thing that specifically?"

"It would take some time."

"Get on it."

"Surprise, surprise," Abdullah said. "Camel jockey come up with one."

David's cell phone rang. "Readout says *urgent* from Hannah."

"Take it," Mac said.

"Hey, what's up?" David said.

"You're 100 percent certain this connection is secure?"

"Absolutely. You all right?"

"I'm in a utility closet. Did you know Carpathia had a Peacekeeper executed today?"

"Actually, I did. Santiago?"

"Thanks for telling me. I just had to go get the body from Security lockup."

"There wasn't time to tell you, Hannah. Anyway, who knew you'd get assigned?"

"It was awful. I deal with death all the time, but he was shot between the eyes at point-blank range. And they aren't even pretending it's anything but what it was. He was executed by Carpathia himself! You know what for? Well, of course you do. You know everything."

"I heard he talked too much."

"Doesn't sound very technical to me, David, but that's what I heard too. Apparently he told someone something that Carpathia said in a private meeting."

"I'm sorry you got in the middle of it, Hannah."

"Yeah, well, I think I know who ratted him out."

"You do?"

"Do you?" she said.

"Actually, I do."

"David, how can you live with this stuff?"

"Don't think it's easy."

"So, who told? Who got Santiago executed?"

"You said you knew, Hannah."

"You'll confirm it if I'm right?"

"Sure."

"Hickman."

"How'd you know?"

"I'm right, David?"

"You're right."

"He was just delivered to the morgue. Someone found him in his office with a self-inflicted gunshot wound to the temple."

16

BUCK AND ALBIE joined and separated from and joined again a caravan of GC vehicles picking its way through what was left of Ptolemaïs. "Would you look at that," Albie said, nodding toward open trucks carrying guillotines. "They're ugly, but there's really not much to 'em, is there?"

Buck shook his head. "That's one of my sidebar stories, how easily they can be assembled. They're simple machines with basic, pattern-cut parts. Each is basically wood, screws, blade, spring, and rope. That's why it was so easy for the GC to send out the specs and let anybody who wanted work and had the materials to have at it. You've got huge manufacturing plants reopening to mass-produce these, competing with amateur craftsmen in their backyards."

"All for something the GC says will serve as a—what did they call it, officially?"

"Visual deterrent. They put just one at each mark application site, and everyone is supposed to fall in line."

Albie stopped where a GC Peacekeeper was directing traffic. He signaled the young woman over. "I'm working here," she said testily until she recognized the uniform. She saluted. "At your service, Commander."

"We've been assigned the main detention facility, but I left the manifest in my bag. Are we close?"

"The main facility, sir?"

"I think that's what it said."

"Well, they're all together about three clicks west. Take a left at your next intersection, and follow the unpaved road around a curve until it joins the rebuilt highway again. The center will be on your right, just inside the city. Can't miss it. Massive, surrounded by barbed wire and more of us. Better hurry, though, if you want to see the fun. They're going to do some chopping tonight if the rebels don't soil themselves and change their minds."

"Yeah?"

"Word I get is they're lining them up and sorting them out now. The ones who go back to their cells with their heads attached will have a new tattoo tomorrow."

* * *

David was exhausted. It was nearly 2300 hours Carpathia Time as he trudged from his office toward his quarters. He was stunned to hear energetic steps behind him and turned to see Viv Ivins, looking as fresh and gung ho as she did every morning. She carried a leather portfolio and smiled brightly at David.

"Evening, Director Hassid," she called out as she drew alongside.

"Ma'am."

"Great days, hmm?"

He didn't know how long he could maintain the charade. "Interesting days, anyway," he said.

She stopped. "I love when things fall into place."

He thought that an unfortunate choice of words, given her personal coordination of guillotine production and distribution.

"Things humming along, are they?" he said.

"I've persuaded top brass not to display loyalty enforcement facilitators here at the palace."

"Oh?"

"Not the best image."

"They're showing up all over the world."

"And that's fine. I can live with that. In fact, I'm all for it. Outside the capital city and the headquarters in particular, you will have certain elements who need the visual aid, a reminder of the seriousness of this test of loyalty. One would have to be pathologically committed to one's cause to really decide against the mark. Seeing the consequence standing right before you as you make your decision will persuade those who merely want a little attention for stalling with their choice."

"But not here."

"Not necessary. If a person was not loyal to the risen potentate, why would he or she want to work here? What I want to see produced here are pictures, still and moving, of happy, willing, joyful loyalists. The citizenry of the Global Community should see rapture on the faces of those it depends upon to administer the new world order. No enforcement is needed here. We are the examples to the world of the joy of commitment, the sense of fulfillment when one takes his stand. Follow?"

"Sure. And I have to say, I like the idea of those ugly contraptions not dotting the landscape here."

"I couldn't agree more. We start with new hires tomorrow, and there is much enthusiasm among them over being among the first to receive the potentate's mark. All are opting for his image on their foreheads. I plan to go for the simple understatement, but I have to say, Mr. Hassid, it's fun to see these kids today with their eagerness to stand out. You're interviewing a prospect tomorrow."

"Right."

"The Asian prodigy."

"That's him."

"What a family! His father is pleading to have his son be the first to receive the mark. It's too late for that, as we're beginning with political prisoners, but he very well could be the first GC employee."

David blanched and tried to cover. "But he's not been hired yet."

"It's a foregone conclusion though, right?"

"Well, I need to talk with him at length, determine his suitability to take his last year of high school here, be away from his parents for the first time, see where he fits best. . . ."

"But the odds of him not being hired somewhere here are minuscule. We could process him first and he would, in essence, be preapproved to work in any department. Sort of like a preapproved mortgage. First you qualify, then you can make an offer on anything in your price range."

"I wouldn't do that," David blurted.

"Why not?"

"It just doesn't seem as buttoned-down as we like to be. Let's let the process run its course—do it right."

"Oh, Mr. Hassid, honestly. What would be the harm?"

He shrugged. "I was told the boy is scared to death of needles and is fighting the whole idea."

"Even to the point where he would pass up a golden opportunity here? He's going to have to take the mark in the United Asian States anyway, or he'll lose more than a job."

"Maybe he'll get used to the idea by then."

"Oh, pish-posh, Director Hassid. If he's so brilliant, it's time for him to grow up. He may fight it, but it'll be over in seconds and he'll see he made a big to-do about nothing."

"Well, my meeting with him is at 0900 hours. It can wait till after that, can't it? I'd hate to try to interview him after he's been through a trauma."

"A trauma? I just told you—"

"But he'll still be upset."

"I can't imagine them administering marks before 0900 anyway."

In his room a few minutes later, David used his subnotebook to double-check his secretary's schedule. She had not informed him of a time for his appointment with Chang, and a quick look at her calendar showed why. The meeting had been confirmed at the end of the day for 1400 hours, two o'clock. It was something she would tell him in the morning.

David changed it on her calendar to 0900, then hacked into Personnel's computer and did the same. He phoned 4054 and left a voice message: "Chang, our interview tomorrow has been changed to 9 a.m. Please do not go to Personnel or anywhere else until we've met. See you then."

While he was finishing his message, his phone told him he had a call waiting. He punched in to find Ming, distraught. "It's started here," she said. "Has it started there?"

"Slow down, Ming. What's started?"

"Application of the mark! The equipment arrived at Buffer this morning, and they're already using it tonight."

"Prisoners are getting the chip?"

"Yes! I can't imagine it will be much longer for us staff. I need to bolt soon, but I wanted to check."

"Any believers there? Anyone refusing the mark?"

"Not a one. They're lining up for this thing as if they've been loyal scouts forever. I think they're hoping they'll get good behavior points. Truth is, they'll still be rotting here, but with a mark on head or hand."

David told her of his conversation with Viv and what he had done about it. "Oh, no, no," she said. "At nine you must make Chang disappear. Get him out of there."

"We're not prepared to leave yet, Ming."

"What are you going to do?"

"I'll have to make up something, I guess. Some reason why he is just not ready. Maybe I'll say I found evidence of immaturity, that I just think he's too young to fit in."

"You're a director, David. Make it convincing. This has to work."

"I have all night to think about it."

"And I have all night to pray about it."

"I'll take all I can get, Ming. Listen, let me do something for you. I can get you reassigned to USNA."

"You could?"

"Of course. I just do it through the computer and no one questions it. They see it's approved by someone higher than their level, and they don't rock the boat. Where do you want to go?"

"There are prisons all over the States," she said. "But I'm never actually going to get to one, right?"

"Right. We get you assigned, get you on a plane, but then lose you somehow.

You run off and we can't find you. But then you're on your own. You need to get to the safe house in Chicago."

"Would they have me?"

"Ming! Leah has told everyone about you. They can't wait to welcome you. They knew you and your brother would eventually have to wind up there. We can use you both. Now where shall I assign you in the States? Somewhere close enough to Chicago so you can get to the safe house but not so suspiciously close that people start putting two and two together."

"I don't know the States," she said. "There is a huge facility in Baltimore that always needs personnel."

"That's a long way from Chicago. Wait! Can you get to Greece?"

"When?"

"As soon as possible, even tonight."

"I guess that's up to you. Make my transfer highest priority, and if you want GC here to get me to Greece, they'll have to do it. But David, Greece is a hot spot right now, crawling with GC and making an example of political prisoners. I don't want to work or hide there."

David told her how she would get to the States from Greece, and it would appear GC was escorting her.

"There is a God," she said. "Where do I meet these men?"

"Get to the airport at Kozani. They'll find you."

"Can you get Chang there too? Please, David, do it! Get him out of my parents' quarters, get him assigned somewhere, and have one of your pilots get him to Greece. We can go to the safe house together."

"Ming, please. It has to make sense. I pull a stunt like that, your parents lose track of Chang, and it all comes back to me—not to mention you! You *both* are sent somewhere and then wind up lost? Think, Ming. I know you're desperate and that you care, but let me work on the logistics. The last thing I want is for the GC spotlight to turn on us."

"I know, David. I understand. I'm thinking with my heart."

"Nothing wrong with that," he said. "Until we quit thinking at all and make things worse."

+ + +

"We in trouble?" a Greece-based GC Peacekeeping chief at the detention center asked Buck when he saw he was accompanied by a deputy commander. "We do everything by the book."

"This looks like a madhouse, frankly," Buck said, surveying the complex of five rather plain, industrial buildings that had probably once been factories. The windows were covered with bars, and the perimeter was a tangle of fence and razor wire. But the place was crowded with GC in lines, peering at printouts in the night, using flashlights to see where various prisoners were located.

"We do all we can with what we have to work with," the chief said, nervously eyeing Albie.

Buck continued to do the talking. "How many prisoners at this facility?"

"About nine hundred."

"You've got that many GC here."

"Well, not quite, sir."

"What are they all doing? Are they assigned?"

"Most are running the mark center in the middle building."

"What is in the other buildings?"

"Teenagers through early twenties in the first building, males in the west wing, females in the east."

"Individual cells?"

"Hardly. Prisoners are incarcerated in large, common areas that used to be production lines."

"And in the other buildings?"

"Women in the next. None in the center. Men in the last two."

"What are the majority of these people charged with?"

"Mostly felonies, some petty theft, larceny."

"Any violent criminals?"

The chief nodded back over his shoulder. "Murderers, armed robbers, and the like, right there."

"Political prisoners?"

"Mostly in the second building, but religious dissidents, at least the men, are right here too." He motioned to the last building again.

"You've got dissidents in with violent criminals?" Buck said, leaning forward as if to get a better look at the man's nameplate.

"Where they're placed is not my call, sir. I'm coordinating the loyalty mark application. And I need to be in that center building in about five minutes. You want to help—I've got a crew of six moving from building to building, starting with the west, doing preliminary sorting."

"Meaning?"

"Determining whether any plan to refuse the mark."

"And if so?"

"They are to identify themselves immediately. We're not going to waste time letting people wait until they're in line to decide whether they want to live or die."

"What if some change their minds in line?"

"Decide at the last minute they don't want the mark after all? I don't foresee that!"

"But what if they do?"

"We deal with that quickly. But for the most part, we want to know in advance so we don't hold things up. Now, gentlemen, I have orders. Will you help with the culling or not?"

"Will this be going on simultaneously in all the buildings?" Buck asked, not wanting to miss the pastor or Mrs. Miklos.

"No. We're starting in the west building. Prisoners will be escorted to the center building for processing, then back before those in the next building go. And so forth."

"We'll help," Buck said.

The chief shouted, "Athenas!" and a stocky, middle-aged Peacekeeper with a one-inch, black crew cut stepped up, three men and two women in uniform behind him. "Ready, Alex?"

"Ready, sir," Alex said, with a high-pitched voice that didn't match his physique.

"Take Jensen and Elbaz here with you."

"I have sufficient staff, sir."

The chief lowered his head and stared at Athenas. "They're here from USNA, and if you didn't notice, A. A., Mr. Elbaz is a dep-u-ty com-man-der?"

"Yes, sir. Would Mr. Elbaz care to lead?"

Albie stuck out his lower lip and shook his head.

\+ + +

It was two in the afternoon in Chicago, and the remaining Trib Force members crowded around the television. The local GC news reported that mark applications had begun at local jails and prisons.

Zeke sat rocking before the TV, his hands over his mouth. Rayford asked if Chaim's Jerusalem disguise was ready. Zeke kept his eyes on the screen and took his hands from his mouth only long enough to say, "All but the robe. Done by tonight."

Tsion had come up with the idea of letting Zeke change Chaim's appearance exactly as he had been planning, but also outfitting him in sandals and a thick, brown, hooded robe that extended far enough in front of his face to hide his features. The whole garment would go over his head and the hem would settle an inch off the ground, the waist cinched with a braided rope. Everyone agreed it sounded humble and nondescript, and yet ominous enough once Chaim was seen by crowds as in charge and with something to say.

Chaim was slowly accepting the idea, provided he could playact from the shadows of his garb. "I still say Tsion ought to go."

"Let me promise you, my friend," Tsion said. "Allow God to use you mightily to get his people to safety, and I will come and address them in person sometime."

The TV anchorman announced that while the area GC had not expected to need the loyalty enforcement facilitators, one prisoner had reportedly refused to take the mark and had been executed. "This occurred at what was formerly known as the DuPage County Jail, and execution of the dissident was carried out less than ninety minutes ago. The rebel, serving an indeterminate sentence for black market trafficking of fuel oil, has been identified as fifty-four-year-old Gustav Zuckermandel, formerly of Des Plaines."

Zeke buried his face in his hands and toppled onto his side, where he lay crying quietly. One by one the rest of the Force approached to merely lay a hand on him and cry with him. Tsion, Chaim, Rayford, Leah, and Chloe surrounded him and Tsion prayed.

"Our Father, once again we face the wrenching loss of a loved one. Shower our young brother with hope eternal and remind us all that we will one day see again this brave martyr."

When Tsion finished, Zeke drew a sleeve across his wet face, moved to his hands and knees, and then awkwardly rose.

"You all right, son?" Rayford asked.

"Got work to do is all," Zeke said, averting his eyes. And he shuffled back toward his room.

\+ + +

Buck had a bad taste in his mouth. He had been in these situations before, had seen enough depravity and mayhem to last several lifetimes. But he wished he and Albie had brought high-powered automatic weapons so they could at least attempt a rescue. How, in his flesh, he wanted to spray deadly projectiles into the swarming GC. How he would love to have stormed the detention barracks, looking for people with the mark of Christ and ferrying them to safety.

But here was an impossible situation. Prophecy was once again coming to life before his eyes, and he would not be able to turn away. At the west building, the eight members of the culling team were checked in past the outer fence, and then again at the main entrance.

Buck was assaulted by the stench as soon as they had cleared the main corridor. Inside a huge cage milled more than a hundred male teenagers, some looking tough, others petrified. The cage was surrounded with four to five guards on a side, weapons in hand, smoking, reading magazines, and looking bored.

The teenagers jumped and cheered and applauded when the team entered. "Freedom!" one shouted while the rest laughed. "They've come to free us!" And others jeered and mocked.

Athenas stepped away from the others and put up both hands for quiet. Buck sidled to a guard, who dropped his magazine and straightened up. "Sir?" he said.

"What's the smell, soldier?"

"The cans, sir. In the corners, see?"

Buck looked to the four corners of the cage where 55-gallon drums stood. Each had a makeshift wooden set of steps next to it and was covered by an ill-fitting toilet seat. "This building has no facilities?"

"Only for us," the guard said. "Just down that hall."

Buck shook his head. "They can't be led there periodically?"

"Not enough of us to risk that."

Alex Athenas had finally commanded the prisoners' attention. "You are privileged to be among the first to display your loyalty and devotion to His Excellency, the risen potentate of the Global Community, Nicolae Carpathia!"

To Buck's amazement, this was met with enthusiastic cheering and applause that went on for almost a minute. Some teens broke into chants and songs, lauding Carpathia.

Athenas finally quieted them again. "In a few moments you will be led to the central building, where you will tell the staff whether you want your loyalty mark on your forehead or your right hand. The area you choose will then be disinfected with an alcohol solution. When it is your turn, you will enter a cubicle, where you will sit and be injected with a biochip, while simultaneously tattooed with the prefix 216, which identifies you as a citizen of the United Carpathian States. The application takes just seconds. The disinfectant also contains a local anesthetic, and you should experience no discomfort.

"Any acts of disorderly conduct will be met with immediate justice. For you illiterates, that means you will be dead before you hit the floor."

This was met with more hooting and hollering, but Buck found himself staring at a boy in the middle of the crowd. He had black, curly hair, was thin and pasty, and wore tilting glasses that appeared to have one lens missing. The boy looked barely old enough to be in this crowd, but what caught Buck's eye was the shadow on his forehead. Or was it a smudge? Or was it the seal of God?

"Excuse me, officer!" Buck said, striding past Athenas and peering into the cage. The hooting stopped and the prisoners stared. "You, there! Yes, you! Step forward!"

The young man made his way through the crowd to the front of the cage, where he stood quaking. "Someone open this door!" Buck barked. No one moved. He whirled to look at the guard he had spoken to, who shuffled nervously and looked at Athenas.

"The rest of you back off," Athenas said, and he nodded to the guard, who unlocked the cage.

Buck marched in and grabbed the boy by the arm, his ratty, gray sweater bunching under Buck's fingers. He dragged him out of the cage, past Athenas and the other guards, scolding him the whole way. "You mock Global Community Peacekeepers, young man? You'll learn respect."

"No, sir, please—I, I—"

"Shut up and keep moving!"

Buck dragged him past the guards at the entrance, who called after him, "Wait! Who is that! We have to process him out!"

"Later!" Buck said.

"Where are we going?" the boy pleaded with a Greek accent.

"Home," Buck whispered.

"But my parents are here."

"Give me their names," Buck said, and he wrote them down. "I can't guarantee they'll get out. But you're not going to die tonight."

"You're a believer?"

Buck nodded and shushed him.

They blew past the guards at the outer gate, and Buck marched him to the GC Jeep across the road. Past the lights and into the shadows, few heads had even turned to watch. "Front passenger side," Buck said. "Any other believers in the cage?"

The boy shook his head. "Never saw anyone."

"Give me the name of one of the guys in the cage, just one."

"Who?"

"Anyone. Just give me a name."

"Ah, Paulo Ganter."

"Got it. Now listen. You are to sit here, right here in this Jeep, until I get back. What you must not do—are you listening?—is make sure that no one is watching. Because if you discover that, you might be tempted to make a run for it and not stop until you are somewhere safe. Then I would get back out here later and wonder whatever happened to my prisoner. Understand?"

"I think so. You don't want me to do this?"

"Of course not. I don't know what I'd do about an escapee. Do you?"

The boy managed a weak smile.

"You know what?" Buck said. "I don't think anybody's watching now."

Feeling like Anis, the mysterious border guard who had discovered Tsion under the seat of the bus so long ago, Buck put one hand on the boy's shoulder and another on his head. And he said, "And now may the Lord bless you. May the Lord make his face to shine upon you and give you peace. Godspeed, son."

Buck trotted back to the gate, and when he glanced over his shoulder, the boy was gone.

The gate guards let Buck through and the ones at the building asked, "Who was that?"

"Ganter, Paulo," he said. "Transferred custody to the United North American States." They were flipping through their printouts as he hurried back in.

Alex Athenas was finishing. "Are there any here who will be choosing to reject the loyalty mark?"

The group laughed and waved derisively at him.

"None then? No one? Anyone?"

The prisoners looked at each other and quieted. Buck waited and watched to see if the boy had been wrong and there were any other believers who might take a stand.

"What if we say no?" a tough called out, smirking.

"You know the consequences," Alex said. The boy drew a finger across his neck. "That's right," Alex added. "Any questions?"

"No rebels here!" someone shouted. "All loyal, upstanding citizens!"

"That's what we like to hear. No questions?"

"Do we get to choose what image we want?"

"No. Because of your circumstances, you are allowed only the basic chip and number tattoo."

The prisoners groused loudly, and Athenas signaled to his team and the other armed guards to get into position. "This will be done in an orderly fashion," he said. "Or you will wish you had opted to reject the mark."

17

RAYFORD STOPPED TO CHECK in on Zeke, whom he found busy on Chaim's robe. Zeke said, "Got enough material. Thinking about makin' him two."

"You heard what Tsion said about clothes in the safe haven?"

Zeke nodded. "He might want variety though. And I didn't hear Tsion say whether the clothes get dirty."

Rayford shrugged. "I admired your dad, Zeke. You know that?"

Zeke nodded, still working.

"He was courageous, right to the end."

"Didn't surprise me," Zeke said. "I told you he'd do that, didn't I?"

"You had him pegged. I pray we'll all show that kind of courage."

Zeke looked up and shook his head, his eyes distant. "I wish he hadn't got caught. Bad timing. He coulda done a lot more for the believers. Like I'm gonna do."

"I admire you too, Zeke. We all do."

Zeke nodded again.

"Don't forget to mourn and grieve too, you know. There's nothing wrong with that."

"I can't help it. I miss him already."

"I'm just saying, don't pretend—you don't have to look strong to us. We've all suffered terrible losses, and even if the Lord helps us through it, we don't have to like it. The Bible doesn't say we're not to mourn. It just says we're not to mourn the way people do who have no hope. Mourn with all your might, Zeke, because we *do* have hope. We *know* we're going to see our loved ones again."

Zeke suddenly stood and thrust out his hand. Rayford shook it. "I don't s'pose I dare go try to get his body."

Rayford shook his head. "The first thing they're going to want is to know your connection. And you know the second thing."

"Whether I want the mark."

"We're crippled with the loss of your dad, Zeke. I don't know what we'd do if we lost you too."

"I just hate to think what they're gonna do with him. I try not to think about . . . you know . . . his head being . . . you know . . ."

"I know. But no matter what they do with your dad's body, God knows. He has his eye on your father. His soul is in heaven now, and his body will eventually be there too, new and improved. If God can resurrect a cremated body—you know what that means?"

"Burned up, yeah."

"Then he can resurrect anybody. Remember, he created us from the dust of the earth."

"Thanks, Captain Steele. Bad as this is, there's no other place I'd rather have been when I heard about it. I sure love all you guys."

"And we love you, Zeke."

Rayford walked out and shut the door, noticing Tsion just out of sight of the doorway, leaning against the wall, arms folded.

"Excuse me," Dr. Ben-Judah said. "I didn't intend to listen in. I didn't know you were there. You must have had the same idea I did."

"It's all right."

"I'm glad I heard that, Rayford. God has restored you to leadership. You did just what I know the Lord would have wanted you to do, and you did it well."

"Thanks, Tsion. God's been more patient with me than I deserve."

"Isn't that true with all of us?"

They walked back toward the commons. "I spoke with Chloe a few moments ago," Tsion said. "I hope I wasn't out of line."

"You can't be out of line, Doc. You know that. What was it about?"

"I was just checking to see how she was doing with the assignment you gave her. I have a vested interest, you know."

"In the call for planes and pilots? I should say you do! So, save me a conversation. How's it going?"

"She was amused and eager to tell me, actually. She put out the request for brave Commodity Co-op members willing to lend their planes and cars and fuel and time to the cause of Messiah in Jerusalem—and she told them it would be soon. She reports that the response has been overwhelming. The element of danger must make these men and women rally. She says they are more willing to throw caution to the wind for this scheme than they are to make the routine flights that keep the co-op running."

Around the corner Kenny Bruce came chugging, chased by Leah. He appeared lost in the fantasy that he *had* to elude her, though he loved her hugs and tickles. "Grandpa!" he squealed, reaching for Rayford. But at the last instant he changed course, leaping into the rabbi's arms. "Unca Zone!"

Leah laughed and grabbed for him. "That old man can't save you!" she said, and he buried his head in Tsion's chest.

"Old man?" Tsion said. "Miss Leah, you have wounded me!"

Tsion carried Kenny back to his mother, and Leah lingered. "Rayford, I feel useful here, helping Chloe—who's incredible, by the way. That girl could run any size corporation. And I love helping with that precious child."

"But—?"

"You know what's coming."

He nodded. "I'm still finalizing assignments," he said. "But yours includes getting out of here awhile."

"Oh, thank you, Ray. I don't want to be selfish, and I know Chloe is as antsy as I am."

"She has responsibilities here. More than you do."

"It doesn't seem fair to her."

"But she takes her role seriously, and I think she's resigned to it."

"Well," Leah said, "I can't speak for her, but I would feel trapped."

"Trapped by motherhood?"

Leah smiled. "Spoken like a man. As someone who has been there, let me tell you, at times you need a break. It doesn't have to be long, and you can't wait to get back. But, well—it's not my business. But if you find a place for her outside, even a short assignment, I'll be happy to spell her."

"You can do what she does? Both the co-op and looking after the baby?"

"Sure. It's only the men around here who are incapable of that." Rayford shot her a double take. "I'm kidding, Ray. But tell me, am I going to get to go to Israel?"

"You *want* to be there?"

"I was stuck in Belgium last time. All the good stuff happens in Jerusalem."

"The dangerous stuff."

"And your point?"

He cocked his head. "Oh, yeah. You live for that stuff."

"I live to serve, Ray. I'm not bragging. It's what I do. It was, even before I became a believer. I want to be valuable to the cause. I'm not even suspicious. No one's out trying to hunt me down. And with that wacky dental appliance in and if I let Zeke touch up the hair, I'm invisible."

"It would take more than that to make you Middle Eastern."

"Maybe this David character can make me GC then. Give me a reason to be over there."

Rayford raised his eyebrows. "Maybe," he said. "You never know."

* * *

Buck and Albie stood with the culling squad in the female teens' area. Buck found it hard to believe the conditions were the same as for the men. There were two women guards, but the rest were men. The girls were not as noisy and raucous as the boys, but the makeup of the group was similar. There were tough girls and apparent victims, but all were curious.

Buck scoured the group, and a tall brunet stared back at him. He was convinced they had seen each other's mark at the same time. Her eyes grew wide, and he tried to communicate with his that she must not give him away. As Alex Athenas ran through his explanation, Buck casually moved close to Albie.

"I'd better not push my luck. Think you can get one out of here?"

"Maybe," Albie said. "You're not thinking of trying this in every building, are you?"

"I hate doing nothing."

"Me too, but we're going to get ourselves killed. And what about when there's a bunch of 'em?"

"I can worry about them only one at a time."

Albie sighed. "Where is she?" Buck pointed her out. "Watch and learn, buddy boy," Albie said.

Albie rushed the cage, shouting. Alex fell silent and watched with everyone else as Albie prowled up and back before the wire mesh, eyes on his prey. "You! You from the North American States?"

The girl froze, her eyes darting at Buck, who nodded slightly, and back at Albie. "No," she said, her voice a constricted squeak. "I'm—"

"Don't lie to me, dirt ball! I'd know you anywhere." Albie whirled in a rage that almost convinced Buck. "Alex, get somebody to open this cage." He turned back, pointing at the girl. "Step to the door! Now! Hands behind your head."

She advanced, stiff legged and shuddering, as the gate was unlocked.

Albie grabbed her and wrenched her out. "Cuffs," he announced, and a guard tossed him a pair. "Key too," he said. "I'll bring 'em back." He pushed her up against the cage and drew her hands down to hook her up. He slipped the key in his pocket and guided her out.

"Have fun," a guard whispered as they passed.

Albie turned on him, grabbed his jacket, and shoved him against the wall. "Say again, soldier?"

"Sorry, sir. That was uncalled for."

Albie gave him another shove and turned back to the girl, hustling her out. He returned a few minutes later and returned cuffs and key to the lender.

Buck was shocked when a girl with a pronounced Greek accent responded in the affirmative to Officer Athenas's main question. The other girls whirled to see who it was, and Buck leaned in to see if he could detect a mark on her forehead. There was none.

"You're refusing the loyalty mark of the Global Community?" Alex said.

"I'd certainly like to think about it," she said. "It seems a drastic move, not something to enter into lightly."

"You understand the consequences?"

"I'd just like to think it over."

"Fair enough. Anyone else?" No one. "Young lady, because you are the only one in this facility, rather than being sent straight to the confirmation facilitator, you may mull this over while in line. Your male counterparts are almost finished with the procedure, and where you wind up in line will determine how much time you have to decide. When you get to the place in the queue where you are asked where you would like the mark affixed, that will be your final chance to elect not to have it at all."

"And then?"

"You will be directed to the confirmation facili—"

"You know what that is, girl?" a teen called out.

"You're dead!"

"Guillotine! Head chopped off."

The girls quieted and Athenas looked at her. "Still want to think it over?"

"What, are they serious? You're going to chop my head off for wanting to think this through?"

"Not for thinking, miss. For deciding against. If you decide for, you just choose where."

"So I don't really have a choice."

"Where you been?" one of the girls said, and others joined in.

"Of course you have a choice," Alex said. "I believe I've made it clear. Accept the mark or accept the alternative."

"The mark or death, you're saying?"

"Still want to think it over?"

She shook her head.

One of the girls said, "You sure made that harder than it needed to be."

"Well, I didn't know there was really no choice."

Before proceeding to the adult women's lockup, Buck and Albie followed the young women to the lines in the middle building. It had already become a model of efficiency. The prisoners moved along steadily. They were ready with their forehead or hand choices, and the disinfectant/anesthesia was applied quickly.

The injectors sounded like electric staplers, and while some recipients flinched, no one seemed to feel pain.

Almost all the teen males took their marks on their foreheads, and one of the last, as he got back in line, raised both arms and shouted, "Long live Carpathia!" That soon became the custom, as it did with the young women choosing to receive the mark on their hands.

Buck stood staring, wishing he could preach. They had made their choices, yes, but did they *really* know what they were choosing? It wasn't between loyalty and death; it was between heaven or hell, eternal life or eternal damnation.

His heart raced as the line of young women neared its end, and they were herded back. In the next building he expected to see Mrs. Miklos. How many of her friends would be there with her?

The women's facility was surreal, in that there was no cage. The guards, again, were mostly men, and they apparently didn't expect trouble. The women sat, mostly passive, chatting quietly, but their curious eyes also took in the Athenas squad.

Buck strolled around the outside of the group of women, looking for Laslos's wife. Finally he noticed a group of about twenty women in a back corner, on their knees. In the middle of the group, praying, was Mrs. Miklos.

"Shut up and listen up!" a guard bellowed, and most of the women came to attention. "This here's Officer Athenas, and he's got announcements and instructions."

Alex began, but the women in the back—who Buck assumed were Mrs. Miklos's believing friends—paid no attention and continued praying. Some gazed toward heaven, and Buck saw the marks on their foreheads. Others peered up and around the crowd at Alex, and Buck noticed that some of them had no mark. Laslos's wife had apparently been trying to recruit new believers.

Athenas grew impatient with those kneeling in the back. "Ladies, please!" he said, but they ignored him. He nodded to one of his female assistants, who handed her high-powered rifle and sidearm to a compatriot, pulled out her baton, and moved directly into the tough-looking women in the front, heading toward the rear. A young, thick, healthy woman, she stared down the menacing ones, clearly knowing that her comrades had her back.

"As I was saying," Alex took up again, but he stopped when the attention of the women diverted to where his guard was headed.

"Ladies!" the guard bellowed. "You will cease and desist, face the front, and give Officer Athenas your full attention."

Many did just that. Some stood and moved away from the group. Others remained kneeling but looked up. Still others kept their heads bowed and eyes closed, lips moving in prayer. Mrs. Miklos, kneeling with her back to the guard, kept her hands folded, head bowed, eyes closed, praying softly.

The guard poked her with the baton, and she nearly lost her balance. When Mrs. Miklos turned to look up at her, the guard bent close and shouted, "Do you understand me, ma'am?"

Mrs. Miklos smiled shyly, reset herself, and returned to prayer. The guard, clearly incensed, put both hands around the end of the stick, set herself, pulled the baton back, and stepped into her swing.

Buck was barely able to hold his voice, and Albie had to grab and hold him back as the hardwood baton cracked loudly off the back of Mrs. Miklos's head.

Blood splattered several of the women as Laslos's wife pitched forward, arms and legs twitching. Several women screamed. Many of the kneelers, even those with marks on their foreheads, stood and rushed to join the main group. One woman dropped to her knees to check on her injured friend, and the guard caught her just below her nose with a second vicious swing.

Buck heard teeth shatter, and she cried out as the back of her head hit the floor and her hands came up to cover her face.

The guard marched back to the front, the sea of women parting for her. Miraculously, Mrs. Miklos drew herself up to her hands and knees and slowly, majestically returned to her kneeling position, hands folded before her.

With her back to the rest, the gaping wound, emitting great issues of blood that ran down her hair and onto her sweater, was exposed to everyone. Most averted their eyes, but Buck stared at the white of her skull at the top of the laceration. Her skull had shattered and surely bone had been driven into her brain. And yet there she knelt, silently continuing to pray.

The other woman, rolling onto her stomach, also slowly drew herself up, spitting teeth, blood gushing down her chin, and returned to prayer. Buck felt a tingle at the base of his spine, imagining the blinding pain.

The guard retrieved her weapons with a look of satisfaction and exhilaration. The crowd behaved with a who-wants-to-be-next? attitude, and Alex said, "We'll see who's strong enough to stand in the enforcement facilitator line."

Buck, his pulse racing and his breath coming in gasps, stood stock-still as Alex finally reached the pivotal question. "Just so we'll know," he said, "how many will be rejecting the mark of loyalty and choosing the alternative?"

Mrs. Miklos stood and turned to face him. Her face was drained of color, eyelids fluttering. Her chest heaved with the effort of merely breathing. Blood pooled behind her from the ugly wound. She shook like a victim of advanced Parkinson's, and yet she raised both hands, a beatific smile softening her macabre face.

"You choose execution by guillotine rather than the mark of loyalty," Alex clarified.

The woman next to Laslos's wife, her face swelling, her nose red, upper teeth gone, stood and raised both hands, smiling a cadaverous grin.

"Two of you then?"

But there were more, and now the rest of the women stood just to see who was making the choice. From the original group of the kneeling devout stood a half dozen, smiling, hands lifted. "You all want to die tonight?" Alex shouted, as if it was the most ridiculous thing he had ever heard. "I'm counting eight. You eight will—now nine—will go to the extreme right when you—all right, now ten—when you are led to the processing center. OK, you can lower your hands now. Two more. OK, twelve of you. No need to keep your hands up!"

A couple of women in front looked at each other and started toward the back, marks of the believer appearing on their foreheads as they lifted their hands.

"All right," Alex said. "Those taking the mark stay left as we enter the center. Suicides stay to the right." And as he said it, three more lined up behind the bleeding women.

Buck fought tears. He could give in to emotion and wind up a martyr this very night, and in the heat of the moment, that didn't sound so bad. But he had a wife and a child and compatriots who counted on him. He stood blinking, panting, fighting to maintain control. These women were heroes of the faith. They would join the great blood-washed who literally made their bodies living sacrifices, soon to be martyred and appear under the very altar of God in heaven in snow-white robes of righteousness. He couldn't help but envy them!

As the women were led out, Alex shouted over the din, "You can change your mind! If you have chosen this ridiculous option and wish you hadn't, simply step out of one line and into the other!"

But as the courageous filed past Buck, he saw the mark on each forehead and knew there would be no one turning back—no, not one. He fell into step with the female guard leading the doomed to the guillotine line. This proved no end of fascination to the others, who stared as they themselves stood in the loyalty lines, deciding where they would bear the mark of Nicolae.

When the guard moved past the head of the line to talk to the two men who would work the death machine, Buck stepped close to Mrs. Miklos and tried to appear as if he were interrogating her. "Laslos wanted me to tell you he loves you with all of his heart and will see you in heaven."

She turned toward him with a start, blood still oozing down her back. She stared at the uniform and then at Buck's forehead. Then at his face. "I know you," she said.

He nodded.

"I don't believe you have met Mrs. Demeter," she said.

Buck was startled. The pastor's wife had taken the blow to the face. "I'd shake your hand," she whispered through her ruined mouth. "But then you'd be in line with us."

Mrs. Miklos bent close to Buck. "Tell Laslos thank you for leading me to Jesus. I see him. I see him. I see my Savior and can't wait to be with him!"

With that her knees buckled and Buck caught her. The guard reappeared and grabbed her. "No you don't, lady!" she said. "You chose this, and you're going to take it standing up." It was all Buck could do not to punch the woman in the face. She turned to him and said, "What are we going to do with all these bodies? We weren't prepared for anything like this."

Buck headed to the back, where the guards were lined along the wall. This was the first they would see of any executions, and it was clear they weren't about to miss it. Albie joined him, clearly overcome.

"That was Pastor D's wife with Mrs. Miklos."

Albie shook his head. "They're champions, Buck. I don't know if I can watch this."

"Let's get out of here."

"Maybe we should be here with them."

"We shall start with enforcement," Alex Athenas announced. "Any who wish to switch lines may do so at any time. Ladies, once you have been secured in position in the apparatus, no change of mind will be honored. Inform someone before that or suffer the consequences."

Buck stood paralyzed as Mrs. Miklos was led to the ugly machine. "Has that been tested?" Athenas shouted. "I want no malfunctions."

"Affirmative!" answered the assistant, who would trade roles with the executioner with each victim.

"Carry on!"

From thirty feet away Buck read the lips of the executioner. "Last chance, ma'am."

Laslos's wife knelt and the assistant positioned her.

"Turn her around!" someone yelled. "We want to see it happen!"

Albie turned on the man. "Shut up! This is not for your amusement!"

The room fell tomb silent. In the stillness Buck heard Mrs. Miklos's delicate voice. "My Jesus, I love thee, I know thou art mine."

A sob attacked his throat. Seemingly all in one motion, the assistant fastened the clamp and stood quickly with both hands raised to indicate he was clear of the blade path while the other yanked the short cord. The heavy blade raced to the bottom of the shaft. Buck pushed past the others and out into the night air, disgusted at the cheer that met the sickening thud.

He was glad for the vomit that gushed from him, allowing him to sob openly. Tears cascaded as he thought of the cold workmanlike crews that would remove heads and bodies and make room for the next and the next and the next.

As he stood in the cool grass, convulsing now in dry heaves, he covered his ears in a vain attempt to muffle the thuds and cheers, thuds and cheers. Albie emerged and rested a hand on his back. His voice was thick as he bent and gently pulled Buck's hands away from his ears.

"When I get to heaven," he whispered, "after Jesus, those women are the first people I want to see."

18

CHAIM TOOK TO PACING around in the Strong Building, repeating lines over and over. He usually carried a Bible, Rayford noticed, but sometimes a commentary or his own notes.

He didn't sound eloquent or forceful or confident to Rayford. It was as if all he was trying to accomplish was getting the basics down and having some idea what he was talking about. He also looked miserable, and Rayford wanted to counsel him again on where he stood with God, but he didn't feel qualified to make Chaim feel better about himself. Chaim apparently didn't see Tsion as a personal mentor but only as a teacher and tireless motivator.

It struck Rayford that they all had had to endure the same doubts and fears when first they became believers. They had missed the truth, then feared they had come to God only as a last-ditch effort to avoid hell. Was it valid? The Bible said they were new creatures, that old things had passed away and all had become new. Rayford had worked hard to accept for himself the truth that God now saw him, in essence, *through* his sinless Son, the Christ.

But it had been almost impossible. He was new inside, yes. From a spiritual standpoint he knew it was true. But in many ways he struggled with his same old self. And while God's truth about him should have carried more weight than his finite emotions, they were loudly at the forefront of his conscience every day. Who was he to tell Chaim Rosenzweig to just have faith and trust that God knew him and understood him better than Chaim himself ever could?

But if there was someone who seemed healthier more quickly than most, it was Hattie. The irony of that was not lost on Rayford. Fewer than twenty-four hours before she became a believer, she was suicidal. Months before, she had admitted to any Trib Force member who had the endurance to debate her that she understood and believed the whole truth about the salvation gospel of Christ. She simply had decided, on her own, to willfully reject it because, even if God didn't seem to care that she didn't deserve it, she did care. She was saying, in effect, that God could offer her the forgiveness of her sins without qualification, but she didn't have to accept it.

But once she finally received the gift, her mere persistence was wearing. In many ways she was the same forthright woman she had been before, nearly as obnoxious as a new believer as she had been as a holdout. But of course, everyone was happy she was finally on the team.

Chaim, if Rayford could judge by facial expressions, was at least bemused by her. He was the next newest believer, so perhaps he identified with her. Yet Chaim was not responding as she was at all. Was it healthy envy that made him seem intrigued with her patter? Did he wonder why he hadn't been bestowed with such abandonment with his commitment to the truth?

Rayford didn't want to get ahead of himself, didn't want to take too literally Tsion's compliments about his return to effective leadership. But sometimes the surprise move, the one against the groove, was effective. Should he—dare he—conspire with Hattie to get her to see if she could jostle Dr. Rosenzweig off of square one? Tsion had become convinced that Chaim was God's man for this time, and Rayford had learned to trust the rabbi's intuition. But Chaim was going to have to progress a long way in a short time if he was to become the vessel Tsion envisioned.

Hattie had fed and was changing Kenny when Rayford approached her. What a bonus for Kenny that he had so many parent figures! The men doted on him, and even Zeke, though slightly intimidated, was extremely gentle and loving toward him. The women seemed intuitively to know when to spell each other, mothering him, but of course, most of the responsibility fell to Chloe.

"Have a minute?" Rayford asked Hattie as she lay the freshly powdered and dressed boy over her shoulder and sat rocking him.

"If this guy is drowsy, I've got all the time in the world, which—according to our favorite rabbi—is slightly less than three and a half years."

Hattie isn't as funny as she sees herself, Rayford thought, *but there is something to be said for consistency.*

"Could I get you to do me a favor?" Rayford said.

"Anything."

"Don't be too quick to say that, Hattie."

"I mean it. Anything. If it helps you, I'll do it."

"Well, if you succeed, it helps the cause."

"Say no more. I'm there."

"It has to do with Chaim."

"Isn't he the best?"

"He's great, Hattie. But he needs something Tsion and I don't seem to be able to give him."

"Rayford! He's twice my age!"

\+ + +

So as not to draw suspicion, Buck suggested he and Albie get a head start on the next group by heading directly to the building immediately east of the processing center. This housed the lesser criminals, according to the organizing officer. Yet he had also said that the religious dissidents were in with the worst felons in the easternmost facility.

The two approached the guards at Building 4. "Ready for us?" one said with a Cockney lilt.

"Soon," Buck said. "You're next."

"Heard whooping and hollering. Somebody choose the blade?"

Buck nodded but tried to make it clear he didn't want to talk about it.

"More'n one?" the man added.

Buck nodded again. "Wasn't pretty."

"Yeah? Wish I'd seen it. Never saw somebody buy it before. You watched, eh?"

"Told you it wasn't pretty. How would I know otherwise?"

"Sor-*ry!* I'm just askin'. How many you see then?"

"Just the one."

"But there were more? How about you, Commander? You stay for the whole show?"

"Leave it alone, Corporal," Albie snapped. "Several women chose it and showed more bravery than any man I ever saw."

"That right, is it? But they wasn't loyal to the potentate now then, was they?"

"They stood by their convictions," Albie said.

"Convictions and sentences, sounds like to me, mate."

"Would you choose to die if you felt that deeply?"

"I *do* feel that deeply, gents. Only I'm on the other side of it now, ain't I? I choose what makes sense. Man rises from the dead—he's got my vote."

The armed guards led the somber survivors back to the women's building while Athenas's crew caught up to Buck and Albie. Buck noticed that Alex's people seemed as subdued as the women prisoners. But their guards seemed energized.

"Let's get this done," Athenas said, leading the way in.

These were clearly white-collar criminals or small-timers. No bravado, no threats, little noise at all. They listened, no one opted for the guillotine, and they filed out quietly to be processed. Buck was repulsed at the smell of blood that hung in the center. Word quietly spread throughout the men that several women had been beheaded in that very room, and the men grew even quieter. The workers assigned to the guillotine seemed relieved to have a break.

Buck watched the process, despairing at the masses who ignorantly sealed their fate. The workers had grown smooth with experience, and the operation went faster and faster. Line up, decide, swab, sit, inject, back in line, file out. Ironically, real life bloomed at the point of bloody death. Men receiving what looked like an innocuous mark they thought kept them alive sealed their real death sentences. From death, life. From life, death.

Buck was eager to see Pastor Demeter again, but why did it have to be here, why now? He dreaded the confrontation with the worst of the worst criminals in Building 5, knowing that many believing men would choose the right but ugly fate.

His phone vibrated. The readout said, "Top priority. Rendezvous at Kozani no earlier than 0100 hours with GC penal officer reassigned from Buffer to USNA. Urgent. Her papers will specify destination. Early twenties, dark hair, Ming Toy. Sealed."

"We'll have company tonight," Buck told Albie. "It will be refreshing to have a sister aboard who won't remind me of this place every time I look at her."

"I understand," Albie said. "I could have lived a lifetime without having seen this and not felt I missed a thing."

+ + +

It was late afternoon at the safe house, and everyone was busy except Rayford. Zeke was sewing. Tsion writing. Chloe working on the computer. Leah copying. Chaim cramming. Kenny sleeping. And Hattie, with a wink to Rayford, approaching Chaim.

The old man looked up at her from a couch, seemingly intrigued. Rayford sat nearby, ostensibly buried in a book. "Ready for an interruption?" she said. "Because I can't be dissuaded." She sat on the floor near his feet.

"As I don't appear to have a choice, Miss Durham, I could use a diversion. Something on your mind?"

"You're new at this too," she said, "but I've noticed you're not all over the place talking about it."

"I'm on assignment. Heavy study load. You remember from college?"

"Didn't finish. Wanted to see the world. But, hey, you won't let the studying get in the way of the thrill, will you? This has to be more than a class or that would take the fun out of it."

"Fun I don't associate with this. I came to the faith, you and I both did, at the worst possible time in history to enjoy it. It's about survival now. Joy comes later. Or if we had come to the faith before the Rapture, I could see where I might have enjoyed it more."

She scowled. "I don't mean fun fun, like ha-ha fun. But we can let it reach us, can't we? Inside? Get to us?"

He let his head bob from side to side. "I suppose."

"Do you? Your eyes and your body language tell me you're still not with the picture."

"Oh, make no mistake. I'm in. I believe. I have the faith."

"But you don't have the joy."

"I told you about the joy."

"I can't debate a brain like you, but I'm not giving up on this. I don't care if you are ten times more educated—I want you to understand this."

"I'll try," he said. "What do you want me to agree with?"

"Just that we have so much to be thankful for."

"Oh, I agree with that."

"But it has to thrill you!"

"In its own way, it does. Or I should say, in my own way."

Hattie slumped and sighed. "This is beyond me. I can't convince you. But I'm so thrilled that you are my brother, and I am on fire about what God is calling you to do."

"Now see, Miss Durham, that is where I suppose we differ or disagree. I have come to see that Tsion is right, that I am in a unique position to be involved in something strategic. I have resigned myself to the fact that it is inevitable and that I must do it. But I do not warm to it, long for it, look forward to it."

"I do!"

"Listen to me now, Miss Durham."

"Sorry."

"I accept this mantle with great gravity and heaviness of heart. I am working not to be a coward or even reluctant or resistant. This is not something one should eagerly embrace as some sort of honor or achievement. Do you understand?"

She nodded. "You're right; I'm sure you are. But does it also humble you that God would choose you for something like this?"

"Oh, I'm humbled all right. But there are times when I can identify with the Lord Messiah himself when he prayed and asked that if possible, his Father would let this cup pass from him."

Hattie nodded. "But he also added, 'Not my will, but yours be done.'"

"He did indeed," Chaim said. "Pray for me that I will approach that same level of brokenness and willingness."

"Well," she said, standing, "I just want to tell you that I know God is going to do great things through you. I will be praying for you every step of the way."

Chaim seemed unable to speak. Finally his eyes filled and he rasped, "Thank you very much, my young sister. That means more to me than I can say."

+ + +

As Buck trudged into the last building, he found himself next to Alex Athenas, going over his notes. "Ugly work," Buck said.

Alex grunted. "Uglier than I thought. Who'd have guessed those women would be so resolute? We're going to run into some of their husbands now. We'll find out who's tougher."

"I find it hard to believe you've got religious dissidents in with hardened criminals."

"That's not my call. I've got one job here."

"I wouldn't want it."

"I didn't ask for it."

"Don't you agree the mix in this building is strange?"

The others passed as Alex stopped and looked Buck full in the face, making him uncomfortable. "Let me ask you something, Jensen. Have you ever talked to Nicolae Carpathia?"

Buck froze. Why would he guess that? "It's been a long time," Buck said.

"Well, I have. And he sees the dissidents as every bit as dangerous as the criminals. Well, they're both criminals."

"Murderers and people of faith?"

"People of the wrong faith, the divisive faith, the intolerant faith."

Buck stepped closer. "Alex, listen to yourself. You just sent more than a dozen women to their deaths because they don't share Nicolae Carpathia's faith. And you call *them* intolerant?"

Alex stared back. "I've got a mind to turn you in. You make me wonder about your loyalty."

"Maybe I'm wondering about it too. Whatever happened to freedom?"

"We've still got freedom, Jack," Alex spat. "These people can decide for themselves whether they want to live or die."

Buck followed him in. This was by far the largest holding room, men of all ages milling about, talking. Buck noticed at least two dozen men with the mark of God on their foreheads, and they all seemed to be earnestly pleading with small groups of others. Strangely, the others seemed to be listening.

Buck caught Albie's eye. "See all of them?" he mouthed. Albie nodded sadly. It was great to see so many believers, but that meant more carnage was not far off. Buck wondered how he could let Pastor Demeter know he was there.

He asked a guard, "Who's the leader of the dissidents?"

"The local Judah-ites?"

Buck shrugged. "That what they call them here?"

The guard nodded and pointed to where the tall, dark-haired man was surrounded by at least a dozen others. He was speaking earnestly and quickly, gesturing. Rayford had first told Buck of the man's gift of evangelism, and he must have been exercising it with desperation. Buck moved to where he could hear.

"'But God demonstrates His own love toward us, in that while we were still sinners, Christ died for us.' That's you and me, gentlemen. I'm pleading with you not to take this mark. Receive Christ, get your sins forgiven, stake your claim with the God of the universe."

"It could cost us our lives," one said.

"It *will* cost you your life, friend. You think I don't know this is a hard thing? Ask yourself, do I want to be with God in heaven this very night, or do I want to pledge my loyalty to Satan and never be able to change my mind? Tonight you'll be dead for an instant and then in the presence of God. Or you can live another few years and spend eternity in hell. The choice is yours."

"I want God," a man said.

"You know the consequences?"

"Yes, hurry."

"Pray with me." They knelt.

"On your feet, everyone!" Alex called out.

"God, I know I'm a sinner," Pastor D began, and the man repeated it.

"I said on your feet!"

"Forgive my sins and come into my life and save me."

"Don't make me send a guard in there to break your heads!"

"Thank you for sending your Son to die on the cross for me."

"All right, get in there!"

"I accept your gift and receive you right now."

"Don't say I didn't warn you!"

Buck noticed that other men were repeating the prayer too, though their eyes were open and they faced the front, standing.

"Amen."

Just as the guard got to Pastor D, he stood and pulled the other man up.

"You two listen up now!"

As the guard left, Buck heard a man whisper, "Pray that again."

Pastor D started in again, quietly, still appearing to be paying attention as Alex finished his information. All throughout the cage, other men were praying and leading others to do the same. The murmuring floated toward the guards, but it was hard to pin on one person.

"I need to know if any of you will be rejecting the mark of loyalty so we can get you in the right line now!"

"Put me in the other line!" Pastor D called out.

"You're rejecting?"

"Yes, sir!"

"You understand the consequences?"

"Yes. I reject the authority of the ruler of this world and wish to—"

"I didn't ask for your philosophy, sir. Just get in the line to my right as—"

"I wish to pledge my allegiance to the true and living God and his Son, Jesus Christ!"

"I said be quiet!"

"He is the one who offers the free gift of salvation to anyone who believes!"

"Silence that man!"

"What are you going to do, kill me twice? Oh, that I could die twice for my God!"

"Anyone else?"

"Me!"

"Me too!"

"Count me in!"

"Sign me up!"

And one after the other, as the men chose their own deaths, they began to holler their reasons.

"I just became a believer tonight, right here! Do it, men! It's true! God loves you!"

"Silence!"

"I was arrested because I was worshiping God with fellow believers! God will never leave you or forsake you!"

"Guards!"

The guards followed Alex's men into the cage, throwing men to the ground, stomping their heads and faces.

"Do not resist!" Pastor D shouted. "We'll be out of our misery soon! May the very men who beat us listen to our report before it's too late!"

He was smacked atop the head with a baton and crumbled to the floor. A criminal who Buck noticed did not have the seal of God on his forehead grabbed the guard around the neck from behind and threw him down as others climbed atop.

"Don't resist, brothers!" a believer yelled. "Just speak the truth!"

But the unbelievers were rioting. "I'm taking Carpathia's mark!" one screamed. "But stop hurting these men! I'm a coward, but they are brave! Agree with them or not, they have more courage than any of us!"

A guard jumped him and wrapped his arms around the man's head, a hand on his chin. He yanked until the neck snapped and the man fell dead.

Alex, who remained outside the cage guarding his men's weapons, grabbed one and fired into the air, squelching the bravado of most unbelievers. "I will authorize my people to shoot to kill!" he said. "Now get to my left if you are accepting the mark of loyalty to the Global Community and our risen potentate. And get to the right if—"

"There is one God and one Mediator between God and men, the Man Christ Jesus!"

"Silence that man!"

The believers helped Pastor D up, but he could not stand alone. They carried him to the front of the line to Alex's right, and dozens of others fell in behind. Suddenly they began singing, "What can wash away my sin? Nothing but the blood of Jesus! What can make me whole again? Nothing but the blood of Jesus!"

"Herd them out! Shut them up! Guillotine line first! Move! Move!"

"O precious is the flow, that makes me white as snow! No other fount I know! Nothing but the blood of Jesus!"

As the line passed Buck, he grabbed Pastor D by the shirt and pulled him up, as if forcing him to walk. He whispered desperately in his ear, "Jesus is risen!"

Demetrius Demeter, he of the gift of evangelism, eyes rolling back, tongue thick, legs failing, mumbled, "Christ is risen indeed!"

Buck watched the staggering band, each with the seal of God on his forehead, march to the death room, singing of the blood of Jesus and accepting the blows. He could not follow them in, knew he could not endure witnessing the deaths of these saints, old and new. Eyes filling, he found Albie in the crowd and motioned with a nod that he should follow. They strode quickly to the Jeep, but not soon enough to avoid hearing the first slide and thud and the cheering of the bloodthirsty crowd.

Buck fired up the engine to drown out the sounds and squealed off into the night. He and Albie shared not a word as they raced south twenty-five miles to the airport at Kozani. Buck skidded to a stop by the motor pool and they leapt out, hurrying through the gate.

"Key in it?" someone called, and Buck nodded, not trusting himself to speak.

As he and Albie marched across the tarmac toward the runway and the hangar where their refueled jet awaited, Buck saw a tiny Asian woman sitting next to a huge suitcase and a smaller bag on a bench under a light pole. Something about the way the light illuminated her red, GC prison-system uniform made her look angelic.

She appeared tentative when she saw them and stood, pulling her orders from her pocket. She was a sliver of reality, a link to life, to safety, a cup of cold water in a desert of despair.

"Tell me you're Ming Toy," Buck said brusquely, barely trusting his voice.

"I am. Mr. Williams?"

Buck nodded.

"And Mr. Albie?"

"Jensen and Elbaz until we board, ma'am, please," Albie said, and Buck could tell he was just as ragged emotionally.

"Let me see your papers," Buck said, picking up her suitcase while Albie grabbed the other bag.

"Let me carry something, gentlemen. You have no idea how I appreciate this."

"Until we get on that plane, Ms. Toy," Albie said, "we're just following orders and ferrying an employee from one assignment to another."

"I understand."

"Once we're on board, we can make nice."

Buck tossed her suitcase behind the backseat, then helped her aboard and pointed to a seat. As she buckled in, Albie slipped behind the controls. Buck sat next to him but did not strap himself in. He turned so his knees were between his chair and Albie's and grabbed a clipboard.

He faced the silent woman behind him. "Ms. Toy," he said, and he began to sob. "We have to do a preflight checklist and get clearance for takeoff." She squinted at him in much the same way he assumed she must deal with the prisoners at Buffer. She had to be wondering what in the world was wrong with this man. "But once we are airborne," he said between great gasps, "we are going to tell you what a miracle you are and why we so badly needed you to be on this plane tonight." He caught his breath and added, "And we're going to tell you a story you won't believe."

19

DAVID AWOKE EVERY FEW HOURS, peeking at his clock. Finally, at 0600, he rolled out of bed, ran a hard five miles, ate, showered, and dressed. He was in his office by 0730.

"You change this appointment?" his assistant asked.

"Yeah, sorry, Tiff. A conflict?"

"No, just curious."

David called 4054, just to make sure Chang was still there and planning to come at 0900. When David identified himself, Mrs. Wong said, "Missah Wong not here right now. I have him call you back, OK?"

"Is Chang there?"

"No. Chang with father."

"Do you know where they are?"

"See Missah Moon."

"They are with Mr. Moon now?"

"I have him call you back."

"Ma'am, Mrs. Wong, are your husband and your son with Mr. Moon now?"

"I no understand. Call Missah Moon."

David called Moon's office and was told Walter was in Personnel. Personnel told him the executives were in a meeting. "Can you tell me if they have begun applying marks to new hires?"

"Not that I know of, but that *is* supposed to be today, and that *is* what the meeting is about."

"Can you tell me if one of my candidates is there, Chang Wong?"

"I believe I did see him and his father in here this morning with Mr. Moon."

"Where are they now?"

"I have no idea. Would you like their room number? They're staying here at—"

"No, thanks. I really need to talk to Moon."

"I told you, sir, he is in a meeting with personnel execs."

"It's an emergency."

"So you say."

"Ma'am, I am a director. Would you please interrupt the meeting and tell Mr. Moon I need to speak with him immediately."

"No."

"Excuse me?"

"I have been in trouble for just that kind of thing before. If it's that important, you may feel free to interrupt the meeting yourself."

David slammed the phone down and jogged to Personnel. He found the conference room empty, then found the receptionist. She held him off with a raised hand as she handled another call.

"Ask them to hold a second," he said. "This is important."

"Just a moment, please."

"*Thank* you! Now, I—"

"I didn't put this call on hold to help you. I put them on hold to ask you to wait your turn."

"But I—"

She held up a hand again and returned to her call. Another phone rang while she was finishing, and she went directly to it. David leaned across her desk and depressed the cradle button.

"Director Hassid! I'll report you for this!"

"You'd better get me fired before I get you fired," he said. "Now where is this meeting?"

"I don't know."

"It's not here; where is it?"

"Off-site, obviously."

"Where?"

"I honestly don't know, but my guess would be the basement of Building D."

"That's a quarter mile from here! Why didn't you tell me it was there when you told me to interrupt it myself?"

"I didn't know you'd actually do it."

Her phone rang again.

"Don't answer that."

"It's my job."

"Answer it and it'll be your job. Why would the meeting be in D?"

"I don't know that it is. I said it was a guess."

"Why *might* it be there?"

"Because that's where they're setting up the loyalty mark application center." And she answered her phone.

David slammed both palms on her desk, making her jump and then apologize to the caller. As he pushed through the door, she called after him in a singsong tone. "Oh, Director Hassid! You might want to take this call. It's your assistant."

He rushed back, only to get a condescending look. "Like I'm going to let you use my phone." She pointed to a phone on a table in the waiting area.

"This is David."

"Hey. Just got a call from Walter Moon."

"Where is he?"

"I'm sorry. He didn't say and I didn't think to ask. Want me to find him?"

"What did he want?"

"He said he would be delivering your 0900 appointment personally, that he and the candidate's father were most excited about your interest, you know the drill."

"What was he doing with Moon this morning?"

"No idea, sir, but I'll find out if you want."

"Find Moon and call me back on my cell."

David hurried to Building D and found the basement cordoned off. He had to use every line in the book to talk his way past Security. When he was finally able to peek through the double doors that led into a huge meeting room, he got his first glimpse of the setup for applying the mark. Crowd-control barricades were arranged to funnel people to processing points and finally to the cubicles where the last of the injection guns were being plugged in and tested.

"What's all this for?" David asked a woman arranging chairs.

"Oh, come on, you know."

"But why so big? I thought they were just doing new employees first."

She shrugged. "The rest of us will be next. Might as well have everything in place and tested, huh? I can't wait. This is the dream of a lifetime."

"Have you seen Security Chief Moon this morning?"

"Actually he *was* here a while ago."

"With anyone?"

"Couldn't tell you who. Some guys from Personnel, I know."

"Anyone else?"

She nodded. "I didn't pay attention, though."

"Any idea where he is now?"

She shook her head. "I suppose you've heard the rumors, though."

"Tell me."

She smiled. "You poor managers miss the gossip, don't you?"

"We often do."

"I figure you start most of it, or at least your decisions do."

"Granted. What's the word this morning?"

"That Moon's in line for supreme commander."

"You don't say."

"I like him. I think he'd be good at it."

David's cell phone vibrated and he excused himself. "Moon's people now say he's in with Carpathia," Tiffany said.

"Alone?"

"David, I'm sorry. I didn't ask. I'll find out whatever you want, but I have to know in advance what I'm looking for."

"My fault. Did they happen to say whether Walter is still bringing Chang at 0900?"

"Yea! I know one! Yes."

"Really?"

"Honest."

"Is Chang with him and Carpathia now?"

"Sorry. No idea."

"I'm on my way back."

David used his cell phone as he walked and tried the Chang apartment again. This time Mr. Wong answered. Encouraged, David asked for Chang. "He not available right now. He see you at nine, yes?"

"That's right. Is he OK?"

"Better than OK! Very excited! Missah Moon come get us to bring to see you."

"You're coming too?"

"If OK. May I?"

David sighed. "Why not?"

"No?"

"Yeah, sure."

Back in his office, with fifteen minutes to spare, he patched in to Carpathia's office. The first thing he heard was Nicolae's voice. "Hickman was a buffoon! I'm better off without him. I don't know what Leon was thinking."

"Probably that he was going to have your job and Jim would be easy to manage."

Carpathia laughed. "You're a good judge of character, Walter. It came down to you and Suhail. He has an impressive résumé, but he's so new to his current position."

"And can you trust a Pakistani? I don't understand those types."

"Who can you trust these days, Walter? Now listen, I don't know how you stand on pomp and circumstance, but I don't want to make a big deal of this.

You'll have an appropriate office you won't have to share with anyone, but I just want to announce your appointment and not get into a lot of ceremony."

"Perfect," Walter said. "I don't want to take any attention from you, sir."

David thought Walter sounded disingenuous and almost palpably disappointed. He was right, though, in pandering to Carpathia's ego. No one was going to steal that thunder anyway.

"Walter," Carpathia said, "how are we coming with the GCMM?"

Moon sounded surprised. "Sir, the Morale Monitors have been in place for a long time. I get input from them every day, and I know Suhail counts on their intelligence briefings."

It was clear Carpathia was impatient. "Mr. Moon, surely you caught my drift recently when I spoke of mobilizing a great enforcement throng from every tribe and nation who would—"

"Of course, Potentate. I am working with Chief Akbar now to—"

"I don't believe it! You missed it! Walter, I am determined to surround myself with people who understand me intuitively!"

"I'm sorry, Excellency. I—"

"For all of Leon's foibles and idiosyncrasies, he is a man who stays with me, anticipating my needs and desires and strategies. Do you kn—"

"That's the kind of subordinate I want to b—"

"Don't interrupt me, please!"

"I apologize."

"Do you know where Leon is now?"

"I heard he had flown to the United European Sta—"

"He is in Vatican City, Walter! He has called together the ten regional potentates and has asked each to bring his most trusted and loyal spiritual leader to join them in that former great bastion of Christianity."

"I don't underst—"

"Of course you don't! Think, man! At this very moment I imagine Reverend Fortunato is kneeling in the Sistine Chapel, the sub-potentates and the spiritual leader from each region who will represent Carpathianism throughout the globe laying hands on him and committing him to the great task before him."

"I should like to have been there, Excellency."

"You're my chief of security and you didn't even know this! I'm going to make you supreme commander, but you have to get in step!"

"I'll do my best."

"Leon called me at dawn, telling me with great relish that he had ordered destroyed every Vatican relic, every icon, every piece of artwork that paid homage to the impotent God of the Bible. There were those among the potentates and even among the Carpathianists who suggested that these so-called priceless treasures at least be moved here to the palace to preserve their worth and to remind us of history. History! I don't know when I've been prouder of Leon. Before he returns, the Vatican will be left no vestiges of any sort of tribute to any god but the one my people can see and touch and hear."

"Amen, Your Holiness. You are risen indeed."

"Of course, and the whole world was watching! Now when I spoke the other day of a host of enforcers, I wanted you to gather that I meant the very core of my most loyal troops, the GCMM. They are already armed. I want them supported! I want them fully equipped! I want you to marry them with our munitions so their monitoring will have teeth. They should be respected and revered to the point of fear."

"You want the citizenry afraid, sir?"

"Walter! No man need fear me who loves and worships me. You know that."

"I do, sir."

"If any man, woman, young person, or child has reason to feel guilty when encountering a member of the Global Community Morale Monitoring Force, then yes, I want them shaking in their boots!"

"I understand, Excellency."

"Do you, Walter? I really need to know."

"I absolutely do, sir."

"I don't care whom you replace yourself with as chief of security. All I want you to know is that I hold you personally responsible for carrying out this wish."

"Of giving more muscle to the GCMM."

"The understatement of the century."

"Any budget for this?"

"Walter, you report directly to me. I control the globe politically, militarily, spiritually, and economically. I have a bottomless sea of resources. Spare not one Nick in your effort to make the GCMM the most powerful enforcement juggernaut the world has ever seen."

"Yes, sir!"

"Have fun with it! Enjoy it! But don't dawdle. I want a full contingent, at least one hundred thousand fully equipped troops, in Israel when I return there in triumph."

"Sir, that is but days away."

"Do we not have the personnel?"

"We do."

"Do we not have the armaments?"

"We do. Are you lifting the embargo against showing military-style strength in the form of tanks, fighters, bombers, and other such?"

"You're catching on, Walter. I want to crush resistance in Israel before it even arises. From whom should I expect opposition?"

"The Judah-ites and—"

"You've already told me they are unlikely to show their faces. They take their potshots from behind the trees of the Internet. From whom shall I expect flesh-and-blood opposition within, say, Jerusalem itself? You know my plans."

"Not totally, sir."

"You know enough to know who will be outraged."

"The Orthodox, sir. The devout, religious Jews."

David heard chairs squeak, and it was obvious Carpathia had stood and Moon followed suit. "Now, Walter. I ask you. How dangerous to me will be the funny-looking men with their beards and their braids and their skullcaps once they have seen one hundred thousand heavily armed troops, there to protect me and those who worship me?"

"Not very, Excellency."

"Not very indeed, Walter. Good day to you."

David guessed Walter still had time to make their appointment. His goal was to schmooze Walter, flatter Mr. Wong, and somehow get rid of them so he could plot with Chang how to get out of there with the other four believers. He sat, earphones in place, ready to shut down his computer. But then he heard Carpathia humming, then singing, as if he were writing a song, trying a line, improving it, starting over. David listened, transfixed.

Finally perfecting it, to a military-sounding tune Carpathia softly sang:

Hail Carpathia, our lord and risen king;
Hail Carpathia, rules o'er everything.
We'll worship him until we die;
He's our beloved Nicolae.
Hail Carpathia, our lord and risen king.

\+ + +

Just before midnight in Chicago only Rayford and Tsion were awake. All were excited about the expected return of Buck and Albie and their next new member, Ming Toy. Chloe and Leah asked to be awakened as soon as the chopper arrived.

Tsion had been working all day on a new, though brief, message. "I'm about to transmit it," he told Rayford. "But I'd appreciate your looking at it. It's an interesting study, but it's not for the beginners. We have hundreds of thousands of new believers joining our ranks every day, but I have to think also about moving the more mature ones from milk to meat. Perhaps the day will come when someone like Chaim can take over the teaching of the newest."

Rayford eagerly accepted Tsion's hard copy, always feeling privileged when he was among the first to get a glance at something a billion people would benefit from.

Dear ones in Christ:

From your letters to the message board, I sense some questions about certain passages and doctrines, one of which I address today. I am most encouraged that you are reading, studying, curious, and that you so plainly want to learn and grow as believers in Messiah. If you have placed your trust in Christ alone for salvation by grace through faith, you are a true tribulation saint.

While we all rejoice in our new positions before God—we went from old to new, from death to life, from darkness to light—no doubt all are sobered by the reality that we are living on borrowed time, now more than ever.

I have gathered from many that one of your loftiest goals is to survive until the Glorious Appearing. I share that longing but wish to gently remind you that that is not our all in all. The apostle Paul said that to live is Christ but that to die is gain. While it would be thrilling beyond words to see the triumphant Lord Christ return to the earth and set up his thousand-year reign, I believe I could learn to deal with it if I were called to heaven in advance and saw it from that perspective instead.

Beloved, our top priority now is not even thwarting the evils of Antichrist, though I engage in that effort every day. I want to confound him, revile him, enrage him, frustrate him, and get in the way of his plans every way I know how. His primary goal is ascendancy for himself, worship of himself, and the death and destruction of any who might otherwise become tribulation saints.

So, as worthy and noble a goal as it is to go on the offensive against the evil one, I believe we can do that most effectively by focusing on persuading the undecided to come to faith. Knowing that every day could be our last, that we could be found out and dragged to a mark application center, there to make our decision to die for the sake of Christ, we must be more urgent about our task than ever.

Many have written in fear, confessing that they do not believe they have the courage or the character to choose death over life when threatened with the guillotine. As a fellow pilgrim in this journey of faith, let me admit that I do not understand this either. In my flesh I am weak. I want to live. I am afraid of death but even more of dying. The very thought of having my head severed from my body repulses me as much as it does anyone. In my worst nightmare I see myself standing before the GC operatives a weakling, a quivering mass who can do nothing but plead for his life. I envision myself breaking God's heart by denying my Lord. Oh, what an awful picture!

In my most hated imagination I fail at the hour of testing and accept the mark of loyalty that we all know is the cursed mark of the beast, all because I so cherish my own life.

Is that your fear today, friend? Are you all right as long as you are in hiding and somehow able to survive? But have you a foreboding about that day when you will be forced to publicly declare your faith or deny your Savior?

I have good news for you that I have already admitted is difficult to understand, even for me, who has been called to shepherd you and exposit the Word of God for you. The Bible tells us that once one is either sealed by God as a believer or accepts the mark of loyalty to Antichrist, this is a once-and-for-all choice. In other words, if you have decided for Christ and the seal of God is evident on your forehead, you cannot change your mind!

That tells me that somehow, when we face the ultimate test, God miraculously overcomes our evil, selfish flesh and gives us the grace and courage to make the right decision in spite of ourselves. My interpretation of this is that we will be unable to deny Jesus, unable to even choose the mark that would temporarily save our lives.

Isn't that a blessed thought? I could no more do this in my flesh than I could swim the Pacific. I have heard stories of believers from the past who were asked at gunpoint to denounce their faith, and yet they stood firm, dying for it. I never envisioned myself with that kind of fortitude.

Even since writing to you last, I have heard the story of one who was among the first to face this test. We have no eyewitness account, no one to tell us how the scene unfolded. Yet we know that of all the people herded through the mark application process at this specific venue (which I naturally have to keep confidential), only one man rejected the mark. Knowing the consequences, he chose to die rather than to deny Jesus Christ.

My heart is broken for his loved ones. What an awful mental image to season one's bereavement! And yet how thrilling to know that God was faithful! He was there at the darkest hour. And this beloved saint is one of the martyrs under the altar of God, his robe snow white.

As Antichrist and the false prophet spread their message of lies and hatred and false doctrine around the world, forcing millions to worship Satan himself by threatening to behead those who refuse, it would bode well for us if we would memorize a verse from John's Revelation. In chapter 20 and verse 4, he writes as part of his God-given vision:

"Then I saw the souls of those who had been beheaded for their witness to Jesus and for the word of God, who had not worshiped the beast or his image, and had not received his mark on their foreheads or on their hands. And they lived and reigned with Christ for a thousand years."

Your loved ones who have been called to what the world would call an ignoble and gory end shall return with Christ at his Glorious Appearing! They shall live and reign with him for a thousand years! Glory be to God the Father and his Son, Jesus the Christ!

And as for you and me, my friend: might we be among those? Oh, the privilege!

Revelation 14:12-13: "Here is the patience of the saints; here are those who keep the commandments of God and the faith of Jesus. Then I heard a voice from heaven saying to me, 'Write: "Blessed are the dead who die in the Lord from now on."' 'Yes,' says the Spirit, 'that they may rest from their labors, and their works follow them.'"

And what of those who enjoy for a season the favor of the ruler of this world? What of those who avoid the guillotine and seem to prosper? As rousing as the Scriptures can be for those who are washed in the blood of the Lamb, look how fearful it can be for those who choose their own way. In Revelation 14:9-11, John quotes an angel, "saying with a loud voice, 'If anyone worships the beast and his image, and receives his mark on his forehead or on his hand, he himself shall also drink of the wine of the wrath of God, which is poured out full strength into the cup of His indignation. He shall be tormented with fire and brimstone in the presence of the holy angels and in the presence of the Lamb. And the smoke of their torment ascends forever and ever; and they have no rest day or night, who worship the beast and his image, and whoever receives the mark of his name.'"

You don't have to be a Bible scholar to understand that.

Now, precious brothers and sisters, let me try to make plain some passages that have resulted in questions from many of you. In Psalm 69:28, the psalmist pleads with the Lord concerning his enemies: "Let them be blotted out of the book of the living, and not be written with the righteous."

Exodus 32:33 says, "And the Lord said to Moses, 'Whoever has sinned against Me, I will blot him out of My book.'"

These references naturally have caused some to fear that they can lose their salvation. But my contention is that the book referred to in those is the book of God the Father, into which are written the names of every person he created.

The New Testament refers to the Book of Life of the Lamb, and we know that the Lamb is Jesus, for he is the one John the Baptist was referring to (John 1:29) when he said, "Behold! The Lamb of God who takes away the sin of the world!"

Jesus the Christ came into the world to save sinners, and thus the Book of Life of the Lamb is the one in which are entered the names of those who have received his gift of eternal life.

The most important difference between these two books is that it is clear a person can have his name blotted out of the Book of the Living. But in Revelation 3:5, Jesus himself promises, "He who overcomes shall be clothed in white garments, and I will not blot out his name from the Book of Life; but I will confess his name before My Father and before His angels."

The overcomers he is referring to are those clothed in the white garments of Christ himself, guaranteeing that their names cannot be blotted out of the Book of Life of the Lamb.

To me the Book of the Living is a picture of the mercy of God. It is as if in loving anticipation of our salvation, he writes every person's name in that book. If one dies without trusting Christ for salvation, his name is blotted out, because he is no longer among the living. But those who have trusted Christ have been written in the Lamb's Book of Life, so that when they die physically, they remain alive spiritually and are never blotted out.

Rayford had to admit to himself that he had also worried about his own response if he were to face the guillotine. He wanted to be true and faithful to the one who died for him, and he wanted to see his family again. But if he failed and proved a coward, he had wondered whether he would lose his standing before God.

"Tsion," he said, "I wouldn't change a word. This will uplift and comfort millions. It sure helped me."

20

DAVID COULDN'T SIT STILL. How was he going to pull this off? Maybe he should act uninterested in Chang as an employee. Would anybody fall for that? He stood and paced, straightening his tie and buttoning his uniform jacket.

When Moon, Mr. Wong, and Chang finally arrived, David was disconcerted at Chang's appearance. A slight, fair-skinned seventeen-year-old, he wore khakis, a plain shirt, a light jacket zipped to the neck, and a red baseball cap pulled low over his eyes. He was clearly angry, his eyes darting everywhere but at David.

Moon and Mr. Wong were giddy, laughing, talking loudly. "Ever see a boy so afraid?" Mr. Wong said.

"Can't say I have!"

Tiffany ushered them in, and David shook hands, first with Walter, then Mr. Wong, who said, "Hat off for meeting, Chang."

For the first time since he had seen them interact at the Carpathia funeral, David saw Chang ignore his father. The elder reddened and lost his smile, then faked one, pumping David's hand. "Made hat come off for picture!"

Moon laughed at the memory of it, whatever it was.

David thrust his hand toward Chang, who ignored it. He stood looking down. His father nearly exploded. "Shake hands with boss, Chang!"

The boy lazily reached out, but he did not grip when David did, and it was like shaking a fish. David thought he saw a tear slide next to the boy's mouth. Maybe this was for the best. If David were to try to bust him out of the place in a few days, it would be better if they didn't act civil to each other.

Walter Moon said, "He is risen."

Mr. Wong and David responded, "He is risen indeed." David was startled to hear Chang mutter, "Christ is risen indeed."

Chang may have considered that godly courage, but David saw it as teenage recklessness. No one else seemed to have heard it.

"Sit, please, gentlemen," David said. "I'd like to spend time alone with the candidate, but it's probably just as well you're both here, Chief Moon and Mr.

Wong. I've been studying the personnel manual, and frankly, I don't see any way around the age issue."

"Age issue?" Mr. Wong said, looking stricken. "What's that?"

"Good," Chang said and rose to leave.

"Sit! Mind manners! You guest here and interview for position!"

Chang slowly plopped back, slouching and crossing his feet.

Moon dismissed David's concern with a gesture. "His Excellency has already waived that, and—"

"The policy allows no exceptions," David pressed.

"David," Walter said slowly, reminding him of the way he had just heard Carpathia speak to Moon, "the potentate *is* policy. If he determines that this young man and his off-the-charts intellect and computer savvy will be valuable to the Global Community, then it's a done deal."

David took a breath, deciding to go on the offensive.

But Moon wasn't finished. "You're aware that Potentate Carpathia has already cleared Chang to finish his last year of high school here, and of course we then offer college classes as well."

"I was under the impression the school here was for the benefit of the *children* of employees," David tried.

"I don't think the teachers care who the students' parents are. Tell Mr. Wong what you are envisioning for Chang, David."

Mr. Wong, grinning, leaned forward to drink it in.

Here goes nothing, David thought. "I envision him finishing high school in China and at least beginning his career anywhere but here."

Mr. Wong's smile disappeared. "What?" he said, turning to Moon.

"David!" Walter said. "What the—"

"Look at him," David said, and both men turned to see Chang staring at the floor, hands in his pockets.

"Sit up, boy. You know better. You shame me."

Chang made a halfhearted effort to shift and raised his chin an inch, but he remained a picture of insolence. His father reached to tug at the shoulder of his jacket, and Chang wrenched away. Mr. Wong glowered at him.

"He doesn't want to work here," David said. "He's young, immature, simply not ready. I don't doubt his credentials or his potential, but let him work out the kinks on someone else's money."

"Now, let's not be hasty, David," Moon said. "The boy's just been through a bit of a trauma. He was scared, but he went through with it, and he's clearly still a little shaken."

David cocked his head as if willing to consider the excuse. "Oh?"

"Yes," Mr. Wong said. "He upset. He frightened of needle. Didn't want injection. Scream. Cry. Try to get away, but we hold him down. He thank me someday. Maybe tomorrow."

"And he needed an injection for what?"

"Biochip!" Mr. Wong announced proudly. "One of first to get it! See?"

He reached for the boy's cap, but Chang stood again and turned his back on his father. David fought to maintain composure. Now what? *How* had he let this happen?

"When?" he blurted. "How?"

"This morning," Walter said. "I was hoping they'd be ready for him. Took a photog along and everything. But they weren't, not really. We were going to just wait till later, but they could see I had gone to a lot of trouble, so when the first unit was plugged in and ready to go, they tested it and then made him the first recipient here. Not sure the picture's much good though. The boy wasn't any happier there than here."

David said, "Well, that's . . . ah . . . that's—"

"Something, huh?" Walter said. "I think the boy is glad to have it over with, and if he's honest he'll admit it didn't hurt a bit."

"I proud! Son will be soon, you'll see. But he ready for work now. No age problem. No school problem. This is place for him."

"Global Community maybe," David said, his voice hollow. How was he going to explain this to Ming? "But not my department."

"Don't be ridiculous, David. We just explained his attitude. You and I both know there's no better place for him."

"Then you take him. I don't want him. I don't have the energy to try to win him over while training him."

"I'm of a *mind* to take him, David. He's going to make somebody look like a genius. It had might as well be me."

David stood and spread his arms, palms up. "Good to see you all again."

Chang started to rise, but his father stopped him with a hand. The man looked to Walter. "David, sit down," Moon said. "Let us give you a few minutes with Chang, let him win you over."

"There aren't enough flowers or boxes of candy in the United Asian States."

"Find out what's troubling him. If it's just the trauma of the procedure, he deserves another look. What do you say?"

"I suppose you'll go running to the potentate if I don't agree."

Moon stood and motioned David to do the same. He reached for him across the desk and pulled David's ear to his mouth. "This is no way for us to conduct ourselves in front of outsiders, particularly a patriotic GC supporter like Mr. Wong. You're blamed right I'll take this straight back to the top. Now you know Carp—His Excellency wants this boy on staff, so get with the program." He let go of David and turned to Mr. Wong. "Let's give them a few minutes to get acquainted."

Mr. Wong bent to his son as he left. "You make proud, and I mean it." But Chang looked away.

As soon as the door was shut, Chang stood and moved to the center chair facing David. He resumed his defiant posture. David sat and rested an elbow on the desk, chin in hand, staring at Chang, who did not meet his gaze. "Are the blinds open behind me?" the kid muttered, still looking away.

"Yes."

"Close them."

"That would send a wrong signal, Chang. If they're watching, I want them to see me not liking you too much, which is exactly what I feel right now."

"Are they still out there?"

"Yes."

"Then either shut the blinds or tell me when they're gone."

"They're leaving."

"OK, then wait till they're out of sight so you can close the blinds without sending them the wrong signal but I still don't have to worry about anyone else coming by and looking in. Or your secretary."

"Assistant."

"Whatever. Tiffany, right?"

"Observant."

"I don't miss anything, like the fact that she's not a believer."

"I'm trying to figure out a way to work on that."

It was maddening that Chang still sat slumped, looking down. "You can't let her in on where you stand for fear she'll turn you in."

"Of course."

"Could you shut the blinds, please?"

"Not till you tell me what in the world you think you're up to."

"I'll wait," Chang said.

David rose and closed the blinds. "What was I supposed to do, son? I didn't know—"

As David returned to his side of the desk, Chang straightened up. "Don't call me son. I hate that." He whipped off his hat. "Look at me! Look what they did to me!"

David leaned over the desk to study Chang's mark of loyalty. It was the first he had seen other than in a drawing. "That is strange," he said.

"That's news to me?"

"No, I mean, obviously it looks different to me and will to any fellow believers. We can see both marks. The seal of God is still there, Chang." David could barely take his eyes off the small, black tattoo that read *30* and was followed by a half-inch pink scar that would fade to a darker line in a few days. "I still haven't figured the significance of the prefixes," David added.

"You serious?"

"Always."

"Don't tell me you don't even know why Carpathia is so obsessed with 216."

"Of course," David said. "That was rather transparent. Easy."

"Same basic logic as these. Ten different regions or sub-potentateships, as Carpathia likes to call them. We know them as kingdoms. Ten different prefixes, all related to Carpathia. I mean, the fact that one of them is 216 should have been your first clue."

"Don't tell me, Chang. I'll get it."

"Should have had it by now."

"You can lighten up on me. I don't know how I could have prevented this. Your little charade didn't help. Your sister is going to kill me. And, assuming you want out of here as badly as Ming wants you out and as badly as the other four believers want out, how did that help?"

"Can you believe my father and Moon thought I pitched a fit because I was afraid of needles?"

"I'm glad you didn't just scream out that you're a believer."

"Well, what am I now, Hassid?"

"You don't like to be called son—don't call me Hassid."

"Sorry. What's your pleasure?"

"Mr. Hassid or Director Hassid while we're in here. Once we're gone, Mr. or Brother will work."

"You sound like an old guy."

"That's because you're a young guy. As for what you are, with both marks you surely have to be in a special category."

"But all that stuff Dr. Ben-Judah writes about, choosing between the seal of God and the mark of the beast. I chose, and I got both. Now what?"

David sat shaking his head. Chang cocked his head and pursed his lips. "It isn't that I really don't know, *Mr.* Hassid. I just keep testing you. Are you not as bright as they think you are, or are you just short on sleep? Can't figure the prefixes, can't figure—"

"First, I'm *not* as bright as they think I am, but I might surprise *you.*"

"I'm not trying to be disrespectful, sir. I'm really not. But you have already surprised me by how long it takes you to make things make sense."

"I've also been under unusual pressure for months, and worse the last couple of weeks."

"Yeah. I'm sorry about your, ah, were you engaged? Was she your fiancée?"

"Secretly, yes. Thanks."

"That would put anybody off track for a while. That's understandable."

"So, you're mad you got the mark, but you've already made some sense of it?"

Chang sat back and crossed his legs. "You know Ben-Judah personally, huh?"

"Haven't met him, but we work together."

"You have his phone number?"

"Of course."

"Well, you might want to call him to confirm, or let me borrow the number and I'll talk to him myself. . . ."

"I don't think so."

"Fair enough. You call him then and see if I'm right. I'm a believer. That hasn't changed. The Bible says nothing can separate us from the love of Christ, and that has to include our own selves. And God says we're hidden in the hollow of his hand and that no one can pluck us out. I didn't choose the mark. It was forced on me. I see nothing but benefits."

"Then why the big scene?"

"I don't figure *everything* out immediately. I sure didn't *want* the mark. I was trying to figure a way to get out of it right up to the time they stuck me. I don't have to like it, but what's done is done, and a smart guy like you ought to be able to see the upside of this."

"Tell me, oh great intellect."

"So mock me. Forget it. I shouldn't have to tell you anyway."

David stood and moved to the front of the desk and sat atop it, his knees inches from Chang's. "All right, listen. It's obvious you're a mental prodigy, mind like a steel trap, all that. I'd heard you were a Bible-memory freak, which is saying something when you can't risk being caught with one. All that from reading it on the Net?"

Chang nodded.

David continued. "I'm not hung up on being the smartest guy in the room no matter where I am. That didn't used to be so, especially when I was your age. I enjoyed not only overwhelming older people with my brain but letting them know that we both knew who was the king. You want me on the floor, kissing your feet? Fine. You're the best. You're smarter than I am. I'm a journeyman, a plugger compared to you. That what you want to hear? It doesn't bother me that you're a few steps ahead of me—it really doesn't. What bothers me is your assuming it bothers me, because it would bother you if the shoe were on the other foot. Then I get defensive, trying to prove it doesn't bother me, which only makes it appear that it does. You following this?"

Chang smiled. "Yeah, I got it."

"So enlighten me and quit trying to rub it in. What are you going to do with this 'advantage,' as you call it, being bi-loyal for lack of a better term? And how does acting angry with me help that cause, whatever it is?"

"Glad you asked. May I take it from the top?"

David nodded.

"First, I like the term. Bi-loyal. That's the way it appears. This forehead is going to really bother fellow believers. They can only assume the seal mark is fake, because no one would fake the mark of the beast. They're going to take some persuading, and if I were them, I might never trust me.

"But the Carpathia loyalists . . . they can't see the mark of God, and they have no reason to believe the loyalty mark is anything but what it appears. Therefore, I am free to live among them—buy and sell, come and go, even work here—without suspicion and—if I'm careful—without risk."

"You're good, Chang. But that last was very teenage thinking."

Chang appeared to think about that, then nodded his concession. "Maybe so. Too bad I won't have an old guy like you around to keep me from being too tempestuous and impulsive."

"I'm starting to feel ancient."

"You are, Director. Think about how few years you have left on this earth as we know it."

"Funny."

"Question is, how do you and your three friends get out of here, and how do I get your job?"

"You're not going to get my job."

"I could do it."

"Maybe you could, but not even Carpathia is foolhardy enough to risk that. You have to work your way up, and I have an idea who might take my spot anyway. You'd wind up working for him."

"That's too bad; if you're right."

"I'm right. You're so smart, have some common sense. They're not going to put a teenager in a director's chair. They're just not. Think about it. I'm the youngest director now by eight years."

"Congratulations."

"That's not the point. If you're going to stay here and be a better mole than

I was—because the mark gives you unquestioned credibility—you have to be strategic. Pick your spots. Do what you can."

"Which is what, in your opinion?"

"I can teach you everything I know before I leave."

A smile played at Chang's lips.

"What?" David said. "I know you're dying to say something."

"Just that you teaching me everything you know shouldn't take long. It's a joke. C'mon."

"A real comedian. Well, for as limited as I am, I'd like to think you'll be amazed by what I've done here and what I have in place. My biggest worry is that my remote access is only good for as long as they stay with the current system."

"You don't have to worry about that anymore," Chang said.

"Because?"

"I'll be here."

"But you're not going to be a director. It won't be your call what system they stay with or change to."

"But I can adapt what you've put in place to work with it, either way."

"You probably could."

"I know I could."

David covered his mouth with a hand, thinking. Why *hadn't* he recognized the possibilities right away? "Some of your confidence is attractive. Part of it is off-putting."

"Most of it is an act, sir."

"Really?"

"Sure. The whole thing in here was an act. Pushing your buttons was just for fun. I'm just showing you how I'd fit in here. Be a little sarcastic, a little condescending. Tweak people. You think they're going to suspect I'm a Judah-ite?"

"I'm just wondering what's really inside you, Chang."

"What do you mean?"

"Spiritually. Your sister is a tough prison guard."

"She could whip my tail."

"But she glows with a spirituality, a humility. She has a real Christlike quality."

"Not around inmates she doesn't."

"I suppose not. But what about you, Chang? Do you know who you are and who you're not? Do you understand the depth of your own depravity and realize that God saved you while you were dead in your sins?"

Chang nodded, maintaining eye contact. "I know I could use a lot more introspection, but yes, I do know. And I appreciate your reminding me."

"All right, I have a plan, Chang."

"That's encouraging. So do I. But I had a little more time to think about mine, so you start."

"I'll start because I'm older, I outrank you, and I am interviewing you. You're not even an employee yet."

"I defer. Mine's going to be better anyway, so go ahead. . . . Kidding!"

"I say you maintain the attitude in front of the people here and your father, but give him a little slack before he leaves. He needs to believe you're at least OK with being here. Don't act impressed with me."

"That won't be hard."

"All right!"

"I'm listening."

"I'll bet. Come reluctantly to the conclusion that you want to work here and that you figure this is the most logical department to work in, though you're not impressed with it. You don't want to appear too eager. They're all excited about you, so let them stay that way. Play a little hard to get. As for me, I won't act much more thrilled than I did in front of Moon, and I'll just assign you to the guy I assume will replace me. After hours, you and I cram—mostly by phone and e-mail—and I'll show you what I've set up. During the day you work with him. Don't alienate him, because you'll quickly be his number-two guy. You might even want to govern yourself so you don't become too much of a star. Let him forget about you while trusting you. That way you'll be most valuable to our cause. Make sense?"

"You thought of that just now?"

"Don't start."

"I'm serious. Those were my thoughts exactly. And there's nothing I want more than to use every gift God gave me to be, like you said, valuable to the cause. Do I get to be a member of the Tribulation Force? Or would I have to live in the safe house for that?"

"They consider me a member. Of course, this is like the nerve center and they depend on what we do here to pave the way for them to come and go and infiltrate."

"So they ought to adopt me soon enough."

"I would imagine."

"May I shake your hand, as long as no one is looking?" David reached for him, and Chang gripped hard. "Don't take me too seriously. I just like to mess with people's minds."

"And I suppose few can compete," David said.

"Well, you sure can."

"I'm going to let you go and not do or say anything. Let them ask what I've decided. Then I'll reluctantly say I can use you if they insist. That way we keep maintaining distance."

"So when you escape, they won't think I had anything to do with it."

"Sort of. But actually—"

"Excuse me, Mr. Hassid, but have you thought of making your disappearances look like something other than running from taking the mark?"

David shook his head. "You got another few minutes, Chang?"

21

ONE WEEK BEFORE the resurrected Nicolae Carpathia's widely advertised triumphal return to Jerusalem, Rayford Steele called an 8 p.m. meeting of the stateside Tribulation Force at the commons near the elevators in the Strong Building.

Grieving for the Greek pastor he had met only briefly and for Laslos's dear wife, he was nervous and fought to keep it from showing. God had restored him to leadership, and he was determined to fulfill his duty. As the others took their places, Rayford reviewed the dog-eared sheets of his legal pad and cleared his throat. He had not expected to become emotional and worried that it would detract from confidence in his command. But he couldn't control his shaky voice from the first word.

Eleven were there, including Rayford, Buck, Chloe—the surviving three original Trib Force members—and Kenny Bruce. In the order that they joined were also Tsion, Leah, Albie, Chaim, Zeke, Hattie, and Ming.

"It's important," Rayford said, "that we always remember our extended family. In Greece, only Laslos remains. In New Babylon we have David, Mac, Abdullah, Hannah Palemoon, and Chang Wong. Maybe sooner than we think, we will all be together. Meanwhile, I am grateful to God for each one on this team."

Rayford asked Tsion to pray, and everyone in the room spontaneously either stood or knelt when he began. "God, our Father, we come to you weak and frail and wounded. So many here have lost so much, and yet we are grateful to you for your grace and for your mercy. You are a good God, full of loving-kindness. We pray for every member of our family and especially for the plans you have for us in just seven days.

"We are comforted by the realization that you care even more than we do about our loved ones. We look forward to when we shall see you face-to-face, and we pray you will allow us the joy of bringing many more with us. In the name of Jesus Christ. Amen."

As the rest settled back in their places, Rayford began again. "I have assignments for everyone. The following will remain here during what we're calling Operation Eagle: Chloe and Kenny, Ming, Zeke, and Tsion. I foresee using

Ming more, but for now her being AWOL from the GC penal system makes her too vulnerable. Changing her appearance is going to be a true test of Zeke's skills. Meanwhile, he has created new personas, looks, names, and documents for all who need them.

"Albie and I will fly the fighter and the Gulfstream to Mizpe Ramon in the Negev tomorrow to supervise the completion of a remote airstrip and refueling center for the airlift. Buck and Chaim will fly commercially to Jerusalem in disguise and under aliases. Chaim will settle into the rebuilt King David Hotel, waiting to confront Carpathia when he enters Jerusalem. Buck will go on to Tel Aviv and be back in Jerusalem in time for Carpathia's return.

"Hattie and Leah will fly commercially to Tel Aviv, where they will process the volunteer vehicles and drivers who will help evacuate believers from Jerusalem to the planes in the Negev when it becomes necessary. They will also monitor Carpathia's arrival, and, like Buck, Hattie will join the crowd watching the air show our New Babylon brothers and sister plan to perform for the potentate and follow the Carpathia entourage to Jerusalem.

"Leah will use a rented vehicle to rendezvous with the New Babylon four in Jordan at the former Queen Alia International Airport, now known as Resurrection International. She will bring the New Babylon contingent to the airlift site, and they will fly back to the States with Albie and me at the conclusion of the airlift. Questions?"

Chaim raised a hand. "I have only a thousand questions. But is it not time for my teacher, who ought to be respectful of his elder, to reveal the city of refuge?"

Tsion smiled and looked to Rayford. "Soon everyone must know where the fleeing saints are headed after they have reached the airlift location in the Negev. Yes, Chaim, you have devoted yourself to your studies and deserve to know where you will lead the people. It is a city you have known about all your life. You have no doubt heard many stories about it, and it would not surprise me to learn that you have actually visited it as a tourist. It is one of the most famous ancient cities in the Middle East. Some call it the Rose Red City."

Chaim's eyes came alive. "Petra!" he said. "In the ancient land of Edom!"

"One and the same," Tsion said.

"I should have known. It will be difficult for *us* to get into, let alone a pursuing army."

"In fact, Chaim, God will make it impossible for them to get in. He has special obstacles planned, the likes of which have not been seen since the days of the first Exodus. Tell me, have you been to Petra?"

"Twice as a youngster. I can never forget it. Oh, Tsion, this is a stroke of genius."

"It ought to be. I agree with countless scholars who say God has planned it for this very purpose from the beginning."

* * *

Toughest for David was planning the escape of the four believers without being able to meet with Hannah. It made sense to meet with Mac and Abdullah, who ultimately reported to him. And while David had to be circumspect and not too obvious, he got some time with Chang without raising eyebrows. What he really wanted was to meet with the four of them to carefully plot the entire scenario. By secure-connection phone calls and e-mails, he accomplished the same thing.

Chang worked out better than David could have hoped. While young and impetuous, he was more than a computer genius. He was also a good actor and simply lent his skills to the department and impressed his immediate superior with his industriousness. When his parents returned to China, he was assigned permanent quarters, and he and David designed and installed a computer with an impregnable fire wall that could do everything David's computer did.

The Tribulation Force around the world would have access to everything David had built into the palace system. But first and foremost, Chang would monitor the escape and stay tied in with the computers at the safe house in Chicago. Everyone would know where everyone else was and how the mission was progressing.

Hannah's practical suggestions proved valuable. She theorized that none of the four should pack or take anything they wouldn't have taken on a real trip of the same duration. "Resist the temptation," she counseled, "to take everything you need for the rest of your life." There should be no hint of closure or finality in how they left their rooms and offices. Of his many computers, David could justify taking only his laptop.

Each of the four planned to leave change on their dressers, things left undone, pictures on the wall, personal items lying about. They were determined to leave anything they would have left if they believed they would be back in a few days. Maybe even a kitchenette light on, a radio playing, favorite clothes or shoes waiting. To-do lists, half-eaten food in the refrigerator, unopened mail.

Mac made a doctor's appointment for the second morning after he was to return. Abdullah sent two uniforms to the palace dry cleaners that he was to pick up the afternoon he returned. David scheduled staff meetings and briefings with key staff members for his entire first week back. He sent memos to colleagues mentioning issues he would like to discuss, "sometime soon when our crazy schedules settle down a bit."

The announcement of Walter Moon's ascension to supreme commander was made without pomp and went barely noticed. David, reporting to him officially the first time, asked casually if his own Israel-related plans should be scrapped in light of the change in personnel at the upper-management level.

"And what were those plans, Director Hassid?"

"Mac and Abdullah were to pilot the Phoenix 216 to Tel Aviv, where Potentate Carpathia and his VIPs would inaugurate the first loyalty mark application site open to the public. We understand he has a couple of days of meetings there first."

"Right. He and Reverend Fortunato have extended sessions with the sub-potentates and their religious representatives."

"Mac and Abdullah would return to New Babylon and return in one of the Quasi Twos, bringing with them the young woman from Medical Services who has experience with the biochip-injection system."

"I can tell you right now, David, that I would not want to see that changed. His Excellency is proud of that aircraft and loves to have it shown off to the citizenry."

"Our thought was that Mac would do a little air show, letting people know what that baby can do."

"The potentate will love that," Walter said.

"I would too, if you thought it wasn't too extravagant to let me go along."

"Not at all. You go right on."

"Mac can really make that thing sing. He and his first officer can put it through its paces with the young woman and me aboard, along with the equipment for the application site. Then upon landing, he can introduce the nurse and the equipment while people line up."

"Perfect. His Excellency will get that site rolling, and we move on to Israel, where he has something else planned."

When the day came, Mac and Abdullah were up before dawn, and David supervised the loading of the Phoenix 216 for the potentate and his entourage's flight to Tel Aviv. The biggest chore for a cargo crew that had recently lost its chief was the loading of a gigantic pig that had been driven in the night before from Baghdad. "Were there no pigs in the Holy Land?" Supreme Commander Moon wanted to know.

A young Russian who had appointed himself acting loadmaster, with David's blessing, said, "The late Mr. Hickman, rest his soul, insisted on the biggest, fattest one in the database, and you're looking at him. Or her."

David liked the Russian because he was by the book, and that came in handy later in the day when Hannah was sent to the hangar to order the loading of cargo onto the Quasi Two. At last, because she had been assigned to David for the work in Israel, she could meet with him in his office without suspicion.

"Worked like a charm," she said. "Look at this."

She slid across his desk the ordering department's copy of the load manifest. Handwritten under Special Note:

> *Following repeated efforts by the acting loadmaster to dissuade Ms. Palemoon and her insistence that approval comes straight from Director Hassid, this plane was, in the opinion of said chief, overloaded by at least 20 percent. If this bill of lading is not countersigned by said director, cargo crew will not be responsible for the airworthiness of this craft.*

"I like it," David said, scribbling his signature. "When we all go down, the investigation will begin and end with our Russian friend. He'll be the grieving hero who wishes we would have listened, will probably be elevated to the position he wants, and we—along with millions of Nicks' worth of plane and cargo—will be sadly explained away as human error. Mine."

"I'm so proud of you," Hannah said, shaking his hand. "You kill me on my first assignment for you." It appeared she was struck by the lack of humor in that, given David's recent loss.

"It's all right, Hannah," he said. "I catch myself using death references all the time, as if even I can't remember."

She sighed. "This really is quite an ingenious plan. I can say that because I had so little to do with it."

"Me too," David said. "If it works, we owe it to Mac and Abdullah. Mac admits to me, if not to Smitty himself, that the best stuff was Abdullah's."

Two mornings later Mac and Abdullah ran through preflight as David and Hannah boarded the Quasi. The Russian fussed and shook his head, trying to get the pilots on his side. Mac told him, "He's the boss. You can only do what you can do, and then you have to remember you're the subordinate."

"Tell yourself that while your plane is going down," he said.

"If I thought it was life or death, I'd stand up to him," Mac said.

"My hands are clean," the Russian said. "Your funeral."

Actually, Hannah had overstated the weight of every piece of equipment she'd loaded onto the plane. The cargo was big and bulky and strained at the cords, but the center of gravity was perfect and would allow Mac to navigate without adversely affecting the attitude of the craft.

The only cargo heavier than it appeared were the pilots and passengers. Hannah had reminded them that should anything float to the surface from the wreckage, it should be their suitcases with clothes, shoes, personal belongings, and toiletries. Everyone carried an extra suitcase so they could leave evidence in the water and still have necessities.

"Watch this," Mac said as he maneuvered the sleek jet out of the hangar and onto the runway. As he made his first turn he increased his speed just enough to make the plane sway off course. "That ought to give loadmaster boy something to shake his head over."

Sure enough, as Mac waited for clearance to take off, operations asked him if he was aware the acting loadmaster had lodged an overload notice. "Doesn't surprise me, tower," Mac said. "We'll take the heat."

"You know enough to abort if she's not accelerating."

"Roger."

Mac made the plane fishtail slightly as he picked up speed down the runway and heard one more warning from the tower as he lifted off. "Caution noted," Mac said.

He set a course for Tel Aviv, but when they were equidistant from there and Resurrection International in Jordan, he informed both towers that he was going to land in Jordan as a precautionary measure. "To be safe, we have arranged to have some cargo driven to Tel Aviv."

Leah, with a printed order originating from David, had talked her way onto the tarmac in a nondescript van. She pulled alongside the left cargo bay, where the pilots and passengers helped load two guillotines and a half skid of injectors into the van. Mac set the autobrakes and the autopilots, and all four occupants crawled into the van and lay on the floor. Leah slowly drove between two hangars where Mac could peek through the window and still see the plane.

He communicated with the tower via portable radio and remote controlled the plane's taxi and takeoff. As the Quasi gradually faded from sight, Mac communicated to the tower through an intentionally distorted connection that he believed he was losing radio power. He asked if they could inform Ben Gurion Tower that he was on schedule, would still perform the air show, and would appreciate it if they could be cleared for landing immediately following. He also hinted that he wished he had unloaded a little more cargo, but he was confident he could handle the rest of the trip.

"Advise abandoning show, considering," Resurrection Tower said.

"Repeat?"

"Consider abandoning air show and proceed to immediate conventional landing."

"No copy, tower."

They repeated their advice, but Mac turned off the radio. Leah pulled out of the airport, and she and the four bogus victims headed for Mizpe Ramon. "We can all keep our fingers crossed," Mac said. "I've seen those Quasis do amazing things based solely on what the flight management system onboard computer tells it to do. But this is a long flight on its own, and I've asked it to do some interesting stuff, barring turbulence."

"Cross our fingers?" Hannah said. "Only God can make this work. You're the expert, Captain McCullum, but if this thing goes down anywhere but deep in the Mediterranean, it won't take long for someone to discover no one was aboard."

* * *

Buck and Chaim had slipped into Israel without incident the day before and checked into the King David. Chaim still seemed out of sorts, having hid two commentaries in his briefcase. Buck thought he looked like a wise old monk in his costume, but privately he wondered whether the old man could command and hold an audience.

From the first time he met Dr. Rosenzweig to interview him as *Global Weekly*'s Man of the Year, Buck had been impressed with how soft-spoken the man was. He carried a heavy Israeli accent, though he had a strong command of English. But his scientific brilliance, his zest for life, and his passion were borne of an intense, distinct, quiet delivery. Would that convey the authority and command the respect he needed to serve as a latter-day Moses? Could this little man with his quiet demeanor lead the remnant of Israel and additional tribulation saints to the promised land of safety?

He would have to challenge the ruler of the world, defy the armies of Antichrist, stand on the front lines against Satan himself. Yes, Chaim had had the fortitude to carry out a murder plot against Carpathia, but by his own admission, he had not known at that time with whom he was dealing.

Buck kept to himself his misgivings and continued to pray. He had inserted himself in so many precarious spots in this very city that somehow the prospect of having a front-row seat to this bit of prophecy seemed par for the course.

It seemed the entire nation had turned out to welcome the potentate at Ben Gurion Airport, then merely waited as anticipation grew for his speech the next day. The initiation of the first public mark application center was one thing, but to see the risen ruler of the nations return to the very city of his death—well, that was what the country was gearing for.

Rumors abounded that His Excellency would flash the ultimate and final nose-thumbing at the stubborn Judah-ites by using for himself one of their most sacred traditional sites, the very Via Dolorosa itself. No one could imagine the scene. Would there be opposition? Protesting? The majority of the populace would welcome its idol and admire his pluck. Could Carpathia take the place of the object of worship for many devout believers, humbly and with class paying homage to Jesus, one whom many now considered his predecessor?

And then his plan to address the world from within the rebuilt temple in Jerusalem . . . could he risk offending two major people groups on the same day? It was no secret that Christians, Messianic Jews, and Orthodox Jews were the last holdouts against Carpathianism. But hadn't Carpathia himself and Reverend Fortunato proved his ascendancy through his resurrection and the deadly miracles? It was one thing to read the myths and legends and perhaps eyewitness accounts of a resurrection centuries ago. But to have seen with one's own eyes a man come back from obvious death and to see his right-hand man imbued with supernatural powers—well, there was a religion for today.

Buck, whose *The Truth* coverage of some of the most dramatic incidents of the day had found an enormous audience of Judah-ites and Carpathianists alike, had engendered worldwide response by his account of some of the first uses of the loyalty enforcement facilitators. He attributed his account to eyewitnesses without identifying himself as one, so no one had a clue where the leak might have come from. He could hope only that even Carpathia sympathizers would be shocked at the inhumanity.

It seemed the entire world was on its way to the Holy Land. Tsion had urged believers to come. Chloe, through the International Commodity Co-op, had recruited pilots, planes, drivers, and vehicles. Meanwhile, Fortunato had rallied Carpathianists from all over the globe to celebrate the brave return of their idol to the location of his murder.

Somehow Jerusalem civic leaders had found the cash and the personnel to put at least a cosmetic sheen on the city. Banners, signs, and landscaping had sprung up seemingly overnight. While the 10 percent of the city that had been ravaged by the recent earthquake still lay in twisted ruins, the eyes of visitors were redirected to the new. If one didn't look too closely, it resembled again the festive place that had welcomed the Global Gala.

Street vendors and kiosks offered palm branches, perfect for waving or laying in the path of the potentate, for just Nicks apiece. Hats, sandals, sunglasses, buttons bearing Nicolae's picture—you name it—you could buy it.

Tel Aviv was choked with foot and vehicular traffic that led to the seashore and the great makeshift amphitheater that would house the mark application equipment. Everything was in place, including covered areas to blunt the brunt of the sun. All that was left to be installed were the injectors, the enforcement facilitators, and the personnel to man the site. People were already in line, eager to be among the first to pledge their loyalty to Nicolae. Part of Buck wanted to be Moishe or Eli or even Chaim, if he could pull it off. As he parked his rental several blocks from the site, Buck dreamed of abandoning reason and shouting to the uninformed, "Don't do it! You're selling your soul to the devil!"

He looked at his watch and quickened his pace. He wanted the best view of the air show, because he knew how much of a show it would be. As he headed for the shore, he called Rayford. "Four minutes to visual contact," he said. "I allowed just enough time and should be in perfect position."

"Remember every detail."

"Don't insult me, Dad. How will I ever be able to forget this? Are they on schedule?"

"On their way. The airport maneuver was successful. They're worried about the flight management system, since there's no chance to personally monitor it. A malfunction could kill innocents."

"I would be one."

"My point. Mac has communicated with Moon's people by phone, telling them when to expect him and letting him know they have a malfunctioning radio."

"How are things at Eagle central?"

"Amazing. These virtual strangers show up with their parts of the construction plan and no supervision until now, and they simply cooperate, get along, and get the work going. They were further along than Albie and I could believe, and we're ahead of schedule. Dozens of choppers are already here. That'll take care of getting the infirm into Petra without walking the gorge. So far we believe we're still undetected, but that won't last long."

Zeke had done such a thorough job on Buck that he started every time he caught a glimpse of himself. As he camped out near a concession stand, he felt as invisible as he had in the underbrush near where Moishe and Eli had been resurrected. Crowds seemed to materialize from everywhere in anticipation of an actual live appearance by Nicolae himself. And he did not disappoint.

A half dozen SUVs rumbled to the site, and the power elite of the world stepped out and strode quickly to the platform to wild applause. Carpathia was at the top of his game, humbly thanking everyone for coming and for making him and the Reverend Fortunato, the ten sub-potentates, and their respective Carpathianism representatives feel so welcome. He produced his usual blather about the improving state of the world, his renewed energy "after three days of the best sleep I've ever had," and how he looked forward to the rest of his time in Tel Aviv and Jerusalem.

"And now," he said with relish, "before a wonderful surprise for you, I give you the new head of our perfected religion, the Most High Reverend Leon Fortunato."

Leon immediately dropped to one knee and took Nicolae's right hand in both of his and kissed it. When he reached the lectern he said, "Allow me to teach you a new anthem that focuses on the one who died for us and now lives for us." In a surprisingly facile baritone and decent pitch, Leon sang a heartfelt and energetic version of "Hail Carpathia, Our Lord and Risen King."

Buck shuddered. He felt the familiar tingle of expectancy when he caught site of the Quasi in the distance and heard its high drone. The crowd had quickly picked up the lyrics and simple, stirring melody, and as their second attempt at it ended, Carpathia returned to praise the technology evident in the new Quasi Two that was bringing "not only the equipment needed for this site, but also a brief display of its capabilities, ably demonstrated by the pilot of my own Phoenix 216, Captain Mac McCullum. Enjoy."

The crowd exulted as the impressive jet came screaming over the city toward the shore. Buck was surprised how low it was, but the people *oohed* and *aahed,* clearly persuaded that this was part of the show. Buck worried that the computer program had somehow jumped off track and might result in disaster.

The plane surged out along the shoreline, the Mediterranean gleaming in the sun. The craft suddenly picked up speed and rolled up onto one side, then flattened, then onto the other before swooping low again. To Buck it seemed to clear the water by no more than ten feet, and he couldn't imagine Mac's having programmed that thin a margin for error.

A long, low turn brought the frisky craft directly over the dignitaries, who tried to maintain their dignity while squinting into the sky, willing themselves not to give in to the urge to duck, ties flapping in the breeze. The Quasi made another turn toward the Mediterranean, running parallel to the water for a blistering quarter mile, then pointing straight up.

The crowd murmured as the thing ascended like a missile, and they had to wonder as even Buck did, though he knew the craft was empty, what it would feel like to be on board. Any astute spectator knew the plane was in trouble before it became obvious. As it slowed to its apex, it drifted backward, nose over tail for a straight plunge toward the water with its underbelly toward the shore.

People talked excitedly and laughed in anticipation of the pullout that would level the plane at the last possible instant. Just when it appeared there was no more room or time, they knew she would rocket parallel, run out to sea, and then turn back toward Ben Gurion to more applause.

Except that the Quasi never pulled out. This plane was not free-falling toward the Mediterranean. No, this multimillion-Nick marvel of modern technology was accelerating, her burner cans hot, the vapor shimmering in a long trail. The strange attitude and angle sent the craft careening toward the shore approximately three-quarters of a mile south of the crowd.

The Quasi and ostensibly her two-man crew and two passengers slammed the beach perfectly perpendicular at near the speed of sound. The first impression of the shocked-to-silence crowd had to be the same as Buck's. The screaming jet engines still resonated even after the plane disintegrated, hidden in a billowing globe of angry black and orange flames. An eerie silence swept in, followed less than half a second later by the nauseating sound of the impact, a thundering explosion accompanied by the roar and hiss of the raging fire.

First one spectator cried out, then another. No one moved. There was no need to run, not away from the crash or toward it. The plane had been there in all its glory, teasing their expectations before fulfilling their worst fears, and now nothing but glowing pieces, the thing all but vaporized in a sand crater.

Another tragedy in a world of pain.

Numbly, people turned toward the sound of the PA system. Carpathia had returned and was speaking so compassionately and softly that they had to strain to catch every word. "Peace be unto you. My peace I give you. Not as the world gives. Would you please quietly make your way from this place, honoring it as the sacred place of the end for four brave employees. I will ask that the loyalty mark application site be appropriately relocated, and thank you for your reverence during this tragedy."

He turned and whispered briefly to Leon, who then stepped to the mike and spread his hands wide, the folds of his robed arms creating great wings. "Beloved, while this sadly preempts and concludes today's activities in Tel Aviv, tomorrow's agenda shall remain in place. We look forward to your presence in Jerusalem."

Buck hurried to his car and phoned Rayford. "The ship is down on the shore. No one could have survived it. On my way back to the voice that will cry in the wilderness."

Buck was struck by an unusual emotion as he merged into traffic that crawled toward the ancient city. It was as if he had seen his comrades go down in that plane. He knew it was empty, yet there had been such a dramatic finality to the ruse. He wished he knew whether it was the end of something or the beginning of something. Could he hope the GC was too busy to thoroughly investigate the site? Fat chance.

All Buck knew was that what he had endured in three and a half years was a walk in the park compared to what was coming. The entire drive back he spent in silent prayer for every loved one and Trib Force member. Buck had little doubt that the indwelt Antichrist would not hesitate to use his every resource to quash the rebellion scheduled to rise against him the next day.

Buck had never been fearful, never one to back down in the face of mortal danger. But Nicolae Carpathia was evil personified, and the next day Buck would be in the line of fire when the battle of the ages between good and evil for the very souls of men and women would burst from the heavens, and all hell would break loose on earth.

DESECRATION

✠ ✠ ✠

To Murf, Timmy Mac, and Mary,
with gratitude.
Special thanks to David Allen
for expert technical consultation.

1

RAYFORD STEELE SLEPT fitfully and awoke tangled in a prickly woolen blanket, knees drawn to his chest and fists balled under his chin. He bolted from the cot and peered out of his tiny makeshift quarters near Mizpe Ramon in the Negev Desert.

The sun cast an eerie, orange glow, but it would soon grow harsh and yellow, shimmering off rock and sand. The thermometer would exceed 100 degrees Fahrenheit by noon—another typical day in the United Carpathian States.

Engaged in the riskiest endeavor of his life, Rayford had cast his lot with God and the miracle of technology. There was no hiding a jury-rigged airstrip on the desert floor—not from the stratospheric cameras of the Global Community. Ridiculously vulnerable, Rayford and his ragtag team of flying rebels—having arrived by the dozens from around the globe—were at the mercy of the most audacious ruse imaginable.

His comrade in the enemy's lair had planted evidence in the Global Community database that the massive effort at Mizpe Ramon was an exercise of the GC's. As long as GC Security and Intelligence personnel bought the great "lie in the sky," Rayford and his extended Tribulation Force would continue what he called Operation Eagle. The name was inspired by the prophecy in Revelation 12:14: "The woman was given two wings of a great eagle, that she might fly into the wilderness to her place, where she is nourished for a time and times and half a time, from the presence of the serpent."

Dr. Tsion Ben-Judah, spiritual mentor of the Tribulation Force, taught that the "woman" represented God's chosen people; the "two wings," land and air; "her place," Petra—the city of stone; "a time," one year—thus "a time and times and half a time" to be three and a half years; and the "serpent," Antichrist.

The Tribulation Force believed that Antichrist and his minions were about to attack Israeli Christ-followers and that, when they fled, Rayford and his recruited fellow believers would serve as agents of rescue.

He dressed in a khaki shirt and shorts and went looking for Albie, his second-in-command. The helpers, rallied via the Internet by Rayford's daughter,

Chloe, from the safe house in Chicago, had only recently finished the landing strip. They had alternated shifts; some were instructed in flight plans by the same personnel who had checked them in and verified the mark of the believer on their foreheads, while others ran heavy equipment or toiled as laborers.

"Here, Chief," Albie said, as Rayford took in the row after row of helicopters, jets, and even the occasional prop plane lining the far side of the strip. "First mission accomplished."

The small, dark, former black-marketer, nicknamed after his home city of Al Basrah, wore his bogus GC deputy commander uniform and had in tow a large young man who, Rayford was not surprised to learn, was from California.

"George Sebastian," the tall, thick blond said, extending a powerful hand.

"Rayf—"

"Oh, I know who you are, sir," George said. "Pretty sure everybody here does."

"Let's hope nobody outside here does," Rayford said. "So you're Albie's choice for chopper lead."

"Well, he, uh, asked that I refer to him as Commander Elbaz, but yes, sir."

"What do we like about him?" Rayford asked Albie.

"Experienced. Smart. Knows how to handle a bird."

"Fine by me. Wish I had time to socialize, George, but—"

"If you have just another minute, Captain Steele . . ."

Rayford glanced at his watch. "Walk with us, George."

They headed to the south end of the new airstrip, Rayford's eyes and ears alert for unfriendly skies. "I'll make it quick, sir. It's just that I like to tell people how it happened with me."

"It?"

"You know, sir."

Rayford loved these stories, but there was a time and place for everything, and this was neither.

"Nothing dramatic, Captain. Had a chopper instructor, Jeremy Murphy, who always told me Jesus was coming to take Christians to heaven. 'Course, I thought he was a nutcase, and I even got him in trouble for proselytizing on the job. But he wouldn't quit. He was a good instructor, but I didn't want a thing to do with the other stuff. I was loving life—newly married, you know."

"Sure."

"He invited me to church and everything. I never went. Then the big day happens. Millions missing everywhere. Smart as I'm supposed to be, I actually tried calling him to see if my session was called off that day 'cause of all the chaos and everything. Later that night somebody found his clothes on a chair in front of his TV."

Rayford stopped and studied George. He would have enjoyed hearing more, but the clock was ticking. "Didn't take you long after that, did it?"

George shook his head. "I went cold. I felt so lucky I hadn't been killed. I prayed, I mean right then, that I would remember the name of his church. And I did, but hardly anybody was there. Anyway, I found somebody who knew what was going on, they reminded me what Murphy had been telling me, and they prayed with me. I've been a believer ever since. My wife too."

"My story's almost the same," Rayford said, "and maybe one of these days I'll have time to tell you. But—"

"Sir," the young man said, "I need another second."

"I don't want to be rude, son, but—"

"You need to hear him out, Cap," Albie said.

Rayford sighed.

George pointed to the other end of the airstrip. "I brought samples of the cargo that's followin' me, soon as the strip can handle a transport."

"Cargo?"

"Weapons."

"Not in the market."

"These are free, sir."

"Still—"

"Our base trained for combat," George said. "When Carpathia told the nations to destroy 90 percent of their weapons and send the other 10 percent to him, you can imagine how that went over."

"The U.S. was the largest contributor," Rayford said.

"But I'll bet we also held on to more."

"What've you got?"

"Probably more than you need. Want to see the samples?"

\+ \+ \+

David Hassid sat in the front passenger seat of the rented van with his solar-powered laptop. Leah Rose was driving. Behind her, Hannah Palemoon sat next to Mac McCullum, while Abdullah Smith lay on his back across the third seat. They had spent the night hidden behind a rock outcropping a mile and a half off the main road, midway between Resurrection Airport in Amman, Jordan, and Mizpe Ramon. The last thing they wanted was to lead the GC to Operation Eagle.

David found on the Net that he, Hannah, Mac, and Abdullah were still presumed dead from the airplane crash in Tel Aviv the day before, but Security and Intelligence personnel were combing the wreckage. "How soon before they realize we're at large?" Hannah said.

Mac shook his head. "I hope they assume we'd a been vaporized in a deal like that. Pray they find small bits of shoes or somethin' they decide is clothing material."

"I can't raise Chang," David said, angrier than he let on.

"I imagine the boy's busy," Mac said.

"Not for this long. He knows I need to be sure he's all right."

"Worryin' gets us nowhere," Mac said. "Look at Smitty."

David turned in his seat. Abdullah slept soundly. Hannah and Leah had hit it off and were planning a mobile first-aid center at the airstrip. "We all fly back to the States when the operation is over," Leah said.

"Not me," David said, and he felt the eyes of the others. "I'm going to Petra before anybody else even gets there. That place is going to need a tech center, and Chang and I have already put a satellite in geosynchronous orbit above it."

His phone chirped, and he dug it from his belt. "Hey," he heard. "You know where I am, because I'm on schedule."

"You don't need to talk in code, Buck. Nothing's more secure than these phones."

"Force of habit. Listen, somebody missed their rendezvous."

"Just say who, Buck. If we were going to be compromised, it's happened already."

"Hattie."

"She was with Leah in Tel Aviv. Then she was supposed to—"

"I know, David," Buck said. "She was to check in with me at dawn today in Jerusalem."

"The old man's there and okay?"

"Scared to death, but yeah."

"Tell him we're with him."

"No offense, David, but he knows that, and Hattie is a much bigger problem."

"She's got her alias, right?"

"David! Can we assume the obvious and deal with the problem? She's supposed to be here, but I haven't heard from her. I can't go looking for her. Just let everybody know that if they hear from her, she needs to call me."

"She crucial to your assignment?"

"No," Buck said, "but if we don't know where she is, we're going to feel exposed."

"The GC lists her deceased, just like us."

"That could be what they want us to think they believe."

"Hang on," David said, turning to Leah. "What was Hattie supposed to do after you two split up?"

"Disguise herself as an Israeli, blend into the crowd in Tel Aviv, go to Jerusalem, check in with Buck, and watch for signs that Carpathia's people recognized either Buck or Dr. Rosenzweig."

"Then?"

"Lie low in Jerusalem until everything blew up there, then head back to Tel Aviv. Someone from the operation was going to pick her up and fly her back to Chicago while all the attention was on Jerusalem and the escape."

David turned back to the phone. "Maybe she got spooked in Tel Aviv and never got to Jerusalem."

"She needs to let me know that, David. I've got to hold Chaim's hand for a while here, so inform everybody, will you?"

+ + +

A few minutes after midnight, Chicago time, Dr. Tsion Ben-Judah knelt before his huge curved desk at the Strong Building and prayed for Chaim. The former rabbi's confidence in his old mentor's ability to play a modern-day Moses was only as strong as Chaim's own. And while Rosenzweig had proved a quick and thorough study, he had left the United North American States still clearly resisting the mantle.

Tsion's reverie was interrupted by the low tone on his computer that could be triggered by only a handful of people around the world who knew the code to summon him. He struggled to his feet and peered at the screen. "Dr. Ben-Judah, I hope you're there," came the message from Chang Wong, the teenager David had left in his place at Global Community headquarters in New Babylon. "I am despairing for my life."

Tsion groaned and pulled his chair into place. He sat and pounded the keys. "I am here, my young brother. I know you must feel very much alone, but do not despair. The Lord is with you. He will give his angels charge over you. You have much to do as the point man for all the various activities of the Tribulation Force around the world. Yes, it is probably too much to ask of one so young, in years and in the faith, but we all must do what we have to. Tell me how I can encourage and help you so you can return to the task."

"I want to kill myself."

"Chang! Unless you have purposely jeopardized our mission, you need feel no such remorse. If you have made a mistake, reveal it so we can all adapt. But you have satellites to manipulate and monitor. You have records to keep in order, in case the enemy checks the various aliases and operations. We are nearly at zero hour, so do not lose heart. You can do this."

Chang's message came back: "I am in my room at the palace with everything set up the way Mr. Hassid and I designed. My machinations are filtered through a scrambler so complex that it would not be able to unravel itself. I could end my life right now and not affect the Tribulation Force."

"Stop this talk, Chang! We need you. You must stay in position and adjust the databases depending upon what we encounter. Now, quickly, please, what is the problem?"

"The problem is the mirror, Dr. Ben-Judah! I thought I could do this! I thought the mark that was forced on me would be an advantage. But it mocks me, and I hate it! I want to take a razor blade and slice it from my head, then slit my wrists and let God decide my fate."

"God has decided, my friend. You have the seal of God upon you, according to our trusted brothers. You did not *accept* the mark of Antichrist, nor will you worship him."

"But I have been studying your own writings, Doctor! The mark of the beast brings damnation, and the Bible says we can't have both marks!"

"It says we cannot *take* both."

"But the heroes, the martyrs, the brave ones accepted death for the sake of the truth! You said a true believer would be given the grace and courage to stand for his faith in the face of the blade."

"Did you not resist? God is no liar. I have told people that they cannot lose the mark of the seal of God and that they need not worry they will lose heart because of their human weakness, but that God will grant them peace and courage to accept their fate."

"That proves I am lost! I did not have that peace and courage! I resisted, yes, but I did not speak out for God. I cried like a baby. My father says I pleaded fear of the needle. When it became clear they were really going to do this, I *wanted* to die for my faith! I planned to resist till the end, though I knew my father would then find out about my sister and expose her too. Right up until the time they stuck me, I was prepared to say no, to say that I was a believer in Christ."

Tsion slumped in his chair. Could it be true? Was it possible God had not given Chang the power to resist unto death? And if not, was he not truly a believer? "Do me this favor," he tapped in slowly. "Do not do anything rash for twenty-four hours. We need you, and there must be an answer. I do not want to gloss over it, for I confess it puzzles me too. Will you stay at the task and fight your temptation until I get back to you?"

Tsion stared at the screen for several minutes, worried he was already too late.

* * *

Rayford's breath caught when he saw what George Sebastian had apparently already shown Albie. "We're not soldiers," he said. "We're flyers."

"With these you can be soldiers too," George said. "But it's your call."

"I wish it were *my* call," Albie said. "If Carpathia's troops are not our mortal enemies . . ."

George handed Rayford a weapon more than four feet long that weighed at least thirty-five pounds and had a built-in bipod. Rayford could barely heft it horizontally. "Carry it nose up," George said.

"I won't be carrying it at all," Rayford said. "What in the world kind of ammo does this thing take?"

"Fifty-caliber, Captain," George said, digging out a clip of four six-inch bullets. "They weigh more than five ounces each, but get this, they have a range of four miles."

"C'mon!"

"I wouldn't lie to ya. A round leaves the chamber at three thousand feet a second, but it takes a full seven seconds to hit a target two miles away, considering deceleration, wind, all that."

"You couldn't hope for any kind of accuracy—"

"It's on record that a guy put five rounds within three inches of each other from a thousand yards. At two hundred yards you can put one of these through an inch of rolled steel."

"The recoil must be—"

"Enormous. And the sound? Without an earplug you could damage your hearing. Wanna try one?"

"Not on your life. I can't imagine a use for these monstrosities, and I sure wouldn't want to produce a sound that would alert the GC before the fun starts."

George pressed his lips together and shook his head. "Should have checked with you first. I've got a hundred of 'em on the way with all the ammo you'd need, some with incendiary tips."

"Dare I ask?"

"A primer inside makes the casing separate if it hits soft material."

"Like flesh?"

George nodded.

Rayford shook his head. "My flyers would never be able to manage these from the air, and that's top priority."

Albie said, "We'll store them. You never know."

"Wanna see the other?" George said.

"Not if it's anything like these," Rayford said.

"It's not." George carefully set the fifty-caliber back into the cargo hold. "These are designed to use from planes or ground vehicles," he said, producing a lightweight rifle and tossing it to Rayford. "No projectiles."

"Then what—?"

"It's a DEW, a directed energy weapon. From a little under half a mile you can shoot a concentrated beam of waves that penetrates clothing and heats any moisture on the skin to 130 degrees in a couple of seconds."

"What does it do to a man's innards?"

"Not a thing. Nonlethal."

Rayford handed it back. "Impressive," he said. "And we appreciate it. My problem is, I don't have combat troops, and even if I did, we'd be no match for the GC."

George shrugged. "They'll be here if you need 'em."

+ + +

Had the day's prospects not been so dire and Buck not so worried about Hattie's whereabouts, he might have chuckled at the sight of Dr. Rosenzweig. The old man opened his door to Buck's knock at the King David Hotel wearing baggy boxer shorts, a sleeveless T-shirt, and the sandals he was to wear with the brown robe. "Cameron, my friend, forgive me; come in, come in."

Buck was used to Rosenzweig's normal appearance: wiry, clean shaven, slight, in his late sixties, pale for an Israeli, and with hazel eyes and wisps of wild white hair reminiscent of pictures of Albert Einstein. Normally the decorated statesman and Nobel Prize winner wore wire-rimmed glasses, bulky sweaters, baggy trousers, and comfortable shoes.

Buck found it hard to get used to his old friend with burnt amber skin, very short dark hair, a bushy beard and mustache, deep brown contact lenses, and a protruding chin caused by a tiny appliance in his back teeth. "Zeke sure did a job on you," Buck said, aware that surviving a horrific plane crash had also left its effects on Chaim.

Dr. Rosenzweig retreated to a chair near where he had laid out his Bible and two commentaries, which he had hidden in his luggage for the flight from the United North American States. A half glass of water sat next to him on a lamp table. His roomy, hooded, monklike robe lay on the bed.

"Why not dress, brother?"

The old man sighed. "I am not ready for the uniform yet, Cameron. I am not ready for the task," Chaim said, his speech altered not only by the appliance but also from damage to his jaw.

Buck checked the closet and found a hotel robe. "Put this on for now," he said. "We've got a couple of hours."

Dr. Rosenzweig seemed grateful to be helped into the terry-cloth garment, but it was white and a one-size-fits-all. The contrast between it and his new skin color, and the hem bunching up on the floor when he sat again, made him look no less comical.

Chaim lowered his head, then looked at the hotel name on the breast pocket. "King David," he said. "Do you not think we should have 'Patriarch Moses' sewn onto the brown one?"

Buck smiled. He could not imagine the pressure on his friend. "God will be with you, Doctor," he said.

Suddenly Rosenzweig shuddered and slid to the floor. He turned and knelt, his elbows on the chair. "Oh, God, oh, God," Chaim prayed, then quickly tore off his sandals, casting them aside.

Buck himself was driven to his knees with emotion so deep he believed he could not speak. Just before he closed his eyes he noticed the rising sun reach between the curtains and bathe the room. He too slipped off his shoes, then buried his face in his hands, flat on the floor.

Chaim's voice was weak. "Who am I that I should go and bring the children of Israel out?"

Buck, despite the heat of the day, found himself chilled and trembling. He was overwhelmed with the conviction that he should answer Chaim, but who was he to speak for God? He had drunk in the teaching of Dr. Ben-Judah and overheard his counsel to Chaim on the calling of Moses. But he had not realized that the dialogue had been burned into his brain.

Silence hung in the room. Buck allowed himself to peek for an instant before squeezing his eyes shut again. The room was so bright that the orange stayed in his vision the way Chaim's question lingered in the air. The man wept aloud.

"God will certainly be with you," Buck whispered, and Chaim stopped crying. Buck added, "And this shall be a sign to you that God has sent you: When you have brought the people out, you shall serve him."

The old man said, "Indeed, when I come to the remnant of Israel and say to them, 'The God of your fathers has sent me to you,' and they say to me, 'What is his name?' what shall I say to them?"

Buck pressed his fingers against his temples. "As God said to Moses," he said, "'I Am Who I Am.' Thus you shall say to the children of Israel, 'I Am has sent me to you. The Lord God of your fathers, the God of Abraham, the God of Isaac, and the God of Jacob, has sent me to you.' This is God's name forever, and this is his memorial to all generations. 'The Lord God of your fathers has seen what has been done to you and will bring you up out of the affliction to a land of safety and refuge.' They will heed your voice; and you shall come to the king of this world and you shall say to him, 'The Lord God has met with me; and now, please, let us journey into the wilderness, that we may sacrifice to the

Lord our God.' But the king will not let you go, so God will stretch out his hand and strike those who would oppose you."

"But suppose they will not believe me or listen to my voice?" Chaim said, so faintly that Buck could barely hear him. "Suppose they say, 'The Lord has not appeared to you'?"

Buck rolled onto his back and sat up, suddenly frustrated and impatient with Chaim. He stared at the old man kneeling there, and Buck's head was abuzz, his eyes full of the color permeating the room. Buck had not felt so close to God since he had witnessed Dr. Ben-Judah's conversing with Eli and Moishe at the Wailing Wall. "Reach out your hand and take the water," he said, suddenly feeling authoritative.

Chaim turned to stare at him. "Cameron, I did not know you knew Hebrew."

Buck knew enough not to argue, though he knew no Hebrew and was thinking and forming his words in English. "The water," he said.

Chaim held his stare, then turned and grasped the glass. The water turned to blood, and Chaim set it down so quickly that it sloshed onto the back of his hand.

Buck said, "This is so that they may believe the Lord God has appeared to you. Now take the water again."

Chaim timidly reached for the glass, and when he touched it, the blood became water, even on his hand.

"Now turn your hand toward God's servant," Buck said. Chaim set the water down again and gestured questioningly toward Buck. And Buck was paralyzed, unable even to move his lips.

"Cameron, are you all right?"

Buck could not respond, light-headed from having stopped breathing. He tried to signal Chaim with his eyes, but the man looked terrified. Chaim pulled his hand back to his chest, as if afraid of its power, and Buck dropped, gasping, his palms on the floor. When he had caught his breath, he said, "Then it will be, if they do not believe you, nor heed the message of the first sign, that they may believe the message of the latter sign."

"Cameron! I am sorry! I—"

But Buck continued, "And it shall be, if they do not believe even these two signs, or listen to your voice, that you shall take water from the river and pour it on the dry land. And the water which you take from the river will become blood on the dry land."

Buck sat back on his haunches, hands on his thighs, exhausted.

Chaim said, "But I am not eloquent, even now since God has spoken to me. I am slow of speech and slow of tongue."

"Who has made man's mouth?" Buck said. "Or who makes the mute, the deaf, the seeing, or the blind? Has not the Lord? Now therefore, go, and he will be with your mouth and teach you what you shall say."

Chaim turned away again and knelt at the chair. "O my Lord," he cried out, "is there no other you can send?"

Buck knew the story. But there was no Aaron. Tsion was at the safe house, not having felt led to help in person. The only other member of the Trib Force with Jewish blood, though he had grown up in Poland, was David Hassid, and he had his own special skills and assignment. Anyway, there was no time to disguise him. If David suddenly appeared in public, he would expose the others who were assumed dead in the plane crash—at least for now.

Buck waited for God to give him an answer for Chaim, but nothing came.

2

JUST BEFORE 9 A.M. and about an hour east of Mizpe Ramon, David told Leah to pull over. "I'm sorry, everyone," he said, "but I just got something from Tsion you need to hear, and I have to get a message to Chang. It's too hard with this thing bouncing in my lap."

"Better hide the van," Mac said. "We're pretty conspicuous."

Leah checked her mirrors, switched into four-wheel drive, and aimed toward the sand. Abdullah sat up, fastened his seat belt, and said, "You would think it was the end of the world."

"Hilarious," Mac said.

Leah stopped a couple of miles off the road in the shadow of a small crag and two scraggly trees. David set his machine on the seat and stood outside, leaning in. The others stretched, then gathered to hear him read Tsion's copy of his back-and-forth with Chang.

"That does not sound so good," Abdullah said. "What to do?"

"I'd take a tone with that boy," Mac said.

"Just what I was thinking," David said. "Somebody update Rayford while I'm working here."

"Got it covered," Mac said, flipping open his phone.

David wrote:

You've got time to interrupt Dr. Ben-Judah but not to check in with your immediate superior? You think this is a game, Chang? What happened to the smart-aleck know-it-all who was going to handle all this in his sleep? Nobody begrudges you your second thoughts and spiritual angst, but you had better come to grips with the fact that you accepted this assignment.

Bottom line, Chang, is that you don't have time for this right now. Too many people are counting on you, and the very success of a life-and-death operation is in your hands. Doing harm to yourself because you can't figure out why God might have let something happen would be the most royally selfish act you could conjure up.

Now as soon as I transmit this, I want a reply from you that you're still on the job. If it is not forthcoming, I'll be forced to initiate the codes that destroy your setup and all the stuff I built there and explained to you. You know we can't risk your doing yourself in and leaving evidence that something was amiss. We need to know Suhail Akbar's plans on investigating the crash site. You need to hack into Sandra's files and be sure we're up-to-date on Carpathia's schedule. And if he holds meetings anywhere you can tap into, you've got to direct that transmission to Chicago, to Mizpe Ramon, and to me. Where's the 216, who's flying it, and is Carpathia using it for meetings?

Hear me, Chang. Something you wrote to Dr. Ben-Judah reminded me of something you said to me about this whole dual mark thing. I know you didn't take it on purpose, though you wanted me to think you got used to it right away and see, as you called it, the "upside." But it's not so easy, is it, when we're all so new at this and something doesn't jibe with what God seems to say about it? Dr. Ben-Judah's the expert, and you've got him baffled, so I won't pretend to have an answer for you. But obviously something's not right, and I don't blame you for wanting to find out how God sees you now.

There's no doubt in my mind that nothing can separate you from God and his love, but you're not going to have peace until you know for sure what really happened that morning. Now, again, let me be clear: This is not your top priority. Most important for you is to complete the tasks I listed above and make sure we're all safe and still undetected. Last we knew, Carpathia was to make his public appearance in Jerusalem at 11:00 a.m. Carpathian time.

But once you're sure everything is under control and that we are all up to speed, try the coordinates I list below. It's a long shot, but I programmed in a string that might allow access to surveillance equipment I did not install. It's possible there's a record, video or audio or both, of what went on that day. The problem is that Building D was a maintenance facility that the brass rarely, if ever, visited. I didn't bother planting bugs there, but for all I know, something was already in place.

You told me in person, and Dr. Ben-Judah a little while ago, that you were trying to get out of taking the mark and were even prepared to tell the truth right up to the time they "stuck" you. I took that to mean up to the time you were given the mark. Maybe that is what you meant, but that's not the way most people refer to the application of the tattoo and the embedding of the chip. I don't know. Maybe I'm reaching. But maybe something else was going on. You never told me what happened from the time you got to the basement of Building D until you got to my office. Do you remember? And if not, why not?

So, first, tell me you're there and doing your job. Give us everything we need. Then see what you can find for Building D. Answer back as soon as you've read this.

David transmitted the message, then let Mac read it before they headed off for Mizpe Ramon. Mac nodded. "How much time do you give him?"

David shrugged. "Not much, but I don't want to nuke the system because he's on a bathroom break either."

Within minutes of their return to the road, David had a reply from Chang: "Following orders. And, Mr. Hassid, I thought the mark was administered in the basement of the palace. Blueprints show Building D several hundred yards from here. I have no memory of having been there. And by being 'stuck,' I meant the anesthetic they gave me prior to the procedure. I thought that was done in the palace too."

* * *

Rayford was encouraged to hear how close the Quasi Two quartet and Leah were to Mizpe Ramon. He told Mac about the weapons George Sebastian was having flown in.

"Smitty will want to see those," Mac said. "He was a combat man before he flew fighters, you know."

Rayford hadn't known, and he could hear Abdullah in the background, demanding to know what they were talking about.

"Just keep a rein on that camel there, desert boy," Mac said.

"You watch it, Texas-cowboy boy. I will learn some slurs about you and torment your ancestors."

"Just a minute, Ray," Mac said. "Smitty, you mean my descendants. My ancestors are dead."

"So much the better. I will make them turn over in their tombs."

"Albie's a gun guy too," Rayford said. "But I've had my fill. Anyway, I need both him and Abdullah in the air."

He was glad to hear of Leah and Hannah's plans, but he fell silent at the news that David wanted to precede everyone to Petra. In the background he heard Hassid say, "I wanted to tell him that myself, Mac."

But as Rayford turned it over in his mind, David's setting up Petra for Chaim and the Israeli believers made sense. He asked Mac what anyone knew about Carpathia's latest plans. Mac brought him up-to-date on the troubles with Chang.

"I need to know as soon as possible," Rayford said. "The parade or whatever you want to call it, the desecration, and the attack could all happen this week."

* * *

Buck carried his Corporal Jack Jensen GC Peacekeeper ID, but he wore civilian clothes and counted on his own new hair and eye color, not to mention his severely scarred face, to throw off anyone who might otherwise recognize him. He and Chaim left the King David by car at 9:30 and picked their way through heavy traffic to within walking distance of the Old City. Chaim's robe was gathered at the waist by a braid of rope, but the hem brushed the ground and hid his feet, making it appear he was gliding.

The two were soon enveloped by the masses who lined the Via Dolorosa, where Carpathia was expected an hour before noon. Buck was struck by the crowds, despite the waning population around the world. The city still showed residue from the earthquake that had leveled a tenth of it, but nothing stopped the opportunists. On every corner hawkers presented Carpathia memorabilia, including real and plastic fronds to toss before him as he would make what was becoming known as his triumphal entry.

Apparently, Nicolae Carpathia the pacifist was no more. Convoys of tanks, military trucks, fighters and bombers on flatbed trucks, and even missiles slowly rolled through the streets. Buck knew they wouldn't fit within the Old City without choking the tiny thoroughfares, but they were pervasive everywhere else.

Buck kept an eye out for Hattie and a hand on his phone, but he had long since despaired of a reasonable explanation for her disappearance. He tried not to think the worst, but reaching him or anyone else in the Trib Force should have been easy for her.

Chaim trudged along beside him, hunched, hands deep in the folds of his brown robe, his nearly bald head hidden by the hood. He had uttered not a word since the hotel-room experience. He had merely traded the King David terry cloth for the burlap-looking but soft flannel robe and slipped into his sandals.

It seemed the city was short of Peacekeepers, local or international. Many shopwindows were boarded up, and anything and everything served as a taxi, even dilapidated private vehicles. At the occasional open appliance store, TVs blared from the windows as onlookers gathered and gaped. Buck put a hand on Chaim's shoulder and nodded toward such a place. They joined the crowd to watch a replay of the crash of the Quasi Two, coverage of rubber-gloved technicians picking through the wreckage, and the somber statements from Potentate Carpathia, Most High Reverend Father Leon Fortunato, Supreme Commander Walter Moon and, finally, Security and Intelligence Director Suhail Akbar.

"Unfortunately," the latter said, "while the investigation continues, we have been unable to confirm the evidence of any human remains. It is, of course, possible that four loyal patriots of the Global Community were vaporized upon impact in this tragedy. Medical personnel tell us they would have died without pain. Once we have confirmed the deaths, prayers will go to the risen potentate on behalf of their eternal souls, and we will extend our sympathies to their families and loved ones."

The news anchor intoned that further investigation revealed pilot error on the part of Captain Mac McCullum and that a New Babylon–based loadmaster had warned the crew of a cargo weight-and-balance problem and had begged them not to take off.

Buck knew he should dread what was coming, but having felt the presence of God at the King David, he was filled with courage. He didn't know how he and Chaim were going to avoid detection or what might happen once Carpathia had initiated his awful deed. He only wished he detected some evidence that Chaim had derived the same confidence from what had happened while they were on their knees.

* * *

David and the others in the van listened to Suhail Akbar's conclusions on the radio as Leah followed careful directions and pulled to within sight of the landing strip outside Mizpe Ramon. David was moved by the shock and sadness in the voice of Tiffany, his assistant, as she was interviewed about him. He wished he could tell her he was all right, but he feared some might already suspect that.

He embraced Rayford, shook hands with Albie, and introduced Hannah all around. As the rest were briefed on plans wholly dependent on the unpredictable Carpathia, David was pointed to Rayford's quarters, where he cleared a table and set up his computer to monitor Chang Wong's success at keeping up with the potentate.

The young man had succeeded in getting the latest copy of Carpathia's itinerary. It showed a meeting including NC, LF, WM, SA, and LH on the FX at 1000 hours. "I know that's now," Chang reported, "but I'm lost after the initials for the four we know. Help?"

"I don't know LH either," David wrote back, "but come on, smart boy. Go phonetic and assume FX is the Phoenix and patch me in there."

"I've got the Akbar press conference downloaded. You want that first?"

"Priorities, man! The press conference was broadcast internationally."

David rustled through his bag for earphones and was slipping them on just as Chang made the connection to the Phoenix. He felt the ambience of the idle plane, and Chang transmitted an inset screen listing GC replacements for

David, Mac, and Abdullah. "A. Figueroa for you," Chang wrote. "Know him? Apparently they're not replacing Nurse Palemoon. Still no idea who LH is."

"No need to prolong this meeting with Hut." That was clearly Carpathia. "Get on with it."

"Right away, Excellency," Moon said. "Leon, uh, Reverend Fortunato would like to update you on the image and the animal."

"I just saw him. Where is he?"

"The head, sir. Feeling some discomfort."

"What is the problem?"

"I don't know."

"He was sitting right here a moment ago, Walter."

"Squirming."

"About what?"

"I'm sorry, sir. I—"

"Well, find out, would you? And get Akbar and Hut in here now."

David heard Moon on a walkie-talkie, directing someone to "let Akbar and Hut board. And have the purser check on Reverend Fortunato."

"Come back?"

"Fortunato. First-class can."

Carpathia roared with laughter in the background. "An apt description, Mr. Moon!"

"I didn't mean that, sir. I was just—"

"Can we get on with this, Walter? Should Fortunato not find his way back here, what is he going to tell me about the image and the animal?"

"He didn't tell me, Lordship, but he seemed very excited."

"Until he went to the bathroom in discomfort."

"Exactly."

After a few seconds of silence, Carpathia barked, "Walter, tell Suhail if he does not have his new man aboard in thirty seconds—"

"Supreme Potentate Carpathia, sir, Security and Intelligence Director Suhail Akbar of Pakistan and Global Community Morale Monitor Chief Loren Hut of Canada."

Akbar said, "Forgive the delay, Potentate, but—"

"Sit, both of you. Director Akbar, where did you find this tall specimen and why is he not still a rodeo cowboy in Calgary?"

David noticed that Carpathia had pronounced the city with emphasis on the second syllable, just like the locals.

"I enjoy ropin' dissidents more," the young man said.

Carpathia laughed. "I was not speaking to you, Chief Hut, but—"

"Sorry."

"—you saved yourself with that answer. Got everything you need?"

"Yes, sir."

"Yes, *Potentate,*" Carpathia corrected. "*Sir* will not cut it when addressing your risen—"

"Absolutely, Excellency, Lordship, Potentate. I was told. I just misspoke there."

"You would *mock* me?"

"No, sir! Potentate!"

"I asked you a question."

"I would not mock—"

"Whether you have what you need, imbecile! Honestly, Director Akbar, this is the best we could do?"

"He is quite accomplished and decorated, Excellency, and merely too intimidated in your presence to exhibit the loyalty he's known for."

"Indeed?"

"Yes, sir, Potentate. I'm loyal to you and always have been."

"And you worship me?"

"Whenever I can."

Carpathia chuckled. "Is every Morale Monitor armed, Hut?"

"Here in Israel, yes, they are. And everywhere else, they will be by the end of next week."

"Why the delay?"

"The sheer numbers. But we have the weapons. It's just a matter of getting 'em to everyone."

"Your top priority is here, Hut. You understand that."

"Absolutely."

"And then it is to arm every one of your troops."

"Yes."

"What is the male-female ratio among the monitors?"

"About sixty-forty males, Excellency."

"About?"

"It's almost exactly fifty-eight to forty-two."

"Excellent. Leon! You're back!"

"Forgive me, Lordship."

"Sit, please. Meet—"

"I'd rather stand, if you don't mind, Excellency. And I have met Mr. Hut. Impressive young man."

"Yes, well, I am glad you find him so. I will decide for myself by the end of next week when I learn whether he has accomplished his task. And I will be interested to know how he handles incorrigibles here."

"In Israel, sir, Potentate?" Hut said.

"That is what 'here' would mean, yes."

"I just can't imagine anybody givin' you a problem here, but if they do—"

David heard Carpathia suck in a breath. "Yes!" he hissed. "Tell me, Hut, what you have in store for people who would be so impudent as to oppose me here in the Holy City."

"They would be immediately apprehended and incarcerated!"

"Wrong!" Carpathia shouted. "Wrong answer! Akbar, I swear, if you do not—"

David could hear Akbar whispering urgently. Then an earnest Loren Hut: "I would have them killed, Potentate. On the spot. Or I would kill them myself!"

"And how would you do this?"

"Probably shoot them."

"Where?"

"In the street. In public. In front of everybody."

"I mean, where on their body?"

"Their body?"

"Where would you shoot them?" Carpathia was speaking quickly now, his delivery liquid, as if savoring the mere thought.

"In the heart or in the head, Potentate, for a sure kill."

"Yes! No! You have how many rounds in your personal sidearm?"

"Me? I'm carryin' a semiautomatic handgun with a nine-round clip."

"Use it all!"

"All?"

"Start with the hands. First one, and when they grab it, the other. As they scream and dance and turn and try to flee, shoot first one foot, then the other."

"I see."

"Do you? As they lie howling and others abandon them in fear, you still have five rounds, do you not?"

"Yes." Hut sounded terrified.

"Both knees, each shoulder. Particularly painful. Make them change their mind, Hut. Make them say they love me and that they are sorry they opposed me. And you know what to do with the final round."

"Heart?"

"A cliché! No creativity!" David heard the leather seat squeak and imagined Carpathia shifting to act this out. "You put the hot muzzle of the weapon to their forehead, right where their mark should be. And you ask if they are prepared to pledge their loyalty. And even if they scream to the heavens that they have seen the light, you give them their own mark. It will be the only round they do not hear or feel. And then what?"

"And then?"

"What do you do, Hut? With a dead victim at your feet, nine rounds in or through the body, surely you do not leave the carcass in the street."

"No, I'd have him hauled off."

"To the guillotine!"

"Sir? Potentate?"

"The price of disloyalty is the head, Hut!"

"But they are—"

"Already dead, of course. But the world is clear on the choice and the consequence, friend. Dead or not, a disloyal citizen sacrifices his head."

"All right."

"Did you know, Hut, that when a live victim is beheaded, the heart can continue to beat for more than half an hour?"

Apparently Hut was stunned to silence.

"It is true. That is a medical fact. Well, we would not be able to test it with a victim you riddled with bullets, would we?"

"No."

"But one day we will get the chance. I look forward to it. Do you?"

"No."

"You do not? I hope you are not too timid for your job, son."

"I'm not. I'll shoot your bad guys and chop their heads off, but I don't need to check the other victims to see if their—"

"Do you not? I do! This is life and death, Hut! Nothing is purer! I have come to give life! But to the one who chooses to place his loyalty elsewhere? Well, he has chosen death. What could be so stark, so clear, so black-and-white?"

"I understand, Potentate."

"Do you?"

"I think so."

"You will."

"Yes."

"Now go. Big week ahead. Be prepared."

David, chilled and disgusted, scribbled himself a note. It would be just like Carpathia to milk this for days.

He heard Carpathia tell Moon to see Akbar and Hut out and to leave him alone with Fortunato. "Excuse us for a moment, would you?" he said to others apparently attending to them in the cabin. After a beat, "Leon, do you not agree that fear is a form of worship?"

"In your case, certainly, Excellency. The fear of our god is the beginning of wisdom."

"I like that. Biblical, is it not?"

"Yes, Lordship."

"Sit, Leon, please!"

"I'd like to, but—well, all right."

Leon let out a tiny cry as he settled.

"What is it, my friend? Food disagreeing with you?"

"No, excuse me, but—"

Carpathia snickered. "A true friend feels free to scratch himself in front of his risen potentate."

"I am so sorry, Excellency."

"Think nothing of it. You are in such discomfort because your hip itches?"

"I'm afraid it's more than that, sir. But I'd rather not—"

"Bring me up-to-date on your assignments, then."

"The animal is in place."

"You may feel free to call it what it is, Leon."

"The pig."

"Oh, I hear it is much more than a pig. A hog! A sow! A huge, ugly, snorting, smelly beast."

"Yes, sir."

"I cannot wait to see it."

"Anytime you wish."

"Well, I am due aboard her not long from now, am I not?"

"Yes, sir. But you would have slipped off."

"Would have?"

"I had a saddle made for you, Excellency."

"Leon! You do not say! A saddle for a pig?"

"And the biggest pig I've ever seen."

"I should hope so! How did you do it?"

"People are happy to serve you, Potentate."

"It must be wide."

"I worry you will feel as if you are doing the splits."

"You look as if *you* would like to, Leon. Stand if you must. There you go! And yes! Scratch if you must!"

"I'm so sorry, Excellency."

"Why, you are wriggling like a schoolboy at his first dance!"

"Forgive me, I'd better head back to the—"

"Go then, by all means. What is it? A bite? An itch can be terribly annoying."

"I wish that's all it was, Excellency. It's quite painful too. When I scratch it, it hurts worse. I am miserable."

"You must have been bitten."

"Perhaps. Excuse me."

"Go!"

"I wanted to tell you about the image."

"And I want to hear it, but I cannot stand to see you in such agony."

"I will return before you must leave and tell you about it."

David sat shaking his head. How he wished he could see what was going on. But the theater of the mind was that much better anyway. Carpathia called someone to fetch Walter Moon, and then he had Moon "bring me that costume."

Moon told him the caravan to Pilate's court would be leaving inside ten minutes. "Did Reverend Fortunato run down the sites for you?"

"No. He seems to be in considerable discomfort."

"Still? Well, we go from Pilate's court to the street. A ways down we have Viv Ivins in place to meet with you as a stand-in for your mother." David heard the rustle of paper—a map, he assumed. "Here's where we have a young woman come out and wipe your face; then two stops later you exhort the women of Jerusalem. And then, after Golgotha, you see Viv again, playing your mother. Then it's on to the Garden Tomb."

Someone seemed to be making a sound through his teeth, and David couldn't imagine Moon doing that in front of Carpathia. Finally Nicolae said, "All right, cut out half of these. This part, and that one with Viv, and this, and the one with the young woman and the speech to the women, this one, and the last one with Viv."

"May I ask—"

"The point is reenacting, Walter. Half of these never happened."

"We don't know that. They're tradi—"

"They never happened. Believe me. I know."

"You'll want to change clothes now?"

"As soon as Leon is finished in the—ah, Leon! Feeling better?"

"Sadly, no."

"So what is it?"

"I'd rather not talk about this with you, sir."

"Nonsense! So is it a bite?"

"I don't think so, sir. But it's large and painful and infected."

"And it is right there?"

"Yes." Leon sounded miserable.

"Poor man! A sore on your left—"

"Yes. On my, uh—on my behind."

Carpathia seemed to be stifling a giggle. "You must tell me about the image."

"On the way, sir. I was hoping you'd notice."

"Notice?"

"My mark."

"Let me see! On your hand! Striking! Two-one-six! Excellent. Thank you, my friend. Does it hurt?"

"I wouldn't know. Because of the, uh—"

"Yes, well . . ."

"Anyway, I'll show you the chosen image. It's life-size and gold and beautiful. And when I had taken the mark of loyalty, I fell before it and worshiped."

"Bless you, Leon. And may you heal quickly."

3

HATTIE KNELT IN HER hotel room in Tel Aviv, thanking God for all she had learned from Tsion Ben-Judah in such a short time. She thanked him for Leah and for Chaim and especially for Buck, whom she had met even before he became a believer. She thanked God for Rayford, who first told her about Christ. She thanked him for Albie who, for some reason, cared so much for her.

As she prayed, she became aware of someone standing in her room. Here she was, one who always checked everywhere before locking herself in. No one else could have been there. Yet the sound of his words made her lower her face to the floor as if in a deep sleep. Suddenly a hand touched her, which made her tremble. And a voice said, "O daughter, you are greatly beloved of God. Understand the words I speak to you, and stand upright, for I have been sent to you."

Hattie had read Dr. Ben-Judah's story of being spoken to in a dream, and she stood, shaking. The voice said, "Do not fear, for from the first day you humbled yourself before your God, your words were heard. I have come because of your words."

"May I know who speaks to me?" Hattie managed.

"I am Michael."

Hattie was too terrified to say anything eloquent. She said, "What are you supposed to tell me?"

He said, "I have come to make you understand what will happen in these latter days." Hattie felt so privileged she couldn't say anything. And Michael added, "O daughter greatly beloved, fear not! Peace be to you; be strong, yes, be strong! Accept not the blasphemy of the evil one and his false prophet. If you are wise, you shall shine like the brightness of the firmament. Those who turn many to righteousness shall shine like the stars forever and ever. Many shall be purified, and made white and refined, but the wicked shall do wickedly; and none of the wicked shall understand, but the wise shall understand."

Hattie sat panting. She took the message to mean she was to speak out against the lies of Antichrist. She prayed that God would give her the courage, because she could only imagine what would happen. She couldn't sleep and asked God if she was deluded. "Why me?" she said. "There are so many older in the faith and better equipped to do such a thing."

Hattie went to her computer and e-mailed Dr. Tsion Ben-Judah, relaying the entire incident. She set the message to be delivered to him after she would have a chance to confront Carpathia the next day, along the Via Dolorosa, she assumed. She concluded,

Perhaps I should have consulted you rather than scheduling this to be sent to you after the fact, but I feel directed to exercise faith and believe God. I look at what I've written and I don't even sound like myself. I know I don't deserve this any more than I deserved God's love and forgiveness.

Maybe this is all silly and will not happen. If I chicken out, it will not have been of God and I will intercept this before it gets to you. But if you receive it, I assume I will not see you until you are in heaven. I love you and all the others, in Christ.

Your sister,
Hattie Durham

* * *

Rayford gathered the troops at the airstrip. He introduced the Fatal Four and explained their roles. "Deputy Commander Elbaz," he said, referring to Albie, "will ferry Mr. Hassid to Petra, where he will begin setting up the communications center. Jewish by blood, Mr. Hassid plans to stay with the displaced believers."

A hand went up, an African's. "Is Hassid the one we have to thank for being able to stand here today?"

"Among many," Rayford said. "But it's safe to say that without the GC thinking this is their own operation, we'd be getting strafed right now."

Someone else asked, "How realistic is it that this can last?"

"We're in no-man's-land," Rayford said. "Once the fleeing Israelis are followed here, it will be obvious what we are doing. As you know, the healthy will walk. But it is quite a journey, and the GC should quickly overtake them. We believe God will protect them. The elderly, the toddlers, and the infirm will need rides. You will recognize them by the mark of the believer and probably also by the fear on their faces. Anyone arriving here in any manner should be transported immediately to Petra by helicopter. Some of these birds have huge capacities, so fill 'em up. Petra is about fifty miles southeast of here. You all have the flight plans."

"It sounds like a death flight," someone called out.

"By any human standard, it is," Rayford said. "But we are the wings of the eagle."

"The co-op didn't call for food or clothing," someone said. "How will these people survive?"

"Anyone want to address that?" Rayford said, and several talked over each other, explaining that God would provide manna and water and that clothes would not wear out.

Finally Rayford raised a hand. "One thing we don't know is timing. Carpathia is on schedule to begin down the Via Dolorosa at 1100 hours. That will end at the Garden Tomb. Whether he will speak from there or head for the temple, we don't know. We've heard that the winning image of the potentate has been chosen and moved to the Temple Mount, where people are already gathering to worship it and take the mark of loyalty."

"Of the beast, you mean!"

"Of course. And many want to do that with Carpathia present. When he learns the crowds are waiting for him, he'll want to be there."

"Are your people in place, Captain Steele?"

"As far as we know. The only one we have not heard from is not crucial to the operation, unless she has been compromised."

"When will Carpathia be opposed?"

"Our man may debate him before he enters the temple. Who knows? The crowd may oppose him—at their peril, of course. You must remember, it is not just Jewish and Gentile believers and unbelievers in Jerusalem. There are also Orthodox Jews who do not embrace Jesus as their Messiah but who have never accepted Carpathia as deity either. They could very well oppose him and refuse to take the mark. Then, of course, there are many undecided."

"They'll decide soon, won't they?"

"Likely," Rayford said. "And many will decide the wrong way. Without Christ, they will succumb to fear, especially when they see the consequences of opposing Carpathia. Okay, it's time for transportation troops to head toward Israel. When the time comes, help anyone who needs it."

"And if we are stopped?"

"You're on your own," Rayford said.

"I'm going to tell them I'm on my way to get the mark of loyalty."

"That's lying," someone else shouted.

"I have no problem lying to Carpathia's people!"

"I do!"

Rayford held up a hand again. "Do what God tells you to do," he said. "We're depending on him to protect his chosen people and those who are here to help them."

+ + +

Buck found a perch overlooking Pilate's court behind several thousand cheering supplicants. The elderly Rosenzweig appeared to gasp for breath without making a sound. Sweat appeared on his forehead, and Buck thought it a credit to Zeke that it did not affect the old man's phony color. This was more than makeup.

Still, Chaim had not spoken since they left the hotel, even when Buck merely asked how he was doing. He only shrugged or nodded. "You'd tell me, wouldn't you, if there was a problem?"

Chaim nodded miserably, looking away.

"God *will* be with you."

He nodded slightly again. But Buck noticed he was trembling. Was it possible they had chosen the wrong Moses? Could Tsion have miscalculated? Tsion himself would have been so much better, having spoken in public for so many years as a rabbi and a scholar. Chaim was brilliant and fluent in his own field, but to expect this ancient, tiny, quaking man with the weak—and perhaps now nonexistent—voice to call down the Antichrist, to rally the very remnant of Israel, to stand against the forces of Satan? Buck wondered if he himself would have been a better choice. Despite Chaim's almost comical getup, he appeared not even to be noticed by the crowd. How could he command an audience?

Buck had worried what he would say or do if GC Peacekeeping forces or Morale Monitors checked for his mark of loyalty. But loudspeaker trucks threaded their way through the streets, announcing that all citizens "are expected to display the mark of loyalty to the risen potentate. Why not take care of this painless and thrilling obligation while His Excellency is here?"

Many in the crowd already had the mark, of course, but others talked among themselves about where the nearest loyalty administration center was. "I'm taking mine at the Temple Mount today," a woman said, and several agreed.

Buck was amazed at the number of men and women who carried toddlers waving real and fake palm branches. Someone passed out sheets with the lyrics to "Hail Carpathia," and when people spontaneously broke into song, others assumed Carpathia had appeared and began a rousing ovation.

Finally Buck spotted a motorcade, led and followed by GC tanks topped with revolving blue and red and orange lights. Between the tanks were three oversized black vehicles. When the convoy stopped, a deafening cheer rose. The first vehicle disgorged local and regional dignitaries, then Most High Reverend Father Leon Fortunato in full clerical regalia. Buck stared as the man straightened his robe, front and back, and slowly continued smoothing it in back.

Finally he kept his left hand just below his hip as he walked, clearly trying to hide it but unable to keep from massaging an apparently tender spot.

The second vehicle produced GC brass, including Akbar and Moon, and then, to a renewed burst of applause and waving, Viv Ivins. From more than a hundred yards away, she stood out among the dark-suited men. Her white hair and pale face appeared supported by a column of sky blue, a natty suit tailored to her short, matronly frame. She carried her head high and moved directly to a small lectern and microphone, where she held both hands aloft for silence.

All eyes had been on the third vehicle, its doors still closed, though the driver stood guard at the rear left and Akbar at the rear right, hand on the handle. Buck noticed that while the attention refocused on Viv Ivins, Leon went to work on his backside, riffling his fingers over the area. He couldn't stop, even when Ms. Ivins introduced him as "our spiritual leader of international Carpathianism, the Reverend Fortunato!"

He muted the applause with his free hand, then asked everyone to join him in singing. He began directing with both hands, but Buck wondered if anyone in the crowd missed it when he kept directing with the right hand and scratching with the left.

Hail Carpathia, our lord and risen king;
Hail Carpathia, rules o'er everything.
We'll worship him until we die;
He's our beloved Nicolae.
Hail Carpathia, our lord and risen king.

Buck felt conspicuous not singing, but Chaim seemed not to care what anyone thought. He merely bowed his head and stared at the ground. When Leon urged the people to "sing it once more as we welcome the object of our worship," people clapped and waved as they sang. Buck, ever the wordsmith, changed the lyrics on the spot and sang:

Fail, Carpathia, you fake and stupid thing;
Fail, Carpathia, fool of everything.
I'll hassle you until you die;
You're headed for a lake of fire.
Fail, Carpathia, you fake and stupid thing.

Finally Suhail Akbar opened the car door with a flourish and a deep bow, and Carpathia bounded out alone. The crowds gasped, then roared and applauded at the youthful man wearing gold sandals and an iridescent white robe, cinched at the waist with a silver belt that seemed to glow with its own light source. As bodyguards in sunglasses and black suits, hands clasped before them, formed a half circle behind him, Nicolae stood with eyes closed, face beatifically pointed toward the clouds and palms outstretched as if eager to embrace everyone at once.

Buck stole a glance at Chaim, who merely squinted at Antichrist in the distance, his face a mix of sadness and disgust.

As the vehicles discreetly pulled away, a camouflage canvas-covered military truck slowly rolled to within twenty feet of Carpathia. Buck saw Fortunato kneel and reach under his robe to vigorously scratch his ankle.

Two uniformed GC Peacekeepers lowered a ramp from the truck; then one jumped onto the trailer and the other reached for a dangling rope. One pulling, the other pushing, they brought into view a monstrous pink sow that, despite its enormous bulk, daintily stepped down the ramp and turned slowly to face Carpathia. The animal, which had clearly been drugged, reacted lethargically to the mayhem.

A black leather strap with a flat leather pad and rounded, covered stirrups was fastened around its middle. Carpathia approached and cupped the pig's fleshy face in his hands, looking over his shoulder to the crowd, which was now laughing and whooping in frenzy. One of the Peacekeepers handed him what appeared to be a noose, which Carpathia draped around the sow's neck.

Then, with one hand on the rope and the hem of his own garment—which he hiked up to his knee—and the other steadied by a Peacekeeper, Nicolae placed his left foot in a stirrup and swung his right over the pig's back. He let go of the Peacekeeper's hand and smoothed his robe back down over his legs, held the rope with both hands, and looked again to the crowd for a response. The pig had moved not an inch under Nicolae's weight, and as he yanked on the rope, tightening the knot around its neck, the spindly legs felt for purchase on the pavement and slowly turned to move the other direction. Nicolae waved as the crowd exulted.

"I don't get it!" a man in front of Buck said, his accent German. "What's he doing?"

"Putting all previous religions in their places, Friedrich!" his wife said, her eyes glued to the scene. "Even Christianity. *Especially* Christianity."

"But what's with the pig?"

"Christianity has Jewish roots," she said, still not looking at him. "What's more offensive to a Jew than an animal he's not allowed to eat?"

The man shrugged, and finally she turned to look at him. "It's hardly subtle."

"That's what *I'm* thinking! You'd think he'd have more class."

"Hey," she said, "you come back from the dead, and you can define class any way you want."

* * *

The spectacle was broadcast internationally on radio and television and via the Internet. David followed it on his computer as Albie helicoptered him toward Petra. Carpathia's brazenness shouldn't have surprised him, but with relatives in Israel and childhood memories of the place, the whole pageant gave him a headache. David's scalp itched, but he dared not scratch it. He pressed his palm over the healing area, which reminded him of Hannah's treating him. That, of course, reminded him of what he was doing when he had collapsed—searching for his missing fiancée in the aftermath of Carpathia's resurrection—and he felt the familiar ache for Annie. He would see her again in less than three and a half years, but that made the second half of the Tribulation seem even longer. If he stayed in Petra, it would be that long before he saw Hannah again too.

David envied Buck Williams and his marriage. He couldn't wait to meet Chloe, the brain behind the International Commodity Co-op. Besides creating an underground where believers would be able to buy and sell from each other when they were restricted from world markets, she had almost single-handedly brought together the personnel for Operation Eagle without having met them. In a cooler behind Albie was food enough to last David until the fleeing Israelis joined him. Maybe God would feed David with manna before the others arrived. He hoped bringing food was not evidence of faithlessness.

Chloe Williams had arranged for the shipment of the latest high-tech computer equipment from various parts of the world, and that too was in the cargo hold. David could only guess how long it would take him and Albie to unload. He studied an aerial sketch of the area and wondered where he would set up and where he would live. "This place sure doesn't look like it could house all the believers in Israel."

"It won't," Albie said. "We're estimating a million people will need refuge. Petra will hold about a quarter of that."

"What do you plan to do with the rest?"

"Expand the borders, that's all. The co-op has tents for the others."

"Will they be safe? Outside Petra, I mean?"

Albie shook his head. "There's only so much we know, brother. This is a faith mission."

* * *

At a little after three in the morning in Chicago, Tsion lay with his hands behind his head on the cot in his study. He fought sleep as he watched the broadcast on his computer monitor. Hearing voices in the commons area, he padded out to find Chloe, Kenny on her lap, watching television.

"Do you believe this?" he said.

"Dis!" Kenny said, and Chloe shushed him.

She pressed her lips together. "I wish I were there."

"You should be pleased with what God has allowed you to accomplish, Chloe. Every report says things are going like clockwork."

"I know. And I've learned what strangers can do when they have a bond."

Tsion sat on the floor. "The vehicle advance should be underway by now."

"It is," she said. "And it's one of the riskiest parts. We didn't have time to put GC insignias on the vehicles."

"God knows," Tsion said.

"Gott!" Kenny said.

"That's *God* in German, you know," Tsion said.

"I doubt he's bilingual," Chloe said. "But apparently Buck is. Never studied another language and now he's speaking Hebrew without even knowing it."

* * *

It was clear to Buck that Carpathia had decided not to address the crowds until either the Garden Tomb or the Temple Mount. All along the Via Dolorosa he confused many by skipping traditional sites, and the people sang and chanted and cheered. Chaim seemed to move more and more slowly, and Buck worried about his health.

The drugged pig was even weaker, however, and the milling throngs found it hilarious somehow when her front legs buckled and she dropped to her knees, nearly pitching Carpathia on his head. They laughed and laughed as aides rushed to help Carpathia off the animal. He formed a gun with his thumb and forefinger and pretended to pop the sow where she rested. Then he dragged a finger across his own neck, as if remembering the actual plan for the porker.

Nicolae strode on while the military truck pulled into view and half a dozen Peacekeepers worked on getting the pig back on four feet and into the trailer. The potentate jogged from the central bus station area up to the traditional site of Calvary, and it was all Buck could do to watch. He was grateful there was no mock crucifixion, but still it turned his stomach to see Carpathia stand at the edge of the Mount and again spread his arms as if embracing the world.

Suddenly Fortunato stepped beside his boss and tried to mimic his pose. He could hold it only so long before having to scratch his backside or his ankle. Some in the crowd seemed to develop sympathetic itches. "Behold the lamb who takes away the sins of the world!" Fortunato bellowed.

Buck gritted his teeth and looked away, noticing that Chaim's breath now came in short gasps.

The sky blackened, and people pulled their collars up and looked around for shelter. "You need not move if you are loyal to your risen ruler!" Fortunato said. "I have been imbued with power from on high to call down fire on the enemies of the king of this world. Let the loyalists declare themselves!"

Buck froze. While thousands jumped and screamed and waved, he stood stock-still, fearing that just about anyone would be able to tell he opposed Carpathia. Chaim crossed his arms and stared directly up at Fortunato, as if daring the man to strike him dead.

"Today you shall have opportunity to worship the image of your god!" Fortunato shouted, but he could be seen only when lightning flashed. Buck saw rapturous looks on the faces of the crowd. "But now you have opportunity to praise him in person! All glory to the lover of your souls!"

Thousands knelt and raised their arms to Nicolae, who remained with his hands outstretched, drinking in the worship.

"How many of you will receive the mark of loyalty even this day at the Temple Mount?" Fortunato implored, now scratching in three places, including his stomach.

Buck stared at the strobelike image of Carpathia's pitiful sycophant, wondering if he would be revealed and struck dead by the man whose power came from the pit of hell.

Thousands rose from their knees to wave, to assure the leader of Carpathianism that they would be there, taking the mark in the shadow of the image. That at least made Buck and Chaim less conspicuous.

"My lord, the very god of this world, has granted me the power to know your hearts!" Fortunato said. The people jumped and waved all the more.

"Not true," Chaim whispered. Buck leaned close. "Carpathia—Antichrist—Satan is not omniscient. He cannot tell his False Prophet what he himself cannot know."

Buck narrowed his eyes at Chaim. So this was it? This was the opposition? This was Moses standing against Pharaoh? Buck gestured as if Chaim should shout it out, make it clear. But Chaim looked away.

"I know if your heart is deceitful!" Fortunato said between claps of thunder, rubbing his body in the flashing light. "You shall not be able to stand against the all-seeing eye of your god or his servant!"

The hymn to Nicolae spontaneously erupted again, but Buck did not have the heart to sing even his own lyrics.

Suddenly the crowd fell deathly still, and the thunder diminished to low rolls that seemed to come from far away. Fortunato stood surveying the massive throng, still scratching, but his eyes piercing. Carpathia had somehow maintained his pose for several minutes. Heads and eyes turned toward a high, screeching voice from the base of Golgotha. The crowd evaporated from around a woman who stood pointing at Carpathia and Fortunato.

"Liars!" she railed. "Blasphemers! Antichrist! False Prophet! Woe unto you who would take the place of Jesus Christ of Nazareth, the Lamb of God who takes away the sin of the world! You shall not prevail against the God of heaven!"

Buck was stricken. It was Hattie! Chaim dropped to his knees, clasped his hands before his face, and prayed, "God, spare her!"

"I have spoken!" Fortunato shouted.

"Yours is the empty, vain tongue of the damned!" Hattie called out. She lifted her pointing finger from the two on the hill and raised it above her head. "As he is my witness, there is one God and one mediator between God and men, the man Christ Jesus!"

Fortunato pointed at her, and a ball of fire roared from the black sky, illuminating the whole area. Hattie burst into flames. The masses fell away, screaming in terror as she stood burning, mighty tongues of fire licking at her clothes, her hair, enveloping her body. As she seemed to melt in the consuming blaze, the clouds rolled back, the lightning and thunder ceased, and the sun reappeared.

A soft breeze made Hattie topple like a statue. People gaped as she was quickly reduced to ash, her silhouette branded onto the ground. As the fire died and the smoke wafted, Hattie's remains skittered about with the wind.

Fortunato drew the attention back to himself. "Marvel not that I say unto you, all power has been given to me in heaven and on the earth!" Carpathia carefully made his way down the Place of the Skull, and the silent crowds moved to follow. As people passed the smoldering ashes, some spit, and others kicked at the powdery stuff.

Buck was overwhelmed with memories of meeting Hattie, of introducing her to Carpathia. He turned and grabbed the praying Rosenzweig by the shoulder and yanked him to his feet. "That should have been you," he hissed. "Or me! We should not have left her with the responsibility!"

He let go of the man's robe and marched off toward the Garden Tomb, not caring whether Chaim kept up with him. If Rosenzweig would not accept the mantle, despite having been a believer even longer than Hattie, maybe Buck was being called to stand in the gap. He didn't know what Carpathia or Fortunato had in store for the tomb, but this time, if need be, he would be the one to oppose Antichrist.

* * *

Rayford hadn't felt as motivated or useful since he had first become a believer. Supervising the advance of his Operation Eagle troops, he had kept just an intermittent eye on what Carpathia was up to. It would be clear when Chaim revealed himself and sent the remnant toward refuge. That would be his cue to start watching for the return to Mizpe Ramon and the airlift to safety.

But now his phone was alive with messages. He took Chloe's call first. "What was that?" she asked. "Clearly Fortunato zapped someone, but they didn't show who! Was it Chaim?"

"I don't know," Rayford said. "Let me call you back."

David reported the same thing just before Rayford heard from Mac and then Abdullah. "I'll call Buck," he told them.

But Buck wasn't answering.

\+ + +

David spent the next hour setting up near what he knew to be a "high place," a site used centuries before by pagans who believed they were sacrificing to their gods by being as close to heaven as possible. He was lonely already, Albie having headed back as soon as he was unloaded. David didn't know how long it would be before he was joined by as many as a million others. So far he had seen only from the air the stunning red-rock masterpiece of a city carved from stone. He couldn't imagine what it would look like from close-up when he had the time to explore.

No one seemed to know what happened with Fortunato and the crowd at Calvary, and David's occasional glances at the screen merely showed the crowds making their way to the Garden Tomb. Then he heard a tone and stood still in the lofty quiet of the high place. Someone was trying to reach him on his computer. David scrambled from a cave he had decided might be his first living quarters. He reached his computer and sat cross-legged before it. The play-by-play from Jerusalem droned on, commentators filling time before the next event, no one specific about what had gone on at the last site. He checked the encoded Operation Eagle site but found nothing new.

The tone sounded again, and he switched screens to receive a summons from Chang Wong in his apartment at the palace in New Babylon.

"I found the mother lode!" Chang had written. "Uploading so you can celebrate with me."

\+ + +

Supreme Commander Walter Moon was clearly not comfortable in front of a crowd, particularly the size of the one pressing around the Garden Tomb. A microphone and sound system had been hastily rigged up for him, and he read nervously from notes. Buck had been among the first to arrive, and he had lost Chaim.

The attitude of the crowd had changed. The festive, eager anticipation had given way to dread, yet no one seemed to feel free to leave. They had seen the power delegated to Leon Fortunato, and surely no one wanted to give the impression they weren't following through on their commitment to taking the mark of loyalty.

"Thank you for being with us today," Moon began. "As you may know, I'm Global Community Supreme Commander Walter Moon, and I'm filling in temporarily for the Most High Reverend Father Fortunato as he goes on ahead to prepare for Potentate Nicolae Carpathia's address at the Temple Mount an hour from now."

"Is he all right?" someone called out.

"Oh, he's better than all right," Moon said, "judging by his performance at Golgotha." He apparently thought that would elicit a laugh, and when it didn't, he searched his notes again to find his place.

Buck called Chang. "We on secure phones, Mr. Wong?" he asked. "Be sure."

"Yes, sir, Mr. Williams, and I just communicated with Mr. Hassid by computer that—"

"Sorry, kid, no time. Check with Medical and see what's happening with Fortunato."

"I'm sorry?"

"What didn't you hear?"

"I heard you all right, sir, but I was under the impression you were with the pageant there in Jerusalem. That's where Carpathia and Fortunato are, along with—"

"Fortunato's disappeared and they're saying he's gone on ahead for preparations."

"I'm on it." Buck heard him tapping at a keyboard. "Good call, Mr. Williams," he said. Now reading, "'Classified, top secret, director-level eyes only . . . Most High Reverend, blah, blah, blah, under care of palace surgeon in chief, mobile unit, Jerusalem, blah, blah.' Ah, here it is. 'Preliminary diagnosis rash, several boil-like epidermal eruptions, testing for carbuncles.' That's all that's here for now."

4

TSION WORRIED ABOUT CHLOE. She had a lot on her mind, sure, and the pressure had to be enormous. But she seemed so distracted. No doubt she dreaded Buck's being in yet another dangerous situation, but if Tsion had to guess, being so far from the action frustrated her. Everyone in the Trib Force had, at one time or another, tried to impress upon Chloe that she was among its most crucial members and that few people anywhere could do what she was doing. But she was a young woman of action. She wanted to be there in the thick of it. Tsion wished he could dissuade her.

He had enjoyed the respite from his uncomfortable cot, but while he and Chloe monitored the boring TV feed from Jerusalem, waiting for the fiasco to reach the Garden Tomb, Kenny had fallen asleep. Chloe looked at Tsion apologetically as she attempted to rise with the toddler in her arms. She poked out a free hand and he reached to pull her off the couch. As she made her way to Kenny's crib, Tsion thought he heard something from his study. Chang again?

He padded back and found a timed message composed two days before and sent automatically on a schedule determined by the sender. It read:

Dr. Ben-Judah,

Please pass this along to my brothers and sisters in Christ, old friends and new. I don't know what to make of it except that I believe I have been called of God to risk my life for the cause. It certainly was nothing I was seeking, and I hope you all know I have no grandiose view of myself.

I knelt to pray in my hotel room in Tel Aviv . . .

Tsion stood, his spirit recognizing that this was no frivolous imagining from a new believer. He bent over the screen and read, finally groaning and making his way back out to where Chloe was watching the end of a brief speech by Walter Moon. "I have forwarded a message to your computer that you need to read right away," he said, knowing his quavering voice scared her.

"Is it Buck?" she said. He shook his head. "Chaim?"

"No," he said. "Please wake the others. We will want to pray. And you will want to call Cameron."

* * *

David ignored the signal that he had a message from Tsion. That could wait as he checked the upload from Chang. Not only had the young man pieced together recordings from devices in the palace, starting in the Wongs' guest apartment the morning in question, but he had also taken the time to include a translation, where necessary, from Chinese to English. David would check the tape with Ming later to be sure the translation was accurate. Chang began with the news that he remembered "only snatches of this before the so-called anesthetic. You must have known they use no such thing."

David knew. But he hadn't known any more than Chang about what had really gone on. Chang's pieced-together production began with the audio of another loud argument between him and his father. Mrs. Wong kept trying to pacify her husband and son, but she failed.

"You will be among the first to take the mark of loyalty!" the subtitles read, as David listened to Mr. Wong fiercely whisper to the boy in Chinese.

"I will not! You are loyal to Carpathia. I am not!"

"Do not speak such heresy to me, young man! My family is loyal to the international government as I have always been to my superiors. And now we know the potentate is the son of god!"

"He is not! I know no such thing! He could be the son of Satan for all I know!"

David heard a slap and someone crashing to the floor. "That was I," Chang wrote.

"You saw the man resurrected! You will worship him as I do!"

"Never!"

A door slammed. Then a phone call. "Missah Moon! Son talk crazy. Say he not want mark, but he just scared of needle. You got tranquilizer?"

"I can get a tranquilizer, Mr. Wong, but it comes in the form of an injection."

"Injection?"

"Shot. Hypodermic needle?"

"Yes! Yes! I can do."

"You can administer the injection?" Moon said.

"Pardon?"

"Give the shot?"

"Yes! You bring!"

They rang off, and Mr. Wong apparently returned to where Chang had locked himself in a room. "You be ready to go in ten minutes!"

"I'm not going!"

"You will go or answer to me!"

"I'm answering to you now. I'm telling you I'm not going. I don't want to work here. I want to go home."

"No!"

"I want to talk with Mother."

"Very well! Mother will talk some sense into you."

A few minutes later, a quiet knock. "Mother?"

"Yes." The door opened. "Son, you must do what your father says. We cannot survive in this new world without showing loyalty to the leader."

"But I don't believe in him, Mother. Neither does Ming."

A long silence.

"She doesn't, Mother."

"She told me. I fear for her life. I cannot tell your father."

"I agree with her, Mother."

"You are a Judah-ite too?"

"I am, and I will say so if he tries to make me take the mark."

"Oh, Chang, don't do this. I will lose both of my children!"

"Mother, you must read what Rabbi Ben-Judah writes too! At least look into it. Please!"

"Maybe, but you cannot cross your father today. You take the mark. If you are right, your God will forgive you."

"It doesn't work that way. I have already made my decision."

Mr. Wong returned. "Let's go. Mr. Moon is waiting."

"Not today," Mrs. Wong pleaded. "Let Chang think about it awhile."

"No more time for thinking. He will embarrass the family."

"No! I won't! You can't make me."

Silence. Mrs. Wong: "Please, Husband."

"Very well, then. I will tell Mr. Moon not today."

"Thank you, Father."

"But someday soon."

"Thank you for your patience, Husband."

It sounded as if both parents left. Then the door opened.

"Father?"

"You *will* think about it?"

"I have been thinking about it a lot."

The bed squeaked. "Father, I—ow! Don't! What are you doing? What's that?"

"Help you relax. You get some rest now."

"I don't need any rest! What did you do?"

"See? You are not so afraid of needles! That did not hurt."

"But what was it?"

"It will help you calm down."

"I'm calm."

"You rest now."

The door shut.

"How long take, Missah Moon?"

"Not long. Don't wait too long or he won't be able to walk by himself."

"Okay. You help."

They returned.

"Chang?"

"Mmm?"

"You come with us now?"

"Who?"

"Missah Moon and me."

"Who?"

"You know Missah Moon."

"No, I—"

"Come on now."

"I will not . . . take . . . the . . . mmm . . ."

"Yes, you will."

"No, I'm . . ."

The sound continued with the two men encouraging Chang to walk with them and his mumbling in Chinese and English about not wanting to, refusing.

"Now, watch this," Chang wrote. "The surveillance camera from the hallway picks up that they're pretty much carrying me down the hall, and look what I'm doing! Crossing myself! I don't even know where I got that! And look! Here, I'm pointing toward heaven! I know it's impossible to prove what I was doing, since whatever they gave me made me forget even the conversation with my mother. And I can't tell what words I'm trying to form there, but I had to be trying to say I was a believer!"

The whole rest of the way, as Chang tied together the angles from various cameras all the way to the corridor leading to Building D, David watched as Walter Moon and Mr. Wong prodded Chang along. At some point a third man met them, carrying a camera. The boy wept, pointed, and tried to form words. Moon reassured the photographer and any onlookers that the boy was "all right. He's okay. Just a little reaction to medication."

Most shocking was that indeed there was a surveillance camera in Building D, and by the time they got Chang there, he was unconscious, eyes shut, drooling, moaning. "Take cap off," his father said. "Smooth hair."

A woman technician who looked Filipino fired up the device. "This boy, he is all right?" she said.

"Fine," Moon said. "What's the region code for the United Asian States?"

"Thirty," the tech said, setting the implanter. "I worry that I might get into trouble for—"

"Do you know who I am?"

"Of course."

"I'm telling you to do your job."

"Yes, sir."

The woman swabbed Chang's lolling forehead with a tiny cloth and pressed the mechanism onto his skin, producing a loud click and whoosh. "Thank you," Moon said. "Now be sure this place is ready for the lines in about an hour."

The technician left, and Mr. Wong and Mr. Moon took turns keeping Chang sitting up. "Thing wears off almost as fast as it goes to work," Moon said.

"Fix hair more," Mr. Wong said, slapping Chang's cheeks. "We get picture."

The photographer shot Chang with a digital camera. The boy came to, and his father held the camera before his face. "There!" Mr. Wong said. "Look at new employee, one of first to take mark!"

Chang wobbled and pulled back, reaching for the camera and trying to focus on the picture. His shoulders drooped and he glared at his father, his face stony. When Mr. Wong and Mr. Moon stood him up, he said, "Where's my hat?"

He jammed it on and stood there until he regained his equilibrium. He said something to his father in Chinese. "I said, 'What have you done?'" he wrote.

"Someday you thank me," Mr. Wong said. "Now we go somewhere, relax till interview."

"I remember just snatches of the argument from the apartment and my father injecting me," Chang wrote. "I have a vague recollection of the flash of the camera and being angry at my father. After that, I only remember sitting awhile in a side room with Moon and my father and slowly realizing that I had been given the mark of loyalty. I wanted to kill them, but I was also embarrassed. I worried what you would think. I was still out of it for the first part of our meeting, but then I decided to play tough, try to make you see the benefits. You already know, though I didn't, that the meeting in your office was recorded too. I can send that if you need reminding, but that's the end of this upload."

David sat back and realized his legs had gone to sleep. He rolled his head to release tension in his neck. By now, Chang should be busy monitoring the Garden Tomb. David clicked on the message that had been forwarded from Tsion.

* * *

Buck's phone vibrated in his pocket, but he didn't look to see who it was. He was prepared if God was calling him to take Chaim's place, but that was foolish. Surely, the chosen one would be an Israeli believer. Maybe Chaim was calling, lost in the crowd. Buck reached in his pocket and shut off the phone. Let him find his own way. It was long past time for the man to accept his role. Nobody said it would be easy. Nothing was easy anymore. But God's call wasn't hard to recognize. It was clearly on Chaim. If Hattie had the courage to do what she had done, surely knowing she couldn't survive, how could any of them shirk their duties again?

Carpathia stepped from behind a draped curtain near the tomb, smiled, and opened his arms to the crowd. Less animated now, they merely applauded. The cheering, the kneeling, the waving were over. It seemed most just wanted to get on to the Temple Mount and get in line for their mark. That would insure them against the fiery fate of the crazy woman at Mount Calvary.

"I was never entombed!" Carpathia announced. "I lay in state for three days for the world to see. Someone was said to have risen from this spot, but where is he? Did you ever see him? If he was God, why is he not still here? Some would have you believe it was he behind the disappearances that so crippled our world. What kind of a God would do that? And the same people would have you believe I am the antithesis of this great One. Yet you *saw* me resurrect my*self*! I stand here among you, god on earth, having taken my rightful place. I accept your allegiance."

He bowed and the people clapped again.

Moon stepped back to the mike and read from his notes. "He is risen!"

The people murmured, "He is risen indeed."

"Come, come," Moon said, smiling nervously. "You can do better than that. He is risen!"

"He is risen indeed!" the crowd responded, and someone applauded. The ovation slowly built until Moon held up a hand to silence it. "We are providing you with the opportunity to worship your potentate and his image at the Temple Mount, and there you may express your eternal devotion by accepting the mark of loyalty. Do not delay. Do not put this off. Be able to tell your descendants that His Excellency personally was there the day you made your pledge concrete."

Speaking softly now and making it sound like an afterthought but still clearly reading, Moon added, "And please remember that neither the mark of loyalty nor the worshiping of the image is optional."

A helicopter nosed into place and descended to take Carpathia and the rest of the dignitaries to the Temple Mount. Buck still had not seen Chaim since he had left him near Golgotha. The crowd dispersed quickly, and many ran in the direction of the loyalty mark application site.

\+ + +

Unable to reach Buck, Rayford called Tsion. "Hattie was the victim, then, in whatever happened at Calvary?" he said.

"That is what we have pieced together, Rayford. We are grieving and praying, but we are also amazed at how God spoke to her."

Rayford had known Hattie for years, of course, and had once jeopardized his marriage over her. He asked to speak with Chloe. At first neither he nor his daughter could speak. Finally Rayford said, "It seems forever ago that you met her."

"Think she accomplished anything, Dad?"

"That's not for me to say. She obeyed God, though. That seems clear."

"What was he up to there?"

"I don't know. If someone in the crowd was wavering, who knows?"

"They would see what happens when you oppose Carpathia," Chloe said. "I don't see what it was all about. Everybody here is speechless."

Rayford tried to dismiss an intruding thought but couldn't. "Chloe, are you envious?"

"Of Hattie?"

"Yeah."

"Of course I am. More than I can say."

He paused. "Kenny okay?"

"Sleeping." She paused. "Dad, am I a scoundrel?"

"Nah. I know how you feel. At least I think I do. But most people see you as a hero, hon."

"That's not the point. That's not why I'm envious."

"What then?"

"She was there, Dad! Front lines. Doing the job."

"You're—"

"I know. Just put me out there next time, will ya?"

"We'll see. You heard from Buck?"

"Can't raise him," she said.

"Me neither. I imagine he and Chaim are treading carefully."

"I just wish he'd check in, Dad."

* * *

Buck waited at the Garden Tomb until the crowd was gone. He no longer cared how suspicious he looked. He scanned the horizon and worried how he would explain himself if he lost track of Chaim. Buck forgot what he had been trying to prove or elicit by leaving him. He was still frustrated with Chaim, of course, but what should he expect from an old man who had endured so much? Chaim had hardly sought this assignment.

Buck moseyed among the olive trees, drawing glances from guards. He recalled his first meeting with Dr. Rosenzweig. He had known of him years before that. It wasn't common to become friends with story subjects, especially Newsmakers of the Year, but it was fair to say the two had been close.

The afternoon sun was hot. The garden was still a beautiful spot, untouched by the earthquake. An armed guard, so still he could have been a mannequin, stood by the entrance to the tomb. "May I?" Buck said. But the guard did not even look at him. "If I'm just a minute?" he tried again. Zero response.

Buck shook his head and ducked inside as if to say, "If you're going to stop me, stop me."

Still the guard did not move. Buck found himself in the surprising coolness of the sepulchre. The slanting light from the entrance cast a thin beam where Christ's burial cloth would have been left. Buck wondered why Carpathia and his people had left this place untouched.

He looked up quickly when Chaim shuffled in. Buck wanted to say something, to apologize, anything. But the man was weeping softly, and Buck didn't want to intrude. Chaim knelt at the slab of rock where the light shone, buried his face in his hands, and sobbed. Buck leaned against the far wall. He bowed his head, and a lump invaded his throat. Could it be that Chaim would claim here the final vestige of courage to follow through on his assignment? He looked so small and frail in the oversized robe. He seemed so overcome that he could hardly bear up under his grief.

Buck heard a sigh from outside, then the creak of leather, the crunch of footsteps. The entrance filled, the silhouette of the guard nearly blotting out the light.

"Just give us another minute, please," Buck said.

But the guard remained.

"If you don't mind, we'll leave in just a moment. Sir? Do you speak English? Excuse me . . ."

The guard whispered, "Why do you seek the living among the dead? Fear not, for I know that you seek Jesus, who was crucified. He is not here, for he is risen, as he said."

Chaim straightened and whirled to look at Buck, squinting at him in the low light.

"You," Buck said to the guard. "You're—you're a—"

But the guard spoke again. "And the Lord spoke to Moses, saying: 'This is the way you shall bless the children of Israel. Say to them: "The Lord bless you and keep you; the Lord make his face shine upon you, and be gracious to you; the Lord lift up his countenance upon you, and give you peace."'

"'So they shall put my name on the children of Israel, and I will bless them.'"

"Thank you, Lord!" Chaim rasped.

Buck stared. "Sir? Are you a—"

"I am Anis."

"Anis!"

The guard stepped back outside. Buck followed, but the guard was gone. Chaim emerged, shielding his eyes from the light. He grabbed Buck's arm and pulled him to a souvenir shop, where a young woman looked as if she was about to close up. Buck found it hard to believe such a place remained open in the Global Community.

Chaim seemed to know exactly what he was looking for. He picked up a small, cheap replica of the container in which the Dead Sea Scrolls had been found in the caves of Qumran. He took it to the young woman and looked to Buck, who felt in his pockets for cash. "Two Nicks," she said.

He peeled off the bills, and Chaim opened the package on the way out. He discarded the box and the tiny printed scroll and put the palm-sized clay vessel and its miniature top in the pocket of his robe. Suddenly his gait was sure and quick, and he led Buck back the way the crowd had come. Golgotha was deserted now, but Chaim found his way to where Hattie had been immolated. He knelt by what was left of her ashes and carefully scooped a handful into the little pot and pressed the top down.

Chaim put the container of ashes back into his pocket and stood. "Come, Cameron," he said. "We must get to the Temple Mount."

5

DAVID HASSID SAT stunned in the desolate aloneness of a "high place" in Petra. While the pagan religions of the ancient past had used such locations to sacrifice to their gods in a helpless, desperate attempt to gain favor, all he wanted was to express to God his thanks for grace. Nothing he could do or say or give or sacrifice could gain what God had offered him freely.

All he could see were sky, clouds, valleys, and the occasional bird of prey. It was clear this would be the ideal cradle of refuge for the remnant of Israel, for those who recognized that Jesus *was* the long-awaited, prophesied Messiah. It was he who would put the finishing touches on God's love affair with his chosen people.

But David's own field of expertise, the gadgets and marvels of technology, would not allow him the proper reprieve to exult in the holiness of God's plan. He had needed, desperately, to know the truth about Chang. But now the news of Hattie Durham had rocked him. And here was a brief message, laboriously pecked in from Buck's cell phone, that said David needed to monitor activities at the Temple Mount. Yet another message from Tsion announced a final teaching on the next event on the prophetic calendar, Antichrist's desecration of the Holy of Holies.

Well, that was not news, and Tsion had taught on it before. But if the rabbi felt the need to clarify and crystallize it for his billion constituents, who was David to argue? The teaching, according to the worldwide Net announcement, would be posted that evening. The very people who might most benefit from Tsion's teaching could be in flight for their lives the next day.

David tapped in the string that brought up the GCNN coverage of the Temple Mount activities and patched the other half of his screen to an ancient video monitor that kept a twenty-four-hour eye on the Wailing Wall. He was convinced the camera there had long been forgotten, and it was amazing it still functioned, though the fidelity of the picture had been compromised by the years.

David wanted to set his transceivers in strategic spots to maximize the wireless network he envisioned for Petra. But here came yet another urgent message from Chang:

I have been invigorated, encouraged, motivated. Dr. Ben-Judah concurs that the record vindicates me, though he fears Carpathia and his henchmen are devious enough to come up with the idea of doping known believers and forcing the mark on them, and that would be a catastrophe.

I know you're busy, but I thought you'd want to know: I intercepted a private transmission between Moon and the head of both Peacekeeping and Morale Monitor forces in Jerusalem. Apparently Walter was spooked by the change in the attitude of the crowd with the martyrdom of the dissident and the sudden mystery about Fortunato's health. Without informing Carpathia, he has directed that armed personnel lead the way in taking the mark of loyalty. If you haven't checked it out yet, connect with the Temple Mount and look at the chaos.

So that's what had Buck so exercised that he would use his phone to transmit a message to David's computer. The official GC broadcast feed showed news anchors nearly beside themselves with glee. "Look at the hundreds and hundreds of military vehicles lined up for miles outside the Old City. They would clog the narrow passageways leading to the Temple Mount anyway, but these are mostly unmanned. Only a skeleton crew of, we would estimate, perhaps one uniformed Peacekeeper maintains custody over every four or five vehicles. We've learned that the ones left to keep an eye on the rolling stock are personnel who have already received the mark of loyalty. The rest are leading the way today, becoming patriotic examples to civilian citizens. Indeed, by the time the massive crowd followed Potentate Carpathia's pageant through the Via Dolorosa and half of what is known as the Stations of the Cross from the now defunct Christian religion, the loyalty mark application site was already clogged with Peacekeepers and Morale Monitors.

"Many citizens are less than happy about the delay, but the response from Global Community brass, including His Excellency himself, appears to be one of delight. Here's the scene at the Temple Mount, where tens of thousands of GC personnel noisily jockey for position to receive the mark, and civilians, patient for the most part, are lined up all the way outside the city walls, awaiting their turn.

"Here's our reporter, Anika Janssen, with several civilians deep in the long lines."

The tall, blonde reporter exhibited mastery of at least the rudiments of several languages as she guessed nationalities and began the interviews in citizens' native languages. Mostly she asked in their tongue if they understood English so translators would not be forced to employ captioning on the screen.

"What do you make of this?" she asked a couple hailing from the United African States.

"It is exciting," the man said, "but I confess we expected to be among the first in line, rather than the last."

His wife stood nodding, appearing reluctant to speak. But when Ms. Janssen waved the microphone in her face, the woman proved opinionated. "Frankly, I believe someone in authority should insist that the soldiers make way. Those men and women are assigned here. Many of us are on pilgrimages. I do not mean to criticize the risen potentate, and I can hardly blame those who happened to have the privilege of transportation and could get here first, but this does not seem fair."

Other interviews unearthed the same attitudes, though most seemed almost bemused, or perhaps afraid, to complain publicly. "Oh, look at this special privilege," Anika Janssen said. "Here is Ms. Viv Ivins of the potentate's inner circle, working the lines, so to speak. She is greeting people, thanking them for their patience. Let's see if we can get a word with her."

To David it seemed that Ms. Ivins had been directed to a spot where a camera crew would notice her. She was certainly ready with the party line. "I'm so impressed with the loyal citizens and their patience," she said. "His Excellency was overwhelmed at the eagerness of his own personnel to become examples and role models of loyalty."

"Though there is, of course, a visible, prominent guillot—"

"Which we prefer to call a 'loyalty enforcement facilitator,'" Ms. Ivins said with an icy smile. "Of course it represents the gravity of such a decision. In all candor, Anika, our intelligence reports indicated that we might face more opposition here, in the traditional homeland of several obsolete religions. Yet I daresay that except for the lunatic fringe, such as the lone representative of the Judah-ites who recklessly challenged the power and authority of our Most High Reverend Father of Carpathianism, any such stubborn opponents have learned to keep silent."

"Speaking of Reverend Fortunato, ma'am, what can you tell us? We expected to see him here."

"Oh, he's fine, and thanks for asking. He's fallen a bit under the weather, but he passes along his greetings and best wishes and expects to be back at full strength tomorrow for the potentate's blessing of the temple."

"The blessing of it?"

"Oh, yes. We believe that the beautiful temple was constructed with the best intentions to honor god, even though the ancients were unaware that they had misplaced their devotion. They meant to serve the one true god but were misled by their own innocent ignorance and erred only in directing worship to their chosen deity. We now know, of course, that our risen potentate is clearly the god above all pretenders and that his rightful place is in a house built for the one who sits high above the heavens. By making this his own house of worship, he lends credibility and authenticity to it, and it becomes the true house of god."

"Besides the Judah-ites and their seemingly large Internet following—"

"Clearly inflated and exaggerated, of course."

"Of course. But besides that faction, might you expect opposition from holdout Jews who are neither Christ-followers nor Carpathianists?"

"An excellent question, Anika. You do your homework. This should give the lie to those who say that the Global Community News Network is merely a shill for the potentate."

"Thank you. So, opposition?"

"Well, that is what we were led to believe and what we have been prepared for. It is still possible, of course, but I am confident that the display of divine power exhibited a few hours ago, along with the overwhelming enthusiasm on the part of GC personnel and these thousands of civilian pilgrims, will far overshadow any pockets of resistance."

"But should either the Judah—"

"Have you seen the image of the potentate yet, Anika? The Reverend Fortunato judged the entries himself, and the winner is stunningly beautiful."

"I have not seen it yet, but I hope to—oh, I'm getting word that our cameras do have a shot of the image, so let's go there now."

\+ + +

Buck had found the area around the Temple Mount—now dominated by the gleaming new temple itself, of course—so congested that he and Chaim were able to just amble around and observe, drawing little attention despite Chaim's getup. Buck looked for other dissidents and was surprised to see that many Orthodox Jews were allowed at the Wailing Wall. He could not get close enough to see whether anyone in that area had the mark of the believer, but he suspected that these devout men of prayer were prepared to oppose the desecration in more overt ways than merely wearing their own religious garments and assembling to pray at the Wall.

The rest of the Mount had been entirely converted into a virtual factory of efficiency. Dozens and dozens of lines herded the Carpathian faithful, or at least the fearful, to stations where they were registered, processed, prepped, and finally marked. Most accepted the mark on their foreheads, but many took it on the backs of their right hands.

Unlike what Buck had seen in Greece, here it was not assumed that anyone in line would decide against taking the mark. In the middle of all the processing stations stood one gleaming guillotine with two operators sitting patiently beside it. Ten feet behind the contraption was a freestanding frame with a drape hung on it, apparently so that the disembodied could be discreetly hidden once the awful sound and severing had served their deterring purposes. No sense rubbing it in, apparently.

As the supplicants finished showing each other their marks and posing for pictures, they were funneled to the east-facing steps of the new temple, where the winning image of Carpathia stood at the second to the top level. The temple itself, a sparkling replica of Solomon's original house for God, was pristine but simple on the outside, as if modest about the extravagance of cedar and olive wood, laden with gold and silver and brass on the inside.

The image of Carpathia appeared bigger than life, but everything Buck had heard about it confirmed it was as exact a copy of Carpathia himself as it could be. Behind it were two freestanding pillars outside the entrance to the temple, and Buck could see what appeared to be a recently fabricated platform, made of wood but painted gold, in the porch area. "Carpathia leaves out nothing," Chaim told him. "That appears to be a replica of where both Solomon and the evil Antiochus—a forerunner of Antichrist—stood to address the people in centuries past."

Many gasped and fell to their knees upon their first glimpse of the golden statue, the sun bouncing off its contours. Unlike the mark application lines, this one moved more quickly as dozens at a time rushed the steps and knelt—weeping, bowing, praying, singing, worshiping the very image of their god.

Chaim's revulsion mirrored Buck's own. The older man looked more resolute than before, but his carriage evidenced no more authority or promise. And still he limped. Buck wasn't sure how Chaim felt or how he would know when the time had come to reveal himself as the enemy of Carpathia, but the more he watched, the more Buck could barely contain himself. He realized that these people—all of them—were choosing Satan and hell before his very eyes, that he was powerless to dissuade them, and that their choice was once and for all.

Buck estimated it would be hours before the GC personnel made way for the average citizens. He found a ledge where Chaim could rest and asked if he wanted anything to eat. "Strangely, no," Rosenzweig said. "You eat. I could not."

Buck pulled a meal bar from deep in his pocket and showed it to Chaim. "You're sure?"

Chaim nodded, and Buck ate. But he could enjoy nothing while thousands eagerly lined up to seal their doom. He swallowed his last bite and was scanning the area for a water vendor when a cloud shouldered in front of the sun and the temperature dipped. As if on cue, conversation stopped and the colossal crowd stared at the image, which seemed to rock forward and backward, but which Buck was convinced was an illusion.

The voice emanating from it was no illusion, however. Even the rabbis at the Wall stopped praying and moving, though Buck could see they were not in the line of sight of the statue.

"This assemblage is not unanimous in its dedication to me!" the image boomed, and grown men fell to their faces, weeping. "I am the maker of heaven and earth, the god of all creation. I was and was not and am again! Bow before your lord!" Even the workers in the mark application lines froze.

Buck worried that he and Chaim would be exposed. Though the old man had to be as frightened as he, neither, of course, knelt before the evil apparition. He forced himself to look away to see if he could find other believers, and he was amazed at what appeared to be row after row of them at the far edges of the crowd. Some were dressed in fatigues; many could have easily been mistaken for GC. They had to be part of Operation Eagle! They must have driven into Jerusalem, found the schedule delayed, and wandered to the Temple Mount, prepared to help with the evacuation.

Buck wanted to signal them, to wave, to approach, to embrace his brothers and sisters. But who knew how far God chose to extend his protection? The Trib Force believed Chaim would somehow be supernaturally insulated, but other brave believers had been martyred for their faith and courage.

"The choice you make this day," the golden image roared, "is between life and death! Beware, you who would resist the revelation of your true and living god, who resurrected himself from the dead! You who are foolish enough to cling to your outdated, impotent mythologies, cast off the chains of the past or you shall surely die! Your risen ruler and king has spoken!"

The sun reappeared, the people slowly rose, and more and more tourists and pilgrims joined the lines. Buck was jealous that those undecided should hear both sides, yet when he looked at Chaim, he saw passivity.

As if the man could read his mind, Rosenzweig said, "They know their options. No one alive could doubt that a great gulf is fixed between good and evil, life and death, truth and falsehood. This is the battle of the ages between heaven and hell. There is no other option, and no honest man or woman can claim otherwise."

Well, the old man knew how to summarize, but his was still the plaintive, weak voice with the thick Hebrew accent that reminded Buck of Jewish comedians or storytellers or timid scholars—the latter of which Dr. Rosenzweig certainly was. Buck wanted the faith to believe that somehow this modest specimen of a man—so endearing, so engaging—could capture the imaginations, the hearts, and the minds of people on the fence.

And yet that was not Chaim's calling. He was to stand against Antichrist—the evil one, the serpent, that old dragon, the devil. He was to go nose to nose with Carpathia himself, while instructing the remnant of Israel that it was time to flee unto the mountains. Different as Chaim appeared now, whom would he fool? He had been a close personal friend of Carpathia's long before Nicolae became head of the Global Community. Chaim had once murdered the man! Would Chaim not be immediately recognized from his voice alone?

Buck wondered if he himself had the faith to believe this was anything but folly. If there were really a million Messianic believers in Israel, surely they were unarmed. Carpathia was of no mind to let them go! He had more than one hundred thousand armed, plainclothes Morale Monitors and uniformed Peacekeepers. His arsenal of personnel carriers, tanks, missiles, rocket launchers, cannons, rifles, and sidearms was on public display. Buck shrugged. Only God could do this, so that made the thought process simple: You either believed it or you didn't.

Buck had long since chosen to believe it and had to fight a grin. Resting apparently none too comfortably beside him was the most unlikely leader of a million people. He couldn't wait to see how God would manage this.

By now, thousands of GC personnel had received the mark of loyalty and clogged the area, celebrating. Their commanding officers urged them to return to their posts and vehicles, and suddenly the Temple Mount was alive and animated again. Men and women, clearly midlevel managers, stood in a ring near the front of the application centers, using bullhorns to remind the newly tattooed and chip-implanted novices that their spiritual obligation for the day was only half over.

"The worship of the image is not optional!" they shouted. "You are not finished here until you have knelt before the living, breathing, speaking image of your lord."

It wasn't as if they were trying to get out of it, Buck thought. But many of these were young people, excited, flushed with renewed enthusiasm for their work. They had seen the manifestations of power. They had seen the potentate himself. They knew that Nicolae's making the temple of Jerusalem his own was tantamount to setting up residence in the mosque of the Dome of the Rock or moving into what had once been St. Peter's Basilica in Rome. This would establish him once and for all the true god over all. And if the pathetic, weakened resistance had breath left, if they truly believed there was a higher being than His Excellency the potentate, where were they? Did they dare reveal their true loyalties in the face of such overwhelming evidence?

And now the revelers were still again. Those with the bullhorns clicked them off. Activities in the line ceased. Carpathia himself appeared in his white robe and gold sandals and shiny rope belt, smiling, standing one step above his own image, arms outstretched. The silence gave way to a deafening roar. Would he speak? Would he touch the worshipers? Some must have wondered the same, for they slowly rose from their knees on the steps and moved as if to advance upon him. He stopped them with a gesture and nodded toward the center mark application line.

There came his top military brass in all their finery, dress uniforms with white gloves, broad epaulets, buttons with sheens as reflective as their patent-leather shoes, capturing and emitting every staggered ray from the sun. Two dozen men and women, heads high, bearings regal, marched to the front of the line, upon command stood at ease, and removed their uniform caps.

One by one they proudly submitted to the application of the mark of loyalty, each receiving it on the forehead, several asking for the largest, darkest tattoo so their homeland designations would be obvious from far away.

As the last of these were processed, the effusive crowd bubbled over again as the dozen members of the Supreme Cabinet marshaled themselves into the staging area. The last three in this contingent were Suhail Akbar, Walter Moon, and Viv Ivins. While the military brass knelt on the temple steps, worshiping Carpathia and his image, the cabinet waited until all were processed and then moved as one to the worship area.

All the while, Carpathia stood benevolently above and beside the gold statue, gesturing toward these humble shows of loyalty. The assembled masses cheered as Mr. Akbar turned to display the giant black *42* that dominated his olive forehead. Then Mr. Moon displayed his *-6.* Finally Viv Ivins chose to kneel on the pavement as she received the application, then slowly stood and turned. Buck could not make out her number, but he knew her native Romania was part of the United Carpathian States and that her discreet tattoo would read *216.*

The cabinet solemnly filed to the temple steps as the military brass moved away. One by one they ascended the steps on their knees, finishing by wrapping their arms around the statue's feet, their shoulders heaving with emotion. Carpathia watched each one and dismissed them by placing his open palm upon their heads.

Finally only Viv Ivins remained at the base of the steps. The crowd seemed to wait breathlessly as she delicately removed her shoes, tugged up the hem of her suit's smart skirt, and began the slow, awkward climb on her knees. Her hose ran with the first brush against the marble, but people seemed to moan in sympathy and in awe of her willingness to publicly humble herself.

When finally she reached the third step from the top, she only briefly embraced the statue, then detoured slightly and went up one more stair, where she prostrated herself and kissed Nicolae's feet. He raised his face to the sky as if he could imagine no greater tribute. After several minutes, he bent and reached for her, but instead of letting him help her up, she enveloped his hands and kissed them. Then she reached into a pocket and pulled out a vial—Buck assumed perfume—and poured it over Nicolae's shoes.

Again Carpathia feigned a humbly honored look and shrugged to the crowd. Finally, as he pulled Ms. Ivins to her feet, leaving her a step below him, he turned her to face the crowd and rested his hands upon her shoulders.

When the cheering died, Nicolae announced, "I personally will be watching from a secure vantage point, all night if need be, until the last devoted citizen of Jerusalem receives the mark of loyalty and worships my image. And tomorrow at noon, I will ascend to *my* throne in *my* new house. I shall initiate new ceremonies, and you will see again the 'friend' who accompanied me for as long as she could on the journey today. And you shall be led in worship by the Most High Reverend Father of Carpathianism."

Nicolae waved farewell to every side, and the application lines began moving again.

"I'm tired," Buck said. "Shall we head back to the hotel to rest and pray and prepare for tomorrow?"

Chaim shook his head. "You go, my friend. I feel the Lord would have me stay."

"Here?"

Chaim nodded.

"I'll stay with you," Buck said.

"No, you need your rest."

"How long will you be?"

"I will be here until the confrontation."

Buck shook his head and leaned close. "Will that be before or after the desecration?"

"God has not told me yet."

"Chaim, I cannot leave you. What if something happens?"

The old man waved him off.

"I can't, Chaim! Leave you here overnight? I would never forgive myself."

"If what?"

"If anything! You sit here until the last mark has been applied, and it will be obvious you have not taken it. I have reason to think Carpathia is watching, as he said. He doesn't sleep anymore, Chaim. He'll know."

"He will know soon enough anyway, Cameron. Now you go. I insist."

"I need to check with the others. This is lunacy."

"Excuse me? Cameron, you believe God has chosen me for this?"

"Of course, but—"

"He is leading me to stay and prepare. Alone."

Buck pulled out his phone. "Just let me—"

"I will take full responsibility for the consequences. I have my inspiration in my pocket. The young woman who modeled the ultimate obedience once personally encouraged me, though she was newer even than I to the things of God. You are to go back to the hotel to rest and pray for me."

"God told you that too?"

Chaim smiled sadly. "Not in so many words, but I am telling you that."

Buck was at a loss. Should he pretend to go but watch from somewhere? He'd done that before. It was near this very spot where he had seen the two witnesses resurrected and raised to heaven.

"I see your mind turning," Chaim said. "You do what I say. If it is true that I have been assigned this task, it must come with some leadership responsibility."

"Only for a million people."

"But not for you?"

"I am not a Messianic Jew, sir. I am not part of the remnant of Israel."

"But surely you must obey one who is to answer for so many."

"I don't follow your logic."

"Ah, Cameron! If this had to do with logic, what would I be doing here? Look at me! An old man, a scientist. I should be in an easy chair somewhere. But here I am, a stranger in my own mirror, trying to tell God he has made a mistake. But he will not listen. He is more stubborn than I. He uses the simple to confound the wise. His ways are not ours. The sheer illogic of his choice of me forces me to the reluctant acceptance that it must be true. Am I ready? No. Am I willing? Perhaps. After tonight, I must go forward, willing or not. Do I believe he will go before me? I must."

It seemed as if he and Chaim were alone in a sea of people. Buck pawed at the pavement with his foot. "Chaim, I—"

"Cameron, I would ask that you call me Micah."

"Micah?"

Chaim nodded.

"I don't get it."

"I am not foolhardy enough to call myself Moses, and I shall not reveal my real name to Nicolae unless God wills it."

"So you'll tell him you're Micah? Why not Tobias Rogoff? Zeke has provided identification for that and—"

"Think about it and you will understand."

"Should I bring *my* fake ID? You don't have a new name for me, do you?"

"You will not need a name."

"You know this for sure."

"As sure as I know anything."

"So I bring no ID."

"Your papers show you as Jack Jensen. Should that be checked, you would be traced to the ranks of the Peacekeeping forces. How would you explain a GC corporal assisting the leader of the opposition?"

"So I'll come without papers, and if they demand to know who I am, I'll be deemed a vagrant."

"I will identify you as my assistant, and that will satisfy them."

Buck looked away. "I liked you more when you were *less* sure of yourself."

"And Cameron," Chaim said, "you *are* a vagrant. We all are. We are aliens in this world, homeless if anyone is."

Buck thrust his hands deep into his pockets. He couldn't believe it. The old man had persuaded him. He was going to leave his old friend alone overnight with the enemy. What was the matter with him? "Micah?" was all he could say.

"You go," Chaim said. "Check in with our comrades and your family. And think about my new name. It will come to you."

6

THE LATE-AFTERNOON SUN made beautifully interesting shadows on the stunning architecture at Petra. David found a sweater and pulled it over his shoulders as he descended from the pagan high place to one of the most remarkable cities ever built.

The various buildings, tombs, shrines, and meeting places had literally been carved out of the striking red sandstone millennia before, and though its early history was largely speculative, the place had become a tourist attraction in the 1800s. David wondered how the new inhabitants of such a surreal place would make comfortable quarters out of solid rock. Tsion taught that God had promised food from heaven and that clothes would not wear out, but what would substitute for insulation, inner walls, and anything resembling modern conveniences?

The place was spread out, many of its famous edifices—the treasury of the pharaoh, the five-thousand-seat amphitheater, the various tombs—connected by a system of gorges and channels dammed and rerouted by the various civilizations that had inhabited the area.

Because David had arrived by helicopter, he had to hike down to the main level to find the sole passageway leading in. With rock walls over three hundred feet high in places and a trail at points fewer than seven feet across, it was no wonder most visitors rode in on camel, donkey, or horseback. Operation Eagle would fly in the majority of the newcomers, because a million fleeing Israelis would be slaughtered if they had to traverse the roughly mile-long, narrow pass on foot.

David could see why the city had been a perfect defensive location thousands of years before. Tsion taught that the Edomites, who inhabited it at the time of Moses, had refused to let the Israelites pass through. But in this world of high-tech travel, only a miracle could protect unarmed innocents from aerial attack. Rather than a place of refuge, David decided, without the hand of God this place could just as easily be ideal for an ambush.

David's life was no longer about creature comforts. And he had forgotten what leisure time was. Until the Glorious Appearing, this would be where the action was, where miracles would be the order of every day. David's people would inhabit this city, and they would be preserved from illness and death, insulated against their enemies until Messiah liberated them. If witnessing that meant making his bed on a slab of stone, it was a small price to pay.

David made sure his laptop had stored enough solar energy to remain charged throughout his night in a cave. In the loneliness at the top of the only world he knew anymore, reading Tsion's post of what he believed Antichrist was up to, monitoring the Carpathian-fashioned news, and communicating with his confreres would serve as David's only links to humanity.

He expected, within twenty-four hours, the first of more company than he would know what to do with. How a million of them could be contained even in the vast area surrounding the great rock city was a problem only God could solve. David had learned not to wonder and question, but to watch and see.

\+ + +

After checking in with everybody and doing his best to explain how he could leave Dr. Rosenzweig unattended, Buck spent that evening at the King David Hotel, watching television with Chaim's Bible before him. He read through Micah, seeing parallels between the Jerusalem of then and now, and he noticed the reference to Moses. Clearly the book was a dire promise of God's judgment, but Buck was not enough of a theologian to decipher its significance to Chaim. The prophecies seemed to deal more with the first coming of Christ than with the Rapture or the Glorious Appearing, but perhaps Chaim planned to use some of the words and phrases when dealing with Carpathia.

The TV news carried mostly rehashes of the day's events, but at least Hattie's death was not glossed over as it had been during the live coverage. While she was not identified—the death of a woman they thought dead previously would have been a puzzler to the GC anyway—it was clear she had died for her courage to speak against the ruler of this earth. The GC did not spin it that way, of course, but boasted of the event, using it as an example of the veracity of Carpathia's claims of deity and confirmation of Fortunato's role as his designate of spiritual power and wonders.

Buck was exhausted, nearly too much so to sleep. But as he stared at the ceiling in the darkness, eager to get back to the Temple Mount at first light, he rehearsed Dr. Rosenzweig's insistence on being called Micah rather than Chaim. The names floated before his mind's eye. And he slept.

\+ + +

In the middle of the afternoon in Chicago, Dr. Tsion Ben-Judah printed out the message he planned to post on the most popular Web site in history. He asked Ming and Chloe to review it for him. They sat together and read.

To my dear tribulation saints, believers in Jesus the Christ, the Messiah and our Lord and Savior, and to the curious, the undecided, and the enemies of our faith:

It has now become clear that Nicolae Carpathia, the one who calls himself the ruler of this world and whom I have identified (with the authority of the Holy Scriptures) as Antichrist, along with his False Prophet Leon Fortunato (upon whom has been bestowed the audacious title of the Most High Reverend Father of Carpathianism), has scheduled what the Bible calls the desecration of the temple.

As with every other connivance and scheme Antichrist believes is the product of his own creative mind, this event too has been prophesied in the infallible Word of God. The Old Testament prophet Daniel wrote that during this time in history "the king shall do according to his own will: he shall exalt and magnify himself above every god" and "shall speak blasphemies against the God of gods."

The prophet also predicted that "many countries shall be overthrown," but one of those that "shall escape from his hand" is Edom. That, friends, is where Petra lies. Sadly, Egypt will not escape his hand. He will have "power over the treasures of gold and silver, and over all the precious things of Egypt; also the Libyans and Ethiopians shall follow at his heels."

Antichrist has already begun fulfilling the prophecy that "he shall go out with great fury to destroy and annihilate many." Fortunately, someday "he shall come to his end, and no one will help him."

It is also prophesied that the great archangel, Michael, shall "at that time" stand up. He is referred to as "the great prince who stands watch over the sons of your people," referring to the remnant of Israel, those Jews like myself who have come to believe that Jesus is the Messiah. Praise God, Daniel also foretells that "at that time your people shall be delivered, every one who is found written in the book."

You know from my previous teachings that the book referred to is the Lamb's Book of Life, in which are recorded those who have trusted in Christ for their salvation. While I cannot be more specific now, due to the divine experience of a beloved colleague just within the last few days, I believe that Michael the archangel is standing watch and that deliverance is nigh.

Jesus himself referred to the prophecies of Daniel when he warned of "the 'abomination of desolation' . . . standing in the holy place." I believe he was speaking of the very desecration planned by Antichrist.

Many were confused before the rapture of the church and believed that the apostle Paul's second letter to the Thessalonians referred to that event when he spoke of "the coming of our Lord Jesus Christ and our gathering together to him." We may rejoice, because it is now clear that Paul was speaking of the Glorious Appearing. Paul writes, "Let no one deceive you by any means; for that Day will not come unless the falling away comes first, and the man of sin is revealed, the son of perdition, who opposes and exalts himself above all that is called God or that is worshiped, so that he sits as God in the temple of God, showing himself that he is God."

Our hope is in the promise that "the lawless one will be revealed, whom the Lord will consume with the breath of his mouth and destroy with the brightness of his coming. The coming of the lawless one is according to the working of Satan, with all power, signs, and lying wonders, and with all unrighteous deception among those who perish, because they did not receive the love of the truth, that they might be saved."

We often wonder, when the truth is now so clear, why not everyone comes to Christ. It is because of that very deception! People did not, as Paul says above, "receive the love of the truth." He says it is "for this reason God will send them strong delusion, that they should believe the lie, that they all may be condemned who did not believe the truth but had pleasure in unrighteousness." Can you imagine it? There are people who know the truth, know their futures are doomed, and yet still they take pleasure in sin! A warning, if you are one of those: Due to your rebellion, God may have already hardened your heart so that you could not change your mind if you wanted to.

Now, if the following is not a description of the two who would steal the souls of every man and woman, I don't know what is: "So they worshiped the dragon who gave authority to the beast; and they worshiped the beast, saying, 'Who is like the beast? Who is able to make war with him?' And he was given a mouth speaking great things and blasphemies, and he was given authority to continue for forty-two months. Then he opened his mouth in blasphemy against God, to blaspheme his name, his tabernacle, and those who dwell in heaven. It was granted to him to make war with the saints and to overcome them. And authority was given him over every tribe, tongue, and nation.

"All who dwell on the earth will worship him, whose names have not been written in the Book of Life of the Lamb slain from the foundation of the world."

What could be clearer? If you are in Christ, you are eternally safe and secure, despite all that we will have to endure these next three and a half years. If you are undecided, I plead with you to make your choice while you are still able. That many have already had their hearts hardened by God—a truth that may go against what we once believed about him—is nonetheless clearly the danger of putting off receiving Christ.

One day I pray God will grant me the privilege of speaking in person to the Israeli believers who will soon be led to safety and out of the way of harm from Antichrist. Brothers and sisters in the Lord, pray as the final events of this halfway point of the Tribulation period unfold and usher in the rest of the time before the Glorious Appearing.

Your friend in Christ,

Tsion Ben-Judah

Tsion was intrigued that the young women were clearly finished reading, but rather than give him their assessment, they whispered among themselves. He cleared his throat and looked at his watch.

"Ming has a wonderful idea, Tsion," Chloe said. "She believes her brother could pirate his way into the Global Community News Network and counter Nicolae's next message to the world with your own teaching."

"What, put my message text on the screen?"

"No," Ming said. "You. Live. In essence you would debate his every point."

"But how?"

"I will check with Chang, but the little camera atop your monitor, the one you now use only to project your image to the Tribulation Force when they are away from Chicago, could be used to broadcast over television as well."

"But might we risk showing clues that would give away where we are?"

"We would have to work to preclude that, of course."

"But isn't this Dr. Rosenzweig's purview?" Tsion said. "Shouldn't he be the one to counteract Antichrist?"

"He probably will be," Chloe said. "Any showdown between those two will likely be on international television anyway."

"Then what would I be needed for?"

"Once the flight to Petra has commenced, Nicolae will be speaking out against you and us so-called Judah-ites. It would be like a tag-team wrestling match. When Chaim is no longer there to oppose him in person, you will debate him via his own television network," Ming said.

Tsion quietly accepted the manuscript back and keyed in the transmission. "I like the way you think, Mrs. Toy," he said.

"So do I," Chloe said. "I only wish you could have mentioned Hattie by name or said that she was a Trib Force member."

"I did not want to give away that we even have people in the area, though I am certain the GC assumes we do."

"And yet, Tsion," Chloe said, "you mentioned Petra by name."

The rabbi covered his mouth with his hand. "I did, didn't I?"

"I meant to say something before you transmitted it," Chloe said.

"That is why I wanted you to review it."

"I'm sorry, Tsion. I assumed you had a reason."

"It is not your fault," he said, collapsing into a chair. "What was I thinking?"

\+ + +

Rayford's eyes popped open at dawn, and a decision he debated in the night had been made. Leah and Hannah had their mobile medical unit stocked and ready, so Leah could do double duty, also monitoring the incoming and outgoing Israelis. That meant Rayford didn't have to stay at Mizpe Ramon. Surely he would be of more use actually piloting a chopper.

He dressed quickly and found the airstrip buzzing. The sun shimmered over the horizon, and Rayford realized it wouldn't be long until he and his comrades would begin counting the days to the end, the *real* end—the Glorious Appearing and the Millennial Kingdom. Much had to happen first, of course, but the head-spinning pace of the last several weeks would give way to precious lulls between the final judgments of God before the Battle of Armageddon. Then things would pick up again. How he looked forward to at least some rest between crises. Rayford pushed his hair back and put on his aviator's cap. The next few days would determine whether he or his loved ones would even survive to the end.

\+ + +

Buck stood under a shower as hot as he could stand it, but the King David must have installed some sort of a regulator. After a few minutes, the water went tepid, then cold. With personnel and energy decimated, there was only so much to go around.

Buck put only enough money in his pocket to be sure he could top off the tank of the car. Following Chaim's advice, he left his wallet and ID in the room. Finding a place to park was harder than the day before, and he had to walk a half mile farther, finally reaching the streets lined on each side with empty military personnel carriers.

Early as it was, the Temple Mount was already filling. Colossal TV monitors were visible from every vantage point, and people waiting for the noon festivities occupied themselves watching the GC network feed and waving when they saw themselves on-screen.

To Buck's great relief, Chaim was in plain sight, not far from where the two witnesses had traded off sitting while the other preached. Buck rushed to Dr. Rosenzweig, who sat with his knees up, staring into the sky. "Morning, Chaim," he said, but the man did not acknowledge him. "Sorry," Buck added quickly. *"Micah."*

Chaim smiled faintly and turned to him. "Cameron, my friend."

"Did you eat?"

"I remain sated," Chaim said.

"Remarkable."

"God is good."

"And has he encouraged you, strengthened you, empowered you?" Buck pressed.

"I am ready."

He didn't sound ready. In fact, he sounded and looked even wearier than he had the day before. "Did you sleep?" Buck said.

"No. But I rested."

"How does that work?"

"There is nothing like resting in the Lord," Chaim said, as if he'd been doing it all his life.

"So, what happens now?" Buck said. "What's the plan?"

"God will reveal it. He shows me only what I need to know, when I need to know it."

"Terrific."

"I detect sarcasm, Cameron."

"Guilty. I'm a plan-your-work-and-work-your-plan kind of a guy."

Chaim reached for Buck's hand and rose unsteadily. He groaned as joints cracked. "But this is neither my plan nor my work, you understand."

"I guess. So we just stand around waiting?"

"Oh no, Cameron. Even I do not have the patience to wait until high noon."

"And if Carpathia does not appear until then?"

"A ruckus will flush him out."

Buck found that intriguing, but again, this frail, little old man hardly looked up to causing anything. Was he expecting Buck to do something? Without papers? Without the mark? Buck was willing, but he didn't know yet what he thought of Chaim's judgment.

"When did they stop administering the mark?" Buck said.

"They have not stopped. See, two lines remain open over there, but it appears one is about to shut down, despite the number of those waiting. You have noticed nothing this morning, have you, Cameron?"

"Noticed?"

"The difference between today and yesterday."

Buck looked around. "Crowd's bigger, earlier. Military vehicles are still everywhere outside the Old City. But why are they closing a line with people still in it? And why didn't they finish last night? More people showed up?"

"And you a journalist!"

"I'll bite. What'd I miss?"

"You said it yourself. The vehicles are still there."

"So? A show of strength. Carpathia probably expects opposition today."

"But they would not leave and come back," Chaim said. "You think these soldiers slept in those trucks? They would not have to. They have accommodations, centers, places to muster."

"Okay . . ."

"How many soldiers did you see with the trucks today?"

"To be honest, Chaim, uh, Micah, I was focused on making sure you were still here and all right. I was in a hurry and not paying attention."

"You certainly weren't. Now look, they are herding what is left of that line into the only one still open."

"And I suppose you know why."

"Of course," Chaim said.

"And you're not even a journalist. But still, you'll tell me."

"They closed that line for the same reason the Temple Mount is filled with civilians rather than GC today."

Buck spun and took in the whole area. "Sure enough. Where are they?"

"They are suffering. Soon they will be as bad off as poor Mr. Fortunato, who must be miserable almost unto death by now. How utterly ingenious for our Lord to plant in someone's mind the brilliance of having the GC personnel go first yesterday. They received the mark of the beast; then they worshiped his image. And now they are victims of Revelation 16:1-2."

"The plague of boils!" Buck whispered.

Chaim looked at him meaningfully with a close-mouthed smile, then moved away from Buck and into an open area. Buck stumbled and nearly toppled, startled by the huge, deep sounds emitting from the little man's throat. Chaim's voice was so loud that everyone stopped and stared, and Buck had to cover his ears.

"I heard a great voice out of the temple!" Chaim shouted, "saying to the seven angels, 'Go your ways, and pour out the bowls of the wrath of God upon the earth.' And the first went, and poured out his bowl upon the earth; and there fell a noisome and grievous sore upon the men which had the mark of the beast, and upon them which worshiped his image."

The thousands who had been milling about fell back at the piercing voice, and Buck was astounded at Chaim's bearing. He stood straighter and looked taller, his chest puffed out as he inhaled between sentences. His eyes were ablaze, his jaw set, and he gestured with balled fists.

Now the curious began to gather round the old man in the brown robe. "What?" some said. "What are you saying?"

"Let him who has ears hear! Surely the God of heaven has judged the man of sin, and those who have taken his mark and worshiped his image have been stricken!"

"Crazy old fool!" someone called out. "You're going to get yourself killed!"

"We'll see your head rolling before you know it, old man!"

If it was possible, Buck thought Chaim grew louder. He needed no amplification, for it was obvious that everyone within sight heard him. "None would dare come against the chosen one of God!"

The people laughed. "You're a chosen one? Where is your God? Can he do what our risen potentate can do? You want fire from heaven to leave you in a heap of ashes?"

"I demand audience with the evil one! He must answer to the one true God, the God of Abraham, Isaac, and Jacob! He dare not touch the remnant of Israel, believers in the Most High God and his Son, the Messiah, Jesus of Nazareth!"

"You'd better just—"

"Silence!" Chaim roared, and the echo reverberated off the walls and left the crowd speechless.

Three young armed and uniformed guards, including one female, jogged up. "Your papers, sir," she said.

"I neither have nor need any documentation. I am here under the authority of the Creator of heaven and earth."

"Your forehead is clear. Let me see your hand."

Chaim showed the back of his right hand. "Behold the hand of the servant of God."

The woman raised her rifle and nudged Chaim's arm, trying to steer him to the mark application line. He would not budge. "Come, sir. You are either drunk or undernourished. Save yourself the grief and me the paperwork. Get your mark."

"And worship the image of Carpathia?"

She glared at him and pulled back the firing mechanism on her rifle. "You will refer to him as His Excellency or His Worship or as the risen potentate."

"I will refer to him as Satan incarnate!"

She pressed the barrel of her weapon upon Chaim's chest and appeared to squeeze the trigger. Buck stepped forward, fearing both the blast and seeing his dear friend hit the pavement. But the young woman did not move, did not so much as blink. Chaim looked at her male partners. "When did you receive your marks?"

They both cocked their weapons. "We were among the last," one said.

"And you worshiped the image?"

"Of course."

"You too will soon suffer. The sores have begun to rise on your bodies."

One looked at the other. "I do have something inside my forearm. Look."

The other said, "Will you stop? We have cause to shoot this man, and I may just do it."

"Shoot him!" someone hollered from the crowd. "What is wrong with your supervisor?"

Both eyed her warily; then one said to Chaim, "Sir, we're going to have to ask you to get in line to take the mark or bear the consequences."

"I have not been called to martyrdom just yet, young man. When my time comes, I will proudly bow before the blade, worshiping the God of heaven. But now, unless you too want to be stricken motionless, you will get word to the one you worship that I demand an audience."

One turned away and spoke into his walkie-talkie. Then, "I *know,* sir. But Corporal Riehl is incapacitated, and—"

"What?"

"He paralyzed her, sir, and—"

"How?"

"We don't know! He's demanding—"

"Shoot to kill!"

The young man shrugged, and both pointed their rifles at Chaim.

"Give me that!" Chaim said, grabbing the walkie-talkie. He depressed the button. "Whoever you are, tell your so-called potentate that Micah demands an audience with him."

"How did you get this radio?" the voice said.

"He will find me and my assistant in the center of the Temple Mount with three catatonic guards."

"I warn you—"

Chaim switched off the walkie-talkie. Within seconds, half a dozen more guards, two in plainclothes, advanced, weapons drawn. "You don't demand a meeting with Potentate Carpathia," one scolded.

"Yes, I do!" Chaim shouted, and the six studied their paralyzed compatriots.

"Well, sir, may I have your name?"

"You may call me Micah."

"Okay, Mr. Micah, sir. The potentate is at the Knesset, where his Jerusalem headquarters have been established. If you'd like to accompany us there and request—"

"I am demanding a meeting with him here. You may tell him that if he refuses, he will face more than a decimated, suffering staff. I am prepared to return to the plagues called down from heaven by the two witnesses! Ask him if he would like his medical staff to try to treat your boils and carbuncles with water that has turned to blood."

7

DAVID WAS NOT sure what time the noise of heavy equipment woke him, but he knew immediately what it meant. He had been nonplussed by Dr. Ben-Judah's mentioning Petra in his worldwide post, and there was no question the enemy monitored the Web site.

David crept back to the high place in the blackness of the wee hours, the stars not providing enough illumination to keep him from skinning shins, stubbing toes, and falling several times, scraping hands and arms on the rocks. His eyes having adjusted to the darkness, far below he saw the semicircle of GC tanks and artillery forming at the perimeter. Though they kept few lights on, he was able to make out that they had closed the main foot-traffic entrance and were heavily stationed around the most likely airdrop zones as well.

David believed God had promised to protect the children of Israel who would flee the anger of Antichrist, but what of the volunteers who helped them? How were they to escape an enemy already a step ahead? How could Tsion have made such a blunder? David phoned Rayford but got no answer. He tried Albie.

* * *

Tsion could not be consoled. He paced, a hand over his mouth, praying silently. Ming and Chloe had tried to reason with him, reminding him that God was sovereign, but he could not make sense of what he had done. He kept the television on, dreading the news of a massacre once the flight from Jerusalem began.

Tsion finally sat on the arm of the couch in front of the television. The tall, fat young man they incongruously called Little Zeke—his recently martyred father had been Big Zeke—lumbered in with a sketchpad. "Wanna see what I'm thinkin' about doing with Ming? I mean, it's hard to disguise a, um, Asian woman, but I'm gonna try to make her look like a guy, I think. I've got a picture of her brother, and with the right haircut and clothes and, you know, wrappings and stuff—"

"Forgive me, Z, but—"

"Oh, I've already told her I don't mean to insult her or anything. I mean, she's thin and small, but I'm not saying she looks like a guy now. In fact, she's really quite pretty and attractive, and feminine."

"I'm preoccupied here, Z. I am sorry. I have made a terrible mistake and I'm praying that—"

"I know," Zeke said. "That's really why I came out here. I mean, I was working on Ming's identity for real, but I thought maybe talking about that would take your mind off—"

"Off tipping off the other side about where our brothers and sisters are headed? Thanks, but I do not see how the GC could do anything but beat them there and lie in wait for them."

Zeke set his pad on the couch and eased his bulk onto the floor. "You're the Bible guy," he said, "but something about this just seems sort of logical to me."

"Logical? Hardly."

"I mean, there must have been a reason, that's all."

"To humble me, perhaps, but this is quite a price. I never claimed to be perfect, but I pray so hard over my messages, and God knows I would never intentionally—"

"That's what I mean, Doc. God must have wanted this to happen somehow."

"Oh, I do not—"

"You said it yourself, you pray about this stuff. That doesn't make your messages like the Bible, I guess, but God's not gonna let a regular human like you mess up his plan with one mistake, is he?"

Tsion didn't know what to think. This uneducated young man often had fresh insight. "Maybe I have myself overrated."

"Maybe. You didn't seem to when you were just the guy who teaches a billion people. Why didn't you let that go to your head?"

"I do not think of it that way, Z. It's humbling, a privilege."

"See? You could get cocky about having this big Internet church, but you don't. So maybe you shouldn't start thinkin' you're important enough to get in God's way."

"Obviously I am not above mistakes," Tsion said.

"Yeah, but come on. You think God is gonna say, 'I had this deal all figured out till Ben-Judah went and messed it up'?"

Tsion had to chuckle. "I suppose he can overcome my blunders."

"I hope so. You always made him out to be big enough."

"Well, thank you, Z. That gives me something to—"

"But it goes past that, even," Zeke said. "I still think God might have had a reason for lettin' you do that."

"For now I am just trying to take in that God can overrule my error."

"You wait and see, Doc. I bet you're gonna find that either the GC doesn't buy it because it looks like such an obvious phony lead. Or they think they've found something juicy and they try to take advantage of it, only to see it blow up in their faces."

* * *

At dawn Rayford was alarmed to find Albie with Big George, uncrating several of each of the two kinds of weapons the latter had had shipped in. "What're we doing, Albie?"

"Your phone not working?"

Rayford patted his pocket and pulled it out. "Nuts!" he said. "Used it too much yesterday." He pulled the solar pack from it and clipped it to the outside of his shirt pocket, where the sun would rejuvenate it, and put a fresh pack in. He found he had missed several calls.

Albie said, "Let me save you checking all those out and tell you what Hassid's and my calls were about."

* * *

"Everybody back off." The newest arrival to the Temple Mount was a tall, athletic-looking, dark-haired plainclothesman with the outline of a handgun under his jacket. "Who're you?" he said to Buck, as the rest of the Morale Monitors and Peacekeepers, including the three who had been paralyzed, stepped back.

Buck thought he had been prepared for everything, but he felt his pockets as if about to produce his ID, then pointed to Chaim. "I'm with him. Who are you?"

"Name's Loren Hut, and I'm chief of the Global Community Morale Monitors. I have the potentate on the phone for the troublemaker." He looked at Chaim, making the pressing crowd laugh. "For some reason my people can't seem to get through to a demented old man. That has to be you."

Chaim said, "Tell your boss I do not care to speak to him except in person."

"Not possible, Mr.—"

"Micah."

"Best you're going to get is this call, Mr. Micah. Now I'm not feeling well this morning, and you're already pressing your luck."

"Not feeling well how, Mr. Hut?"

"Do you want to talk to His Excellency or—"

Chaim looked away, shaking his head.

Hut scowled and put his phone to his ear. "False alarm. Apologize to the potentate for me. . . . Well, sure, I'll talk to him, but I don't want to waste his—good morning, sir. Yes . . . I don't know . . . I'll be sure to get full reports from everyb—well, yes, I can get it done. . . . You want me to do that? I—yes, I know, but it's not as if he poses a real threat . . . yes, sir. Nine in the clip . . . if that's what you want . . . I don't disagree, it's just that he's a frail . . . I could do that. . . . Affirmative, you can count on me."

Hut slapped his phone shut and swore. "You," he said to Buck, "keep your distance. Be glad for your sake I kept you out of this. And you people—" he gestured toward the crowd—"stay back!" Some moved; most didn't. "Don't say you weren't warned!"

"Sores starting to get to you, young man?" Chaim said.

"Shut up! You're about to die."

"That will not be up to you, son."

"Actually, yes it will. Now be quiet! Corporal Riehl, are you all right?"

"A little foggy," she said flatly. "What do you need?"

"Find a GCNN camera crew and get 'em over here. The potentate wants me to put nine in this guy, but he wants to see it."

"So do I," she said, trotting off.

"Mr. Hut," Chaim said, "will you be able to do your duty? You are getting worse by the second."

Hut bent over and vigorously scratched his abdomen and belly. "I don't have to be a hundred percent to kill a man at point-blank range."

"That will not happen."

"You think you can paralyze me?"

"I never know how God will act."

"Well, I know how *you* will act. You'll be squirming and screaming and pleading for your life."

"My life is not my own. If God wishes it, he may have it. But as I have further responsibilities, including talking in person to the coward who would ignore me, God will spare me."

Corporal Riehl returned with a turbaned man with a camera on his shoulder. With him was a short black woman carrying a microphone. "What are we doing?" she asked with a British accent.

"Just tell me when you're rolling," Hut said. "This is for His Excellency."

"Live or disc?"

"I don't care! Just cue me!"

"All right! Hang on!" She spoke into a small radio. "Yes!" she said. "Carpathia himself. Just a minute." She turned to Hut. "Central wants to know your authority."

Hut swore again and scratched himself from abdomen to shoulders. "Hut!" he said. "GCMM! Now let's go!"

"Okay," the woman said, stepping in front of the camera. "This is Bernadette Rice, live from the Temple Mount in Jerusalem, where we are about to witness an execution ordered personally by His Excellency Nicolae Carpathia. Behind me, Loren Hut, new chief of the Global Community Morale Monitors, will administer the sentence to a man known only as Micah, who has refused the mark of loyalty and resisted arrest."

When people from other areas of the Temple Mount saw on the giant TV monitors what was going on, they flooded the area around Chaim and Buck and Hut.

+ + +

"Don't let Kenny see this!" Zeke called out. "But come quick, both of you!"

It was after midnight in Chicago, and Tsion had slipped off the arm of the couch to a cushion, where he sat hunched forward, peeking at the screen between his fingers. "God, please . . ."

"There's Buck!" Chloe said, pointing.

Tsion thought Cameron looked weird, standing casually, hands in his pockets.

The GCMM chief pulled his sidearm from its holster, paused to scratch himself with his left hand and right elbow, then prepared the weapon. He spread his legs and held the gun in both hands, aiming at Chaim's hands, which were clasped in front of him. Hut's angle would make the bullet pass through them without hitting his body.

The explosion of the first shot made Buck skip out of the way and the crowd recoil, but Chaim didn't move, except to flinch at the sound. Hut stared in disbelief at Chaim's unmarred hands and moved to his opposite side, aiming the second shot at them again. The crowd scattered. *BLAM!* Another apparent miss from just inches away.

Hut, scratching himself all the way to the knees between shots now, aimed at Chaim's foot and fired. Nothing. Not even a hole in the robe. Hut lifted the hem with his left hand and fired at the other foot. Moaning in agony and apparently fear, Hut scratched with his free hand, pressed the muzzle onto one of Chaim's knees, then the other. The shots produced only noise.

The crowd laughed. "This is a joke!" someone said. "A put-on! He's shooting blanks!"

"Blanks?" Hut screamed, whirling to face the heckler. "You'd bet your life on that?" He fired shot number seven into the man's sternum. The back of the victim's head hit the ground first, the sickening crush of his skull clear on the TV reporter's microphone.

With the crowd running for cover and Bernadette Rice falling out of the picture, Loren Hut fired at Chaim's left shoulder from six inches, then pressed the gun to the unharmed old man's forehead. Chaim looked sympathetically at the shaken, writhing Hut, and casually plugged his ears. The barrel of the gun left a small indentation on Chaim's skin. The bullet proved harmless.

Hut tossed the gun away and threw his arms around a tree, rubbing his body against it for relief. He cried out in agony, then turned and summoned Corporal Riehl. He reached for her rifle and pointed it under his own chin. Chaim approached calmly.

"No need for that, Mr. Hut," he said. "The death you have chosen will overtake you in due time. Put down the weapon and summon Carpathia for me."

+ + +

Hut threw down the rifle and staggered away, but already Buck heard the thwocking of chopper blades. Two helicopters touched down, and the crowd—which had largely retreated—cautiously returned, avoiding the corpse that lay in a pool of blood.

Carpathia was the only civilian in either bird, and he wore his jet-black, pinstriped suit over a white shirt and brilliant red tie. He strode directly to Chaim and Buck while seven uniformed Peacekeepers formed a semicircle behind him, weapons trained on Chaim.

Nicolae smiled at the crowd and turned to locate the GCNN cameraman. Bernadette was still on the ground, trembling. "Keep rolling, son," he said. "What's your name?"

"R-R-Rashid."

"Well, stand right here, R-R-Rashid, so the world can see who dares mock my sovereignty."

Carpathia approached Chaim and faced him from three feet away, arms crossed. "You are too old to be Tsion Ben-Judah," he said. "And you call yourself Micah." He cocked his head and squinted at Buck, who feared that Nicolae recognized him. "And this is?"

"My assistant," Chaim said.

"Does he have a name?"

"He has a name."

"May I know it?"

"There is no need."

"You *are* an insulting dolt, are you not?" Carpathia spoke to a guard, nodding at Buck. "Get him out of here. The mark or the blade."

Buck set himself to resist, but the guard looked petrified. He cleared his throat. "Come with me, please, sir."

Buck shook his head. The guard looked helplessly back at Carpathia, who ignored him. Suddenly the guard dropped, wriggling on the ground, scratching himself all over.

"All right," Carpathia said. "I concede I have you to thank for the fact that nearly my entire workforce is suffering this morning."

"Probably all of them," Chaim said. "If they are not, you might want to check the authenticity of their marks."

"How did you do it?"

"Not I, but God."

"You are looking into the face of god," Carpathia said.

"On the contrary," Chaim said, "I fear God. I do not fear you."

\+ + +

Rayford spread a topographical map on the hood of a truck. "Let's get Mac and Smitty in on this too," he said. Albie phoned them.

Big George leaned in. "Anywhere we could hunker down within a couple of miles of Petra?"

Rayford shook his head. "I don't know. Whole area looks a lot different on paper than from the air. I know you're gung ho ho and everything, but I'm not prepared to do any killing."

"All due respect, Cap," George said, "but they're going to be killing our people. You might change your mind when you see that."

"We're here to get people to safety, not to kill the enemy."

Albie slapped his phone shut. "What if killing the enemy is the only way to get the Israelis to safety?"

"That's God's job."

"I agree," Albie said, "at least from what Dr. Ben-Judah says. But I'd hate to see us lose one brother or sister, and if these weapons are what it takes, I say use 'em."

\+ + +

Buck would never forget a detail of this macabre meeting, and the entire world was watching.

"So, Micah," Carpathia said, shifting his weight, "what will it take for you to lift this magic spell that has incapacitated my people?"

"There is no magic here," Chaim said, in a voice that sounded as far from his own as Buck could imagine. "This is the judgment of almighty God."

"All right," Nicolae said, smiling tolerantly. "What does *almighty God* want in exchange for lightening up—" and here he made quotation marks with his fingers—"on this *judgment*?"

Chaim shook his head.

"Come, Micah. If you would negotiate on behalf of *God*, surely you can think of something!"

"Those who have taken your mark and worship your image shall suffer."

Carpathia moved close, his smile gone. "Do not tell my beloved not to accept the mark of loyalty or worship me!"

"They know the consequence and can see it here."

Rashid began to pan the camera around to take in many agonized loyalists. "Do not!" Carpathia whispered to him, grabbing his shoulder and swinging him back. Then to Chaim, "If anyone refuses my mark, I will put him to death myself!"

"The choice then," Chaim said, "is life with excruciating pain or death at your hand."

"*What* do you want?"

"You will carry out your plan for the temple," Chaim said, "but many will oppose you for it."

"At their peril."

"Many have already decided against you and have pledged themselves to the one true God and his Son, the Messiah."

"They will pay with their lives."

"You asked what I wanted."

"And you propose that people be allowed to shake their fists in my face? Never!"

Rashid dropped to one knee, trembling. Carpathia shot him a look. "Get up!"

"I can't!"

"I see the *42* on your forehead, Rashid! You need not fear!"

"I am not afraid, Excellency! I am in pain!"

"Agh! Set the camera on a tripod and tend to your sores!"

Chaim continued calmly. "A million of God's chosen people in this area alone have chosen to believe in Messiah. They would die before they would take your mark."

"Then they shall die!"

"You must let them flee this place before you pour out revenge on your enemies."

"Never!"

"The recompense for stubbornness is on your hands. The grievous sores on your followers shall be the least of your troubles."

Buck looked past Carpathia to where the mark application lines had been replaced by makeshift medical tents. Lines of people waited in misery for treatment. Some held their friends as they gingerly moved about, only to collapse under their own pain. Bernadette had crawled away. Rashid was headed toward the tents. Every guard who had accompanied Nicolae staggered away. One of the helicopters stopped idling and the pilot tumbled out, whimpering. The pilot of the other was slumped over the controls.

Civilians, many of whom had been among the last to take the mark and worship the image, tried to run from the Temple Mount, only to stumble with sores appearing all over their bodies.

Chaim said, "Your only hope to avoid the next terrible plague from heaven is to let Israelis who believe in Messiah go."

Finally Carpathia appeared shaken. "And what might that next plague entail?"

"You will know when you know," Chaim said. "But I can tell you this: It will be worse than the one that has brought your people low. I need a drink of water."

Carpathia caught the eye of a loyalist and told him to "fetch Micah a bottle of water." Chaim stared at the potentate as they waited.

"You are nothing but a thirsty old man in an outsized robe."

"I am not thirsty."

"Then why—"

"You shall see."

"I can hardly wait."

The man came running with the water. He gave it to Carpathia, who handed it to Chaim. The old man held it up and peered at it. "I could not drink this anyway," he said.

"What is wrong with it?" Nicolae said.

"See for yourself."

Chaim handed it back, and the bottle turned nearly black as the water turned to blood.

"Ach!" Carpathia said. "This again? Do you not know what happened to your two associates at the Wailing Wall?"

"Any advantages you gain are by God's hand, and they are temporary."

Nicolae turned to see the disaster at the Temple Mount, nearly everyone writhing. He turned back to Chaim. "I want my people healthy and my water pure."

"You know the price."

"Specifics."

"Israeli Jews who have chosen to believe Jesus the Christ is their Messiah must be allowed to leave before you punish anyone for not taking your mark. And devout Orthodox Jews must be allowed a place where they can worship after you have defiled their temple."

"The Orthodox Jews do not even agree with you, and yet you speak for them?"

"I reserve the right to continue to attempt to persuade them."

"Would you take them to Petra with the Judah-ites?"

"I would propose Masada as a site for them to gather. Any we are able to persuade would then join us."

"In Petra."

"I did not say where."

"We already know where, you fool, and it required no intelligence on our parts."

"You tread on dangerous ground when you call a fool one who has been granted the power to turn your water to blood."

Carpathia screamed into the air, "I need the assistance of loyalists who have not yet taken the mark or worshiped my image!" A few civilians came running. "Follow me to the Knesset Building. Obey me, and I will reward you."

+ + +

David made his way from horizon to horizon, trying to gauge the extent of the GC presence at Petra. While there seemed to be countless vehicles and weapons, the personnel seemed to be in trouble. Most languished on the ground or on the beds of trucks, being ministered to by others thus far less affected. He called Albie to report.

+ + +

Rayford headed east toward Petra in a vehicle carrying three each of the weapons George had brought to Mizpe Ramon. Albie and Mac followed in identical vehicles, similarly laden. George and Abdullah rode together in a vehicle carrying DEWs. Rayford hoped to find a spot to set up and, using David Hassid as their eyes, see how many vehicles he and Albie and Mac could destroy with the fifty-caliber rifles.

There would be no need to kill any GC, if David's reports were accurate. As the enemy fled, George and Abdullah, from closer proximity, would try to overheat their skin, making their sores all the worse. Rayford's biggest concern, after avoiding any intentional killing, was the five of them getting back to Mizpe Ramon in time to ferry the first escapees from Israel into Petra.

8

BUCK FOLLOWED CHAIM to the temple, where, within twenty minutes, civilians without the mark of the beast scurried to set up TV cameras and make arrangements, apparently following hastily written and reproduced instructions. From where he and Chaim sat, Buck saw others tidying up the Temple Mount, some carting off the slain heckler, some directing people either to spectator locations for what they called the "temple festivities" or to first-aid lines, and still others replacing in the medical tents GC doctors and nurses who had themselves fallen too ill to help out.

"Pray for me," Chaim said.

"Why? What? Carpathia is not even here yet."

Chaim stood and began to speak, again in a huge voice. "Citizens! Hear me! You who have not taken the mark of loyalty! There may still be time to choose to obey the one true and living God! While the evil ruler of this world promises peace, there is no peace! While he promises benevolence and prosperity, look at your world! Everyone who has preceded you in taking the mark and worshiping the image of the man of sin now suffers with grievous sores. That is your lot if you follow him.

"By now you must know that the world has been divided. Nicolae Carpathia is the opponent of God and wishes only your destruction, regardless of his lies. The God who created you loves you. His Son who died for your sins will return to set up his earthly kingdom in less than three and a half years, and if you have not already rejected him one time too many, you may receive him now.

"You were born in sin and separated from God, but the Bible says God is not willing that any should perish but that all should come to repentance. Ephesians 2:8-9 says that nothing we can do will earn our salvation but that it is the gift of God, not of works, lest anyone should boast. The only payment for our sins was Jesus Christ's death on the cross. Because besides being fully man, he is fully God, and his one death had the power to cleanse all of us of our sin.

"John 1:12 says that to as many as received him, to them he gave the right to become children of God by believing on his name. How do you receive Christ?

Merely tell God that you know you are a sinner and that you need him. Accept the gift of salvation, believe that Christ is risen, and say so. For many, it is already too late. I beg of you to receive Christ right now!"

\+ + +

David Hassid, hiding in the rocks atop Petra, tried to coordinate with Rayford and his cohorts two miles away. They were so well hidden that he couldn't see them, though he thought he had seen plumes of dust south of the village of Wadi Musa, immediately east of Petra. They conferenced up on their secure phones, and Rayford told him George and Abdullah were trying to get close enough to use the directed energy weapons. David couldn't spot them from his perch either.

"We can see the GC hardware from three different locations," Rayford reported. "Anybody manning those weapons?"

"Not that I can see," David said, whispering because he had no idea how his voice might carry down the mountainside. "They're likely waiting for word from Jerusalem that the Israelis are on their way."

"It's hard to tell the location of personnel," Rayford said.

"To my right and your extreme left," David said, "the first six or so vehicles appear unmanned. Only a few of all the soldiers are still ambulatory, and they seem to be tending to the others either directly below me or to my left."

"Take cover," Mac said, cutting in. "These things take a while to aim. It's going to be hit-and-miss at first, and probably more miss than hit."

"Just don't overshoot," David said. "I've got a small cave staked out. When we're done, I'll be incommunicado for a while."

"We'll each fire two rounds from the big guns," Rayford said. "After you've heard six, come out and try to reconnect. We're trying to drive the personnel to your left so we can safely take out some of the vehicles. If we can get the soldiers on the run, George and Smitty will try to make 'em miserable."

"They're already miserable," David said. "But I hear you. If they think staying put is going to get 'em killed, they'll start walking back to Israel! Okay, I'm out."

He ducked into the cave and sat waiting for the first blast.

\+ + +

Rayford tried to remember everything George had told him about the fifty-calibers. He set up two in the truck bed, side by side and loaded. Fifty yards away, Albie had the same setup. And fifty yards farther, Mac was ready. They would fire once in that order, then start over for the second round. Each would watch through high-powered telescopes to try to gauge the adjustment for the second shot. Six rounds were perfect to start, Rayford thought, because at some point the miserable GC would wonder if the barrage would ever stop and whether they had a prayer of surviving. All he wanted was to destroy their weapons and their transportation, send them running, and discourage any hope of ambushing the Israelis.

George had told him it was impossible to judge the wind between weapon and target and so to aim high, accounting for the effect of gravity over two miles, and to not expect accuracy within more than twenty or thirty yards. Rayford worried that an errant shot would kill someone, including David. He lay on his stomach in the bed of the truck, made his final adjustments, and locked in on the leftmost vehicle. If he missed left, the bullet would at least spook the soldiers. If he missed right, he had all kinds of vehicles he might hit, yet he should still avoid hitting personnel.

Rayford had his finger on the trigger and the stock pressed hard against his right shoulder. The scope showed him dialed up forty feet above the target. Just before he squeezed, he reminded himself to keep his eyes open—not that it would make any difference in trajectory. Only amateurs shut their eyes.

Thinking about his eyes reminded him of his ears and George's desperate admonition to plug them somehow. How close had he come to deafening himself? Rayford rolled to his side, ripped a strip from his shirttail, tore it in half, and forced a bunched-up wad of material into each ear. As he was settling in again, hoping he had not affected the aim, his phone chirped.

It was Albie. "You going first or what?"

"Yeah. Almost forgot my earplugs."

"Oh, man! Thanks for reminding me!"

"Ten seconds."

"Give me thirty," Albie said. "We want to fire in close succession, but I've got to get something in my ears too. Remind Mac, eh?"

Rayford dialed Mac. "Another half minute while we get earplugs in."

"Say again?"

"Did you remember earplugs?"

"Just a second. Let me get this out of my ear! Now, what?"

"A few more seconds. Ready?"

"Been ready, boss. Let's commence."

Rayford looked at his watch and settled back in. How loud could it be? How much recoil? The stories had become legends. People shot these all the time. Should be interesting, that's all. He would squeeze off the round and stay put, watching through the scope to see where it hit.

It was as if he had not protected his ears. If his eyes were open when he pulled the trigger, they were driven shut when the stock drove deep into his shoulder, sending him sliding on his belly until his boots slammed into the back of the cab. The explosion was so loud and the heat so intense from a six-inch burst of fire shooting out the side that Rayford found himself dazed, ears ringing, head buzzing, hands vibrating.

The weapon flew forward off the resistance from his shoulder until the legs of the bipod dropped off the edge of the truck. Rayford had meant to count one-thousand-one up to one-thousand-seven while looking through the scope, but all he could do was groan, hearing himself as if in an echo chamber, his ears not really working yet.

His other weapon had rattled off its bipod and lay on its side, and Rayford was glad it had not gone off. Albie was to wait three seconds from the sound of Rayford's shot, and Mac another three after that. Rayford heard the boom from Albie's rifle and figured he had four seconds to get the second weapon into place and still see where his first bullet hit.

He yanked it up, but the scope seemed cockeyed, and Mac's weapon sounded only a little farther away than Albie's. Rayford should be shooting again within a few seconds, but he was desperately searching with the scope for his first shot while trying to line up the second. He hurt all over, and his body resisted putting itself through that again.

He saw a huge cloud of pink smoke, assumed he had hit the rock face above the vehicles, quickly aimed lower and more to the right, and squeezed, the concussion driving him back yet again. Rayford knew he had closed his eyes with that shot, but a cloud of sand and a black plume told him their first three rounds were high, low, and luckily right on. His second shot sent a shower of sparks and more red dust, Albie's brought back the sound of twisted metal, and Mac's seemed to still be in the air.

By now, George and Abdullah should be shooting the directed energy weapons, but as DEWs had no projectiles, they emitted only a clicking sound Rayford was unable to hear. He pulled the cloth out of his ears, then crawled to the second weapon and removed the scope. He sat up and tried to survey the results. Without anything to support the powerful lens, it moved around too much. He went to his knees and lodged it against the side of the truck bed, then scanned slowly until he got his bearings. No GC personnel in sight.

Three vehicles from the left and about twenty feet up, a hole bigger than a truck had been blown deep into the rock wall. The fifth and sixth armored carriers appeared to have been blown away from the wall by a shot that may have gone between them. The next vehicle was aflame. There were two dug-up troughs of sand and another obvious hole in the face of the rock.

David called. "Whoa, ho!" he said. "Do that again and we're home free!"

"Don't count on it," Rayford said. "I don't *ever* want to do that again."

"It sounded like World War IV, man! The GC had to have started moving away with the first explosion, and by the time I looked over the edge, they were mostly at the other end. A lot of them were just pleading for their lives, but a few dozen lit out across the desert. The directed energy thingies must have worked, because it wasn't long before those guys were rolling around in the sand. Some are coming back to the trucks now, though, so you might want to think about a couple more rounds each."

Rayford slumped and groaned. And reloaded.

* * *

Tsion was still despairing at just before four o'clock in the morning in Chicago, so he was grateful for the report of the attack on the GC. "They knew where we would be, so we knew where they were," David wrote him. "The area will soon be secure for the fleeing remnant of Israel."

Tsion knew he should sleep, but he also knew the rest of the second half of the Tribulation would not all be this dense with activity. As he had often reminded an exhausted Rayford, there would be time to rest and breathe between Carpathia's breaking of the covenant and the Battle of Armageddon. If they could keep up their strength while trying to stay atop everything now, they could endure.

Tsion turned on the television to discover that the plague of sores had swept the world. Even the reporters on TV were in pain, and one entire special channel was devoted to advice for the sufferers. While the potentate's visit to the temple at noon Carpathian Time was next on the network schedule, Tsion switched to the auxiliary channel to see what they were saying about something that was not of this world anyway. There was little relief for a plague sent by God, but the Global Community tried to put the best face on it.

* * *

In New Babylon, Chang worried he would be found out if people realized he was the one among them not afflicted with the sores. His boss had e-mailed him to see how he was, and Chang intimated that he had better stay in his room for several days. His boss granted that permission, provided Chang was sure to put in place what was necessary for the senior medical staff person in the palace to go live on the special channel with treatment advice.

Chang was able to do that without leaving his apartment. He watched a bit of the feed, reminding himself that at 1:00 Palace Time, Nicolae would enter the temple.

Dr. Consuela Conchita, with dark circles under her eyes and seeming to struggle to sit up straight, walked people through their own treatment. "The fact is that we have thus far been unable to specifically diagnose this pandemic affliction," she said. "It begins as an irritation of the skin, most often in areas normally covered by clothing, though it has been known to spread to the face and hands.

"In its initial stages it progresses to a serious itch, soon becoming a running sore that acts like a furuncle or a boil and sometimes even a carbuncle. But whereas the usual such maladies are caused by acute staph infections, these have not responded to conventional symptomatic treatment. While staphylococcal bacteria are naturally found in these sores, because such are found on our skin surfaces anyway, some as yet undetermined bacteria make this outbreak much more serious and difficult to treat.

"While these do not appear life threatening, they must be carefully managed to keep from becoming deeply infected abscesses. We have ruled out any causal relationship between the sores and the methods used to administer the mark of loyalty. So while the sores seem to affect only those who have the mark, the connection seems entirely coincidental.

"These types of skin problems can lead to permanent scarring, so it is important to keep the affected areas clean and use any anti-itching recipe you find helpful. Antibiotics have not yet proven effective at containing the infection, but are recommended nonetheless.

"Wear loose clothing to allow for good ventilation of the skin. Avoid intravenous drug use, and invest in a good antibacterial soap. Use hot or cold compresses, whichever best alleviates your discomfort. Fever and fatigue are common side effects."

Chang didn't know if it was the power of suggestion or just his own irrational fear. But he noticed an itch on his shin, leaped from his chair, and pulled up his pant leg. There was nothing visible, but he couldn't keep from scratching the spot. That made it redden, but was there something deeper? He told himself it couldn't be, that even if he *had* the mark of Carpathia, he had neither chosen it, nor had or would he ever worship the image of Nicolae, let alone Nicolae himself.

* * *

Buck could hardly believe it when dozens of unmarked civilians approached Chaim and asked to pray with him. "You realize you could pay with your life," Chaim told them. "This is no idle commitment."

People knelt before him, following him in prayer. The mark of the seal of God appeared on their foreheads.

"Those of you who are Jews," Chaim said, "listen carefully. God has prepared a special place of refuge for you. When Carpathia's plans to retaliate reach their zenith, listen for my announcement and head south out of the city. Volunteers will drive you to Mizpe Ramon in the Negev. My assistant here will tell you how to recognize them by something we can see that our enemy cannot. If you cannot find transportation, get to the Mount of Olives where, just as from Mizpe Ramon, you will be airlifted by helicopter to Petra, the ancient Arabian city in southwestern Jordan. There God has promised to protect us until the Glorious Appearing of Jesus when he sets up his thousand-year reign on earth."

As noon approached, the men from the Wailing Wall made their way toward the temple. They were serious-looking, and clearly not happy. Many were in traditional Jewish garb and stood at the edges of the crowd that pressed in on Chaim. They listened, but none approached or spoke. Several glanced over their shoulders at the temple and at the monitors, apparently to be sure they missed nothing.

Chaim finished with the new believers, and as they slowly dispersed, he gestured to those who had come from the Wailing Wall. "You holy men of Israel," he said, "I know who you are. You remain unpersuaded that Jesus bar Joseph of Nazareth is the foretold Messiah, yet neither do you accept that Nicolae Carpathia is of God. I urge you only to listen as a man enters your Holy of Holies and defiles it in his own name. I shall tell of Scriptures that foretold this very event. Then I will beg your indulgence yet again as I seek refuge for you at Masada, where I will present the evidence for Jesus the Christ as the Messiah of Judaism."

The holy men scowled and murmured.

"Gentlemen!" Chaim called out with authority. "I ask only for your attention. What you do with this information is entirely up to you. Without God's protection you run the risk of death opposing the ruler of this world, and yet his desecration of this holy site will enrage you."

Buck felt his phone vibrate and saw that Chang was calling. "Make it quick," Buck said.

"Are you aware of my sister's idea of my cutting in on Carpathia's broadcast and superseding it with Dr. Ben-Judah's?"

"Chloe told me. Can you do it for Chaim as well?"

"With your help."

"What do you need?"

"A camera and a microphone."

"Where do I get that?"

"You're there, Mr. Williams. I'm not. Obviously, Carpathia will have cameras in the temple and wants the world to see what he does there. My schedule says he's going to speak afterward, but I can't tell if that's inside or outside. If you can somehow commandeer a camera and mike while he's inside, I can put Rosenzweig on instead of Carpathia, and he won't know it until someone gets to him."

"I like that."

"I do too," Chang said, "but if he makes his speech outside, he'll see what we're doing."

"We've got to take that chance. And here he comes now. Chaim thinks he will speak outside on a replica of Solomon's scaffold. He's got an entourage of civilians around him carrying an extravagant throne, and some are dragging that pig from yesterday. Carpathia just told 'em, 'You will all be rewarded. Soon the world will know beyond doubt that I am god.'"

"No GC brass with him?"

"Yeah, I see Fortunato and Moon and a few others, but they look terrible. They're not going to be much help to him."

"There have to be unmanned GCNN cameras around, with all the technicians down with sores."

"I see a few on tripods, aimed at the temple."

"Can you grab one?"

"Who's going to stop me?"

"Go for it. I just need to know the number on the upper left in the back, and be sure a monitor and a mike are attached."

"Hang on."

Buck hesitated as Carpathia stopped near them, Fortunato, Moon, Ivins, and others mince-stepping behind, pale and haggard. The holy men turned and glared at them. Nicolae pointed at Chaim. "You I will deal with later," he said. "This spell of yours is temporary, and what happened to your two crazies at the Wailing Wall will befall you as well. And as for you," he added, gesturing to the angry men, "you will regret the day Israel turned her back on me. A covenant of peace is only as good as either side's keeping its word."

"Boo!" one shouted, and others hissed and clucked their tongues. "You would dare blaspheme our God?" Still more joined in, raising their fists.

Carpathia turned toward the temple, then spun back. "Your God?" he said. "Where is he? Inside? Shall I go and see? If he is in there and does not welcome me, should I tremble? Might he strike me dead?"

"I pray he does!" a rabbi shouted.

Carpathia leveled his eyes at the men. "You will regret the day you opposed me. It shall not be long before you either submit to my mark or succumb to my blade."

He strode up the temple steps, but his suffering followers had to help each other ascend. The holy men followed several feet behind. When Carpathia and his people followed a contingent of his loyal civilians past the pillars and into the porch area, the men stood outside, rocking, bowing, crying out to God.

Buck jogged to an unmanned camera and mike, his phone to his ear. A small monitor and headphones dangled beneath the camera, fastened between two of the tripod legs. The monitor carried the network's global feed and just then showed Carpathia entering the temple. The camera operator must have been newly recruited, because he fumbled for the correct lens opening.

"Got it," Buck told Chang and read him the information.

"Good! Wireless. Get it as close to Rosenzweig as you can, and set the mike in the cradle beneath the lens."

Buck tried to wrestle the tripod, but the wheels were locked, and working with just one hand, he barely kept it from toppling. He told Chang he'd call him back and went to work on the wheels.

Meanwhile, Chaim unloaded on Carpathia again. "If you are God," he railed, "why can you not heal your own Most High Reverend Father or the woman closer to you than a relative? Where are all your military leaders and the other members of your cabinet?"

The attention of the crowds moved from Chaim to the temple entrance again. His ploy had worked. Carpathia had reappeared. Many of the holy men rushed down the steps, effectively blocking Nicolae's view of the camera now in front of Chaim, but Buck feared it appeared they were scared of the potentate.

"Where are your loyal followers," Chaim continued, "those who have taken your cursed mark and worshiped you and your image? A body covered with boils is the price one pays to worship you, and you claim to be God?"

To Buck it appeared Nicolae was merely trying to stare down the old man. The Rosenzweig Buck knew would not have been able to withstand that kind of psychological warfare, but Micah—this new Moses—held Carpathia's gaze so long without even blinking that Nicolae finally turned away.

Buck studied the monitor. It looked like the last exchange had not been broadcast. The picture now showed someone in the studio in New Babylon announcing that GCNN was "returning to Jerusalem, where His Excellency will tour the famous temple. With the illness affecting much of our staff as it has so many around the world, we ask your indulgence, as many of the technicians helping bring you this special event are volunteers."

* * *

David worried when it took several rounds from the big guns and strategic use of the DEWs to finally dislodge from Petra the already boil-crippled GC forces. He was certain he had not been detected, and now he hoped the enemy's military brass would rule out reinforcements.

Rayford told him that he and Albie and Mac were okay except for sore shoulders and ringing ears, and that George and Abdullah had reported a few more hits with the flesh-heating weapons as the fleeing GC passed within a quarter mile of their blind. "I wouldn't be surprised," Rayford added, "if you started getting a wave of new residents by late this afternoon."

That was as close as David had ever been to live combat, but it had almost not seemed fair. He couldn't imagine trying to stage an attack while most of your personnel were suffering from nasty sores.

Not knowing whether Chaim would lead or follow the escaping Israelis to Petra, David considered that he might be in charge until Dr. Rosenzweig arrived. He could think of no better plan than first come, first served, and he tried to scope out where the first quarter million would begin to settle. By the time he got back to his computer to see what was happening at the temple, a message was waiting from Hannah Palemoon.

David, there is a lull here, and of course we never know how long those last. We're praying that the small party that answered your call to thwart the GC there comes back healthy and successful.

This is not easy to write, but I feel I must get it off my chest. Besides that you are still grieving the love of your life, neither of us would likely have considered a relationship during this period of history anyway, and we barely know each other. So, please, please don't think I'm writing this in the context of any feelings I think either of us should have for the other.

We're friends, aren't we? That doesn't obligate us much, if at all. For both of our sakes, let me just say it. I was hurt at how cavalierly you treated me regarding your decision to not return to the United North American States at the end of Operation Eagle. It was a huge, complicated thing, a major crossroads in your life. I need to say too that it probably is the right decision.

But I learned about it along with everyone else. You apparently discussed it at length with Captain Steele, and next thing we know, it's announced, you're shaking hands and bidding farewells, and off you go. My friend, my buddy, the one I assumed I would lean on, is gone, just like that.

I'm sorry to lay this on you, but I just don't feel you have treated me like a friend. I would have felt honored to help you make the decision or at least have been informed of it privately, as if you cared what I thought. I could be making you glad you didn't see this neurotic nurse as a better friend. If this is crazy and you know without doubt that I will regret having sent it, pretend I didn't. And thanks, really, for some cherished memories.

Love in Christ,
Hannah

9

BUCK FOCUSED ON CHAIM, framing him close to keep from giving clues to his whereabouts to anyone monitoring in New Babylon. If this worked the way Chang seemed to hope, the Global Community News Network people would try to pull Chaim off the air and, short of that, try to locate and reclaim the pirated camera.

Buck turned the monitor so both he and Chaim could keep track of Carpathia and also be able to tell when Chang switched to them. When GCNN moved to the camera inside the temple, they found a commotion. Nicolae barked at the volunteer cameraman's volunteer assistant, and the picture wobbled. Buck jammed on the headphones and heard the assistant. "I'm sorry, Excellency, but I don't want to do that."

"You would disobey me?" Nicolae whispered.

"I want to obey, sir, but—"

"Sir?!"

"Holiness! But I'm not supposed to even be in here, and they aren't going to listen to me."

"You are speaking for me, and if they are not out of here by the time I get to their stations, *their* blood will be used for the sacrifices."

"Oh, sir—Potentate!"

"Now, or you face the same fate."

GCNN in New Babylon broke in. "His Excellency's entourage has passed through the Court of Women, where Ms. Viv Ivins will wait. The rest have entered the Court of Men and apparently have come upon priests refusing to leave the temple for Potentate Carpathia's private tour, as was clearly stipulated.

"From the time he negotiated with the Muslims to move the Dome of the Rock mosque to New Babylon, the potentate made it clear that all activity in the rebuilt Jewish temple would be allowed only with his approval. It is no secret that Orthodox Jews have continued with the daily rituals and sacrifices of their own faith even after Enigma Babylon One World Faith was instituted as the only legal international religion, designed to incorporate the tenets of all faiths.

After His Excellency resurrected himself from the dead, he became our object of worship, resulting in the dissolution of One World Faith and the establishing of Carpathianism. Still, the Jews and a faction of fundamentalist Christians known as Judah-ites—after their leader, self-proclaimed Messianic Jew, Dr. Tsion Ben-Judah—remain the last holdouts against our true and living god.

"His Excellency will eventually enter the Holy of Holies, but first he is insisting on the removal of the dissidents. Let's go back."

"Anyone not here in honor to me may be shot dead," Carpathia said. "Are you armed and prepared?"

"No!" the assistant cried.

"I am armed," Walter Moon said.

"You," Nicolae said, pointing to the assistant, "take Mr. Moon's weapon and do your duty."

Buck was riveted to the monitor as Nicolae stared not into the lens but past it to the volunteer. The camera turned jerkily to show the man refusing the gun. There was a rustle, a shot, a cry—and the man fell. The camera turned back to show Carpathia himself with the gun. "Show him," Nicolae said, and again the camera moved toward the body on the floor.

A change in ambient noise in Buck's headphones preceded Chang's voice. "Here we go," he said.

Chaim stepped back into position, and the red light shone on Buck's camera.

"Not only does the evil ruler of this world want to rid the priests of their rightful place in their own temple," Chaim said, "but it also appears he has personally committed murder at this holy site." What Buck heard did not match the movements of Chaim's mouth, and he realized the man was speaking in Hebrew and he was hearing in English.

The protesting holy men watching the monitors outside shouted and pumped their fists, bringing others crowding up the steps. Many of these, Buck noticed, had no marks of loyalty either, and their number was growing. He peeked at the small monitor beneath his camera. GCNN was broadcasting Chaim, though through his headset he could hear chatter about technical difficulties. Chang broke in again, assuring Buck, "I've got the New Babylon people muted off the air, but they're trying to get a bead on your camera. I'll switch back to Carpathia and let them wonder awhile."

"Hold till Chaim finishes this thought," Buck said.

"As Carpathia continues," Chaim said, "you should be able to see the laver where the priests wash their hands before they approach the main altar. The temple was creatively placed over a series of underground waterways where gravity allows constant water pressure for the various cleansings. Of course, he has no business in this place, and even a ceremonial washing of his hands will not exonerate him for defiling it."

"Switching," Chang said, and the monitor showed Carpathia signaling to his cameraman to follow.

"We were idle there for a moment," the man said.

"What did you miss?"

"I don't think we picked up the, you know . . ."

"My touching the blood?"

"No, Excellency. Shall we go back?"

"No!" Carpathia said, disgust in his voice. He held his black-red hands before the lens. "My faithful get the message." He raised his voice till it echoed and was distorted. "Any who dares interrupt my pilgrimage will find his blood on my fingers!"

Pounding footsteps made the cameraman whirl, and the screen filled with robed priests, charging Carpathia.

"See where this blood comes from!" Carpathia shouted, and the camera went to the faces of the priests, who stopped and paled.

Looking to where the body lay, they moaned and cried out, "Does your evil know no bounds?"

"Are you the god-haters," Nicolae raged, "who do not know me as a god, a god acknowledged by all others, but not named by you?"

One spoke up. "It should not surprise you that we showed our loyalty by offering daily sacrifices on your behalf."

"You have made offerings," Carpathia said, "but to another, even if it was for me. What good is it then, for you have not sacrificed to me? No sacrifice shall ever again be made in this temple except to me. Not *for* me, *to* me. Now leave or face the same fate as this unlucky one who was foolish enough not to believe that I have been allotted the nature of god!"

"God will judge you, evil one!"

"Give me your gun again, Supreme Commander!"

"We retreat not in fear but rather because you have turned the house of God into a killing field!"

"Just go! I shall have my way in my home, and should you be found without proof of loyalty to me by week's end, you shall offer your heads as ransom."

The priests left with shouts and threats, and Buck saw their colleagues outside greet them with sympathy and encouragement. "Lovers of God, unite!" one shouted, and onlookers picked up the chant.

Buck's camera light went on, and Chaim began again. "The inner court inside the pillars has stairs that face east and lead to the main altar. Priests who revere God march around the Court of Priests and the Holy Place with their left hands closest to the altar. This one who would trample holy ground has already begun the opposite way, so his right hand will be closest to the altar. The Scriptures foretold that he would have no regard for the one true God. What plans he has for the beast with which he ridiculed the Via Dolorosa will be revealed only as he invades deeper into God's own territory.

"What a shameful contrast this is to the Shekinah glory of God, which has thrice appeared, the last time at this very temple. God appeared to Moses on Mount Sinai when the Ten Commandments were handed down. He appeared again when Moses dedicated the Tent of God. And finally he showed himself at the dedication of Solomon's Temple on this very site. Should God choose, he could reveal himself even today and crush under his foot this evil enemy. But he has an eternal plan, and Antichrist is merely a bit player. Though Antichrist has been granted power to work his horror throughout the world for a time, he shall come to a bitter end that has already been decided."

"We were off the air again, Excellency," the cameraman reported when they came back on.

"What are you doing wrong?"

"Nothing, Potentate! My red light merely goes off, and no matter what I do, it returns when it returns."

"Show that! Show the beauty of the construction that was for my benefit, even though the architect and the craftsmen did not know it at the time." The camera panned to the cypress, the cedar, the gold inlays and coverings, the silver and the brass. "No expense was spared in my house!" Nicolae exulted.

Leon Fortunato, apparently feeling left out, said something not picked up by the microphone. "Speak up, my friend!" Carpathia said, removing his lapel mike and holding it to Fortunato's mouth.

"You, my lord," Fortunato rasped, obviously weak and wasted, "are the good spirit of the world and source of all good things."

+ + +

David Hassid sat high above Petra, with the solar panel of his laptop facing the sun and the screen shadowed. Chang was amazing. But the drama being played out on international television and over the Internet made David wonder how Chaim was going to gain the ability to free the believing Jews. He wished he could somehow communicate with Chaim that the time was now to put out a call for everyone to flee before Carpathia finished the desecration and returned to retaliate.

But scheming was not his place, David knew. God had had this worked out since the beginning of time, and he alone could prompt Chaim.

The crowds outside the temple looked dangerous. Carpathia supporters tried to shout down the Orthodox Jews, but those who had received the mark and worshiped the image could barely stand. The growing opposition to Carpathia seemed to gain confidence with its numbers, especially considering that the potentate's inner circle and military personnel were so clearly incapacitated.

Still, David knew, Nicolae was a mortal incendiary, flaunting his temporary power. He instructed his ersatz camera bearer to set up behind him as he waited outside the veil hiding the Holy of Holies. David could only imagine the God of heaven watching with the rest of the world as, with a flourish, Nicolae removed a long knife from his belt and sliced the veil from as high as he could reach all the way to the floor, then pushed back each side. Over Carpathia's shoulder—already waiting near the brass altar—David could see Carpathia's own gaudy throne and the gigantic pig from the day before, now without a saddle and clearly no longer tranquilized. It fought two ropes around its neck, held by more Carpathia loyalists who had not yet received his mark. Fortunato and Moon shuffled into position behind the pig, as if only to be sure to be in the picture.

Suddenly the feed switched to the camera outside, and David knew Chang had to have tipped off Buck. He had turned his lens on the opposition watching the monitors. Many fell to their knees and tore their robes.

The scene switched back inside, where the pig squealed and strained and Carpathia laughed, approaching with the knife. He lunged at the animal and it dodged, making him slip. "Want to play?" Nicolae roared and leaped aboard, knocking the pig to its knees. It quickly righted itself, and the potentate nearly slid off. He caught himself on one of the ropes, pulled himself back up, and reached with the knife, slashing the animal's throat.

The pig went wild and dumped Carpathia to the floor. The animal thrashed as Carpathia struggled to his feet, his clothes covered in blood. The handlers held on, and the pig soon slowed and lost its footing.

Nicolae, abandoning any semblance of ritual, resheathed his knife and cupped both hands under the blood pouring from the dying pig's neck. Before he was even upright again, he flung blood toward the altar and splattered the pig handlers, who ducked and howled in hysterics. Fortunato and Moon were caught in the melee and appeared to force smiles, though they also looked as if they were about to collapse.

David sat with his mouth open, wondering how anyone could take seriously a man who not only thumbed his nose at God, but who also acted like a drunken reveler at a frat party.

When the pig finally stopped moving, Nicolae attempted to butcher it with the knife and found neither himself nor the blade equal to the task. "Pity!" he cried, to the laughter of his people, and plopped himself down in his throne. "I wanted roast pork!"

Carpathia seemed to quickly tire of the silliness. "Get the pig out of here," he said, "and bring in my image." He stood and hurried to a spigot of rushing water. The camera stayed on his face, but it was clear he disrobed under the spray. "Cold!" he shouted, finally reaching for a towel provided by yet another lackey. Someone handed him the robe, sash, and sandals from the day before, and he looked directly into the lens. "Now, once my image is in place," he said, "we are out to Solomon's scaffold."

Chang patched in Chaim. "Is this not the most vile man who ever lived?" Rosenzweig said. "Is he not the antithesis of whom he claims to be? I call on all who have resisted or delayed in accepting his mark and plead with you to refuse it. Avoid the sentence of grievous sores and certain death."

David shifted and stretched his legs, eager to interact with someone about what everyone had seen. The most logical person he could think of was Hannah.

\+ + +

Buck feared his appropriated TV camera would be revealed when the small contingent of Orthodox Jews who had unintentionally worked together to shield it from Carpathia and his minions suddenly bolted away. The Temple Mount had become a roiling stew of angry citizens, and not just those without the mark of the beast. Loyalists had apparently come to the end of their patience with the loathsome sores all over their bodies. And the fiasco Carpathia had just perpetrated in the temple could not have amused more than his basest, most rabid supporters.

Messianic believers, new Christ-followers, the Orthodox Jews, and seemingly even thousands of undecided among the general populace had seen the new Carpathia. It was as if he had abandoned any attempt to persuade or convince anyone. He was to be revered and worshiped and followed because he was god, and anyone who didn't agree would suffer. But those who agreed most wholeheartedly were suffering the most.

But to have murdered a man in cold blood on international television, to literally drench his hands with the man's blood, to have announced the end of ceremonial sacrifices—except to himself—and then to not just claim the temple as his own house but to also defile it in such a graphic, disgusting way was more than the natural mind could comprehend.

Men in flowing beards cried out, "He would sacrifice a *pig* in the Holy of Holies and cavort in its blood?" They fell to their knees, weeping and moaning. But even more people crowded the pillars at the top of the steps, calling for Carpathia's own blood.

It became clear to Buck when Carpathia finally irrevocably tipped the scale against himself. The holy men shushed the crowd when Nicolae's small contingent of healthy men fetched the golden statue. A low rumble of dissent grew as thousands seemed unable to control themselves, while trying to hear what dastardly thing he would do next.

"Why worship at an altar of brass?" he said, his sneer filling the monitors. "If this is indeed the holiest of holy places, every supplicant should enjoy the privilege of bowing to my image, which our Most High Reverend Father has imbued with the power to speak when I am not present!"

Carpathia waited inside the temple for delivery of his statue, but when the assignees appeared to carefully tip it horizontally and bear it inside, they were surrounded by the mob. "Even GC personnel are fighting this, Chaim," Buck said, and the old man nodded. Buck shot him a double take. Chaim seemed more than solemn. He appeared distracted, probably running over in his mind his next step. This situation had turned uglier than anyone in the Tribulation Force had expected, from what Buck remembered of all their discussions and planning sessions. Something had to give—and soon.

When the protestors rushed the men carrying the statue, other loyalists from inside rushed out, brandishing weapons. A few fired into the air and the crowd backed off, waving their fists and cursing. When the monitors showed the men transporting the life-size image to the west end of the temple and up the steps to the Holy of Holies, the crowd had had enough and began rioting. If a person wore a GC uniform and was not part of the melee, he or she was a target of it.

Most uniformed personnel were too weak even to fire their weapons, but when some did and a few fell under their bullets, the throng erupted and attacked. The medical tents toppled, benches and chairs were upended, the guillotine was knocked over and stomped into pieces. Morale Monitors and Peacekeepers were trampled, their weapons yanked from their hands, and soon the TV monitors came crashing down. All over the Temple Mount people raged, screeching, "Down with Carpathia! Death to the monster! May he die and stay dead!"

Buck pulled Chaim to a safe spot and tried to shield the contraband camera. His monitor showed that the cacophony had reached Carpathia, and he appeared pale and shaken. "I am coming out to calm my people," he said into the lens. "They need only be reminded that I am their risen lord and god."

Few heard that over the din, but those who did must have spread the word quickly, because as Buck followed Carpathia's march back to the entrance of the temple, he looked up to see the Orthodox Jews leading the way to the fake Solomon's scaffold, which was quickly reduced to splinters.

A band of zealots spotted Buck's camera, and before he could convince them he was on their side, they grabbed it and smashed it to the ground. Desperate to see what would happen in front of the temple, Buck scampered up a tree and saw Viv Ivins meet Carpathia near the entrance. Something kept the rioters outside, and Buck guessed it could be only their reluctance to assassinate a man in the temple, despite what he had done there.

Nicolae looked petrified while trying to appear otherwise and kept looking back to find the rest of his entourage. They finally caught up, but simply remaining upright seemed to take the last vestiges of strength from Fortunato and Moon and many others. Carpathia pointed and shouted, and someone found him a microphone that was connected to loudspeakers in the outer court.

Like a madman choosing the wholly wrong approach to winning back the crowd, Carpathia held the mike in one hand and raised his other for attention, crying out, "You have breached the covenant! My pledge of seven years of peace for Israel is rescinded! Now you must allow me and my—"

But the rest was drowned out by the mutinous multitude. While they would not cross the threshold of the temple, they pressed right up to it, creating a human barrier between Carpathia and his freedom to step out. Suddenly they quieted and began to chuckle, then laugh, then roar with pleasure at what they had accomplished. It was as if they had cornered a helpless pest and now didn't know what to do with him.

"My brothers and sisters of the Global Community," Carpathia began again, "I will see that you are healed of your sores, and you will again see that it is I who love you and bring you peace!"

"You'll not leave here alive, pretender!" someone shouted, and others took up the cause.

Then, crystal clear in the early afternoon air, came the piercing voice of the little man in the brown robe, and all eyes and ears turned toward him. "It is not the due time for the man of sin to face judgment, though it is clear he has been revealed!"

The crowd murmured, not wanting to be dissuaded from killing Carpathia.

Chaim strode slowly toward the bulk of the group, and they respectfully, silently parted. "As was foretold centuries ago," Chaim continued as he angled toward the temple steps, "God has chosen to allow this evil for a time, and impotent as this enemy of your souls may be today, much more evil will be perpetrated upon you under his hand. When he once again gains advantage, he will retaliate against this presumption on his authority, and you would do well to not be here when his anger is poured out."

"That is right!" Carpathia hollered, his voice sounding tinny compared to Chaim's authoritative tone. "You will rue the day when you dared—"

"You!" Chaim roared, pointing at Nicolae. "You shall let God's chosen ones depart before his curse is lifted, lest you face a worse plague in its place."

Buck, still wedged in the tree, phoned Chang. "Camera's trashed," he said.

"So I gathered."

"You getting this?"

"The GC's trying to talk over it. It's as if they can't decide whether Carpathia would want it on the air. Heads are going to roll."

"What'd Carpathia just say?" Buck said. "I missed it."

"Something about his being at the Knesset, available to negotiate or to answer honest inquiries from his subjects."

"They'll never let him get out of the—"

But they did. The crowd backed away for Nicolae and his people as they had for Chaim.

"Any chance of tapping into the Knesset?" Buck said.

"Not that I know of," Chang said. "Are you going?"

"If Chaim goes, I go."

"Leave your phone open. I'll patch it to everybody else."

But before Buck could get down from the tree, Chaim raised his arms and gained the attention of the angry mob. "Let those who are in Judea flee to the mountains. Let him who is on the housetop not go down to take anything out of his house. And let him who is in the field not go back to get his clothes."

"Why should we flee?" someone yelled. "We have exposed the potentate as an impotent pretender!"

"Because God has spoken!"

"Now we're to believe *you* are God?"

"The great I Am has told me. Whatsoever he even thinks comes to pass, and as he purposes, so shall it stand."

Buck was sure the people would have none of it, but Chaim had apparently spoken with such authority that they were instantly calmed. "Where shall we go?" someone asked.

"If you are a believer in Jesus Christ as Messiah," Chaim said, "leave now for Petra by way of Mizpe Ramon. If you have transportation, take as many with you as you can. Volunteers from around the globe are also here to transport you, and from Mizpe Ramon you will be helicoptered in to Petra. The weak, the elderly, the infirm, find your way to the Mount of Olives, and you will be flown in from there."

"And if we do not believe?"

"If you have an ear to hear, make your way to Masada, where you will be free to worship God as you once did here at his temple. There I will present the case for Jesus as Messiah. Do not wait! Do not hesitate! Go now, everyone!"

Buck was stunned to see many with Carpathia's mark stagger into the throng that was quickly forming to depart the Temple Mount. He knew they could not change their minds, that they had once and for all turned their backs on God. But they were now in no-man's-land. They were without the protection of God, and yet they had publicly crossed Antichrist. Should the plague of boils be lifted, surely GC forces would cut them down. The Orthodox Jews and the undecided were allowed at Masada, but no one who had taken the mark of the beast could enter.

+ + +

David had been unable to raise Hannah on his computer, so he wrote his response to her e-mail and transmitted it just before watching the goings-on at the Temple Mount. Excitement coursed through him as he anticipated the first arrivals. He had spent hours setting up the basic framework of the wireless computer system, and now all he could do was wait.

+ + +

Buck didn't want to lose Chaim, but he needn't have worried. The Temple Mount was soon empty and left a mess. Chaim descended the temple steps and motioned to Buck to follow. As they walked in the direction of the Knesset, Jerusalem seemed to explode around them. Looters smashed windows and knocked over merchandise kiosks in the streets. Drunken revelers sang and danced and sloshed drinks as they cavorted outside bars and clubs. Those suffering with boils wailed, and many tried to kill themselves in broad daylight.

Meanwhile, the Jewish believers, the undecideds, and the Orthodox Jews hurried along, seeking rides to the Mount of Olives, Masada, or Mizpe Ramon. Operation Eagle vehicles abounded, unidentified other than by eager drivers encouraging others with the mark of God on their foreheads to quickly get aboard. Drivers who saw Buck and Chaim either saluted or pointed to heaven. Everywhere people called out, "He is risen," and were answered by, "Christ is risen indeed!" Many were singing.

Buck suffered from sensory overload. He mourned Hattie. He missed Chloe and Kenny and feared for their safety. He was both horrified and thrilled by what he had seen, and he was also puzzled yet hopeful. He had not expected Chaim to have to persuade people to flee Carpathia while they believed they had already gained the upper hand. And of course he had no idea what to expect at the Knesset.

* * *

As a commercial pilot Rayford had thrived on the schedule, the predictability of his days. But on this mission he had had to adapt at a moment's notice, depending upon how God led Chaim. This could have been as simple as driving people from Jerusalem to Mizpe Ramon—roughly a hundred miles—then airlifting them about fifty miles southeast to Petra. But somewhere along the line both Masada and the Mount of Olives had been added to the itinerary, and it was Rayford's job to stretch his personnel to fit the task. One responsibility he carved out for himself was picking up Chaim and Buck once everyone else was safe. Dr. Rosenzweig insisted on their being among the last to arrive at Petra, akin to a captain and his first mate's being the last ones off a ship, but Rayford wouldn't know until the last minute where to pick them up.

* * *

"Binoculars?" Z said. "I can do ya one better'n that, Chloe. You lookin' up or out?"

"Mostly out," Chloe said, yawning. "Nothing specific." She didn't want Zeke to know what was on her mind. It wasn't that she didn't trust him. She simply didn't want any input. The adults had sat watching the temple debacle, and the flight to Petra was under way. Once she was satisfied that Buck was safe, she would be able to sit idle no more.

Zeke had come up with an interesting idea weeks before. Like everyone else, she liked the way he thought, though his way of expressing himself might fool a stranger into thinking he was less than bright. He had encouraged Chloe to clone herself via the Internet. "You know, recruit other people like you. There have to be lots of young moms who are feeling left out of the action. Teach 'em what you do, get 'em to do it in their areas and regions. You can't do it all yourself anyway."

The concept had ignited like a gaslit fire. Chloe uploaded manuals and lists of duties, procedures, cross-referenced contact databases—everything a regional director of the International Commodity Co-op would need. She was virtually working herself out of a job.

Now she had gone to the jack-of-all-trades and the one man besides her father who had inventoried the entire Strong Building. Zeke had gone further than Rayford, however. He had computerized a list of everything he had found.

A tower that huge bore a mother lode of treasures. "I mean, there *are* binocs," he said. "Some really super-powerful, top-of-the-line types too. But knowin' you, you want the most powerful eyes I can find ya, am I right?"

"As usual."

"It'll be dawn soon. You want it like right now?"

"If possible."

"Be right back."

Zeke took several minutes. His computer told him where this item was, and he headed for the elevators.

Ming headed back to bed while Tsion reported that Chang had informed him he would try to patch Chicago in to the Knesset meeting of Chaim and Buck with Carpathia. "I need to sleep," Tsion told Chloe, "but I will keep an ear open for that . . . unless you want to."

"I've had enough of St. Nick for one night," she said. "Why don't you just record it and get some rest?"

Tsion nodded with a look that said her idea had scored with him. "That way I can listen if I want and not worry if I nod off."

Zeke returned, looking as if he couldn't wait to see Chloe's reaction. He handed her a plain white box that surprised her with its weight. She sat and opened it, producing a huge, squatty telescope about a foot long that took two hands to pull from the wrapping. "Wow," she said. "Will this need a tripod?"

"Not supposed to," Zeke said. "But you gotta brace it on somethin'. The window ledge will do. Want any help?"

"No thanks, Z. I appreciate it. Let me figure it out for myself. It's way past your bedtime too, isn't it?"

"Way past."

10

THE SORES HAD so decimated Carpathia's staff that Buck thought anyone could walk right past security at the Knesset and take him out. The weak, scratching, wincing crew looked up wearily at Buck and Chaim but barely acknowledged their presence. Not only was Buck not searched, but he was also not even asked his name. He and Chaim were ushered into a small conference room, where Nicolae sat with Fortunato on his right and Moon on his left. They looked like refugees from a quarantine camp, both hunched over the table, heads in their hands, barely able to keep their eyes open.

As the door shut behind Buck, Carpathia said sarcastically, "Forgive me for not standing." He pointed to two chairs. Buck sat quickly, then felt conspicuous when Chaim remained standing.

"I represent the one true God and his Son, Jesus, the Christ," the old man said. "I prefer to stand."

Carpathia appeared so angry he couldn't speak. His jaw muscles protruded as he ground his teeth, glaring. Chaim merely met his gaze.

"All right," Nicolae said, "I am letting these people run off to the hills. When do the sores go away? I upheld my end of the bargain."

"We had a bargain?" Chaim said.

"Come, come! We are wasting time! You said you would lift this spell if I—"

"That is not my recollection," Chaim said. "I said that if you did *not* let them go, you would suffer yet a worse plague."

"So I let them go. Now you—"

"It is not as if you had a choice."

Carpathia slammed an open palm on the table, making his cohorts jump. "Are we here to play word games? I want the sores on my people healed! What do I have to do?"

"Make no attempt to stop Israeli Messianic believers from getting to Petra."

Carpathia stood. "Have you not noticed? I am the only full-time employee of the Global Community not suffering from the plague!"

Chaim remained calm. "And that only because you have not taken your own mark, though I daresay you worship yourself."

Nicolae rushed around the table and bent to face Chaim from just inches away. "Our medical experts have determined there is no connection between the application of the mark of loyalty and—"

"Why does your bad breath not surprise me?"

"You do not dare to lift the curse for fear your fate will be the same as that of your two associates at the Wall."

"If your medical experts know so much," Chaim said, "how is it that they have been able to offer no relief?"

Carpathia sighed and sat on the table, his back to Fortunato and Moon. "So you are not here to negotiate? You are here to tell me I am at your mercy and that there is nothing I can do to ease the pain of my people?"

"I am here to remind you that this script has already been written. I have read it. You lose."

Carpathia stood again. "If I am not god," he said, "I challenge yours to slay me now. I spit in his face and call him a weakling. If I remain alive for ten more seconds, he, and you, are frauds."

Chaim smiled. "What kind of a God would he be if he felt compelled to act on your timetable?"

Buck loved seeing Carpathia speechless. He seemed to tremble with rage, staring and shaking his head. Behind him, Moon tapped Fortunato's shoulder, making the reverend recoil. "Sorry," Moon whispered and leaned close to his ear.

"Excellency," Fortunato rasped, "a word, please."

"What? What is it?"

Fortunato struggled to his feet, clasped his hands before him, and bowed. "Please, Your Worship. A moment."

Nicolae looked as if he were about to detonate. He moved back behind the table, making Moon stand too. Fortunato pleaded with him in a voice too faint for Buck to hear.

"I suppose you concur, Moon," Nicolae said.

Moon nodded and Fortunato added, "It was *his* idea," which made Moon's face drop, and he shot Leon a look.

"You two get out of here. I want a meeting, you know where, with the full cabinet."

"Not here?"

"No! I said you know where! These walls have ears!"

The two gingerly made their way out. Carpathia looked down at Buck. "This one makes me nervous," he said. "Does he have to be here?"

"He does."

"My people are pleading for respite," Nicolae said. "I recognize that I am forced to concede something."

"And that would be?"

Carpathia's eyes danced, as if he hated with his entire being what he had to say. "That . . . I . . . must . . . submit to you in this. I am prepared to do what I have to do to enable a lifting of the plague." He lowered his head as if pushing against an invisible force.

"You are under the authority of the God of Abraham, Isaac, and Jacob, maker of heaven and earth. You will allow this exodus, and when I am satisfied that the people under my charge are safe, I will pray God to lift the affliction."

Buck wouldn't have been surprised to see smoke rise from Carpathia's ears. "How long?" Nicolae said.

"This is a huge undertaking," Chaim said. "Six hours should be telling."

Carpathia looked up hopefully.

"But should you attempt to lay a hand on one of the chosen," Chaim warned, "the second judgment will rain down."

"Understood," Carpathia said, a little too quickly. He thrust out his hand.

Chaim ignored it, glanced at Buck, and left.

Buck rose to follow and wondered if Carpathia recognized either of them. He avoided eye contact, but as Buck slipped past Antichrist, Nicolae growled, "Your days are numbered."

Buck nodded, still looking away. "That's for sure."

* * *

Chloe scraped a three-inch hole in the black paint at the bottom of a window. Then she placed a cushion from the couch on the marble floor and set the telescope lens against the glass, bracing it on the frame. Several minutes of trial and error finally resulted in her discovering an image in the predawn haze. She thought she had seen something in the middle of the night several days before, but she had not been able to locate it again and thus told no one. Now she slowly scanned the horizon, trying to keep the hugely powerful apparatus steady and the image in front of her eye. The image was so magnified that she guessed she was viewing just a few feet square from more than half a mile away.

The problem was, of course, that such a lens required as much light as she could find. It was designed to bring stars into focus on clear nights. All she saw were the dark silhouettes of a ravaged skyline, and no light anywhere. Frustrated, she set the scope down and refocused with the naked eye, trying to get a bead on what she had seen faintly once. At about two o'clock in her field of vision and maybe three-quarters of a mile away, a speck of light stopped her. So it wasn't her imagination. The question was, what light would be on in a city the world thought was radiation contaminated? Was it possible Tribulation Force members were not the only intelligent life-forms in this alien universe?

She shook her head. Probably just a streetlight that somehow was still hooked up to power. Still, the scope might offer more clues. Keeping the speck in sight, she raised the instrument to the window and carefully studied the area. After a minute or two she realized she had aimed too high and was taking in the foreboding waters of Lake Michigan. Keeping the apparatus in place, she looked past it again and adjusted, then peeked through the eyepiece again.

The image jumped and moved, appeared and disappeared. It was more than a streetlight, but the harder she tried to focus on it, the more elusive it became. Her neck stiffened, her wrists cramped, her eye wearied. She realized she'd been holding her breath to minimize her movement, but that just caused her heart to beat harder. Finally she had to put the telescope down and move. But when she was ready to try again, the sun teased the eastern horizon. Chloe would have to try again another night.

+ + +

"Mount of Olives?" Buck said, as he caught up to Chaim.

"Of course. Then to Masada to see what kind of a crowd we have attracted."

"Question. Why six hours? You trust him?"

Chaim shot Buck a look. "Trust him? Of course! He was willing to shake on it."

"Okay, dumb question. But there's no way everybody will be safe by nightfall."

"We already know he will break the agreement, Cameron. Revelation 12 is clear that Israel is given two wings of a great eagle, that she might fly into the wilderness to her place, but that the serpent spews water out of his mouth like a flood after her. No question he will attack somehow, plague or not. Tsion believes the 'flood' is Antichrist's army. That same chapter says the earth helps the woman by opening its mouth and swallowing up the flood. May the Lord forgive me, but I want to see that. Don't you?"

Buck nodded, finally grabbing his phone and listening to see if Chang was still monitoring. "You there?" he said.

"Working on the Phoenix connection," Chang said. "Thanks. That was spooky."

"You're the best."

"I'll call you when I'm ready to patch you in."

Chaim waited till Buck was finished, then asked, "You know what happens after God thwarts Antichrist's armies, do you not?"

"You mean before or after you drop the second judgment on him?"

"Before *I* drop it? I am merely the messenger, my friend."

"I know," Buck said.

"The Bible says the dragon becomes enraged with the woman and goes to make war with the rest of her offspring, 'who keep the commandments of God and have the testimony of Jesus Christ.' To me that sounds like the other believing Jews around the world."

"And what do we do about that?"

"I have no idea," Chaim said. "We obey, that is all."

* * *

Rayford was too antsy to sit at Mizpe Ramon waiting for the first arrivals. He set a course for the Mount of Olives and phoned Tsion in Chicago on the way. Rayford felt bad when it was obvious from Dr. Ben-Judah's voice that he had been sleeping. But he said, "You are never an intrusion, Captain Steele."

"I confess I'm troubled, Dr. Ben-Judah. My military training was during peacetime, so this is the first time I've been responsible for so many people in a dangerous situation."

"But you have been through so much with the Tribulation Force!"

"I know, but I just wish I could be assured I will see no casualties."

"We certainly have had no such guarantees in our inner circle," Tsion said, "have we?"

"That's not reassuring."

"I just want to be honest, Captain. I assume that is what you want."

"What I want is what I asked for, I'm afraid—the knowledge that I will lose no one."

"I believe we will lose none of the 144,000, but most of those are scattered throughout the world. I am also fairly certain that the prophecies indicate that God will protect the Messianic believers who are fleeing Jerusalem. But you are asking about your operation personnel."

"Right."

"I can only pray and hope."

"I'm committed to not engaging the enemy in kill strikes."

"I am sympathetic to that, and yet you wish for no deaths on your side either. I do not know how realistic that is. Would you not feel justified in an all-or-nothing situation?"

"You mean if it's my guy or theirs? I guess I would permit firing."

"You know, Captain, the enemy will most certainly suffer losses. The way the verses read, many will perish in the calamities God puts in their paths."

"I prefer leaving that work to him."

* * *

David checked for a response from Hannah, and seeing none, keyed in a connect to Chang, who had the bugged Phoenix 216 online for the Trib Force.

The first voice was Walter Moon's. "I should be in bed, Excellency. I hate to complain, but I might have wished this meeting had been held at the Knesset. The incessant moving about—"

"Oh, stop your blubbering, Walter. I am not discounting your discomfort, but you make it sound as if you are at death's door."

"It feels like we are, Lordship," Leon said. "I am not one to—"

"Of course you are! Now I laid down the law to this Micah character and got him to guarantee a lifting of this disease by nine tonight or there would be consequences."

"You did? Well, how—"

"He had better tread lightly with me."

"But I thought—"

"That is your problem, gentlemen. Sometimes you must act viscerally and do what needs to be done. Is everyone here?"

"Many are being pulled from sickbeds," Walter said. "Which is where—"

"You should be, yes, I know. Here are Viv and Suhail. Let me know when we are all here."

"How long will it take to recover, once the affliction has been lifted?" Viv asked.

"I do not know," Carpathia said. "But even if there is residual fatigue or pain, you must all fight through it and encourage your people to do the same."

"Mr. Hut completes the contingent, Potentate."

"You look terrible, son," Nicolae said.

"I feel worse," Hut said.

"I cannot imagine. So how is my inaccurate-shooting friend?"

"Very funny."

"Excuse me," Nicolae said, "but was that two times consecutively you addressed me without title?"

"Well, pardon me, your highness."

David heard movement and assumed Carpathia had stood. "You would employ sarcasm with me?"

"I shot that man eight times at point-blank range, *worshipfulness!* The heckler I killed from two feet away. You couldn't have killed Micah yourself."

"Mr. Akbar, your sidearm, please."

"Oh, Excellency, is this nec—"

"Is *everyone* planning to disrespect me? I have death pills enough for the lot of you, and I deliver them through the barrel of this gun."

"If you could have killed Mr. Micah," Hut said, "why didn't you?"

"Oh, you honor him with a title, but not me—no, not your risen lord."

"You are nothing to me, Carpathia."

"On your feet, boy."

"I wouldn't give you the satisfaction."

BOOM!

Cries and gasps followed the sound of the body's tumbling. "Walter, have the stewards get him out of here. Now who is next?"

Silence.

"Is there then someone here who would care to fire upon me?"

"No!"

"No, Excellency!"

"Please, Potentate!"

"No!"

"Is there another among you who retains some notion that this is not serious business? I remind you that I was dead three days and raised myself! I have demanded your freedom from these sores, and though we cannot be certain until the time comes, I believe you will enjoy immediate healing. Regardless, you and yours will be ambulatory and able enough again to carry out my battle plan."

"Wouldn't an attack bring back the plague, Excellency?" Moon asked.

"Viv, do you see what I have to work with here? Mr. Moon is my supreme commander, my executive vice president, if you will, yet he wants to know if—" and here he mimicked Moon with a ridiculous plaintive whine—"an attack wouldn't bring back the plague! Honestly, Walter, do you think I am new to the negotiating game?"

"No, sir, I—"

"Spare me! The curse will be lifted at 2100 hours, and the hundreds of thousands of cowards will be in one of four places. Anyone? Come on! Someone?"

Suhail Akbar said, "The Mount of Olives, en route to Mizpe Ramon, Masada, or Petra."

"Excellent! Someone is thinking! And what is unique about so many people in so few places? Suhail?"

"They are together, and they are vulnerable."

"Precisely. I want the whole of Israel declared a no-fly zone for all but Global Community aircraft at 2115 hours."

David heard Suhail calling his people.

"And while you are at it, Director," Carpathia said, "establish a curfew at the same time in all of the United Carpathian States for civilian vehicular traffic. Prepare a retaliatory strike for the damage we suffered at Petra earlier today, assuming until further knowledge that that wanton ambush was initiated by the Judah-ites."

"Where will we attack, Potentate?" Akbar said.

"Masada at 2130 hours. Did you not predict attendance of more than one hundred thousand?"

"But those are not Judah-ites, Excellency."

"They are potential converts, man! And this Micah himself will address them! He will surely have followers with him, but he has unwittingly put them all in one box for us and tied a ribbon around it. What would it take to ensure annihilation?"

"We have the firepower, sir."

"No arrests on the road. No warnings in the air. Illegal vehicles will be destroyed on sight and invading planes shot from the sky. This Mizpe Ramon site was camouflaged to somehow make it appear a GC operation. Let us make use of it then. And if anyone remains on the Mount of Olives after 2100, they are fair game."

"Sir?" Moon said. "What if Mr. Micah does call down the plague of sores again?"

"He will know the consequences if we act with dispatch."

"But what if he follows through on his threat to turn the water—"

"The what-ifs will do you in one day, Walter. You serve the ruler of the universe, and we shall prevail. I have tricked this wizard into breaking his spell, and before he realizes his mistake, we will have regained the advantage. We can virtually eliminate the Jerusalem Orthodox Jewish population and cripple the Judah-ites to the point of extinction. Ideally, we will flush out Ben-Judah himself, and this time he will not find me so hospitable."

"What about those who reach Petra?"

Carpathia laughed. "Petra as a place of refuge is ludicrous! It is as defenseless as Masada. They will be on foot, stuffed into a bowl of rock. An air attack should be over in minutes, but for that we shall wait until the last of them are there."

"The Judah-ites did display heavy firepower today," Akbar said.

"That merely justifies whatever level of retribution we deem appropriate. Any casualties?"

"No reports of anyone actually hit. Two unaccounted for."

"Missing in action?"

"If you wish."

A long pause. Then Carpathia: "Two MIAs."

* * *

Buck and Chaim sat under an ancient tree on the Mount of Olives and watched thousands find their way in. Within an hour the Operation Eagle choppers began floating into position, Rayford himself among the first. The birds were loaded to capacity but were in no way keeping up with the growing crowd.

Buck had relayed the Carpathia meeting word for word to Chaim as he listened by phone, but Dr. Rosenzweig had remained expressionless. In the end he said, "I am not surprised. I will pray that God will lift the plague of boils completely and restore everyone to full strength. I want them overconfident, full of themselves when they try to take vengeance. And when the second plague rains down, I pray it will carry God's full potency."

"Doctor, do we risk catastrophe at Masada?"

The old man shook his head. "I do not know, but I do not feel we should back down. We will finish before nine o'clock and warn the Jews of Carpathia's plan. They may leave or stay and fight, but I hope they will feel even more urgency to make their decisions for Christ too. As people are sealed by God, we will rush them to Petra."

* * *

Rayford felt alone in the packed chopper. Listening in on the Carpathia meeting had confirmed his worst fears. The only location he was confident of was Petra, and even there, he had to wonder if it was the place or the people who would be protected. He used his secure radio to reroute all air traffic directly to Petra. "No stops, repeat, no stops at Mizpe Ramon. Ground vehicles will deliver their charges to the foot passage into Petra. Those who can walk in, will. Those who cannot—or when the passageway is too crowded, those who are left exposed—will need to be air-hopped inside. Continue the routes to and from the Mount of Olives. And ignore an expected air curfew. Take evasive and defensive action as necessary, but do not fail these people."

Rayford conference-called Albie, Mac, and Abdullah. "Wish we could get our heads together," he said. But each was either flying a load to Petra or returning to pick up another.

"Rethinkin' your no-shootin' policy there, Chief?" Mac said.

"I hope so," Albie said.

Rayford let out a heavy sigh. "I just don't want to lead anyone to slaughter."

"Arm us, Ray," Albie said. "George has enough weapons for—"

"Tell me George was not privy to the Phoenix patch-in," Rayford said. It wasn't that he didn't trust the man, but keeping need-to-know circles close was important and had been made clear.

Silence.

"Tell me, Albie!"

"Ray, you know me better than that. You said nobody but Trib Force, and that's the way we played it."

"How many of our pilots would know how to handle a fifty-caliber?"

"None of 'em, Ray," Mac said. "You issue those to drivers. Too erratic and dangerous from the air. Give us the DEWs. Somebody stops us on the ground, we heat 'em up."

"They're planning to shoot us out of the air, gentlemen!"

"Only way to prevent that with the fifties is to shoot first," Mac said. "It means a change of policy. Is that where you're goin', Ray?"

Rayford stalled. "Haven't heard from you, Abdullah. You there?"

"Here, boss."

"Well?"

"Not bad, thank you, sir."

"I mean, well, what do you think?"

"About what?"

"Smitty! Come on! I need some counsel here."

"We cannot shoot the big guns and fly too, Captain. That would take two pilots to a chopper. And out of what hole do we shoot such a weapon?"

"He's right," Mac said. "As usual."

"I am willing to trust God with my life," Abdullah said. "And if he would allow me, I would happily use a DEW to make toast of the enemy."

Rayford peeked over his shoulder at the believers huddled behind him, fear and hope etched on their faces. They could not hear him over the noise of the engine and the whirring blades.

"All right, gentlemen," he hollered into the phone, "after you unload your passengers, swing by Mizpe Ramon and pick up a third of the DEWs each and distribute them to your respective squadrons. Albie, get George involved too. And the first one there, get Ms. Rose and Ms. Palemoon evacuated if they're ready. You'll need room for all their supplies too."

"You think the GC is going to waste the landing strip and our quarters?" Albie said.

"Likely."

"Where are we EVACing these women?"

"Masada for now."

"You gonna distribute fifties to ground drivers, Chief?"

"Still noodling that one, Mac," Rayford said.

* * *

David guessed it would be two hours from Chaim's speech at the Temple Mount until he saw his first arrivals. He called Rayford. "What gives with our nurses? Hannah owes me an e-mail response. They okay?"

"No reason to believe otherwise. Did you try calling them?"

"No response."

"I'll check in on them." He told David what was happening with the weapons and the med center.

"Need my help on that?" David said.

"You've got to hang in there and coordinate until Chaim arrives, and that could be a couple of days."

"I could appoint one of the first to get here. There's no science to this. How are you going to handle those big guns by yourself?"

"I'll get Leah and Hannah to help."

"They done tearing down and packing up?"

"Should be."

"You regret having the airstrip built and then having to abandon it?"

"Sure, but we needed it on the front end anyway. Where else were all our birds going to land?"

"Got any prospects on board?"

"For your job? I don't know, David. Why don't you stay put?"

"If they speak Hebrew and can elicit trust, that'll free me up to hop back to the strip with you and load the guns."

"I'm not even sure I'll issue the fifties," Rayford said.

"Well, I'm willing if you need me."

Late in the afternoon David climbed to the high place and scanned the horizon. Nothing yet, but he heard movement in the rocks below. No way anyone on foot could have arrived before the choppers. He knelt and crept to the edge, holding his breath to listen. His heart banged against his ribs. He guessed two sets of footsteps, slowly moving.

David pulled out the only weapon he could think of, his phone, and readied himself to speed-dial Rayford. He rose to where he could peer over the side. Resolutely and gingerly picking their way through loose rock not fifty feet below him were two sickly, stumbling GC Peacekeepers, uniforms drenched in sweat. Each carried a high-powered rifle. David punched the speed-dial button for Rayford, and the Peacekeepers both looked directly up at him at the same time. Before he could get the phone to his ear, they dropped to their knees and angled their weapons at him.

David dropped the phone and dove for cover, sharp rocks digging deep into his knees and hands. The soldiers, obviously left for dead by their compatriots, must have felt a surge of adrenaline. They couldn't have expected to find anyone here after surviving the fifty-caliber assault from the other direction, but now they advanced with vigor.

David scrambled to his feet, only to discover something seriously wrong with his ankle. He tried hopping toward a cave, but unarmed he would be easy prey there. He heard his pursuers separate just below the ridge, the sounds of their boots in the rocks coming from about twenty feet apart. If they rushed him, David had nowhere to go.

He was no match for them, but retreat wasn't an option. He hopped toward the edge, bent to scoop a handful of jagged rocks, and reared back to fire at the first head that popped up.

\+ + +

Rayford glanced at his ringing phone and saw who was calling. Again. So soon. David had never proven to be a pest. "Steele here," he said.

All he heard were sounds of boots on rocks.

"David? You there?"

From a distance, "God, help me!"

"David?"

A desperate cry, a shout in Hebrew, burps of gunfire from at least two weapons, a fall, a grunt. David's hoarse whisper, "God, please!" Liquid splashing.

\+ + +

David lay on his back, his body numb, no pain even in his ankle. The cloudless blue sky filled his entire field of vision. His heart galloped and his panicked lungs made his chest rise and fall in waves. Though he could feel nothing, he heard blood gushing from his head.

The soldiers leaned over him, but he could not move his eyes to focus on either of them. If only he could appear already dead . . . but he couldn't stop his heaving chest. David could pray only silently now. He pleaded with God to let him neither hear nor feel the kill shots as the two pointed their muzzles at his heart and pulled the triggers.

\+ + +

Rayford's phone was still open, but all he heard after more deafening rifle shots were expressions of effort and what he could only imagine was the lifting of a body and the flinging of it over the side of a mountain. Then footsteps away from the phone, until they faded out of range.

Besides dreading what he would find at Petra, Rayford couldn't deliver a chopper full of believers to a spot that could be teeming with the enemy lying in wait. Hating himself for already thinking past what sounded for all the world like David Hassid's death, Rayford knew he had to keep that phone from falling into the wrong hands.

11

LEAH DIDN'T UNDERSTAND HANNAH, but that was okay. She didn't always understand herself either. They had secured the last of the medical supplies into hard-sided boxes that would fit into a cargo hold and were now monitoring Hannah's computer.

"You know for sure it was Hassid who called?"

Hannah nodded.

"And you want to talk to him, so why didn't you—"

"I'm not sure I want to talk to him until I know how he's going to respond to my e-mail. He should have written me back. Then I'd know and I could take his call. Maybe."

Leah shook her head. "Even if we didn't have only three and a half years, I'd tell you life's too short and you ought to call him. He's a busy guy. When would he have had time to write you back?"

"I found time to write."

"Hannah! We're not building a computer system here that has to serve a million people."

Hannah was staring at the screen. The news was nothing but Carpathia propaganda, pundits trying to spin his temple folly into something that made sense. Leah leaned in to look at the scroll across the bottom of the screen. "His Excellency the potentate guarantees healing from the affliction of sores by 2100 hours Carpathian Time."

"I'm stupid," Hannah said.

"I know."

"Stop it! We hardly know each other."

"Sorry. Why are you stupid?"

Hannah pointed to the computer's status bar below the scrolling message. It showed she had mail. "Bet that's from David," she said.

"Let's find out," Leah said, but before either could switch screens, their phones rang simultaneously. "Rayford," Leah told Hannah.

"Mine too," Hannah said.

Leah held up a hand. "Let me," she said. "Med center."

"Leah, Rayford. You two okay?"

"Yeah, except it looks like you called us both at the same time."

"I did. Hannah there?" Leah nodded at her and Hannah answered too. "You packed up and ready to go?"

"Yes," Leah said. "But where—"

"Just listen. I'm short on time. You know George?"

"Big guy? Calif—"

"That's him. I just pulled him off another assignment. He's gonna land there within three or four minutes and he's going to need help setting up a nest of fifty-caliber rifles. Smitty will join him soon."

"Don't they each have a load of passengers?"

"Yes, and we need to get them as far from the airstrip and the buildings as we can."

"They're not going to Petra?"

"Eventually. Just listen. By the time it's dark, those people need to be isolated and invisible from the air. After I land there briefly and take off again, any other aircraft over Mizpe Ramon will be GC, and George and Smitty will be defending the airstrip."

"And we'll be babysitting two loads of passengers until someone comes for them?"

"Three. I've got a load too, and I need to pick up a fifty myself."

"Where are you going?"

"I've got a situation at Petra, and I'm going to need one of you to go with me. Leah, that would be you."

"Hold on!" Hannah said. "Who's at Petra besides David?"

"We've delivered no one yet. I want to be sure the area is secure before we—"

"Why wouldn't it be? What's the problem?"

"I don't know yet, but—"

"But there's a problem or David could tell you."

"I just can't reach him right now is all," Rayford said. "Let's not jump to any—"

"Then I'm coming. Leah can help George and Abdullah and herd these people somewhere."

"Hannah," Rayford said, "I—"

"Don't try to talk me out of this, Captain Steele. I—"

"Hannah! This is a military operation and I am your superior officer. I decide who will do what, and I've told you who is going and who is staying. Do you understand?"

"Yes, but—"

"Any questions?"

"No, but, well, I think I just heard from David."

"Either you did or you didn't. Did he call?"

"He e-mailed."

"You're sure?"

"Not entirely," Leah said. "Check it, Hannah."

She switched screens. "Yes, it's from him!"

"When was it sent?"

"Just a sec—oh!"

"Just now or . . . ?"

"No. Some time ago."

"Anything pertinent? Problems? He need help?"

"No," Hannah said, scanning it quickly. "Just personal stuff."

Leah put a hand on Hannah's shoulder and raised her chin at Hannah in encouragement. The younger woman looked terrified.

"Okay, Hannah? We clear?"

"Yes, sir."

"Let me talk with just Leah now, all right?"

Hannah slapped her phone shut while reading David's message.

"Leah," Rayford said, "I don't know what we're going to find at Petra, but David tried to call me and all I heard sounded like him being shot."

"Oh, no!"

"Bring heavy-duty, first-aid stuff and a stretcher."

"Got it."

"If we have to load him on the chopper, can you and I do that?"

"Worry about your end, Captain," she said. Then, whispering and turning away from Hannah, "And you'd better start worrying about that phone and those computers."

"Way ahead of you," Rayford said. "Be there in a few minutes."

* * *

Chang was studying the itchy spot on his leg under a light in his New Babylon palace apartment when Rayford called. After a fast briefing, Chang said, "Don't worry about the phone. I can neutralize that from here."

"What do you mean?"

Chang began tapping keys as they spoke. "I can nuke the innards, erase the mother chip. In fact, I just did."

"Now let's hope they haven't found it yet."

"When you connect with David," Chang said, "I need to talk with him."

"I didn't like what I heard, Chang."

"I know, but you can't be sure what you were hearing."

"I know David was unarmed."

"I'm checking on those computers."

"Right now? You can do that?"

"Thanks to David, we can do just about anything from here. Luckily, there's no way they can break into the software. That's on a revolving encoder that can only unravel itself, and it's programmed not to."

"Well, I don't understand all that, but I'm more worried we've got a bunch of crazed GCers up there who think they'd be helping their cause by just destroying all the hardware."

"They *would* be helping their cause. And they would set us way back. But there wouldn't be a bunch of them, would there?"

"How would we know?"

"These have to be leftovers from your attack, right?"

"Probably."

"You heard the Phoenix meeting," Chang said. "There were two unaccounted for."

+ + +

Rayford put down well off the south end of the airstrip at Mizpe Ramon and sat talking with Mac and Albie by radio as Hannah and Leah met the chopper with medical supplies and a stretcher. As Hannah led the escapees away from the craft, first finding out who understood English and Hebrew and using them to interpret for her, Leah tossed the supplies aboard and waited outside. "Mr. Smith is bringing your weapons," she mouthed.

Rayford nodded and told Mac and Albie to fly their charges to Wadi Musa, near Petra, and to assume they would be both seen and heard by the two GC suspected at Petra. "Tell your people to stay with the choppers until you come back for them, and then get to the footpath entrance as soon as you can. Don't go in until I get there with weapons for you."

"Question," Albie said.

"Make it quick."

"Have we been all wrong about this being a place of refuge?"

"Albie, all I know to do is to clear it for the people, get 'em in there, and trust God to take care of them."

"And if you find Hassid's body?"

Rayford hesitated. "Then I'm gonna assume it's them or us, and let me tell both you guys something: It's going to be them."

When Rayford leaped from the chopper, Abdullah was already hurrying across the sand from the munitions storage unit. He was bent under the weight of three fifty-caliber rifles on his shoulder with a huge belt of ammunition draped over them. His other arm pointed straight out from his body for balance. Rayford and Leah ran to him and helped carry the weapons to the helicopter.

"You all right, Smitty? You ready?"

"George is giving me a course crash," he said, "whatever that means."

"Crash course. Quick, fast."

Abdullah nodded. "I liked the DEWs, but I will shoot these too. George is setting up at a steep angle to take the enemy planes out of the sky, but I worry about accuracy."

"All you'll have to hit is one and the rest will run."

"I hope you are right, Captain. I will be praying for you, and I am hoping you are wrong about Mr. Hassid. He is a wonderful man."

Rayford hoped so too. He and Leah boarded, and as he guided the chopper up and away, he gazed at the Jordanian sprinting back to where George was setting up to defend the airstrip. Rayford was in the middle of exactly what he had hoped to avoid. People were going to die. One may already have. Knowing he would again see these beloved martyrs, along with all the others he had lost in so short a time, did little to console him. There had to be a limit to the trauma a man could endure. He should have long since blown past his.

\+ + +

Buck had helped Chaim board one of the choppers bound for Masada, and they arrived to find tens of thousands of curious Israelis streaming up the steps into the fabled fortress. Buck had been getting sketchy reports that the airlift had hit a few snags and that the return runs from Petra to the Mount of Olives would be delayed. Rayford was undoubtedly busy and in contact with his people, because he was not answering his phone or returning Buck's calls. Chang reported that he would rather Buck wait and talk with Rayford personally.

It was around nine in the morning in Chicago, so Buck called Chloe while Chaim was pacing behind him. Just before Chloe answered, Chaim bent and whispered, "I shall speak when this place is full."

\+ + +

Rayford could not think of a way to avoid detection by whatever GC might be waiting at Petra. Three choppers would land close by inside several minutes of each other, and it wouldn't be long before dozens more showed up. He considered rerouting the others to Mizpe Ramon, but he feared Carpathia might order an attack there even before the lifting of the plague, in retaliation for the firing upon his forces. Fearing the airstrip was targeted made him wary to risk more than the three chopper loads already waiting near there. Who knew? Maybe Carpathia or Akbar were smart enough to delay their attack until dark.

With just himself and Leah to worry about, Rayford decided to set the helicopter down on the narrow Siq that led pedestrian and hooved traffic into Petra. He carefully positioned the craft close enough to the outside walls that even if they had been seen, it would be impossible to be fired upon from inside the city.

Unless the enemy was asleep or deep in a cave, they had to be aware that outsiders were coming. Mac and Albie jogged up, the latter gasping for air. "He is so much older and yet in such better shape," Albie said.

"I jog every day," Mac said. "'Sides, I got about a foot on you."

"Catch your breath," Rayford said. "We've got about another mile to go on foot, and that just gets us into the city. Unless we want to be just targets, we're going to have to climb, and you remember how heavy these babies are."

He handed fifties and ammo to each man while Leah dragged out her box of supplies. "The stretcher," she said. "Bring it or leave it?"

"We can always come back for it," he said, reminding Mac and Albie to carry the weapons vertically to focus the center of gravity. "When we get inside, we're going to split up. If there are only two of them, we'll even the odds a little. I'm assuming they'll be above us, which gives them the first advantage. Resist the urge to call out for David."

"That's your urge?" Mac said.

Rayford nodded. "I want to know what happened to him, even if it's what I fear."

"Let me look for him," Leah said. "I'll leave my stuff at the other end of the gorge. I don't know why you couldn't have spared another of those rifles."

"Too much to carry," Rayford said. "Anyway, I hope you're busy with a patient."

"I won't be much good to him if I'm dead," she said.

Mac handed her his sidearm. "It's only a .45," he said.

"I'll take it."

"You know how to use it?"

"Safety on the left?"

Mac nodded.

"I know more than Captain Steele thinks I do," she said.

"We're only as good as the slowest man," Rayford said. "Albie, lead the way. We need to hurry, but don't waste all your energy."

Albie pulled up his trousers, tightened his belt, and retied his boots. Hoisting the weapon, he swung it vertically and leaned it back into one shoulder. He started off at a fast walking pace, frustrating Rayford, but soon enough he seemed to catch a second wind and began to trot. Mac dropped in behind, loping easily. Rayford let Leah slide in front of him and had to admit he was amazed that she could lug the medical box in one hand, keep her other arm out for balance, and still trot along apace. Rayford himself had little trouble keeping up, but he felt every one of his years—and every joint as well.

A little more than ten minutes later, the narrow, high-walled gorge opened into the stunning sight of Al-Khasneh—the Treasury, once purported to hold the riches of the pharaoh at the time of the Exodus. Under different circumstances, Rayford would love to have gawked at the towering façade cut out of solid rock, but he and his people—not to mention the million that were to follow—were at a point of no return.

Albie stopped and bent over, sucking for air. The rest quietly set down their loads. Rayford moved ahead of them and squatted, peeking out into the vast opening. It was then that he realized that either by dumb luck or the subtle leading of God, he had done something right. He heard the thwocking of at least one more helicopter and knew that more could not be far behind. All those birds had to give the GC, if that's who was here, pause. Where would *they* hide but in a cave? Unless they went on an immediate offensive, they would be quickly outnumbered and had to assume they would be easily overrun.

Rayford turned and whispered, "Leah, leave the med box here, take a hard right, stay low and out of sight as much as you can. Circle around as far as you can go before having to ascend. If that gives you too much exposure, find a place to stay hidden. Our main objective is to find David and get him out of here. He usually called me from one of the high places for best reception."

"Have you tried calling him again?" Leah said.

"Chang already nuked his phone to be safe."

"Safe for whom? What if he's trying to contact us?"

"We couldn't risk it, Leah," Rayford said. "Albie's going to be going left. Mac and I will cover each other and try to see what's straight ahead past the main monuments. We're all trying to get as high as we can without becoming targets. If you find David, click your radio twice and we'll find you. If you encounter the enemy, keep clicking till you see us. Questions?"

They looked at each other in the cool dimness of the gorge and shook their heads. As they moved out into the brighter but fading sun before twilight, Rayford was overwhelmed with the feeling he was in someone's crosshairs. It was nothing unique. He had felt the same way years before in weekend paintball games. There was just something about knowing you were likely beneath your enemy that made you feel you could be seen without being able to see.

Rayford must have seemed as slow to Mac as Albie had to Rayford, because as soon as they reached a clearing wide enough for him to get by, Mac easily moved on ahead. He was headed for the shadow of an outcropping of rock, and Rayford accelerated to stay with him. They knelt there, panting, and Mac squinted across the high horizon behind them. Two more choppers flew over, and almost immediately, Rayford heard two clicks on his radio. He and Mac caught each other's eye. "Who?" Mac mouthed, leaning out and looking to his left, where Albie would have gone.

Rayford leaned the other way and saw Leah behind a rock maybe a hundred yards away and thirty or forty yards up a rocky path. He elbowed Mac and they stared at her as she held up an open palm to them and kept her eyes in the direction of whatever she had seen. She pulled the .45 from her belt with her free hand, but her open palm and her gaze did not stray.

Finally she turned and looked directly at Rayford and Mac. She pointed two fingers at her eyes, then her index finger above her and to the left, which would put the target almost directly above the men. She held up two fingers. "Two directly above us?" Rayford whispered.

Mac nodded. "I'm guessin' she's lookin' a couple hundred yards up."

Rayford kept his eyes on Leah as he started to scoot out from under the rock overhang, but she held up her palm again, stopping him as she continued to watch. Suddenly she showed him the back of her hand and beckoned him out with her fingers. He hesitated, and she looked at him and nodded, then looked back up.

Rayford duckwalked out and turned to look. He stared at the sheer face of a rock wall and looked back at Leah to see if he could keep coming out. She nodded, and he heard two more clicks on his radio. That made him and Mac and Leah look to where Albie was climbing. He signaled the same as Leah from his vantage point. Rayford backed away from Mac, who stayed in position, until he saw the two GC with their backs to him on a high ridge. Both were uniformed and armed, but they looked lethargic, following the helicopters and checking the valleys below too.

Rayford signaled to both Leah and Albie to keep moving, then nodded to Mac to follow him. They hurried out and between building walls to a small gorge that led to a path toward higher ground. They waited at a bend where they were out of the line of vision of the two on the ridge far above. "They're too far from Leah and Albie to hear their radios," Mac whispered.

Rayford mashed the button and said, "How sure are we there are only two?"

"No idea," Leah said.

"They're not on assignment," Albie said. "They're hurting, and they don't seem to be answering to anyone. They're not doing anything specific. Just hanging around, waiting."

"You'd bet there are no others?"

"Not sure I'd stake my life on it," Albie said.

Mac clicked in. "That's exactly what we're doing," he said. "Make the call."

"If we had to decide, I'd say it's worth the chance. But what's the rush?"

"Hundreds of people starting to line up outside," Rayford said. "And they've got to be an hour above us."

Two clicks interrupted and Leah came on. "I see about a hundred yards I can advance without their seeing me. Shall I go for it?"

Rayford glanced at Mac, who nodded. "Affirmative. Three clicks when you're in place, but don't speak unless you know they're far enough away."

As soon as he said that, Leah began a long but smooth ascent, the sidearm in her hand. The two GC abruptly turned and walked the other way. "They're headed your way, Albie," Rayford said.

"I hope they keep coming," he said, and he lay on his stomach, unfolding the built-in bipod and loading his weapon.

"That's not a bad idea," Mac said. "We can set up right here."

"We've got Leah up there without us then, Mac. We using her for bait?"

Mac shook his head. "Not unless they turn back toward her." He nodded at her. "She'll reach a flat area up there in thirty minutes." Mac thrust a round into the chamber of the big gun and stretched out on his belly.

A little more than twenty minutes later a chopper approached, and the GC stopped and stared at it, not even attempting to hide. Like mirror images, they raised their weapons and followed the trajectory of the craft. "Don't even think about it, scumbags," Rayford muttered.

Mac scooted to his left and sighed. "I've got a bad angle here. You still got a bead on 'em?"

Rayford sat up and peered through his scope. "Yeah." He punched the radio. "See 'em, Albie?"

"Do I ever! They've both got that big old mark with Carpathia's mug on it, about two inches high over their right eyes."

"Hold," Rayford said. "Maybe they've got David somewhere."

"I lost 'em," Albie said.

"Me too," Mac said.

"I've still got 'em," Rayford said.

Click.

"Go, Leah."

She clicked again.

"They're far enough away," Rayford told her. "What've you got?"

But Mac grabbed his arm. "Maybe she can't talk. Maybe she's got more company."

"Did I give her away by talking to her?" Rayford felt sick.

"Let me check," Mac said. "You got another weapon?"

"Nine millimeter is all."

Mac reached for it. "I got no angle anyway, and Big Bertha will slow me down."

Rayford dug the weapon from his belt in the back and handed it to Mac, who quickly rose and hurried off.

Another twenty minutes and Leah came back on. "You don't want to know what I found," she said.

Rayford almost collapsed from relief. "You're okay there?"

Mac heard the exchange and stopped on the path, his back to a wall.

"I'm okay," Leah said, her voice quavery. "Found David's phone."

"Good."

"Not so good. Lots of blood here, and it leads over the side of a ridge."

Rayford let his eyes shut for several seconds. "Better stay put."

"I've got to know, Ray. Permission to proceed."

"Denied. Those two come any farther around a crag and they'd be able to see you."

"Thought you said they were closer to Albie."

"They are, but there's a clear visual line if they come around."

"I'll risk it."

"Negative."

"C'mon, Rayford! They couldn't hit me from there anyway."

"Leah! Stay . . . put."

From as far away as she was, Rayford felt her glare. He wanted as badly as she did to know just whether the trail of blood led to David's body, especially if there was a chance he might still be alive.

"Where are they now?" she asked.

"I'll let you know if and when you may proceed. Any hope he's alive?"

"Not if this is his blood."

"How can you know that?"

"You sure you want to know?"

"Give me your professional opinion."

"There's an awful lot of blood here, Ray. If it's all one person's . . ."

"And you think it is?"

"One pattern shows a pulsating spray. You want me to go on?"

"Yes."

"Another shows exit wound drainage and no pulse. And the blood leading to the edge looks like a drain too."

"So whoever it was, was dead before he went over the side."

"Affirmative."

"I want to know if it was David, Leah."

"So do I. Say when."

"Hold."

12

HANNAH FOUND THE ISRAELI believers remarkably low maintenance. Many had brought food, which they shared with others. All they wanted was to know when they might be transported to Petra, and the best Hannah could tell them was that she believed it would be that very evening. The people paced or sat and talked about Carpathia, what had gone on at the temple and the Temple Mount that day, and how excited they were about this new adventure. They wanted to meet Micah.

Big George, who proved shy around Hannah, and Abdullah, who was shy around everyone, busied themselves setting up their weapons nest where they could be seen neither from the sky nor by the Israelis, who did not need to be unduly troubled.

Hannah found herself praying for David, for Leah, for Rayford, and for the entire operation. When she had a moment, she stole back into the medical quarters and reread David's e-mail.

> *Hannah, forgive me. What can I say? You are right. I was insensitive. And don't give a second thought to your worry that I might misinterpret your feelings. The truth is, if there was one thing that niggled at the back of my mind in this whole decision, it was that I was going to miss you. I didn't know how to express it because I didn't want to be misunderstood either.*
>
> *I don't know why we feel we have to tiptoe around these issues, especially now. No, we didn't know each other well enough to be thinking about anything but a friendship, and I am still in deep pain over Annie, of course. I would not likely have even wanted to consider a new romance with such a short time left.*
>
> *On the other hand, I suppose it's understandable that we were awkward about this because we were, suddenly in my case, "available." It was stupid of me to fear you would misunderstand. We had become such good friends so quickly that, who knows, maybe I feared something deeper would develop just as quickly. Naturally, I was wary of that, and you should have been too.*

We should have been able to simply let our bond of friendship grow and prosper, assuming nothing would have come of it. What I especially appreciate about you, Hannah, is how much you love God. It seems everything you do—how nice you are to people, what a servant attitude you have, your cheerfulness and encouragement during such dark, dark times—well, that is clear evidence of the work of Christ in you. You are an example to me and to anyone else who pays attention.

You're also right that there is likely no need for medical personnel here, and you're certainly not an Israeli. :-) You know, despite being ethnically Jewish, I am not purely an Israeli either, though I have distant roots here. Regardless, it's almost certain we won't see each other again until heaven or the Millennial Kingdom. That alone should have made me invest the time in a proper farewell, and if you would allow it, I'd like to try to make up for that by phone.

Because of what we have been able to put together using satellite and solar technology, it is just as easy—not to mention free—for me to call you in the States as it is to call you here, from about fifty miles away. When we have worked through the mess I caused by leaving without so much as a heart-to-heart talk, would you let me call now and then? I know the time difference is significant and we would have to pick our spots. We'll both be busy, but I'd like that if you would.

Speaking of busy, I recognize that by taking so long to deal with this, I may be getting back to you so close to the time when our real labor-intensive duties kick in that you'll barely have time to read this, let alone respond to it. It's kind of lonely here, no surprise, so if I find myself doing nothing but waiting for the choppers to start arriving, maybe I'll call to make sure you got this and to save you the time of having to keyboard a response.

Anyway, because of who you are, I know you'll understand and forgive me, and I look forward to starting over again.

Your friend,
David

* * *

Rayford felt a fool. He was no military strategist. While his preys were clearly weak and bumbling, he had allowed all three of his people to move into untenable positions. Albie had no line of fire and dared not move. Mac was out of position with only a handgun. Leah had to substitute obedience for patience or she might get herself killed. Rayford himself was the only one with the angle and a shot at the two GCs, but the fifty-caliber he cradled was a one-shot wonder.

And besides, he had only reluctantly concluded he would actually kill someone if it came to that. Nothing said he had the nerve or the ability.

The weapon, however, brought to the table everything he needed. He lay over it, delicately framing through the powerful scope a spot on the rock face his targets would pass if they continued on course. His right hand brushed the trigger while his left palm lay atop the scope, steadying the piece. And now Leah was on the squawker again, pushing to be allowed to approach the edge of the ridge.

Rayford didn't want to risk losing his aim, so he slowly reached for the radio with his left hand and drew it to his lips. "Negative. Don't call me; I'll call you."

He dropped the radio and cupped the stock of the rifle in his left hand . . . waiting . . . waiting. The GC had stopped and sat together on a rock. Rayford carefully pivoted the rifle until he had them both in his sights. He turned his head slightly and saw Leah waiting. Their backs were to her. There was no reason she couldn't take her look, if she hurried. He picked up the radio, while focusing on the targets again. They looked up and a second later he heard what drew their eyes. Yet another chopper.

"Leah, go and return quickly. Don't reconfirm, just move."

Rayford gently set down the radio and tried to regulate his breathing. The two logy GCs filled the lens, and he believed he saw sores on their sweaty necks from two hundred yards. He aimed inches above the head of the one on the right. They both slid off the rock and knelt on one knee, aiming their weapons at the bird about to fly directly over them. It was an oversized job, a personnel transporter from United North American States Army surplus—a multimillion-Nick machine that no doubt carried at least two dozen fleeing Israeli believers. Well-placed projectiles from as high as the GCs knelt could conceivably bring it down. The mere sound and fury of Rayford's weapon putting a hole in the rock above them should save the helicopter, but he needed more incentive to take the risk.

It came from the radio and Leah's flat, halting news. "It's David . . . they butchered him . . . the birds are already upon him."

The GC tensed as if ready to fire, and Rayford slightly dropped his sight just as the soldier on the left leaned in front of the other. If he had only let David come back to Mizpe Ramon when he wanted to, Rayford wouldn't be in this mess. He remembered to roll up onto his toes and bend his knees, so when he squeezed the trigger the recoil merely sent him sliding back a yard or so. He had forgotten to plug his ears, however, so the explosion tearing against his shoulder was the least of his worries.

The blast stunned and deafened him. Without even the sensation of sound now, he slowly rolled his head, retrieved the toppled rifle, and looked through the lens. He feared he had permanently damaged his eardrums, but his vision had not been affected. In his periphery the big chopper continued past, and across the way both soldiers slumped, motionless, a cloud of rock dust rising behind them.

Rayford picked up his radio. "Be alert for others," he said, aware he was speaking too loudly. His words reverberated inside, but he heard none of them. "Let's see what we've got," he said.

Albie was the first to the targets. Then Leah, Mac, and finally Rayford. He expected Leah to turn away from the carnage, but she didn't. She said something and he asked her to repeat it. She took him by the shoulders and turned him to face her. "David looks worse than they do," she shouted, and he read her lips.

If that was true, he didn't want to see Hassid. But he knew they should bury the body. "Can we get him out?"

She shook her head. "Impossible."

"That's where these two should go too," Mac said, or at least that's what Rayford thought he said.

The bullet had ripped through the spine and heart of one soldier and the neck of the other before blowing a two-foot-diameter hole in the rock face. Rayford spun and caught himself, afraid he would be sick. Isolated by his deafness, he was overcome with remorse. He had done this. He had killed these two. He had lost a man in a place that was supposed to be a refuge. Now his airstrip was vulnerable, and the entrance to Petra swarmed with chopper loads of people waiting to be let in.

Rayford's knees buckled, but he was borne up by Mac, who held him and pulled his face close. "This is war!" Mac said. "These men murdered our unarmed guy, and they would have killed any one of us. They were drawin' a bead on that packed chopper. You saved us all, Ray!"

Rayford felt his face twist into a grimace, and he tried to form words to express that he couldn't allow these mutilated bodies here when the place began to fill. But he could not speak, and Mac was already ahead of him. He said something to Albie, and the wiry little man stepped forward without hesitation. He stretched, then squatted to pick up the first victim. Bouncing once to settle the corpse in his arms, he moved ten feet toward the ledge and launched him into the unknown. He returned to do the same with the other.

"Get on the horn, Ray!" Mac said. "Let's get these people in here!"

Rayford shook his head and handed the radio to Mac, pointing at him. "With pleasure," Mac said. "Let's gather up and get out."

Rushing down and out was sure easier than coming in had been. Leah stayed close to Rayford, and he believed she looked the way he felt. Before they even reached the passageway, choppers were popping over the ridge and setting down to disgorge passengers. By the time they had traversed the mile through the narrow Siq back to Rayford's craft, a huge crowd had formed at the entrance. Mac had spent much of his time on the radio on the way out, and now he and Albie were urging people not to walk but to accept the helicopter lift into Petra.

Leah helped heft the fifty-caliber, her medical box, and the stretcher into the chopper, then pulled Rayford off to the side. "You can't fly until you can hear," she said.

"Yes I can," he said.

"You can hear again already?"

"You can hear for me."

She shrugged. "Well, I sure can't fly," she said.

+ + +

Despite his youth and his grief, Chang had the maturity and presence of mind to carefully dole out the awful news about David Hassid. The Tribulation Force agreed that neither Chaim nor Buck need know until Chaim finished his work and was safe at Petra. Chloe said she would inform Buck at the appropriate time.

For the next several hours Chang monitored the Trib Force activities. Leah treated Rayford's ears back at Mizpe Ramon, informing everyone that time would be the best healer. The Israelis left there by George and Abdullah and Rayford were worked into later runs, and Rayford settled in with the other two in their fifty-caliber lair. They had seen nothing of the GC.

Leah reported that Hannah had taken the news of David's death so hard that she was unable to speak. Apparently she had steeled herself to join Leah on a flight to Masada with Mac, where they would reassemble the medical center in a tent. Meanwhile, it seemed to Chang one of God's clear miracles that not one mechanical failure was reported on the ground or in the air during the massive relocation effort.

When night fell in Jerusalem and the world seemed to wait for the nine o'clock reprieve from the plague of boils, Chang finally stood and stretched. He stared at himself in the mirror and thanked God for clear skin all over his body. Even the itch on his leg had disappeared, and he attributed it to either an insect bite or something psychosomatic.

He returned to his computer to check his e-mail, idly wishing the Masada event had not been an afterthought. There had not been time even to arrange for a speaker system, let alone anything Chang could tap into besides Buck's phone.

Chang was taken aback to discover a message from his mother. He quickly accessed it. It was filled with mistakes and retries, but plainly she had painstakingly taught herself how to compose and send the message, and from what she had to say, she had learned how to access Tsion Ben-Judah's Web site too.

> *Father upset over Carpathia's shameful exhibition in Jerusalem. Not know what to think. Wants me to ask what you think. What do you think? I will send this before he sees and will erase from storage. You answer careful in case he see. Carpathia seem bad, bad, bad. Ben-Judah very interesting, a prophet. How does he know in advance? I need to know how to send to Ming. Tell her I will.*
>
> *Mother*

+ + +

Not long after dark and still an hour before 2100 hours, Chaim surveyed the packed fortress of Masada, and Buck looked out over the overflow crowd below. He agreed with the old man that almost everyone who was to come was likely there. Buck put an arm on Dr. Rosenzweig's shoulder and bowed his head.

"God, grant me the wisdom to say what you want me to say," Chaim said, "and may these dear ones hear what you want them to hear."

"And God," Buck added, "anoint his voice."

There was neither a stage nor special lighting. Chaim merely stood on high ground at one end and raised his arms. The place immediately fell silent, and it seemed all movement stopped. Buck whispered into the phone to Chang, "At least record this. We can worry about enhancing fidelity later. The whole Trib Force will want to hear it."

"How are you on power?"

"One and a half packs left. Should be okay."

Chaim spoke in Hebrew, but again, Buck understood him perfectly. "My friends," he began in a voice of vigor and authority but, Buck feared, not enough volume, "I cannot guarantee your safety here tonight. Your very presence makes you an enemy and a threat to the ruler of this world, and when the plague of sores upon his people is lifted at nine o'clock tonight, they may target you with a vengeance."

Buck stood and looked to the far reaches of the fortress and outside below. No one seemed to have to strain to hear. No one moved or emitted a sound except Leah and Hannah, quietly arranging the small, makeshift medical center. So far no one seemed to need their services.

"I will keep my remarks brief," Chaim said, "but I will be asking you to make a decision that will change your destiny. If you agree with me and make this commitment, cars, trucks, and helicopters will ferry you to a place of refuge. If you do not, you may return to your homes and face the gruesome choice between the guillotine or the mark of loyalty to the man who sat in your temple this very day and proclaimed himself god. He is the man who defiled God's house with murder and with the blood of swine, who installed his own throne and the very image of himself in the Holy of Holies, who put an end to all sacrifices to the true and living God, and who withdrew his promise of peace for Israel.

"I must tell you sadly that many of you will make that choice. You will choose sin over God. You will choose pride and selfishness and life over the threat of death. Some of you have already rejected God's gift so many times that your heart has been hardened. And though your risky sojourn to this meeting may indicate a change of mind on your part, it is too late for a change of heart. Only God knows.

"Because of who you are and where you come from, and because of who I am and where I come from, we can stipulate that we agree on many things. We believe there is one God, creator of the universe and sustainer of life, that all good and perfect things come from him alone. But I tell you that the disappearances that ravaged our world three and a half years ago were the work of his Son, the Messiah, who was foretold in the Scriptures and whose prophecies did Jesus of Nazareth, the Christ, fulfill."

Not a murmur or a word of dissent from all these Jewish people, Buck thought. Could this be Chaim Rosenzweig, the diminutive, soft-spoken scientist, commanding an audience of tens of thousands with the mere power of his unamplified voice and the authority of his message?

+ + +

It was darker than dark at Mizpe Ramon, so Rayford couldn't even read lips. Fortunately, if George or Abdullah spoke directly at him, he was starting to be able to make out their words.

"I realize I'm the new guy and everything, Captain," George said, "but I been wonderin'. Is there anything here worth protectin' from the GC? I mean, let 'em concentrate their efforts on tearin' up the dirt we worked so hard to smooth out. And these temporary quarters aren't worth a nickel either. What say we get back where the action is and start flyin' some more people to safety instead of lyin' here waitin' for an enemy that might not show?"

Rayford rolled onto his back and stared at the star-filled sky. Abdullah waded in with his opinion, and Rayford had to push up on one elbow and get him to start over louder.

"I was just saying, boss, that I agree. As much as I would enjoy shooting the big guns and maybe knocking someone out of the sky who deserves it anyway, why waste ammunition? We might need it to protect ground troops or flights later."

Rayford's chopper was the only one left. George's and Abdullah's had been pressed into service. The captain rolled onto his back again and ran it all through his mind. The truth was, he didn't care if the GC attacked here. Let them waste their time. He was burned out, desolate, and needed the break. If someone else would fly his craft, and if perhaps Mac would take over running the operation, at least for a while, he could hang on till daybreak. Mac was temporarily in charge anyway, with Rayford's temporary—he hoped—handicap.

"Let's break camp," he said finally, and the other two quickly broke down the weapons and loaded them. Rayford asked George to fly and Abdullah to tell Mac what was going on. He lay on the floor of the chopper and covered his face with his hands. The problem, Rayford told himself, was that he had a hero complex. He knew anything good that happened in a time such as this was God's doing and not his. But running out of gas before a mission was over was not his idea of what a leader would or should do.

Was it possible that God had allowed him to forget something so simple as earplugs just to put him out of commission long enough to restore his strength? He despaired over losing David and having to kill two men. But it all worked together to drain him. He was not even aware of dozing, but a moment later Abdullah woke him with a yank on the arm.

"Please to forgive me, but we are needed at Masada. Mr. McCullum believes that many, many more will need rides to Petra."

* * *

Buck found himself thrilled to the point of bursting. Much as Tsion Ben-Judah had done on international television years before, Chaim made the case for Jesus as the Messiah the Jews had sought for so long. As he ticked off the 109 prophecies fulfilled by Jesus alone, first one, then another in the crowd stood. Soon the entire crowd was on its feet. Still they were silent and no one moved around. A holy hush filled the place.

"He is the only One who could be Messiah," Chaim proclaimed. "He also died unlike anyone else in history. He gave himself willingly as a sacrifice and then proved himself worthy when God raised him from the dead. Even skeptics and unbelievers have called Jesus the most influential person in history.

"Of the billions and billions of people who have ever lived, One stands head and shoulders above the rest in terms of influence. More schools, colleges, hospitals, and orphanages have been started because of him than because of anyone else. More art was created, more music written, and more humanitarian acts performed due to him and his influence than anyone else ever. Great international encyclopedias devote twenty thousand words to describing him and his influence on the world. Even our calendar is based on his birth. And all this he accomplished in a public ministry that lasted just three and a half years!

"Jesus of Nazareth, Son of God, Savior of the world, and Messiah, predicted that he would build his church and the gates of hell would not prevail against it. Centuries after his public unmerciful mocking, his persecution and martyrdom, billions claimed membership in his church, making it by far the largest religion in the world. And when he returned, as he said he would, to take his faithful to heaven, the disappearance of so many had the most profound impact on this globe that man has ever seen.

"Messiah was to be born in Bethlehem to a virgin, to live a sinless life, to serve as God's spotless Lamb of sacrifice, to give himself willingly to die on a cross for the sins of the world, to rise again three days later, and to sit at the right hand of God the Father Almighty. Jesus fulfilled these and all the other 109 prophecies, proving he is the Son of God.

"Tonight, Messiah calls to you from down through the ages. He is the answer to your condition. He offers forgiveness for your sins. He paid the penalty for you. As the most prolific writer of Scripture, a Jew himself, wrote, 'If you confess with your mouth the Lord Jesus and believe in your heart that God has raised him from the dead, you will be saved. For with the heart one believes unto righteousness, and with the mouth confession is made unto salvation. For the Scripture says, "Whoever believes on him will not be put to shame." For there is no distinction between Jew and Greek, for the same Lord over all is rich to all who call upon him. For whoever calls on the name of the Lord shall be saved.'

"For years skeptics have made fun of the evangelist's plea, 'Do you want to be saved tonight?' and yet that is what I ask you right now. Do not expect God to be fooled. Be not deceived. God will not be mocked. Do not do this to avoid a confrontation with Antichrist. You need to be saved because you cannot save yourself.

"The cost is great but the reward greater. This may cost you your freedom, your family, your very head. You may not survive the journey to safety. But you will spend eternity with God, worshiping the Lord Christ, Messiah, Jesus.

"If you choose Christ, pray this prayer with me: Dear God, I am a sinner and separated from you. I believe Jesus is the Messiah and that he died on the cross to pay for my sins. I believe he rose again the third day and that by receiving his gift of love I will have the power to become a son of God because I believe on his name. Thank you for hearing me and saving me, and I pledge the rest of my life to you."

All over the vast historic fortress—where legend said Jewish parents chose to slay their own children and themselves rather than fall into the hands of the Romans—men and women prayed that prayer aloud. The mark of the seal of God on the believer appeared on their foreheads, and thousands and thousands of them followed Chaim as he strode through the crowd and down the steps to where hundreds of vehicles and helicopters waited in long lines. Hannah and Leah and their equipment were among the first to go. Buck saw Mac assign his chopper to another flyer and help load the medical stuff into an idling truck. He got behind the wheel as Hannah and Leah herded about a dozen new believers in.

Thousands of others, despair on their faces, ran from the scene and looked for rides back to Jerusalem.

Buck caught up to Chaim and stood next to him, watching as the cars and trucks and choppers filled and took off. The old man breathed heavily and leaned over on Buck as if his last ounce of strength had been sapped. "Praise God," he whispered. "Praise God, praise God, praise God."

Buck looked at his watch. It was minutes before nine, and already the loudspeakers on GC vehicles began spreading the news that was being broadcast on television and over the Internet. "The entire state of Israel has been declared a no-fly zone by the Global Community Security and Intelligence director. All civilian aircraft, take fair warning: Any non-GC craft determined to be over Israeli airspace runs the risk of destruction.

"The potentate himself has also decreed martial law and has instituted a curfew on civilian vehicular traffic in Israel. Violators are subject to arrest.

"Due to the severity of the affliction that has befallen GC personnel, these curfews are required. Only a skeleton crew of workers is available to maintain order.

"His Excellency reminds citizens that he has effected a relief from the plague as of 2100 hours, and the populace should plan to celebrate with him at daybreak."

\+ + +

Abdullah woke Rayford again. He sat up, his hearing still gone. "Your son-in-law has requested transportation for Dr. Rosenzweig and himself from Masada to Petra, and he says you personally requested permission to convey them. Is that still your wish?"

Rayford nodded, wiped his face, and climbed into a seat. George descended to the staging area outside Masada, and they sat waiting until nearly everyone was gone save Chaim and Buck and a man standing behind them in a robe similar to Chaim's.

"Who is that?" Rayford asked, pointing.

"Dr. Rosenzweig and Mr. Williams," Abdullah said.

"No, the other," Rayford said.

"I do not understand."

"Who is with them?"

Rayford saw Abdullah glance at George, and George meet his gaze. "I see no one," Abdullah said, but Rayford assumed he meant he didn't know either.

Later, when GC vehicles began arriving at the site and finally only Buck, Chaim, and the other man remained outside, Abdullah stepped out of the chopper and held the door open. Chaim walked wearily, Buck with a hand on his arm. The third stayed a pace behind. As they boarded, it seemed to Rayford that Abdullah very nearly slammed the door on the unknown man.

They sat as George turned in his seat and Rayford introduced Chaim and Buck to him. "And introduce your friend," Rayford said.

Buck smiled. "I'm sorry?"

"Your friend. Introduce your friend. Who is this?" Rayford gestured toward the third man, who merely looked at him. Chaim and Buck looked to where he had gestured and then back to Rayford. "Well?" he said.

"What are we missing?" Buck said.

Rayford wondered if he was dreaming. He leaned toward the man as the man leaned toward him. "So, who are you?" Rayford said.

"I am Michael," he said. "I am here to restore and heal you."

Rayford stiffened as Michael cupped Rayford's head in his hands, his palms over the ears. Rayford's hearing was restored, and he felt a surge of life and energy that made him sit up straight. "You mean Michael the . . . I mean, *the* Michael?"

But the man was gone.

13

RAYFORD FELT TWENTY YEARS younger and wished he were piloting his own chopper. But George was doing fine. Abdullah sat next to him, scanning the sky and the ground with a serious, worried look. Buck sat next to Chaim on the long side bench, his head back, mouth open, sound asleep.

"You must be exhausted too, Dr. Rosenzweig," Rayford said.

"For the first time today, yes, and you know I was up most of last night."

"I heard. God has stood by you, hasn't he?"

"Captain, I confess I am famished! It is as if I have been fueled by the energy of the angels to whom God gave charge over me."

"Did you see them, sir?"

"Me? No. But you know Miss Durham saw Michael the archangel."

Rayford nodded. There would be time to tell his own story. "Abdullah?" he said, and the Jordanian turned. "Were there any foodstuffs in what we loaded?" He had been heating something over a flameless stove just before they left Mizpe Ramon.

"There were! Yes!" Abdullah was shouting and enunciating.

"I can hear, Smitty. I've been healed."

"Really!?" He leaned back and quit shouting, but still talked loudly enough to be heard above the din of the craft. "I have pita bread warm in an insulated box, along with sauce for the dipping."

"You sound like a waiter in a swanky restaurant."

"How would I know?"

Chaim leaned in. "That sounds like milk and honey to me."

Abdullah unbuckled himself and squeezed back between them, kneeling to retrieve the box. He pivoted and opened the lid, revealing a stack of nearly twenty round pitas about ten inches in diameter, steam rising.

The aroma permeated the helicopter and woke Buck. Big George even reached back without looking. Rayford slapped a couple of pitas into his open palm. "That's what I'm talkin' about!" the pilot said, though he hadn't said a word for an hour. All dug in, tearing at the chewy bread with their teeth.

"Lord, you know we are grateful!" Chaim said, his mouth full, and the others *amen*ed.

Abdullah was still kneeling by the box when he nudged Rayford and nodded outside. The sky was full of Operation Eagle choppers and GC craft, both fixed-wings and whirlybirds. Below, the streets were jammed with fleeing vehicles, careening around corners, bouncing over curbs and torn-up streets, pursued by GC vehicles with flashing lights.

The others turned to peer out. "How are we doing on fuel?" Chaim asked.

"Several hours' worth," George reported.

"Captain Steele," Chaim said, "could we remain in this area and monitor this?"

Rayford told George to find a friendly altitude, and they hovered in a wide-box pattern. A GC chopper moved in behind them at one point and summoned them with an all-frequency transmission. "Civilian chopper, you are advised to leave Israel airspace immediately."

"Captain," George said, "what frequency can they hear me on?"

Rayford told him and asked what he had in mind.

"I just think I should be courteous, don't you?"

"Don't antagonize them."

Everybody in the chopper laughed at that, and Rayford realized how absurd it was. The GC couldn't be any more antagonized.

George switched to the frequency Rayford suggested. "GC chopper, this is the civilian bird. Over which part of your populated city did you plan to send our flaming wreckage?"

"Civilian, you are violating a curfew established by Potentate Carpathia himself."

"I don't recognize the authority."

"Repeat, Carpathia! His Excellency himself!"

"I recognize the name, GC. I repeat, I don't recognize the authority."

Abdullah's eyes were alive. "You Americans are crazy brave!"

The radio crackled again. "By authority of the Global Community and its risen potentate and lord, His Excellency Nicolae Carpathia, you are commanded to land at once in the first available area and surrender yourself, your passengers, your cargo, and your craft."

"No thanks," George said.

"That is not a request, civilian. That is an order sanctioned by the potentate."

"Sorry, GC, but we're on a mission from the real risen Lord, and we have both human and edible cargo we don't wish to surrender."

"Repeat?"

"The part about the people or the pita bread?"

"Be forewarned, civilian chopper, we are fully armed and prepared to destroy your craft if you do not comply immediately."

"Right now?"

"Affirmative."

"Just a minute."

"You request time to comply?"

"No, I just need a minute."

"You have sixty seconds."

"I can't have a minute?"

"Fifty-five seconds, civilian."

"Let me make sure I get over the busiest streets here, GC, in case I'm not as invulnerable as I think I am."

"Coming up on forty-five seconds. Put that chopper down."

"We're eating and we have no airsick bags. If we have to use evasive measures, we could make a mess."

"Final warning. Thirty seconds."

"We won't be hearing from you again, then?"

"Negative."

"Not at all?"

"Correct."

"Not one word?"

"Twenty seconds."

"That's two words."

Rayford had to wonder if George was as scared as he was. The big man obviously believed they were safe because Chaim was aboard, and Rayford had more than enough reason to trust God. But when he saw the GC chopper back off to where a missile explosion would not damage the shooting craft, he believed they were about to be fired upon. "Buckle in, Smitty," he shouted.

Abdullah leaped into his seat while Rayford secured the food box. Buck looked as focused as Rayford, but Chaim seemed bemused. "We belong to God," the old man said. "His will be done."

* * *

Mac hadn't had this much fun since he was a schoolkid and his pet snake found his sister's room. He bounced along Jerusalem streets with a truckload of Israeli believers and two nurses from America. The scene reminded him of the Keystone Kops. Operation Eagle drivers simply would not be stopped. They swung around barricades, over boulders, through earthquake residue, and past GC Peacekeeper vehicles.

Back in Texas when Mac was a kid, you could drive a farm vehicle at twelve. By the sixth grade, he was driving tractors and combines, pickups and dump trucks. And now he had drawn a new personnel transport from France, driven in by an International Commodity Co-op volunteer who had ridden back to get another.

This was a fancy rig with power and the ability to be driven in automatic or manual. The former would come in handy on the open road, once they got south of the city, but in the chaos in which he now found himself, Mac enjoyed the six-speed stick. Even more, he was entertained—though that seemed too light a word for it under the circumstances—by the spectacle of the freshly healed GC personnel thumbing their noses at the Micah-Nicolae agreement and trying to get in the way of the exodus of a million people.

Nearly all the Operation Eagle vehicles were four-wheel drive and could pick their way around any obstacle. When the road filled with stopped cars and trucks, those in the back just swung out and around and made their own routes and paths. GC Peacekeepers and Morale Monitors—the former in uniform, the latter wearing their badges and bright orange sashes—tried to direct traffic, stop civilian cars, check papers, and inform everyone they were violating the martial-law curfew. They were ignored, and Mac wondered how God was doing it. He saw a lot of weapons but heard little gunfire. No one allowed himself to be pulled over, and when GC vehicles blocked the path of a civilian car or truck, the latter just backed up and went around.

Mac wondered why the GC didn't shoot or ram these vehicles, but he figured he'd learn when he was singled out. For now, Leah was asking an Israeli in the passenger seat if she could switch places with him so she could talk to Mac.

"We going to make it?" she asked.

He shot her a glance. She was pale and her eyes darted about the scene around them. "Looks like it," he said. "You see any of ours who are *not* making it?"

She shook her head and fastened her seat belt, then sat with her hands balled into fists in her lap. "Uh, Mr. McCullum, Hannah is wondering why we're going to Petra, she and I, I mean. Obviously there's no need for medical personnel there, and neither of us is an Israeli."

"Me either," Mac said. "Obviously we're takin' these people to their new home. Chloe's got shipments of building materials and such that will need to be processed. Maybe you can help coordinate that while we're gettin' the last of the refugees delivered. That's gonna take a while."

"Okay."

"That a problem?"

"No, it's just that—"

"You're not gonna tell me it's not what you signed up for. I mean, we all do what we gotta d—"

"No, I know, it's fine. It's just that being at Petra is going to be real hard on Hannah with what happened, you know."

"I was there."

"So you see."

"Have her join me up here, would ya?"

"She can hardly talk, Mr. McCullum."

"I don't need her to talk. I need her to listen."

* * *

Rayford leaned as far to his right as he could and kept an eye on the GC chopper behind them. They apparently cared not a whit about who or what was below.

"Everybody secure?" he said. "Prepare for incoming." The pursuing craft was directly in line with them in a can't-miss situation. Rayford considered barking evasive maneuvers at George, but it would be futile. The GC flew a smaller, more agile bird. Even if George eluded the first fusillade, it would be only a matter of time.

"They're firing!" Rayford hollered, and buried his face between his knees. He had seen the orange bursts and the white tracers and expected the instantaneous ravaging of metal and Plexiglas and fuel tanks, the gush of cold air, the ball of flame, and the free fall.

He felt the blazing, screaming bullet tips shoot past between him and Buck and Chaim, and the white-hot streaks made him look up. The ammunition flashed through the bird, and the force of the air pushed George's head to the left and Abdullah's to the right as both involuntarily ducked and covered their ears. But there had been no damage to the back or front of the chopper.

Rayford stared as the shots found the tail rotors of a GC craft ahead of them and sent it spinning to the ground. He shuddered and realized he was gripping the seat so tightly his fingers had locked into position.

"Why are you so fearful? How is it that you have no faith? Be of good cheer! Do not be afraid."

Rayford turned slowly to see Michael next to him again. "You all see him this time, don't you?" he said.

"We saw him," Chaim said. "Praise God."

"I heard him," Abdullah said, turning. But again, Michael was already gone.

* * *

Mac saw the flashing lights in his side rearview mirrors. "You're not going to stop, are you?" Hannah asked quietly.

"Take more'n that to stop me now." The GC behind him started in on their PA system. "I don't want to talk to them," he said. "I want to talk to you. Did you lose a loved one today?"

"Of course. Didn't you?"

"Yes, I did."

"Then you should understand."

"That's why I don't, Hannah. I'm not sayin' this is easy. But did you see David fold up and hibernate when he lost his fiancée? No, ma'am. I know you and David were close, but what do you think he'd want? Do I hafta remind you that Rayford lost two wives and a son? That Tsion lost his whole family? I'm not discountin' it, and I'm not sayin' you don't have a reason for wanting to stay away from Petra. But David was my boss and my friend, and this is no picnic for me either."

"I know."

"We're all going to need some grieving time, and we won't likely get it until we head back to the States. Meanwhile, we need you, Hannah. We don't have the luxury of grieving the way we used to. Too many people countin' on us. Now there may be nothin' for you and Leah to do inside Petra, but you know well as I do that none of us helpers are guaranteed safety. Who knows what kinda walkin' wounded we might have showin' up to drop people off?"

She nodded. "Mac, um, you'd better pull over."

"Ma'am?"

She pointed past him, out his window. A guard hung out the passenger side of a GC vehicle with a submachine gun pointed at Mac.

\+ + +

"Well," George said, "that was just about the most amazing thing I've ever seen. Do we keep testing our luck or do we get on to Petra?"

"If you think that was luck," Rayford said, "maybe—"

"Just an expression, Cap. I know good and well what that was."

"Let's stay here and watch," Abdullah said, craning his neck to see the chopper that had fired on them.

"No need to be in the middle of everything," Rayford said. "Get someplace where we can observe without unduly drawing more fire."

\+ + +

Chang phoned Tsion early in the afternoon Chicago time and walked him through how to broadcast live over international television from right where he was. "Is your monitor somewhere that you can stand behind it and survey the room?"

"Yes."

"Have someone sit where you're going to sit, and see what you can see past them. Anything that would be a clue to your whereabouts, get rid of it."

Tsion asked Ming to sit in his chair at the keyboard, and he squeezed between the back of the monitor and the wall. On the opposite wall a clock would give away what time zone they were in. "Chang," Tsion said, "let me get rid of the clock, and then the background will be a blank wall."

"Good. And then, can you tell me how long your message—wait, sir?"

"Go ahead."

"Why not just change that clock to Carpathian Time and let people wonder where you are?"

"Interesting."

Ming broke in. "Won't they see it as an obvious trick, Chang?"

"They might if we made it prominent," he said. "Put it in the corner of the shot, and I'll make sure it's out of focus. People will think they have discovered something unintended."

"My message will be short, Chang," Tsion said. "Just enough to encourage the believers before you transmit Chaim's salvation message audio."

"Excuse me, Dr. Ben-Judah, but I'm getting something on my Phoenix 216 bug. Stand by."

"You go and get back to me later."

+ + +

Mac held up a finger to the GC as if requesting a moment before he pulled over. He had speed-dialed Rayford. "Permission to fire upon the GC before they shoot out our tires."

"Denied, Mac. Just elude. Let God work."

"He can work through your nine millimeter, can't he?"

"You still have that?"

"Sorry."

"Just don't stop," Rayford said.

"Even with a flat?"

"Call back if they flatten your tire."

Mac stopped in the middle of the road with the GC next to him, but he refused to roll down his window. The GC pulled in front of Mac. When the passenger got out, Mac backed up and pulled around the vehicle, and the pursuit began again. When the GC got close, Mac slammed on the brakes. "Sorry, friends!" he yelled. "Shoulda told y'all to buckle up!"

The GC stopped within inches of Mac's bumper and they both jumped out, shouting and waving weapons. Mac took off again, and as soon as they jumped back in and accelerated, he swung left, popped a U-turn, and swung in behind them.

\+ + +

Apparently Carpathia still suspected the Knesset Building and thought his own plane was most secure. Chang followed an indication on the audiometer from the patch to the bugs there, and sure enough, it sounded as if workers were setting up for yet another meeting in the first-class cabin.

A couple of stewards were speaking in an Indian dialect, so Chang quickly fed it through a filter David had recommended and an immediate interpretation came up as captions.

"They will not destroy the rebel airstrip, then?"

"It appears the GC will use it for its own purposes. They will take out the buildings and clear it of the enemy, of course, but then they will fly in their own troops, who will be trucked to Petra to head off the fleeing insurgents. They will try to—shh, they are coming."

"Mr. Akbar, sir."

"Pakistani?"

"No, apologies, Director."

"Speak English?"

"Yes, English."

"This will be a small gathering, just the potentate, Reverend Fortunato, Mr. Moon, Ms. Ivins, and myself."

"Oh, thank you, sir. We had already made room for too many, had we not?"

"No problem. You know what everybody likes. Have it out and available. And don't forget Ms. Ivins's fondness for ice."

"A thousand thank-yous for reminding me, sir. 'More ice, please,' she says constantly. Water for you and Mr. Moon, juice for Mr. Fortunato, and—"

"*Reverend* Fortunato."

"Oh yes, humble apologies."

"I do not care. But you do not want to make that mistake in front of His Excellency."

"Or the Most High Reverend Father, ha!"

Chang heard Suhail Akbar chuckle. "Make yourselves scarce once everything is in place."

Chang formatted the program to record and then switched back to Chicago. "Ready?" he said.

"I am," Tsion said. "How do I look?"

"Scared."

"I do not wish to look scared."

"Can't help you there, Doctor. We're pirating the only show in town all over the world. If anyone is watching TV, listening to radio, or surfing the Net, you're what they're going to get."

"*That* sets my mind at ease!"

"Just trying to explain your nerves, sir."

"Say when."

"Now."

"I am on?" Tsion said. "Seriously?"

But Chang didn't dare answer for fear of his voice being traced. He held his breath, grateful Tsion had not used his name.

"Greetings," Tsion said. "It is a privilege for me to address the world through the miracle of technology. But as I am an unwelcome guest here, forgive me for being brief, and please lend me your attention . . ."

Chang checked in on the Phoenix. It sounded as if everyone was there and settling in. "Commander Moon, get someone to turn off that television. Wait! Who is that?"

"You know who that is, Excellency," Leon said. "That's the heretic, Tsion Ben-Judah."

"More than a heretic," Carpathia said. "He is behind this Micah, thus the plague of sores. So now he consolidates the Orthodox Jews with him. How did he get a television network?"

"That is GCNN, Potentate."

"Well, get him off there!" Carpathia raged. "Walter!"

The TV in the Phoenix went silent, and Carpathia exploded. "I mean get him off the air, you imbecile. Call whom you have to call, do what you have to do! We have overcome the plague and now we will look like buffoons, allowing the enemy on our own network!"

Moon was on the phone, his voice shaky, sounding to Chang as if he feared Carpathia would put him to death if Tsion was aired a minute longer. Moon swore and demanded to be put through to the head of broadcasting. "No excuses!" he cried. "Pull the plug! Now!"

"Give me that phone!" Carpathia said. "Cut the feed! Cut the signal!" It sounded as if the phone was flung across the cabin. "Turn it on! Let me see!"

Moon: "I'm sure they've at least gone to black, Excellen—"

"Turn it on! Ach! Still there! What is it with you people? Suhail, come here. Right here!"

"Excellency."

"No restrictions on curfew enforcement." Carpathia spoke so quickly that his words ran together and Chang had to strain to understand. "Shoot to kill at the Mount of Olives, at Masada, on—"

"Those locations have been cleared, Highn—"

"Do *not* interrupt, Suhail! Every civilian plane destroyed and—"

"We have suffered casualties on the ground from crashing planes, sir—"

"Do you *hear* me? Do you understand what I am saying? Do I need to have you executed the way I will execute Walter if this Ben-Judah *is not off the air when again I look at the screen!?"*

Moon wailed, "What more can I do, Excellency?"

"You can die!"

"No!"

"Suhail, a weapon."

"Please, sir!"

"Now, Suhail!"

Scuffling. *BLAM!* A scream.

"Hold out your other hand, Walter!"

"Please!"

BLAM! More screaming. More shots, fresh cries with each. The banging of shoes against seats and tables as Moon, Chang assumed, frantically tried to crawl to safety. More rapid shots in succession, wailing like a terrified baby, finally a last shot, and silence.

"You're doing the right thing, Nicolae," Viv Ivins said. "You should kill them all and start over."

"Thank you, Viv."

Fortunato: "I worship you, risen master."

"Shut up, Leon. Suhail, put a fresh clip in this."

Sounds of the snapping in of more ammunition.

Fortunato: "I bow in respectful silence to your glory. Oh, for the privilege of kissing your ring."

"Now give it to me, Suhail."

"As you wish, Excellency, but I will execute anyone you wish. I have always carried out your directives."

"Then do what I say!"

"Anything, Potentate."

"I want dead insurrectionists! Run them down. Crash their vehicles. Blow their heads off. As for Petra, wait until we know for certain Micah is there, then level it. Do we have what we need to do that?"

"We do, sir."

"In the meantime, someone, anyone, get—Ben-Judah—off—the—air!"

"I will pray him off, Your Worship," Fortunato said.

"I will kill you if you do not shut up."

"Quieting now, Highness. Oh!"

"What!?"

"The water! The ice!"

Chang jumped up and turned on the faucet over his sink.

Blood.

14

THE TAILLIGHTS AHEAD went bright red, so Mac slammed on his brakes. But suddenly the GC vehicle disappeared from his vision. In the distance, Operation Eagle cars and trucks roared on, but behind them a great cavern opened and the pursuing GC dropped into it.

Mac jumped out and realized his front tires were on the edge of the gigantic crevasse. Amazingly, the lights of the GC cars grew smaller as they continued to fall. The cavity in the earth was hundreds of feet deep, and his idea to sneak behind the GC had almost been fatal. His knees rubbery, he climbed back into the truck and carefully backed away, looking for a way around.

Roaring up past him came yet another GC car, but as it neared the drop-off, its two occupants leaped out and rolled, their weapons clattering onto the pavement. Their car hurtled into the great beyond. The Peacekeepers slowly rose, retrieved their rifles, and took aim at Mac's truck. "Duck!" he shouted, and his head banged Hannah's shoulder as they both leaned toward the middle of the front seat. In the back, the Israelis tussled for position.

The bracketing of gunfire made Mac shut his eyes and cover his head, but it stopped almost as soon as it had started, and he rose and stepped out to see the Peacekeepers sprawled dead. No one else was around. He could only surmise that their own bullets had somehow killed them. Mac's Operation Eagle truck stood unscathed. His phone rang.

It was Rayford. "Tsion's on the air right now," he reported.

"Well, that's good, Cap. Nothin' I could use more right now than a little broadcast entertainment."

"Say again?"

"Nothin'."

"What's your location?"

"The Grand Canyon."

"I don't follow."

"Good idea not to."

"Mac, you all right?"

"Yeah. 'Cept for almost drivin' my people into the netherworld, I'll make it."

"Sounds like you'll have a story, as usual. Can you see what's happening in the air over Jerusalem?"

"Guess I been lookin' the other direction, Ray."

"Well, look up and listen."

The air battle had moved away from Mac, but in the distance he could see it, and its low rumbling echoes came rolling back. "They hittin' anybody?"

"Only each other," Rayford said. "Look out below."

"I heard *that*!"

✠ ✠ ✠

Chang was overcome by a feeling so delicious it made him tingle to the top of his head. All over his computer were frantic codes and messages and attempts by the broadcasting division in the next building to yank GCNN off the air. But nothing they did worked. He hoped Tsion would finish soon so he could go to the Chaim audio. That would drive them crazy. With no visual to worry about, they would catch each other coming and going trying to mute the sound.

With one ear monitoring Tsion to know when to make the switch, Chang was also still listening to the cockpit of the Phoenix. Carpathia had turned his verbal guns on Fortunato.

"What good is a religion if you cannot come up with some miracles, Leon?"

"Holiness! I called down fire on your enemy just yesterday!"

"You cooked a harmless woman with a big mouth."

"But you are the object of our worship, Excellency! I pray to *you* for signs and wonders!"

"Well, I need a miracle, *Reverend*."

"Excellency," Akbar interrupted, "you might consider this phone call miraculous."

"While that infernal Ben-Judah remains on the air, the only miracle is that either of you remains alive. So, thrill me."

"You recall we lost two prisoners in Greece recently?"

"Young people, yes. A boy and a girl. You have found them?"

"No, but as time and manpower allowed only a cursory investigation, the best we came up with were witnesses who said a Peacekeeper named Jensen may have been involved in both disappearances."

"Yes, yes, and though he was our man, you lost track of him. So you have found him now?"

"Maybe."

"I hate answers like that!"

"Forgive me, Excellency. You know how this Micah and his sidekick seemed to appear out of nowhere."

"Get to the point. Please! You are making me crazy!"

"We got a tip that the two were seen at the King David Hotel, but when everyone fell ill, we didn't have time to pursue it. Now we have, and we even know what rooms they occupied."

"And this is a miracle?"

"We have combed both rooms. One contained a wallet that appears to belong to Jensen. The photo, however, does not match the photo in our personnel files."

"Why would he be foolish enough to leave his identification behind? It is clearly an attempt to mislead."

"We're comparing with our international database fingerprints lifted from each room."

Chang's fingers flew. He was into the GC Peacekeeper personnel file in seconds and eradicated all vestiges of Jack Jensen.

"Suhail, there must be dozens of different people's fingerprints in a hotel room, from every recent guest to the staff to—"

"The predominant prints in the one room trace to Chaim Rosenzweig."

Carpathia laughed. "The man who murdered me."

"One and the same."

He laughed again. "Well, which do you think is Rosenzweig? The one in the robe or the one with the scarred face?"

"Excellency, the prints from the scarred man's room do not lead to Peacekeeper Jensen, interestingly enough. They match the prints of a former employee in your inner circle."

Back Chang went into the system, and seconds later Cameron "Buck" Williams, former media czar for the Global Community, was gone as if he had never been there.

"I did not study the sidekick," Carpathia said, "but he did not remind me of anyone."

"He was your first media guy."

"Plank? Nonsense. Confirmed dead."

"My mistake. Your second media guy but first choice."

"Williams?"

"That's the man."

"Micah's assistant is not Cameron Williams, Suhail. I would know. And let me tell you something else—Micah is *not* Dr. Rosenzweig."

"All due respect, Excellency, but miracles of disguise can be wrought today."

"He may be approximately the same height, but that voice? That look? That bearing? No. That could not be playacting." There was a long pause. "Anyway," Carpathia said quietly, "I pardoned my attacker publicly."

"And that protects him from whom?"

"Everyone."

"Including yourself?"

"Excellent point, Suhail."

"Anyway, you yourself installed Walter Moon as supreme commander. That apparently didn't give *him* tenure."

Chang heard the men laugh, while in the background Viv Ivins supervised the removal of Moon's body and the cleanup of the area.

Chang switched to Tsion's broadcast, which closed with Dr. Ben-Judah's promise to travel to Petra to personally address his million strong "brothers and sisters in Messiah."

Someone called Suhail. Chang heard him ask Carpathia's permission to take it, then: "Ben-Judah is coming to Petra, Excellency."

"Delay its destruction until his arrival."

"And the blood problem is international."

"Meaning?"

"Intelligence is telling me the waters of the sea are 100 percent blood."

"What sea?"

"Every one. It's crippling us. And we have a mole."

"Where?"

"At the palace. And connected here somehow."

"How can you know that?"

"Jensen and Williams? Their files have disappeared from our central database since you and I began discussing them."

"Quarantine this plane, Suhail."

"Sir?"

"We will kill the mole, of course, but we must find the leak first. Lie detector tests for everyone. How many is that?"

"Fortunately, not many. Two stewards, myself, and Leon."

"You were wise to leave me out and diplomatic to leave Viv Ivins out. Do not be diplomatic."

"You want her polygraphed, Excellency?"

"Absolutely."

"Perhaps I'll conduct it myself," Suhail said.

"And who will conduct yours, Mr. Akbar?"

"Actually, Excellency, lie detecting has become quite streamlined. We now merely use a computer program that detects changes in the FM frequency of the voice. A person has no control over it. He or she can speak at a different pace or even volume, but the FM frequency will change only under stress."

"*Real*-ly."

"It's gold, sir."

"Do include me in the testing."

Chang hacked into the personnel files and created a record showing him in the infirmary and treated symptomatically for boils for the last two days. He saved everything from his computer to the secure minidisk in the bowels of the palace, then purposely crashed the hard drive on his laptop, erasing everything in it. He created a phantom auxiliary hard drive buried under such massive encoding that only another computer working twenty-four hours a day for years could even hope to crack it. He accessed the miniature archive and downloaded everything he needed, then pulled the cords and packed up the machine, putting it deep in a closet. David—the only other person on the planet who could have detected a thing on his hard drive—was actually no longer on the planet.

Chang would be at his desk in his department the next morning, right on time and ready for work. Not only would they not find the mole, but they would also strike out in their search for a contact person in the executive cabinet.

* * *

George put down well outside the growing throngs at Petra, opened the door for ventilation, and Buck and the others dozed as load after load of more escapees was delivered. Rayford and Chaim had decided to keep Chaim's presence a secret for as long as possible so as not to interfere with the massive move into the safe place. Though some had begun walking in and others were airlifted, by daybreak, hundreds of thousands clogged the Siq, awaiting their helicopter hop inside. They sang and rejoiced and prayed.

Buck left the chopper and walked among the people, keeping an eye on the skies and the western horizon as he listened to the radio. Global Community forces had been decimated, nearly half lost in firefights in the sky that never touched Operation Eagle or during ground pursuits that left GC vehicles and bodies buried so deep that rescue operations were abandoned.

The GCNN radio network had switched back to Carpathia's auspices sometime in the night, after Chaim's case for Jesus as the Messiah had been broadcast around the world, followed by his prayer of allegiance to Christ. Buck believed Tsion's prediction that a worldwide revival would break out in the midst of the worst terror of the Tribulation. Reports from around the globe revealed tragedy and death related to the seas having turned to blood.

Ships that counted on processes that made the waters of the ocean drinkable found it impossible to convert the blood. Rotting carcasses of all species of aquatic life rose to the surface, and crews of ships fell deathly ill as many boats radioed their inability to get back to land.

Carpathia announced that his Security and Intelligence forces already had determined the true identities of the impostors who claimed to represent the rebels and that it had been their trickery that resulted in the great seawater catastrophe.

* * *

Night had fallen in Chicago, and Chloe found a way to excuse herself during a lull in the news. She took her new telescope and set up at a window far from curious eyes. Waiting until the sky was black, she first scanned the city with the naked eye. The tiny beacon she had noticed some time before still shined from about three-quarters of a mile away.

Chloe carefully settled and steadied herself, bracing the instrument and aligning it with what she had seen. At long last she was able to bring the illusive beam into focus and calm the jumpy lens. To her astonishment, the source of light was at ground level. She sat and sat, cramping again but forcing herself to stay still so she could study the image until it made sense to her overtaxed brain.

She ran the various shapes and images through the grid of her life's memory, and gradually Chloe thought she came to understand what she was looking at. One window on the ground or basement floor of a big building, maybe ten or twelve stories, emitted light from inside. And the more she sat staring, the more convinced she was that there was activity inside. Human activity.

* * *

At eight in the morning Palace Time, Chang was assigned by his supervisor to help monitor reports of deaths and casualties attributed to the oceanic disaster. To the wonder of everyone involved, lakes and rivers had not been affected.

In the large office where Chang and some thirty others sat at desktop computers, he made it a point to only occasionally grunt a response to coworkers who tried to draw him out. He neither looked anyone in the eye nor smiled. His boss, a tall, bony Mexican named Aurelio S. Figueroa, proved an officious loner who treated his superiors like kings and queens and treated his subordinates like servants.

"How are we today, Wong?" Mr. Figueroa said, his Adam's apple protruding.

"Okay, sir."

"Happy in your work?"

"Happy enough."

"Have you heard the news?"

"About?"

"Supreme Commander Moon."

"I saw nothing on the news about him."

"Come, Master Wong, I know you are a Carpathia pet. Surely you have inside knowledge."

Chang shook his head.

"Moon is dead."

"Dead? How?"

"Shot to death outside the potentate's plane."

Chang tried to appear stunned and curious, but he hated being drawn in as Figueroa's confidant. "The enemy?"

"No! Don't be naïve! Our people at that level are surrounded by security."

"Who then?"

"They suspect the stewards." Figueroa leaned close. "Both Indians."

"But why?"

"No one else would have done it."

"Why would *they*?"

"Why not? You know the Indians."

"No, I do not."

"They have a contact on the inside."

"On the inside of what?"

"Here."

"Why?"

"You *are* naïve, aren't you?"

Chang bit his tongue. He hated stupid people, especially ones twice his age. "Not too naïve to guess your middle name."

Figueroa's eyes turned dark. "What does that have to do with anything, Wong?"

Chang shrugged. "Forget it."

"You couldn't know it anyway."

"Of course I couldn't."

"Unless you saw my personnel file."

"How would I do that?"

"You couldn't. Not without my knowing. Everything done on these computers is recorded, you know."

"Of course."

"I could see if you have been snooping."

"Feel free."

Figueroa broke into a wide grin. "But I trust you, Wong! You are a friend of His Excellency."

"Well, my Father is."

"I suppose you have heard they have asked for lie-detecting software. I uploaded it this morning."

"How would I know that?"

Figueroa clutched Chang's shoulder, and it was all Chang could do to keep from recoiling. "Because you are connected, my friend!"

"I'm not."

"We are all going to be subjected to searches, you know. Interrogations."

"Why?"

"I told you! The Indians, the stewards, have a connection here, a leak."

Chang shrugged.

"You want to be first or last?"

"To what?"

"To be interrogated."

"I have nothing to hide. They can interrogate me anytime they want."

"They will search your apartment, want to see your personal computer."

"They may feel free. The hard drive has been worthless for some time."

"Then you have nothing to worry about."

"I was not worried."

Figueroa looked around, as if realizing he might be criticized for paying too much attention to one worker. "Of course, you weren't, Wong. You're connected."

Chang shook his head. "Who will replace Moon?"

"Akbar is too important where he is. Fortunato has already had that job. Maybe Ms. Ivins, who knows? Maybe no one. Maybe Nicolae himself. One thing is certain, Wong," Figueroa added, turning to leave, "it won't be you or me."

"Don't be so sure," Chang said, hating himself for playing these games.

As Chang expected, Figueroa stopped. "What are you saying? What do you know?"

"Nothing to speak of, sir," Chang said. "Have to protect my connection, you know."

"You're putting me on. You know nothing."

"Of course."

"Seriously, now. I mean it."

"Me too, sir."

Five minutes later, as Chang was collating reports from around the world and assembling them for a briefing, Figueroa called from his office. "You swear you've never tapped in to see my personnel files?"

"I swear."

"If I ran a review on your computer, the one here and your own, it would bear that out?"

"This one would."

"But your personal computer?"

"I told you. The hard drive crashed."

"Then this about knowing my full name . . ."

"Would be guessing, sir."

"Want to guess?"

"I'm busy, sir."

"I'll give you one guess."

"I was just talking. I don't know."

"Come now, Wong. Take a shot. Tell you what—you get it right, I'll leave your name off the interrogation list."

"How could you do that?"

"I have my ways."

"Why would I care about being interrogated?"

"It's a waste of time, a nuisance, stressful."

"Not if you're innocent. I never even heard of the Indian stewards."

"The offer stands."

Chang sighed. Why had he started this? And who would believe Figueroa gave a rip anyway? "I know it starts with an *S.*"

"Everybody knows that. It's on my nameplate. But maybe it's like the *S* in Harry S Truman and stands for nothing."

"You use the period after it, so it stands for something. I'd just be guessing."

"Unless you're lying about hacking into my file, a hundred Nicks says you couldn't guess in ten tries."

"I have only one guess."

"Let's hear it."

"Sequoia."

A long silence. Figueroa swore. "You couldn't know that!"

"I'm right?"

"You are and you know it, but how did you know? It's not even a Mexican name. Not even Spanish."

"I'm guessing Indian. American Indian, I mean."

"Tell me how you knew that."

"Guessing, sir. I thought it made sense."

\+ + +

Why would a light be on in Chicago? Was it possible, Chloe wondered, that someone else had somehow discovered that David Hassid had planted the radiation readings in the Global Community database computer? That reminded her she had not yet told Buck the horrible news.

Chloe tried to plot where she would find the lighted window, then put up the telescope and phoned Buck. It broke her heart to hear that he was at Petra and as excited as she remembered him being in a long time. She let him go on and on about what had happened, how Rayford had seen and been healed by the angel, and how he and the others in the chopper had eventually seen him as well when he protected them from gunfire.

Chloe could only agree with Buck about the signs and wonders, the confrontations with Carpathia, the supernatural change in Chaim, the thrill of pirating the network for the spreading of the truth. Finally he must have noticed her enthusiasm did not match his. "You okay, babe?"

"I have bad news for you, Buck. Two GC MIAs murdered David Hassid, and we all agreed not to tell you and Chaim until your work was almost finished. . . . Buck? Are you there?"

"Give me a minute," he said finally.

"I don't know when Daddy was going to tell Chaim. It ought to be soon if he's right there on-site."

"Yeah," Buck managed. "He'll probably somehow get everybody else out of the chopper first. We don't want the people to see Chaim yet."

"Of course."

"Chloe, what're we going to do?"

"I don't know. The most awful part is, it's only going to get worse. Before I fall asleep I run over in my mind everybody we've got left and I can't help but wonder . . ."

"Who'll be next, I know. I didn't know David as well as some of the others did, but just from a practical, logistical standpoint . . ."

"He was so crucial," Chloe said. "And how much do we know about Ming's brother?"

"David was high on him, but he is still a teenager. And he'll never be in the same position, have the same access David had. I hate to talk about it only in terms of what it means to the Trib Force, but—"

"The mourning process has to be so blunted, Buck. Everything's life and death now. Each loss makes it harder for the rest of us to survive, and it's only natural that we look at it that way. I just want you all back here and safe one more time."

"Soon," Buck said. "Your dad wants to use Abdullah's underground contacts to get use of a supersonic plane that will hold eight or so. Albie's credentials are still intact, so he would fly us all back to the States and pick up Tsion for a personal visit to Petra."

"I want to go," she said.

"You just said you wanted us back in one piece."

"I need babysitters."

"Be serious. We all need some R & R before Armageddon."

"I don't."

"What're you talking about?"

"Dad promised I could go on the next mission if all the bases were covered. I took that to mean if there were enough people here to watch Kenny."

Buck was silent.

"You don't approve."

"No," he said. "Kenny could stand losing me more than you."

"Don't be silly."

"I'm being silly? Listen to yourself. You're his mother."

"So I get the whole responsibility."

"That's not what I'm—"

"And you're so crucial to the frontline work of the Trib Force that we can't risk losing me and leaving you to be Kenny's primary caregiver."

She could tell Buck was angry. "I can't believe I'm standing here in the middle of the desert, arguing with my wife about who's going to watch the baby. Listen, you can't come back with Tsion, because the GC is waiting till he returns before they make an air strike here."

"Yet you send Tsion into that, and a billion people a day are dependent on him."

"We believe he'll be protected here."

"And I won't?"

"We don't know. David wasn't."

"I don't want to fight about this on the phone, Buck. Please don't be closed to it until we get a chance to talk it through. And be careful. I love you and I couldn't live without you."

With her phone in her pocket, Chloe nonchalantly chatted with Zeke out of the hearing of the others. "If I were to go out for a walk, would you keep an ear out for Kenny and not feel obligated to mention to anyone else that I'm gone?"

"This time of night? Ma'am, it's—"

"Z, please. I'm a grown woman and I need to get out of here. I'll have my phone with me."

"I couldn't lie for you."

"I didn't ask you to. Just don't volunteer anything. I don't want anyone to worry."

+ + +

Buck headed back to the helicopter. The transfer of people into Petra was slow but steady. He wanted to let Rayford know he knew about David and give him a chance to tell Chaim. But as he worked his way through the enthusiastic crowd, beautifully bronzed children, exhausted by the flight and sleeping on parents' shoulders, distracted him. How he missed Kenny!

The crowd suddenly shifted and smiles froze. Their attention turned to the east, and Buck jogged to where he could see. Billowing across the desert came three huge clouds of dust that threatened to blot out the diminished sun. The two on the left continued to separate themselves from the one on the right. Buck dialed Chang, only to find out he was temporarily incommunicado. He dialed Rayford.

"Chloe told me about David. Get rid of the others for a minute and tell Chaim. And what do you make of what's coming?"

"Abdullah's figured it out," Rayford reported. "GC ground forces. They're going to separate until they can come at the people simultaneously from three different directions, forcing them into the Siq, which will hold only so many."

Buck began sprinting toward the chopper. "The news of David can wait. Are the rest of us safe, or just Chaim? And are the people safe outside the entrance?"

"I'm going to switch places with George and get up where I can get a look at these troops," Rayford said. "When I come back down, be close by. We may have to take up arms."

"Arms?" Buck said. "I heard about those. Count me out."

"You may change your mind if the GC opens fire."

I just might, Buck thought.

15

CHLOE SLIPPED OUT in dark slacks and a black jacket. Besides her phone, she carried an ancient Luger she found among Rayford's keepsakes. She had experimented with it until she figured out how to load it and work the safety. She only guessed how it might fire, but it gave her a measure of security she hadn't known was available.

She walked five blocks in the pitch-blackness of unlighted streets and heard nary a sound. Chloe looked to her left at every cross street now, imagining she was close to her target. How far off could she be? Maybe a quarter of a mile, she decided. So she went left two blocks and started looking both ways at each corner.

* * *

Rayford ascended and hovered at less than a thousand feet, just high enough to allow himself a sense of what the Global Community Security and Intelligence forces were sending their way. "George," he said, "switch seats with Dr. Rosenzweig, please."

"What are we looking at?" Chaim said as he settled in. Rayford told him and pointed to where the two other columns of tanks, armored trucks, personnel carriers, and rocket launchers peeled off to circle around the massive crowd of Israelis.

"I worry that only you Israeli believers are safe," Rayford said. "But are even you safe outside the walls of Petra?"

"Captain, the question must be academic. Without a miracle of God, we are still hours from having more than half our people inside. How long before these attackers reach us?"

"They're probably within firing range right now," Rayford said. "In twenty more minutes they will all be in position. If they advance as soon as they are mustered, they would be able to fight hand to hand within ten more minutes of that."

"So half an hour . . ."

"Maximum."

"My people are neither armed nor prepared to defend themselves. We are at the mercy of God."

"I'm tempted to have you urge all believers who are not Israelis to get into Petra as quickly as they can," Rayford said. "Do you think your people would defer to them, allowing them to get to the front of the helicopter lines and make way for those who would walk in?"

"Not without understanding, and how would there be time to explain?"

"The alternative is that Operation Eagle suspend the airlift and every able-bodied believer, except those from Israel, be armed and prepared to stand against this attack."

"You will be hopelessly outnumbered, Captain."

"But we would inflict damage, and we would not go down without a fight."

"I would not begin to try to advise you," Chaim said. "You must do what you must do. What is God telling you?"

"He's telling me I am as afraid as I have ever been, but I cannot stand by and allow a massacre. Are you able to operate a weapon, Doctor?"

"Forgive me, but I am not here to resist with arms. I am to take charge of these people in Petra and prepare the way for a visit from Tsion. And when he again leaves, I will remain."

Rayford looked over his shoulder and shouted, "George, Abdullah, find out where Albie and Mac are. Tell them our situation and to connect with us as soon as we're on the ground, if they can. Stand by to load weapons and set up a perimeter a hundred yards in front of the Israelis."

"I am only guessing, Captain," Abdullah said, "but if we are to surround them up to the walls on either side of the Siq, we will likely stand more than fifty yards apart each."

"I didn't say this would be easy or even successful, Smitty. I'm open to suggestions."

"I have none."

"Then round up our guys and tell the rest that all Operation Eagle personnel are on combat duty effective immediately." He turned back to Chaim and motioned him to lean close. "Doctor, I need to tell you what happened here yesterday. . . ."

+ + +

Chang had been the fastest keyboarder in his Chinese high school, regardless of whether they were inputting in Chinese or English. Now he sat speed-typing code into a secondary window every chance he got. He maneuvered his monitor in such a way that it faced neither the surveillance camera in the corner nor his coworkers if they remained at their stations. He also forced himself to look not at the characters he was typing but at the reflection off the screen, which told him when Figueroa or anyone else happened to stroll within view.

The secondary window, as he designed it, would show up on any check of the machine as a local notepad, but he programmed his codes so they would appear as random keys rather than any sensible strings. If questioned, he could attribute the gibberish to residue in translating from Chinese to English or even a computer language. He was building and formatting an independent drive he could access from anywhere and which would duplicate the capability of his laptop.

* * *

Chloe kept peeking at her watch and asking herself if she was a fool. What did she expect to find? Was she just satisfying her curiosity? Being out by herself, especially in the dark, gave her a wholly satisfying sense of freedom, which in turn made her wonder if she was too young for the responsibilities she bore. She was a wife and mother, head of an international co-op that meant the difference between health and starvation for its millions of members. And yet she needed this kind of an escape? One with perhaps more danger than she knew?

Finally she reached a corner, where she looked right to no avail and then left, which made her stop. Could that be her source of light, that faint strip of a lighter shade that seemed to color the darkness four or five blocks away? Did she have the time or energy to see if she had been that far off in her calculation? Of course. What else was she out here for? It was clear Buck and probably her dad were not really going to let her journey to Petra with Tsion when an air attack was certain. This might be her only mission, and of course, the odds were it would prove to be nothing. But even if it was folly and turned out to be nothing but a game of hide-and-seek in the dark, it was better than nothing.

She turned left.

* * *

Rayford banked and circled to drop back down, and as the craft leveled and settled, he saw Buck hurrying toward him, motioning with a finger across his neck to cut the engines as soon as possible. From all over the area, other drivers and chopper pilots emerged from vehicles and aircraft and headed his way, awaiting instructions and weaponry for the stand against the GC.

The crowd, however, seemed to ignore both the Operation Eagle personnel and the GC, though the clouds of dust and the sounds of engines drew closer. Rather, the people all seemed riveted to where the Siq led into the high-walled path into Petra. Rayford had dropped too quickly to see what they could be looking at.

Buck reached the chopper, more frantically signaling the cut-engine message, and Rayford quickly shut down and reached past Chaim to push open the door. "Everybody out," Buck said. "You've got to see this!"

"Do we need weapons?" Rayford called, and they tumbled out.

"Doesn't look like it. Follow me. Chaim, you all right?"

"Call me Micah, but yes. Lead the way."

"Aren't we afraid of people recognizing him?" Rayford said.

"No one's looking," Buck said.

"So I noticed," Rayford said, sprinting behind Buck and realizing that Chaim had hiked up his robe and was somehow keeping pace. George and Abdullah pounded along behind.

Buck led them to an incline, then bent and charged up to where a giant boulder offered a flat surface from where they could overlook the hundreds of thousands. "There," Buck said, "near the entrance. See?"

+ + +

Chloe grew more excited the farther she walked. The contrast between the light and the darkness grew stronger, and she knew she had found what she had seen from the safe house in the Strong Building. The possibility that it represented anything more than a rogue light left on by some quirk of the power grid was, she knew, likely only in her head. But as she came within a block and a half of the window, which was barred and indeed at street level, she saw the camera. It sat directly above the window, hooded by a thick metal box that she would not be surprised to learn was covered with graffiti. A tiny dot of red light glowed from it, and the lens, though she could barely make it out, swiveled in a 180-degree arc.

Chloe was certain she was too far from any light source to have been picked up by what appeared to be an old camera, but she slowed and stayed close to buildings and the rubble of buildings, stopping whenever she detected the lens pointing in her direction. When it swung away, she hurried to get closer.

Finally she crossed the street away from the camera and pressed her back up against a wall. Again she stopped when the camera seemed to find her, and when it swung the other way, she edged closer. Eventually she was within three feet of where the light from the window reached the wall next to her across the street. Inside the window she saw only a fluorescent ceiling unit with three of its four tubes illuminated. When next the camera scanned her way, she realized the light barely touched her left sleeve. She stood stock-still, wondering if the camera had any kind of a motion sensor.

Here came the rotation of the lens again. Chloe remained where she was but moved her arm slightly in the edge of the light. The camera stopped rotating and the light in the window went out. Now all she could see was the dot of red, and it remained stationary. She imagined the lens opening to try to decipher what stood across the street there in the darkness.

Should she run? Was it possible that whoever or whatever controlled the camera and the light was as scared as she was? Did it or they want to catch her or scare her off? or simply be aware of what was out there? Chloe took a deep breath and, trying to relax, worked to regulate the rise and fall of her diaphragm. One thing she was sure of, if she could trust David and Chang, this was not GC.

Chloe tiptoed halfway across the street and noticed a faded sign on the wall, but still it was too dark to make out. She stood there, the camera seeming to study her. Finally the fluorescent light came back on. She did not move, except to raise her eyes and read the sign. It was some sort of currency exchange. That meant that behind the bars was a window likely made of bulletproof glass.

She put her hands in her pockets, the handgrip of the Luger nestled in her right palm. The camera stayed on her as she moved closer to the window, and the lens moved only enough to keep her centered, the faint whine telling her it was also adjusting constantly to keep her in focus. At long last, throwing caution to the wind, she bent at the waist and peered inside the window.

A squawk box crackled to life. "Identify yourself and explain your mark."

+ + +

There, just above the heads of the people at the front of the crowd, stood the man Rayford knew to be Michael. He was dressed similarly to Chaim, though he was taller. He held both hands aloft, and such a hush fell over the Israelis that everyone could hear him, though he spoke in normal, conversational tones. Rayford stood far beyond the edge of the throng, yet it sounded as if Michael spoke directly into his ear.

If the effect on the crowd was the same as on Rayford, they were filled with a sacred peace.

Michael began, "Fear not, children of Abraham. I am your shield. Fear not, for God has heard your voice. He says to you, 'I am the God of Abraham your father: fear not, for I am with you, and will bless you.'

"Behold, the Lord your God has set the land before you: go up and possess it, as the Lord God of your fathers has said unto you; fear not, neither be discouraged. Hear, O Israel, you approach this day unto battle against your enemies: let not your hearts faint, fear not, and do not tremble, neither be terrified because of them; be strong and of a good courage, fear not, nor be afraid of them: for the Lord your God, he it is that goes with you; he will not fail you, nor forsake you.

"Peace be unto you; fear not: you shall not die. Turn not aside from following the Lord, but serve the Lord with all your heart. God your Father says, 'You shall eat bread at my table continually. Be courageous, and be valiant.' Fear not: for they that be with us are more than they that be with them.

"You shall not need to fight in this battle: set yourselves, stand still, and see the salvation of the Lord with you, O Judah and Jerusalem, for the Lord will be with you. God shall hear you, and afflict them because therefore they fear not his name. Say to them that are of a fearful heart, 'Be strong, fear not: behold, your God will come with vengeance, even God with a recompense; he will come and save you.'"

Michael stepped down and began walking through the masses, who backed away and followed with their eyes. As he strode past, he continued to encourage. "For the Lord your God will hold your right hand, saying unto you, 'Fear not; I will help you, people of Israel.' So says the Lord, and your redeemer, the Holy One of Israel.

"Thus says the Lord that created you, O Israel, 'Fear not: for I have redeemed you, I have called you by your name; you are mine.' It shall be well with you. Be glad and rejoice: for the Lord will do great things. The very hairs of your head are all numbered. Fear not therefore: you are of more value than many sparrows.

"The Lord God says, 'Fear not, for I am the first and the last.' Stand firm then, remnant of Israel. Fear not! Fear not! Fear not! Fear not!"

The crowd began to take up the chant, louder and louder, as Michael found his way to the edge of the people, facing what was now the middle column of desert dust, fast approaching. He stood grasping his robe at the chest, chin raised toward the advancing armies of the evil one, and behind him the teeming thousands matched his pose.

Rayford and Buck and Abdullah and Chaim hurried down and fell into the crowd behind Michael. Rayford couldn't know how the others felt. As for him, fear was gone and he had never rested more surely in God.

* * *

Chloe found her throat constricted, but they could see her mark! She was able to croak, "If you can see it, it does not need to be explained."

"Identify yourself."

"What more do you need to know than that I am a sister in Christ?"

"How are you able to survive the radiation? Are you supernaturally protected?"

"I will answer only when I know whether you are all brothers and sisters."

"Persuade us you are not radioactive and we will welcome you inside."

"I must know if any enemy is among you."

"We are all believers. No Carpathianists, no GC."

"The radiation is a ruse perpetrated by the Judah-ites." Chloe had crossed a line she could not retreat from. Any more information that might be secreted to the enemy, and she would be giving away the safe house and her comrades.

"To what purpose?"

"You should be able to surmise."

"Are you alone, sister?"

"You mean—"

"Is anyone with you now?"

"No."

There was a long silence. The camera remained on her, the light on in the empty room. It had a ratty, gray, short-nap industrial carpet, a green countertop built into a wall, and three Plexiglas-windowed transaction stations, all long since retired from use.

A door in the far corner opened slowly, and a black man in bare feet, beltless suit pants, and a white, sleeveless T-shirt emerged. Maybe in his late twenties and muscular, he moved cautiously across the carpet, standing directly under the light, looking out, not smiling but not scowling either. Chloe detected hope, curiosity, perhaps bemusement in his eyes. He invited her closer to the window with a wave, and she lowered her face to within inches of it. He broke into a huge grin. "Greetings, sister!" he called out, and she saw the mark of God on his forehead.

He hurried back to the door and called to others. A black girl came out, about Chloe's age, wearing shorts and socks and an oversized man's white shirt. Chloe felt on display, as if at the zoo. And here came two middle-aged Latino women—one big boned but gaunt, the other thin and short.

"You're okay?" the young black woman called out. "How long you been outside?"

"Almost an hour. But I've been out before. Lots of times."

"And you're okay?"

Chloe smiled. "I'm okay! Not contagious!"

"Let her in!"

"Yeah, let her in!"

"Get Enoch! He'll decide."

* * *

First in line, Rayford noticed, in each of the three massive divisions of GC battalions, were full-track tanks, chewing up rocks and dirt and sand, bouncing and rolling over the uneven ground. Behind them, beyond the clouds of dust, from what he had seen from the air, were missile launchers. Then came cannons, then armored personnel carriers, trucks, Jeep-type vehicles with gun-toting soldiers, then smaller cars.

Rayford judged their speed at about thirty-five miles an hour, and he assumed they would soon synchronize a stopping point where every weapon in their arsenals would have maximum kill power. But there seemed no slowing as they drew within half a mile, then a quarter mile. They bore down on the unarmed civilians.

Rayford suddenly had a sinking feeling. He had only assumed the rest of the Operation Eagle forces would merely stand in confidence behind Michael. But what if they acted on old information? What if Albie or Mac or someone else had provided them weapons and they returned fire, or worse, initiated it?

He wanted to grab his phone and his walkie-talkie and confirm with his people that they were to stand down, to remain unarmed. But the GC were nearly upon them now. The noise reverberated off the rock walls and the dust blew all around them. Still, neither side opened fire. Rayford finally ducked and turned, covering his eyes against the dust and peeking back to be sure none of his people took overt action. As far as he could see, the Israelis and the Operation Eagle forces remained calm, standing firm, trusting in God's protection.

Rayford had to fight a smile. In his humanness he allowed that he could be in heaven within seconds, and his survival instinct wanted him to defend himself. But the promises of God also rang in his ears. He shook his head at the lunacy of Carpathia's ego. Clearly this three-pronged army had been instructed not to fire unless fired upon, and they intended to run over the Israelis and grind them into the ground!

They were within a hundred feet now, yet Rayford heard not a sound from behind, not a cry from anyone's lips. This flood from the serpent's mouth was going to hit an invisible wall or be swept away by some wall of water from nowhere, or the Israelis and their helpers would prove so ethereal that the weapons of destruction would pass harmlessly through them.

Ten feet and ground zero, and suddenly the entire mass of God's people fell to their knees and covered their ears at the thunderous peals that resounded like mountains falling. All around the sea of people, right at the feet of those in the front on every side, the earth split and ripped open for a mile in every direction away from Petra.

The echoes from the shattering of the earth were as loud as the actual cleaving, and as the tanks and missiles and cannons and personnel armaments were fired in panic or from being shaken to their core, the projectiles rose vertically and eventually dropped back down onto the plunging armies. Smoke and fire rose in great belches from the colossal gorge that appeared to reach the bowels of hell. The roar of racing engines, whose drivetrains propelled steel tracks or wheels that merely spun in thin air, could not cover the screams of troops who had been just seconds from squashing their prey and now found themselves hurtling to their deaths.

Rayford and all those around him pulled their hands from their ears and thrust them out wide to keep their balance as, still on their knees, they were rocked by aftershocks. It was as if they surfed on unsolid ground as the earth slowly healed itself. The walls of the chasm came back together as the Red Sea must have millennia before, and the loose, rocky topsoil was suddenly new. The dust settled, and quietness wafted over the assembled.

Michael was gone. Chaim slowly rose and addressed the people. "As long as you are on your knees, what better time to thank the God of creation, the God of Abraham, Isaac, and Jacob? Thank him who sits high above the heavens, above whom there is no other. Thank the One in whom there is no change, neither shadow of turning. Praise the holy One of Israel. Praise Father, Son, and Holy Ghost!"

* * *

Enoch turned out to be an incongruously named Spaniard who carried, of all things, a cheap, hardbound Bible, the kind you would find in a hotel or a pew. He too was strangely dressed, wearing expensive shoes with missing laces and no socks, khaki pants, and a tank top–type shirt. These people, Chloe decided, looked like they had raided a Salvation Army barrel.

Enoch conferred with the others, then motioned Chloe around the corner to the main entrance, where she waited while he released lock after lock. Finally the inner door was open, and Enoch crossed the shallow lobby to push open the outer door. "We have limited food supplies," he said, as he held the door for her.

"I'm not looking for food," she said. "I was just curious about the light."

"We thought we were the only ones left in the city," he said. "We run the camera just in case but are just days from shutting it down to conserve energy."

"I have so many questions," Chloe said.

"So do we."

"I'm afraid I can't say much," she said. "I'll understand if you choose not to, either."

"We have nothing to hide," Enoch said.

"What is this place?"

"It was once a currency exchange. But it adjoins the basement of an old office building that was abandoned. Since they were connected, we thought it would be safer for us to stay largely underground, especially since there was a safe standing open. We never found the combination, so we do not close it all the way, but some prefer to sleep in it."

Enoch led Chloe through the old exchange lobby, where the curious who had eyed her through the window now shyly greeted her and stared. Just past the door and down the hall stood the huge, walk-in vault, and she had to assume this was a bank in one of its first manifestations. No currency exchange, even in Chicago, would need a vault that large.

"How many of you are there?" Chloe asked.

"As of last night, thirty-one."

"You're not serious."

Enoch cocked his head and smiled. "Why would I not be?"

"What are you doing here? How did you get here?"

"Well," he said, pushing open a door that led to a large-pillared basement room, "I'm sure that's what my friends and I want to know from you." She stepped in to meet everyone's curious and wary eyes.

* * *

Rayford was on his walkie-talkie to Operation Eagle personnel. "Let's step it up, people. I want constant rounds of chopper hops to get these people inside Petra. Building materials and miscellaneous stuff flown or carried in. We believe Carpathia made a major blunder and used our Mizpe Ramon airstrip rather than destroying it, so we can use it to take off and get back to our homelands before he finds out what happened here. No one is left to tell him, so for now he has to assume he has simply lost radio contact.

"When Micah is inside, our mission is accomplished. Good-bye and Godspeed."

Rayford clicked off the walkie-talkie and conference-phoned Trib Force members, old and new, among the crowd. "Let's be ready to get home and get Tsion. He's got a speaking engagement scheduled here."

16

CHLOE SAT IN a cheap metal folding chair surrounded by a wide-eyed mix of cross-cultural people in their twenties and thirties. She had many questions, but they insisted on asking theirs first. Clearly they were true believers, but still she prayed silently, pleading with God for peace about telling them of the Tribulation Force.

"None of you have been outside since the bombing of the city?" she said.

They shook their heads. Enoch carried the conversation. "If we come to believe it is safe, all of us will take a walk before dawn. Now tell us more."

Chloe took a deep breath. "You vouch for everyone in here, Enoch?"

"Check our marks," he said.

Chloe knew that was unnecessary. And she saved her two biggest revelations till last. "The spiritual mentor I have told you about is Jewish. He was a rabbi. He is Dr. Tsion Ben-Judah."

The group sat, obviously stunned, many smiling, others shaking their heads. Finally a Latino said, "Ben-Judah lives in Chicago?"

She nodded. "And I am Chloe Steele Williams."

Enoch leaned toward her, trembling. "And we are hungry," he said, making the others laugh.

"You look it," she said. "What have you been living on?"

"Canned goods and dry goods. We've been slowly rationing them, but they're fast running out. If Dr. Ben-Judah is right and we have three and a half years to go, we're not going to make it. Do you think the co-op might—"

"Send a couple back with me and I'll load them up with enough to feed you for a month. Then we'll figure a way you can contribute to the co-op and start trading for food and supplies."

Several stood to volunteer. "We also want to travel," Enoch said, "to help other people, to tell them the truth. We're desperate for a chance to do that."

"We ought to be able to manage it, in time," she said. "Now tell me your story."

* * *

Laslos Miklos had been used to an affluent lifestyle, owning a lucrative lignite-mining business in Ptolemaïs, Greece, before the disappearances. But when he and his wife became believers in Christ, his hundreds of trucks and dozens of buildings became fronts for the efforts of the Greek underground church, which became the largest in the United Carpathian States.

The Greek Jesus-followers lived on the edge of danger, but for a time it seemed Nicolae Carpathia was more interested in projecting an image of tranquillity in the region named for him than in rooting out dissidents. Laslos did not think he and his fellow believers became overconfident, but somehow one of their secret meeting places had been discovered, someone caved, and the largest assembly had been raided. Many were martyred, the rest scattered.

Laslos lost his wife to the guillotine—also his pastor and his pastor's wife, plus dozens more adults and many teenagers. He had not been at the meeting the night of the raid and now lived with guilt. Was there something he could have done? Though he still felt the hand of God on his life, the Lord was strangely silent about his blame. Laslos was the most prominent among those who had escaped and immediately went into hiding, north of the city.

He feared that a hideout connected in any way to his business would easily be discovered. But he knew of a long-abandoned dump surrounded by mountains of debris, including soil and gravel and chunks of concrete. With the help of trusted friends, he dug himself a dirt-walled chamber where he slept during the day, far below ground and with just enough room for plumbing, a cot, and a small television. In the dead of night, when the walls seemed to close in on him, he would steal away to connect with other believing desperadoes, who then hooked up with clandestine members of the International Commodity Co-op, where they were supplied with food and other necessities.

From those brief, terror-filled meetings grew tiny replicas of the former underground church that had been so vibrant. Laslos and his friends shared with each other what they knew of the rest of the surviving church and passed precious messages back and forth. The few who had wireless computers and enough power downloaded and printed Tsion Ben-Judah's daily messages and Buck Williams's *The Truth* cyberzine. To Laslos these were more priceless than food and water.

The squat, heavyset, fifty-six-year-old widower retained huge, rocklike muscles from his early days of manual labor in the mines. Now he stayed out in the night for as long as he dared, keeping to side and back streets. Sleeping during the day helped keep his claustrophobia in check. More than once he found himself praying that he would wake up in heaven, reunited with his wife and other loved ones.

Late one morning he was awakened by footsteps in the gravel above his hideaway. As quietly as a man of his girth and age could manage, Laslos moved to the edge of his bed and slipped onto all fours on the wood floor. He painfully crept a few feet to where he could reach his handgun, a classic revolver he had never fired, not even on a practice range. It was, however, loaded and—he believed—in working order. A man of peace all his life, he no longer wondered whether he would shoot to kill a Global Community Peacekeeper or Morale Monitor who threatened him or any believer.

The sun cast dusty beams between the cracks of the door over the top of the chamber and the rickety wood planks leading down into the space. The door was level with the ground, and its topside had been inlaid with gravel to blend in. As Laslos stood near the bottom plank, his neck awkwardly craned, staring at the underside of the door, he cocked the revolver and held his breath. The footsteps were atop the door now, tentative, as if aware of the subtle difference between a metal surface with rigid, glued-on stones and the hard-packed but loose gravel of the real ground.

Laslos used his free hand to guide himself and started slowly up the planks, listening over the thud of his pulse for any clue to whether his intruder was alone. When he drew within inches of the door, he leaned to peer through a peephole undetectable from the other side and found himself looking from the boots to the head of a teenage boy, bare armed and wearing neither uniform nor badge nor gun.

Suddenly the boy squatted, as if studying the door. "Mr. Miklos?" he whispered.

Laslos had to calculate countless options at once. If this boy was undercover GC, Laslos had been found out. He could pretend to be fooled, open his door to the boy, and surprise him with a bullet between the eyes. But if the boy was a believer and had been directed there by one of Laslos's friends, he should threaten the comrade with a bullet for stupidity. Either way, for some reason this lad believed Laslos was there, and he was.

He couldn't risk slaughtering his visitor without cause. "Who goes there?" Laslos said quietly in Greek.

The boy dropped to all fours, as if overcome. "Oh, Mr. Miklos!" he rasped desperately. "I am Marcel Papadopoulos! My parents—"

"Shh!" Laslos interrupted, uncocking the weapon and tossing it down onto his bed. He unbolted the locks and grunted as he pushed up the door. "Are you alone?"

"Yes!"

"Hurry!"

The boy turned and nimbly backed down the steps. Laslos returned to refasten the locks. When he came back down, the boy was sitting in a corner on the floor, his knees pulled up. Even in the low light of the underground, the boy's mark was plain on his forehead.

Laslos sat on the bed, realizing the gun was gone. How could he have been such a fool? "I knew your parents, of course," he began carefully. "I knew you too, did I not?"

"Not really," Marcel said. "I was in a different house church from my parents."

Laslos *had* seen this boy with his parents occasionally, he was sure of it. "Did you not think I'd notice you took my fake pistol?"

"Oh, sir! I was just looking at it!" He held it out and Laslos wrenched it away. "It looks and feels so real, Mr. Miklos! Is it really fake?"

"Hardly. How can you be so stupid and survive on the street? What made you think I would not just grab another weapon and shoot you dead?"

"I don't know, sir. I wasn't thinking."

"Who sent you?"

"The old toothless one with the car. He calls himself K."

"I should wring his neck."

"Don't blame him, please, sir. He warned me not to come during the day, but I have run out of places to go. The GC is thin here with so many assigned to Israel, but they are on their way back, and there is no more grace period for taking Carpathia's mark. I have seen people dragged off the street."

"Your parents, weren't they with Pastor Demetrius and—?"

"They were. And so was I. But a believer who had infiltrated the GC accused me of being an American and dragged me out, then let me go. I gave him my parents' names, and I have been praying ever since that he got them out too. But I know they would have found me if he had."

"He did not. We know who he is, Marcel. He also was able to get a young woman out."

"I have met her! Tall, brown hair. Georgiana something. But she was not from our church. She found her way to one of the co-op stations. Her story was just like mine. How did this man do it?"

Laslos sighed heavily. "Frankly, he blundered with you. He used another boy's name for you. . . ."

"Yes, I told him the only other name I knew from in there. Paulo Ganter."

"Well, this fake GC told authorities at the prison that you were Paulo and that he was deporting you back to the United North American States. But when Ganter took the mark of loyalty, his ID checked out, and they quickly realized someone else was gone. By process of elimination, they know your name. He must have done the same with the girl. You may not have marks they can see, but you are marked young people. Fortunately your liberator was gone before they realized what he had done."

"How I would love to thank that man. He's American."

"I know," Laslos said. "I know him."

"Could I get a message to him?"

"It could be done."

The boy sighed and his shoulders sagged. "What am I going to do now, Mr. Miklos? I am out of options."

"You can see there is no room for you here."

"We could expand."

"*We?* Let's not get ahead of ourselves, son. This is no way to live. You need a new look, a new identity, and you must continue to keep from being seen by the GC at all costs."

* * *

Rayford assigned Leah and Hannah to search out the computer savvy among the Israelis. "Tell them that once they have located the computers in Petra, our man in New Babylon will contact them online and provide information on how to get the network up and running."

Rayford, Albie, Mac, and George joined dozens of others to resume chopper duty, making run after run to get Israeli believers inside. Chaim was in seclusion, preparing to address the entire populace when they were settled. Buck had temporarily taken the duties David would have had: getting building and miscellaneous supplies in and organized so builders and finishers could get started. Already volunteers were passing out blankets and helping people get settled.

Rayford was nearly overwhelmed with the attitude of the Israelis. Maybe because of their faith, maybe because of the miracles, maybe because of the novelty of what they were about, they displayed cooperation and a camaraderie Rayford found unique. Considering they were uprooted from their homeland and targeted by the entire evil world system, he would not have been surprised to see manifestations of impatience and anger.

Rayford sent Abdullah bouncing over the desert in one of the most able four-wheel-drive vehicles they could recruit to rendezvous with his co-op contact from Jordan. The contact was bringing in a long-range jet with room for everybody heading back to Chicago. All the co-op guy wanted in exchange for the loan of his plane was to be delivered to Crete on the Trib Force's way to the States and to be brought back from there on their way back.

That gave Rayford the idea that they should stop in Greece to check on their brothers and sisters. Trouble was, Albie was the only one left with other-than-suspect papers. During one of his hops into Petra, Rayford phoned Lukas Miklos.

+ + +

Chang noticed on his monitor evidence that his bug of the Phoenix 216 had kicked in. He couldn't wait till the end of the workday to get back to his apartment and see what had been recorded. He switched to the GCNN feed and learned that Carpathia was already on his way back to New Babylon. Hiding his trail, Chang hacked into the encoded schedule for surprise inspections of GC personnel's private computer systems. The encoding was so elementary he nearly laughed aloud. He discovered he was third on the list and could expect a "random" visit that evening at around 2000 hours.

His screen suddenly came alive with a flash from Figueroa's office, and for an instant Chang thought he might have allowed himself to be caught using the office desktop for unapproved purposes. He covered his tracks with a burst of keystrokes and informed Figueroa he was coming.

Chang hurried to the office that had been David Hassid's. Figueroa had rearranged the furniture and redecorated it within hours of moving in, and now he glided about in it as if he were the Global Community potentate himself.

"Have a seat, Wong," he said. "Cigar?"

"Cigar? Do I look like a smoker to you? Anyway, isn't the whole complex smoke free?"

"A director's office is his domain," Figueroa said, lighting up. Tiffany, who had also been Hassid's assistant, looked up quickly from just outside the office window and scowled. Shaking her head, she left her desk and loudly slapped a switch on the wall between her office and Figueroa's. A ventilation fan came on, sucking the blue smoke into the ceiling. "I love when she does that," the director said, but Chang thought he looked embarrassed.

Figueroa leaned back in his chair and put his feet up on the corner of his desk. Apparently he miscalculated, because as he pulled the huge cigar from his lips, his heel slipped off the desk and his center of gravity shifted. His boots slammed the floor and he nearly flew out of his chair. He dropped the cigar in the process and leaped from his chair to keep from burning himself.

He picked it up and brushed off the seat, quickly licking a finger that had found a hot ash. It was all Chang could do to keep a straight face when Figueroa smoothed himself, put the wet end of the cigar back in his mouth, and sat again. He leaned back but thought twice about putting his feet up and merely crossed his legs. This shifted his weight back more than he expected, and he had evidently not yet learned how to tighten the chair's tilt, for he was suddenly leaning back, legs still crossed, but with both feet in the air.

Figueroa seemed to try to subtly lean forward, but failing that, tried to appear that this was the way he wanted to sit. He pulled the cigar out again and rested an elbow on the arm of the chair, blowing smoke toward the ceiling while trying to maintain eye contact with Chang. "So," he began, the effort to keep his head erect clearly straining his neck. He let his head fall back as if searching the ceiling for what he wanted to say, and suddenly he was inches from toppling over backward. He quickly reinserted the cigar, gripped both arms of the chair until his knuckles were white, and pulled himself up again. He leaned forward, careful to keep his weight centered.

"I, uh, spoke too soon when I exempted you from being interrogated," he said.

Chang made a teenager's face at him. "What? I thought you were in charge here."

"Oh, I am. Make no mistake. But I would have to answer for it, probably to the potentate himself—we talk, you know—if I made an exception for anyone, especially in my own department."

"So you're going back on your word."

"I didn't exactly give my word."

"No, you just said it, and apparently that doesn't mean anything."

"Of course it does, but you're going to have to roll with me on this one. I'll owe you."

"It's not that big a deal. Forget it."

"No, now I want to be known as a man of his word. Tell you what—I'll conduct the polygraph myself."

"Now it's a polygraph?"

"Well, not really. The type I told you about is all."

"Fine."

"You're a good man, Wong."

"Yeah, I'm great."

"No, really, you are."

Chang pressed his lips together and looked away, shaking his head.

"I'm trying to be friends here," Figueroa said.

Chang looked back at him. "You are? Why would you do that?"

"You intrigue me, that's all."

"Oh, no. You're not—"

"Wong! I'm a married man!"

"Thank goodness."

"No, like most everybody else around here, I'm intrigued with your gifts and skills."

"Which I'm not using as long as I'm sitting here."

"Don't be a hard guy, Wong. I'm in a position to do you some good."

"You're not even in a position to keep your word."

"Hey, that was uncalled for."

"Come on," Chang said. "What's this about? That would have been uncalled for only if it weren't true."

"Okay, fair enough. It's just that you're bordering on insubordination, and you don't seem to care that as your boss, I hold your destiny."

"What, you're going to fire me if I don't make nice?"

Figueroa took three short puffs and studied him. "No. But I might fire you if you don't tell me how you knew my name."

"I told you, I guessed."

"Because to tell you the truth," Figueroa continued, as if not listening, "I can't think of a way in the world you would know that."

"Me either. You could have denied it and I wouldn't have known the difference."

"Now see? That's a level of thinking I have to admire. That's intuitive."

"Whatever."

"No, because you know what? I started thinking about my personnel file, and I had to wonder if I ever gave *them* my full name. So, know what I did? Huh? I checked it myself. Not there."

"What do you know."

"So you really did guess."

"Wow. I'm something."

"You are."

"Can I get back to work now?"

"One condition."

"I'm listening."

"Promise you won't say anything about my telling you I've got your destiny in my hands or that I could fire you, any of that."

"Already forgot it."

"Good man. Because I know your dad and you-know-who are tight, and . . ."

"Already forgot it."

"You want to be a project leader, a group head, anything?"

"Just want to get back to work."

"Fair enough."

+ + +

"Three and a half years ago there was, like, a church in here," Enoch said. "Some of us—" he turned to the group—"how many went to the church thing at least once?" About half a dozen raised their hands. "The rest of us had just seen a flyer, a brochure, about the place. We still have those, don't we?" Someone went to get one.

"It's kinda simple, just a regular piece of paper folded in half and then printed on the four pages in black and white."

Someone handed Chloe one. On the front it read "The Place." Inside, it said "Jesus loves pimps, whores, crackheads, drunks, players, hustlers, mothers with no husbands, and children with no fathers."

On the next page it told who made up the people of The Place, mostly people who had once been like those listed on the previous page. "We talk about Jesus and what the Bible says about him and you. Come as you are. Address and time on the back."

Chloe looked at the back, where, besides the address and times, the brochure also said "Food, clothes, shelter, work, counseling." She looked up at Enoch and realized she was blushing. Everybody in the room seemed amused.

Enoch reached for the brochure and faced his people. He read off the list of who Jesus loves, one by one, pausing after each for a show of hands. Everyone raised a hand at least once, and several did many times, always with huge smiles. Enoch carefully set down the brochure, looked meaningfully at Chloe, and rose. With lips trembling and tears streaming, he gestured to the assembled and whispered, "And such were some of you."

They nodded and *amen*ed.

"But you were washed . . ."

"Amen, hallelujah!"

"But you were sanctified . . ."

"Praise Jesus!"

"But you were justified in the name of the Lord Jesus and by the Spirit of our God."

And they stood with hands raised, humming and singing,

"Amazing grace, how sweet the sound,
that saved a wretch like me;
I once was lost but now am found,
was blind but now I see."

* * *

"Rayford, my friend, how are you?" Laslos exulted. "You will not believe who is here with me. Is Cameron there?"

"Unavailable just now. So who is with you?"

When Laslos told him, Rayford said, "I'll have Buck call. He wondered what happened with those kids."

"Marcel tells me Georgiana remains on the run too. It is as if God himself told you to call. You must come get these children and get them out of here."

"Nowhere is safe, Laslos."

"But your safe house! Your man with the disguises and the papers! We are literally one wrong look from death here."

Rayford hesitated. "We're stopping on Crete. If you could somehow get them there . . ."

"Captain Steele, you have not seen the oceans! There is no water travel. None. Could we not somehow try to get them to the airport your people flew into last time? It would be risky, but we could—"

"It would be a death trap for us, Laslos. We will have virtually everyone with us."

"There must be some way. Someone."

"Let me noodle that," Rayford said.

"I don't understand 'noodle.'"

"I'll think about it."

* * *

"Almost every one of us has the same story," Enoch explained to Chloe. "The streets, these neighborhoods, were our lives. A lot of us had some kind of religious background as kids, but obviously we moved a long way from that. More than half of us served time, and almost all of us should have. The line between legal and illegal didn't exist for us. We called everything we did a matter of survival.

"Most of us had seen this place and knew something churchy went on here. What surprised us were the people who came and went. All colors and nationalities and people we'd known. We all saw the brochure and, though we didn't admit it then, it enticed us, you know? Something that straightforward, that in-your-face, calling things what they are. When you're at the end of yourself, wondering in the night what's to become of you in the morning, you start wondering if there's hope anywhere or if you are too far gone. You remember yourself as a kid and recall that there was something still innocent about you, and you wonder what happened to that person.

"Any of these people will tell you that they either came here once or twice to try to work the system and get something free, or they even came sincerely and sat through a meeting or two. But all of us, even those who never came once—me, for one—were fixin' to get around to it. One of these days, we were going to check out The Place.

"You know the rest. End of the world. People disappearing. We all lost somebody, and this place just about lost everybody. Well, where did we run to first? Right here. Empty clothes all over the place and nobody to tell us what was what. But this poor little church must have had some money from somewhere because they thought to record everything they did. Audio and video. Here we are—two, three dozen no-account street people, some of us women who lost babies—and somebody finds those discs, man, and the players. It didn't take us long to learn the truth. It was all there.

"Most of us stayed, sleeping in here, watching, listening, studying, praying to get Jesus, and all of a sudden, World War III. Chicago's toast. We've got one TV and one computer hooked up. First we hear it was not nuclear; then the next wave is, and we expect to die of radiation poisoning. It doesn't happen, but we don't dare test the atmosphere outside. We knew if it was full-blown radiation, we were not protected just because we were inside some basement, but we figured we were safer in than out. Till now."

\+ + +

Rayford called George and asked if he wanted a mission on his way back to San Diego. "I thought you'd never ask," he said.

Rayford gave him the gist of the assignment and said, "I can't give you papers on short notice, but if I can reach our guy in New Babylon, you can bluff your way around in Greece. If they check on you, you'll appear to be in the system."

"I can come up with some reason why I don't have papers. And you want these kids delivered to Chicago?"

"Unless you're prepared for them in California."

\+ + +

Knowing what was coming that evening, Chang felt out of touch with the Trib Force. Not until after his "surprise" visit at about eight o'clock could he key in the stuff Rayford wanted for this George Sebastian, nor could he find out what had happened on the Phoenix 216. He made sure he was watching GCNN and reading a book at the time, but even he was surprised at the nature of the drop-in.

Chang thought Figueroa's assignee—a cocky, condescending Scandinavian named Lars—would have at least knocked. But at a few minutes after eight, as Chang watched coverage of Carpathia and his senior cabinet being enthusiastically welcomed back to New Babylon, he heard a key in his door. It was just as well. He quickly turned up the TV and pretended he didn't hear a thing until they burst in. This was the best cover. He was relaxing, watching TV, reading, not even thinking about his worthless laptop.

The door swung open and two uniformed Peacekeepers marched in. "Mr. Chang Wong?" one said.

"That's me," he said, rising. "Did I forget to lock my door?"

"Turn off the television, please, sir, and join us over here, if you would."

"What if I wouldn't?"

"Now, sir."

"Thanks for making me feel welcome in my own place."

"This is not your place, Mr. Wong. This is the property of His Excellency, the potentate, and you serve here at his behest."

Chang made a show of turning off the TV and dropping his book onto a chair. As he approached, the Peacekeepers moved aside and one of them announced, "This, sir, is Mr. L—"

"Lars!" Chang said, smiling, though he had barely done anything more than greet the guy. "How are you, man? I know him! We're in the same department."

"We need your cooperation and silence, Mr. Wong," the Peacekeeper said.

"Ooh, okay! What's up?"

17

THE PEACEKEEPERS ASKED if they could search Chang's apartment. "For what?" he said.

"Routine," they told him.

"You won't find any routine here. I am studying English words new to me and my current favorite is *serendipity.* That's what you'll find here, the opposite of *routine.*"

"Funny. We don't need your permission. We were just being polite."

"Of course. My clue was your use of a master key to get me to answer the door."

While they searched the apartment, Lars set up a high-powered laptop on Chang's small kitchen table. "I'll be asking a few questions," he said.

"No, you won't."

"Stop being a smartaleck," Lars said. "This is my assignment."

"Do the questions relate to finding a leak from the palace to the suspected mole?"

Lars turned ashen. "You've already been interrogated?"

"No, but I have my reservation in with another *interlocutor*—another new word. You like?"

"Computer!" the other Peacekeeper called out. "Looks like his personal laptop."

"If you had told me what you were looking for, I could have directed you to it."

"This your only one?"

Chang was tempted to pretend there was another, but the fun of watching them try to locate it wouldn't be worth their leaving the place in more of a shambles. He nodded.

"Over here with that," Lars said.

"I'm so glad you're here, Lars," Chang said. "I had everything on that hard drive, and I mean *everything.* Maybe you won't feel so bad about losing the interviewing assignment to our boss if you have this project to work on."

"Project?"

"I crashed the hard drive, and I've tried everything."

"Everything *you* know."

"That's right! That's why I'm so glad you're here. I must be missing something, and even if it's something complex, I know you can solve it."

"You bet your life I can."

Chang, of course, was betting his life Lars couldn't. "I don't want to be up late, Lars."

"Oh, this shouldn't take long."

"I'm just saying maybe you want to call Mr. Figueroa so he can do whatever he has to do with me while you're retrieving my information."

"What're you, serious?"

"He promised."

"Why?"

"You'll have to ask him that."

"He'll ask you the same questions I would, and you'll answer into the same mike."

"Only with him, I'll answer. With you I won't."

"Then you'll be suspected as the leak, and you don't want that, guilty or not. You hear what happened to the stewards today?"

Chang didn't like it when he was asked a question to which he didn't know the answer. "Shock me."

"Sentenced to death."

That did shock Chang. "For what?"

"Subversion. Treason. They flunked the lie detector test. They were feeding information to a mole here. Conversations between the potentate and his people were acted upon before they were through talking." Lars handed him a lapel microphone. "Put this on."

"Not for you," Chang said.

"For Figueroa then."

Chang applied it to his shirt, praying silently. The key, he knew, was how the questions were worded. In his mind, a mole was an animal; he was a human being. If the questions were too specific and unequivocal, he'd be in trouble. "Start with my computer, will you? I'd really love to see all that stuff I had stored."

"You don't back up your stuff?"

Chang shook his head. "Nah. Do you?"

"Not as much as I should, but you gotta know you're going to fry something—hard drive, motherboard, whatever—every few years."

"Guess I've been lucky."

Lars dialed, tucked his phone between his cheek and neck, and started pecking furiously at Chang's laptop. "Yes, Mr. Figueroa, sir. I'm at Chang Wong's apartment and he says—oh, you did. Well, yes, right now. I'm helping him with a computer problem, so we'll be here. Thank you, sir."

Slapping his phone shut, eyes still on Chang's computer, Lars mumbled, "On his way. My, you *have* fried this thing."

"Really, Lars? You can tell already? Wow."

"Yeah, it won't let me in at all. Let me try this." He appeared to try everything. "Nothing. Believe me, Wong, if anything was here, I could get it for you."

"No doubt."

"But this acts like it's been exposed to some super electromagnet."

"Haven't heard that term in a while."

"You know the drive is all about electricity and that a magnet can wreak serious havoc."

"Really?"

"Oh yeah, it's quite simple."

"For a brain like yours, maybe," Chang said. "I just know what buttons to push."

"Well, there's a lot more to it than that."

"I suppose. It's Greek to me."

"Thought you were supposed to be some kind of a genius," Lars said.

"Live and learn. Look what I did to my own laptop. Ten gigs somewhere in the ether."

"Should have called me at the first sign of trouble. There had to be warnings."

"Yeah, I saw a lot of strange stuff, but you know, laptops are temperamental."

"Not if they're treated right. Did you defrag and run ScanDisk and all that?"

"Not often."

"Obviously not. I don't think there's anything here."

"You can't help me?"

"If anyone could, I could. But there's either something on the drive or there isn't, and in this case, there clearly isn't."

"What if it was on a different drive, named something else?"

"You couldn't do that by accident," Lars said. "I could do it, but you have to know what you're doing."

"Which I don't."

"Obviously. Here's what I *can* do for you. While you're being interviewed, I can format your whole drive for you so you can start rebuilding."

"That's got to be hard. Complicated."

"Nah. Won't take much."

"You'd do that for me?"

"What are friends for?"

* * *

Chloe had sneaked two of her new friends into the Strong Building in the wee hours of the morning. Only Zeke was stirring, and he blanched at the new faces. Chloe introduced the young man and woman with such enthusiasm that she knew he'd understand they were okay, without wondering if she was covering and he should go find a weapon.

Once he heard the story, Zeke offered to help them transfer a serious amount of foodstuffs to their place. Chloe wrote every detail she could remember and e-mailed it to the rest of the Trib Force before collapsing just before dawn and sleeping till almost noon. She assumed she would be scolded for taking such a risk, but she was so excited she was amazed she was able to sleep at all.

* * *

No surprise to Chang, Figueroa arrived looking all business and gave him a stare that communicated he should avoid any familiarity in front of Lars.

"Ignore me," Lars said, taking Chang's laptop to a couch and settling in with it. "Just making sure this is ready for a whole new protocol." Chang wondered if Lars *could* affect his encoded drive with his clumsy efforts.

Figueroa pointed to a chair and sat across from Chang. He dismissed the other Peacekeeper, then whispered, "I didn't think you were going to hold me to this."

"I could have let it slide," Chang said. "Proved you were completely untrustworthy. Mind if I take a peek at that software?"

Looking bored, Figueroa pivoted the machine to face Chang. He sighed. "Newfangled stuff. Supposed to be better than the bulky old hardware."

Chang knew it wasn't all that new. He had seen it in China and even played with it. He made a show of tilting the screen so the light was just right. "Interesting," he said, and as Figueroa leaned closer, Chang added, "Sequoia, ah, I mean, Aurelio."

Figueroa sat back, obviously peeved. "I'd appreciate your addressing me by my last name."

"Excuse me, of course," Chang said.

Figueroa grabbed the laptop and pulled a small notebook from his pocket. "State your name," he began, then walked Chang through a series of banal, obvious questions. "Is today Sunday?"

"No."

"Is the sky blue?"

"Yes."

"Are you a male?"

"Yes."

"Do you work for the Global Community?"

"I am employed by them, yes."

Figueroa looked up at Chang. "That's the answer you want to give?"

"Yes."

"Are you loyal to the supreme potentate?"

Chang closed his eyes and reminded himself that Jesus Christ was the only person who fit that definition. "Yes," he said.

"Have you ever done anything that would be considered disloyal to the supreme potentate?"

"Not intentionally, no."

"Stick to yes or no answers."

"No."

"Do you get confidential information from someone who leaks it to you from the inner circle around the supreme potentate?"

"No."

"Is the supreme potentate risen from the dead and the living lord?"

"Yes."

"Can His Excellency Nicolae Carpathia personally count on your continuing loyalty for as long as you serve as an employee of the Global Community?"

Chang hesitated, making Figueroa look up again. "Understand the question?"

"Of course."

"Then your answer is yes?"

"No."

"Don't start playing games now, Chang, or we'll have to do this all over again."

"Well, Mr. Figueroa, I can certainly say in all sincerity that I will continue to show the same level of loyalty to the Global Community leader that I have shown him since the beginning."

"So that's a yes?"

"It merely is what it is."

"What would he think of this?"

"Probably that you're wasting your time, and mine."

"You don't want to just say yes and be done with it?"

"That's the last question?"

"Yes."

"How'm I doing so far?"

"It looks fine," Figueroa said.

"Then let it ride."

"That last answer could look evasive."

"To whom?"

"To anybody who's got a question."

"Do *you* have a question, Mr. Fig—"

"Man, do you ever just give a straight answer?"

"Should I?"

"Agh!" Figueroa swept up the equipment. "Let's go, Lars."

"Yes, sir. Laptop's ready to go, Chang."

"Find any of my stuff on it?"

"No, but you can rebuild from here with a clean slate."

"You have no idea how I feel about what you've done for me here, Lars."

"Well, you're welcome."

✢ ✢ ✢

It was time for the Trib Force assignees to Operation Eagle to head for Mizpe Ramon and the flight home. The overflow crowd of Israelis was bivouacking outside Petra, and Chaim was about to be airlifted to a spot where all could see and hear him, from both inside and outside. Rayford, Buck, Mac, Leah, Hannah, and Albie stood in a circle with Chaim, holding hands. Big George from San Diego sat in an idling chopper fifty yards away, waiting to lift Chaim into Petra, then transport the Trib Force to Mizpe Ramon, from where he would also fly his own plane to Greece, then to Chicago, then to San Diego. "Let's get George in on this," Rayford said, beckoning him with a wave. "I have a feeling we're going to be seeing more of him."

George jumped out and jogged over. "Micah ready?" he said.

"In a minute, George," Rayford said. "Get in here with us." As they bowed their heads, Rayford told everyone of George's assignment in Greece later that night.

"Wish I could go too," Buck said. "But I'm too hot right now. You'll love those kids, George."

"We should pray," Rayford said.

"One moment, please," Chaim said, letting go of Rayford's hand on one side and Hannah's on the other. He pulled from his robe the miniature urn containing Hattie's ashes. "We do not worship the remains of those who go to God before us, and my wish is to one day toss what is left of these to the winds from a high place of worship to the one true God here at Petra. I believe that is what our impetuous but sincere young sister would have wanted. But first I want to entrust these to you, Captain Steele, to take back to her new brothers and sisters in the safe house, back to some who knew her and loved her even long before she gave herself to the Christ. Then bring them back with Tsion Ben-Judah, and we will remember her one last time before he addresses the remnant of Israel. And as we think of David Hassid, we wish only that we also had a token by which to remember our courageous brother, who knew so few of us personally but who contributed so much to the cause."

"I have a token," Leah said, producing David's phone.

"Would you take that, too, to our comrades in Chicago for a moment of remembrance, looking forward to the day when we shall see this dear one again?" Chaim said.

Leah handed it to Hannah. "I would like his friend to take it," she said. Hannah thanked her with a hug.

"And now," Chaim said as they joined hands again, "to those who are called, sanctified by God the Father, and preserved in Jesus Christ: mercy, peace, and love be multiplied to you, beloved, building yourselves up on your most holy faith, praying in the Holy Spirit, keep yourselves in the love of God, looking for the mercy of our Lord Jesus Christ unto eternal life.

"Now to him who is able to keep you from stumbling, and to present you faultless before the presence of his glory with exceeding joy, to God our Savior, who alone is wise, be glory and majesty, dominion and power, both now and forever. Amen."

* * *

Finally alone again, Chang waited a few minutes, then moved a chair to his door, stood on it, and secured a latch he had built in along the top that would keep out even those with a master key. He dropped into his chair with his laptop and typed in "Christ alone." That brought up a screen with a grid of two hundred dots square. He counted in eighteen rows from the bottom and thirty-seven from the right and clicked on it. A fifteen-digit counter appeared, the numbers ascending at a rate of several hundred a second. Chang keyed in a multiplier, factored in the current date and time, and sent the product hurtling toward a synchronous number ninety seconds away. Four more minutes and three complex, moving targets later, Chang was back in business. He was connected to every Tribulation Force computer, including those at Petra, and anything he wanted at the palace and on the Phoenix 216.

Chang transmitted hundreds of pages of instructions encoded for the Petra machines, checked the locations of reporting gadgets from phones to computers to handhelds, and let everyone know he was up and running. Then he checked Rayford's specifications for the man he called Big George and planted GC credentials in the main palace database. They had decided to use his real name in case his prints or other details were cross-checked. George Sebastian of San Diego, California, in the United North American States, would be transporting a teen male prisoner and a teen female prisoner from Greece to the States. He would fly a high-speed, transatlantic, four-seat Rooster Tail and would be traveling WOP—without papers—due to a recent undercover mission, but for identification purposes he was six feet four and weighed two hundred forty pounds, dark complexion, blue eyes, and blond hair. He had level–A-minus clearance and reported directly to Deputy Commander Marcus Elbaz. Chang entered a six-digit code that George was to memorize and recite if asked.

Chang understood that Rayford had planned all this with Lukas Miklos, who would inform Mr. Papadopoulos, who would inform Georgiana Stavros. Lukas was to use his own contacts and resources and be responsible for making sure that the two young people rendezvoused with George.

Chang then located the newest Phoenix 216 recording since last he had listened in. He put on his headset.

The bug first picked up Akbar. "I assume you are pleased with the new pilot, Excellency."

"All I care about is getting out of this godforsaken country, Suhail. Can he accomplish that?"

"Oh, Supreme Potentate," Fortunato sang out, "Israel is no longer godforsaken. It is now *truly* the Holy Land, because you have been installed as the true and—"

"Leon, please! You have conferred upon your underlings the power I have imbued you with, have you not?"

"I have, Your Worship, but I prefer not to refer to them as underl—"

"Have any of them, one of them—you, for instance—come up with a thing to match the oceans-to-blood trick?"

"Well, sir, besides the calling down of fire from heaven and the, uh . . . I'd like to think I played some small role—whether just the influence of my presence in part of the meeting with Mr. Micah or . . . anyway—in the healing of the sores."

"I do not believe you realize, Leon, the scope of the tragedy on the high seas. Do you?"

"Enough to hope it's not a permanent thing, Excellency."

"You hope? Think, man! Suhail, does the right-reverend-whatever get the cabinet briefings? Does he read the—"

"Yes, sir, he's on the list."

"Leon, read the reports! Our ships are dead in the water! Our marine biologists tell us every creature in the water is surely dead by now! If this *is* temporary and the water turns pristine tomorrow morning, do you think all the fishies will come flopping back to life too?"

"I certainly hope so!"

"Imbecile," Carpathia muttered, and Chang assumed Fortunato didn't hear him. The potentate tended to murder people he referred to that way, and Leon would have been pleading for his life. "Suhail, can we not get this plane off the ground?"

"We're waiting for Ms. Ivins, sir."

"Where is she?"

"If I may speak to that, Potentate," Leon said.

"Of course, if you know where she is."

"She wanted one last visit to the temple. She wants to be the first woman to go into the main part and see where you went, worship your image in the Holy of Holies, sit on the, uh, in the—"

"What?! You are not saying she would dare sit on the throne of god!"

"No, sir, I misspoke there, sir. I'm certain she wanted only to see it, to perhaps touch it, take a photograph."

"Why are you not there with her?"

"She wanted only security. She plans to walk in alone and, I believe, just violate a few traditions."

"I like that."

"I thought you might. She thought you might too."

"Find out if she is en route."

"In the meantime, Potentate," Akbar said, "we have received the software for lie detection."

"Yes, get that started now and begin with the stewards."

Chang heard dread in the voices of the Indians. They answered with conviction and earnestness. "You both test entirely truthful," Akbar concluded. They wept, expressing their gratitude.

"Been tested, have you?" Carpathia said, as the sounds of their bustling about and serving came through the system.

"Yes, sir. Thank you, sir."

"Indeed." Carpathia sounded skeptical and dismissive. "Test the pilot, Suhail."

"Ms. Ivins is on the tarmac, sir."

"There is time. First him, then Leon, then her. And here is a question I want added to her session."

The pilot sounded unconcerned, almost bored, answering quickly and matter-of-factly. "He's clean," Akbar reported. "Reverend Fortunato, are you ready?"

"I have nothing whatever to hide," Leon said. But when he was asked the day of the week, he asked if it was a trick question. His answers became more whiny and pensive, but of course, he was cleared too.

The plane took off; then Suhail could be heard talking with Ms. Ivins. "I'm assuming, ma'am, that you are willing, just as a matter of procedure, to submit to the truth test."

She chuckled. "And what do we do if I am revealed as the leak to the mole?"

"Please clip this on, ma'am."

"Ready."

"State your name."

"Ms. Vivian Ivins."

"Is today Sunday?"

"No, but I would like to know if I got the first question right."

Akbar laughed. "Is the sky blue?"

"Yes."

"Are you a male?"

"No."

"Do you work for the Global Community?"

She hesitated. "Yes."

"It showed okay, ma'am, but just out of curiosity, why the hesitation?"

"I have never really considered myself an employee of the Global Community. I serve Supreme Potentate Nicolae Carpathia, and I have most of my adult life. I would, even if I were not compensated, but yes, I also actually am part of the personnel of the Global Community."

"Are you loyal to the supreme potentate?"

"Yes."

"Have you ever done anything that could be considered disloyal to the supreme potentate?"

"No."

"Do you leak confidential information from the supreme potentate to anyone at GC headquarters?"

"No."

"Is the supreme potentate risen from the dead and the living lord?"

"Yes."

"Can His Excellency Nicolae Carpathia personally count on your continuing loyalty for as long as you serve as an employee of the Global Community?"

"Yes, and beyond."

"Did you sit on his throne in his temple in Jerusalem today?"

"I—no."

"Thank you, Ms. Ivins."

Chang heard Akbar unbuckle and leave, but it was clear Viv Ivins immediately followed. "Director Akbar, wait, please. Before you share the results with His Excellency, let me have a word with him."

"Certainly."

"My lord," she said quietly.

"Yes, dear one," Carpathia said.

"May I kneel and kiss your hand?"

"That depends. How did you do on the little test?"

"I don't know, but regardless of the results, I answered truthfully until the very end."

"You were deceitful in your answer to *my* question?"

"I was, sir, but I immediately regretted it and have come to beg your forgiveness."

If Carpathia responded, Chang couldn't hear it.

"I told Reverend Fortunato what I intended to do," she said, "and he advised me against it."

"Did he? Did you, Leon?"

"I did, sir."

"Good for you! But it should not be only the Most High Reverend Father of Carpathianism who knows what a defilement it would be to presume to sit on the throne of god!"

"I am so sorry, Nicolae," and Chang got the impression she said his name the way she had when Carpathia was a small boy. Nicolae again fell silent.

"I did not do it as an act of insubordination, I swear. I merely envied your moment and felt a deep need to share it. I would like to think I earned the right with—"

"Earned the right? To sit on *my* throne? To take *my* place?"

"—with my years of service, with my uncompromising devotion, with my love for you. Oh, don't dismiss me, Your Worship. Forgive me. Please! Nicolae!"

Chang heard her weeping. Then Nicolae: "Suhail, let's administer the test to each other." Ms. Ivins's crying faded as she must have moved back to her seat.

Akbar was brief and confident, and when it was Carpathia's turn, of course the questions were slightly revised. But Carpathia was in a testy mood.

"State your name," Akbar began.

"God."

"Is today Sunday?"

"Yes."

"Is the sky blue?"

"No."

"Are you a male?"

"No."

"Do you serve the Global Community?"

"No."

"Are you loyal to the citizens under your authority?"

"No."

"Have you ever done anything disloyal to the Global Community?"

"Yes."

"Do you leak confidential information to someone inside GC headquarters that undermines the effectiveness of your cabinet?"

"No. And I would personally kill anyone who did."

"Did you rise from the dead and are you the living lord?"

"Yes."

"Can the Global Community count on your continuing loyalty for as long as you serve as supreme potentate?"

"No."

"You astound me, Excellency."

"Well?"

"I don't know how you do that."

"Tell me!" Carpathia said.

"Your answers all proved truthful, even where you were obviously sporting with me and saying the opposite of the truth."

"The truth is what I say it is, Suhail. I am the father of truth."

18

ON THE FLIGHT HOME, Buck called Lukas Miklos.

"I imagine you want to talk to the young man whose life you saved, eh, Cameron?"

"I do, Laslos. And I'm sorry all my other messages to you about what happened that night had to come electronically and not even by phone. I wish I could have given you your wife's message in person, but—"

"I understand, my friend," Laslos said, his voice quavery. "I remember every detail of it. I wish only that I could have gone to heaven with her."

"I can't imagine how hard it is," Buck said. "But the church needs you there, and—"

"Oh, Cameron, I am useless. I am not free to help in any real ways anymore. Sometimes I wish they would just find me so I could testify for God before they kill me."

Buck wanted to counter him, but what could he say? "We sure appreciate your help in getting those kids out of the country."

"I'll do what I can. I look forward to getting them connected with your pilot, but it's unlikely I can risk coming out of the shadows to meet him. I will get them as close to the airport as I dare. Here, let me have you talk to the boy."

"Hello, sir?" Marcel said, and Buck remembered the voice from their only encounter.

"I'm so glad to talk to you again, son. I didn't expect I ever would."

"I can't thank you enough, Mr. Williams. I know you got in trouble for that. Will I meet you in Chicago?"

"You sure will."

"Mr. Miklos has told me so much about you and your family and friends. I hope I will be safe there."

"Safer than where you are, I guess. And the girl?"

"Georgiana, um, Stavros," Marcel said. "I was so surprised when I heard she had the same story as mine. We finally were introduced at a co-op center."

"And you have been able to communicate with her?"

"It's all set. We will meet her on the road. Mr. Miklos will stay with us for as far as he can."

"That's quite a journey on foot."

"He has arranged for someone to drive us, at least until we are a couple of miles from the airport. Then the pilot, Mr. Sebastian, is it—?"

"Yes."

"—will come find us and walk us in as prisoners."

"We'll be praying for you all."

* * *

Chang listened to several minutes' worth of small talk, then a pitiful effort by Viv Ivins to again reconnect with Nicolae and get his forgiveness. Finally Nicolae summoned Akbar. "Suhail," he said, "I am not going to replace Mr. Moon as supreme commander."

"I see."

"The job and the title are redundant."

"Whatever you say, Excellency."

"I will count on you more and more, and you may inherit duties that might otherwise have been carried out by a supreme commander."

"As you wish."

"First assignment: Take action on our security leak."

"I'm, we're—sir, we are already conducting a full investigation at the palace, but as you know, we turned up nothing on the plane. . . ."

"How does that make sense? You told me it was as if someone were relaying our very conversations to someone with access to the central database."

"That's what it seemed. We are scouring headquarters for weaknesses in our fire walls, but the late Mr. Hassid put the system in place, and there was not a better person in the world for that job."

"His replacement, the South American—"

"Mexican, sir. Figueroa."

"You have confidence in him?"

"A stellar record. Not the technician Hassid was, but capable. He is overseeing the testing, and he himself will also be tested, of course."

"I want to send a message to whoever is subverting us from inside. Get them to panic, put them on the defensive."

"I'm open to any suggestion, Potentate."

"Charge the Indians."

"Sir?"

"The stewards. Convict them of treason."

"Uh, on what evidence?"

"They are the only logical ones, Suhail. The pilot was not even on board during most of our meetings. They were."

"But they tested clean."

"Who knows that but you and I?"

"Um-hm."

"No one, am I correct?"

"You are."

"Whisper it to Leon. And to Viv. Then release it to the media. They should disembark in New Babylon in handcuffs. Do you have two pair on board?"

"I do, but—"

"A problem?"

"I'm at your service, sir, but I'm missing something. The mole will see we fingered the wrong perpetrators. Rather than put him or her on the defensive, it may make us look like soft opponents."

"So much the better. Let him grow overconfident. Still, he will see what we do with people we believe are insurrectionists."

"If convicted, the penalty is death."

"Oh, Suhail! If they get off this plane in shackles, consider them convicted. The executions should follow within forty-eight hours."

"Done."

"And your conscience, Director?"

"My conscience?"

"Knowing the truth, does this give you pause?"

"No, sir. You are the father of truth. My conscience is at your service."

There was a long pause. "They do good work, though, do they not?" Carpathia said at last. "The stewards?"

"Quite."

"No need to inform them or cuff them until we touch down. But do get the information trail started. And then we need to discuss the final solution for the Israeli dissidents and the Judah-ites. Let me know as soon as you have casualty statistics on Operation Petra."

\+ + +

Laslos wished he could go with the two young people all the way to the safe house in America. What an adventure! But how could he justify abandoning his brothers and sisters in Greece? The net was tightening and few of them would survive until the Glorious Appearing, but no one would question giving the teenagers a better chance.

Being involved in getting them connected with this pilot made Laslos feel alive again. He dreaded the end of the caper when his friend K would drive him back to Ptolemaïs. He would then walk the last mile and a half to his secret place and settle into his awful routine.

The plan was for K to pick up the boy and him in the country at the north edge of town. They would stay on the outskirts, getting Marcel close enough to the co-op to where he could walk there and get his meager bag of belongings. Georgiana Stavros would wait for them on the southern end of town, off the road that led to the airport. Cameron Williams and Marcel had told him she was a tall brunette, fair-skinned for a Greek, and pretty. Laslos liked to imagine that she looked like his wife when first he met her more than forty years before.

* * *

Chang noticed that Carpathia's plane sounded as if it was descending when Suhail Akbar returned to talk with the potentate. "Ah, Director," Nicolae began, "we are planning something very special for Petra when Ben-Judah is confirmed present, no?"

"Sir, we need to talk."

"Answer my question, Suhail."

"Yes, of course, but I have bad news."

"I do not want bad news! Everybody was healthy! We had plenty of equipment for the Petra offensive. You were going to ignore the city—waiting to destroy it when Micah and Ben-Judah were both there—and overtake those not yet inside. What could be bad news? What do we hear from them?"

"Nothing. Our—"

"Nonsense! They were to report as soon as they had overtaken the insurgents. The world was to marvel at our complete success without firing a shot, no casualties for us versus total destruction of those who oppose me. What happened?"

"We're not sure yet."

"You must have had two hundred commanding officers alone!"

"More than that."

"And not a word from one of them?"

"Our stratospheric photo planes show our forces advancing to within feet of overrunning approximately five hundred thousand outside Petra."

"A cloud of dust and the enemy, in essence, plowed under."

"That was the plan, Excellency."

"And what? The old men in robes and long beards fought back with hidden daggers?"

"Our planes waited until the dust cloud settled and now find no evidence of our troops."

Carpathia laughed.

"I wish I were teasing you, Potentate. High-altitude photographs ten minutes after the offensive show the same crowd outside Petra, and yet—"

"None of our troops, yes, you said that. And our armaments? One of the largest conglomerations of firepower ever assembled, you told me, split into three divisions. Invincible, you said."

"Disappeared."

"Can those photographs be transmitted here?"

"They're waiting in your office, sir. But people I trust verify what we're going to see . . . or not see, I should say."

Carpathia's voice sounded constricted, as if he'd rather explode than speak. "I want the potentate of each of the world regions on his way to New Babylon within the hour. Any who are not en route sixty minutes from now will be replaced. See to that immediately, and when you determine when the one from the farthest distance will arrive, set a meeting for the senior cabinet and me with the ten of them for an hour later. And these Jews," he said slowly, "we expect them all to be in Petra as soon as they can be transported there?"

"Actually, they will not all fit. We expect Petra itself to be full and the rest to camp nearby."

"What is required to level Petra and the surrounding area?"

"Two planes, two crews, two annihilation devices. We could launch a subsequent missile to ensure thorough devastation, though that might be overkill."

"Ah, Suhail. You will one day come to realize that there is no such thing as overkill. Let the Jews and the Judah-ites think they have had their little victory. And keep the failed operation quiet. We never launched it. Our missing troops and vehicles and armaments never existed."

"And what of the questions from their families?"

"The questions should go *to* the families. We demand to know where these soldiers are and what they have done with our equipment."

"Tens of thousands AWOL? That's what we will contend?"

"No, Suhail. Rather, I suggest you go on international television and tell the GCNN audience that the greatest military effort ever carried out was met by half a million unarmed Jews who made it disappear! Perhaps you could use a flip chart! Now you see us; now you do not!"

* * *

"I'm scared," Marcel told Laslos as they stole out of the hideaway at nightfall.

"There is no need to be, son. You are just excited. You have endured tragedy, as we all have, but you are being given a second chance. If you are not safe with the Tribulation Force, you will never be."

They walked the mile and a half in the dark on dirt paths Laslos had come to know well. Though he walked more than he rode and never drove anymore, he still felt the pain and weariness of his age. Marcel seemed to have to wait for him, and Laslos wished he could tell him to go on. But he wanted to feel useful. He was part of the escapade, part of the plan. These precious young people would be in his charge until he sent them off with Godspeed to rendezvous with George Sebastian.

Half a mile outside Ptolemaïs, Laslos spotted K's tiny white car well off a rarely used road. Laslos stopped Marcel with a touch, then made a birdcall. K tapped the brake and the taillights went on briefly. "That means no one is around," Laslos said. "Run to the car. I will be there."

He knew Marcel wanted to stretch those lanky legs, and as Laslos shuffled along as quickly as he could, he enjoyed watching the boy lope to the car. K had long since removed the inside light, so when the door opened, the car still looked dark. When Laslos arrived, K was behind the wheel, Marcel next to him.

Laslos squeezed into the minuscule backseat, directly behind Marcel. K, older than Laslos, bald and bony, wore a small black stocking cap and spoke with difficulty because most of his front teeth were missing. He said, "He ith rithen," and the boy and Laslos—though wheezing—said, "Christ is risen indeed."

K drove carefully to the edge of the city and parked on a dark street. "You know where you are?" Laslos asked the boy.

"I think so," Marcel said. "The co-op is in the cellar under the pub a block and a half that way?"

"And you know the password?"

"Of course. They have my stuff."

"And they will confirm that the girl—"

"Georgiana."

"—yes, is waiting."

Marcel nodded and jumped out of the car. Laslos quickly cranked down his window. "Psst! Do not run," he whispered. And the boy slowed.

K turned and grinned at him. "Young people," he said.

"How long until our luck runs out, K?"

K shook his head and his smile faded. "We are already living on next month'th time, Lathloth."

"What happens if you ever get stopped?"

"Thath the end of it," K said. "They'll take me to get the mark but I'll tell them to jutht kill me, becauth I'm through fighting."

Laslos clapped his friend on the shoulder. "But you're doing damage until the time comes, eh?"

"Muth ath I can."

Marcel returned, a canvas bag over his shoulder. "Any problem?" Laslos said.

He shook his head, tossing the bag in the back, leaving just enough room for the girl. "She's supposed to be there, and nobody followed me. Look for one small stone on top of two others, eight kilometers from the airport. She'll be in the underbrush near there. Just pull over and she'll find us."

K stayed outside the city and headed toward the airport road. They saw no GC Peacekeepers or vehicles, but still Laslos found his right leg bouncing, his hands clasped tightly in his lap. When they passed the 10K sign, Laslos leaned forward and helped K watch the odometer. A few minutes later Marcel said, "There!"

K's headlights showed two small stones on the left side of the road with another laid casually atop them. No one would have noticed if they hadn't been looking for them. K checked his mirrors, and Laslos shifted so he could look out the back too. "Nobody," he said.

K pulled off to the side, his right front tire crunching the three stones. He sat with the engine idling and the lights on, squinting into the rearview mirror. "Let's go, young lady," Laslos muttered. "We don't want to be seen."

"Want me to call for her?" Marcel said.

"She was supposed to find us, right?"

"Right."

"Always stick to the plan. If the plan changes, you don't improvise. You leave."

K nodded. "Ten thecondth," he said. "I won't thtay here longer."

"There she is!" Marcel said.

Georgiana ran up to the car, and Laslos leaned across Marcel's bag to open her door. She was shivering in jeans and a white, short-sleeve shirt, and a ratty, red baseball cap hooding her eyes. She carried a small, dark green satchel, barely a foot long. "Marcel," she said. "Good to see you again."

"Yeah, hi! Let's go!"

She jumped in and put her bag between her feet. "You must be Laslos," she said. "I'm Georgiana." She squeezed his arm. Her dark fingers were cold. She put her hands on K's shoulders. "And this must be K."

Marcel raised a hand, and she gripped it. "This is exciting," she said, then rubbed her palms together.

"He ith rithen," K said.

"Amen!" she said, nearly squealing. "He is risen indeed!"

"Is that all you brought?" Laslos said.

"It's all I have, sir," she said, smiling. "And all I need."

"Venturing out into the new world with hardly a thing to your name."

"God is able," she said. "Marcel tells me you have a gun."

"Marcel has the mouth of a young man," Laslos said. "You must both learn to say little and listen much."

"I'm sorry," she said. "Am I talking too much? Just excited, that's all. I haven't felt this way since the day Mr. Williams let me go."

Marcel nodded.

"So I can't see your gun, Mr. Laslos?"

"Miklos. I do not bring my gun out of my home. I am not looking to hurt anyone. It is for my safety, that's all."

"But K has a gun," she said, squeezing his shoulders again. "Don't you, young man?"

K smiled shyly and shook his head as he pulled the car back onto the road.

"You watch too much television," Laslos said. "American TV, am I right?"

"Not for a long time. When I do see it, it's all Carpathia, Carpathia, Carpathia."

Laslos's leg was still bouncing, his hands still pressed together. "You're both clear on the plan, then?" he said.

"If Marcel is, I am," Georgiana said. "He's the one who told me. We're meeting this George guy off the road up from the airport. He'll take us in like we're his prisoners, and the computer will show that's what he's there for."

"Yes, and you must avoid eye contact, look sullen, and just go directly to the plane with him. Maybe you could let Marcel wear your hat low enough to cover his eyes and you could let your hair hang in your face."

She was still rubbing her hands together. "This thing wouldn't fit him. Anyway, we'll recognize the pilot how again?"

"He should be the only man on the road looking for you," Laslos said.

"But he's a big man, right? An American?"

"Way over six feet tall and almost two hundred and fifty pounds," Marcel said. "Light hair, blue eyes, and—"

"You'll know him," Laslos said. "We should pray."

"Yes," Georgiana said. "Please."

"Why don't you pray?" Laslos said.

"I'm too nervous," she said.

"All right," Laslos said. "Lord, we thank you for these young people and ask you to go before them and protect them. We—"

"There he is!" Georgiana said. "Is that him?"

A big, young man strode purposefully up the right side of the road. He wore big boots, khaki pants, and a light, zippered jacket. His hair looked almost white, his face dark. Laslos couldn't make out the eye color, but the man stopped and looked directly into the car as K slowed and passed, pulling over fifty yards beyond him.

Marcel reached for his door handle, and Georgiana reached for her bag.

"Wait!" Laslos said. "He's early." He rolled down his window and leaned to stick his head out, aware that Georgiana was digging in her bag and ready to go.

"Mr. Miklos?" the man called out, but Laslos thought he detected a European accent.

"Hey, Mr. Sebastian!" Marcel shouted before Laslos could shush him.

Now jogging and having cut the distance between him and the car, the man hollered, "Marcel? Georgiana?"

"Keep rolling, K," Laslos said. "This isn't right."

"Why?" Georgiana said. "What's wrong?"

"If that's Sebastian," Laslos said as K slowly pulled back onto the road, "he'll find us."

"No!" Georgiana whined. "Stop!"

"We'll not make this transfer in the middle of the road," Laslos said.

"K, pull over," Georgiana said with sudden authority. She pulled a huge handgun with a silencer from her bag and pressed it against Laslos's temple. "I'll kill him if you don't stop."

"Don't stop, K!" Laslos cried. "Marcel is for real! I know him!"

K stopped accelerating but coasted. "Stop now," she said. "I mean it."

Marcel whipped around, kneeling on the seat to face her. He yanked her cap off, and as the silencer pulled away from Laslos's head, he turned to see Georgiana's forehead and the mark of the beast. The whistling, abbreviated punch of the shot filled the car with the acrid smell of gunpowder, and Marcel was driven back with such force that he folded under the dashboard. The windshield was covered with gore, and Laslos grimaced at the gaping hole in the back of the boy's head.

"Stop now, K!" she wailed, pointing the gun at the back of his head. The older man wrenched the wheel back and forth, pushing the accelerator to the floor. The little car rocked violently, and Laslos felt himself bang into his door handle before his bulk went flying back over Marcel's bag toward the girl.

She fired through K's neck and he went limp, the car losing speed and angling toward the gravel. Laslos wrapped his massive arms around the girl and pressed the bottoms of his feet against the door on his side, trying to smash her against her own door. He could only hope the gun was buried somewhere in the crush, but the sounds of more than one set of running footsteps told him that unless he wrestled it away from her, he would soon join his wife in heaven.

The car thudded to a stop, and they both rolled forward into the back of K's seat. Two other men had joined the Sebastian impostor, and all carried weapons. One jerked the girl's door open and dragged her out with one hand. Laslos tried to hang on, but he had no leverage. He lay on Marcel's bag across the backseat, his arms leaden, gasping.

"You all right, Elena?" one of the men said.

Laslos saw her nod with disgust. "He's the only one left," she said, pressing the gun to his forehead. He turned his hands over, opening his palms toward heaven, and closed his eyes.

\+ + +

"We're short-staffed tonight, sir. Hard copy is quicker than the computer, if you don't mind."

"I hear you," George said. "But I told you, Old Man Elbaz had me on recon runs over rebel territory in the Negev, and we were all required to leave our IDs at the field HQ. It's all in the computer."

The airport GC clerk swore. "They never think about what those decisions mean to us little guys."

"They never think at all," George said. "Sorry."

"What're ya gonna do?" the clerk said, sighing as he tapped his fingers atop the monitor, waiting for the info. "Hey, what about all the guys goin' AWOL in Jordan?"

"Don't think I wasn't tempted," George said. "Strangest deal I've ever seen."

"You get the boils?"

"Who didn't?"

"Here it is. You're good. You got a number for me? Six digits."

"Zero-four-zero-three-zero-one."

"That's it. And where're your prisoners?"

"Being held up the road."

"Need a vehicle?"

"That would be great."

"You're coming right back?"

"Right back. I'll secure 'em in the plane and bring the wheels directly to you."

The clerk tossed him a set of keys and pointed to a Jeep. George decided he could get used to Trib Force work, if it was all this easy. Couldn't be.

He sped a mile and a half up the road and pulled over. What was that in the distance? The girl? Alone? He turned on his brights. She was running toward him. Screaming.

He stepped out. "Georgiana?"

"George?"

"Yes!"

"We were ambushed!"

As she got closer he saw she was covered in blood. He reached for her. "What happened? Where are the oth—"

But as the girl slumped against him, wrapping her arms around his waist, she called out, "Unarmed!" Two men, one about his size, rushed from the bushes with weapons trained on him. Another pulled a Jeep into view, doors standing open.

The big man jumped into the car George had borrowed at the airport. The other kept a weapon on him as the girl handcuffed and blindfolded him. He was tempted to drive his bulk into her, make her pay for whatever she was involved in. But he wanted to conserve his strength for any real chance to escape. They pushed him into the Jeep, and as it took off, he heard the other vehicle behind.

"We're going to have fun with you, Yank," the driver said. "By the time we're through, we'll know everything you know."

Fat chance, George thought—and wanted to say. But he had already blundered enough, leaving his plane and his weapons unprotected and venturing unarmed into enemy territory, trusting a risky plan devised by well-intentioned brothers, but civilians after all. Maybe the proverbial horse had already escaped the open barn, but too late or not, his training kicked in. Not only would he not say, "Fat chance," but he would also not say anything. The only way these people would know he was capable of uttering a word was if they remembered he had spoken to the girl. Unless he somehow escaped, his next word would be spoken in heaven.

He bounced and lost his balance as the Jeep accelerated, and he kept bouncing off the door, then almost into the lap of the captor to his left. The man kept pushing George back upright. He could have planted his feet more firmly and kept from jostling so much, but he didn't mind being a two-hundred-forty-pound irritant to the enemy.

"So, George Sebastian of San Diego," the driver said, "and a newly recruited Judah-ite. A little information will buy you some dinner, and a lot will have you on your way back to the wife and little one before you know it. Hungry?"

George did not respond, not even with a nod or shake of the head.

"Lonely then, perhaps?"

The man next to George, less fluent in English, said, "Do you know who is really Elbaz? Because we think we do."

"We *do*!" the girl said.

George let the next curve throw him into the man, who pushed him back. "Sit up, you big stupid person!"

19

SOUND ASLEEP OVER the Atlantic and never so happy to be heading home, Rayford at first thought the incoming call was a dream. Then he wished it were.

The caller ID showed it originating in Colorado. Before Rayford could speak, a weird, nasal voice said, "I believe I followed your instructions on how to call you securely, but could you confirm that before I proceed?"

Rayford sat straight up. "Stand by," he said, believing he knew whom he was talking to. He checked the tiny LCD readout as David Hassid had instructed him. "You're secure," he said.

"You've got trouble," the voice said. "Do you have anybody inside at New Babylon to replace your guy that died?"

Rayford hesitated.

"Hey, it's me."

"Who?"

"Ah, you may know me as Pinkerton Stephens. GC stationed in Colorado."

"I need to be dead sure, Mr. Stephens."

"Aka Steve Plank."

"A little more, please."

"Your grandson's name is Kenny Bruce."

"How did you know our guy died?"

"Everybody knows, man. Didn't he go down with three others right in front of Carpathia?"

"Not really, Steve."

"Not bad, Captain. But anyway, New Babylon thinks he's dead, so he's clearly not inside."

"We're covered inside."

"Good. Then maybe you know this."

"What?"

"About your trouble. Where are you?"

Rayford told him.

"And you have not been brought up to speed by the palace?"

"I thought I had."

"You've been compromised."

"Me personally?" Rayford said.

"Actually, no. Depending on what alias you're using, I think you're okay. But I just got a high-level, for-your-eyes-only briefing from Intelligence, and for the first time I thought I'd better take you up on your request to be informed."

"I'm listening."

"The alias your friend, the one I met, is using has been exposed. I and S is speculating that Deputy Commander Marcus Elbaz is actually a former black marketer out of Al Basrah."

"How?"

"This is mostly coming out of Greece, Rayford."

"Oh no. Tell me we weren't wrong about the guy we sent in there."

"Sebastian? No, he's solid. But they've got him."

"Oh no. Start from the top."

"First, you've got your Elbaz character flying your plane right now, right? And the craft is ostensibly a GC issue."

"Right."

"His name and that bird are on everybody's screens, so don't—"

"Got it. Don't land as GC or as Elbaz."

"You're scheduled into Kankakee, right?"

"You got it. What happened in Greece, Steve?"

"Stay with me. First, I think I've found a way to get you close to where you want to go. Back to Chicago, correct?"

"Affirmative."

"Okay, listen up. I put in a request for cargo out of Maryland with a stop at the auxiliary field near where Midway used to be. That's as close to Chicago as they'll let anybody land, due to the radiation, you know."

"Right."

"You know as well as I do that you could put down at Meigs."

"On the lake?"

"Sure."

"We're not going to draw any suspicion from heat-seeking stratospheric GC recon planes?"

"Not if your guy keeps the phony radiation levels up to speed on the database."

"This is a pretty big jet to land at Meigs, the way I remember it."

"You've got reverse thrusters, don't you?"

"Of course."

"It can be done. But there's nobody on the ground there, of course. But listen, Ray, if your guy is still keeping track of Chicago and what the GC thinks about it, he'd better get in there and tinker."

"What're you saying?"

"I doubt anybody else has checked lately, but just to be sure I wasn't leading you into a trap, I looked up that area, and something was giving off moving heat signals down there within the last several hours."

"We always tell him before we go out, walking, driving, or with the chopper. That way he can head off any readings we emit."

"Well, somebody's on the move down there. Not much, but it'll arouse suspicion like it did with me."

"So back to Greece, Steve. We know Buck's Jack Jensen ID is history."

"That's not the worst of it. He cut loose a couple of kids from a detention center and one of 'em—the girl, Stavros—got herself caught. You can't blame her; she's just a teenager, but apparently she cracked and gave up a lot. Story she told matched up with what they figure happened with the boy, who had used the name Paulo Ganter. 'Course Ganter was still in there, so they figured out by process of elimination who got sprung. Kid named Papadopoulos. His parents both refused to take the mark. GC in Greece plants a young woman with similar looks to this Stavros in the underground. She starts askin' around about the boy, somebody gets 'em connected, and she tells him her story—which is just like his. Bada-bing, she had to be freed by the same guy, nobody checks her out, she stays away from people who would know she wasn't who she claimed to be, and—"

"—she walks our people into an ambush."

"Yeah, and it's bad, Rayford."

"Just tell me."

"GC says the ruse went squirrelly at the end and their operatives wind up having to kill an old man named Kronos, a big fish—name of Miklos—and the boy."

Rayford sat in the screaming jet with the phone to his ear, head in his hand, eyes shut. "And Sebastian?"

"Alive and well, but they're confident they can get what they need from him to lead them to Ben-Judah. He's former military, so he might be tougher than they think."

"Plus he doesn't know that much."

"He was supposed to bring the kids to you, though, right? He's got to know enough to hurt you."

"He does. Any idea about the disposition of the real Stavros?"

"I think that goes without saying, now that they have a connection to you guys. She's served her purpose."

"We don't have to assume the worst."

"Oh, sure we do, Rayford. Of course we do. I always do."

Plank asked if Rayford had anybody on board whose face was not known to the GC. "Well, I've got three people aboard who are thought dead."

"Can any of 'em look like a Middle Easterner?"

"One's a Jordanian."

"Perfect. Does he have a turban?"

Rayford leaned over and woke Abdullah. "Do you have a turban, or can you make yourself one?" Abdullah gave him a thumbs-up and went back to sleep. "That's affirmative, Steve."

"Can you put him on the radio and pretend he's your pilot?"

"He flies."

"Perfect. Here's his new name and a refueling docket number for Maryland. Your next stop after that should be Resurrection Field here, south of Colorado Springs. I won't expect you."

"No, but you'll log us in as if we made it."

"Of course."

"Words aren't adequate, Steve. . . ."

"Hey, one of these days I'm gonna need a place to hole up . . . if I survive that long."

With Buck, Hannah, Leah, and Mac also asleep, Rayford chose to tell only Albie what was going on. There would be plenty of time for Abdullah and Albie to switch seats. Rayford called Chang.

* * *

Twelve hours later Chang sat at his terminal in the office, grateful he'd been able to sleep after a flurry of emergency activity in the night. He wondered how David had managed this on his own and prayed that God would either deliver him or send someone to help him. Chang was unaware of any other believers in New Babylon, but still he held out hope. While he sat monitoring the overwhelming reports of death and ruin on the bloody high seas, he was recording the meeting of the ten regional potentates with Carpathia, Akbar, Fortunato, and Viv Ivins.

The workday was interminable, but Chang walked a fine line. He had to appear above reproach while maintaining a typically irreverent attitude. David had warned him that if he appeared too good to be true, someone would assume he was. And new as he was in assisting the Tribulation Force, he feared he would be unable to keep pace emotionally. Losing David had rocked him. He couldn't imagine how the others dealt with the loss of Miss Durham, then their main contact in Greece. Things were supposed to get worse and worse. Fear and loneliness didn't begin to describe his feelings. He prayed that until he was rescued from this assignment, God would somehow allow him to stay rested, stay strong, and be able to carry on despite the danger and tragedy.

\+ + +

In Petra Chaim felt as if he were already in heaven. How was it that God could make it so that a million believers could live together in harmony? Chaim reminded the people that Tsion Ben-Judah had promised to come and address them in person, and they lifted such a roar that he himself could barely wait for that day.

"You know, do you not," he said, unamplified yet miraculously able to be heard by all under his charge, "that the Word of God tells us we will live here unmolested, our clothes not wearing out, and we will be fed and quenched until the wrath of God against his enemies is complete. John the Revelator said he saw 'something like a sea of glass mingled with fire, and those who have the victory over the beast, over his image and over his mark and over the number of his name, standing on the sea of glass, having harps of God.' Beloved, those John would have seen in his revelation of heaven and who had victory over the beast are those who had been martyred by the beast. Death is considered victory because of the resurrection of the saints!

"Sing with me the song of Moses, the servant of God, and the song of the Lamb, saying: 'Great and marvelous are your works, Lord God Almighty! Just and true are your ways, O King of the saints! Who shall not fear you, O Lord, and glorify your name? For you alone are holy. For all nations shall come and worship before you, for your judgments have been manifested.'

"John said he heard the angel of the waters saying, 'You are righteous, O Lord, the One who is and who was and who is to be, because you have judged these things.'

"And what," Chaim continued, "of our enemies who have shed the blood of saints and prophets? God has turned the oceans into blood, and one day soon he will turn the rivers and lakes to blood as well, giving them blood to drink. For it is their just due.

"But what shall we his people eat and drink, here in this place of refuge? Some would look upon it and say it is desolate and barren. Yet God says that at twilight we shall eat meat, and in the morning we shall be filled with bread. In this way we shall know that he is the Lord our God."

That evening a great flock of quails invaded and a million saints enjoyed roasting them over open fires. In the morning, when the dew lifted, there on the rocky ground were small, round flakes as fine as frost. "We need not ask ourselves, as the children of Israel did, 'What is it?'" Chaim said. "For we know God has provided it as bread. Take, eat, and see that it is filling and sweet, like wafers made with honey. As Moses said to them, 'This is the bread the Lord has given you to eat.'

"And what shall we drink? Again, God Almighty himself has provided." Chaim raised both arms, and springs of fresh, cool water flowed from rocks in every quarter of Petra, enough for everyone.

+ + +

The refueling had gone without incident in Maryland, but Rayford wondered when their supply of impostors would run dry. A couple of hours later, Rayford took the controls for the landing at the tiny airstrip by Lake Michigan near what was left of downtown Chicago. His passengers were rested but stunned by the news related in his call from Steve Plank.

The news had also proved devastating at the safe house. Chang reported from New Babylon that he had been able to cover in the computer for the motion and heat activity of Chloe's movements that might otherwise have raised a red flag, and Tsion told Rayford by phone that Chloe was sick about having been responsible. "But she has exciting news," Dr. Ben-Judah said. "She is insisting on being the one to pick you up. And yes, we have the young Mr. Wong covering for your landing and your transport here."

The landing was a test of Rayford's skills, and as he touched down as close to the water as possible, he wondered if he would have been smart to let Mac handle it. But the thrust reversers and carbon brakes left him with room to spare, and he maneuvered the jet between two abandoned buildings, where it could be recognized from the stratosphere only from an angle available just a few seconds a day.

The others allowed Buck out first to greet Chloe. She drove a Humvee from beneath the Strong Building and had brought Ming to hold Kenny. Rayford stretched and watched the reunion as the other five clambered out and unloaded luggage. Finally safe again in the building, introductions were made all around before they knelt and prayed and wept over lost and endangered loved ones. Rayford showed them the urn of Hattie's ashes, and Hannah passed around David's phone.

"'Course we ain't leavin' this George guy by himself in Greece, right?"

"Exactly, Zeke," Mac said. "But we've got a lot of planning to do in a short time, and you're gonna be as busy as any of us."

"I know some people I'll bet would want to help," Chloe said.

* * *

Chang's day had been filled with coworkers' rumors and gossip. Two Indian stewards from Carpathia's plane were to be put to death for leaking secrets to a mole in New Babylon. Everyone was under suspicion and tested. The general invitation for all employees to visit the spectacular new office of the supreme potentate had been suspended with his earlier-than-expected return from Israel. But those who saw it gushed about the ceiling that rose to the now transparent roof, so it was as if the office itself looked into heaven. It had been widened, the walls of adjoining offices and conference rooms demolished to make one gargantuan space in which the king of the world could relax or conduct business or hold meetings. Which he had done all day with the potentates of the ten world regions.

Chang hurried to his apartment to hear the recording of that meeting, but first he checked copies of what the assembled computer whizzes had sent around the world from their secure system in Petra. What a thrill to see Chaim's pronouncements and accounts of the miracles retold and broadcast to the globe. Reports had come back immediately of people on every continent printing these out or passing them on electronically. Secret house churches were encouraged, and many people were becoming new believers. People undecided and disillusioned with Carpathia sought out the believers, and international revival was happening right before Chang's eyes.

And it was none too soon, considering Carpathia's high-level meeting. He had quickly quelled the cooing over his new digs and gotten down to business. "The world has changed, gentlemen," he said, "as much in the last several days as in the last three and a half years. Please, no hands. I know all your problems and want to talk about mine today. Without some miraculous intervention, the oceanic catastrophe will not soon be remedied. We must be creative in our approaches to it. But have you noticed something, my friends? Is it as obvious to you as it is to me? We have the Jews to thank for our current predicament.

"Yes, the Jews. Who have been among the last to embrace Carpathianism? The Jews. Who is their new Moses? A man who calls himself Micah but whom we believe to be none other than the Jew who vainly assassinated me, Dr. Chaim Rosenzweig.

"Who are the Judah-ites? They claim to be Jesus-followers, but they follow Ben-Judah, a Jew. Jesus himself was a Jew. They are fond of referring to me as Antichrist. Well, I will embrace Anti-Jew. And so will you. This is war, gentlemen, and I want it waged in all ten regions of the world.

"For my part, we are planning to stagger and ultimately eradicate the so-called Jesus-believers who are nothing but Judah cultists. Tsion Ben-Judah himself, who claims a billion adherents, has publicly announced what will prove to be his fatal blunder. He has accepted an invitation from the brash Micah you-know-who—whom we have to thank for the plague of sores and the seas of blood—to personally speak at Petra to the million cowards who refused to express loyalty to me and yet ran like children when they had the chance."

"Excellency," someone said, "could you not have stopped them before they reached Petra?"

"Please do not interrupt! Of course we could have easily overrun them, but they have made it much easier and more economical for us. They are now all in one location, and as soon as Ben-Judah makes good on his promise, we will welcome him with a surprise. Or two. Or three. Security and Intelligence Director Suhail Akbar . . ."

"Thank you, Your Worship," Akbar said. "We are carefully monitoring the activities of the Judah-ites, and while we have not infiltrated the Jews at Petra, they have confined themselves to that area, saving us the work. We are prepared to rally two fighter-bombers when we know Ben-Judah is en route—we believe him to be only one or two hours from Petra anyway—and we should be able to drop one annihilation device from each craft directly onto Petra, literally within minutes of his arrival. We will follow with the launch of a missile that will ensure total destruction. That was scheduled to be launched from an oceangoing vessel but will now be launched from land."

Chang had to chuckle at the Intelligence area's falling for the clock ruse from Tsion's pirated TV appearance.

Carpathia took over again. "The Judah-ites have proven to be such hero worshipers and so dependent on the daily Internet babblings of Ben-Judah that his death alone may mean the end of that nuisance. While we are aware of other pockets and strongholds of Judah-iteism, we do not believe any other leader has the charisma or leadership required to withstand our unlimited resources.

"But make no mistake, my loyal friends. The Jew is everywhere. Is there one potentate here who would aver that you do not have a significant Jewish population somewhere in your region? No one, of course. Here is the good news, something to make you forget the inconvenience of this journey I required on short notice. I am opening the treasury for this project, and no reasonable request will be denied. This is a war I will win at all costs.

"Maintain your loyalty mark application sites and make use of the enforcement facilitators. But, effective immediately, do not execute Jews discovered without the mark. I want them imprisoned and suffering. Use existing facilities now but build new centers as soon as possible. They need not be fancy or have any amenities. Just make them secure. Be creative, and share with each other your ideas. Ideally, these people should either long to change their minds or long to die. Do not allow that luxury.

"They will find few remaining Judah-ites to sympathize with them. They will be alone and as lonely as they have ever been, even though their cell mates will be fellow Jews. There are no limits on the degradation I am asking, requiring, you to inflict. No clothes, no heat, no cooling, no medicine. Just enough food to keep them alive for another day of suffering.

"I want reports, gentlemen. Pictures, accounts, descriptions, recordings. These people will wish they had opted for the guillotine. We will televise your best, most inventive ideas. From time immemorial these dogs have claimed the title 'God's chosen people.' Well, they have met their god now. I have chosen them, all right. And they will not find even death a place they can hide.

"Apply for all the funds, equipment, rolling stock, and weapons you need to ferret out these weasels. The potentate who demonstrates the ability to keep them alive the longest, despite their torment, will be awarded a double portion in next year's budget.

"Questions?"

20

GEORGE SEBASTIAN HAD planned to wait to eat until he had his charges on board and was free in the air again, leaving Greece. Now, of course, hunger was the least of his problems, but weakness wouldn't help either. The Greeks, particularly the thugs who had ambushed him and—he assumed—the people with whom he had been expected to connect, hoarded their water supply. The news from the high seas had everyone rushing to lakes and rivers to stock up on freshwater fish. Water would soon be more valuable than gold.

His captors were well connected, he could tell that. After they drove more than forty minutes north, then about twenty east, if he still had his bearings, they plowed through softer soil, and he heard leaves and branches brush heavily against the Jeep. It sounded as if the vehicle he had appropriated was still behind them.

George was grateful for his training, which had included blindfolding and mock torture. He had been astounded at how helpless he felt, even when he knew his own people were in charge. To be bound and blind, even knowing you weren't going to die, was a dreadful, sickening, fearful thing. He had been allowed to get hungry and thirsty, and the most harrowing part was being left alone long enough for his mind to play tricks on him. Back then he knew he was still in California, not far from San Diego, not far from home. But his timekeeping techniques, his mind games to keep himself calm and sane, quickly dissipated with the passing of the minutes, and the young, strong, healthy recruit began imagining it had been hours.

He wanted to take what he had learned from that trauma and use it in this one, but he hated to even recall it. Having no resources had been the worst. George had been considered one of the most creative and innovative soldiers in his platoon. When they were dropped into the middle of the woods thirty miles from base, wearing only shorts and boots, he was always the first one back. He could improvise, find his way based on shadows, foliage, intuition. He knew how to protect himself from the sun, to keep from walking in circles—somehow a common malady for people who had lost any sense of direction.

But being left in a dark room without so much as the sound of one other person breathing, no muffled sounds outside of officers or fellow recruits gossiping about how long he'd been there, that had been true torture. Though he had quickly freed himself from the bindings, he could not free his hands from each other. But he was able to stand and walk, getting a measure of the room, helping time pass by remembering songs and poems and birth dates and special occasions.

But when he ran out of all that and began losing count after two hours, he had been tempted to call out, to tell his fellow GIs that he had had enough, that he got the point, that it was time to return him to normal. But who did that, other than the weaklings, the washouts? He had to face that he too wanted to cry, to scream, to beg and plead, to kick at the wall, to ask if they hadn't forgotten him. He had succumbed to the temptation at long last to make noise so at least if he *had* been forgotten, they would be reminded and could save face by pretending it was all part of the drill.

He remembered what it was like to be hungry and thirsty and desperate, but there had always been that fail-safe. Deep in the recesses of his fast-unraveling mind had been the knowledge that this *was* training, this *wasn't* real, there was no real threat to his life and health and mind. No one was going to inflict permanent injury, no one would threaten his new bride, nothing would happen to his parents.

His superiors had trained the men in basic transcendental meditation, which most of them passed off as something for weirdos, druggies, and holy men from the East. Yet George had seen some benefit to thinking beyond his consciousness, or at least trying to. Even back then, even before becoming a believer in Christ, he didn't want anything to do with any religious aspects of meditation. But he did long to transcend this life, to reach a point beyond himself, to be able to park his senses and emotions on a plane where they would be safe from the threat of mere mortals.

It hadn't worked long then, and that was what he feared now. This was the real thing. While he regulated his breathing and told himself not to think about his hunger and thirst, they were things he could not blot from his mind. The more he tried, the worse they invaded.

He was nudged along in the night—no light whatever peeked through his blindfold—by the butt of a rifle, and as much as he tried to catalog all the information he could remember since the girl had clumsily frisked him and he had been jumped, his overriding emotion was shame.

No, he had not been the one who got the teenagers caught—along with anyone helping them. But while the assignment excited him, he had not treated it like a military operation. Back in the Negev, that was war, pure and simple—except when they had been surrounded by superior firepower and it went from armed conflict to no fair. It had done his soul good to see what happened to anyone who thumbed his nose at God. *Our general is better than your general,* he thought, *so game over.*

That almost made him smile. Why should he worry about the people who held him now when Michael the archangel could step in and make them faint dead away—if they were lucky?

He was held up briefly, then heard two doors open. He was nudged inside and sensed a light come on. A few more steps, another door, a musty smell, a shove from behind, steps leading down, but how many? He started carefully, feeling with his foot, but he was bumped again, rushed his feet hoping he would come to the bottom before he lost balance, and failed.

George didn't know how far he might tumble down these wood stairs. The best he could do was tuck his chin to his chest, clamp his eyes shut as tightly as possible, and draw his knees up to his chest. He counted two, three, four stairs, then hard-packed dirt. His momentum carried him a couple of rolls, and the whole way down, he expected to hit a wall or who-knows-what with some part of his body.

When he finally came to rest on his right side, he could hear from their footsteps that his feet faced his captors. He kept his knees drawn up and feigned more pain than he had. He groaned slightly and did not move. He waited until steps drew close to him, then thrust out both feet with all that was in him.

No one on his base could do squats with more weight, and no one could touch him in leg presses. Had he been able to see the man before him, he could have broken both his legs. But his thrust had found purchase on only one of the man's legs. The man cried out, something giving way in the knee, it seemed to George. The man went flying and rolled, his weapon clattering.

"Idiot!" the other man said, and George heard the girl stifle a laugh.

"I'll kill him!" the one on the floor said, grunting and whimpering in pain as he struggled to his feet and cocked his weapon.

"Stop it!" the other said. "He's our only link."

"Well, she didn't have to drop all three of them."

"What's done is done. He's it, so don't do anything stupid again."

"Again?"

"You don't think that was stupid? What are you doing over there?"

A muzzle at his neck. "Keep still there, big boy. Up we go." A hand on the cuffs, pulling until he had to get up or injure his arms. He was led to a chair and pushed back onto it. He had the impression only two of the men and the girl were downstairs with him. Footsteps upstairs. He tried to slow his breathing so he could hear. The one upstairs was talking, but no one was responding. He was on the phone, talking about the car—probably to the clerk who had lent it. Then he said something about the plane. George decided it would serve him right if they shot him right there. He had treated this assignment like a game and now had exposed the entire Tribulation Force. And, if these men had any credibility, the others in Greece had been killed.

Cigarette smoke. Blown in his face. *Please,* he thought. These people had seen too many movies. Maybe cataloging their gaffes would help. Someone squatted next to him, he assumed the second one down the stairs. The other would be wary for a while.

"We can make this hard or make this easy," the man whispered, and George couldn't help himself. He pressed his lips together hard, but he couldn't keep from giggling. He wanted to ask if they were going to try good-cop, bad-cop too, but he had resolved to say nothing.

"We know who you are, Mr. Sebastian," and George lost it. He laughed aloud, knowing what the next line had to be. "We know who you work for."

Trying to keep from laughing only made it worse, and he sat there, shoulders heaving, squealing to keep from guffawing. He took a backhand directly on the mouth, splitting his upper lip against his teeth.

George was almost relieved when that sobered him. He wiped his mouth on his shoulder, tasted blood, and spat. At least he wouldn't get himself killed for being unable to stop laughing. When the man said he would cut to the chase, trying to make it sound normal with his thick accent, George almost laughed again. But his stinging lips were swelling, and he had a hunch that would be the least of his pain by the time this was over.

"All we need to know is where we can find your people. Your information proves correct; you are free to go." As if they wouldn't kill him for not having the mark of loyalty. "We have them narrowed to the United Carpathian States."

George cocked his head ever so slightly. That had surprised him, and he didn't mind it showing, because he knew they would think he was shocked that they knew. It was no secret Tsion Ben-Judah would soon be on his way to Petra, so why did they care about anyone else?

"You might be more surprised by how much we know. Rosenzweig is no threat as long as he stays in the mountains. His assistant we know to be Cameron Williams, who illegally transmits over the Internet material subversive to the Global Community, a crime punishable by death. We know there is a mole connected to the Judah-ites somewhere within the GC. And the pilot who has disguised himself as a GC officer has pushed his luck too far. He has been linked with another Williams identity, who also passed himself off as GC and temporarily freed two rebel prisoners. We have reason to believe a former guard at the Buffer, now AWOL, may be connected with these people."

George wondered if they had made the connection between Ming Toy and Chang Wong. Maybe the fact that she had been married and now had a different last name would delay that realization. It would be only a matter of time, of course. Chang had to get out of New Babylon.

George's captor sounded as if he believed George was surprised by how much they knew. In fact, the opposite was true. Apparently they had never connected the crash of the Quasi Two with the Trib Force, and no one even knew it had been empty.

More smoke in his face. "So, you just tell us where to look, and when you are proved trustworthy, you go home to your family."

Most ironic of all, George would not have been able to give away the Trib Force if he'd wanted to. For his own safety, Rayford had told him only to fly Marcel and Georgiana to a Kankakee, Illinois, airstrip and that he would meet George there. Whether George accompanied them to the safe house, wherever it was, or flew on home to San Diego, would have depended on timing, weather, and any suspicion that might have arisen over whether the GC were onto him.

The man near him tried the next strategy in the hostage-taker's guidebook. He laid a hand gently on George's shoulder and whispered, "All we need is a specific location. No one knows where we got it, you go free, and everybody's happy."

The man had been so full of clichés that George was tempted to answer with one of his own: a bloody spit to the face. But if there was one thing he knew well, it was that apathy was more offensive than resistance. As long as he resisted, his captors knew they were getting to him. When he ignored them, they had nothing to grab on to, and the insult of not being taken seriously had to drive them crazy.

Ironically, George had learned that from his wife. He didn't mind when she argued with him. But when she gave up and said she didn't care, *that* got to him. Disengaging, he knew, was a cruel strategy. And he employed it now with a vengeance. He didn't shake his head. He didn't try to kick. Since he had shown a modicum of surprise over the man's asserting that he knew the Trib Force was in the local region, George had barely moved a muscle. The man had to wonder if he was even listening. In fact, he wasn't.

To keep from even the temptation of responding nonverbally, George began reciting silently the books of the Bible. Then his favorite verses. Then his favorite songs.

The Greek nudged him with his weapon, and George didn't want him to think he had dozed off. He raised his chin.

"Well, what will it be, Sebastian? You're refusing? At least say so. No? Tell me you've chosen not to say anything. You just want to give me rank and serial number? We already know your name. Come on. Not even that?"

+ + +

Chang monitored all the various feeds and sites as he continued to listen to the Carpathia meeting recording. Most alarming was a list directed to Suhail Akbar that informed him of all the AWOL GC employees his department was aware of. Chang found his sister's name and deleted it, but he knew he might have been too late. How many knew that she was his sister? Perhaps not even Akbar. Moon had known. And Carpathia himself had known. Chang could only hope that such detail stayed below the potentate's radar level. Who knew what could come of it? Yes, he appeared to be loyal, even to the point of the mark. But if investigated, how long could he keep his parents and his sister out of it? Now wasn't the time, but one day soon he would have to raise the issue with Rayford Steele. He believed he could monitor the palace and GC headquarters from the safe house.

In the Carpathia meeting, someone responded to Nicolae's new emphasis on the Jewish question with a question of his own. "Does this mean you no longer want videodisc records of our beheadings?"

"Oh, no! That remains a more than enjoyable pastime. As you know, I no longer require sustenance or rest. I am able to take advantage of unlimited time while others eat and sleep. One of the benefits of godhood is the time to revel in the folly of my opponents. Sometimes I sit for hours in the night, watching head after head drop into the baskets. These people are so smug, so stubborn, so pious. They sing. They *testify.* Do you not just *love* that word? They testify to their god and against me. Ooh, that makes me feel so bad, so jealous. But then what happens? From fifteen feet above, that heavy, gleaming, razor-sharp blade is released. It takes one-seventieth of a second to reach the bottom of the shaft—did you know that? And the last two-hundredths of one second is all it takes to slice through the neck as if it were not there.

"I love it! The only problem, dear friends, is that if anything, the guillotine is too humane! For certain it is far too quick and deadly for the Jew. How far can you go in inflicting pain upon a man or woman before he or she dies? I want to know! I want you to report it to me with all the visual and audio evidence you can. And you know whom I want you to use as test subjects.

"For a special treat today, during our break we will witness the execution of the two insurgents we discovered serving on my own plane. We still search for the mole here at headquarters, but perhaps he or she will also see the beheadings today and will be flushed from hiding to plead for his or her life."

"The guillotine then, for these two?" someone asked.

"I know," Nicolae said. "Pedestrian. But we do not have a lot of time, and it will be a nice respite from the meeting."

Many of the others expressed agreement and excitement. Chang was sickened. He was tempted to download some of this bile for his mother, but it was too risky with his father still being such a Carpathia loyalist. He held out a modicum of hope for them both, having not heard whether his father had followed through yet on their taking the mark in their own region. Until he was able to convince his mother and get to his father with hard evidence, he was persuaded that his father would turn him in in a heartbeat if he thought Chang was subversive.

* * *

Rayford called a meeting of the three remaining original members of the Trib Force, plus Tsion, in Tsion's study. "I hope we're talking about who's going to Petra with Dr. Ben-Judah," Chloe said.

"We are," Rayford said, "among other things." Tsion looked deep in thought as they settled in. "You all right, Doctor?"

"Troubled, I confess," the rabbi said. "I should not be surprised, but it seems we have come to a crossroads. I know we will lose more and more as we head toward the end, but it seems as if our tenuous bit of safety is unraveling fast."

"It is," Rayford said. "We know George can't give us up beyond pointing them in the direction of Illinois, but I don't think he'll do even that."

"Neither do I," Buck said. "They're not going to get a thing out of him."

"Except perhaps his life," Tsion said, sighing.

"What are we going to do about our new friends?" Chloe said.

"That's one of the reasons we're here," Rayford said. "It seems to me, as exciting and encouraging as it is to discover these wonderful new brothers and sisters, your escapade was reckless and could have cost us everything."

Chloe shot him a double take and looked as if she'd rather argue with him as her father than have to respond to him as head of the Trib Force. "All due respect, but I didn't know what stratospheric detection could tell the GC. Shouldn't we all be told that kind of stuff?"

"How were we to know you would venture out on your own?"

"Last time, I discovered the new safe house. And look what has come of this foray."

"You're lucky what came of it," Rayford said. "What if they had been GC or just lowlifes? We'd have lost you, probably the safe house, and thus our whole reason for being."

"I'm sorry, but now we have people we can help and who can help us."

"Did you think about sensitivities, Chloe, such as maybe they don't want to move to our building, even though it would provide infinitely more safety and advantages? Maybe they don't want to become part of the Tribulation Force. They have been self-governing and self-sufficient up to now. Maybe they don't want to be used for dangerous missions, using aliases and all that."

"They *do* want to move here," Chloe said. "They *do* want to help with travel and assignments. But you're right. They want to maintain their own organization. They're comfortable with each other, and while they would like to have Dr. Ben-Judah's involvement, Enoch is their pastor and they want it to remain that way."

"So," Rayford said, "all the benefits of the Trib Force, but none of the responsibilities."

"Oh, they'll pay," Chloe said. "They'll work. They'll travel. They'll exchange all kinds of things for food and necessities, just like any other co-op members. It's not like they should owe us rent on a building we don't own."

"They've made a point about not answering to us?"

"No, I'm making that point. Is it a requirement that they be subordinate to you?"

"That's not it at all, Chloe. We just don't have time for squabbles, lack of organization, confusion about responsibility."

Tsion held up a hand. "These are wonderful brothers and sisters, Captain Steele. I believe they will be a vibrant addition to the building and that we should take it a step at a time. See how it works while you and I are gone. I would not recommend using anyone new on this trip."

Chloe shook her head. "It's already been decided that it's you and Tsion?"

"No—"

"What's the point of a meeting about it if—"

"I said no, Chloe. Yes, Tsion and I are going. But others will go."

"Me included, I hope."

Rayford stared at her. "I might have hoped the same before you risked exposing us."

Chloe stood. "I don't believe this," she said. "The co-op can't go on without me? Buck can't watch Kenny?"

Rayford looked to Buck, not wanting to be parental when Chloe's husband was right there. "Careful, Chloe," he said. "Daughter or not, there's protocol."

Buck reached up and took her hand. "Don't talk yourself out of an interesting assignment," he said.

"I'm not looking for interesting," she said. "I'm looking for crucial."

"How does Greece sound?" Rayford said, and she sat. "I'm going to Petra with Tsion. I'll have a new look and a new name. As soon as the GC recognizes that I'm not Buck, we're guessing their attention will be on Tsion anyway. We need another flyer for insurance over there, so Abdullah will go. I wanted you and Hannah to go to Greece. You're the least exposed people we have, at least until we know for sure whether the GC still suspects Hannah and the others from the plane crash being at large. You would be less suspicious and threatening, being women."

"Who would fly us?"

"If we can get the logistics done, Chang will have a GC plane delivered to Crete. You two and Mac would split off there and head into Greece while Tsion and Smitty and I go on to Petra. You'll be posing as GC, and it'll be dicey without the mark. Mac will trail you and keep an eye on you, also posing as GC. Ideally we want at least one of you to talk your way into overseeing the Sebastian situation for the senior cabinet."

"How long will it take them to catch on to that?" Chloe said.

"It would work only as long as you made it work. We all need to get with Zeke for new identities, papers, looks. All but you anyway. I don't think anybody knows what you look like. But how do I explain giving such an assignment to someone who pulled—"

"Captain," Chloe said, "let me do it to prove myself."

+ + +

On instructions from the safe house in Chicago, Chang began building dossiers on everyone traveling to Crete, then to Greece or Petra. Rayford's height and weight and a close enough birth date were entered, along with identification that showed him to be a brother to Abdullah Smith's phony persona. Both would pose as Egyptians in full regalia. Fortunately, Abdullah had not shaved for nearly two weeks, and he would craft his long stubble into a goatee, which Zeke would tinge gray. Rayford would have his skin chemically darkened, allow a mustache to grow thick and dark, and wear glasses with small, round lenses.

Taking advantage of Hannah's dark coloring, Zeke was transforming her into a New Delhi Indian, rather than a Native American. Chloe could go as she was, but with a new name and Canadian roots.

Mac was the challenge. He would be easily recognized as Carpathia's former pilot, so his coloring was altered to eliminate his freckles and the hint of red in his hair. He would also be issued glasses but would have to rely on bluster as a GC commander with a new name to throw off overzealous clerks.

"The biggest advantage you all have," Chang wrote Rayford, "is the decimated state of the GC around the world. 'We' are so understaffed, ill, and dying that maintaining strict security has become virtually impossible. Fortunately, in many areas, there are surplus vehicles, except in Israel, of course."

Once everything was in place in the computer, Chang listened to more of Carpathia's meeting while composing a nuanced—he hoped—message to his mother. The trouble was, she was not normally a woman attuned to nuances.

"We have our engineers working around the clock," Carpathia was saying, "on the water issue. All saltwater marine industries are dead, of course. We have lost hundreds of thousands of citizens, who may never be retrieved off the high seas. Vessels can go only so far through a liquid with such a thick, sticky consistency, and the diseases brought by the rotting carcasses of sea creatures may be our most serious health issue ever. Yes, worse than the boils and sores. People only wished they could die from those. The water crisis is again decimating our citizenry."

"Holiness," someone said, "in our region we have seen an alarming trend. Even those with your mark of loyalty are beginning to speak out in protest against you. We counter with the fact that this is not your doing, but you know people. They want to blame someone, and you become the target."

Before Carpathia could answer, Fortunato jumped in, and Chang thought he sounded like his old self. "This shall not be tolerated," he said. "I hereby decree and shall pass this word along to the priests of Carpathianism in all ten regions of the world that from this day forward, every citizen of the world shall be required to worship the image of their supreme potentate, their true and risen lord, when they rise in the morning, after they eat their midday meal, and before they retire at night."

"How shall we enforce such an order?" someone said.

"See to it," Carpathia said. "This, from the Most High Reverend Father, is inspired!"

"But, sir, there are still many who have not yet even received the mark of loyalty!"

Fortunato again: "They shall surely die!"

"Reverend!" Carpathia said, admiration clear in his tone.

"I have spoken," Leon said, warming to his point. "The time is long past for delays and excuses. Take the mark of loyalty to the god of this world or die! Anyone found without the mark on his or her forehead or right hand shall be given immediate opportunity to receive it, and upon their rejection, shall be put to death by guillotine."

There was silence as Chang sensed the regional potentates were considering the ramifications.

Finally Carpathia spoke. "With one notable exception," he said.

"Well, of course, Excellency," Leon said. "You need not take your own mark of loyalty!"

"Oh, Reverend!" Carpathia said, clearly disappointed. "You were doing so well!"

"Forgive me, Your Worship. The exception?"

"The Jew! The Jew, Reverend Fortunato!"

"Of course!" Leon said. "As the potentate himself has clarified, the blade is too good for the Jew."

Chang finished his letter to his mother with the following:

Assuming that you and Father have yet to take the mark of loyalty, ask Father how he would feel about a ruling that said he must take it immediately or die. What does that do in the heart and mind of someone who would otherwise be a loyalist? Does it rob him of any satisfaction he might get out of pledging allegiance to a leader?

That is what is coming, Mother, and you and he may hear it soon after receiving this. As soon as the regional potentate for the United Asian States returns from New Babylon, you may expect just that ruling. The time has never been riper for seeking another object of one's devotion. It may seem riskier at present, but in the end it will make the difference between eternal life and death.

21

RAYFORD HAD NEVER doubted Zeke's brilliance or artistry, but the young man outdid himself over the next several days. Around the Strong Building, various members of the Tribulation Force and members of The Place shot double takes at the soon-to-leave crew as their looks changed daily. Rayford caught himself studying his own visage in the mirror, wondering how such a transformation was possible.

"Your young brother keeps going with this, Captain Steele," Enoch said, "and you'll find out what it's like to be a black man."

As the people from The Place moved in on another floor in stages, the two groups began to share meals and prayer times. Enoch promised that his people would pray for the Trib Force entourage every minute they were gone. "And then some of us want in on one of your trips. We wouldn't even have to be disguised. Nobody's expecting to see us."

The day before the flight overseas, the Global Community News Network announced a special appearance of Carpathianism's Most High Reverend Father Leon Fortunato. He had a message for the entire world, and it would be broadcast live over television, radio, and the Internet at noon Palace Time and every hour on the hour for twenty-four hours so all the peoples of the world would be able to see it.

At three in the morning in Chicago, per Rayford's invitation, everyone in the Strong Building, except the babies, padded out and gathered in the commons near the elevator, where they watched television. The announcement would have proved anticlimactic, because it only reiterated what had been announced regionally anyway, save for what happened—which would be blamed, unfairly in this case, on the ubiquitous but elusive palace mole.

"We go live now to the sanctuary of the beautiful Church of Carpathia off the palace court here in New Babylon and the Reverend Fortunato."

Leon had assembled a massive choir behind him, and as he stepped into the pulpit, clearly standing on a small riser to make himself look taller, he was in his finery. He had added to the purple and gray and gold busyness of the robe and tassels. On his pate perched an Islamic-looking, flattopped, head-hugging cap. It seemed to try to incorporate the sacred symbol of every historical religion Leon could remember, but the effect made him look like an exploding ringmaster.

He stood there feigning solemnity and dignity while the choir sang "Hail Carpathia"; then he spread his notes before him.

"Fellow citizens of the Global Community and parishioners of the worldwide church of our risen lord, His Excellency, Supreme Potentate Nicolae Carpathia . . . I come to you this hour under the authority of our object of worship and with power imbued directly from him to bring to you a sacred proclamation.

"The time has expired on any grace period related to every citizen receiving and displaying the mark of loyalty to Nicolae Carpathia. Loyalty mark application centers remain open twenty-four hours a day for anyone who for any reason has not had the opportunity to get this accomplished. Effective immediately, anyone seen without the mark will be taken directly to a center for application or the alternative, the enforcement facilitator.

"Furthermore, all citizens are required to worship the image of Carpathia three times a day, as outlined by your regional potentate, also under threat of capital punishment for failing to do so.

"I know you share my love for and dedication to our deity and will enthusiastically participate in every opportunity to bring him praise. Thank you for your cooperation and attention, and may Lord Nicolae Carpathia bless you and bless the Global Community."

Fortunato tried to finish with a half wave, half salute, but suddenly the lights went out in the church. They came back on just in time for everyone to see the choir stumbling over each other to flee and Fortunato falling off his little platform, trying to get up, and having to billow out the skirt of his robe to do it. All eyes seemed to be on something in the ceiling, but as the camera panned that way, something happened to the camera operator, and the picture shook and wobbled.

Text rolled across the bottom of the screen: "Please stand by. We have temporarily lost picture and sound." Yet the interior of the church was in plain sight. And while the camera seemed to be at a cockeyed angle, showing only the empty platform and choir loft, the sound of people stampeding out the doors was clear as well.

Suddenly superimposed over the screen was a face so bright it lit the room from the television. The voice was so loud that a woman sitting near Enoch reached up and turned the volume off. Yet the voice could still be heard.

"If anyone worships the beast and his image and receives his mark on his forehead or on his hand, he himself shall also drink of the wine of the wrath of

God, which is poured out full strength into the cup of his indignation. He shall be tormented with fire and brimstone in the presence of the holy angels and in the presence of the Lamb.

"And the smoke of their torment ascends forever and ever; and they have no rest day or night, who worship the beast and his image, and whoever receives the mark of his name.

"Here is the patience of the saints; here are those who keep the commandments of God and the faith of Jesus.

"Blessed are the dead who die in the Lord."

The scene changed to the GCNN anchor desk in New Babylon, where a woman said, "We apologize for that malfunction, which should be ignored. We will now show again Reverend Fortunato's message in its entirety."

This time, as soon as the video rolled, the message from the bright visage overwhelmed it. Again the error message flashed but could not overcome the angelic announcement. Back at the GCNN desk the anchorwoman said the network would be off the air until further notice. But the instant the screen went dark, it came back on again with the message. Script from the network announced technical difficulties, but nothing could eradicate the shining face and the loud pronouncement.

* * *

Chang checked his computer, and there too the message played and played. He went outside into the hot sun, and there in the sky was the overpowering image of the angel of God. Chang dropped hard to his knees, panting, astounded that anyone anywhere in the world could doubt that Carpathia was the enemy of the one true God, and after this, they could doubt it only out of stubborn rebellion. He ran back in to e-mail his parents, only to discover they had already written him.

> *Your father says we will risk our lives, live in hiding, or face the death machines before we will take the mark. He is nearly suicidal over forcing you. I tell him you already sealed by God, and so is Ming. I will connect to Ben-Judah Web site. We will be worshipers of God and fugitives. Pray.*

* * *

Rayford knew it was folly to expect his people to rest during the day in anticipation of an early-evening flight from Chicago to Cyprus, then to Jordan. But they tried. Having their new friends from The Place in and out all day—singing, praying, and having church—was like a prelude to heaven. Before they piled into the Humvee, in which Buck would deliver them to the aircraft, the whole group huddled in a huge circle on their knees, praying.

* * *

George Sebastian's training was out the window by now. The resolve, the meditation techniques, the strength of character had been scraped away, replaced by hunger, thirst, loneliness, and, yes, fear. His silence had brought blows, none enough to do permanent damage, he knew, at least not yet. But his forehead and the back of his head had been butted enough times by the stock of a rifle that pain echoed through his skull.

George had been laced across the shoulders and shoulder blades repeatedly by what felt to him like the chain off a bicycle or motorcycle. Finally a fist struck him in the cheek and the jaw so many times that he knew he would never look the same. He tried and tried to time the swings and punches from his captors so that he could move with the blow. Finally he got the idea to do the opposite. When he sensed a fist was coming, heard the inhale of the assailant, felt the air movement, he lifted his chin and took it square. Just before he hit the floor and lost consciousness, he knew he had succeeded. Sleep, in any form, had to cover his body's ravaging need for food and water.

They had not been able to get to him with talk of his family. He knew better than to think his family would be any safer if he talked. If they really knew where his wife and child were, they could easily already be dead. He had despaired of his own life by now too. As long as he would wake up in heaven, there was no sense in giving up a thing.

The power to maintain silence had not come from within, but from without. He had, at long last, surrendered to God even whatever resources he thought he had. He came to on the cold floor in a corner with no idea of the passage of time, only that his middle was racked with hunger, his throat desiccated.

His captors argued. "Do you want him dead? You get us killed if we lose him. Give him some water. Enough to keep him alive anyway."

A few drops on his lips felt like a fresh spring, but he forced himself not to drink it in for fear they would think it was enough to satisfy him. He let most of it dribble until they quit being stingy with the bottle. He grasped the neck of it with his teeth and sucked as hard as he could, filling himself with enough to refresh him before they twisted it away. Then they pulled him back to the chair and resumed.

* * *

Abdullah landed at what was left of the airport at Larnaca on Cyprus midmorning. Albie's contact had recommended it as one of the least patrolled airstrips in the United Carpathian States. He proved dead-on. And he was waiting with a craft, appropriated by Chang's computer magic, that Mac would fly to Greece and land at an abandoned strip Chang had located some eighty miles west of Ptolemaïs. He had forged an order to a local GC operative, requiring him to deliver six Peacekeeper vehicles to an earthquake-damaged vacant lot a half mile from there. The memo came back to the bogus New Babylon commander: "You're out of your mind. Best I can do is one."

"Watch your tone," Chang's imaginary brass had answered. "One will do for now."

Rayford had not begun to seriously worry until he saw the stress on Chloe's face as they parted in Cyprus. Of course, it wouldn't have been natural if she wasn't scared. He wanted her on edge. But the open-endedness of their mission concerned him most. She and Hannah and Mac would fly in there, drive toward Ptolemaïs, and what? Start asking around and trust their GC identities? It sounded like suicide, but there was no way they would abandon George Sebastian as long as there was a chance he was still alive.

Rayford embraced her fiercely before she disembarked, wondering, his throat constricted, whether he would see her again. Chloe held on the way she had with Buck and Kenny in Chicago, and when finally she turned to go, Rayford feared he had not said enough. In fact, he had said nothing.

Toward Amman, Albie's friend took over the flying. As far as anyone knew, he was alone. Once he was in and down and hangared, Tsion, Rayford, and Abdullah would emerge from the plane and walk across the runway to the tarmac, as if appearing from nowhere. When accosted, as they would surely be, Tsion would ask to talk directly with Carpathia, offering hope for an end to the blood in the oceans if he and his two anonymous companions could borrow a helicopter for the trip to Petra.

All Rayford could think of was that the last non-Israeli he had sent into Petra had not come out. And yet he and his Operation Eagle forces had proved invulnerable to the attack of Carpathia's army. Whether it had to do with timing or location, he could not know. He just didn't want to jeopardize Abdullah's life, or his own, if he could help it. But he couldn't. The risk was there, and they were going.

* * *

Chang furtively monitored Suhail Akbar's and Nicolae's offices as he sat at his terminal. With the heat turned up and security forces combing the place for a mole, he had to be more careful than ever. He kept an eye on Figueroa's office and constantly covered his tracks. Finally pay dirt.

Director Akbar's secretary informed him that GC Security in Amman was calling, ostensibly with Tsion Ben-Judah on the line for Carpathia. "Put them on," Suhail said. When they were patched through, he insisted on talking with Ben-Judah personally. "How do I know it's really you?"

"You do not, sir," Tsion said. "Except that your own people are telling you it is I. I have a request of Carpathia and will ask it only of him."

"You would be wise to address him appropriately and formally, Dr. Ben-Judah."

"And then he will overlook the fact that I refer to him daily to a billion people as Antichrist, the enemy of God, and to Fortunato as his False Prophet?"

"Hold on."

Suhail told his secretary to give him time to get to Carpathia's office and to then transfer the call there. Two minutes later, Akbar sat panting in Nicolae's office when he hit the speaker button.

"Dr. Ben-Judah!" Nicolae began, as if to an old friend.

"I am requesting helicopter transport to Petra for myself and two associates without interference, in exchange for considering asking God to withdraw the plague of the seas having turned to blood."

"And why should I contemplate this?"

"You do not need me to tell you that. Surely your people are telling you that there has never been a time of greater resistance to you around the world. Renaming all of the oceans the Red Sea could not be in your best interest."

"If I have someone ferry you to Petra, the seas will return to water?"

"I do not speak on God's behalf. I said I would consider asking him."

"You would only consider it?"

"I will ask. He will consider it."

"Granted."

"But we need only the aircraft. Not a pilot."

"*Real*-ly. Granted."

Tsion hung up. Carpathia said, "You are welcome. Suhail, how long to Petra from Amman by helicopter?"

"I will see to it that they are issued one that will get them there in no more than an hour."

"And everything else is in place?"

"Of course."

"I want the area leveled within minutes after his arrival and the missile to make sure within moments after that."

"I will merely give my fighter-bombers time to get out of the way. They will make visual confirmation that he is there, drop their payloads, clear the area, and we will launch."

"From?"

"Ironically enough, Amman."

"Excellent. And the planes are equipped with videodisc recording devices?"

"Of course, but not only that."

"Something more?"

"We have arranged for you to watch live."

"Do not tease."

"A monitor will be in your office."

"Ooh! Oh, Suhail! Something to enjoy."

* * *

Had Rayford not been petrified, he might have enjoyed that Tsion looked the same in the Jordan sun as he did around the Strong Building. It was Abdullah and Rayford who looked like Middle Easterners in their robes. Tsion looked more like a rumpled professor.

"Who is your pilot?" a GC guard asked.

Tsion nodded to Abdullah, and they were led to a chopper. Once in the air, Rayford called Chloe. "Where are you?" he said.

"We're on the road, Dad, but something's not right. Mac had to hot-wire this vehicle."

"Chang didn't tell the guy to leave the keys?"

"Apparently not. And of course you know Mac. He's going to hop out and thumb a ride with some other GC while we drive merrily into town, trying to pass ourselves off as assignees from New Babylon to check on the Judah-ite raids."

"You ready?"

"Am I ready? Why didn't you make me stay in Chicago with my family? What kind of a father are you?"

He knew she was kidding, but he couldn't muster a chuckle. "Don't make me wish I had."

"Don't worry, Dad. We're not coming out of here without Sebastian."

* * *

When Abdullah came within sight of Petra, Chaim was in the high place with a quarter million people inside and another three-quarter million round about the place, waving to the helicopter. A large flat spot had been prepared, but the people covered their faces when the craft kicked up a cloud of dust. The shutting down of the engine and the dissipating of the dust were met with applause and a cheer as Tsion stepped out and waved shyly.

Chaim announced, "Dr. Tsion Ben-Judah, our teacher and mentor and man of God!"

Rayford and Abdullah climbed down unnoticed and sat on a nearby ledge. Tsion quieted the crowd and began: "My dear brothers and sisters in Christ, our Messiah and Savior and Lord. Allow me to first fulfill a promise made to friends and scatter here the ashes of a martyr for the faith."

He pulled from his pocket the tiny urn and removed the lid, shaking the contents into the wind. "She defeated him by the blood of the Lamb and by her testimony, for she did not love her life but laid it down for him."

Abdullah nudged Rayford and looked up. In the distance came a screaming pair of fighter-bombers. Within seconds the people noticed them too and began to murmur.

* * *

In New Babylon Chang hunched over his computer, watching what Carpathia saw transmitted from the cockpit of one of the bombers. Chang layered the audio from the plane with the bug in Carpathia's office. It became clear that Leon, Viv, Suhail, and Carpathia's secretary had gathered around the monitor in the potentate's office.

"Target locked, armed," one pilot said. The other repeated him.

"Here we go!" Nicolae said, his voice high-pitched. "Here we go!"

* * *

Tsion held out his hands. "Do not be distracted, beloved, for we rest in the sure promises of the God of Abraham, Isaac, and Jacob that we have been delivered to this place of refuge that cannot be penetrated by the enemy of his Son." He had to wait out the roar of the jets as they passed over them and banked in the distance.

* * *

"Yes!" Nicolae squealed. "Show yourselves; then launch upon your return!"

* * *

As the machines of war returned, Tsion said, "Please join me on your knees, heads bowed, hearts in tune with God, secure in his promise that the kingdom and dominion, and the greatness of the kingdom under the whole heaven, shall be given to the people of the saints of the Most High, whose kingdom is an everlasting kingdom, and all dominions shall serve and obey him."

Rayford knelt but kept his eyes on the bombers. As they screamed into range again, they simultaneously dropped payloads headed directly for the high place, epicenter of a million kneeling souls.

* * *

"Yessss!" Carpathia howled. "Yes! Yes! Yes! Yes!"

EPILOGUE

REJOICE, O HEAVENS! You citizens of heaven, rejoice! Be glad! But woe to you people of the world, for the devil has come down to you in great anger, knowing that he has little time.

Revelation 12:12, TLB

About the Authors

Jerry B. Jenkins, former vice president for publishing at Moody Bible Institute of Chicago and currently chairman of the board of trustees, is the author of more than 175 books, including the best-selling Left Behind series. Twenty of his books have reached the *New York Times* Best Sellers List (seven in the number-one spot) and have also appeared on the *USA Today*, *Publishers Weekly*, and *Wall Street Journal* best-seller lists. *Desecration*, book nine in the Left Behind series, was the best-selling book in the world in 2001. His books have sold nearly 70 million copies.

Also the former editor of *Moody* magazine, his writing has appeared in *Time*, *Reader's Digest*, *Parade*, *Guideposts*, and dozens of Christian periodicals. He was featured on the cover of *Newsweek* magazine in 2004.

His nonfiction books include as-told-to biographies with Hank Aaron, Bill Gaither, Orel Hershiser, Luis Palau, Joe Gibbs, Walter Payton, and Nolan Ryan, among many others. The Hershiser and Ryan books reached the *New York Times* Best Sellers List.

Jerry Jenkins assisted Dr. Billy Graham with his autobiography, *Just As I Am*, also a *New York Times* best seller. Jerry spent 13 months working with Dr. Graham, which he considers the privilege of a lifetime.

Jerry owns Jenkins Entertainment, a filmmaking company in Los Angeles, which produced the critically acclaimed movie *Midnight Clear*, based on his book of the same name. See www.Jenkins-Entertainment.com.

Jerry Jenkins also owns the Christian Writers Guild, which aims to train tomorrow's professional Christian writers. Under Jerry's leadership, the guild has expanded to include college-credit courses, a critique service, literary registration services, and writing contests, as well as an annual conference. See www.ChristianWritersGuild.com.

As a marriage-and-family author, Jerry has been a frequent guest on Dr. James Dobson's *Focus on the Family* radio program and is a sought-after speaker and humorist. See www.AmbassadorSpeakers.com.

Jerry has been awarded four honorary doctorates. He and his wife, Dianna, have three grown sons and four grandchildren.

Check out Jerry's blog at http://jerryjenkins.blogspot.com.

Dr. Tim LaHaye (www.timlahaye.com), who conceived and created the idea of fictionalizing an account of the Rapture and the Tribulation, is a noted author, minister, and nationally recognized speaker on Bible prophecy. He is the founder of both Tim LaHaye Ministries and The PreTrib Research Center. Presently Dr. LaHaye speaks at many Bible prophecy conferences in the U.S. and Canada, where his current prophecy books are very popular.

Dr. LaHaye holds a doctor of ministry degree from Western Theological Seminary and a doctor of literature degree from Liberty University. For 25 years he pastored one of the nation's outstanding churches in San Diego, which grew to three locations. It was during that time that he founded two accredited Christian high schools, a Christian school system of ten schools, and San Diego Christian College (formerly known as Christian Heritage College).

Dr. LaHaye has written over 50 nonfiction and coauthored 25 fiction books, many of which have been translated into 34 languages. He has written books on a wide variety of subjects, such as family life, temperaments, and Bible prophecy. His most popular fiction works, the Left Behind series, written with Jerry B. Jenkins, have appeared on the best-seller lists of the Christian Booksellers Association, *Publishers Weekly*, the *Wall Street Journal*, *USA Today*, and the *New York Times*.

Another popular series by LaHaye and Jenkins is The Jesus Chronicles. This four-book novel series gives readers rich first-century experiences as John, Mark, Luke, and Matthew recount thrilling accounts of the life of Jesus. Dr. LaHaye is coauthor of another fiction series, Babylon Rising. Each of the four titles in this series have debuted in the top 10 on the *New York Times* Best Seller List. These are suspense thrillers with thought-provoking messages.